Southern Spirits
Book Three in the Southern Series

By Shelley L. Stringer

To Karen.

Best,

Shelley L. Stringer

Table of Contents

"For it was not into my ear you whispered, but into my heart. It was not my lips you kissed, but my soul."

Judy Garland.

Chapter One

Loneliness is a funny thing. I was surrounded by family and friends, but my loneliness and longing for Banton trumped everything else in my life. Married only six months, my husband had been deployed twice. Apprehension had almost become a sickness as the days passed with no news from Banton or the rest of his SEAL team--Ty or Ben. The fact John had been excluded from this latest mission to allow him a period of mourning only made me worry about Banton's safety more. I'd always considered John and Sam Banton's protectors, and their absence from this mission made Banton the oldest and most experienced of the team.

John moved some things down from his house and took up residence in the nursery. Everett and Stephan stayed at the house too, taking turns as our resident Aldon protectors.

As if I didn't have enough to worry about, my dreams returned. I was determined to handle them on my own, and I'd become quite successful at waking myself up.

My house was a cold, gray tomb. The light eerily played tricks through the mottled, broken glass at the front door. I stood, dumfounded, clutching the doorknob in the front hallway. Ghostly shapes greeted me as I peered into the living room. All of the furniture in the once-cheery room had been draped with white sheets. The house was cold, tomblike and empty.

"Banton? Kids...where are you?" I called and called, but only the lonely sound of my echo in the shadows answered me. Where was everyone? What had happened to my family...my life? I moved back toward the stairway, and sensed someone behind me. I heard the dreadful low, deep guttural voice from my past.

"Everyone is gone. You are my last victim," the Tariq rasped out as he raked his teeth down my neck. "I've waited a lifetime to have you, and now you are mine! You will taste as sweet as your babies did,"

"No...NO! I screamed as I fought against the arms crushing around my ribcage. His teeth hovered against the vein in my neck, his hands roughly grasped my breasts. My chest heaved with sobs

as I pushed against his chest, trying to break free from his hold on me.

"Give in, little girl...you have no one left...your lover is dead..." *The words were more painful than his hands digging into my flesh. I hung my head in defeat.*

"Banton...no...please, Banton...I love you," I sobbed. I felt his teeth sink into my neck...

"Andie-girl, hey...you okay?"

My eyes opened to the soft moonlight of a southern Louisiana night shining across the foot of my bed. John pushed my bedroom door open wider, slipping through and then making his way across the room to stand beside me. I sat up and rubbed my eyes. It had only been a dream. As I took a deep breath, the tears had gathered behind my eyelids in sleep pooled and spilled over.

"Hey...Chandler. What is it? What's wrong?" John questioned softly, sinking down on the bed.

"I just had a nightmare, that's all."

"Want to talk about it? You were calling to Banton," he whispered.

I shook my head. He reached up and wiped a tear from my cheek and then added, "It's just because you can't talk to him right now. He'll call soon, I just know it. They can't stay on communications lockdown forever."

"It's been two weeks! Two weeks since he left that morning for a simple meeting. I need to hear his voice," I sobbed as I let go of the emotions I'd been holding in.

He sighed, and then pulled me into his chest. "I'd give anything if Reed had sent me instead. Banton would be here with you right now. I don't have anything left here," he whispered wistfully, stroking my hair as he tried to soothe me.

"Oh, John, I don't wish that. And you are wrong. You have me, and you have Constance and Everett. I know it's not the same, but if Banton has to be gone at least I still have you here. I'm sorry you're on babysitting duty." I sniffed and wiped my eyes with the back of my arm.

"Okay, now, don't start that. If I can't be deployed with my team, then at least I have a job here protecting you. There isn't anything I'd rather do right now, I promise."

I shivered; the cool air conditioned draft through the vents in my ceiling blew a fresh blast of air as the unit kicked on. As I pulled the comforter up under my chin, John readjusted on the bed and pulled both his legs up, relaxing back on the pillows beside me on top of the comforter.

"Snuggle down here and go back to sleep. Banton will have my hide if he calls tomorrow and you aren't well-rested."

"Kay," I answered sleepily. Just like that, John's calming presence was enough to relax me.

* * *

"I never heard her. I wonder if her stalker is back. We might need to stay with her when she sleeps."

"Stalker? Are you talking about the Orco Banton killed? He said something about her dreaming about him," John's voice drifted quietly through my closed bedroom door.

"Yes, but it's a bit more than that."

"She didn't say. I only heard her call out for Banton. I hope we hear something soon."

"And so do I, dear boy. So do I." Everett sighed as he pushed the door open.

"Well good morning, Sweet Bebe! I see you are awake!"

I sat up in bed and flung the covers back to rise.

"Yes, I'm waking up earlier and earlier these days. The babies won't let me sleep late anymore," I grumbled as Everett chuckled. I padded over to the bathroom to dress and meet another long, tedious day sans Banton.

I returned from brushing my teeth and dressing in our little bathroom nook, finding Everett had already made my bed and tidied my room.

"Everett! Why do you do that? You act like my maid sometimes, and it makes me feel bad," I scolded.

He raised an eyebrow. "You ought to know by now; it's just a nervous habit. My hands always have to be doing something, and I wanted to wait for you to come back so I could talk to you. How would you like to go to lunch with me today and maybe go and visit our secret patient? I think she needs a little push toward her reunion with John." Everett's eyes sparkled.

"Yes, yes I would. I would love it! Maybe it would get my mind off Banton."

"Good. Then I will meet you downstairs."

After Everett the cheery godmother left, I picked my laptop up off the nightstand and sank down on the bed. I said a silent prayer, and then flipped it open to check my e-mails. I scanned my inbox hurriedly --one from Laurilee, one from LSU admissions, nothing from Banton or Ty. I let out my breath and picked my cell up to check. No missed calls, no text messages. I teared up again, just as I had every morning for the past ten days. After closing my laptop gently and placing it back on the nightstand, I grabbed my purse and slid my cell in the side pocket.

I found Everett waiting for me at the foot of the stairs.

"All set? Let's be on our way," he urged cheerily, motioning me out the door. John honked and waved, backing out of the driveway.

"Where is he off to?" I asked as Everett escorted me over to his Mercedes.

"Gym. He said he wanted to get a little workout time in while you were with me."

"Oh. Everett, how much longer? How much longer do you think it will take Brie before we can finally reunite her with John?" I pleaded with him for the hundredth time.

"Bebe, I just don't know. We take two steps forward and then three steps back. All last week, she fought human scent issues again. She fanged on numerous occasions and her emotions were all over the place. We couldn't seem to put a finger on it. Then this week, she seems much better again. She is like a roller-coaster, and I'm beginning to wonder if she will ever level out. She fangs without warning now, and I thought we'd almost conquered that."

"Oh, no. I should have been spending time with her every day."

"I don't know if this is the best idea. We'll see how it goes. I don't want you taking any unnecessary chances," he warned as we pulled up into the driveway at the safe house.

"I promise. I will be careful."

Once inside, I could sense an aching feeling. The closer we came to the basement stairs, the more aware of it I became. The hair stood on the back of my neck as I realized the same fear and emotion I'd felt inside the funeral home when my parents had died. *Why was Brie emitting these emotions?*

Everett jiggled the keys in the knob loudly, announcing our approach. When he finally opened the door, Brie stood facing us in the center of the room. She stood tall, her shoulders pulled back in a silent show of strength.

"Hey, Brie...it's good to see you. How are you?" I asked softly.

Staring at me for several moments, she seemed as if she were trying to decide on the most appropriate reply. *Oh no, she's having trouble putting responses with feelings*, I thought.

Then her eyes lit up, sparkling like she just remembered some delicious secret.

"How am I? Let's see --I'm a newbie, blood-sucking horny-as-hell vampire, locked away in a stinking basement going on month four. My newly-married husband, love of my life, thinks I'm dead...and I have no idea how he's doing. The life I knew is slipping though my grasp and I doubt I will ever be able to make any of it right. If I have one loving thought of John, I fang. If I smell a human, I fang. If I get mad, I fang. If I cry, I fang. I fang, fang, fang, fang...and I have nothing to bite. If I fang once more, I think I will go mad. That about sums it up, how are you?"

"Good," I replied softly as I shrugged. What could I say to that?

We stood silently staring at each other. Giggles erupted from her as I smirked.

"I feel better already." She moved toward me and held her hand out timidly to me. "I've missed you."

"Oh, Brie...I've missed you too!" I took her hand, and as she breathed in I could see her upper lip quiver, her teeth trying to fang. I knew the scent of my blood was having an effect on her.

"Is this too much for you today? I can go," I hesitated. Everett placed his hand on Brie's shoulder as a precaution.

"No, please! I'm in control physically, it's just these darned fangs. It's an emotion I can't control, much like your tears. Once they start, I can't seem to get them to stop," she muttered as I nodded.

"Do you want to sit?" I asked as I pulled her over to one of the sofas.

"Actually, Bebe…we have a courtyard outside. Mr. Philippe will be along any minute with Olivia and Patrick. We thought we might take Gabriella outside for some fresh air and sunshine today."

Brie took several steps back and dropped my hand. "What…no, no I can't," she shook her head slowly, terror evident in her eyes.

"Why are you afraid, Gabriella? The Aldon would never let anything happen to you."

"It's not me I'm worried about. What if I…what if I escape? What if I smell a human! What if I can't control…"

"Whoa, slow down, mon chere. We will be with you every step of the way. We won't let you get in any trouble," Everett assured her as I nodded.

"I think it would be good for you, Brie. Really. You need to do this."

I watched her panic level rise.

As if on cue, Mr. Philippe, Olivia and Patrick appeared in the doorway.

"Ladies, we have wine, cheese and sparkling water waiting on a blanket in the garden. If you will follow me," Mr. Philippe offered, and I took his hand. Over my shoulder, I observed Everett as he pulled Brie along reluctantly, with Patrick and Olivia urging her forward.

We moved through the house to the backyard. I'd never been back this far into the safe house before. Several glass patio doors opened into a garden room, and then that room spilled out to a large courtyard surrounded by ten foot ivy-covered stone and brick walls. We seemed quite secure and secluded.

Once outside, Brie seemed to relax. She took a turn around the small yard, and then came to sit down on the quilt Everett had laid out on the patio.

"I'd forgotten what the sun felt like," Brie murmured as she held her face up to let the dappled light through the trees above bathe her face. She took in a breath of fresh air, and then released it slowly.

"Wine, Gabriella?' Everett asked as he held the bottle up for her inspection.

"Please," she replied, continuing to gaze around the courtyard in wonder. She seemed like a small child, taking in something wondrous for the first time.

"Brie, are you okay?" I asked after a few moments.

She turned back to me and nodded. "I'd forgotten how the outside smells…I thought…I really thought I'd never get to see it again," she murmured. Her eyes filled with tears.

"Everything is going to be all right, Brie. I just know it. We just have to work with you more," I began as she held her head up higher, appearing to catch a scent. Every muscle in her body stiffened as she turned to full-alert mode. I glanced hurriedly up at Everett, alarmed in the subtle change in her mood. He was talking in low tones to Mr. Philippe, totally oblivious to the changes taking place. Before I could call to him, Brie bolted, flying to the wall opposite where we sat in the courtyard.

"Brie, NO!" I screamed as she clung to the top. Everett moved almost simultaneously, reaching her in a split second and pulling her down from almost scaling the wall. They both fell to the ground, Brie on top of him. He struggled to keep her contained in his arms - she seemed to be much stronger than Everett. Mr. Philippe and Patrick reached him, helping him to subdue her. As the situation came under control, I realized Olivia stood at my side, my hand in hers. She was ready to pull me from the courtyard.

"Brie, what's going on?" I finally managed to breathe out.

Everett helped Brie up. As I made eye contact with her, I gasped. Her eyes were wild, like the fiercest Orcos I'd encountered. Her eyes looked…*oh God*, they looked like Lucien's had looked, the night he'd taken her life. Visions of his gaze, the blood on his teeth as they'd hovered over her neck, came flooding back.

She gazed at me for several moments, not herself at all, but seeming more like one of the creatures the SEALs hunted. She focused on me, and without warning, lunged toward me. Olivia flew toward her, grasping her by the neck and flinging her

13

backwards violently just as Brie reached within an arm's length of me. Her fangs throbbed with her need for blood. I stood frozen, horrified at her reaction to my presence. This was not Brie. She was not the Brie I knew, but an Orco. I was sick to my stomach.

"Chandler, back away! Go inside, NOW!" Everett yelled, struggling toward me. I was frozen, unable to move. Patrick and Mr. Philippe streaked toward Brie and managed to help Olivia pull her back into a corner of the courtyard. Everett grabbed me up in his arms and flew inside the house.

Once we were indoors, Everett sat me down on a sofa in the main room.

"Bebe, are you hurt?" he asked as he checked me for injuries.

"No," I whispered. I was still in shock from Brie's violent reaction to being outdoors.

"What was she feeling?" Everett asked calmly.

"What?"

"Could you feel her emotions, when she bolted for the wall?" he probed as I realized his game.

"You knew how she would react. You wanted me there as a sensor," I accused, feeling angry when his plan became clear to me.

"No! Well, not exactly. Bebe, don't be angry with us. I was hoping you could sense some inner emotions for us, so we could push her further. I thought you might be a barometer for us in respect to how she reacted to sounds, smells, sensations. But I never thought she would fly at you. We wouldn't have tried this if I'd known."

I nodded slowly. "It was so sudden. She was apprehensive, but happy to be with me. All I sensed was her fear as we went outside. Then, it was like...like her mind went blank. I saw her mood change, but didn't feel it. It was as if her emotions left her body."

Everett studied me for several moments, and then grasped my hand.

"As I suspected. Orcos behave as they do, because they lose their human emotions. Brie has retained a great many of hers, but she still battles the beast...the beast that has killed a part of her."

I shuddered as I considered his words. "Will she be able to suppress it?"

14

"Bebe, if I could answer that question, I could tell you her future. I just don't know." He shook his head sadly, and then pulled me up from the sofa. "Let us be off...we'll try this again in a day or two."

We drove in silence on the way home. I was a depressed after Brie's episode, and Everett sensed my melancholy. He insisted I rest and walked me upstairs to make sure I took a nap.

After he'd left the room, I turned my attention to my laptop. I had an e-mail from Banton! I clicked on it hurriedly, my heart in my throat.

Chandler,
I finally had a few minutes and access to a computer. I'm fine. We've been out on two missions. I don't know how much longer we will be deployed, but we haven't had the success we'd hoped. I have a brief window of time to contact you, so stay close to your laptop. I'll try you around 4:00 this afternoon your time.
I'm worried about you and the babies. I'm so sorry we had to leave like we did, and didn't get to give you a proper goodbye. Please, please take care of yourself, and keep John and Everett close. I love you,
Banton

Finally! Just hearing from him put my world back on track. I smiled as I picked my laptop up and carried it over to the bed with me. Checking the clock beside the bed, I decided I had just enough time to nap before our video date. For the first time in almost three weeks, I smiled, hugging my laptop to me as I drifted off to sleep.

"Chandler, wake up! Did you get an e-mail?"

I opened one eye, finding Constance hovering over me.

"Um, yeah, I did," I mumbled. I tried to clear my throat. I pushed up in bed to I checked the clock on the nightstand. Four o'clock.

"Well...what did Banton say?" she urged.

"Just that they'd been on two missions and things weren't going as planned. He said he would have some time this afternoon, and that he would try to contact me on the computer around four."

"Yeah, that's pretty much what Ty said. But Ty sounded kind of frustrated. I couldn't put my finger on it," Constance said as she sighed, flopping down on the bed beside me. "You look tired, Andie. John told me earlier he heard you having nightmares last night. You aren't sleeping?"

"No, I'm not. Until Banton comes home, I'm not going to sleep well. I can't relax. And anyway, the babies flip so much! I swear one of them has a foot right in my ribs and waits to start kicking when I'm in bed."

She laughed as she pushed a strand of hair behind my ear. "I think you have little versions of Cade and Drew in there."

The subtle ping of my inbox alerted us to an incoming message. Constance's eyes widened, and she dashed across the room and out to the landing as I flipped my laptop open. Banton's tired but smiling face greeted me.

"Banton! God, I'm so glad to finally see you!" I gasped out, my heart pounding. He looked really scruffy and tired, showing three or four days' worth of beard growth. It was still the sexiest thing I'd ever seen.

"Sweetheart, what's going on? You look so pale, and tired. What's up with the dark circles under your eyes?" Banton scolded as I rubbed my eyes, still trying to wake up from my nap.

"Nothing...I just miss you so much, that's all. Everything is fine."

"You don't look like you have had any sleep. Are you resting?"

"Sometimes. I just had a bad night last night. The babies are getting so big it's hard to rest. I just woke up from a nap, though. Everett made me lay down this afternoon."

"Good. I'll be sure and thank him. By the way, I've been worrying about your shots. Since I'm not there, who's been giving them to you?" He frowned into the camera as I hesitated. "You are still taking the shots? You have to have them," he reminded me.

"Yes. Constance gave me the three last week and two this week. But she's going to be gone for a few days, so I don't know. I guess I'll have to go and see Dr. Lane to get them."

"Andie, I don't want you to have to drive far, and I don't trust your SUV. I had it serviced before I left, but it has so many miles on it. I guess..." he hesitated, and then continued, "I guess you could ask John to give them to you," he suggested, his tone sounding hesitant.

"Banton, you don't need to be worried. I'll figure the shot thing out. How are you doing? When are you coming home?" I almost begged. I ached so deep inside. Just watching him on the monitor was torture, not being able to touch him.

"I honestly don't know, sweetheart. I wish I did. Reed runs a whole different show and right now, we feel like...well, I can't really talk about it, without revealing too much. You know I can't even tell you where we are. I do know I'm going to be away from communications for a while, so don't worry if I don't call for another week or two."

He ran his hand through his hair, his agitation and frustration showing. I'd never seen him so out of sorts and it frightened me. He was usually so in control.

"It's all right, Banton. Don't worry about me. I just miss you. I just want you to keep your mind on your mission and get home safely. You just have to be here when the babies come," I whispered, frightened at the thought he might not make it home in time.

"What did Doc Lane say at your last appointment? Is everything good?"

"Everything is still fine. One of the babies still isn't gaining like they'd hoped, but there isn't anything else to do other than the shots. The other baby is way ahead...almost too big. He said if he continues to gain like that, they will take them early, maybe as early as the fifth of August. So you have a little over one month, mister...or else!"

He finally grinned at me, flashing his signature dimple in the sexiest manner imaginable. "I promise I will be there. And the doctor said 'he'?"

"Just a figure of speech, Banton," I shook my head and grinned back at him.

"Are you sure you don't know what sex the babies are?"

"No. Nothing more than what Aunt Chloe told us," I replied. He touched his screen with his fingers and sat silently for several moments, gazing at me, saying nothing. When a tear slipped down my cheek, he finally broke the silence.

"Baby, please don't cry. I want to touch you and hold you so badly. I hate we left like we did. I'd planned to take you out on the town before we left. I wanted to make love to you in every room in the house; hold you all night. I had all sorts of plans," he murmured. I smiled through my tears.

"Not a night goes by I don't go to sleep with some memory of you. I was just remembering our night in front of our fireplace when you took my pregnant pictures. That night was one of my favorites," I whispered as he nodded.

"Mine too. That night and the night you said you'd marry me – when I first made love to you. They rank right up there with our honeymoon. But they won't compare to the night I come home," he finished. I smiled at his promise.

"Oh, and about that night…you should be getting a box soon. I ordered a portrait. Hang it in our bedroom and think of me. I'll be home before you know it."

I nodded, too overcome to answer him without my voice failing.

"The pool contractor will be calling any day, and I don't want you to wait on me. I know whatever you decide on the construction will be beautiful, so go ahead with everything. We'll have one hell of a party when I get home and we'll break it in. And one more thing," he said as he rubbed his forehead, "There will be a delivery coming any day. I ordered something for your and the babies' safety. I was hoping to be there to surprise you with it, but it doesn't look like I'll make it back in time. Just know I love you, and I can't wait to see you again."

"Oh, Banton…I can't stand this! I love you so much," I whispered, about to lose the control in my voice.

"Baby, I miss you too. The one thought that makes me smile and keeps me going is thinking about you…you, holding your tummy, rocking my babies on our front porch swing, waiting for me to come home. I love that picture…the one I have in my head."

I could only nod at him and smile, a Texas-size lump in my throat.

"Sweetheart, I have to go now. Keep John and Everett close, and I'll call when I can. Hold the babies for me. I love you, you are my entire life."

"My love forever," I whispered, touching the dimple on his cheek. As I gazed at him lovingly, the screen went blank.

* * *

I cried harder for him that evening than the day he'd gone missing after he'd proposed. I was miserable. Pregnant hormones in the last trimester were definitely not conducive to waiting patiently for one's husband on deployment.

A light rap on my bedroom door brought me upright in bed. I wiped my eyes and cleared my throat as I called out, "Come in, it's open."

John pushed the door open and crossed over to the bed. "Andie-girl, Constance told me you were having a hard time. I thought you were up here napping," he scolded, sitting down on the bed beside me. "Oh, come here, darlin'," he murmured. He immediately folded me in his arms. Kissing the top of my head, he continued, "Banton is going to kill me if he comes home and finds you in this state. We have to take better care of you."

He reached over to the nightstand and handed me a bottle of water. I nodded as I took a drink. Feeling better in his company, I smiled up at him.

"Actually, I do need for you to start doing something for me," I remembered. He looked at me curiously.

"Anything at all. What do you need?"

"Constance has been giving me my shots three times a week…injections the doctors say I have to have because of the babies and the complications and all. I can't give them to myself. Banton used to do it. Anyway, Constance will be gone next week, and I need someone else. Banton suggested I ask you." I explained, embarrassed. It seemed like a really intimate thing to ask him, since I had to take them in my hip or leg because of the kind of injection it was.

"Of course. When is your next shot?"

19

"Well, I need one tonight...but Constance is still here." I raised my eyes to look up at him.

"I'll give it to you and see if I'm as good as Constance," he teased. "Where is your medicine?"

"Everything is in the refrigerator door with the syringes. I'll go down and get it," I replied, starting to get out of bed.

"Stay put, Andie. I'll go and get it," he scolded.

I sighed as I watched him go out the door. He and Everett were being as attentive as Banton would be if he were here. I felt really lucky to have such good friends. As I waited for him to return, I could hear their voices downstairs. Everett and Constance were talking in low tones, John answering as I heard his footsteps on the staircase once again.

"Constance says I can have this job for good. She didn't want to say anything, but it really bothers her to give it to you," he informed me as he entered the room. He sat down beside me on the bed and asked, "Okay, where do you want this?"

"Why, does it bother her?"

"She knows it hurts you, and it makes her light-headed to watch you," he answered, his eyes wide. "Andie, I don't know about this," he began.

"It's fine. I'm getting used to it. My backside is still pretty bruised up. We'd better do it in my thigh," I whispered as I began to turn red. This was going to be harder than I thought. I pulled my gown up, uncovering my right thigh. I looked at him hurriedly, and his eyes widened as he contemplated the spot I indicated.

"I'm sorry. I should have told you where you would have to give them to me," I began, more embarrassed than ever.

"No, it's not that. You're just so bruised," he murmured. He glanced back up at me. Shaking his head, he pulled the medicine from the bottle and then removed the needle. Watching me warily, he blew out a deep breath. "Okay, ready? Here goes."

He inserted the needle gently as I grasped his shoulder. He finished the first shot and removed the needle as he watched me. I released my breath and nodded to him.

"The first one isn't so bad...it's the second one that gets me. You're doing fine," I assured him as he filled the second syringe.

"Okay, same leg?"

20

"Let's move to the other one," I replied as he nodded. He reached over and inserted the second shot. I winced, holding my breath again. Just when I thought I couldn't stand another second, he was through, pulling the needle out and then gently rubbing the spot on my leg with his thumb.

"God, I'm sorry, Andie. I know it hurt. Now I know what Constance meant," he exclaimed as I breathed out in relief.

"I'm okay. The last shot is just kind of intense," I assured him as he placed everything back in the baggies.

"What are they for, anyway?"

"Some sort of concoction Dr. Renault came up with for the babies. One of them isn't gaining like they want, and their blood was lacking in nutrients. It's iron and other stuff," I explained as he pulled the comforter back over me.

"You need anything else?" he asked as he started to leave.

"No, I'm good. I think I'll turn in."

He leaned over and kissed my forehead. "Night, then. Get a good night's sleep, and I'll see you in the morning." He brushed my cheek with his thumb and pulled away.

"Night, John. Thanks."

As John started to leave, Everett entered.

"Bebe, are you still awake? Something came for you this afternoon, and Constance and I just opened it." He pushed the door open, and John followed him back into the room with Constance close behind them.

"What is it? Banton said to be expecting something," I replied, pushing up in bed once again.

"Only the most beautiful photograph I've ever seen!" he exclaimed. He flipped a large canvas around. It was my pregnant portrait.

"Oh, my." I was stunned. I'd seen it on the camera, but on canvas it was breathtaking. Banton had converted it to sepia tones, and the effect of the firelight dancing around our silhouettes brought the picture to life. My body, much to my surprise, looked lean and supple, with the sheet draped discretely around me. With just my tummy and shoulders bared, it showed just enough skin to be tasteful. But the most beautiful part was Banton's hand across my abdomen, his hand twined with mine, both our wedding rings showing. I gazed at his profile as my eyes filled with moisture once again. In the portrait, Banton gazed down at our hands, his lips pressed to my bare shoulder.

"And when did you take this, Miss Thing? I didn't know you'd had a photo session," he scolded. "I had a photographer in mind for you for this. I had no idea you'd already taken them."

"Actually, we never had a photo session. Banton just suggested it out of the blue one night, and he grabbed my camera and staged it. He set it on self-timer and propped it up across the room," I explained. I continued to study the picture. My face grew red remembering the sex that preceded the photo. Banton looked as hot in the photo as he had that night--his chest bare, torn jeans unbuttoned at the top and hanging on his hips.

"Wow. Chandler, that is some picture," Constance commented as she looked back at me.

"Maybe it's a little too...Just put it there by the dresser," I replied. I felt my face redden further.

"No, it's not. It's beautiful. You need to hang it," Constance urged as Everett sat it down in front of the dresser.

"Here, Bebe. There was a card from Banton inside."

I took the note from Everett and tore it open.

> *Just as beautiful as I knew it would be. The perfect portrait to look at every morning as I wake up – my beautiful wife, pregnant with my babies.*
> *I love you with all my heart,*
> *Banton.*

"Well?" Everett stood waiting, tapping his foot with his hands on his hips.

"He wants me to hang it on that wall, so he can see it when he wakes up every morning," I replied, folding the card and handing it to Constance.

"That would be my vote," John joked as Everett chuckled.

"Holy crap, Chandler! He couldn't take the romance up another notch if he tried, could he?" Constance asked incredulously. She slapped the card back into my hand and said, "Ty can't be that romantic when he's in the room with me and wantin' some ass," she added flippantly as Everett gasped at her crude remark.

"It's beautiful, Andie-girl. We'll hang it for you tomorrow," John grinned, moving to leave.

"Yes, Bebe…it's late. You need to get some sleep. Mr. Philippe and I are just downstairs watching some old movies, if you need us. 'Night, Constance darlin'."

"Night, Ev. Love you," Constance kissed him on the cheek in passing when she moved to sit down beside me.

"Chandler, it is so beautiful. You are so lucky," she commented, looking over at the portrait again. "You know, he has to be about the hottest guy on the planet, aside from Ty, of course!"

"Of course," I replied, grinning at her.

"Seriously. He is so in love with you. You can see it in the picture. It gives me goose bumps." She shivered for effect and we giggled.

"Yes. It's hard to look at…that was some night," I added. My face flushed again. Constance turned to study my expression as I continued, "That was the night everyone left us here alone and we christened the sheepskin rug in the living room."

"Eww! I was on that rug watching television last night," she made a face as I laughed at her.

"Yep. The very one."

"So did Banton tell you anything?"

"Not really. Did Ty?"

"No. I could just tell he isn't happy about the way things are going, and he was vague about when they would be back."

"Mmm. Same with Banton," I replied.

"Well, at least we heard from them. Ty told me he has a surprise for me when he gets home," she announced as I grinned.

"They're just full of surprises, huh?"

"I'd better hit the hay. Remember, I'm going to Denham Springs for the week? Momma and I are helping with my friend's wedding."

"Yes, I remember. I'll be fine here. I have the two mother hens downstairs to look after me. Just go and have fun," I urged her.

"I will. Maybe the guys will be back soon after I get back."

"Let's hope so," I replied, crossing my fingers.

* * *

Banton's other project, the swimming pool, began when the contractor and designer showed up a couple of mornings later. It was as if Banton had scripted it. It made me a nervous wreck to make decisions of this magnitude without Banton there. Everett walked outside with me as we watched the construction crew stake out the outline of the pool.

"So fill me in. What style did you decide on?" Everett queried as he tucked my arm into his.

"A Grecian "L." The contractor suggested it, since we were working with the back corner of the house and yard. He suggested a shape to work into the corner, and I thought the classical feel of the style of the pool, thinking in terms of antique statuary, might fit in with the theme of the house and greenhouse." As I glanced up at him, a smile tugged at the corner of his mouth.

"What?" I asked, wondering what amused him.

"You were so apprehensive to make these decisions, yet you easily plan something architecturally pleasing to the house and the period. You really should be more confident, Bebe!" he teased, pulling me into his side to kiss the top of my head.

"Oh, I know what I want. It's just hard. I finally forced myself to make a decision based on what I would have done if I was still single and spending my own money."

"Whatever do you mean?" Everett asked disbelievingly.

"You know...spending so much of Banton's money. I feel guilty," I murmured, a little embarrassed.

"You have got to be kidding! Banton would be irritated to think you feel that way. He has told me on more than one occasion he wished you would let him spend more money on the house. He still feels like it's your house. The more you let him do, the more he will feel like it's his, too."

"Hmm. I really hadn't thought of it that way." I grinned up at him, feeling better about the sixty thousand dollar contract which I'd signed thirty minutes before.

24

A horn honking in the driveway turned both our heads. A pearly-white SUV pulled up, followed closely by another car. Everett and I changed our direction to greet the visitors.

A man in khaki pants and a white button-down shirt bounded out of the SUV with a clipboard in his hand. As he neared us in the driveway, I noticed a red ball cap on his head with a car dealership logo emblazoned on the front.

"Mrs. Gastaneau?" he asked.

"Yes, I'm Mrs. Gastaneau," I replied as I glanced at Everett. He shrugged and turned his gaze back to the man.

"I'm with the dealership. Mr. Gastaneau came in a month or so ago and special-ordered this SUV for you. It just came in this morning, and I had instructions to bring it to you. If you could just sign here," he directed, handing me the clipboard.

I stared at him, my mouth open. Banton bought me a new car without telling me. I took the clipboard, and absent-mindedly signed the dotted line.

"If you have a few minutes, I'll go over the features," he rattled on, opening the doors for me, pointing out the back-up camera, all the latest safety features…custom built-in child safety seats, side air-bags in front and rear, voice-activated GPS system.

After a few moments, I found my voice. "And my husband special ordered this?"

"Yes, Ma'am. He'd researched everything in the Luxury SUV class, and insisted on this one. The Lincoln is one of the safest models on the market."

As I ran my hand over the luxurious leather on the seats, I smiled, remembering our conversation a couple of days before. He'd said he'd ordered something for my and the babies' safety. I shook my head as I'd remembered the last time we'd driven my car together. He'd been checking out the tires, wondering at what kind of baby seats we'd need for it. I shook my head…he'd been plotting this then.

After the salesman had finished going over the features, he handed me two sets of keys and then left with the other dealership employee.

Everett joined me by my new car and cleared his throat.

"Well, are you going to give me a ride?" He grinned as I turned to stare at him, shaking my head.

"Why didn't Banton say anything to me? This is all so overwhelming," I stammered.

"Bebe, he loves you. You just got married, and he moved into your house. He needs to feel like the man, you know. He needs to know he's taking care of you."

"But my car is just fine," I interrupted.

"Your safety is everything to Banton. How old is your little SUV anyway?" he asked, raising an eyebrow at me.

"I don't know…seven or eight years. It belonged to my mother," I muttered. I considered the luxurious vehicle in front of me.

"Well, I know the old car is another link to your mother, Bebe. You don't have to get rid of it."

"I know. I just feel uncomfortable sometimes. Banton's spending so much money," I argued as he shook his head.

"You are stubborn, ma cherie. It's part of your charm. Come, give me a ride," he urged as he helped me to the driver's door.

My mood lifted tremendously the further we drove. The Lincoln drove like a dream, and the interior was so luxurious. Before I knew it, we'd spent almost two hours tooling around Baton Rouge playing with all of the gadgets and features.

As we pulled into the driveway, John bounded out of the house with an expression that urged me to hurry.

"John, what is it?" I asked breathlessly, I hurrying around the front of the vehicle.

"Nice wheels! Is that yours?" he asked. I met him on the steps.

"Yes. Banton ordered it and just had it delivered. What's wrong, John?"

"Um, I was just watching the news, and there's a story breaking about the SEALs."

I took the steps as fast as I could and hurried into the house and around the corner into the living room.

John followed close behind and picked the remote up from the coffee table. I sank down on the sofa, my eyes glued to the TV. Just when he turned the volume up, a newscaster broke in on a scheduled talk show.

"This just in…a team of Navy SEALs ordered to the coast of Somalia by the U.S. has taken control of the private yacht taken hostage a few weeks ago. Casualties have been reported, but reports are sketchy, and there is no official word yet from the pentagon. We will keep you informed as we receive information."

I struggled to see a familiar face. Flashes of men aboard the luxury yacht continued to play across the screen. Pictures of a navy gunship shown now and again, and I was sure Banton and the SEALs were assigned to that ship.

"Andie-girl, breathe…" John caught my attention as he sat down beside me and took my hands in his.

I didn't realize I'd been holding my breath. I sighed and tried to relax as I gazed at him.

"I don't know whether to be terrified at the thought they've been engaged with the pirates or relieved something is finally happening," I whispered, glancing back at the television.

"Have you heard anything from Singleton?" I asked. As John shook his head, his cell rang in the pocket of his jeans. He fished it out and answered, "Calder. Yes, Commander…I was wondering," he glanced at me as he held his finger up to me, crossing the room into the foyer where he could talk more privately. Relief washed over me when I knew he was talking to Commander Singleton. Everett came to sit beside me on the sofa.

"Bebe, maybe this means he'll soon return to you," Everett took my hand and pressed the back of it to his lips. I smiled at the thought.

John finished his conversation and then came back into the room.

"Well? What did Commander Singleton say?"

"Not much. The SEALs are all okay, and casualties were kept to a minimum. According to what little information he's been able to get, Reed is keeping them there. He's hoping he'll get one more chance at the leader. It seems they have some more information about where he's hiding."

My heart sank. This was the opportunity Banton had been waiting for, and I was afraid none of them would stop until they ended this. The only way to end it was to destroy Lucien and Dante.

We watched the television for an hour or more, flipping channels, hungry for any glimpse in the news footage about the SEALs. Everett popped some leftovers in the microwave, and we camped out for the night on the sofas.

"Have y'all been watching? It's on all the cable news channels," Constance called out, blowing into the foyer with a bag in each hand.

"Here, Diva...let me help you with those," John called out as he got up from the sofa.

"Actually, there are three more in my car. Would you be a doll?" she fluttered her eyes at him as he rolled his. After he bounded out the front door she turned to me.

"Has Banton texted you? I got a text from Ty a few minutes ago," she said breathlessly as she plopped down in a chair.

"Hello, you beautiful doll you! How was the wedding?" Everett bounced out of his chair and leaned down to kiss her cheek.

"Over the top, but I knew it would be. My mother will be in full bride-wars armor for the next three months just trying to figure out how to beat it, and I'm not even engaged yet!" she answered sarcastically.

"You heard from Ty?" I asked as I grabbed my phone from the coffee table. The screen flashed, *No new texts.*

"He said he would meet me on Skype in an hour or so, so I bet you'll hear from Banton too," she smiled as she plopped down beside me.

I pulled her in and kissed her. "I'm glad you are back. I wallow better with a partner."

"Diva, what the hell...what do you have in here, a dead body?" John called out, dragging her hanging bag in the front door. She had packed it so full it bulged to the point it couldn't fold to hang it. He just dropped it on the floor, trying to readjust everything.

"Well, I needed a few things from home," she replied. John snorted. He proceeded upstairs with the bag thrown over his shoulder and a suitcase under each arm.

My phone buzzed and jumped on the table, signaling an incoming text. Grabbing it up, I read it hurriedly and then looked up at Everett and smiled.

"Skype in ten to fifteen minutes, baby…"

"You girls go on up, and I'll bring you some ice tea." Everett waved us upstairs.

"Come on, Preggers, let's get you upstairs," Constance grabbed my hand and pulled me up from the sofa. John met us on his way down.

"Andie, I'll be up in a while and bring your shots," he called over his shoulder.

"Okay," I called back as I hurried into my room. No sooner had I flipped my laptop open, Banton's face popped on the screen.

"Oh, Banton…hey!" I called out, caressing the screen. He looked so tired. I just wanted to reach through the screen to him.

"Hi, baby. You are the best thing I've seen in days," he said as he reached his hand out toward mine.

"Are you okay? Was anyone injured?" I asked.

"I guess you've seen news reports," he said, raking his fingers through his hair. *He needs a haircut*, I thought, watching him.

"Yes. We've been watching all night. Are you any closer to coming home?"

"I really don't know. We've got a couple of things more to clean up here, before we wrap everything up."

I nodded. I knew what the two things were…Dante and Lucien.

"Banton, please be careful. Please!" I begged as my eyes began to water.

"Hey, I'm going to be fine. There's nothing wrong with me a night with you won't cure!" he replied in the sexiest tone possible.

"I love you so much," I whispered.

"Me too, Sweetheart. How are my twins?" he grinned, looking more lively.

"Rolling and tumbling like tom-boys. One of them has a foot in my ribs, and decides to kick-box every morning about two a.m."

"Well, when daddy gets home, I'll have a talk with her, all right?" he grinned, and flashed me the dimple.

29

All I could manage was a nod. I was choked up again. I swallowed hard, and then remembered the presents.

"Banton, the Lincoln arrived today. I can't believe you spent so much money on me," I admonished him as he grinned wider.

"I never even asked them how much it was. I just wanted the safest SUV I could find. We can't put a price tag on your safety. You are so precious to me."

"Banton," I choked up again.

"Hey, don't cry. Did you get the picture?'

I nodded at him. "Mmm, Wow...Banton, it's...it's so," I stuttered.

"Yes, it is. I love it. Did you put it where I told you to?"

"Of course. Ev hung it for me this morning. I'm looking at it now."

"Let me see," he commanded. I giggled at him, and then flipped my laptop around to face the picture.

"Yep, just like I remember. I can't wait to lie in bed and look at it. I can't wait to lie in bed and look at the real thing! You know, I actually had a jealous moment tonight."

"What do you mean?" I asked.

"When we got back here today, we were all talking about calling our wives, girlfriends...and the pictures came out like they always do. The two new guys fell in love with your picture. Boston...he's one of the newbies...he said, 'Wow, you get to tell her goodnight every night?' Then he called me one lucky son-of-a-bitch."

"I guess I'm flattered."

"Believe me, it was a compliment."

There was silence for several moments. We just gazed at each other. I had this weird feeling, like I should be memorizing his face...his beautiful bright brown eyes; the flecks of gold that seemed to shimmer when the light hit them just right...the sexy shadow of stubble on his cheeks, the dimples that appeared every time his eyes crinkled into a smile.

"Well, tilt the screen so I can see the baby-bundle."

I giggled and then picked the laptop up so he could see my belly.

"Good night little girls. Let Mommy get some sleep tonight, okay? Bedtime for you," he murmured, stroking the screen with his finger.

"Come home to me...please?"

"You know I will." He paused as he looked down, unfolding something and pressing it out to read. "I found this on a website the other day and copied it down to read it to you."

"Oh." I smiled through my tears at him when he continued.

"You know that place between sleep and awake...the place where you can still remember dreaming? That's where I'll always love you. That's where I'll always be waiting," he whispered as he looked back up at the screen.

"Tinkerbelle," I whispered back.

He grinned devilishly. "My favorite fairy next to Everett," he chuckled.

"Banton Matthew Gastaneau!"

"Hey, I couldn't resist..." He grinned even bigger. I shook my head.

"I can't imagine anything more romantic than a man who quotes Disney," I sighed as I gazed at him. After another pause he cleared his throat.

"Baby, I have to go now. I'll meet you later in our dreams..."

And he was gone.

Chapter Two

My eyes snapped open the next morning. *Wow, that was intense...*I sat up, not believing what had just happened. I shook my head...I'd read about it in books and mentioned in movies, but didn't believe it.

I'd just had the most intense *dream* ever. *What brought it on?* I was missing Banton so much when I went to bed. I stared at our picture on the wall...just looking at him, his muscles bare across his chest, his hand on my belly, the way his jeans hung just under his hipbones, the sexy "v" that trailed down to...

I'd sprayed some of his cologne on his pillow and snuggled down in one of his flannel shirts. Then I drifted off.

"Banton, you're home!" I squealed as he picked me up off the floor in the foyer and swung me around.

"God, I've missed you, Andie!" he exclaimed, twisting his hands in my hair.

I still wore the flannel shirt.

"You look really sexy in that shirt," he murmured, grasping the collar. The buttons went flying in different directions as he ripped it open down the front.

"Banton!" I protested.

His eyes were burning as he looked at my naked form. As soon as he picked me up, I found myself seated on the round table in the foyer; the books and pictures usually perched there swept into the floor. I lay back on the hard surface and looked up at him, amazed and aroused at the same time. This was so hot!

He unbuttoned his jeans slowly, watching my eyes. Grabbing my legs under my knees, he pulled me forward until he rested between my thighs.

"Your tummy is the sexiest thing I've ever seen," he murmured as he splayed his hands across it. He leaned over to place a kiss between his hands and I moaned, grasping his hair with both my hands. He rose to look into my eyes as he slowly pushed against me...

Wow. I blushed, remembering my quick reaction, my breathing still heavy from the dream. *He can do that to me, even in my dreams!*

"Why couldn't I have dreams like that all along?" I asked his picture on the wall. I stuck my tongue out at his smiling face, shook my head, and then climbed out of bed.

The inspiration struck! *This was just what Brie needed*! I began to form a plan, jazzed about a project I knew might take up three or four of my lonely days. After I showered and dressed, I decided to put my scheme in motion. I descended the stairs and peeked around the doorway into the living room.

I took a deep breath. I'd never been good at acting. In drama, I was always part of the stage and set building crew. I watched the play from the wings. Now trying to help with Brie, keeping her secret... I felt like I was center stage.

Now or never, Andie-girl. Now or never.

"John?" I called to him as I entered the living room. He was stretched out on the sofa, watching a sportscast on TV.

He turned and grinned at me. "What's up, Andie-girl?"

"I have a favor to ask. It's a bit much, and kind of awkward..." I trailed off.

"Anything for you, lady. Ask away." He grinned bigger, moving over for me to sit.

"Well, there is this charity fundraiser Aunt Sue is working on. It's a calendar they're putting together...different pictures for each month. They're going to sell them, and the proceeds go to the charity."

"Sure, I'll buy a few," he agreed hurriedly.

"No, that's not...I don't need you to buy them. I need for you to pose for the pictures."

"Huh?" His jaw dropped. I remembered his aversion to having his picture taken when we'd done the photo shoot in our dresses before Mardi Gras, so I rushed on.

"I would ask Banton, but he's not here. Sam's agreed to do it, and I need one more. Aunt Sue talked Cade into doing a football athlete kind of thing. You would do a Navy SEAL Mr. September pose...nothing too revealing. It will be tasteful. Just some chest-bared glamour shots..." I trailed off, so embarrassed I wished the

33

floor would open up and swallow me. *Remember, Chandler. This is for Brie. Brie needs this.*

"And Sam's already agreed?"

"Yes." *Shoot, I'd have to talk to Sam and clue him in to my plan so he would go along.*

"I…I guess so. Who is taking the pictures?"

"A photographer who is a part of the charity. Then you will do it?"

"Sure. I'll do it for you," he agreed grudgingly as he leaned over and kissed me on top of the head.

Why do I feel so guilty? This is for Brie…

"Great! Thanks, John. I knew I could count on you." I jumped up and bounded up the stairs, relieved I had that big lie out of the way.

Everett's accusatory gaze met me in my bedroom doorway.

"And just what, may I ask, are you up to?"

"What?" I asked innocently. My face gave me away; I was sure it was crimson.

"You know what. Photo shoot, Mr. September?' He cocked an eyebrow at me in the most dramatic fashion.

"How did you hear that, all the way up here?"

He rolled his eyes at the absurd question. Of course he heard me.

"Oh, yeah…I forgot. With those big Aldon ears," I retorted as I pushed around him into the room.

"You haven't answered my question."

He followed me over to my desk. I opened my laptop to fire it up, and then glanced up at him.

"Okay, it's a ruse. I need some sexy pictures of him to give to Brie," I whispered, glancing toward the door.

"Oh?"

"I figured she might need some visual aids. I thought some pictures of him might help. And I thought I might buy her a toy or two," I almost whispered as Everett's eyes widened.

"Hmm. Better than a John blow-up doll. I see. This might actually be a good idea, Bebe." He smiled and then bent down to kiss me on top of the head.

Everett was on board, giddy with anticipation.

"I know just the photographer…a friend of mine. We will clue him in on the secret. You'd better talk to Sam, though. We don't want to blow our cover."

I grinned at him and nodded as I picked up my cell.

*   *   *

Four days later, I held the eight by ten envelope in my hands. I waited until I was upstairs alone in my room, and then pulled the photographs out slowly. *Holy Crap! He is serious male-model material.* There were several poses of John--shirtless, in cutoffs walking in sand, lying back on pillows, his hands under his head. All of them showing his tanned chest off, his jeans unbuttoned, hanging on his hips. I blushed, appalled at my own bodies' reaction to the photographs.

I looked down at myself. "Stop that, you are a pregnant, married lady!"

Yeah, these would definitely work. Now, I just needed something else for the senses. I snuck into the spare bedroom, hoping John wouldn't come home before I was through. Rifling through his drawers, I finally found what I was looking for. I spritzed some of his cologne on one of his t-shirts, and then folded it and placed it in the envelope with the pictures. *This is perfect!* With the purchase I'd made for her at the lingerie party store, I was all set.

I was a woman on a mission. I just had to get Brie ready for her reunion with John. The more time I spent with him, the more my heart hurt for him. I was determined I would push her progress and end this before Banton got home.

After I'd worked on Everett, he agreed to take me to see Brie.

"Bebe, are you sure about this? She has made a lot of progress since you were here last, and there were extenuating circumstances last time that caused her reaction. But I think I need to be with you." He paused and looked at me as we began our descent down the stairs.

"I can already sense her emotions. She is calm and in control today," I assured him.

"I will be just outside the door if you need me," he replied.

I paused at the door to her little basement apartment, watching her as she sat alone staring at a book.

She turned, sensing my presence.

"Hey, Chandler! I was just thinking about you, and then I smelled you and Ev as you entered the house. How have you been?" She crossed the room and then stopped abruptly about two feet away from me. She held her hand out tentatively, and then her face broke into a smile as I took it.

"I promise, no attacks today."

"I know. Everett says you are doing really well, and he thinks you are passed that hurdle," I assured her.

"Where is he?" she asked curiously, knowing he would never let me come to see her alone.

"He's just in there, in the other room. I told him I had to see you in private," I whispered conspiratorially.

She cocked her head at me, wondering what I was up to. Taking her hand again, I pulled her over to the sofa and sat down beside her. I took a deep breath, and then went determinedly where I thought this prim and proper Texas girl would never dare to venture, even in a conversation with a best friend.

"Brie...I want to help you, and I think we need to drop all the barriers. You and I are probably as close as two friends could possibly get, emotionally, I mean...am I right?"

"Yes. You are my best friend. Now as a vampire...and before, when I was alive."

"This is going to be hard, but you and I need to go there. We have to have a heart-to-heart discussion about sex."

"Oh. Chandler, I'm a freak now, but I'm just not attracted to you that way. Sorry," she said, just as serious as she could be.

"You are a freak! No, I'm talking about you and John!" I exclaimed as she laughed. "I think I actually like you better as a vampire. You have such a dry sense of humor!" I shook my head when she continued to laugh at me.

"John loves you, Brie. He loves you on so many levels. If all he could have was your touch, your companionship...I know he would choose that in a heartbeat. What you have to do is imagine being with him up to the point you would normally become intimate, and then stop yourself. Stop yourself at intervals until you can grasp your level of control. Am I making sense?"

"Sort of. But how are we supposed to do that without him here?"

"Well, hear me out. I've given this a lot of thought from the perspective, of course, that it was me and Banton."

"Of course," she chirped at me as she grinned. *Almost human again...*

I took another deep breath, and then continued, "Have you, I mean, did you ever, when you were human...have an orgasm, well...alone?"

"Haven't we all?" she grinned at me, and it all became easier.

"Well, it just so happens I have your own special visuals, made just for you. I'm going to leave them with you, along with a tape of his voice, something with his scent... and you do with it what you will."

I pulled the portfolio out of my purse and dropped it on the table for her. "And just so you know, I told him he was taking these for a Navy SEALs Mr. September sort of thing, to raise money for a charity. He would have never agreed otherwise. You and I are the only ones who have seen these."

She stood motionless, suddenly serious. "I'm afraid. What if I can't do this? What if I can't control...it's not like there will be someone real there, with a beating heart to resist."

"I didn't say this would be easy. Just work with it, and then we will talk tomorrow. Bring yourself to the brink and stop. Take it all the way, test your emotions. But no matter what, talk to me about it. I know you can do this, Brie. You have to. For John," I added as she looked back up at me with tears in her eyes.

"So what made you think of this? How did you..." she began.

"Banton's absence. I miss him so much, and I am so lonely at night. I was staring at his picture the other night, and then I sprayed some of his cologne on his pillow...well, you get the picture. It has me thinking, maybe we could work you up to something."

"Chandler, thank you. Thank you for being my friend. I don't think anyone else would...could get this close to the problem with me. I love you, you know. I owe you so much," she said. I pressed my finger to her lips. She drew her breath in, and as she did, I pulled her to me and held her closely. We held each other several seconds, my being aware of her face only inches from the artery in my neck. I was confident she could handle it-- I was becoming so good at feeling her emotions. As I pulled away she smiled at me, the biggest I'd seen her smile since she'd transformed.

"You trust me. You really trust me?" she asked incredulously.

"More than you trust yourself. That is the problem. Trust yourself, Brie. Trust yourself, and love John enough to trust you too," I whispered.

* * *

Upon arrival at home on Rue Dauphine I found visitors. Recognizing Claudia's car, I grinned, jumped out of my new SUV, and hurried up the steps of the front porch, Everett right behind me.

"Where's my Doodle-Bug! Ava, Claudia!" I yelled out breathlessly as I kicked my shoes off right inside the front door. Ava came running down the hallway, followed by an ecstatic Beau.

"An Andler! Aba came to see you!" she exclaimed. I knelt to hug her. Beau immediately sped the cadence of his tail beats, licking us both in the face as we tried to hug each other.

"Beau, get back! I can kiss you anytime," I admonished him. Ava Grace giggled.

"Where's your Mommy?" I asked her as I stood up.

"I'm here. Hello, you…Oh my, Chandler…you look as if you are about to pop!" she exclaimed, moving toward us, wearing my apron.

"And just what are you up to?" I asked.

"I just thought I'd try out a new recipe on you tonight. You always cook for us when we come, so I thought I'd return the favor. Sorry we dropped in unannounced, but Will had to fly out unexpectedly for a three-day trip this morning, so I thought we'd get a little sister-in-law time in," she smiled as she leaned in to kiss me, placing her hands on my belly. She leaned over and spoke to the babies, "Aunt Claudia is ready for you to come out now, hurry it up!"

"Mommy, can my babies hear you inside An Andler's tummy?" Ava asked. Everett chuckled behind us.

"Yes, I think they can, Ava. You need to start talking to them, so they will know your voice when they get here."

Ava placed her mouth against my tummy and yelled, "Hewoo in deair! Aba's weady to see you!"

"That's good, Ma Petit! The babies will love you," Everett exclaimed, picking her up and swinging her around. "I've been waiting for you to come and visit, Miss Ava! I have a surprise for you." Everett swung Ava up on his shoulders and then skipped down the hallway with her. "Uncle Everett made a tire swing in our tree, just for you," he told her as they made their way outside.

Claudia laughed and shook her head.

"So what are you cooking for me?" I asked as I tucked my arm in the crook of Claudia's.

"It's a meat pie, much like a chicken pot pie, but with different cuts of beef and pork with a homemade crust. I thought with your new cravings and all, the meat would be appealing to you. Ev said you still struggle with eating enough for the babies," she admitted as I frowned.

"The doctor has me on shots, but one of the babies isn't gaining like they would like," I said as we entered the kitchen.

"What do you hear from Banton?"

"He called a few nights ago, the day they took the yacht back from the pirates. He sounded...I don't know...tired and discouraged. He said they had a couple of loose ends to tie up."

"Are they still trying to get at the leader coordinating the attacks against you?'

"I'm afraid so. The longer he is there, the more I worry about his safety. It's time for them to come home to us," I said as I sighed. "But I'm so glad you are here! Your visits help pass the time."

"Chandler, you should call me when you get lonely! You know I'll come whenever you call."

"I know, but you need to be home when Will is there. How is everything with the new house?"

"It's coming along. We are still at Momma and Daddy's right now. You know them, they would be happy with us just staying there forever. But I'm ready to have my own house again."

As I watched Claudia putter around my kitchen, I began to feel a dull ache in my lower back. I pulled a chair out at the bar and sat down. Claudia turned, watching me as I rubbed my hip and lower back.

"Chandler, is something wrong?"

"No, my back is just a little tight. Probably been on my feet too much today."

"Well, why don't you go upstairs and lie down, and we'll come and get you when dinner is ready," she urged, tucking my hair behind my ear.

"Okay, I think I will." I rose and slowly made my way back up the hallway to the staircase. I started up the stairs and a sharp pain radiated across my lower abdomen, seeming to pull straight through to my lower back and tailbone. I gasped, clutching the banister. I took a deep breath and it subsided. Just as I took the next step, it hit again, only twice as intense. As I sucked my breath in trying to control the pain, I fell to one knee.

"Chandler!" John called from the doorway, having just entered the house. "What's wrong?" He was quickly at my side on the stairs.

"I can't catch my breath, the sharp pains...Ah-ow!"

John picked me up and carried me the rest of the way up the staircase. Pushing the door open with his foot, he carried me to my bed and sank down with me.

"Do I need to call Doc?" he asked worriedly.

"Yes. I've never felt anything like this, since our honeymoon," I whispered, still holding my breath trying to control the shooting pain.

"Is his number on your cell?"

"Yeah. It's on the table in the foyer."

He rushed out of the room as he called over his shoulder, "I'll be right back."

God, please...don't let the babies be in danger, I thought silently over and over as I waited. After a couple of moments, I could hear Claudia and Constance on the stairs.

"What's wrong? What happened?" Constance called out as she rushed into the room.

"Chandler, is it the babies?" Claudia asked worriedly.

"I don't know, I just started having pains," I breathed as John came back into the room.

"I've called Dr. Lane, and he's on his way here. He said for you to lie still and take it easy."

I nodded silently, my eyes closed.

"Sweetie, can I get you anything? How about some tea, maybe something warm would relax you. Or some water?" Claudia asked, feeling helpless.

"Some hot tea would be nice, thanks." Claudia hurried from the room.

"Did this just start?" John asked. He moved over beside me and sat down on the edge of the bed.

"Yeah. I thought maybe I'd been on my feet too much today. But when Claudia suggested I might need to lie down, that's when the pains really started...when I started up the stairs."

"Okay, just rest," he murmured, leaning over to kissed my forehead. Here is your phone. I'm going to put it here beside you. Doc should be here in less than thirty minutes."

Constance sat down at the foot of my bed, watching me helplessly. I could hear Everett and Ava as they came in from the yard downstairs, and Claudia's voice as she told Everett where we were.

"Do you want me to call Momma?" Constance asked. I shook my head.

"No, not yet. There's no need to worry her until we find out what's wrong," I answered as John brushed my hair from my eyes.

After Claudia brought my tea to me, John helped to prop some pillows behind me. When the pains finally began to subside, Dr. Lane arrived.

"Hey, Doc...thanks for coming," John rose to greet him as he walked into my room.

"Well, Chandler...what's all the commotion? You just didn't want me to play my nine holes this afternoon, did you?" he teased, placing his bag down on my bed. "Let's see what is going on with you and those babies. If everyone will step out for a moment, I'm just going to check her." He motioned everyone out of the room.

"I need to give you a thorough exam. I know this is awkward, without my nurse here. Would you feel better if we asked Constance to come back with you?" he asked in a fatherly tone.

I blushed and nodded at him. He smiled and stepped out into the foyer. "Constance, could you come back in with her a moment?"

"Sure," Constance replied. She appeared through the doorway ahead of Dr. Lane.

"Want me to hold your hand?" she joked as she stood by the head of the bed, taking my hand in hers.

I just nodded at her, the tears beginning to pool in my eyes. I was terrified Dr. Lane thought the babies might be in danger with his having made a house call.

Dr. Lane pulled the covers off the end of the bed into the floor, and then helped me scoot to the end. He opened his bag as Constance helped me place the sheet so he could examine me. She discretely turned her back to Dr. Lane, facing me so I could look at her. After hearing him snap his gloves on, he placed one hand on top of my tummy, while he pushed two fingers inside to check. I gasped. The examinations before this had never hurt like this one. After a moment or two of prodding and feeling, he removed his hand, and snapped the gloves back off. He then felt over my abdomen, and then checked the babies' heart rates the old fashioned way with a stethoscope. He then removed the ear pieces and pulled the sheet back down over me.

"I suspect the placenta is torn again, but the babies seem fine, for now. You have some slight bleeding. I'm a little concerned, Chandler. A tear this late in the pregnancy might lead to an early labor. You are just going to have to stay down for a while. Nothing strenuous, no climbing the stairs. With these twins getting big, we don't want to put much stress on that tear."

I nodded at him as the tears slipped from my eyes.

"Doc, since Chandler does the fast healing thing since the transformation, why does she have trouble with these tears," Constance asked.

"Well, it's not quite that simple. Her body is actually fighting being pregnant. The tears are due to her body trying to reject the babies, but she's still human, so it's kind of push and pull," he tried to explain, and then shook his head.

"The babies are okay for now. They have good, strong heartbeats, and good movement. I want you to take something to help you rest tonight. Call me if your pain comes back, or if you bleed any heavier than you are now." He patted my leg. I nodded to him as Constance opened the door for him, and then shut it behind him.

"Here, let's get you settled back and the bed straightened," Constance urged as she put the covers all back on the bed. After she had me back in place, she opened the door and let John and Claudia back in.

"Doc says you are fine, we've just got to keep you down," John smiled at me as he sat down on the edge of the bed. "Here, take two of these and drink some more of your tea," he urged. He shook two of the pills out of the bottle which Dr. Lane had left on the nightstand.

"Chandler, I'm going down to check on Ava and Everett and finish supper. I'll be back up a little later. Call me if you need me," Claudia called as she left the room.

Constance's cell rang, and she left to answer it.

"Andie-girl, don't worry. You are going to be fine," John murmured, brushing a tear from my cheek.

"I have to be. I have to carry these babies till Banton gets home," I choked out as he leaned over and put his arms around me.

"We're going to take care of you till he does get home. And I know it can't be too much longer now," he said, his breath blowing into my hair. He laid me back into the pillows and smoothed my hair from my face. As he handed me my teacup my cell phone rang. He picked it up and handed it to me. Not recognizing the number, I answered it hesitantly.

"Hello?"

"Chandler Ann, are you all right?" Banton asked worriedly. "Constance got a call through to command, and they told me to call you.

"Oh, Banton! I'm so glad you called," I sobbed into the phone, emotional at hearing his voice.

"Sweetheart, what happened?"

"Another tear in the placenta. I'm bleeding, but not heavily. Dr. Lane put me back on bed rest for now," I said as I heard him draw a deep breath.

"Are you at the clinic?"

"No, I'm at home. John carried me up to our room after I started having the pains. He called Dr. Lane, and he came here and examined me. He just left."

"John carried you?" There was an awkward pause, and then he continued. "Just do what Doc tells you and stay down. What about the babies?"

"He said their heartbeats and movements are good. He just said we need to watch the tear, and not put too much stress on it this late in the pregnancy," I explained. I wiped my eyes.

"Oh baby, I wish I was there. I can't stand being this far away when you need me."

"When are you coming home?" my voice quivered.

"Not much longer, I hope. Then I'll be there to carry you. That's my job, you know."

I nodded as I smiled, like he could see my reaction.

I have to go, Chandler...I'll call back as soon as I can. Please take care of yourself...God; I love you so much,"

"I love you too," I managed to whisper. Then the connection clicked off.

John had discretely left the room while I was talking to Banton. I could hear him talking to Constance in the hallway. I choked back a sob...this would only take Banton's mind off his mission. Right now he needed to be focused. I almost wished Constance hadn't called him. I took a deep cleansing breath and wiped my eyes. Being emotional would not help the babies.

John stepped quietly back into the room. He sat down in the chair by the bed and reached out to lay his hand over mine.

"Any better?" he asked hopefully.

I smiled at him. "John, you don't have to stay in here and babysit. I know you have better things to do...I'll call you if I need something."

44

"Don't have anywhere I need to be, just now, Andie-girl. So if it's just the same to you, I'll camp out here and see to my best friend's girl."

He drew my hand up and kissed my knuckles as he wiped my hair from across my forehead.

"What did Banton say?" he asked softly.

"Not much. I guess Constance called command and got a message to him. I almost wish she hadn't. He doesn't need the worry or distraction."

He shook his head. "You're wrong. He can compartmentalize when he needs to, it's part of the training. He's better off knowing. He has the assurance you'll call if you need to."

I relaxed a little at his words.

"I know he's dying to get home. I would be, if I was in his shoes. Let's just keep those babies in there till he gets back."

I nodded and then glanced up just as Claudia came into the room with a tray.

"Well, I'm glad I showed up to help take care of you, Sweetie. Here is your supper…and you have a visitor. I've invited him to eat with us, so we are going to have a little picnic up here in your room! Is that all right?"

"Sure. Who is it?"

She moved to set the tray on the nightstand as John helped her make a place for it.

"Mr. Jackson came by with some things to give you, and he's out on the front porch now, sprinkling some more of that dirt stuff around," she said, rolling her eyes.

"Brick dust. It's brick dust, for protection. It's an old Creole superstition," I explained as she raised an eyebrow.

"Whatever. I'm just going to go down and Everett is going to help me bring the rest of our dinner up here. We'll be right back," she called over her shoulder as she left the bedroom.

"Now Mister Ev, I's doin jes fine. Don't you go a'frettin 'bout me none," Mr. Jackson's voice came up the staircase. "I kin climb dem stairs jes like you young folk kin. I's a bit spry fo my age," he chuckled as he gained the top of the stairs, his cane under his arm. After he let go of the bannister, he walked into the room.

"Miss Chandler, you done gone and done too much and put yoself back in dat bed now, hadn't you, Missie?" he shook a withered finger at me.

"Yes. I have to take it easy for a few days, but I'll be fine. How are you?"

"I's doin jes fine and dandy, now dat de weather is set in on summer. My old bones like de summer!" he chuckled, settling down in the chair by the dresser. "I done brought you some mo gris-gris makins from my Auntie Chloe. And she done sent you somethin' real special." He leaned forward, handing a box to John for me. John sat it down in my lap. I removed the lid, finding three small drawstring bags wrapped in tissue. The lavender and sage smell drifted out of the box, cheering me up immediately.

After I'd placed the bags out on the bed, I removed the tissue. Underneath, I found an ancient, worn leather Bible. I looked up at him questioningly, and then back down at the fragile book as I opened the cover. I flipped over a handful of pages to a place where a flower had been pressed. Several passages were marked with ink. As I scanned the pages, I found many more of the same.

"Dis is one of many of dem Bibles dat Auntie Chloe has. She said dat dis one here is special, dat she wants you to study des here passages dat be marked wid de herbs and such. All of dese here has a meaning, and every passage done been marked wid a date. It might be da birthin' of a new baby in my family histories, or a death. A war, a trial of some kind…it all be here. She said to study it, and it will help you through yo trials, chile. God don't give us dat which we can't deal wid…it makes us strong, makes us seek him. Dat be what she wanted me to tell you."

I looked up at him in wonder. A family Bible was a sacred thing, and I felt like she was bringing me into her family, spiritually, with the loan of the precious book. I hugged it to my chest.

"Thank you, Mr. Jackson! Please thank her for me, and tell her I will take good care of it."

I placed it back in the box, and then handed it to John to place on the dresser. Claudia soon reappeared with the rest of our dinner and placed a quilt in the floor for her, Everett, Constance and Ava to spread out on.

"Bebe, I'm so worried about you. I shouldn't have kept you out so long today, Ma Petit. We have just got to take better care of you," he fretted as he placed a kiss on my forehead.

"Nonsense, Ev. It's just one of those things. I'll be all right," I assured him.

"Mister Ev, it sho be good to sees you. You haven't been down to sees me in days. I done got a whole notha mess of dem greens to gives you outta my garden," Mr. Jackson said.

"Oh, good. I'll be down there tomorrow and work that ground a little for you while we visit," Everett replied as he leaned over and patted Mr. Jackson on the knee. He turned back to me, and I raised an eyebrow at him. I had no idea Ev had been going down to see Mr. Jackson by himself. He winked back at me in a silent reply.

"Mommy, I get to eat on my bankie?" Ava Grace turned her big brown eyes back to Claudia.

"Yes, Ava…we are going to have a picnic in Aunt Chandler's room tonight. Isn't that fun?"

"Yay! Can I make Aba and Daddy Will's pway tent?" she asked excitedly, clapping her hands together.

"Well, maybe after we eat, if Aunt Chandler feels like it. Come here, now, and sit down and eat," she urged her. Ava plopped down between Claudia and Constance and took her bowl in her hands.

John helped me, placing the tray in my lap and then handing me my tea. I looked around the room and it hit me. One year ago I knew none of the people in this room, except for Constance. And as I looked at each one slowly…Everett, Mr. Jackson, Claudia, Ava Grace, John…I couldn't imagine my life without any of them. God had certainly placed some special people in my life at a time when I'd needed them. Maw Maw Irene's words rang in my head, "God doesn't make mistakes."

"No, he doesn't," I murmured.

"What was that, Bebe?" Everett asked.

"Oh, nothing." I smiled at him. "I was just thinking about what I needed to thank God for in my prayers tonight," I replied as he smiled warmly at me.

Chapter Three

"I was mad at you at first, but I'm glad you called Banton," I said to Constance.

"Well, you'll just have to get over it, sister...'cause I'm callin' him whenever we need to. After the time you broke your arm, I'm never keeping anything from him. He was so pissed at me it kind of scared me," Constance replied warily.

"What? What do you mean?"

"When he called me and grilled me that next day, he made me tell him what was really wrong with you. You know me, Andie...no guy is going to tell me what to do. But Banton...he's different. I love him like a brother, but I wouldn't want to cross him. And I won't ever lie to him again, not even for you. He's like a man possessed when it comes to your safety," she said as she folded my covers back.

She'd never told me that. As I thought about what she said, Claudia came in the room.

"Do you feel like a bath? I'll help you, and then you can lay right back down," Claudia offered.

"Y'all are making me feel guilty. You are doing so much for me," I complained.

"Yeah, yeah...wait till I get my chance. You'll pay me back, someday," Constance shot over her shoulder as she went to run my bath. After they had me soaking in the tub full of bubbles, Claudia stripped my bed and made it up with clean sheets. I could hear Ava Grace's voice as she came up the stairs.

"Hey, Doodle-Bug! What are you doing this morning?" Constance called out brightly.

"I want to see my An Andler," she demanded.

"Well, come in here, Bug...she's taking a bubble-bath. You can come in here and keep her company."

"Kay."

Ava tiptoed around the door and around beside the tub where I could see her.

"An Andler, are my babies in the bubbles?" she asked.

"Yes, Ava...see, here they are," I replied as I wiped the bubbles away from my tummy.

She leaned over the side of the tub, and traced the faint stretch marks forming under my belly button. "Does it hurwt?" she whispered, pointing to the marks.

I smiled at her and tucked a curl behind her ear. "No, sweet girl, it doesn't hurt. Those are just because my tummy is getting so big my skin is stretching over the babies."

"But my Mommy said you hurwt wif the babies wast night," she answered, her eyes wide.

"Well, yes I did, a little bit. But I'm better, now you and your Mommy are here to take care of me."

"I take carew of you, An Andler," she said, patting my shoulder. She reached over and picked up the bar of soap, and then got a washrag off the counter. As I watched her in wonder, she dipped the rag into the water and squeezed it out, and then ran it over the soap. Placing the soap in the dish carefully, she then began to rub the soapy rag on my arm and shoulder. I watched her, totally captivated by my little niece as she played out her nurturing instincts.

"Well, Ava...are we ready to get Aunt Chandler out and back in the bed?" Claudia asked.

"Yes, Ma'am. I help An Andler take a bafth!" she replied happily as she slopped water on the bathroom floor.

"I think she's clean enough. Here, Chandler...easy, stand up slowly, and I'll help you dry. I've got your robe here," she offered, taking my arm when I pushed up to stand.

"An Andler! You have big chi-chi's wik my Mommy Cwadia!" Ava Grace squealed. I heard Constance bust out laughing in the bedroom.

"She doesn't miss a thing," Claudia rolled her eyes as I shrugged into my robe.

"Where on earth did she hear the term, 'chi-chi's?'" I asked.

"Wewl, that's what my Daddy Will calls dem," Ava replied, matter-of-factly.

"Out of the mouths of babes," Claudia commented.

"I'd love to hear what else Will has taught her," I teased as Constance came to the door.

"Well, if we have Chi-Chi Mamma all ready, I've got her bed ready."

"Ha, you are so funny," I shot back. Ava skipped into the bedroom after us.

"Chi-Chi Mamma," Ava sang out as she giggled.

Everett floated into the room. "What have you all taught this sweet child now?"

"We are just havin' a little 'ole anatomy lesson, Uncle Everett," Constance sang in her best southern belle drawl.

"Well, I'm going to take Ava and do a little shopping. Ev, are you going to be here a while?" Claudia asked as she finished tidying up in the room. Everett's eyes followed her every move…I watched him curiously. When he realized I was watching him, I could have sworn I saw him flush.

"My plan is to be here with her all day," he replied, taking the chair beside me.

"I think I'll come with you," Constance told Claudia as they left the room together.

"And what are you up to, today?" I asked, sensing Everett wanted to talk to me.

He leaned over, looking out the door and then rose to close it. Pulling his cell from his pocket, he sat back down in the chair beside me.

"Bebe, this is a secured cell. It's for Gabriella only. Just hit "one," and send. It's her speed-dial. If you are up for it…she really needs to talk to you. Since you can't go and see her today maybe you can help her by phone."

"Why? Has something happened?" I asked, worried about her.

"She just called me a little while ago, and she seemed emotional. I'm going to give you some privacy," he replied. He rose and placed a kiss on my forehead before he left the room.

I dialed her number and waited. She answered on the first ring.

"Everett?" she said breathlessly.

"No, it's Chandler, Brie. What's going on with you?"

"Oh, Chandler! I've been so worried. Ev told me about last night," she said, almost sobbing.

"Brie, I'm fine. I just have to stay in bed, for now. What's wrong? Why are you upset?"

50

"Andie, can we talk…I mean, on the phone?"

"Sure! Brie, what is it?"

"I…I tried what you suggested…I tried it last night…"

"Go on, Brie. You can tell me. You can tell me anything."

"Well, I looked at all John's pictures. I miss him so much! And you know, after you are bitten how your feelings…how out of control everything is," she said.

"Um, yes, I understand what you are saying. Go on," I urged her.

"It wasn't long before I was so…and looking at him, his body…remembering how he was, what he would do to me…I decided I could handle it. So I used what you brought me, you know…the battery thing," she said, embarrassed.

"It's all right, Brie…go on."

"It was so intense. And…" she began sobbing so hard I couldn't understand her.

"Brie! It's all right…calm down."

"My fangs…Chandler, it was awful. I can't. He would never understand," she cried inconsolably into the phone.

"Oh, Brie. Don't you think eventually you can learn to control them, just like when you are thirsty?"

"No, you don't understand. I'm like a monster," she whispered into the phone. "The venom…it's so gross. It's awful. I'm like a salivating dog. I couldn't control it, and it drips…he can't see me like this," she sobbed. "This is never, ever going to work. He can't see me like this! Ever!"

"Oh, Brie…listen to me! We can get through this. This was just the first time you tried it. Brie, are you there?"

"Yyyess," she stammered as she answered me.

"Please, Brie. Will you keep trying, for John? Brie, you just have to. John is grieving so hard for you, and he is inconsolable. We have to do this for him. I've never seen anyone mourn for someone the way he has for you. You just have to get better, so we can tell him. Please? Will you do this for John?"

After a long pause, she drew a ragged breath. "Yes, for John."

"Good girl. I'll call you tomorrow and check on you. Call Ev if you need me," I told her.

"Okay, Andie. I will," she replied.

"I love you, Brie. Get better because I need you too," I whispered.

"Oh, I love you too. Bye."

I laid the phone down on my chest and sighed. I wondered if her experience was really as repulsive as she said it was, or if she was being overly sensitive and hard on herself. After several moments, Ev came back into the room.

"Ev, did I do the right thing, urging her to try this? Or did I make it worse?"

"Oh, Bebe…who knows? We have to try something, or she won't ever try to come back to him. Let's just give her some more time. That is the one thing we seem to have plenty of," he said as he shook his head.

I wrapped my arms around my tummy, and then circled my abdomen with the palms of my hands.

"Yes, I guess so," I sighed.

Everett settled down on the bed beside me and pulled me into his side.

"So now that we need to keep you down again, what would you like to do to pass the time?"

I cocked an eyebrow at him and decided now was the time to pump him for information.

"You can entertain me with some trivia about yourself. Ev, have you ever been in love?" I widened my eyes and gave him my best attempt at a true southern belle pout. Evidently, it wasn't good enough.

"That would not be a very entertaining story, Ma Petit. That's a story better left for an afternoon of mourning. What else can we talk about?" he urged, kissing me on top of my head.

"Ev, you mentioned once you thought Lucien was after you and wanted to hurt someone you love. Why do you think that?"

"I don't think…I know. He is evil, pure and simple."

"But why you? What is your history?" I continued to urge him, sensing he might open up today.

"My father. It has to do with my father," he answered finally.

"And he was an Aldon? You said he drank," I added, remembering our conversation long ago when he told me a little about his family.

52

"He was an Aldon, of sorts…or he tried to be for a time…" he trailed off sadly.

"What do you mean, he tried to be?" I asked curiously.

His brow furrowed deeply as he seemed to be reaching far in the past.

"My father was a renegade, card-playing ladies' man. Around 1840, he was working the Mississippi, jumping from steamboat to steamboat making a small fortune at playing cards. He met my mother on a trip into N'awlins at a party. They fell in love, and his plan was to go out one more time on the river and make enough gambling that he could marry her and settle down. On his trip back, he was attacked by Orcos in a river town and left for dead. He transformed," he tried to continue, but I interrupted.

"He wasn't born an Aldon? He was human?" I asked incredulously.

"No, he was human, until the attack. He went through a painful transformation by himself out in the swamps. An old Creole woman, who was Sange-Mele, found him still battling, and sensed he already hated himself and what he had become. She helped him to hunt and to curb his appetite with small animals and animal blood. Her brother came to visit her and vowed to help my father as he was a Sange-Mele as well. He had a friend who was Aldon, and they brought my father back to N'awlins to work with him. The friend who helped to work with him was Mr. George, my mother and grandmother's butler.

"That's some coincidence," I muttered. He glanced over at me.

"No, he didn't work for them then. He didn't know my mother and grandmother at the time. He was a young man, and he lived with other Aldon. They worked with my father, until they were sure he had the control of an Aldon. Then they let him return to my mother. He was truthful with her, and Grandmother Wellington was quite impressed with everything he'd gone through to be reunited with her. They soon married, and mother gave birth to Evangeline first, then me. Everything seemed fine, until there was an attack one day from two boys down the road from our house. They were trash, and while my father was gone they broke into the house and raped my mother and Evangeline." His voice softened, his eyes staring off in the distance.

I drew my breath in...poor Mrs. Henrietta! I was nauseated, sickened at the picture in my head. As I studied Everett, I sensed an inner struggle and regret. "Everett, how old were you when this happened?"

"Six or seven."

"Were you there when it happened? Did you witness any of it?" I asked quietly.

"Yes. I was there. I was so young, and I couldn't do anything except hide my eyes! I've always wished I had been older, that I could have fought them,"

I placed my arms around his shoulders and pulled his head over on my shoulder.

"Oh, Ev...a boy that young, even an Aldon, couldn't have done anything."

"I know. I've come to terms with that, over these many years. It's my father's reaction which still troubles me. He returned home and of course, became enraged. He lost the control he'd worked so hard to achieve. He went on a rampage, and he attacked the two boys and their family, leaving them all for dead.

I studied his reaction curiously. "Ev, I certainly understand his reacting that way. If it happened to me, to our girls...Banton would certainly do the same."

He shook his head. "No, after that. When he came back to us, he was changed. Drinking human blood did something to him. He began to drink, and to stay gone for longer and longer periods of time. He lost control of his inner beast. Nothing my mother did seemed to bring him back to us. Grandmother Wellington can be somewhat trying at times, and when he lost control with her, he bit her, transforming her. Mother ordered him out of the house. We haven't seen him since."

"Oh, Everett...how traumatic!" I reached out and cupped his cheek in the palm of my hand.

"So your father transformed your Grandmother. What about your mother?"

"She transformed much earlier when they were first married. He lost control, in a fit of passion, you might say. It was an accident."

"Oh." I could tell he was a little embarrassed to tell me. "I'm confused. How does all this tie in with Lucien?"

"Lucien was one of the brothers who attacked my mother and sister. My father bit them and left them for dead. Only, they didn't die. My family and anyone who I love, they seem to become a target. This has just resurfaced since I met you. I hadn't seen Lucien since I hunted him, long ago."

"Why did you hunt him?' I asked, studying him again as he seemed to be a million miles away.

"Oh, Bebe…that's a story better left for another day. I have already told you enough for a novel's worth. Just chew on all of it and write it down. Change the names, of course…"

"Of course! You really don't mind if I work it into a story?" I asked disbelievingly.

"It was another lifetime ago. No one would believe it, anyway." He paused, and then smiled his handsome, all-knowing Aldon smile. "C. Collins Gastaneau, Supernatural Author."

"Hmm. It does have a certain ring to it, doesn't it?"

After he left me to check on Beau and fix us some lunch, I pulled my laptop out and checked for messages. Nothing from Banton.

I settled down and then lost myself in journaling everything Everett had revealed. I was engrossed in the story for at least two hours before I drifted off, the computer still perched on the baby-bundle.

Chapter Four

The middle of June marked seven months of pregnancy and over a month since I'd seen Banton. Sensing my frustration, Everett and John made it a point to carry me anywhere in the house they thought might lift my spirits and break up the boredom. My favorite place to be was on the front porch in the early morning, while the dew still kissed the kudzu and the oppressive heat remained at bay until at least eleven o'clock. John would carry me down the stairs and place me on the front porch swing, where I spent the morning watching Constance teach Ava Grace the finer points of hopscotch and stair-hop.

This morning my trip down brightened my day tremendously. Smiling, I pushed the porch swing off with my foot, the motion soothing my jangled nerves. It had been a week since we'd heard anything from Banton and Ty. Constance sat beside me, sharing my mood.

I thought of Banton and something he said in one of our last conversations. *Baby, I miss you too. The one thought that makes me smile, that keeps me going, is thinking about you...holding your tummy, rocking my babies on our front porch swing...waiting for me to come home. I love that picture...the one I have in my head.*

I smiled even bigger. I hoped I would have warning as to when he would come home. I planned to wait for him right in this spot, to give him the picture in his head.

Ava Grace giggled as she ran up and down the stairs to our front porch, singing the little ditty Constance and I had taught her the morning before. I was so glad she and Claudia had come to stay with us; she made the house so much happier and warmer with Banton gone. Ava had blossomed the eight months since her mother had died, and the shyness had totally disappeared. She was a typical, precocious three-year-old, and I was overjoyed to know I'd helped in her transition.

"An Andler, can I teach my babies to pway hopscotch wike Aba?" she called out. She jumped at the end of her little chalk boardwalk Constance had drawn for her.

"They will be too little at first, Doodle-Bug, but when they get bigger." Claudia answered her as she hopped back toward her. She giggled as Claudia swept her up into a big hug, covering her little face with kisses.

Everything became silent…a static, strange sort of silence. The leaves on the trees stilled. A hush fell over everything. No car horns honked, no motors sounded. The birds ceased to chirp, and a shadow fell across the entire street, the lawn, and up to the front steps.

Everything stalled into a kind of a slow motion, a time warp, of sorts, where voices slowed and sounded like they had been stretched. There was a ringing of the ears, like a different frequency you can't quite pick up. Sounds began to intrude, coming from an alternate universe. Car doors slammed, and then I detected the sound of footsteps on the pavement. One pair, then two, then three. I raised my eyes, and my brain began to scream out, *NO! NO! This is not happening.*

A dark navy-blue Suburban with a United States Navy logo was parked across the street. Three uniformed officers made their way up the sidewalk to where the three of us sat motionless. One of the men wore a chaplain's collar.

This was not happening. I'll wake up soon, and I'll laugh, and roll out of bed. Wake up, Chandler…Wake up…

"Is one of you Mrs. Gastaneau?" The first officer asked us. I heard Claudia's sharp intake of breath as she cuddled Ava closer to her chest.

"Yes. I'm Chandler Gastaneau," I replied in a whisper, barely audible. I grasped the chain on the porch swing so tightly my hand began to bleed. I stood, sensing I needed to brace myself.

"Mrs. Gastaneau, we regret to have to inform you, your husband and two of his SEAL team are missing, presumed dead. We can't give you any details yet, someone with family services will contact you tomorrow with more details. The Navy extends our deepest condolences, Ma'am, and we ask you call us, if there is anything we can do. I'm so sorry."

Missing, presumed dead. Presumed dead. Dead. The Chaplain came forward, and asked if we could go in and sit down. I realized I was shaking from head to toe, and I couldn't put a name to the sensation. Oh, it was rage. That's what it was. *Find your voice, Andie. He expects a response.*

"You can leave a card with us, Chaplain. I'm sure I have questions, I just can't think right now..." I whispered.

"Which other two SEALs are missing?" Constance asked, gripping my hand.

"We can't say, Ma'am, until we know their next-of-kin have been notified."

"*All of us* who live in this house **ARE** their next of kin!" Constance exploded as I began to weep silently. "You can give me some names, or you can limp back to that car! Your choice..." she threatened, choking back sobs.

The second officer cleared his throat, clearly shaken. "Lieutenants Ty Preston and Ben Oakley. I'm sorry, Miss. I'm truly sorry."

The Chaplain leaned in to give his card to Claudia, and then they turned to leave.

I continued to sob silently, turning to go into the house. Claudia picked Ava up and followed as Constance pulled me into her arms. As I reached the bottom of the stairs, I sank to the floor.

"NOOOOO!" I screamed, breaking apart inside. "NOOOOOO! He can't leave me like this, he promised me..." I looked up at both of them, their faces twisted with grief like my own. "He can't leave me with these babies! He has to come back; I can't live without him!" I continued to scream.

Constance took charge and pulled me up to help me up the staircase. I heard the door slam behind us.

"Bebe, what's going on...what is all the commotion?" Everett hurried through the door, searching our faces as the horror dawned on him. "Oh, no..."

"Banton, Ty, and Ben. They're gone. Missing, presumed dead." Claudia whispered. I continued to sob. Everett picked me up and turned to Claudia. "I'm taking her upstairs. Have you called your parents yet?" he asked her softly.

"Oh, my God..." the realization of the conversation she'd have to have dawned on her. Everett turned then and hurried up the staircase with me.

He placed me on the bed and then went into the bathroom. I curled up into a tight ball, trying to hold myself together. My mind went numb. I had a déjà-vu kind of feeling, like when my parents had died. My mind began to separate from my heart, a strange, funny sensation, like a coping mechanism. I remembered the sensation...like I couldn't find my feelings.

Everett came back to the side of the bed with a wet washrag. He sat down on the edge of the bed and began to bathe my face.

"Bebe, what do you know? What did they say?"

I lay silently. I couldn't find my voice, couldn't feel anything. I just lay there like stone. Everett rose and met Constance at the doorway.

"I called mom and dad. They're on their way. Everett, you'd better call John. I don't know if he knows."

"All right. You stay in here with her," Everett instructed.

I could hear Everett outside in the hallway as John picked up on the other end.

"John, I...I'm not sure how to say this. I have some bad news..." He began. "It's about Banton...yes, you've heard the report. No, I haven't been watching the news...No, it's Banton, Ty and Ben. They're missing, presumed dead. The Navy just showed up here, and informed Chandler and Constance... Yes, please. I think she needs you now. They both do," Everett spoke quietly into the phone as he pushed the door open, glancing in at us. Constance lay on the bed beside me holding one of my hands, sobbing and stroking my hair back from my face. I lay like stone, feeling nothing.

Everett flipped his phone shut, and then walked back into the room. I could hear Claudia sobbing downstairs, trying to break the news to their parents. Ava Grace began to wail, trying to get Claudia's attention. Everett hurried out of the room, apparently moved to help Claudia with Ava.

Constance rose and walked silently over to the television on the wall, flipping it on as she turned to me.

"There's something on TV," she began. "Do you want to see?"

I continued to lie like stone, feeling nothing.

The news reports were just beginning to come in, a Navy gunship, blown up by short range missile fire. What was left of the ship was featured on every news station, CNN, FOX, CNBC, and Headline News...Every station the same story. *Casualty reports are yet to come in...came under attack without warning...missiles fired from the coastline...some Navy SEALS missing, presumed dead.* The names were being held pending notification of the next of kin. Constance flipped through the channels, scanning the news stories.

"They could be wrong," she said. "They said missing, presumed dead. They don't know for sure," she sobbed as she continued to flip, her eyes glued to every image of every angle of the burning debris.

I continued to lie like stone. I felt nothing.

"Bebe, John is here, he wants to see you," Everett began. John pushed through the door behind him, and hurried over to the bed. He pulled me up into his arms like a rag doll, holding me closely.

"Andie-girl, I'm so sorry. I can't believe it...I'm here. I'm so sorry," he repeated, over and over again, his voice racked with sobs. He kissed the top of my head as he held me close to his body. "Chandler, talk to me," he pulled me back to see my face. I was terrified to look up into his eyes. John's eyes would make it all real.

"Chandler!" John shook me slightly. I slowly raised my eyes, and met his tortured gaze.

"He's gone," was all I could say. The tears began to pour, then. My chest ached, my insides ached. There was a hole that opened wide, nothing in the world, no amount of time, not even eternity could heal. I was gone, too, gone with him.

"When he died, he took everything," I whispered.

John pulled me back against his chest, and held me tightly. I couldn't respond. I couldn't hug him back. I couldn't feel anything but an empty burning ache.

John eased me back down across the pillows and continued to stroke my arm as he watched the news reports. I cried silently until there were no tears left to shed. Then I became like stone again. Like when my parents died. Someone had to move me – I had no will of my own. After an hour or so, I fell into an exhausted slumber.

I floated through the clouds, over the river, and down the mighty Mississippi for miles and miles. The river rolled, ebbed and flowed as the trees hung their branches out down low as if they wanted to catch a drink. The moss hung down from the trees in curtains, concealing what lay at the water's edge. Being able to fly was exhilarating, and a feeling of euphoria washed through me as I glided easily wherever I wanted to go. But where? I was confused. I wanted to go somewhere but I'd lost my way. Banton, where was he? I couldn't find the house, I couldn't find him. I landed, walking by the edge of the river as a tree stump floated by, and turned over in the current. Not a tree branch, but a man...Banton's face stared at me, his skin a sickly ashen gray, his eyes dead black, lifeless...

I gasped and sat up in bed. I blinked hard; I couldn't focus my swollen eyes. It was dark in the room, *where was I?* Then I remembered as I heard sobs in the next room, the subdued voices down the staircase. Everett's voice drifted in and out among others I recognized the familiar voices of Sam and Patrick...Mr. Jackson answered someone. His lyrical Cajun accent was somehow like a warm hug. It was so like him to come to the house when he sensed a crisis. I sank back into the pillows and wanted to die. I wanted to be with Banton.

There was a knock at the door. "Bebe, are you awake?" Everett pushed the door open, and Beau pushed his way into the room and padded over to the side of the bed, laying his head on the mattress beside me.

"Sweet Bebe, Banton's parents are here. They want to see you. Is it all right if I send them up?" he asked, sitting down beside me.

"Umm," I tried to clear the hoarseness from my throat, and then whispered to him. "Yes."

Claudia came in first, her face swollen from the shedding of tears and unbearable grief. Mrs. Elaine was ashen, all of the color gone from her beautiful complexion. She seemed more in shock than anything else. Mr. Matt appeared to be in control. The only clue to his grief was his red-rimmed eyes.

"Chandler, Sweetheart…" Mrs. Elaine flew to my side, and I threw my arms around her neck. As she sobbed into my neck, Mr. Matt sat down slowly on the other side of the bed.

"Everett says you haven't eaten or drank anything since you heard the news. You have to at least drink something, Sweetheart…for the babies…" Mrs. Elaine whispered to me as she pushed a strand of my hair back behind my ear. *Just like my mother used to do.*

"I can only imagine what this is doing to you. This is harder for you than any of the rest of us. Sweetheart, there are some decisions to be made; we have to make some arrangements…" Mr. Matt began, his voice breaking.

"No," I looked up at him.

"All right, we…we can talk in the morning. Our pastor is coming from N'awlins in the morning, and we can make arrangements then…"

"No!" I said louder.

"Chandler…" Claudia began, in a reasoning tone.

I wasn't having any of that. "I said, no. Not until they find him. He's only missing. I won't do anything while he's only missing. They could still find him, he's not dead…" I stared at them. "He's not dead. He's alive. Like Sam. He's ALIVE! He's NOT DEAD!" I screamed at them to understand me.

"Bebe, calm down. Shhh. Calm down, please," Everett pleaded, pushing around Mrs. Elaine to comfort me. Mr. Matt began to sob softly. Claudia put her arms around him and pulled him from the room. John came running up the stairs as he heard my outburst.

"What's wrong? What happened?" Everett glanced up at him, shaking his head.

"Banton's parents tried to talk to her about arrangements, and she won't…" he began.

"HE'S NOT DEAD! He's only missing! Why won't any of you believe me?" I screamed, grabbing my stomach as pains shot across my abdomen. I gasped and fell over, curling into a ball. I tried to stop the onslaught of pain.

"I think we need to call Doc. Maybe he can give her something," John said, sitting down on the bed beside me.

Banton's mother followed Everett out of the room as I let John pull me into his arms. He eased back into the pillows, pulling me up to rest on his chest. I continued to catch my breath as spasms broke across my abdomen and lower back.

"What's wrong? Are you hurting?" he asked, stroking my hair.

I sucked in my breath as another pain hit. "Yes, I'm…I think I'm in labor," I managed to gasp, my voice breaking on my sobs.

"Oh, God," John pulled my face up to look at me. "Hold on, Andie-girl, we're going to get you to Doc Lane's." He picked me up off the bed and flew down the staircase, my head buried in his neck.

"Everett! Ev!" John yelled as he reached the front door.

"John, where are you going with her?" Everett exclaimed. He, Claudia and Constance rushed into the entry. I glanced over John's shoulder and noticed Mr. Jackson standing silently inside the living room, twisting his hat in his hands.

"I'm taking her to Doc. Help me, Everett. I need for you to call ahead. Tell Doc she's in labor."

"Oh, no. It's way too early," Constance interrupted.

"I know. Come on, Ev, hurry!" John insisted as Everett opened the front door. John ran down the steps and over to his truck. Everett opened the back door, and John slid into the seat with me in his lap. He handed Everett the keys, and Everett ran around to get into the driver's seat. As he started the motor, Constance opened the passenger door.

"I'm coming with you!" she exclaimed, crawling into the front seat.

I had no concept of time, just that I was in pain. My head felt as though it was exploding with thoughts and memories I couldn't bear to dwell on. Pains continued to draw my stomach into contractions, and my back ached horribly. The physical pain I could stand. The mental pain was unbearable. My mind began to slip, leaving reality behind. Banton…I closed my eyes, and I could see him like the last time I'd studied his face. It was so clear…the shadow of stubble on his face as he gazed at me on the computer screen, the way his lashes curled against his lower lids, the flecks of gold in his eyes, his deep, soft sexy voice…*"Baby, I have to go now. I'll meet you later, in our dreams…"*

63

I drifted. I was warm and comfortable. No longer in pain, I was in a sort of restful limbo. Sleep… peaceful, dreamless sleep. The numbness was tolerable. I couldn't remember why I was supposed to be hurting. I was just relieved I wasn't any more. I slept and slept.

* * *

Slowly but surely I began to wake. Someone stroked my cheek. I could smell his cologne, a familiar guy smell. He stroked his thumb across my cheek, up my jaw line, and whispered softly in my ear.

"I'm here, Chandler. I'm here. Sweetheart, I'm here."

"Banton." I opened my eyes and turned my head toward him.

John's eyes filled with tears as he answered me. "No, Andie-girl. It's not Banton. It's me. I'm sorry," he continued to stroke my cheek as he spoke.

"How are you feeling?" Constance's voice came from across the room.

I just turned and stared at her. She looked like hell.

She continued, "You've been asleep quite a while. The doctor put you on a drip to stop the contractions. You're all right for now, and the babies are good. Momma and Daddy just left to go back home and clean up and change."

"How long have I been asleep?" I asked groggily. I didn't even recognize the sound of my own voice.

"Twenty-four hours," she replied.

"Has there been any…any more news?" I asked, searching both their faces.

"Just confirmation the Navy only found a few survivors. They found Colin and he's on a Navy hospital ship. He's going to be fine. I talked to his sister last night," she explained quietly.

"Has anyone talked to him? What about the others?" My voice rose, my heart beating faster. The monitors attached to me went wild.

"Shhh, Andie, stay calm, please, or we will have to give you something to calm you down," John pleaded as he rested his head down across his hand, resting it just beside mine.

64

"He remembers seeing Banton and Ty, just before..." her voice broke. "He didn't offer much hope," she finished.

"But they haven't found their bodies. They haven't found them," I insisted.

"No, Chandler. They haven't found them," John answered, moving his hand to rest beside my cheek.

I lay my head back silently and took a deep breath. Denial was my new strategy. I had to hold on, just had to keep him alive, in my own mind. I had to, for me and for his babies.

Taking a deep breath, I decided to plunge forward. It was time to wake up. "What does the doctor say, about the babies?"

"They're good. We've made it to twenty nine weeks. He wants to try to hold you till we can get them to thirty-four. Their lungs have a much better chance," Constance answered me in a much cheerier voice. She rose and crossed the room to the side of my bed.

"Well, I guess I'd better get going again on the nursery. I don't have much time left. We've got furniture to put together," John grinned at me just like Banton used to.

I had to look away. It hurt too much to look John in the face. It seemed as though he were trying to take Banton's place. I couldn't stand it.

"Mrs. Elaine and Mr. Matt want you to call them, when you feel up to it. They've been so worried, and they were here all day yesterday. We need to call and update them," she answered.

"Have they, I mean, did they insist on...on making arrangements?" I whispered.

"Yes, they did. They've planned a memorial service in conjunction with Ty's father at their church on Friday morning. They're hoping you'll be able to go."

"No, I'm not going. I'm not." I fixed my eyes on the window and watched the rain as it ran down the panes.

"All right, Sugar. We'll talk about it later."

"Constance, if you want to go home and rest, take my truck. I think I'll camp out here with Andie a while. You look tired," he commented.

"I guess I need to. I need to call Momma and Daddy to let them know I'm coming home. We'll all be back tonight."

"Don't rush, Constance. You need to rest. I'll be fine. John's here with me," I insisted as she leaned over to kiss my cheek.

"Okay, I'll call you when I get home. I love you, darlin'," she said, turning to leave.

"I love you too," I whispered. John rose from the side of the bed, and walked over to the doorway, intercepting Constance as she started to leave. He took her in his arms. I'd never seen them embrace before. Her shoulders shook with sobs as she held him close.

"I'm here for you, Diva Doll. We'll get through this together. I love you, you know," he pulled back and smiled at her.

"I love you too, John. Bye."

He shut the door gently, and then turned back to me. "Can I get you anything?"

I turned my gaze back to him. I'd been watching the rain drizzle in zig-zag patterns down the windowpanes. "No, nothing. I'm fine."

He strode back over to the bed and commanded, "Scoot over. I'm coming in." He settled down beside me, pulling me over to rest my head on his chest. We lay like that the rest of the afternoon, saying nothing, just watching the rain outside the windows. He knew, and so did I, that there was nothing to say. Both of our lives had been ripped apart, and there was nothing we could do but hold each other.

*　*　*

Doctor Lane kept me in the clinic until Saturday, for observation and to keep me off my feet. I suspected he was also giving me an excuse not to have to make the decision about going to the memorial service for Banton, and I was relieved. I didn't want any more confrontations with Banton's family. They were resigned to his death, and I wanted them to stop pushing me. I was angry. I couldn't understand how they could just take everything at face value, when there was no body, and the Navy hadn't even declared Banton, Ty or Ben dead. Not in my mind, anyway. They all thought I just couldn't deal with the reality, but I just wasn't

66

convinced he was gone. As long as there was no body, there was still hope. I would not give in.

Aunt Sue and Uncle Lon took turns with Constance and John staying with me, reluctant to leave me alone. Saturday morning when Dr. Lane released me, everyone was on hand to bring me home, creating somewhat of a circus-like atmosphere. Even the evil cousins Cade and Drew were in the group cheer-up session. They were all smothering me.

"Come on, Andie! Let's get this show on the road. Waddle on through, and we'll get your bags," Cade teased as Drew picked my suitcases up and then tossed them one at a time into the hallway to Cade.

"I don't waddle!" I shot back, standing to stretch my back. I was definitely off balance these days, not used to all the weight out front, but I was determined I wouldn't show it as I walked. I was a little stiff and unsteady, having been on strict bed rest for days.

"Leave her alone, boys! She's doing fine." Everett steadied me at my elbow.

"If we hurry, we can catch the last three or four innings of the Rangers game on TV. Hey, Andie, we're actually pulling for a Texas team for a change."

"That's a first. I might even let you watch it on my TV," I offered. Cade grinned at me. He was trying too hard to be nice and keep the atmosphere light, and my eyes began to water at his effort.

"Well, I know she'll be glad to get home," John added, joining our little group on the way out to the car. "Beau's really missed you. He'll be glad you are back." He leaned over to kiss my forehead as he helped me into the car.

We made a little train down the interstate with Aunt Sue's SUV, Everett's car, and John's pickup. Everyone chattered away in Aunt Sue's car as I remained silent, falling into somewhat of a state of what I liked to call "hovering." I hovered over the conversation, the people there, my reactions. It was like I was watching the world around me, detached, too afraid of my responses to join in the world of the living. It was to be my state of being for the next several days.

67

I thought I'd be relieved to be home, but walking through the front door I found Banton's absence was everywhere. The house was the thing that brought us together, and it was as if the structure was in mourning as well as its inhabitants. Beau howled during the commotion of our arrival, and I spent a good deal of time holding and petting him, assuring him I wouldn't leave him for quite a while. After what I figured was an acceptable amount of time to visit with everyone, I made my excuses, and retired upstairs to our bedroom with him close at my heels. I sank down into the down comforter and pulled it up over me. I just wanted to disappear into it and block the world and consciousness away.

After a while, I heard the bedroom door open and shut, and then felt the mattress give way on Banton's side of the bed. I could smell Constance's perfume, and I turned over to her tear-stained face.

"When I'm in here with you, I feel...I feel like I did when Ty and Banton were deployed, and we were just waiting for them to come back to us... when we'd both sleep in here, Everett babysitting us. I like that feeling, like we just rewound the clock."

I pulled her into my chest and held her there. "I know. You are the one person besides John who understands how I feel. You are the one person who I can stand to share my feelings with. I just wish for your sake that wasn't the case. I'm sorry. I feel like your grief for Ty is lost in all the commotion over the grief for Banton, and everyone's concern for the babies," I whispered into her hair as she cried into my chest.

The babies chose that particular moment to try to change positions, and Constance got an elbow or knee in the side.

"Wow, I can't believe they are that strong! That's amazing!" She giggled through her tears. "The way they fight in there, it's just got to be twin boys. Oh, boy, they'll probably be just like Cade and Drew! What did you possibly do in a former life to deserve that?" She laughed again and wiped her eyes.

I just sighed and placed both hands across my large tummy, feeling the babies kick as they rolled inside. I couldn't wait for their arrival; the babies would be a place to channel all the love I had for Banton, which I couldn't give to him now.

"Knock knock, can I come in?" A voice came through the doorway.

"Yes, it's open," Constance called out. The door opened and John's face appeared.

"I just wanted to check on you two, and to see if Andie was sleeping." He crossed the room silently, and then sat down on the bed beside me.

"I was just resting. I can't sleep. I close my eyes, but I can't go to sleep," I lay watching Constance as I spoke to John; she just nodded, apparently having the same problem I had.

"So, what was all the giggling I just heard before I came in?" he asked, stretching out beside me.

"This." Constance grabbed his hand, and placed it against my tummy. The twins picked that exact moment to tumble around again, and he pulled his hand away slightly as he jumped and then grinned.

"Wow, that's amazing! Do they do that a lot? No wonder you can't sleep." He grinned as he watched my reaction.

"Yeah, they are pretty active the last few days. I imagine they are getting pretty cramped in there. Dr. Renault says according to the sonogram, the biggest one weighs about four pounds already, and by his calculations, if they continue to gain at this rate, they will be almost seven pounds each by the due date."

"That's really big, for twins, isn't it?" Constance asked, and I nodded.

"Doc thinks he might need to take them early, I think he's afraid you might pop!" John said.

"I might...I can't believe the stretch marks. My stomach will never be the same again!" I exclaimed, pulling the comforter back over my tummy.

"Oh, Andie-girl, give it up. You are still the most gorgeous brunette on the planet, pregnant or not! You know it used to drive Banton nuts, when you started all that *I'm so pregnant, I'm so out of shape* stuff." John paused and glanced down at me. The silence in the room was overwhelming. His use of Banton's name hung heavy in the air.

The tears began to appear silently in fresh streams down my cheeks.

"I'm sorry, Chandler. I'm…" John pulled me in to his chest as Constance began to sob, spooning her body behind mine. John pulled us both into his arms, and we lay holding each other the rest of the afternoon.

Chapter Five

"This just came for you, Chandler." Constance shut the front door and walked into the living room where I'd been camped out on the sofa for a week. I'd decided our bedroom had too many memories, and all of the Aldon in and out of the house helped to fill the empty void.

"What is it?" I asked, peering over the laptop screen.

"I don't know, a small box the postman just left out front with one of the Aldon," she replied as she placed it in my lap. Checking the label, I found nothing but my name and address. I tore the tab label across the end and a letter and DVD fell out.

"What's on that?" Constance asked as she picked them up.

I opened the letter, and read aloud.

> *Dearest Chandler:*
>
> *Banton's father and I want you to know we understand your feelings and we respect them. We love you so much; we were upset about your decision regarding Banton's service, but Sweetheart, we had to go on, and we had to have some closure. Matt and I planned the service at the suggestion of the Navy Chaplain and our own Pastor. We know the Doctor kept you in the hospital until Saturday, and whatever the reason, we don't want you to ever regret your decision not to attend. When you are ready, please call us. We want to come to see you. Until then, we are sending you a copy of the service provided to us by the Church. You may keep it, until you are ready for it.*
>
> *Claudia, Will, Ava Grace, Julia, Matt and I send our infinite love to you, and hope you will call us soon. We are worried about you and the babies.*
>
> *All our love,*
> *Elaine*

I folded the letter, and then placed it back into the cardboard envelope along with the DVD I retrieved from Constance.

Aunt Sue came around the back of the sofa. She'd been listening from the foyer. She sat down quietly beside me on the sofa and put her arms around me.

"Chandler Ann, don't you dare feel a bit guilty about not going. It was your decision, and we stand by you, Sweetheart. You are entitled to deal with this however you decide," she stated firmly as she looked into my eyes.

"Absolutely. I can't believe she would just send this and not come in person, or call." Constance shook her head.

"Oh, I don't think she meant it that way. I'm not angry with them anymore. I feel a little guilty. Not about my decision, but my not answering their phone calls. I just couldn't talk about having a service for Banton; he's not dead. They just don't believe it like I do. I know they love me." I began to tear up as I held the envelope.

"Well, I'll just take this and put it away. You can call them in your own time. You will know when you can handle it." She smiled and patted my leg as she rose.

"So, what are you working on now?" Constance asked, leaning over on my shoulder.

"I just thought I would organize my notes on the house and put it in a narrative. I want to write a history on the Johnson and DeLee families and a history on my house and the cemetery."

"I think that's neat, Andie. But, why now?" she asked, twirling a section of my hair that had fallen lose out of my pony-tail.

"I feel like I need to give the house closure. However mine and Banton's story ends, I want to have all the rest on paper. I…I think I might sell the house."

"What? Chandler, you love this house! It's you…you've put so much of yourself into it. I even feel like its home, now," Constance exclaimed. I pulled back and studied her face. It was so unlike her to become attached to something inanimate. And she had certainly never indicated she was in love with this old house. I raised an eyebrow at her.

"So, I'm attached. There, I said it. I've grown to love it here, and all of the people in it. And the memories I have here…" She began to tear up as well.

"That's exactly why I can't stay, if..." I couldn't finish the sentence. After a long pause, I added "It's a good project anyway, to keep me busy. Otherwise I think I would climb the walls!"

"What can I do to help?" Constance asked, sitting back upright again. "I need a diversion too."

"Well, there are some things I need cleared up, some things I think Mr. Jackson might still be able to help us with. Do you think maybe you might go down and see if he feels like walking down to visit? I could make us some lemonade, and I miss talking to him."

I shut my eyes, remembering the night the Navy had paid us the visit. Mr. Jackson had hurried right down and paid his respects, just before I was rushed to the clinic. I hadn't visited with him since.

"Sure, I'll just go and check on him, and if he doesn't feel up to it, just jot some questions down, and I'll take a recorder down to his place," she brightened up at the little assignment. She'd just stepped out the front door, when I heard it open again.

"Bebe, hellooo, you have visitors, are you up?" Everett called from the foyer. I popped my head above the sofa and waived to him.

"Oh, there you are. Ma Petit Bebe, you aren't supposed to be up! Whatever are we going to do with you?" Everett exclaimed as he came into the room. John, Sam and Patrick followed close behind him.

"I'm resting like I'm supposed to, and I'm staying off my feet. I just can't stay cooped up upstairs. I have to stay down here, around people." I paused, and then asked, "What are the four of you up to?"

"Well, since it's a lazy afternoon, we just thought we might get a little work done upstairs in the nursery."

"Yeah, I need a project, and we've got some little shelves to build, Andie-girl. We need plenty of places to store those mitts, baseball bats and Tonka trucks!" John grinned as he dropped down on the sofa beside me. He leaned over and pulled me into his chest, placing a kiss on the top of my head. *The hug felt really good*, I thought.

"Chandler, I need...Oh, hey, Everett, John...just who I need." Constance came breathlessly through the front door.

"What's up, Diva-doll?" John asked as he rose from the sofa.

"Mr. Jackson. I went down there and knocked and knocked, but I couldn't get him to the door."

"Maybe he went somewhere, or to the doctor," Sam answered.

"On a Sunday afternoon? I'm worried he might be sick and can't come to the door." She wrung her hands, and I began to get anxious. He was always there.

"We'll go down there and check on him for you. Come on, Cowboy. Let's go see about our sweet little neighbor."

The four of them left just as Aunt Sue came back into the living room. "I thought I heard voices," she inquired, wiping her hands on a cup towel.

"Yeah, I went down to check on Mr. Jackson and couldn't get him to come to the door. Everett, John, Sam and Patrick went down to see if they could get him," Constance answered her.

"Well, when they get back, invite all of them to dinner. I'll have etouffee ready in about thirty minutes."

Constance went upstairs to change clothes as I continued to work away on my laptop, organizing my existing notes in a narrative format. After a few minutes, Constance ran back down the staircase.

"Oh, no, Chandler, there's..." She didn't finish her sentence.

"What? I looked up. She crossed over to the window, pulling the curtains back.

She turned back to me, and then slowly walked back and sat down gently beside me, tears gathering in her eyes.

I glanced back over to the window, and realized Everett and the others had been gone a suspicious amount of time. Then I heard a siren.

"There's an ambulance at Mr. Jackson's apartment," she whispered softly, taking my hand in hers.

The front door opened silently, and then closed, Everett, John, Sam and Patrick returning home. I raised my eyes as the all came around the sofa, Everett and John kneeling in front of us.

"Oh, Sweet Bebe, I have some sad news. I'm so sorry; I don't know how to tell you, it's so untimely..." Everett began. I nodded, for I already knew.

"Darlin', we forced the door open when we couldn't get Mr. Jackson to the door. I could see him through a window. He was lying on his bed; he looked to be resting," John began. "When we got inside, we checked him and he'd passed away in his sleep. I don't think it had been long. He was still warm." He smiled gently and placed his hand on my cheek as I nodded, the tears streaming down my face.

"Andie-girl, I have to tell you something. Do you remember a while back when we visited with him?" I nodded again. "He'd said it was a lucky man who could die peacefully, surrounded by the sweet images and memories of your beloved...those you loved most in your life." John reached over and took my hands.

"Yes," I took a deep breath as I replied.

Everett finished for him. "Bebe, we found three pictures clasped in his hands...a picture of his wife from the living room wall; the picture of his children, and a picture of you, dancing with him at your wedding."

Everett embraced Constance as John pulled me from the sofa into his arms. He held me in his strong arms for hours that night as I cried for the loss of my dear, sweet friend.

* * *

Mr. Jackson's family held a small, graveside service for him. I was determined to go, and Everett finally relented after several arguments and phone calls to Dr. Lane. I donned the only black dress I had...a short, black sleeveless dress and black hose. I hadn't worn makeup in weeks, and I felt I owed it to Mr. Jackson to look my best. He'd said a body always needed to dress up for their loved ones and for the Lord on Sunday, if nobody else. So I curled my hair and took the time to put makeup and jewelry on.

I rode with Everett to the cemetery. It was a hot, sunny, beautiful July day, and as we rode along the shaded road to the burial site, I was thankful it was to be an early morning service, for the heat after noon would be oppressive. I wondered if Mr. Jackson had left a list of his wishes, or if his children just known exactly what he would have wanted. The casket was a plain wooden variety, with a simple swag of ferns, magnolia blossoms, and roses.

75

A lone trumpet played "When the saints go marching in" and "Lord, I'm coming home".

As I glanced up over a grassy knoll overlooking the site, I saw several of the Aldon who had been guarding our little neighborhood the past six months. Mr. Stephan was in their midst. Sam, Olivia and Patrick joined us as well as John and Constance. There were at least a hundred other people there besides his rather large gathering of children and grandchildren, and I thought, *you shouldn't be surprised, Andie...He was such a special man. Just look how he touched your life.*

When the crowd began to form a line to speak to Mr. Jackson's family, I walked down with Everett and John at my side. I waited patiently until I could speak to his daughter and Aunt Chloe, who stood by her side.

"Oh, Mrs. Chandler! It sho be good to sees you, even at a time like dis!" Aunt Chloe embraced me as Everett patted her shoulder.

"Mrs. Chloe, I'm so sorry about Mr. Jackson! I'm going to miss him so much," I assured her as Mr. Jackson's daughter took my hand.

"Are you the little lady down the street who Daddy told us about?" she asked as I nodded. "He sure did enjoy your "front porch sits" as he called them. It was so nice of you to check in on him when he was sick and all," she continued.

"It was my pleasure. He made my first year in the house a pleasant one, and he helped me so much with the history of the house. Everyone in our neighborhood will miss him!"

"I sho is sorry 'bout yo troubles, chile! Red tole us 'bout Mr. Banton done gone missin. You keep a'prayin to the good lord and study dat bible like I done tole ya. De Lord, he don't give us mo dan what we can handles."

I nodded at her and smiled through my tears.

"Well, we thanks you for a'comin' today! I'm sho dat he is a lookin' down from heaven, and a grinnin' at all these here folkses dat come to pay dey respects," Aunt Chloe replied as Everett took my hand. "You two will jes have to come and see me, chile, and let me knows when dem babies come...and stays strong, like I done told ya."

I whispered as I answered her, "I will...I promise."

76

After the service, we joined John and Sam and the others at my house, and Everett insisted we all go out to eat somewhere before they had to put me back on lockdown at the house.

"Let's go to that little Cajun place off-campus...I feel the need to suck the heads off some crawfish, laissez les bon temps rouler!" John whooped. We all loaded into the cars. I visited with Constance in the backseat, and it wasn't until we pulled up and started up the stairs to the little restaurant that it occurred to me where we were. I stopped cold...It was the restaurant Banton brought me to on our first date.

"Do you feel all right?" Constance asked as she turned to see why I'd fallen behind.

"Andie-girl, if you don't feel up to it, I can run you home so you can get off your feet, maybe this was too much for you," John commented as he hurried back to my side.

"No, I'm good. I just..." I began to tear up.

"What is it?" John looked back at the restaurant, and then back to me. "Oh, gosh, Andie, I'm so sorry!" His face had gone white. Apparently Banton had told him about our first date at some point.

"No, John, I promise, it's all right. Let's eat," I said, decidedly, climbing the stairs to go in. I was determined I was going to put all of these firsts behind me and get on with things. We entered the restaurant, finding most of our party had already been seated at the back part of the restaurant right by the windows looking out on the patio and the river. A jazz band played, and several couples danced on the dance floor. The memories of the little white dress I'd worn, Banton's hands on my bare back for the first time, our kiss on the dance floor that had almost made me pass out, the way he'd held me at the table...all came flooding back. I sat mesmerized, watching the couples as they swayed to the music. I could remember thinking that night, *If I die tonight, my life would be complete...I am so in love with him.*

"Andie?" Constance asked, peering over her menu at me.

"What?" I asked. Everyone looked up at me.

"The waitress is ready to take our order. Do you know what you want to order?" she asked softly as she pushed a glass of water over to me. I took a couple of swallows, and then since I hadn't even looked at my menu, I asked the waitress, "Do you have some sort of grilled chicken salad?"

"Sure, is that what you would like?"

"Yes, please." It was all I could think of, and I knew I wouldn't eat it, anyway. I'd had no appetite since the Navy visit.

Somehow I made it through dinner. I listened to the light chatter around me, and even managed to giggle a couple of times when Everett and John bantered back and forth across the table, sparring with the other Aldon and teasing Constance. Everett asked Constance to dance as the band picked up on a Dixieland number, and Sam and Olivia joined them. We laughed as we watched Everett and Constance. What he lacked in modern dance skills Constance more than made up for.

I was so tired; I hadn't really slept in days. As we drove back across town to go home, John pulled me over on his shoulder and I fell asleep. I roused slightly when I felt him lift me from the car…The smell of his cologne wafted through my head as he carried me into the house and up the stairs to put me in bed. I felt him place a soft kiss in my hair as he tucked the comforter around me. I feel into a deep sleep, deeper than I had since we'd gotten word of the accident. And I began to dream again…

I was back in the sewers. It was oppressively hot and muggy, and the stench was overpowering. Some light filtered through from above, and I could hear shuffling noises behind me. I pushed on, struggling to keep from getting sick from the heat and the stench in the air. A muffled cry broke the silence in the distance, and I began to run, kicking up water as I pushed forward. I turned a corner, and I saw them…my babies, tiny, helpless…in the arms of the Tariq. His teeth glistened in the shaft of sunlight streaming through the grating overhead. I flew at him, pulling one of the babies free, and turning to find somewhere to put her, so I could fight him for the other. He laughed and bent his head as if to bite the baby…

"NO!" I screamed. "Please, no, leave them alone! Take me; I'm the one you want! Please!" I pleaded as his teeth hovered over her.

"Give me the baby, Chandler, so you can fight him," My mother commanded from behind me. I turned and hurriedly handed my baby to her, and then flew at the Orco, grabbing the other baby and shoving him backward. My mother flew to my side, and took the second baby as I continued to fight the Tariq. I shouted to her, "Run, Mamma, get them to safety!"

I shoved him against the wall, and then he pushed me down, crushing me with his weight. He pushed my head downward, and then slammed it against the wall with the full force of his brute strength. I heard a crack, and I could feel the blood as it ran down my forehead and down to my shoulder.

"You may be a half-breed immune to the change, but you aren't immune to my feeding on you." He smiled and then sank his teeth into my shoulder, opening the old wound where he'd bitten me before. As he drank, my world began to swirl out of focus, and I lost the strength and the will to fight him. I realized my mother had the babies and if I just gave in, the Tariq could take me and I wouldn't have to miss Banton anymore...

Out of the darkness, I heard a familiar voice.

"Mrs. Chandler, don't you go a-givin in to dat trash Loogaroo, you got's to fight him. I won't let him win, you jes let me at him..." Mr. Jackson came out of the darkness, and swung a large two by four at the Tariq, striking him across the chest, causing him to release his hold on me. I sank down on the ground as Mr. Jackson continued to work him over. As the Tariq fell, Mr. Jackson pulled me from the ground, and then said firmly, "You wake up now, Mrs. Chandler. You's all right, now. Dem babies, dey be all right, too. I'm here, now, and I's ready to fight. I's gonna protect you, now, so you go on ahead. Go on, now, Chile..."

"Andie-girl, wake up. You're dreaming...Oh, God, Everett. Everett, get up here!" John shouted as he pulled me up into his arms. I opened my eyes, and his face hovered over me as he held my head in his hands.

"Can you hear me?" John asked as he frantically searched my eyes.

"Yeah, you're screaming, I hear you. What's wrong?" I asked, wincing. My head was throbbing with every sound.

"Andie, you are bleeding. How did you hurt yourself?" he asked disbelievingly.

"I didn't," I began as I touched the side of my head, feeling the gash and wet blood in my hair.

"Bebe...Oh, he's back, isn't he?" Everett asked from the doorway.

"He who? What the hell is going on?" John demanded.

"The Tariq. He stalks her in her dreams. I thought they'd stopped, and she had control. I guess we were wrong," Everett said as John examined my head.

He leaned back and called to Constance. "Bring me something to clean the wound and a bandage or sterile pad. I don't think she needs a stitch, Everett?" John asked as Everett bent over me to examine the wound.

"No, I think she'll be all right. The blood looks worse than it really is. Head wounds tend to bleed a lot." He stood back and looked into my eyes. "How is your vision?"

"Fine. I'm fine. My head just throbs a little," I replied.

"Banton told me, when we were in N'awlins, that Andie had a stalker in her dreams, but I didn't realize..." John began.

"We'd been staying with her, either Banton or me, when she sleeps. We can usually wake her before the Tariq hurts her. I guess we'll have to keep better watch," Everett answered as Constance came back into the room, with the clean cloths and bandages. When she had me cleaned up and placed a bandage on the side of my forehead, John sat down beside me.

"What is that smell? It smells like sewer," he wrinkled his nose in disgust.

"It is. That's where we were, in the dream," I answered.

"And your mother was there," Everett added. "I can smell her perfume."

John turned and gawked at Everett.

"There was someone else there too, this time," I replied softly. "Constance, you were right." I began to tear up as I told them.

"Right about what, Andie?" Constance asked.

"About no one who is living is ever in my dreams. My mother took the babies, so I could fight the Tariq, like she always does. But when I started to lose the fight, Mr. Jackson showed up. He fought him, so I could get away," I continued to cry as I glanced up at them. John sat down beside me on the bed and pulled me into his side, stroking my arms to comfort me.

John continued to stay close, not letting me out of his sight. Constance went to bed early. I dozed on the bed, Everett watching me from a chair across the room, John beside me, lounged out on the bed. They spent the evening watching a baseball game on the television, bantering back and forth as they always did with their sports trivia. At bedtime, Everett's phone signaled a text.

"Oh, my fannie-ass, here's another emergency," Everett announced, reading the text.

'What's the matter?" John asked.

"Oh, nothing…just an Aldon thing. I need to leave for a while. Can you stay here with Chandler?" he asked as he started out the door.

"Sure, no problem. I have nowhere to go," John answered, glancing down at me. He didn't realize I was awake. I lay studying his face.

"I'm sorry, John. I can get up and find something to do till Ev gets back. The Aldon are outside. I'm protected," I stated, not wanting him to have to stay on my account.

"No way. I'm staying. Besides, there isn't anywhere else I'd rather be, I promise." He pulled me in to hug me and kissed the top of my head. The shirt I wore slid off my shoulder, and the bite mark that had transformed me was visible, the jagged edges of the bite looking fresh since the dream.

I glanced back up at John, and he lifted his hand toward me I felt my breath catch. He looked angry as he slowly traced the outline of the mark with his index finger. My skin burned where his fingers lingered. When he looked back into my eyes, my heart beat faster and my mouth was dry as though I were having a panic attack. I felt so strange. I'd never felt uncomfortable with John near, but now the closeness felt different.

"Andie, is something wrong?" John asked, studying me.

"No, no. Everything is fine," I assured him as I took a deep breath. He reached up and pushed a stray strand of hair back behind my ear.

"I can hear your heartbeat. Are you frightened?" he urged, his brow furrowed.

"No, I'm fine. I just feel badly, I mean…you having to watch over me. The place is like Fort Knox, and well, the dream thing…I can find plenty to do till Everett gets back. He's used to having to watch me, and he doesn't sleep anyway."

John pulled back to look at me. "I was serious, Andie, when I said there was no place I'd rather be. This feels like home, and I'm not lonely when I'm with you. Sometimes, I can't stand going down to our house alone at night. In the daytime it's not so bad. I'm enjoying the remodel. But at night…I really miss Brie at night. I'm good when I'm here with you." He leaned over and kissed me softly. I was so startled, I hardly breathed as he continued. "I love you, you know. You've been such a good friend, and you've been babysitting me in a way. So it's good for both of us." He slid his hand lightly down my check, caressing my skin with his fingers. I fought the desire to lean into his touch.

"Then I'm glad…" I stammered, still not knowing what to say. His kiss had been like the kind between best friends, but my reaction wasn't. *What was wrong with me?* I was so lonely. I missed Banton so much tonight it hurt. John continued to flip channels, settling on an old romantic black and white movie. Normally, it would have been my favorite kind of movie to watch, but lately I couldn't stand to watch anything involving love or romance. It just made me sad. My chest began to ache like it had a large hole in it. I shut my eyes and silently began my nightly crying jag, snuggling down for the night.

"Andie, are you hurting? What's wrong?" John asked, stroking my bare shoulder.

"I'm…nights are just hard. I do this, sometimes," I replied softly.

He pulled me back into his chest and wiped the tears from under my eyes. "I'm here, Andie. I'm not going anywhere. I don't want you to ever feel like you're alone. I'm here for you, darlin'." He pulled my hair back and placed a soft kiss on my neck as he laid his cheek against mine on the pillow. His nearness was comforting, and I allowed myself to relax. I finally drifted off to sleep.

Several hours later, I woke to the sound of John whispering softly in my ear.

"Chandler, I think maybe I need to move."

My eyes snapped open as I realized the problem. My head lay on his shoulder, and I had my knee hitched across John's midsection, much like Banton and I had always slept. The rather large bulge I felt under the inside of my thigh let me know our position was just a little too intimate for good friends.

"Oh, John, I'm so sorry," I offered hastily as I removed my leg and rolled on my side. I was so embarrassed, I was sure he could see my red face even in the darkness.

"No, I'm sorry I don't have better control," John chuckled in the darkness. "I'm just a guy, after all. You don't have to move that far, it's all right." He pulled my shoulders back toward him, and put his arm around me as he kissed me on the forehead. "I'm sorry I woke you, go back to sleep, Andie-girl."

Yeah, like that was going to happen now. I was so embarrassed. I didn't know how I was going to face him in the daylight. Thankfully, Everett showed up about ten minutes later.

"Sorry, Bebe. That took longer than I thought. I'm back now, so I'll take over now, John. You go home and get some sleep," he commented as he plopped down on the air mattress beside the bed, book in hand.

"Yeah, guess I'd better get going. I'll see you tomorrow, Andie. Call me if you need anything. I can be here in two minutes." He leaned over and kissed me lightly on the lips.

"Kay. Night, John," I replied. He strode out the door, shutting it behind him.

"Everything all right, Bebe?" Everett asked.

"Um, yeah, why?" I asked.

"Just checking. There was quite the static electricity in the atmosphere. Just seemed a little strained when I came in, that's all."

"Ev, how could you possibly..." I began.

83

"Oh, it's that Aldon – taste the turn of your emotions and thoughts thing, that's all. Is everything all right between you and John?"

"Yes, Ev...goodnight!" I exclaimed. Everett chuckled in the darkness.

Chapter Six

Now I really began to feel like I was living in a fish bowl. Everett said fighting the Orcos was easier than trying to keep me in the bed lying flat. There was always someone with me, and while the Aldon continued their patrols at the house, Everett watched over me when I slept. Aunt Sue was back and forth between Denham Springs and my house, spending as much time as she could with Constance and me. Constance was having a hard time, for her grief at Ty's disappearance had hit her full-force. She cried herself to sleep most nights, and Aunt Sue was wearing herself out trying to take care of us and snap us out of our depression.

All of this confinement was not helping my depression. I was sick of staying in the house and having people waiting on me. I was so bored, and determined I wouldn't let myself wallow in grief and Banton's absence. I'd even planned my schedule for the fall semester, and then looked the reading lists of novels and short stories up on the computer for the literature class I'd planned to take. I was well into the third novel, when Constance approached me one hot July afternoon.

"Knock knock, are you sleeping?" Constance murmured, peeking around the door to my room.

"No, I'm not allowed to sleep unless Ev is up here with me. Come in. I thought you'd gone shopping with Aunt Sue."

"No, I didn't much feel like it. I wanted to talk to you," she replied as she crawled up on the bed and lay her head down on the pillow beside me.

"What's on your mind?" I asked, closing my laptop.

"Andie, I don't want to upset you, but I just have to…"

"What is it, Constance? It's all right, you don't have to be on pins and needles around me," I smiled and brushed my hand down her cheek. She'd been so quiet about her mourning for Ty, and she rarely broached the subject.

"I…I think you are right," she said finally.

"I usually am, but about what?"

"Banton and Ty. I think…I agree with you. I don't believe they're dead," she said finally.

85

"I'm glad someone does…but what has convinced you?"

"Your dream the other day. Your dream when Mr. Jackson appeared, and fought the Tariq. Chandler, if Banton and Ty were dead, wouldn't they…wouldn't they be there, to help you?" she asked as she played with the lace on the pillow.

"Yeah, I've been thinking about that, too. I hope you are right, Constance. I have to believe it…I just have to," I replied as I hugged her.

* * *

Constance's belief Banton and Ty were alive did wonders for my morale. I had renewed interest in decorating the nursery and enlisted Everett's help for the finishing touches. He even let me help in the painting of one of the murals on the walls, letting me sit on a pillow in the floor and paint the ocean under the "rub-a-dub-dub, three men in a tub…" nursery rhyme wall.

"Everett, this is just beautiful. I can't imagine growing up in this room. It's like a magical wonderland!" I exclaimed as I glanced around at the nursery.

"I'm making sure our babies have the best of everything. I just can't wait for them to get here. I'm just giddy!" he shivered for effect.

He was so dramatic, and he never failed to make me laugh. I lay back in the floor and surveyed the room. The cribs were beautiful, draped in the antique fabrics his mother had produced for us. They would make any designer drool. The dressing tables on each wall were painted to match the antique chest he'd bought at the estate sale, and every custom-built shelf held a multitude of whimsical toys. Clouds drifted on the ceiling, and the interior wall was painted with nursery rhyme murals straight from mother goose nursery rhymes. I could just imagine sitting in the antique rocker in the corner, singing to my beautiful babies, one in each arm…

Then I couldn't help but think of Banton. The empty ache began anew in my chest. He would be so sweet with them. I could just imagine him, picking up one of the twins as I picked up the other, placing a kiss on their foreheads, both of us rocking them together. My eyes began to mist as I glanced down at the basketball that used to be my tummy. I put both arms around my babies, their kicks unusually active today.

"Are you all right?" Everett asked, reading my expression. He'd been so wonderful, watching my every move, staying with me every moment, entertaining me, keeping me from wallowing during this period of mourning.

I sat up, determined as always I wouldn't go there, not yet.

"Yeah, I'm good. Let's go downtown and eat at that fabulous new restaurant. I feel like one of those thousand calorie desserts!"

I knew how much Everett was worrying about my appetite, and I knew it would make him happy to see me devour a chocolate volcano dessert or two.

After a wonderful lunch at our favorite tea room, and a dessert I was sure contained enough calories to get me thru the next week, Everett and I walked arm and arm back to my SUV.

"Ev, I'm feeling great. I know I'm not supposed to push things, but could we go to the park, for just a little while? We can just sit on a bench and watch the kids play in the fountain. I just don't want to go back to the house yet." I sighed as I watched him. It didn't take much to talk him into anything I wanted these days.

"All right, Bebe, but we have to take it easy," he cautioned.

As we drove to the park, I rolled the windows down. It had just stopped raining and the grass smelled so sweet. The air had cooled down to a pleasant temperature for July. Everett parked and then walked me over to a bench close to the fountain.

I sat down and relaxed into the corner of the bench as Everett pulled my feet up, propping them in his lap.

"Darlin', all of your research on your house is making for quite an interesting story. I daresay, might even be worthy of a look by a publisher or agent. I hope you don't mind, but I sneaked a peek on your laptop the other day. You are a really good writer," he commented as he raised an eyebrow at me.

"Well, don't act so surprised!" I teased as he grinned.

"But, you need an ending to your little tale about the builders of the house, and I feel it is time I complete the circle. It's time, Bebe. I need to tell you a story… not to make you sad, but to let you know I *feel* how you are grieving."

"I'm not grieving," I gritted through my teeth. "Banton is not dead. He's just missing. I know in my heart, he's coming back to me."

"Oh, Ma Cherie, I know you don't want to give up hope." He cupped my chin in his hand and made me look into his eyes; beautiful, sea green eyes full of unshed tears. I'd never seen him like that, so emotional, such raw passion evident on his face. It was yet another layer of Everett that was foreign to me.

"It's time to set the stage for you, to unfold before your eyes the drama that created my persona, that which made me who I am. I once loved so deeply, so completely, I haven't been able to open my heart to another."

I sat motionless, alert to the fact he never spoke seriously about himself, about his own relationships. I felt as if the entire world needed to cease its hurried pace and lay down for the telling.

"You know, Ma Petit, things are often not as they appear. The last century I have buried myself in varied loving, delightful friendships that are very fulfilling. I have been blessed with such deep friendships most others would surely be envious. My relationship with you alone has brought me such joy…I could have only imagined. Living as I did for many years with an eccentric mother and grandmother programmed certain, shall we say, characteristics many misread. The conclusions they draw I find extremely humorous, but not in the least offensive."

"Everett, are you finally going to tell me if you are gay or straight?" I raised an eyebrow.

He chuckled and then began. "Let me set the stage for you. I was a young man, barely out of my teen years, when the war broke out between the states. I immediately rushed off to join my brethren in gray, and saw much action at the first of the war. After one particularly brutal battle, I found myself at the outskirts of the battlefield, wounded, weak from the loss of blood. A bayonet had separated two of my ribs and my heart, barely missing the latter. Being an Aldon, I knew I would survive, but I was in a weakened state." His eyes traveled far into the distance, and his voice was tired. He gazed back at me, and continued, "A young woman, only nineteen or so, happened upon me before the enemy did. She helped me back to her farm and nursed me back to health. After two short days I was fully healed and in love." He paused to look up at me, and my mouth was hanging open. I shut it, and he smiled as he continued. "She was beautiful, silky jet-black hair, and deep blue, grief-saddened eyes. Her young husband had been killed in a battle only two months before, and she carried his child."

"That's so sad," I replied, watching the emotions on his face.

"She was extremely strong willed, and had already taken in a widow and a small orphaned boy. She had an extremely caring heart, my Marie-Claire," his voice broke as he whispered her name.

My heart skipped a beat. "Marie…Marie-Claire as in…Marie-Claire Johnson? The judge's daughter, who built my house?" I asked incredulously.

He shut his eyes and nodded slowly. "The same."

"But why…why didn't you tell me? Why did you keep this a secret all of this time?" I asked, irritated with him.

"Because I didn't know. I didn't meet her here; we were down just north of Clinton. She found me on the battlefield there. She was staying with one of the widows who she'd befriended, and she told me her plantation was over-run with Yankee wounded. The small farmhouse where she was hiding out was outside of Clinton, and I never found out where her plantation was or what her family name was.

"Why not?" I asked, mesmerized by his account.

"I guess I might as well weave it all out for you, you know you are the only person on the earth I've ever told this story to. I've kept it over one hundred and fifty years."

"Your mother never knew about her?" I asked, almost in tears sensing the raw emotion that seemed to radiate from him.

"She knew, but I never told her the whole story or any of the details. After I told her of my broken heart and the loss of my true love, we never spoke of it again. Aldon, Bebe…Aldon love fiercely. That love, it never dies. Never diminishes over time. The pain of loss doesn't fade, like it does for a human." He smiled sadly and touched my cheek.

Everett sighed, and then began slowly, like he'd transported himself back in time…

When I finally roused to full consciousness the next day my wounds were almost fully healed. I glanced around. I was in a small cabin, a dogtrot cabin, no more than two or three rooms, I guessed. I spotted her in the corner...my dark beauty, the angel who had come to me on the battlefield. I thought I'd only dreamed of her, but there she was.

I asked her, almost in a whisper... "Who...who are you?"

"My name is Marie. Marie-Claire. I'm a widow, and I'm living here with these two other women until it is safe to go home. I found you yesterday after the battle. What is your name, Sir?" she asked.

I began to rise, and she cautioned me. "Stay in bed, you still need to rest. I know you are an Aldon, but you aren't fully healed yet. And there are Yankees around, looking for stray confederates like you. They took many prisoners, but some of them escaped, and they are turning every household upside down looking for them," she cautioned.

I smiled at her. "My name is Everett. Everett Lee Samuels. If you know I'm an Aldon, you needn't worry. I can take care of myself with these mere mortal Yankee soldiers."

"That's just it, Captain. There is more afoot than soldiers," she replied in her soft, sweet southern drawl. By this point, I was mesmerized. The way she moved, she was so graceful, everything about her was swanlike. As she moved about the room, straightening up, plumping my pillows, straightening my bed linens, checking my wounds, I found myself attracted to her like I'd never been by a woman before. I watched her silently as she worked.

"What more is there...how did you know I'm an Aldon?" I asked her.

"Elois. She is a young Creole maid I brought with me. She is schooled in the voodoo ways, and she said you were 'C'est bon Loogaroo' the first night I brought you here. She cautioned me the Yankees have many like you, and they would be able to sense your presence. She urged me to get rid of you as soon as possible.

"How does she know there are Aldon in the Yankee ranks?" I asked.

"Not Aldon, but the others...the ones she calls "The guilty ones. Orcos Loogaroo," she replied, almost in a whisper. "She says you will draw them here, and then I... my baby and I will be in danger," she finished as my eyes widened.

"You are with child?" I asked, glancing at her tummy. I hadn't noticed before, but her skirts did look a bit full around her middle, compared to her tiny torso and arms.

"Yes, I am...well along. I haven't but two months to go before the little one comes. Ms. Eloise, she says I am to birth twins, but I don't know how she can tell." She lowered her eyes, like she was ashamed to tell me.

"When was your husband killed?" I asked softly as she sat down in the rocker at my bedside.

"I received word about a month ago, but I don't know how long he'd been gone, before..." her voice began to shake as she relayed the series of events.

"I'm so sorry for your loss. Do you have family, or his people, who you can go to?" I asked her, suddenly afraid for her burden.

"My husband has no family here in the South. He has an aunt up North. My mother and father live close by, but they're up in Savannah, staying with friends until things calm down here. I refused to go with them. I wanted to stay near my beloved Hiriam. Now he is gone, I will be traveling to be with my parents after the baby is born."

"It's not safe for you here; no women are safe here without men to protect them," I asserted as she shook her head.

"There is a Yankee captain who has been by here before. He has assured me we will not be harmed as long as his men are in the area. It's only the Orcos who they have in their ranks, who hunt the prisoners. They are the ones who we are frightened of, and some local Orcos have joined in their search. There is a band of them who roam the countryside. They have been drawn here, Ms. Eloise says, because of the carnage...of all the blood on the battlefield. She says the dead make easy feeding," she shuddered, imagining the picture in her head.

I reached out and took her hand and held it as she turned to look at me. Her eyes were so beautiful, I caught my breath, and I *knew...I was in love with her. I'd never felt this way before, ever. I struggled with my thoughts...which question to voice next.*

"If there is so much carnage, blood on the battlefield, easy feeding...Why are you afraid of the Orcos? Are they a threat to you, for a reason?" I asked her softly.

"Eloise seems to think so, because of the baby," she replied, fear apparent in her eyes.

"Why? Why would they want the baby?"

"Eloise thinks I'm having twins, and the Orcos will want them. She says twins possess special powers, and are two parts of the same soul, that they each retain half. The Orcos believe as the Creole Voodoo worshipers do, spirits, either good or evil, will inhabit the other half of the soul. She says they believe if the spirit is good, the baby will be a threat to them. If it is an evil spirit, then the child can be used to their advantage," She became silent, and as I watched her, I realized the level of fear she had for her unborn babies.

I'd already made up my mind in the short time I'd listened to her story that I had a new mission in life, that I had a new purpose. I'd been brought up to believe I was put on this earth for one purpose... to use my talents and abilities to help humans, and to be the protector our name proclaimed us to be. The cause ceased to exist, the cause I'd fought so hard for these past three years. My cause was suddenly this beautiful young girl I saw before me.

The next few days, I gained my strength back. I had to go hunting. Obviously I didn't have a butcher friend handy to help me with my food source. In those days I had to be self-sufficient. I left the small cabin several times over the next days, hunting in the nearby woods and fields, killing small animals. When I fully regained my strength, I killed a deer, and after I'd had my fill, I brought the meat back to the cabin to cure and store for her and the ladies living with her.

Marie made a venison stew with some of the meat. After we'd all eaten, the other ladies retired for the evening, and the small orphan boy she'd taken in sat playing in the floor at her feet.

"Marie, if I can arrange for a buckboard or wagon and horses, would you agree for me to take you to stay with my mother and grandmother before I go back to my regiment? I know I

couldn't get you through to your father, but the way to N'awlins would be the easiest. You would be safe there," I asked as she sat knitting.

"I don't know. I don't think you can find..." she began.

"Believe me, I can. I have many friends down in N'awlins. I can get there and back in no time. I will take you back there, and you can stay with my mother and grandmother until it is safe for you to return."

"I could never ask you to do that, they don't even know me," she replied as she covered my hand with hers. My heart leapt. Her touch set me on fire. I could imagine taking her in my arms, kissing her...But I knew she thought of me as an Aldon. A blood-drinker. She wasn't afraid of me, I was sure, but she would certainly be repulsed by what I was and how I lived. I was tormented, I was so afraid she saw me for what I was, and not how I wanted to be.

"My mother would love to take you and your maid, your widow friend, and the lad here...she would love and protect you, until we could get you to your father. You saved me, helped me to heal. Now let me help you. Think about it. I can leave day after tomorrow and secure a wagon for you and the others to travel in."

"I...let me think about it. I would need to get word to my father..."she trailed off as she stood. She tried to take a step, and was unsteady on her feet. She tripped over the toys the small boy played with in the floor, and became tangled in her skirts. I was up in a flash to catch her before she hit the floor and injured herself. As I held her, time stood still. She looked up at me, and I was lost in the deep blue translucent pools fringed with thick, black lashes. I hesitated, my face only inches from hers. While I tried to keep my emotions in check, she did the unthinkable...she raised her lips to mine. I held my breath, not wanting to frighten her, and unsure I could control myself if I gave in. But the minute I began to move my lips, we were both swept away. I kissed her with a passion I'd only dreamed of, and she returned that passion, winding her arms around my neck as I pulled her into my chest.

We could hear gunfire and cannons that night. The war raged on, outside, just beyond the fields next to the little cabin which sheltered us. I kept my gun close by, and spent the night in the rocking chair with Marie-Claire safely in my arms. As I held her, I knew she was my heart's true love. I'd never felt like that about anyone. As she slept, I could feel the tiny babies moving in her belly, and I fell in love with them as well. At dawn, I decided I had to sneak back to N'awlins for the supplies we would need for the trip to my mother's house. Being an Aldon, it only took me a day to make it there, but it took a little over two days coming back; I had to stop frequently to hide the buckboard and horses I'd procured for the journey. When I arrived back at the cabin, the battles that had been fought close by had moved on, and the country looked deserted. As the buckboard pulled up outside, the small lad met me outside, his tear-stained face alarming me.

"What is it? What has happened?" I asked him as I shook his shoulders.

"The Missus, Suh, The Missus...she's..." and he didn't have to finish. I could hear the wails of Elois, the young Creole maid, from inside the cabin. I flung the door open, and my heart truly stopped beating.

Marie-Claire lay on the bed; the Orco bite glaringly apparent on her neck. Her dress was torn and bloodstained, and the two small babies who had been born just after lay wrapped in blankets beside her. According to her maid they'd lived about an hour after, and then died, their little lungs not fully developed. I turned and saw the rogue band of Orcos outside in the yard, and saw him...Lucien, the Ocro responsible for killing my beautiful Marie.

All I could see in front of me was blind, searing rage. I was so full of hate and hungry for revenge I saw no other course of action before me. I killed two of them instantly, and then I hunted Lucien for days, coming close several times to killing him but I was never able to finish the deed. When I finally gave up and returned to the cabin, it had been burned to the ground, and there was no sign Marie or her two baby girls had been buried. The Creole maid and her widow companion were long gone, and as I searched for them, the only thing I ever found to tie me to them was the small lad hidden in the woods. He was only four or five years old, and somehow he felt responsible for her death. He was an Aldon like me. He'd been orphaned when his Sange-Mele mother had been killed, and the Creole maid and Marie-Claire had taken him in. I took him to my mother and grandmother, and they raised him as their own. That is how Stephan came into our family.

I realized, after a few moments of silence, Everett had returned to the present. As I gazed at him, the one-hundred and fifty years of grief he'd suffered were painfully apparent on his face. His eyes glistened with unshed tears, and his expression was as if the whole tragedy had just played out in the last few minutes. I reached up and cupped his cheek in my hand. I realized my own cheeks were wet with tears.

"You see, sweet Bebe, I know how you are suffering. I know the pain, the loss, the agony of knowing you are forever separated from your soul mate. To have loved that deeply, that completely, no matter for how short a time – you loved a lifetime. It only comes but once for most of us," he finished sadly as he raised his eyes to mine.

We sat there several minutes, saying nothing, listening to the breeze sweeping through the trees beside the large fountain. I finally broke the silence.

"So you really aren't gay?" I asked, the rude, absurd question breaking the ice. He chuckled his light, Everett chuckle.

"I can always count on you to make me laugh, Ma Petit. No, I'm not. I'm not anything, really. Ever since, I've walled my heart off from everyone. Friendship is the only thing I've let myself feel, since her. If I was ever going to fall for someone again, it would have probably been you, Bebe, but we were the best of friends instantly, and I instinctively knew that is what you needed from me," he finished as he studied my face.

"Then why do you let everyone think…" I began.

"Being an ancient relic of the past, and as eccentric as I am, still possessing the Old South's gentlemanly qualities, people just assume. I guess I could practice the ass-hole crotch scratching, cold-hearted jerk thing most men exude these days, to blend in, but that just isn't me, Bebe. I fit in with Philippe's crowd. They seem gentler, somehow."

"Don't you think it's time to open yourself up to a new relationship?" I asked, wanting to see my best friend happy.

"If there was ever a terminal bachelor, it would be me. I'm too set in my ways. I might make an exception for Constance, but she's just too much woman for me." He smiled, and then placed a kiss on top of my head. "Besides, I've already fallen for someone, but she's off-limits, so I'm doomed to unrequited love. Just as well, I'd probably scare her out of her wits!" He grinned down at me.

"Who? Everett, you have to tell me…" I began.

"No way, sweet girl. I'll take it to the afterlife, if I have one, the good Lord and Mother Mary above willing. Now, let's get you home. You have a story to finish, and the babies need rest, I think." He pulled me from the bench and we walked arm in arm back to my SUV.

I studied him the entire way home. I saw him in a new light. I'd always thought of him as beautiful, his dishwater blonde hair, flawless complexion…he was almost too perfect. I realized how handsome he was, and my heart almost skipped a beat. He was so perfect --beautiful, thick eyelashes and very pouty lips for a man. I'd thought of him as gay for so long, I was almost having trouble processing the new information. After several moments he glanced sideways at me and laughed, putting his hand over mine.

"I absolutely love your inquisitiveness, Bebe. You know that is what makes you such a good writer." He winked at me, and then drew my hand up and kissed the back of it.

"Everett, all this time…all the times you've seen me undress, at the shop, the nights you spent on the mattress on the floor, lay beside me on the bed…all that time, you were straight?" I asked incredulously, being slow to process everything.

"I do feel a little guilty about that, but I assure you, my intentions toward you have always been as a best friend --a brother, really. I don't want my telling you the truth to make you uncomfortable in any way. If this changes our little relationship, I'll slap my mama and kiss John's ass!" he exclaimed in the most flamboyant way. My Everett was back!

Chapter Seven

Our little outing did wonders for my spirits. Upon our arrival back at home, I spent an hour or so playing with Beau and giving him the attention he'd been lacking the past several weeks. Like me, he too had fallen into a state of depression. Although I knew he missed Banton, my mood was having a greater effect on him. After a romp in the living room with his favorite rubber ball, he followed me closely up the staircase to nap beside the bed on his rug.

"Okay, Bebe...I was just about to come in and give you one of my best lectures. I just won't have you overdoing," Everett scolded as he gained the top stair and drifted into my room. "Oh, and remember, Constance left to go to N'awlins with Aunt Sue. They'll be back tomorrow."

"Oh, Ev...I'm fine. I'm taking my afternoon nap like a good girl. I promise I'll spend the next couple of days on bed rest, all right?"

"Yes, you will. Dr. Lane will have a fit if I let you do too much. We've worked so hard to get you this far. Now, can I get you anything before you nap?" He flitted about my room tidying up.

"No, Ev. I'm fine."

"Are you going to work on your book?" he asked when I picked up my laptop.

"I just thought it might be good for me to work on it. It might help me to get sleepy. And about that..." I trailed off as I watched his expression.

"What's rolling around in that beautiful brunette head of yours?"

"I just feel like I need your permission," I started.

"Oh, pishhhhaw. You go ahead. I told you the story for that very reason. You needed the information to be able to fill the holes in for your story," he stated.

"But some of it is so intimate, but it would be hard to tell, without...and what about the Aldon thing? I can't," I stopped and watched his reaction.

"You go ahead, and write it smack out of your little head. Be passionate. Tell it in your own beautiful, mesmerizing style. Let me be the judge after you've written it. We can come up with some middle editing ground together. Just write it!" he commanded as he bent over to place a kiss on my head. He straightened and then became serious.

"You know, Bebe…someone once said of a writer, 'You have the power to say at any time, 'This is not how my story is going to end,' and I want you to bring that chapter of my life to a close. It will help me come to terms with it after all of these years. I think it will help you too," he finished as I nodded slowly.

All of the raw emotion was still fresh in my head. I wrote the story down he'd laid out for me earlier in the day, and my own emotions got the best of me. I typed and cried, and then typed and cried some more. I'd felt his raw passion, his despair, the devastation he'd felt when he lost Marie. I glanced around the room, wondering for the first time which bedroom had been hers and Hiriam's. I wondered which one was to have been her own babies' nursery, and if the babies had been conceived right here in this house. I placed the laptop beside me, and gazed out the window into the cloudy afternoon sky. Soon the storm clouds began to darken and thunder rolled in the distance. I wondered aloud, "I wonder if they were as in love as Banton and I when the babies were conceived."

"Wonder if who was as in love as you and Banton?" John asked, entering through the open bedroom door.

"Oh, hey, John," I greeted him as I pushed up in bed.

"Andie-girl, don't get up, stay there." He crossed the room and sat down on the bed beside me.

"I was just wondering about the couple who built this house during the Civil War. I found her grave in the cemetery down the road, you know," I informed him as he took my hand and rubbed it between his.

"No, I didn't know that," he answered, studying me.

"She died as she was having twins. The twin baby girls are buried beside her," I finished sadly. "I'd just never thought about it before, about her living here with her new husband, and the war breaking out and all. I just wondered which room was hers," I finished.

"No wonder this place seems haunted at times. It has every right to be." He brushed the hair back away from my eyes.

"So what brings you up here? I thought Everett and Mr. Philippe had babysitting duties this week," I joked.

"I don't consider this a duty, Andie. I love spending time with you," he declared solemnly.

"I know, I was just kidding. I feel the same way about you."

We sat for several minutes; the only sound intruding on the moment was the click-tock-tick from the clock on my nightstand. I watched as he made circles on the back of my hand with his thumb, and then he cleared his throat.

"Umhum...Andie, there is something I need to give you, to tell you," he finally offered.

"John, what is it? You can tell me," I urged him.

"Sweetheart, it's about Banton. Singleton called me this morning, and the Navy has officially closed the search. They've given up on finding our three boys."

"Oh." I was determined to stay calm at the news and maintain a casual demeanor, like it had no bearing on how I felt. Inside, the strings that held my heart connected to my head had just splintered into a million pieces. The transition was almost complete, the detachment to help me not to feel...my defense mechanism of old.

"Chandler, did you hear me?" John asked gently.

"Yes."

"I think we have to face facts. I don't think he's coming back to us."

I continued to watch him caress the back of my hand, not wanting to raise my eyes to his. Once I did, I would be giving in.

"Andie-girl, Banton made me promise to give you this, if anything were ever to happen to him. He gave it to me the morning he left. I've kept it, but now I think it's time you read it. I'm going to leave it here, and leave you alone for a bit." He almost whispered as he let go of my hand. Leaning over, he pressed his lips firmly to my forehead and then left the room. I sat for a long time, not wanting to raise my eyes. I took a deep breath, and finally gazed upon the small white envelope with Banton's handwriting…the last thing he would ever write to me. I picked it up with trembling hands, and opened it slowly, folding the paper out gently that held his beautiful handwriting.

Andie…

If you are reading this, things must be pretty bad. I've given this letter to John, in case   anything was to ever happen to me. Chandler, I never, ever imagined I could love someone as much as I love you. You are everything to me, and I can't imagine ever being separated   from you. I can feel your love, even across the miles when we are apart. So I know, no matter where I go, no matter what happens that my love will stay with you. I'm a part of you, and you are a part of me.

I wanted to put pen to paper, and give you a forever record of just how I fell in love with you. I've never told you, and I'm sorry. I always had the feeling like there was someone missing, that there was someone I was supposed to love, that there was a missing   piece. That feeling stopped, ceased to exist when you opened your front door the night Beau went missing. You smiled at me, and I melted. It was the way you looked so innocent, your   hair   curling   around   your   neck glistening with sweat, your curvy little figure lost in the   baggy sweats, the obvious way you were throwing yourself into your new house.

I couldn't breathe. I followed you down that hallway, totally mesmerized by you. As we talked, I began to form a plan, a plan to see you again. When you gave me an opening about not having any friends to help you renovate, I had my plan, and I couldn't wait to get back to John to enlist his help. As you shut the front door when we parted, my   heart ripped apart. I almost made up an emergency, so I could come back, some ruse I could concoct to make you let me stay with you, to protect you. I knew there were Orcos around your house, and I couldn't stand the thought of leaving you unprotected. I never slept that night or the next, and I ended up out in my pickup watching your house.

I don't know if you remember, but something woke you in the early morning hours, and you flipped the lights on in the foyer. It took every ounce of strength I had not to come running down that sidewalk to check on you. You told me later you'd had a bad dream, and imagined noises. I knew exactly the time it happened, for I was watching over you. I loved you, even then.

Every minute I spent with you I fell deeper and deeper in love. Our first kiss, the night you told me about your parents, I almost couldn't control myself. I was so afraid I'd frightened you off, that you might not want me since I was so much older. Then the night Beau was bitten by the snakes and I sensed you were angry with me, my heart broke in two pieces. I confronted you, and when I realized you were upset, that you wanted a relationship with me and thought I was involved with someone else, my heart soared! I sat down and planned out how to take things slowly, to make sure you would fall in love with me, too. And my life began, truly began, when we kissed under our tree, and you told me you loved me. I knew at that moment, somehow I had to marry you and to spend the rest of my life with you.

I was the happiest man alive when I found you in the tunnels. And when the doctor said "and so is the baby's..." in the emergency room, the whole world became silent. You became my whole universe at that moment. I know you will give our babies all of the love we wanted to give them, together.

Chandler Ann, you are my soul mate. My love, the mother of my children. I'm so sorry I have failed you...I know I have, if you are reading this. Please know this, my love for you will never die, my love will have to go on, across any barrier, from this life to the next. I want you to be happy, sweetheart.

My love is yours, forever and for always.
Banton.

101

I lay for hours, holding his precious note in my hands. As the last of the rain cleared and the clouds parted, afternoon sunlight began to fade across the floor in my room. A faint knock at the door brought me back to the present.

"Come in," I called out, not even turning my head.

"Andie-girl, are you awake?" John asked, crossing the room to the bed.

"Yeah, I'm awake."

He sat down slowly, and then I felt his hand rest gently on my back, and then down my arm. I turned over slowly to face him as he reached to wipe the tears from under my eyes.

"I'm sorry. I was torn between wanting to give you his letter, and wanting to keep it from you a while longer," he began.

"No, I'm glad you gave it to me, John. Thank you," I whispered as I watched his eyes. I could tell by the way he looked at me, the depth of emotion his eyes held, he'd accepted Banton's disappearance as final.

"But you still don't think,"

"No. I don't," I answered quickly but firmly. He nodded quickly, reaching down and pulling me up into his arms. I lay my head against his chest and could hear the rapid beating of his heart. He tightened his arms around me, and I felt safe for the first time in a long time. I released my breath as I slid my arms around his waist. He lay his cheek over on top of my head, and then placed his lips in my hair, kissing the top of my head, *just like Banton used to do*, I thought. I pulled away, and he looked down at me with a puzzled expression.

"What is it, Andie?"

"This...I'm...I guess I'm just tired." How could I possibly admit to him it felt good for him to hold me? That I felt lonely...that our closeness felt like it was morphing into something else? I wasn't ready for that yet. I wasn't ready for anyone to hold me like Banton did.

"Let me hold you, please?" he asked, reading my thoughts as he pulled me back over into his arms. Sliding his hand into my hair, he pulled my face to his neck, holding me tightly as my shoulders began to shake with sobs. It seemed he was determined to make me let go.

"It's all right to cry, Sweetheart. Shhh, I'm here, and I'm not leaving you," he murmured as he continued to stroke my hair. A heavy sense of guilt enveloped me when I relaxed in his arms, letting sleep overtake my tears once again. I'd held my eyes open as long as I could...my eyelids felt as if someone had weighted them with fishing line. Sleep was the last thing I wanted to do, for somehow I sensed my dream would return. I finally gave in...thinking as everyone does, if I just closed my eyes for a minute and rested them, I would be all right. When I finally drifted, my last thoughts were filled with Banton's silky voice.

"You know that place between sleep and awake...the place where you can still remember dreaming? That's where I'll always love you. That's where I'll always be waiting," he whispered.

I ran as fast as my legs would carry me. In daylight, with the sun streaming over the open field, one would think that it was a cheery, hopeful place, free of threat or worry. But my heart was pounding, and I felt vulnerable. I was supposed to have my babies, but I couldn't find them. I could hear their faint cries somewhere in the deep grass...but where? I pushed on, searching through the tall fronds and reeds swaying in the breeze.

"Hurry, Chile, afore he gits here to hurt you," I heard Mr. Jackson call from behind me. "You gots to find dem babies quick," he warned.

"Where? I can't find them," I called out frantically. I kept searching, my legs getting heavier and heavier. It seemed I kept searching over and over again in the same spots, finding nothing. The sun overhead became unbearable, and the babies cried harder and harder as though they were in pain.

"Help me! Help me find them," I screamed as I heard my mother's voice.

"Chandler, Calm down. Look for them, they are here," she called out from somewhere behind me. I pushed on as the rank smell in the air caught my attention.

"Miss Chandler, dem Loogaroo, dey is here! You got's to find dem babies!"

103

I was on my hands and knees, crawling now. Just as I was about to reach them, rough hands drew me up, squeezing the air from my lungs.

"Here she is, right where I want her," The Tariq from my dreams stood over me, crushing me into his chest. I looked down, my babies lay at his feet.

I pushed against him, beating him with my fists.

"Let me have them," I screamed as he dropped me to the ground. I fought to pick the babies up before he could get to them. I cried out in frustration. I could hear Mr. Jackson and my mother, but I couldn't see them. Why weren't they helping me?"

"You've got to have faith, Miss Chandler. You've got to draw on yo love...You gots to accept it."

"What? I do have faith...I do," I sobbed out. I pulled at the babies, drawing them up into my arms. As I clutched them to me, sitting at the Orco's feet, I murmured, "Please, God, help me! Banton, I'm so alone! Where are you?"

The Orco laughed, pulling his hand back as if to strike at all of us. I knew he would kill the babies, and I was frozen, unable to move.

And then I heard him.

"Andie, look out!" Banton's voice called out. He dove from behind me toward the Tariq. I watched, mesmerized while he fought the assailant who haunted my dreams. Banton strained against him, trying to get the upper hand. As he changed his grip, moving the Orco around his body, he had the creature in a headlock.

"You've hurt my wife for the last time. You'll not hurt her again! I'm sending you back to hell, where you belong, where the evil belongs," Banton ground out through his teeth as he snapped the Tariq's neck. As he fell, Banton placed his boot on the Orco's chest, pulling his torso apart and dismembering the horrible creature in one swift motion.

I sensed my mother and Mr. Jackson at my side, helping me by taking the babies from me. I rose and ran to Banton.

He held me at arms' length, and cupped my cheek with his hand as he spoke. "Chandler, you are safe now. You and the babies are safe. He'll never hurt you again, I will see to it. You mean the world to me. You are safe and forever loved. Chandler Ann, you were right, I feel your love across the miles...across time. All my life, my love ...forever," he whispered as I turned my face to kiss his palm. And then he was gone.

I opened my eyes and stared at the ceiling in my bedroom.

Banton had appeared in my dream and killed my night stalker. Banton was in my dream with my mother and Mr. Jackson. Banton was gone.

The tears began to slide down my cheeks, and I began to sob, the ache in my chest growing with each passing moment.

Banton was in my dream. Banton was dead.

"No! Why, God? Why? Banton, No! No!"

My chest heaved as I tried to drink in large gulps of air, then releasing it in violent bursts. "Banton!" My screams vibrated across the room, shaking the window pane.

The door swung wide open as John entered in a panic.

"Andie-girl, what's wrong? What happened?" he asked as he crossed the room, frantically searching me for injuries.

I shook my head at him disbelievingly, just like I'd just received word of Banton's death. I took a deep breath, and then let it out as I responded, "Banton...he's gone, isn't he? He is dead. I know it, he's dead."

John sat down gently on my side of the bed. "Andie,...Shhh, it's okay. Sweetheart, I'm so sorry. But what's changed your mind?" He stroked my cheek with his hand.

I raised my eyes to his. "I know because Banton just woke me from my dream. He was there...and he told me everything was over, and the babies and I would be safe now. He'd seen to it, and he killed the Tariq once and for all," I whispered

"And why..." John began.

"Why do I...finally accept he's dead? Because he came to me in my dream. No one living has ever been in my dreams. Mr. Jackson came into my dream the night after he died. Banton..." My voice broke on his name. "Banton's gone, John. I know it in my heart, now." The tears finally flowed, and my shoulders shook with the sobs. "I want to die, too."

"Oh, Andie, come here. Come here, sweetheart." He pulled me into his arms, and held me against his chest. "I know, I miss him too," he whispered as the tears rolled down his cheeks and into my hair.

"How can I ever feel happy again? I can't stand this, to know I had a perfect love, a perfect life, for one brief moment...then I had it taken away. I'm so grateful...that I even had him, had his love, for that long. I know you are the one person who understands ... who knows what I feel." I looked up into his eyes, and I knew we both shared the same kind of loss.

"I'm just glad you will have the babies. You will always have a part of him. I know you are scared, but I'll always be here for you. You won't raise them alone, I promise you." He pulled my face back up with both his hands and wiped the tears from my eyes with his thumbs.

He pulled me in close and held me. I could hear the beating of his heart, and I felt so peaceful. "There is life beyond this grief. I know there is, for both of us," he said softly.

"I just can't imagine there would ever been anyone who could love me like he did. So completely, like I was his whole world," I whispered as I lay my head over on his shoulder.

"Andie?" John asked softly as he caressed my back.

I turned my head to look up at him, our faces only inches apart. His eyes bore into mine.

"I...I do love you like that," he whispered, lowering his gaze to my lips. He angled his mouth slowly to mine and kissed me, barely touching my lips. I held my breath, shocked at his response and shocked at my own. As I opened my lips to him, his kiss became hungrier. I wrapped my arms around his neck, and he lowered his body down beside mine as he slid his hand over to rest on my abdomen. I wanted to throw myself into the kiss; it was as if every nerve in my body screamed out to feel his touch. I hesitated for one split second, and then remembering Brie, I pulled away and studied his face.

"John, I...I can't do this. I..."

"Chandler..." he breathed my name softly.

I pulled away and took his hands from my face, holding them with my own.

"John, you know I love you. We've been through a lot together. But this, it would be wrong... for all the wrong reasons.

We're both grieving for the people we've loved most in our lives. I believe you want this, and it would be so easy to give in to these feelings. But I won't do that to you," I whispered, searching his eyes. "I would have to know we were together because we wanted each other, and not because you're my link to Banton. And John, I truly think that is part of the reason you want this. I'm your link to Brie," I smiled at him through my tears. "Believe me, soon, very soon, you would regret this."

"I'd never regret this. And I meant it, when I said I love you, and you won't raise these babies alone. I want to be there for you, every step of the way, if you will let me." He reached up and cupped my cheek in his hand.

"John, I have to tell you something. Everett asked me not to, but I think it's time." I switched on the lamp beside the bed, and pushed up, pulling an extra pillow from across the bed and propping it behind me.

Could I do this? I knew if I told him, there would be no going back. I was forcing Brie back into our world, whether she was ready or not. But the need to ease our pain was fierce. There was nothing I could do about my own pain, but I could do something about John's. For one brief moment, the thought flashed through my mind that I was making the decision to tell him about Brie so I wouldn't be tempted to give in to my own feelings for John. I couldn't go there, so I took a deep breath.

"You have to promise me you will keep an open mind, and you have to promise you won't judge me or Everett from keeping this from you. But I think it's time I forced the issue." My emotions got the better of me, and the tears streamed down my face. I was about to give him the news I couldn't even wish someone could give me.

"What is it? I could never be mad at you," he assured me as he leaned his arm across my legs and placed his hand over mine.

"That awful night in New Orleans, the night Brie was taken…" I began. A dark shadow came across John's face, and the tortured look returned to his eyes. He looked back up into my eyes, and urged, "Go on."

"The Aldon...John, the Aldon intercepted the Orcos who took her. They took her body, and John...her heart was still beating," I breathed out, almost in a whisper.

"What?" He stared at me, incredulous, the meaning of my words barely sinking in. "What are you saying?"

"Everett came to me about a week afterward. I was grieving, like you, and he was afraid I was going to lose the babies. He told me in confidence the Aldon had Brie, and she had transformed into one of them...into an Orco," I revealed as I studied the expressions that crossed his face.

"Brie...Brie's alive?" he asked me in a whisper.

"Everett made me promise not to tell you, until they knew for sure she could be rehabilitated. You remember what Dr. Lane said about his wife? About how he had to destroy her himself, that she couldn't overcome the transition?"

"Are you saying Brie's become one of those Orcos?" he asked, horror apparent on his face.

"She had a horrible time, John. At one point, Everett didn't think she was going to make it. He didn't want to tell you and then have to take her so far away. He was afraid it would be worse than thinking she was dead. So they had to keep her existence a secret."

"Where is she? Chandler, I have to see her, I have to help her! My God, she's alive! Brie's alive!" he cried out as he shook my shoulders.

"Yes, John. And I'm convinced she's going to be fine. She's finally turned the corner, and I've been with her myself. They were giving her more time to work through some other issues. She is so unsure of herself, and she still refuses to let everyone know she's alive. But John, her love for you is what has pulled her through this far. She and Everett and the other Aldon holding her, they still don't think she is ready to see you...to see her parents. But I think it's time for you to make that decision and force her." I smiled at him through my tears; the relief on his face was overwhelming. I knew at that moment I'd done the right thing by telling him. As he processed this new revelation, his brows creased and the unthinkable happened. He turned on me.

"Brie...Oh, God...why? Damn you, Chandler...Damn you! How could you keep this from me?! Knowing I wanted to die, too." he shouted at me. "My Brie...I could have been helping her! She's been going through this hell, alone! How could you? And how dare Everett! How could both of you, let me think, and all the time..."

I shut my eyes. My greatest fear was this reaction to the news. I couldn't blame him. And at that moment, a hole more jagged than the one already there tore open in my heart. I opened my eyes, and all I could see on his face was his fury and contempt for me.

He stood up, and his angry strides echoed in the house long after the front door slammed downstairs. I lay back down in the bed and pulled the covers up over me. It hurt so badly...his reaction to my silence over the past few months. And then the most selfish thought of all pushed forward. I'd just lost my last link to Banton. The hole in my chest burned like someone had tossed a lit match into it.

But I had to be happy for him, and for Brie. I shut my eyes tightly against my tears. I just hoped he could forgive me and Everett for what we'd had to do.

After a few hours of attempting to sleep, I finally gave up and rose to get dressed. I realized for the first time I was alone in my house, no one watching over me. I didn't care. I felt empty inside. It was after five in the morning, and the sun would be up in an hour or so anyway. After I'd showered and dressed, I went downstairs with Beau close on my heels. Playing with my cell phone in my hands, I finally decided I'd better call and warn Everett about the storm headed his way.

"Bebe, what are you doing up so early? Is everything all right?"

"Actually no, that is why I'm calling," I sighed, and then continued. "Ev, I had to tell John about Brie last night. I'm sure he's probably headed over there soon."

Everett chuckled on the other end. "Bebe, did you really think he would wait until sunrise? He showed up here in the wee hours this morning and demanded I take him to Brie. I have to say, that moment was one sight it was worth living one hundred and fifty years to see. They've already had their happy reunion, she is in full control, and they're spending a little quality time together. And she assured him most of our silence was due to her wishes, and she gave him one hell of a hard time about how he reacted to your involvement in the secret. I'm supposing you will hear from him real soon."

"Oh, I'm so glad." The tears began to pour again.

"Bebe, I'm headed that way. I'll be there in five minutes. Just hang on."

I turned my cell off and curled up in a ball on the sofa. I was so angry. I was ashamed of myself. I was actually mad at John and Brie. They were having the reunion I would never have with Banton. I hated myself for having those thoughts, and it made me sob even harder. The raw emotions John had uncovered last night were still so fresh. I ran over the scene in my head, when he'd kissed me, how I'd responded to him, to his touch…and couldn't even begin to imagine how awkward everything would be between us from now on.

My chest ached anew. I was so confused about how my feelings for John had changed. As I lay on the couch in the early morning light, I realized he would have been a crutch. I missed Banton, and I was just reaching for those emotions John had stirred up. About ten minutes had passed when I heard Everett's light steps cross the front porch, and his key in the lock on the front door. *Okay, Andie, it's time to stop feeling sorry for yourself.* I wiped the tears from my eyes and sat up on the sofa.

"Bebe, are you okay?" Everett hurried across to where I was still seated on the sofa.

"Yeah, I'm fine, Ev. Or I will be. I've just decided it's time to join the world of the living." I smiled and steeled myself against emotion. It was time to be strong, to get past all of this grief and wallowing. It was time to get ready for my babies.

"Well, all right then. What shall we do today?" Everett smiled at me, my savior once again. He instinctively knew I needed to move on, and we didn't need to talk about John and Brie. We busied ourselves with plans about the nursery and plans for shopping for more maternity clothes. He pointed out to me everything I'd been wearing was getting a little stretched, and I knew shopping was the one thing we shared that lifted both our spirits.

"All right, one shop, Bebe, and then the tea room! Home for an early nap, and then you, me, Constance and Mrs. Sue and the big screen! I've got some old black and white Katherine Hepburne and Spencer Tracy movies we've just got to watch tonight!" Everett gushed. I tried as hard as I could to get excited about our little "girls day out."

We spent the morning at our favorite boutique with Everett wearing the sales girls out as usual. After he'd loaded his car down with our purchases, we walked together down to the tea room for lunch.

"Bebe, you've hardly touched your salad. I know the babies are growing, and getting what they need, but I'm worried about you. I swear you've lost weight since you got pregnant! What am I going to do with you?" he exclaimed.

"I'm sorry, I'm just not hungry," I replied, placing my fork across my plate.

"Well, will you a least split a piece of southern pecan pie with me?"

"Now sugar, you know I will," I replied in my best southern drawl. "But I'm not sharin'. Please, would you bring us each a piece, with ice cream?" I asked the waiter as he paused at our table.

"Certainly, Ma'am," the young waiter replied, picking our dishes up. He looked at me for a moment and then blushed. Everett smiled at me over his wine glass.

"That's so cruel, Bebe," Everett said, his eyes sparkling.

"What?"

"Don't play innocent with me, Scarlett. You just sent that poor boy into convulsions in the kitchen."

"Don't be ridiculous, Ev. Look at me, I'm eleven months pregnant!"

"You have no idea the effect you have on men, do you?" Ev asked. He batted his eyelashes at me comically.

I tried to suppress my giggle and failed miserably.

"Now, that's my sweet Bebe. Your smile just warms my heart," he said as he grinned at me and covered my hand with his.

111

After we'd cleaned the pie and every last crumb up, Everett escorted me home. As we turned the corner on our street, I spotted a new Lexus SUV parked in my driveway.

"How beautiful...wonder who it belongs to, Bebe? Were you expecting company?"

"Just Aunt Sue and Constance. Their cars are already here."

Before I could get my door open, Everett was around the car and at my side to help me in the house. "Just leave those packages in the back. I'll bring them in and lay them out later," he instructed as I heard the front door open.

"An Andler! Aba's here!" Ava Grace ran down the front steps and across the lawn to us. I knelt down to hug her.

"Ava...where on earth did you come from? Oh, Ava Grace, I've missed you so much!" I hugged her to me. It felt like such a long time since I'd held her.

"Come, sweet Ava, let's get Aunt Chandler in the house where she can rest," Everett urged as Ava chattered away at us. I raised my eyes when we reached the front porch. Claudia met us at the door with tears in her eyes.

"I just had to come and see you. I've missed you so. I hope it's all right, maybe I should have called," she said, fighting her tears.

"Of course it's all right! I'm so glad you've come. I've really missed you!" I exclaimed as I embraced her. We held each other for several moments just inside the foyer to the house. I pulled away first and smiled at her through my own teary eyes.

"So, I guess that beautiful new car outside is yours?" I grinned at her as she nodded.

"Yes, an early birthday present from Will. He surprised me with it last weekend. He left on a business trip this morning, so I thought maybe Ava Grace and I might come and visit you for a couple of days?"

"I'd love it!" I exclaimed, pulling Ava in close to me again.

"Where are Aunt Sue and Constance?" I asked. Everett maneuvered around us, placing some of the packages from the car down in the foyer.

"Oh, they're out back on the patio. Constance is catching a little sun, and your Aunt Sue is watering for you." Claudia informed us as she hugged me again.

112

"Bebe, let's get you upstairs. You really aren't supposed to be on your feet like you've been today," Everett suggested.

"Oh, don't let us keep you up. Come upstairs, and we'll get you comfortable so we can visit. It's Ava's naptime anyway, so we'll see if we can get her down.

"Can Aba sweep wif An Andler in Unca Banin's bed?" Ava asked innocently. I teared again at the mention of Banton's name and thought *get a hold of yourself, Andie. You have to be able to say his name without crying.*

"Of course, Doodle-Bug. That's your spot!" I pulled her along with me up the stairs with Everett and Claudia close behind.

After we were all settled, Everett lounged on the window seat with the latest Nicholas Sparks, and Ava Grace, Claudia and I piled in my bed with my mother's softest afghans thrown over us. Claudia and I caught up on all the family gossip.

"...and Mrs. Elaine and Mr. Matt, how are they?" I asked her.

"They're fine. Mother and Daddy both still have moments when they struggle, but they're doing amazingly well. They miss you, though, Chandler."

"I know. I miss them too. I need to call them; it's just hard for me. I need to apologize to them for everything," I whispered over Ava's head as she played with her doll.

"Oh, sweetie, you have nothing to apologize for. We have all dealt with this thing in different ways, and I'll not have anyone question yours. We are the ones who need to apologize. I feel like we have abandoned you and left you alone in this." She placed her hand over across mine and left it there. We lay there in silence for several moments, watching Ava as she played.

"How is Julia holding up?" I asked her.

She shook her head slowly. "Not good. She is grieving so hard for Banton, they were so close. And then there's Ben. No one anticipated how hard she would take his death. I think she was more serious about him than any of us suspected. His family lives way up north, and they had a service immediately. There was no way Julia could go, so she hasn't had any closure."

"Oh, Claudia, I'm so sorry. What are your Momma and Daddy doing to help her?" I asked.

"She spent a week at a hospital in N'awlins. They did some grief counseling. Momma and Daddy brought her home yesterday, and talked her into going back to college this fall. She's enrolled in Tulane, and she's resigned to going. I think it will help her once the semester starts.

"So how are you and Will adjusting to life in N'awlins?" I asked.

"Man, you've got that accent down, darlin'," Claudia quipped. "You say 'N'awlins' like a true Coon-Ass!"

Everett chuckled as he turned a page in his book.

"We're settled in, and we love our house. I want you to come and stay a while after the babies come. I have a suite of rooms that will be perfect for you, and I'm looking for some baby furniture to put in there for you to use. It's right across the hallway from Ava's bedroom. She'll love having the babies there," she said as her eyes sparkled.

"I'd love it. I can't wait!" I assured her.

"An Andler?" Ava asked.

"What, Doodle-Bug?"

"Are my babies in your tummy?" she asked as Claudia smiled at me.

"Yes, sweet girl, they are, but they are going to come out real soon to meet you! They're going to love you so much! You'll be their cousin, did you know that? Cousin Ava Grace!"

"I know," she exclaimed proudly. "An Andler, where is Unca Banin?" Ava asked, taking me by surprise. I looked up at Claudia, and there were large tears threatening to slide down her cheeks.

I took a deep breath. I knew she would ask, but I still wasn't sure how I was going to answer her. I hadn't had much time to think about it since I'd accepted his death.

"Well, Doodle-Bug, Uncle Banton had to leave us to go and fight with the SEALs. There was an accident and Uncle Banton…" I shut my eyes, dreading the pain I knew would come with the words. I hadn't said the words out loud to anyone but John.

"But where is Unca Banin? Is he coming home?" she asked innocently.

"No, Sweetie, Uncle Banton …Uncle Banton went to be with Jesus. Uncle Banton went to live in heaven. He loves us very, very much, but he can't come back," I whispered to her as the tears welled up. Everett silently shut his book, and crossed the room to sit down on the edge of the bed beside me. I felt him touch my shoulder, and I reached up to put my hand over his.

"Is Unca Banin wif Miser Jackson?" Ava asked, gazing up at me.

"Yes, I think he is."

I took a deep breath, and then let it out, trying to get my tears under control. Glancing back up at Claudia, I realized she was having the same problem, the tears rolling down her cheeks. She took a deep breath as well, and smiled when she said, "Ava, remember…we talked about this. Uncle Banton is in heaven, where your Mommy Jess had to go. They are where Jesus can take care of them, and we'll all see them again, someday. Now it's time for you to snuggle down here, and take a little nap." She patted Ava on the leg and pulled her down between us.

Several moments passed as I wiped the tears from under my eyes and stilled the ache that had begun again in my chest. Everett remained still beside me, sensing my longing and staying near. A strange sound broke the silence and then began to grow as I realized it was coming from Ava.

"Noooo, I want my Unca Banin! Unca Banin wooved me, and he needs me! I want my Unca Banin to come home, pweeze, Mommy…call him and tell him to come home, An Andler needs my Unca Banin!" she wailed,

"Oh, Chandler…I'm so sorry, I…let me take her in the nursery and get her down for her nap. Come on, my Ava, let's go in the babies' room," she whispered to her as she clutched her little body close. Ava continued to wail when they stepped out into the foyer. I lay perfectly still, afraid to move, afraid to look at Everett. Several more moments passed and I took a deep breath, held it, and then let it out slowly.

"Bebe, are you all right?" Everett whispered. He slid down on the bed beside me and put his arms around me. I just nodded and curled up against him, willing myself to sleep.

Chapter Eight

I woke with a new determination. I had some of the firsts behind me. The first time I had to say it out loud. Banton was never coming home. I was alone again. He was gone. I lay for an hour or more staring at the ceiling, amazed at the calm that had come over me. I'd prayed long and hard during the night, praying as I'd heard my mother do when she'd lost my grandmother. I'd heard her pray for the strength to believe through him, all things are possible. I'd heard her pray for the peace that passes all understanding. I found the family bible Aunt Chloe had loaned me, and as I opened it, the old, yellowed, tattered pages fell open to the book of Matthew. Circled in pencil was a single passage --"I am with you always."

I felt calm for the first time since Banton had left that day in May. I sat for hours flipping through their family history…all of the trials, the grief, the celebrations outlined in the passages. After I'd absorbed all she had tried to convey to me, there was nothing more I could ask for, than to ask for strength and his guidance in helping me to bring the babies into the world.

After I'd accepted my resolve, I decided I needed to act. The first thing I had to do was to mend my relationship with Mrs. Elaine and Mr. Matt. After I'd showered and dressed for the day, I sat back down on the bed and dialed Mrs. Elaine's cell. She answered on the second ring.

"Chandler, sweetheart…is that you?"

"Yes, Mrs. Elaine. How are you?" I asked in the cheeriest voice I could manage.

"I'm doing well. How are you? What does the doctor say?" she asked anxiously.

"The babies are doing fine. I'm still on course, but I'm still supposed to take things easy, so I'm staying pretty close to home and resting most of the time."

"Oh, I'm so glad to hear it. Banton's father and I would love to come and visit you, if that would be all right?" she asked, her voice shaking with emotion.

"Of course, you are both more than welcome. Mrs. Elaine, I just called to ask your forgiveness about before...when I was so difficult about Banton's service," I almost whispered into the phone. "I know it was hard for you, and my reaction couldn't have been easy," I continued.

"Shh, I'll hear no more, now. You have nothing to be sorry for. We just stayed away, not wanting to upset you any further. Our only concern is for you and the babies right now."

"Please tell Mr. Matt for me and give him my love," I finished, beginning to choke up.

"I will, sweetheart. You know you are our daughter too," she whispered into the phone as I nodded silently. "I'll call you back soon when I find out from Matt when we can visit. Please take care and call us if you need us," she finished.

"I will, I promise. Goodbye," I replied.

Hanging the phone up, I stared at it in my hand for several minutes until I sensed movement in the room. I glanced up and found Everett studying me from the doorway.

"I'm so proud of you, darlin'. And now I have a wonderful surprise for you," Everett announced, rounding the foot of the bed to sit down beside me.

"What surprise?"

"You have a visitor, Bebe. Brie would like to see you. Are you up for it?" he asked gently, squeezing my hand. I'd never spoken to Everett about what had transpired between John and me, but I knew he'd guessed at least part of it. He certainly knew my emotions were raw where Banton was concerned, and he sensed I was a bit jealous of John and Brie's reunion.

I took a deep breath. I was determined I would not be that person.

"Oh, yes...please. I want to see her," I assured him. He nodded, and then rose and left the room. Several moments later, there was a soft knock on my bedroom door.

"Yes, it's open," I called out.

"Chandler...hey." Brie called out in her new, raspier, sexier voice. "How are you feeling?" "I'm good, I just tire out quickly," I replied. "How are you doing? I've been wondering about the two

117

of you. Everett says you've had quite the reunion," I smiled at her as she grinned and dropped down on the foot of the bed.

"Oh…yes, you could say that," she said sheepishly, studying her hands. As she glanced back up at me, I realized she was blushing.

"Brie! I didn't know vampires could blush!" I teased. "Then everything is going well?"

Brie nodded. "Better than I could have imagined. I still have trouble, sometimes. But John has the patience of a saint. He is so sensitive to my feelings and at the first sign that I might be weak he always knows what to do. He's been wonderful."

I watched her carefully trace patterns on the bedspread with her finger. She paused, and then looked back at me with a careful expression.

"Chandler, he needs to come and see you. He has been absolutely tortured, knowing he hurt you terribly with his reaction about me. He feels guilty now, and I really let him have it. I told him I was the one who wanted you and Everett to keep quiet until I was sure about my control. After he'd calmed down, we talked, and he admitted to me part of his anger was due to his confusion over his feelings," she paused, and then whispered "about you."

"Me? What about me?" I asked slowly. When her eyes met mine once more it dawned on me. John had told her about what had almost happened between us.

My eyes began to water as I thought about his kiss. I'd put the entire thing out of my mind. It was too painful to deal with added to all of the raw emotions since I'd accepted Banton's death.

"Oh, Brie…I'm sorry," I breathed out. "I'm sorry for what happened that night, and I'm sorry it still bothers John. He shouldn't be tortured about it. He just missed you, and I knew that. He misses Banton, and we both felt lonely. That's all it was. His anger over my keeping you a secret was understandable. I even expected it, I think. Please tell him it's all right, and I miss him. I wish he would come and see me," I finished as I tried to hold myself together. My insides ached with a raw emptiness I'd become accustomed to whenever I thought about my loneliness.

"Oh, Chandler. You are a better friend than either one of us deserve," she exclaimed, leaning up to embrace me. I held her

118

tightly for several moments and the babies chose that moment to kick and roll.

"Wow, the babies are getting big, huh? I can't believe you can feel them like that," she said, placing her hand on my tummy.

"Um, yeah, it's getting to the point I can't rest or anything. They seem to always be moving."

Brie's smile faded as she raised her eyes back to mine. She seemed to be changing the subject with her expression.

"What can we do for you? I'm so sorry, John told me the Navy has called off their search and closed the files."

I just nodded at her. "Oh, Brie, there's nothing anyone can do. Just promise me you two will be around when the babies get here," I said as I sighed. I took a deep breath. I had to make the ache go away until she was gone and I could cry in private.

"So tell me, what have the two of you been doing? Have you crossed all your hurdles yet?" I asked with a twinkle in my eye.

"Well, we stayed together at the safe house for a couple of days, and then John took me home. I've been staying in until yesterday. I finally got my courage up and went to see my parents...to let them know I was alive."

"How did that go?"

She sighed. "It was really hard. I had my story all arranged, how I'd been held hostage, and how they'd finally released me with the help of the SEALs. They don't believe all of it and suspect I'm holding back. And then there is the problem with my eyes being a different color..." she began.

"How did you explain them?" I asked.

"I told them they'd been damaged in the attack, and I'd had to have surgery, and special lenses. They're skeptical, but they've accepted my explanations for now. They're still extremely hostile to John, and I told them if they continue, I won't have anything else to do with them. My mother backed off immediately. But they both still seem angry with me...I'm not sure why."

"Brie, I'm sure they will come around. Just give them time. They've been through so much," I assured her. "So what about you and John? Are you intimate yet?"

"Well, yes, I can't believe it. I put him off as long as I could. We'd been together for three or four nights. He just held me and assured me he could handle anything. Whenever he'd kiss me passionately, or things would heat up..." she trailed off as she watched me.

I grinned at her. "Go on, you know I'm dying to know," I said.

"I would stop him and tell him I couldn't handle it. Then a couple of nights ago, he woke in the middle of the night. We sleep together like we always did, and I doze, but you know Aldon don't ever really sleep. It's more like sort of a trance."

"Yes, I know a little, with Everett staying with me all the time," I replied.

"John began kissing me slowly and then started to caress me, and before I knew it, we were undressing. I steeled myself against feeling anything. I couldn't let myself go. I was so afraid of losing control of my eyes, of the fangs," she almost whispered as she watched me.

"So, what did you do?"

"I decided I could give in to him without letting myself go, so I didn't stop him."

"And how did that go?"

"I was fine, until he...he was determined to get me to respond! He was so passionate, and the things he did to me! And when our bodies started to move together I lost control. I couldn't stand it, not letting myself feel anything. And it happened," she breathed out as she watched my reaction.

"What happened?" I asked innocently.

"I was so lost into his touch. It had been so long, and we both reached that certain point at the same time...and well, the orgasm, it was so intense I couldn't control it, and I bit him," Brie whispered.

"You what? How did you...I mean, did you have trouble stopping?" I asked carefully, not wanting to upset her.

"No, I realized immediately, and I stopped myself. It's different than feeding, or drinking for thirst. I was horrified I lost control with him, and I was so afraid he would be repulsed by me, but Chandler," she paused and looked up at me.

"What?"

"He told me it was all right. I kept waiting for him to get sick or something, to fight my venom, but he never did. He acted like it was nothing. The next night, he wanted to be intimate again, and I stopped him."

"Did he get upset?" I asked.

"No, he kept urging me to try again. He's so…so passionate. The things he does to me," she paused as she blushed once again. "So we tried again. But this time he pulled me to his neck, wanting me to bite him."

"What?" I whispered. "You're kidding."

"He said it's a part of me, and he can handle it, and…well, he admitted it's really a turn on."

"Okay, we just crossed the 'too much information' line." I held my hands up in horror.

Brie giggled, and then she had me giggling. "Sorry. I just can't believe he does not only so understand about my new baser instincts, but he's actually encouraging them! Chandler, that's the hottest sex we've ever had," she admitted.

"Brie, that's great. Now you have crossed this hurdle, I know there isn't anything you two can't do together. I'm really happy for you," I told her as I held her hand. I could feel her relief and her complete joy flowing through her like a tidal wave. It was almost more than my nerves could handle, being such a complete opposite of what I was feeling at the moment. It took every ounce of strength I possessed to sit quietly and encourage her.

I could tell she sensed my struggle. She sat quietly for several minutes, just holding my hand and watching me.

"Chandler, I'm sorry. I'm sure a conversation about our love life is the last thing you need. You are my best friend. There isn't anyone else who I can talk to. You have been so good to me, and I would have never been able to get through the transformation without you and Everett. I owe you so much," she whispered as she raised her hand to my cheek.

I raised my eyes back to hers, such a beautiful deep emerald green, brimming with emotion.

"Just be happy and love John with all your heart. Believe me, when the babies come, you'll pay me back with interest. I'll need your help…and if they turn out to be fully transformed, we'll all have our hands full. I'll be calling in those favors," I joked as I squeezed her hand.

121

Rising to leave, Brie turned and placed a kiss on my cheek, lingering there. "I feel your sadness, and the hollow ache in your heart, Chandler. I'm so sorry, please let us know if you need anything,"

I just nodded at her. There was nothing they could do for me.

After Brie left, I let the ache take over and sobbed into my pillow until exhaustion finally brought the numbing sleep that was my only refuge.

* * *

There is a time in everyone's sorrow when they reach the point they don't want to grieve anymore. I wanted to feel for someone else. My emotions were all-consuming. I'd been working on my research and notes for the book on my house when I remembered the diary Aunt Chloe had given to me. After searching through my closet I finally found the box I'd stored it in. Checking out my window and finding Aunt Sue and Constance on the patio, I settled back down on my bed with my computer and notes scattered about. I opened the diary and had to study the first few pages slowly. Mrs. Johnson's handwriting proved to be artful and full of flourishes, but not legible. After a bit I finally got the hang of deciphering it, sort of like developing an ear for an accent. The diary seemed to begin sometime around the time of Marie-Claire's engagement.

May 1, 1860   Today Mrs. Montalba stopped by for a fitting for dear Marie's dress. To my distress, we seem at odds about every detail regarding her nuptials, from the ceremony to the reception party, the guest list and the dress. Her father is over-indulgent as usual, and especially so since his hand has been in this courtship from the beginning. I pray this union will be a happy one for our dear girl, and love will follow this alliance her father has made with this family of good standing. I fear it is more to mend his own stormy reputation than to make our daughter happy...

I skipped forward a few pages.

June 25th, 1860   Talk of war dominated the entire day, and I fear spoiled the mood for my dear Marie Clair and her wedding. The DeLee family was represented by one Aunt, who seemed detached from the whole affair. Frederick made quite a show of gifting our daughter and her betrothed with a fair piece of the vast amount of property we have accumulated these past years, and is to have a beautiful new house built on the property just adjacent to town.

March 30th, 1861   My dear Marie-Claire's house is complete! Much grander than our own, it has a beautiful parlor and dining room for entertaining as well as servants quarters across the back and in the attic. There are three large bedrooms up the grand staircase I hope are overflowing with grandchildren soon. Hiriam is away much of the time, and this war will surely put their plans on hold for a family. Marie's mood is much improved of late, and now she is mistress of her own home, seems much more willing to meet me on friendly terms and not to see me as a rival for her father's affections. I believe my dear daughter has grown up at last.

April 16th, 1862   The Judge and I are finding life here in Savannah quite tedious. News of the war and battles fought ever near drive us north to stay with family here in Georgia. Marie's letters are a comfort, but she still refuses to leave. She has abandoned her large home for a time, choosing to stay at a small house in the country. I have sent my beloved Elois to stay with her and the widow Bondreaux, to be of some company to them, and to help Marie through this pregnancy I fear is in jeopardy. The union between Marie and her father's business partner has been a strained and stormy one. I just hope the time apart and distance this conflict has imposed upon their young relationship might help in some part...

October 20th, 1863   These dark days since we lost our beautiful daughter find me in a deep despair I cannot share with my husband. I find solace in writing my feelings on paper; he finds comfort in the bottle. I fear he will find death in his spirits, and I believe that is his wish, his drinking has become such a burden. I cannot find fault, if I were turned to

123

such, would I do the same? I find myself wishing for a sleep deep enough I will never wake, so I can be with my precious Marie-Claire and her sweet babies forever as I am when I dream. I see them, happy and giggling, singing the childhood songs taught by me to their mother, their beautiful dark tresses falling down their little backs much like their mother's did at their age. My dreams are the only place free of pain, free of longing. I'm not lonely in my dreams.

I paused, and placed the opened book across my swollen abdomen. Her description of grief sent chills up my spine. It was as if I'd written it. Over one hundred and fifty years separated us, but we shared a secret, an ache in our hearts. I lay back into the pillows and stared at the ceiling. Some of Banton's last words to me came back hauntingly.

"You know that place between sleep and awake...the place where you can still remember dreaming? That's where I'll always love you. That's where I'll always be waiting,"

I wondered, *did Mrs. Johnson lie in this very room and mourn for her daughter? Had she watched her beloved Elois work out this window?* I felt a connection to both her and Marie-Claire like I'd never felt before.

July 16th, 1865   The War is coming to an end, a dark weave in the fabric of our lives. My life is in ruins as is the South around me. There isn't a family in East or West Feliciana Parish who is not in black, grieving for a son, brother, father...lost in the name of the cause. Daughters lost during the occupation, or to sickness...There seems to be a gray cloud that hovers over the entire country...

August 14th, 1865   I have sold the main house and a fair piece of the property left to me by my late husband. As my daughter's house is closest to town and the newest, I will make my home there. Elois has graciously agreed to stay with me as most of her people have agreed to stay on and sharecrop a piece of the remaining land. My husband's holdings in the north sustain me now, though I suspect it is those holdings for which many held him in contempt. Elois says not to question his decisions, which provide for us now, supporting four

124

families in our time of need. Elois is of the greatest comfort as she has become my one and only lasting friend. She has confided in me of the last days of my dear Marie's life, and for that I am eternally grateful. Elois tells of a handsome sandy-haired young Army captain my Marie helped nurse back to health, who held my Marie's young, grieving heart for a time. The happiest and most in love she'd ever seen a young girl, that is what Elois says. He was away, providing for a way to get her out of this wretched country ravaged by war when she was murdered, her and my two precious unborn grandbabies. I just wish I could hold the dear boy's hand, and express to him my gratitude at making her the happiest in her life, if for only the briefest of moments. This young man, this Captain Samuels, has my eternal love and gratitude.

I slowly made my way back to the present. Rain made patterns down the windowpanes...*when had it started raining*? I had been so absorbed in reading Mrs. Johnson's words I had lost all concept of time. I reached up and wiped a tear from my cheek. I had to give this to Everett, but I had no idea how I would bring it up to him.

As if on cue, Ev picked that exact moment to knock softly.

"Helloooo, Ma Petite...are you awake? Everett needs a little Bebe time," he flirted, plopping down unceremoniously on the bed beside me. "Have you been working all this time?"

"Yes, I have. I have to be doing something...I have to stay busy. The more I write about my house the more I am fascinated by it. The story you told me the other day," I began.

"Yes, how is that coming?" he asked softly as he pushed a stray strand of hair back behind my earlobe, placing a kiss there.

"Flowing as if I experienced it myself. But now I have a different point of reference."

He pulled back to look at me more clearly. "What do you mean, Ma Petit?"

I pulled the diary around and handed it to him, opened to the page I'd just read. "Ev, I think you should read this. Here, or in private. It's Mrs. Johnson's diary, one of the gifts Aunt Chloe brought to us."

125

Everett nodded and began to scan the page. After a few moments, he raised his eyes slowly to mine. "Miss Elois?" he began. I nodded.

"Miss Elois – Mr. Jackson's great-grandmother, and Marie-Claire's Creole maid," I whispered. He nodded his understanding. He continued to read until he'd finished the entire entry.

We sat in silence for several minutes. I knew when he'd finished the last entry, and then had time to read it again. When he lifted his gaze to meet mine, there was a depth of emotion there I'd never seen before. His eyes were the deep, effervescent green of an emotional Aldon, but with a velvety passion that could never be described. He shed no tears, but held the book close to his chest as he exhaled the breath that he seemed to be holding throughout his study of the journal.

"Everett, would you like to take the diary, and keep it for a bit? I will need to borrow it again, for my research. But, I think you should have it. It should stay with you," I whispered.

Everett rose without a word, leaned over to place a kiss on my forehead as he cupped my cheek with his hand, and then left my room silently. I realized Marie's mother's diary was to Everett what Banton's letter had been to me.

* * *

As if I hadn't had enough emotional closure in the day, I had an unexpected visitor that evening. As I was getting ready for bed and for Everett to give me my shots, there was a knock on my bedroom door.

"Come in, it's open."

When no one answered, I looked up. John stood silently in the doorway, his unease draped on him like a cloak.

"Chandler, is this okay?" he cleared his throat and began again, "I...I'm so sorry about the way I behaved the other night...Can I talk to you?" he almost whispered. I'd never seen John so unhinged.

I nodded to him as he closed the bedroom door and walked over to sit down beside the bed.

"Andie, I...I came to apologize for the other day. I don't even know where to begin," he stammered.

"John, don't. I love you so much. Besides Everett and Constance, you're my closest friend. You were Banton's best friend. There is no need for any apologies between us." I reached over and took his hand.

"But the things I said to you, after I'd just..." he paused, running his hands through his hair. "I was so confused about how I felt...how I still feel, about you," he murmured as he looked back into my eyes.

"We've been through hell and back, together. You finally have Brie back, and nothing that happened before matters. I just want my friend back. I miss you, friend," I assured him. I uncharacteristically kept my eyes dry. I had no more tears to shed.

He watched me intently for several moments, and then nodded slowly.

"Everything is good with you and Brie?" I questioned.

"Yes. Better than good," he responded. "I love her so much, even more than before. Things are better than I could have imagined."

I smiled at him, and forced myself to be joyous for him. "Then I just need my friend back and the world will be right again between you and me," I whispered as he finally smiled at me. He stood silently, bent over, and kissed me softly on the forehead. Walking silently to my door, he turned and gazed at me for a brief moment, and then he was gone. I knew we'd never speak of what had transpired between us again.

Chapter Nine

"Darlin', where are you waddling to? I swear you're going to have those babies on this staircase any minute! And Miss Scarlet, I don't know nuthin' 'bout birthin' no babies," Everett sang out as he threw his arm over his shoulder dramatically. "What are you doing out of bed?" he scolded as he rounded the bottom of the staircase from the hallway. "It's impossible to get you to rest! We simply have to get you a couple more weeks down the road, before you go into labor."

"Constance just wheeled in the drive like a bat out of hell. Something's up," I said anxiously, just as the front door flew open.

Constance stood breathless, trying to compose herself enough to talk. Her face was white and stained with tears. She looked up at me when I descended the last three steps and found her voice.

"I don't know how to say this, I don't believe it..."

"What's wrong, Constance?" I demanded. It was inconceivable we would have any more bad news now. "Has something happened to Aunt Sue or Uncle Lon?" I asked, my voice rising.

'No, no. It's...I can't believe it, but just now..." It was like she'd just run out of air, and couldn't go on. She sank down to her knees, dropping everything in the floor.

"Constance! Answer me, what is it?"

"Ty...Ty just...Ty just called me," she began, gazing up into my eyes.

"What?" I whispered. I shook my head as my heart thudded painfully in my chest. This was cruel. She was either confused or was finally losing it.

"I heard him...he was cutting out, and I lost him. I heard him!" she yelled at us, frustrated we didn't believe her. Everett walked over to her and placed his hand on her shoulder. I couldn't believe what I was seeing. Constance was always so matter-of-fact, usually so level-headed.

"Okay, darlin'. You just thought it was him." Everett soothed, picking up her phone. It suddenly rang and vibrated in his hand.

Looking at the number on the front, frown lines appeared in his forehead. He glanced up at me and flipped it open.

"Hello, this is Everett Samuels," he answered, holding his finger up. "Who? What...You're...You're cutting out, I can't hear," and then he looked up at me again with the most incredulous look on his face. His jaw dropped as he walked closer to me and handed me the phone. I placed it to my ear, my hands shaking so I could barely hold it.

"Hello? Hel...Hello? I asked. The signal cracked on the other end, and then faint voices began to clear and get stronger. "Constance, is that you? Can you hear me! It's me, baby, it's Ty! We're coming..."

"What! No, this is Chandler..." I whispered, my eyes rising to meet Everett's. I'd never seen him cry openly, but there were tears brimming. Constance continued to sit like a statue in the middle of the foyer. I held the phone tightly to my ear, straining to hear the voice on the other end.

"...ton, we're on...home,...how...babies...need..."

"What? Ty, I can't hear you...You're cutting out!" I screamed into the phone, desperately trying to hear what he was saying.

"...call back, just hold on,..."

And then I heard him.

A flash of light, my world had light in it again. A warmth spread over me as his voice came, dreamlike, over the small cell phone.

"Sweetheart...ndie......love you so..."

"Banton? Ban...Banton, is that...is it really you?" I whispered, not even able to make myself utter the words. I was afraid I was going to wake up, and this was another vicious, horrible dream.

"...call back, try...get another chance..." and then silence. The line went dead. I slowly dropped my hand, and sank to the floor. I heard him. I knew it. Banton was alive.

"Chandler? Did you hear him?" Constance asked, the tears still streaming down her face.

129

"Yes," I whispered, barely able to speak. I raised my eyes to meet hers. "And Banton. I heard Banton," I whispered as Everett embraced me, rocking me back and forth in the floor.

"Everett," I choked out. "Ev, it's not possible...but I heard him!"

"Yes, Bebe. I believe you did."

Constance shook her head back and forth, crying out loud. Swallowing hard, she looked back up at Everett. "They'll call back. Surely they will call back!"

"How is this possible?" I whispered as Everett pulled me back to look into my eyes.

The doorbell ringing startled Constance back into reality. She stood to open the door.

"Uh-hum, Mrs. Gastaneau, are you Mrs. Gastaneau?" A uniformed Naval Officer stood behind Constance on the front porch. I looked beyond, another officer stood behind him. I could see the same dark blue suburban that had turned my world upside down just weeks before.

"Yes, I'm Mrs. Gastaneau," I answered. He looked around Constance toward me and smiled.

"Mrs. Gastaneau, we have some news, about your husband and another one of the SEALs. Could we come in and talk with you?"

Everett stood and pulled me up. "Certainly, come in, gentlemen."

"It looks as though someone else may have beaten us here to break the news to you."

"Um, yes, I believe we just received a phone call from her husband, and Lieutenant Preston." Everett smiled as he guided me to the sofa. The second officer steadied Constance with his hand under her arm.

"Mrs. Gastaneau, I know this news is a shock, but we've received word just this morning your husband and Lieutenant Preston have been found alive in Somalia. They've both been wounded, but they're going to be all right. They're on shipboard now, on their way home as we speak. They're being de-briefed and should be home by tomorrow evening." He smiled at me, and all I could do was cry. Banton was coming home.

130

Banton was alive. He was coming home to me.

"I must apologize, there is no way to do these things without shocking everyone, but we need for you to inform your immediate family before the news breaks on the television. These things always leak out, even as we try to shield the family." He patted me on the knee and then rose to leave.

"Someone with family services will be in contact with you soon. There will be some red tape to work through."

Constance found her voice. "Commander, did they find anyone else? What about Ben…Lieutenant Oakley?"

"I'm sorry, no. We've found no one but Lieutenants Gastaneau and Preston."

"Thank you, Commander. Thank you so much" I whispered, hardly able to breathe. Everett rose and walked the officers back to the front door.

I sat in stunned disbelief for several minutes, unable to find my voice or to form a coherent thought. All at once, my emotions seemed to take over, having been suppressed for weeks. It all came pouring out at once.

"Constance, you have to call Aunt Sue and Uncle Lon. I'll call Banton's parents and Claudia…" The adrenalin rushed into every part of my body. My hands shook as I pulled my cell from my pocket.

Mrs. Elaine answered on the second ring. "Chandler, what's wrong? Are you in labor?" Mrs. Elaine immediately jumped to conclusions.

"No, Mrs. Elaine. Everything is fine. I…I need for you and Mr. Matt to come here. I need to see you, and I need you here. Could you come right away?" I smiled, wiping the tears from my eyes as I glanced at Everett. This was news I couldn't break over the phone, not to his parents.

"Certainly, dear. Are you sure you are all right?" she asked in an apprehensive tone.

"Yes, I am. I'm great. Please, just hurry. I need to see you," I said, barely able to keep the emotion out of my voice.

"We're on our way! We'll be there in a few hours," she answered, hanging up. Constance grinned at me as she wiped away tears, and then flipped her cell open to call Aunt Sue and Uncle Lon.

I stood and walked shakily back into the entry. Everett had just dialed his phone.

"John, hey, this is Everett...What do you mean, I sound funny? You say I sound funny all the time...Yeah, funny, ha ha. Hey, I need a favor. Could you come over here for a few minutes? It will only take a little while. I just need to talk to you and Brie for a minute...Okay, yeah. See ya in a minute."

He grinned as he pocketed his cell.

"Bebe, are you all right? Can I get you anything?" Everett asked.

"No, I'm..." I couldn't even talk. *Banton was Alive. He was on his way home. He was on his way home, to me. I would see him in less than twenty four hours.* I continued to walk toward Everett, and my knees buckled, my world fading to black.

* * *

"Bebe, can you hear me? Sister, you need to wake up." Everett shook my shoulders as I focused on his face.

"Where...where am I?" I asked as I glanced around, my eyes focusing on my bedroom.

"Well, when you decided to faint in all the excitement, I brought you back upstairs where you belong, darlin'. I don't want you having those babies before their daddy gets home. We've gotten you this far, and we are going to see you through until he can take over." He smiled at me, and I smiled back.

"Then it is true. I didn't dream it." The tears pooled in my eyes as I whispered a reply.

"You've got to stop, Andie-girl. You know how your eyes swell, and you don't want Banton to see you like this," John moved into my view and sat down on the bed beside me.

"He's really coming home! I'm...I'm so scared, John," I began to shake uncontrollably.

"What do you mean? Why are you scared?" he asked as he helped me sit up in bed.

"I'm afraid to believe it. I'm afraid to hope. I'm afraid something will happen, or I'll wake up."

"He's really on his way home, Chandler. You can believe it, I promise." He drew me in and hugged me. "I'm the one person here who knows how you feel. I've been through this too, you know. I still can't believe I got Brie back, but here she is." He grinned, and took Brie's hand and pulled her over next to the bed. "You know, Andie, you and I, we've been through a lot together. I'll help you. It's a hell-of-a-ride, this emotional roller-coaster we've been on." He leaned over and kissed my forehead.

"Yeah, I guess you do know how I feel," I sighed, and then glanced up at Everett. He hadn't stopped smiling since he'd heard Ty's voice.

"Commander Singleton called me before I got over here. He's confirmed the news too, darlin'," John continued to grin the goofiest grin I'd ever seen.

"I wish I could talk to Banton. I want to hear his voice!" I exclaimed as Everett walked across my room.

"Here, Bebe, I got your cell off the charger downstairs. I'm sure whenever they are able to call, you'll hear his voice." He placed the phone in my hand.

I closed my eyes. Visions of Banton walking up the sidewalk, coming through the front door and seeing me after so many weeks had my pulse racing. My eyes popped open.

"Oh no…" I breathed out.

"What?" Everett asked as he perched on the foot of my bed.

"Banton hasn't seen me since May. I'm so big, he won't recognize me! How could he possibly want me," I whispered, looking back to Everett.

"Chandler! I can't believe you are even thinking about that! All he is going to be thinking is how beautiful you are, and how much he's missed not being with you these past months. You can't possibly think he would be disappointed with how you look. You are the most adorable pregnant woman I have ever seen," Everett assured me.

"Besides, you haven't gained an ounce of weight anywhere but your little tummy!" Brie exclaimed, taking my hand in hers.

"Chandler, turn your TV on. The news is breaking." Constance came bursting through the doorway and grabbed the remote, switching the flat screen on.

"FOX news has obtained information from an unnamed source that two Navy SEALs who were previously reported missing/presumed dead in the deadly attack on the Navy vessel a few weeks ago have been found alive in Somalia. No official word has been released from the Pentagon. We will bring you updates as they're received."

I smiled at Constance, and she ran over and flopped on the bed beside me. We all settled in…John on one side, Constance and I on the other, Brie and Everett curled up on the foot. None of us could take our eyes from the television, scanning the ticker across the bottom for any updates about the SEALs. We stayed that way for an hour or more, glued to the screen. The doorbell downstairs broke the silence, and Constance jumped up and bounded down the stairs to answer it.

After several moments of flipping through the news channels some more, Banton's parents burst into the room.

"Chandler, what's going on? Constance wouldn't tell us anything," Mrs. Elaine began as she took in all the faces gathered in the room. Mr. Matt came over and took my hand in his.

"Have you seen any news today?" I asked. Their eyes traveled to the television screen.

"No, what is it?" Mr. Matt asked. My cell phone rang. I picked it up, and it was a number I didn't recognize so I answered it quickly.

"Hello?"

"Chandler, it's me. It's Banton. I'm so glad to hear your voice. They told us we were presumed dead. I'm so sorry! Are you all right?" he asked in a rush. "Sweetheart, are you there?"

"Yyesss," I stammered. "I'm here and I'm fine! I…I can't believe it! It's you…" I sobbed out.

"Baby, I love you so much. Calm down, it's all right. The pregnancy, are you still on schedule?" he asked as I tried to get control to speak coherently.

"Yyesss, I'm …on bed rest, to keep from going into labor. Sweetheart, there is someone else here who needs to hear your

134

voice," my voice quivered. I handed the phone to his father. He looked at me inquiringly and took the phone from me, placing it to his ear as he continued to hold my hand in his.

"Hello…" he asked cautiously. "Ban…oh, my God…Banton?" He looked at me with a shocked expression, and then his knees gave way. John caught him and gently sat him down on the floor. Mrs. Elaine swayed and grabbed the doorway as tears gathered in her eyes. I nodded to her and smiled. Mr. Matt struggled out of his dazed state.

"Son! Oh, my God! Son, we thought you were dead! When, how did you…" He couldn't control the flood of emotion enough to formulate his first question. He glanced around to everyone in the room as they waited, holding their breath.

"Sure, son. I understand. I'll put her back on." He turned back to me and handed the phone back up to me in the bed, his hands shaking as badly as mine were. I had the presence of mind to hit the speaker button, so everyone could hear him.

"Chandler, are you…Are the babies all right?" he asked frantically.

"Yes, Banton, we're all fine. I'm perfect, now I know you are alive. I didn't want to give up hope…I just knew it!" I sobbed.

"Sweetheart, calm down. I love you so much. I can't wait to see you."

"Banton, a Commander and Chaplain who came by this afternoon after you called, they said you'd been wounded…" I took a deep breath. "How badly are you hurt?"

"I'm going to be fine. One of my legs was broken, and my arm, several ribs…They healed without being set, and the Doctors had to re-break some bones and set them. I'm on crutches temporarily, but I'll be good as new, I promise."

"Oh, Banton…I…I don't know what to ask first! When will you be home?"

"This hurricane off the coast is a factor we might have to deal with, but if everything goes well, we should beat it there and be home by tomorrow evening. If necessary, we will re-route and they will fly us in. Either way, I'm coming home to you as soon as possible. Darlin', are you still on track with the babies? How many

135

more weeks does the doctor say?" he asked. I began to sob again. "Sweetheart, it's all right. I'm coming home. Sweetheart?"

I took a deep breath. "I went into labor a few weeks back, when we got word about the missile strike, but Dr. Lane got the contractions to stop, and he's pretty much kept me on bed rest until now, trying to get me to thirty-four weeks for the babies' lungs. I...I can't believe it! You're going to be here when they come," I whispered as the tears continued. I couldn't breathe. My nose was completely plugged from all the crying I'd done the past two hours. I glanced at Constance, and everyone had forgotten her in all the excitement. I knew she needed to talk to Ty, so I just handed the phone to her.

"Banton, Chandler's such a bawl bag, she can't breathe through her nose to talk to you. You know how she swells up, so she gave the phone to me. Is Ty...Can I talk to him?" she almost whispered as though it might make everything disappear if she said it too loud. I smiled at her, knowing exactly how she felt.

"Yeah, he's right here. Ty..." we heard the phone exchange hands, and then Ty's voice.

"Constance, darlin', I'm coming home...I can't wait to see you!" he exclaimed as the tears began to flow from her eyes as well.

"I can't wait...Oh Ty, I can't believe it. I'm so afraid someone is going to wake us up, that this isn't real. We thought you both were dead!" she exclaimed into the phone.

"Hey, it's all right. I'm coming home. I can't wait to see you, to hold you...Hey, stop crying, it's all right, baby...I love you."

"I love you too. I sound just like Andie now, I can't stop crying, either!" she exclaimed into the phone as everyone around the room laughed and cried with her.

"Baby, the connection is beginning to break up again. One of the guys on the ship is trying to set up a video conference through the base, so maybe we'll contact you both on Chandler's laptop a little later...love you all..." then the connection went dead.

Constance turned my phone off, and then glanced around the room. "I forgot to ask him how badly he was wounded!" she exclaimed, tossing the phone back to me.

136

"His wounds probably aren't any different from Banton's or they would have said something. I'm sure he'll be fine, too." John rose and went around the bed to hug her. I surveyed the room. Banton's parents sat in the floor, their arms around each other. Everyone else bounced around hugging each other, stopping to watch the television, and talking on their cell phones.

After he'd had time to calm down and process all of the information, Mr. Matt pulled his cell out and called Claudia and Will to break the news to them, and to ask them to go and get Julia and bring her to Baton Rouge. Everyone in the room could hear Claudia's squeals, and her promise they were on their way. Soon the house overflowed with guests. Sam and Olivia arrived, and Aunt Sue and Uncle Lon followed soon after. All of our Aldon friends who weren't already there on guard duty arrived, and I was sure no Orco would dare come within miles of our little neighborhood tonight. We all watched television until the wee hours of the morning, everyone milling around the house. No one wanted to leave until Banton and Ty were home.

Sometime after three in the morning, my room began to clear as everyone began to settle down. I was exhausted, and my eyes drooped. I was fighting to stay awake. I didn't want to miss a minute of the celebration.

"Bebe, you are exhausted. You need to get some rest," Everett commented, flipping the lamp off beside my bed. The television continued to flicker lights in the darkness.

"No, don't leave me, Everett. I don't want to be alone. I'm afraid I'll wake up and everything will change - that all of this will have been a dream! Promise me you won't leave me," My eyes were closing as I spoke.

Everett sat back down beside me on the bed, drawing me close. "I promise you, my dearest friend, I will not leave you. I'll be here when you wake up, and it's not a dream. Sleep, Bebe. We'll still be celebrating when you wake."

His promise was the last thing I heard before I began to drift.

Chapter Ten

Noises intruded…muffled voices, light banter and laughter. I could hear the soft clicking of my laptop keyboard close by. I slowly opened my eyes, and Everett sat beside me on the bed, focused on my laptop, in the exact same place he'd been when I fell asleep,. As usual my eyes were swollen. I felt them as I pushed up in the bed, but at least they weren't swollen shut this time.

"Good morning, sweet Bebe. I was beginning to worry I needed to wake you, but I wanted to make sure you got enough sleep." He smiled as he pushed a lock of my hair out of my eyes.

"What time is it?" I glanced at the bedroom window realizing it had to be late morning; the sun was streaming through my window.

"It's noon. Are you hungry? I'll go and get you something to eat." He rose and placed my laptop back down on the bed.

"Noon! Why didn't anyone wake me? Has anyone heard from Banton?" I asked frantically.

"No, darlin'. Constance has been in here every ten minutes all night and all morning, checking your cell phone and your computer. I'm sure when they get your little conference arranged you will hear from him. I think maybe they've been a little busy, trying to work out the details of how to get our boys home quickly and safely. We have a little storm moving into the Gulf, you know," he said as he threw his hand out dramatically like he was tossing the information my way. Normally I would have laughed at him, but I was too distracted to notice his little idiosyncrasies today.

"What storm?" I asked, perplexed.

"Did you forget, Bebe, they've been talking about it on the news for days, the little tropical depression out in the gulf. It's now a category three hurricane headed this way. They aren't sure about how it is tracking, but it looks to make landfall sometime early in the morning tomorrow, anywhere from N'awlins up to Alabama. N'awlins is evacuatin' north. My mother and grandmother are already here, stayin' at my apartment for now."

"What will they do about Banton and Ty? Will they wait and come in later?" I asked as Everett patted my shoulder.

"John thinks they will probably make landfall far ahead of the storm, and bring them in to port at either New York or Norfolk, and then fly them down here before the storm hits. He said if he knows Banton, if they close the airport he'll rent a car. Nothing will delay his trip home to you."

"Can't we find out where they're going to make landfall? I'll fly there and wait!" I exclaimed, not wanting the storm to come between me and my reunion with Banton.

"Andie-girl, calm down. Dr. Lane and Dr. Renault aren't going to let you fly anywhere." John appeared at the top of the staircase. He strode into the room, and flopped down on the foot of the bed. "As a matter of fact, Dr. Lane is downstairs right now, talking with Mr. Matt and Mr. Lon. He seems to think with the storm coming, he needs to move you somewhere else. He has a theory about pregnant women and hurricanes."

Everett flipped the laptop shut.

"What theory, Cowboy?" Everett asked as I threw the covers back on the bed, determined to get up.

"Dr. Lane said it's a phenomenon. Dozens of women will go into labor during these storms - something about the drop in the barometric pressure. He doesn't want to get caught unprepared. He wants to get Chandler locked down at his clinic where he has all the equipment he needs. Dr. Renault is already on his way there now."

"No way, I want to be here when Banton arrives! We have to wait," I argued as Dr. Lane came into the room, followed by Banton's parents.

"Chandler, I think it's a good idea. We'll go with you, but we don't have to go until late this afternoon. Dr. Lane is going to enlist John and Sam to set up some back-up generators in case we lose power and you go into labor. He'll need the equipment at the clinic, and we can't chance having to rush you to a hospital with all of the unknowns and your medical history," Mr. Matt reasoned as he and Mrs. Elaine sat on either side of me on the bed.

"We promise, we'll make arrangements, and we'll make sure Banton comes straight to the clinic to be with you." Mrs. Elaine patted my hand, and as I glanced around the room, it seemed it was all settled.

"Well, I guess I'd better get your little bag packed...and just where do you think you are going, Miss Thing?" Everett scolded when I tried to stand up.

"Well, it just so happens I've been in bed for more than eight hours, I'm pregnant, and my bladder doesn't seem to function well with two babies laying on it," I shot over my shoulder. Mrs. Elaine stood and hurried to my side to help me.

"Oh, I'm sorry, Bebe. I'm just used to policing your every move." He smiled and hugged me as I passed.

When I emerged from the bathroom after I'd showered and dressed, my room was full. It seemed I was going to be the entertainment while everyone waited for the boys' homecoming.

"What? Is everyone waiting for me to go into labor?" I grinned at them as Aunt Sue and Uncle Lon filed in with everyone else in the room. Someone had pulled extra chairs into the room the evening before, and it would be the gathering place for the remainder of our stay in the house.

"Yep. It's kind of like watching the microwave popcorn pop!" Cade quipped from the doorway. "The harder you watch, the longer it seems like it takes." He shot me a lopsided grin as he flopped down in the floor in front of Uncle Lon.

We all watched the weather updates together on the television, and I kept my laptop handy in case the video conference was sprung on us in a hurry. While the afternoon drug on, everyone became apprehensive. We assumed there would be at least a phone call from Banton with an update. Sam and John left to go on to the clinic to help Dr. Renault and Dr. Lane with the equipment, and Aunt Sue and Uncle Lon took Constance, Cade and Drew to buy supplies, water and food for us in case of a prolonged power outage while we were at the Clinic. As the house quieted down, Everett tried to get me to lie down and rest, but I was too wired.

"Bebe, you need to get all the rest you can with this storm coming and all the excitement. We'll probably be up late tonight."

"I can't sleep anyway, Everett. My back is really aching from all the laying around." I rubbed my tailbone down low. It seemed with every passing minute my back pain got worse.

"Lean up. Let me rub it for you." He began to rub my lower back and my shoulders as we continued to watch the news. There was a commotion down stairs, and voices drifted up the staircase.

"Sounds like your family is back," Everett observed as he looked down at his watch. "It's five o'clock, so I think we might need to get you to the clinic soon. I'll just take your bags down to load them."

"Thanks, Everett. Thank you for everything. You're a doll."

I leaned over and kissed his cheek.

"Oh, don't I know it." He rolled his eyes heavenward, and I giggled as he bounced up to pick up the suitcases. I heard his footsteps descending the staircase, and then hushed voices...

I frowned as I resumed my search on the computer.

"Chandler, sweetheart...I've waited so long to hear you giggle."

I raised my eyes from my laptop and gasped as I heard his deep voice. Sam and John stood at the top of the staircase with Banton's arms around their shoulders, the two of them helping him to the top step and then through the doorway to our room.

"Banton..." I breathed in a whispered prayer. I could hardly believe my eyes. "Oh, Banton!"

I focused on his face. His beautiful brown eyes were brimming with tears. He had the slightest sexy shadow of a beard, and as he grinned and shot his dimple at me, I gasped. I finally tore my eyes away from his face, to appraise the condition of the rest of his body. I could see the outline of bandages around his ribs under his t-shirt, and one of his legs was in a boot-type cast. They helped him hobble over to the bed and turned him so he could sit beside me. He pulled me into his arms and I collapsed into them, laughing and crying at the same time. I heard the bedroom door shut, Sam and John were giving us time for a private reunion.

He pulled my face back to look at me as we gazed at each other. I couldn't believe my eyes.

"You're here. You're really home!" I began to cry again. He covered my face with kisses.

"Sweetheart, don't cry. Yes, I'm home!"

He grinned, and for the first time in months, I touched his dimple, winking at me from the corner of his mouth. He pulled

141

back and placed his hand on my stomach, rubbing it as he leaned over to kiss the basketball that used to be my abdomen.

"I've dreamed of this moment...seeing you so pregnant." He raised my shirt to look at my belly. "You are so beautiful. I've...I've missed so much time with you!" he exclaimed angrily as he caressed my skin, expanded across the babies.

I watched him take in the changes to my body, and then his eyes rose slowly back to hold mine.

"I can't believe it!" I breathed. "I've never been so relieved...so happy," I whispered. He held his hand out to my cheek. We sat staring at each other for several minutes. I was lost in his deep brown eyes. He slowly pulled me to him as he covered my lips with his, gently at first, then deepening his kiss. I wound my fingers in his hair while he caressed my lips, pulling back every so often to look at me, and then drawing my lips back up to his again. The babies kicked furiously as he held me. Pulling away, he looked down at my stomach and smiled when he placed both of his hands there to feel them.

"They're welcoming you home...they must sense the excitement!" I exclaimed. Banton looked back up into my eyes, and then rose back up over me, kissing the tears as they slid down my cheeks.

"I kept expecting you to call. I was afraid you'd been held up because of the storm." I stammered. He pulled me into his lips again. He kissed me deeply, drawing me up fully into his arms as I wound my arms around his neck.

"You are so beautiful, Chandler. I love you so much! It's been torture not to be able to get word to you, to talk to you," he whispered, placing kisses down my neck. Stopping abruptly, he slid his thumbs under my eyes and wiped the tears away. "I've never been so frustrated...knowing you needed me and I couldn't get word to you I was alive and coming home to you."

All I could do was stare at him and nod. His eyes were so beautiful, seeming to be three different shades of brown at once. They sparkled with unshed tears as he continued to flash his dimple at me. He embraced me again, pulling my cheek up against his lips as his breath brushed inside my earlobe.

"How can you possibly be more beautiful than when I left? You are glowing, Chandler. You have to be the most stunning pregnant woman I've ever seen."

As he slid his fingers into my hairline, catching the long curly tresses fully into his grasp, his mouth covered mine again, his kisses long, intense gulps as he seemed to drink in the memory of my lips.

He pulled away when we heard a knock on the door.

"Go away!" I called out as he chuckled and pulled me in close, folding his arms around me. With my face in his chest, I inhaled deeply...I'd missed his smell.

"I'm sorry to interrupt, but we need to move Chandler to the clinic now. We're under a severe thunderstorm and tornado watch, and they're expecting the weather to deteriorate rapidly in the next two hours. We don't want to get caught on the road with her," John warned. He and Sam came back in the room with Everett directly behind them.

"Yeah, let's get you to Dr. Lane's," Banton agreed with them as I peeked out from under his arms and started to protest.

"I promise, we won't separate the two of you for a second. We've got the Lincoln running, and you two can have the back seat all to yourselves," John promised. He took Banton's hand to help him up.

As Banton started to push off the bed to stand, John just swung him up into his arms. "This will be much quicker, Brother, don't argue...I'll just run you to the bottom of the stairs and plop you down." He started out of the room with Banton.

"I'll get Chandler." Sam leaned over to pick me up from the bed.

"Oh, I'm sorry, wait, I need to go to the bathroom again," I stalled. The pain in my lower back was getting worse, and when I rose, pains shot across my tailbone and everything seemed to tighten. A sudden gush of water between my legs soaked my tights and the side of the bed. Startled, I looked up at Sam as Everett exclaimed, "Sweet Holy Mary, Kids...Chandler's water just broke!"

"What?" Banton whipped his head around over John's shoulder at the top of the stairs. John whirled, just as a spasm

143

ripped across my abdomen, seeming to pull my tummy down to the floor with the contraction.

"Sam, pick her up, and get her downstairs!" Banton yelled. His frustration at not being able to do it himself was apparent. Sam did as instructed. He scooped me up in his arms and hurried down the staircase with me.

"Wait, let me get something dry on," I complained as he carried me out the front door and into the front yard.

"We'll take care of all that in the car, Bebe, don't worry," Everett called from somewhere behind us. We were quickly surrounded by family in the front yard as everyone talked at once. Sam and John made the announcement my labor had started as I was loaded into the car. John shoved Banton in on the opposite side and then jumped into the front seat. Everett climbed in beside me with a blanket. Within seconds we were off, our little circus caravan of family, SEALs and Aldon trailing down the interstate toward the clinic. Banton glanced worriedly back and forth out the window at the black clouds beginning to gather overhead, then back to my face as I fought to control my breathing. The contractions intensified.

"Here, Bebe, let's get those wet things off – we'll just wrap you up in the blanket." Everett threw the corner of the blanket across me to Banton as Banton helped me off with my tights. After he had my clothes off under the blanket, he wrapped it around me and pulled me over into his lap, cradling me in his arms. I lay my head on his shoulder.

I gritted my teeth when another contraction hit. "As bad as this is, I'm so happy…you're here, and the babies are coming." My voice rose, the pain grabbing me again, doubling me over as Banton tried to soothe me. He slid his hand under the blanket, and placed it on my abdomen as he watched my expressions. When the pain subsided, I relaxed and smiled up at his concerned face.

"This is nothing, compared to the pain of losing you."

"Boy, Dr. Lane nailed this one. He said hurricanes seem to bring on labor early," John commented from the front seat.

"Is he concerned…I mean, this is too early, isn't it?" Banton asked as Everett wiped my forehead with a cool rag.

144

"Just a month," I panted out breathlessly. "We are only about a week and a half away from where the doctor really wanted me to be."

I began to breathe faster. I could feel the next contraction beginning, and my lower back and abdomen were beginning to tighten in to a hard contraction.

"Sam, get us the hell to that clinic! These contractions are only about four minutes apart!" Banton exploded as he glanced at his watch. In spite of the pain, I couldn't help but smile. Banton seemed so serious and frustrated. This was one situation he couldn't control. Even in the middle of the contractions, warmth tingles spread over me with the knowledge Banton was home, and I was in his arms.

I reached up and wiped the sweat that had begun to form on his brow. Banton leaned down, pressing his lips softly to my forehead.

"Bebe, did the contractions just start when your water broke?" Everett asked, pouring fresh water over the washrag out of his water bottle and bathing my face again. I held my breath, waiting for a contraction to pass.

"No, I guess they started earlier. I thought it was just a backache, but now I know it must have been my labor starting," I gritted through my teeth as the pain began to subside.

"How long ago did your back start hurting?" Banton asked, stroking my cheek with his thumb. His brow creased. I began to wince again, the pain coming back much faster this time.

"When I woke up, about noon," I gasped out. A hard contraction hit. This time, I let out a moan and then a scream, the pain becoming unbearable. I watched the helplessness on Banton's face as everything began to snow out of my vision, the pain causing me to become light-headed. I fought to stay conscious as the SUV came to a halt outside the clinic doors.

"Hang on, sweetheart, we're here," Banton pleaded. The doors flew open. I was losing my grip on awareness. I felt two sets of arms pulling me out of the door and then laying me on a gurney. I watched over me as we passed under the awning and through the doors into the emergency room entrance to the clinic.

Dr. Lane's voice broke through the confusion around me. "She's bleeding, there's too much blood..." he exclaimed, pulling the blanket from me. Banton was at my shoulder, his face coming into view as he grabbed my hand and held it.

I could feel cold hands on my abdomen. "She's not dilated, and she's hemorrhaging. Don't bother with the fetal monitors. We need to get them out, now." Dr. Lane cautioned.

"Hurry, please! Banton, don't leave me," I pleaded, scared I was about to lose them.

Banton gently took my face in his hands, and leaned over to kiss me. "I love you...you and the babies are going to be fine. I'm not going anywhere." He continued to gaze at me as Dr. Renault spoke.

"You're going to be fine, Chandler. The babies will be all right. We're going to take them, but we've got to do a C-section now. We don't have time for an epidural, so we're going to put you under. Just calm down," Dr. Renault's face came into view as he placed the rubber mask over my mouth.

Banton leaned over me and kissed my forehead. "I promise you, I'll be right here when you wake up."

"Just count backwards from ten, Chandler," Dr. Renault commanded as I nodded.

I watched Banton's beautiful face as he counted with me. "Ten, nine, eight..." And his face faded from view.

Chapter Eleven

Voices drifted around me as I fought the fog in my brain... "Sleeping!"... "Look just like Banton!"... "Chandler is still out."..."Sirens are sounding...lost power..." Loud noises intruded as the excited voices continued to drift in and out. I could hear the loud wind and rain and huge claps of thunder that seemed to rock the room I was in. I pushed myself to wake up as I heard someone say "tornado on the ground, south side of the city... get the generators running!"

I was panicked. *Where were my babies? Were we safe from the storm? Banton, where was Banton? Oh, God...had I just dreamed he was alive? Banton...* I couldn't see. I fought to open my eyes, and all I could make out was darkness and shadows. A bolt of lightning ripped through the sky, lighting the room with a flash.

Someone hovered over me. I fought to focus my eyes. *The medication they'd given me must be affecting my vision,* I thought. As I struggled to focus, Banton's face took form. When he caught sight of my opened eyes, he grinned down at me. His dimple made my world brighter than the lightening had.

"Banton...you're here!" I tried to shout over the thunder, but croaked instead.

"Of course I am, Sweetheart. I've been right here the whole time."

"Where are the babies?" I asked hoarsely.

"Shhh. Rest, now," he soothed me, placing his lips in my hair. "The babies are fine. They're here in the room with us, Chandler. Momma and Daddy are holding them right now." His face split into a huge smile as he stroked my cheek with his thumb.

"They're sleeping. Oh, God, Chandler, they're so beautiful -- and so are you." He leaned over and kissed me gently on the forehead, and then moved down to my lips, placing a more lingering kiss there. He leaned his forehead into mine, and I was momentarily lost in his gaze.

"Thank you, baby. I love you so much," he murmured softly.

I began to relax, realizing from his manner everything was fine. "Two girls?" I asked sleepily. He shook his head slowly and grinned.

"A girl and boy. One perfectly matched pair, just like Aunt Chloe predicted."

"Why is it so dark in here? Banton, I want to see our babies. I want…" I winced as I tried to raise my head. My abdomen felt as though I'd been sawed in half, every muscle in my body ached.

"Shhh. We'll let you see them, just let us get some lights on. Wait a few minutes, John and Sam are trying to get the generators hooked up to get some power on." He reached down and cradled my face with his hand, stroking my cheek again with his thumb.

The fog began to lift in my brain enough to begin to worry. "Are the babies' lungs good? How is their breathing?" I asked anxiously.

"They seem fine, but Dr. Renault wants to put them under oxygen tents until they consult with an Aldon pediatrician. Sam and John are rigging something up now."

He continued to stroke my cheek as I asked questions. "How much did they weigh?"

Banton chuckled. "Our big boy weighed in at seven pounds and nine ounces! Mrs. Sue said he looks like a three month old, that he is every bit as big as either one of her two boys were, and they weren't twins. We'd all hate to see how big he would have been, if he hadn't been a twin, and early…" he trailed off.

"And our daughter?" I asked. I watched his eyes sparkle.

"Six pounds, two ounces. That's fourteen pounds of babies, Sweetheart! I don't know how you did it!" He leaned over and kissed me again. "So, what are we naming them?"

"I don't know. I guess I'll have to see them first." I smiled as I watched his face in the dark. Lights flashed in the other room, and the lights on the foot of my bed flashed.

"Sam must finally have us hooked to a power source," Banton commented.

"They're so perfect, Chandler. The most beautiful babies I've ever seen!" Mrs. Elaine exclaimed as she walked over closer to the bed. I could see one of the babies bundled in her arms, but I couldn't make out a face. Banton reached over and took the control to the bed.

"Here, let me raise your head just a bit." When he moved to prop more pillows behind me, I winced.

"I'm sorry, did I hurt you?" he asked anxiously.

"No, I'm just sore, that's all. Please, raise me a little more. I want to hold them." I held my arms out, and took my baby just as the reserve low-lights blinked and came on in the room. The tiny face that greeted me could not have been more angelic.

"Meet our beautiful daughter, Mommy," Banton whispered, touching her cheek.

"Oh, wow! Hey, sweet girl," I whispered to her. "So you're one of the culprits who's been kick-boxing me in the ribs." I took her tiny hand in my fingers, and pressed my pinky finger into her grasp as she clenched it tightly. I looked up at Banton through my tears.

"Ellyson...Elly. I think it fits. Ellyson Marie Gastaneau," Banton whispered as I nodded. She had a head full of jet black hair curling around her face. She was sleeping, but I could tell she resembled Banton. Her lashes curled downward and touched her chubby cheeks. I took my finger out of her grasp and touched the corner of her little mouth. She puckered her mouth at first, and then scrunched her tiny cheeks into a grin – the slightest hint of a dimple showed at the corner of her mouth.

I gasped, "Look at her dimple!" and then glanced up at Banton as he grinned down at me, showing me his.

"Yes, you marked both of them good, you little stud-muffin, you!" Everett teased, waltzing into the room. "Good to see you awake, Bebe! You sure had everyone hopping there for a little while. I've never seen Sam so unhinged, or our cowboy John pace more. Even the Aldon were unsettled!" He leaned over to kiss my cheek.

"So our baby boy has the same dimple?" I asked, grinning up at Banton.

"He sure does. Here, give Ellyson to me," Banton urged. I handed her up to him. Then Mr. Matt leaned over and handed me our son. He picked that exact same moment to open his eyes and yawn, a precious squeak escaping as he closed his little mouth. My

149

eyes began to tear again as Banton whispered, "And both of them definitely have your beautiful almond shaped eyes." He placed a kiss gently on Ellyson's forehead.

Aunt Sue and Uncle Lon pushed through the doorway as everyone else craned their necks in the hallway to see in.

"I can see both of you in their features. They're beautiful!" she exclaimed when she pulled the receiving blanket away from our son's face.

"Oh, crap, Mom, you say that about all babies. You can't tell who they look like until they're walking!" Cade called out from the hallway.

"Yeah, they all look wrinkled and fat, like little Sumo wrestlers!" Drew chimed in as everyone laughed.

"I can't tell if his eyes look blue or green in this light," I whispered. I glanced up at Banton. He reached over with his hand and touched my face, smiling reassuringly. He knew what I was asking, and I knew he was unsure as well.

"Well, you've named our baby girl. What are you going to name our grandson?" Uncle Lon asked as Aunt Sue put her head over on his shoulder. *He said our grandson...like it was the proudest moment of his life.*

"Chandler insists on this one, but I'm still not sure." Banton handed Elly to Aunt Sue, and then placed one hand under our son's head and the other on my cheek. I looked up into his eyes as he smiled. He knew I'd made up my mind so he nodded.

"Banton Matthew Gastaneau IV. I refuse to mess with tradition, and I think it's a name worth aspiring to live up to. But since it's such a mouthful for such a little boy, I think Matty will do just fine for now." I watched Mr. Matt's reaction, and he snapped his head up and grinned at me.

"Banton Matthew and Ellyson... Marie?" Everett whispered Ellyson's second name as his eyes watered. Matty and Elly...That's beautiful, Bebe." Everett smiled at me, adding his approval.

"I'm sorry to interrupt, but we need to take the babies for just a little while. We want the pediatrician to check them, especially their lung function, just to be sure. We'll bring them back to you as soon as we're finished," Dr. Lane assured us when he reached for

Matty. I gave him up reluctantly as Aunt Sue handed Ellyson to Dr. Renault.

"Let's everyone come back into the camp-out area. We have food prepared, and we'll get everyone settled in. There's another storm moving through in a few minutes and Chandler needs to rest." Aunt Sue herded everyone out of the room, except for Mr. Matt and Banton. Mr. Matt hesitated beside the bed for a moment and then leaned over, kissing me on the forehead.

"Thank you, my sweet daughter. You have made me a, very happy grandfather today. We love you with all our hearts." He raised back up, and the light from the lightening through the window made the tears in his eyes sparkle. Then he whispered softly, "You never gave in...Even when his mother and I gave up hope and accepted his death. You knew he was alive. You are truly his soul mate. I thank God every night in my prayers for sending you to my son." The tears spilled over as he turned and touched Banton's cheek and silently left the room.

Banton turned to me after he shut the door. "Sweetheart, what was he talking about? What did he mean, *you never gave in?*" he asked as he sank down in the chair beside the bed.

"Oh, I was just difficult...I...I still have a hard time, talking about that day," I whispered as he took my hands in his. He lifted them to his lips, and pressed a kiss there.

"What day, Andie?" he urged me to continue.

"I was on the front porch with Constance and Claudia. We were playing with Ava Grace, swinging on the porch swing, waiting on news from you." I took a deep breath. "A Navy Suburban drove up, and a chaplain walked up to the front porch and asked for Mrs. Gastaneau. He told us you and two other SEALs had been listed as missing, presumed dead. Everyone fell to pieces, Everett had to carry me upstairs, and John came over to try to help Everett hold us all together. Claudia called your parents, and when they arrived they tried to talk to me about making arrangements with their pastor, and to make plans for a memorial service. I picked that moment in time to be obstinate, to get really angry, and resigned myself that you were not dead. You were only missing, and I wasn't having any talk about your death."

I took a deep breath, and gazed up at him. He was studying me with a rather stunned look. "I really upset your parents and Claudia. We really didn't speak until two weeks after the memorial service."

"I didn't know...I didn't know they held a service," he answered. "Oh, God, Chandler! What you must have gone through!"

"I waited for news. I kept thinking they would find you like they had Colin. I told everyone until I had a body to bury, I wouldn't consider you dead." I returned his gaze and he smiled. "That strategy worked until the night I had the dream..." I sucked in my breath, trying to control the sobs I felt rising in my chest as I watched him closely. This was the one thing I was so confused about. He studied my face and then nodded to me.

"You were in my dream," I whispered.

"Yes, I was. You dreamed you were in a field, and you were standing in the middle, and your Mother and Mr. Jackson were behind you, unable to come any further. You seemed out of options...the Tariq stood in front of you with the babies at his feet, totally unprotected," he stated as he studied me.

"How do you...how do you know that?" I whispered incredulously.

"Because I was there, Andie. I shut my eyes at that moment, and I saw what you saw in your dream. I flew at him to protect you and the babies. I fought him. I killed him again in the dream, and then I told you that you were safe, that he would never hurt you or the babies again."

He smiled at me, and then his smile faded as he watched the tears stream down my face, my chest heaving with sobs. The memories of that night tore my chest open again.

"What is it?" he asked as he placed his hands on my cheeks and wiped the tears away with his thumbs.

"When you came to me in the dream, it convinced me you were really dead. No one living had ever been in my dreams. Mr. Jackson passed away and appeared right after in my dream with my mother. When you showed up in my dream..." I gasped and caught my breath, reliving that awful night when I had accepted his death.

"Oh, God, no…Andie, I'm so sorry. I can see why you thought that. I'm so sorry." He leaned over, pulling me into his chest.

I pulled away and released all of the emotion. The tears released when I revealed my inner thoughts to him. "I died too, Banton. I truly died on the inside, and my dreams ended with you. I wanted to curl up and die to be with you. I relived it every day after that." I paused as he continued to watch me, concerned. Then I added, "And now, I feel like I have to tell you everything."

I dropped my eyes, not knowing how I was going to put into words what had almost happened between John and me, and knowing if I didn't tell him, it would eat away at me.

"Tell me what, Andie?" he asked softly.

"First, you have to know John saved me many, many times. He and Everett never left my side after you went missing. Then, when the Tariq began stalking my dreams again, they took turns staying with me. One of the hardest things was trying to help John. He was still mourning Brie, and he was trying to get me to accept your death. He'd given me your letter, and then I had the dream. That was the night I told him about Brie."

He continued to watch me intently, and I sensed he was putting two and two together.

"What are you trying to tell me, Chandler?" He closed his eyes as he continued, whispering as if in pain. "Did something happen between you and John?"

"He thought he'd lost Brie, and we both thought you were gone, that we'd lost you. He was downstairs when he heard me sobbing, when I woke from my dream. He came up to check on me and I told him why I'd finally accepted you were dead. We were both hurting…both so lonely, and we shared a brief kiss," I whispered, watching in terrified silence when a tortured expression crossed his face.

I placed my hand on his cheek as he looked back up at me.

"I realized in the flash of a second, all I was feeling was he was my link to you. And I told him it would be a mistake, because that is all I was to him, besides a friend…I was his link to Brie. That's all both of us were feeling," I finished. I spent several tortured moments waiting for him to react. Finally he seemed to relax as he took my hand in his, and then looked back into my eyes.

"I wish it hadn't happened. It's difficult for me to wrap my head around. But I understand you both thought I was dead," he said, tears glistening in his eyes.

"That's when I told him he'd regret it if anything at all happened between us. Then I told him about Brie. It was the hardest thing aside from accepting your death I've ever done. Once it dawned on him Ev and I had been keeping Brie's existence a secret, he became furious and he turned on me."

My tears began to fall again as he watched me intently. "It broke my heart. We'd become such good friends, but in a second, it had changed from that to contempt. All I could see in his eyes was hate when he stormed out of the house. Then I felt really guilty. I knew he was having the sweet reunion with Brie I would never be able to have with you. I wanted to be happy for them, but really, all I wanted to do was to go to sleep and never wake up... so I could be with you." I whispered as his expression changed from pain to anger.

"Never say that! I couldn't stand the thought," he stammered as he pulled me in to his chest. "I wouldn't. I had the babies to think of. That's all that pulled me through. That, and your memory. I had to go on for you. The babies were yours, and I was determined they would know you, and you would be proud of me." He tightened his embrace, tighter than he'd ever held me.

"Please, don't be mad at John. Things were a little awkward after that, it was something we've put behind us. He and Brie were so happy when they reunited, and then when we found out you were alive, well...aside from me and your parents, John was the most emotional. It was like he was complete again, when he found out you and Ty were coming back. He truly loves you, Banton."

He waited several moments, gathering his thoughts, and then finally he sighed and spoke. "Sweetheart, I'm glad you told me. This is all so strange, and we've been through so much. It's a lot to process, but I'm trying to understand." Then he pulled me in to kiss me deeply. As he finished, he pulled away slowly and breathed, "I love you even more, if that is possible."

Watching him was so surreal. I'd been mourning him for so long, I couldn't process that he was sitting here in front of me, alive and well. I began to cry again, trying to smother the sobs erupting out of my chest.

"Sweetheart, what is it? I told you, everything is all right," he began, wiping the tears from my cheeks.

"I can't...I just can't shake the feeling of mourning that is still hanging over me. I can't convince myself you're really alive and you aren't going to disappear!" I almost shouted at him.

Banton rose and scooted onto the bed and pulled me up into his arms.

"I'm so, so sorry. Shhh. I'm sorry." He rocked me for quite a while as my breathing returned to normal.

"So how, how did you finally come into my dream?" I asked as he released his hold on me.

"Some fishermen pulled Ty and me out of the water, and they took us to a small village to hide us from the pirates and the Somali band of Orcos. After what they considered was a safe amount of time, they sent for a voodoo leader - a medicine man to help with our wounds. He couldn't do much for the broken bones which had already begun to heal, but we were able to communicate enough for me to ask him questions about your dreams. I confided in him. I was so worried about you. He brought in some of his tribal leaders and they prayed with me, and then they prayed to the voodoo saints. That night, I dreamed about you. I felt really close to you, and I missed you so much, worried about you so much my chest ached. I woke in a sort of trance. That is when I saw your dream."

I reached up and touched his cheek, and drew his face down to mine. "You said in your letter you could feel me even with the distance between us. You said you would always be with me. You were right. I felt you with me, even when I convinced myself you were dead."

He leaned down and kissed the tears left on my cheeks.

"I'm not leaving you, ever again. I promise. I'm here, and I'm all yours." He drew me up to kiss me passionately. He moved his lips over mine, his breath sweet in my mouth.

I drew back and held his face in my hands. "I still can't believe I have you back." I gazed back and forth at his eyes as he dropped his eyes back down to my lips. I sighed as he kissed me again, sliding his hands down my shoulders as he moved his mouth across my cheek, down my neck to my bare shoulder. I shivered as the familiar warmth spread over my body Banton's touch always stirred.

I was euphoric. I just couldn't grasp the reality of the miracle. So much had happened in just one day...*Banton back from the dead, and, I was a mother!*

After a few more moments, the doctors came back into the room with the babies.

"How are they, Doc?" Banton stood and took Matty from Dr. Renault.

"They're perfect in every way. Their lungs are good, no need for any respirators." Dr. Lane answered him.

"And thanks to your decision, the cord blood is stored and waiting for our tests," Dr. Renault said as he patted Banton on the back.

Dr. Lane handed Elly back to me, and then tucked the blanket in around her.

"Dr. Renault, can you tell anymore about...how they will be? Are they like Banton and me, or will they be more like Aldon children?" I asked nervously.

"It's too early to tell, Chandler. We'll just have to wait and see. We should know by the time they're four or five months old. Their eyes will give them away by then."

"Chandler, are you going to try and breast-feed the babies, or do you want me to give you something to dry your milk up?" Dr. Lane asked.

"No, I want to breast feed," I said determinedly.

"Then you need to pump today because of the drugs in your system from your surgery. I think by tomorrow, you can start feeding them. We have a special formula for you to feed them until you can nurse, with lots of protein they will need. Would you like to feed them now?" He smiled as the nurse brought in the bottles they had prepared.

"Oh yes, please."

The nurse handed a bottle to each of us, and Banton sat down in the chair beside the bed, offering the little bottle to Matty as he cradled him in the crook of his arm. Matty latched on and sucked noisily, apparently hungry. Banton grinned up at me. "Oh, wow. This is great. It's wonderful...I had no idea how this would feel."

I looked down at Ellyson and touched the bottle to her lips. I had to urge her several times to take the nipple, but she finally latched on as well. She'd hardly taken two ounces before her little eyelids became heavy and she drifted off to sleep.

"You may have to wake them often to feed them the first few weeks. I'll have the nurse bring a breast-pump in to you later and show you how to use it. I encourage you to eat as much protein as possible so they will get the nutrition they need. You need rare steak, for yourself and them."

"Okay, thank you, Dr. Lane. Thank you for everything."

He touched my cheek, and then Ellyson's, before looking back at my face. "It was my pleasure, Chandler. I so rarely get to experience this part of the job, with all of my patients being half-breeds. And twins...this is a first for me."

Banton stayed at my side, feeding Matty until he drifted off like his sister, and then rose to put him down in his bassinette. He hobbled back to my bed to take Elly and I shook my head.

"Please, let her lay here a little while. I love this." I grinned up at him as Ellyson continued to sleep, curled up in her little baby-ball, her face planted firmly against my heartbeat.

"You two are so beautiful." Banton gazed at me as he straightened the little blanket around her. He sat back down in the chair at my bedside and lay his head over on the pillow beside me, watching her little face as she slept. Every so often she would make sucking noises in her sleep, and Banton would chuckle and caress her tiny cheek with his finger.

I finally relented and let him take her and put her in her bassinette. The nurse came back in to take them back to the other room.

"Oh, please...leave them in here with us. I want to take care of them," I requested as she shook her head.

"Doctor's orders. He wants you to rest. And you have two very determined grandmothers out here who are dying to take care of them tonight. We'll bring them back to you first thing in the morning, I promise." She smiled as she turned to push the bassinets back through the doorway.

"She's right, Andie. You need to rest. How is your pain, are you hurting?" he asked, placing his hand over mine.

"I'm all right," I lied. The pain across my abdomen and lower body was excruciating, but I knew if I asked for pain meds it would be even longer before I could nurse the babies.

Banton watched me as I hesitated. "You're lying, Chandler Ann. I know you are hurting. I'll get Dr. Lane to give you something.

"No!" I replied, pushing up in the bed. "No, I don't want them to give me anything else! I don't want to mess up being able to nurse the babies tomorrow."

"Chandler. Please, for me?" He watched my expression, and then resigned himself to the fact I wouldn't give in.

"You are really, really stubborn, you know? Now, lay back and try to rest, Chandler. It's been a long day." He stroked my cheek as he lay his head back down on the bed beside mine.

I nodded and closed my eyes. I couldn't seem to get into a peaceful sleep. My brain wouldn't turn off. The sound of my family and friends drifted through the doorway to my room, Everett's laughter, excited chatter between Mrs. Elaine and Aunt Sue, and the sound of Cade and Drew arguing.

* * *

I stood on the shoreline, watching as the gunboat that carried the SEALs drew nearer to the dock. I started down a flight of stairs that would take me down to meet them, and a flash and shockwave stopped me in my tracks. The ship lit up like a roman candle, debris flying in all directions.

"BANTON! Please, dear God, no!" I screamed out as I sat up in bed. I looked frantically around the room in the moonlight, and struggled to focus on Banton when he rose and hobbled across the room to me.

"Shhh. Chandler, it was only a dream. I'm here, sweetheart," he soothed, sitting down on the edge of the bed. I stared at him for a moment as I remembered he was home.

I took a deep breath, and then smiled at him, shaking the dream. "Get in with me, please?" I begged. I pulled the blankets back and invited him in beside me. He kicked his boot off his good foot and flashed his dimple at me, snuggling down beside me and gently pulling me over to lay my head on his shoulder. I inhaled as I nuzzled against his t-shirt. The scent of his cologne wafted through my head, instantly relaxing me.

"I've dreamed of smelling your scent again," I sighed, closing my eyes.

He chuckled as he answered me, "Sleep, Chandler. It's almost dawn, and this will be a busy day. You need to sleep now," he commanded, kissing the top of my head as I relaxed and drifted off again.

After a couple of hours, I woke to the sounds of our babies crying. I moved my head and glanced up at Banton. He was awake, watching me sleep.

"You are so beautiful. I love you," he mouthed to me.

"And I love you," I mouthed back.

"It sounds like my babies are hungry," he chuckled as the door opened to my room, the nurse wheeling the babies back to us. Banton stood and stretched, and then moved over to pick Elly up. The nurse picked up Matty and brought him over to me.

"Here, Mommy, he's hungry and ready for his morning bottle." She turned him gently to hand him down to me.

"Can't I nurse them yet?" I asked. She shook her head. "Dr. Lane wants to check your blood before you start. I'll be in to draw it after they've been fed." She handed us the bottles and left the room.

"Hey, little man. You sure are making a fuss," I cooed to him, offering the bottle. He took it immediately, sucking noisily as I looked up at Banton.

"She doesn't seem to be hungry. She keeps falling asleep," he worried, urging Elly to take the nipple in her mouth.

"The Doctor said we might have to wake them to feed them the first few weeks. Just keep trying," I urged. I watched our son suck his first four ounces down immediately.

"Hey, how are Aunt Constance's babies this morning?' Constance bubbled. She slipped into the room followed closely by Ty.

"I wondered what happened to you two after we got here last night." Banton arched an eyebrow at her as Constance walked over and kissed his cheek.

"Sorry, we got lost in the shuffle at the house. Then after everyone left, we kind of got caught in the storm at home, so we rode it out alone at your house. Besides, someone had to watch Beau," Constance grinned as Ty put his arm around her.

"Oh, yeah, I'm sure your main concern was Beau," I teased.

I pulled the bottle from Matty's mouth. He'd sucked it completely dry, taking all six ounces and then proceeding to scream at the top of his lungs again. I placed him on my shoulder and gently patted his back, and he burped loudly after only a few seconds.

"That's my boy!" Banton exclaimed as he set the bottle down on the nightstand.

"Did she eat anything?" I asked, cradling Matty back against my chest.

"Just two ounces. I couldn't get her to stay awake." He frowned as he leaned down to kiss her forehead.

"Can I hold him?" Constance asked. Tears brimmed in her eyes.

"Sure." I handed Matty up to her. She gazed at him, mesmerized. Ty leaned over her shoulder and pulled the blanket back away from the baby's face.

"What did you name them?" she asked, gazing back up at me.

"Well, you are holding Banton Matthew Gastaneau IV. Matty. And this is your niece, Ellyson Marie Gastaneau. Elly." Banton held her up as Ty moved over to hold her.

"They're perfect, Chandler. I can't believe they are finally here. Wow, I want a baby!" Constance looked up at me as Uncle Lon cleared his throat behind her in the doorway.

160

"Um, no you don't. You can wait…you can wait, a lot!" he answered. Then he moved behind Ty. "Ty, it's so good to see you, son. Sue and I are beside ourselves you are safe and home." Uncle Lon placed his hand on Ty's shoulder.

Matty began to squirm and whimper. Constance shot me an alarmed look, and quickly handed him back to me.

"See, you can't do that when you have one of your own." Uncle Lon chuckled as she turned to him.

"Uncle Lon, would you hand me one of those diapers in the bassinette please?"

Uncle Lon located one and then handed it to me.

"You know how to do that, Andie?" Ty asked, handing Elly back as Banton chuckled.

"Are you kidding? Andie's watched every baby video that exists, and can spout home remedies for any ailment you throw at her," Banton replied. I untaped the tiny diaper around Matty's waist. The minute the diaper was pulled away from him, he pee'd a stream across the side of the bed into the floor.

"Oops, equipment works, man!" Ty laughed as I quickly covered him back up.

"You have to be quick, Chandler. Here, let PaPa Lon do it." Uncle Lon walked over and took Matty's little legs in one hand, pulled the diaper quickly, and slid the new diaper under his little butt. He then unfolded the front and covered him in one motion, taping the tabs firmly at the sides of his little legs.

"All done. It's all in the wrists!" he grinned, pulling the blanket back up around him.

"Wow, you are good at that," Constance commented.

"You had two little brothers, remember? It all comes back to you."

Banton rose to place Elly in my other arm, and for the first time I held them both at the same time.

Constance sat down in Banton's chair and pulled up close to the side. "Wow, Chandler, you're a mom. I can't believe it," she whispered as she played with my hair.

"Yeah, my life sure has turned around in the last seventy-two hours. I went from being a widow, to my husband alive, and two babies. It still seems so surreal."

161

"I know what you mean." She glanced up when Uncle Lon put his arm around Ty.

"You know, son, we felt like we lost three of our own children, when the three of you went missing. Now, we almost feel complete," his voice choked up as Aunt Sue walked into the room.

Constance watched him in wonder as he continued to hug Ty.

"Well, I'm glad you feel that way, sir, because we have something to tell you," Ty answered, gazing at Constance. She rose, walked over and held her hand out to Aunt Sue. As Aunt Sue took Constance's hand, she gasped. There was a stunning diamond ring on the third finger of her left hand.

Uncle Lon looked back when Ty cleared his throat.

"I'm sorry. I should have spoken to you first. After I came home last night, I decided that ring was going on her finger before the world turned one more time. Mr. Lon, Mrs. Sue...I'd like to ask you for your blessing."

"You'd just better be glad, son, the shock of your homecoming hasn't worn off yet. You have a couple of days before this sinks in, and then you'd better start running," Uncle Lon said seriously as Aunt Sue slapped his shoulder.

"We couldn't be happier, Sweetheart. Of course you have our blessing. We've learned over the past months, love and relationships are so much more important than any life plans you might have laid out for yourself." She smiled through her tears at Ty. Constance looked back at me, and I nodded my head for her to move closer to me as I leaned in and kissed her cheek.

"I'm so happy for you. I just knew you two would get married!" I exclaimed as Banton hugged Ty.

As I thought about another wedding in the future, I remembered my promise to Laurilee and Dan. "Wow, I've got to call Texas! Laurilee and Dan will be pissed if they find out the babies have been here for fourteen hours and I haven't even told them yet."

"Oh, they know already. I texted them three baby videos last night while you were sleeping. I realized you hadn't told them about me being alive when she texted back wanting to know who the proud father was who took the video. I think I scared her at first," Banton chuckled as he sat back down beside me. "I had some explaining to do. Texting kept me busy till about 2:00 am."

Banton played with my hair as I continued to gaze down at the babies. After both babies were sound asleep on my chest, Dr. Lane and the nurse came back into the room.

"I hate to run everyone out, but the Pediatrician is back, and we also need to draw blood on Chandler and take her catheter out."

"Chandler, we'll be back later this afternoon." Constance leaned over and kissed both the babies and me.

"Banton, you did good, man. Congratulations!" Ty gushed as he kissed me on the forehead.

"Banton did good? Who carried those big babies around in her tiny body for eight months, did the morning sickness thing, went through labor..." Constance berated Ty all the way down the hallway as we all laughed at her.

Aunt Sue moved toward us. "We're going to go too, Chandler. We need to get back home and check to see what kind of damage we have at our house. If you will let me, I would like to come to your house and stay the first few nights after you bring the babies home, to help you until you've healed. I know your mother would do it if she were alive." She smiled at me and kissed my forehead. "I'd love to do it for you, if you want."

"Of course. We'd love it," Banton answered her as he helped the nurse take the babies from me.

"Sweetheart, we are so proud of you. We love you." Aunt Sue leaned over and hugged me.

"I love you both so much," I replied. Uncle Lon reached to touch my foot as he rounded the foot of the bed to leave the room.

Banton sat and watched the nurse draw the vials of blood from my arm, and then silently stepped out as Dr. Lane removed the catheter.

"Chandler, the nurse will help you in the shower," he offered as the door opened.

"Won't be necessary, she can go," Banton stated as he came back with two glasses. "I've got this. Here, Chandler, I brought you some ice water. They're getting you something to eat. It'll be here in a few minutes." Banton set the glasses down on the nightstand, and then came around to the side of the bed as Dr. Renault slipped out the door.

"You are awfully bossy, mister."

"I've done this before." He leaned over and kissed me as he pulled the covers back to help me from the bed.

"Yeah, I seem to remember a shower in a hotel in N'awlins."

"But I didn't have the privileges I do now, Mrs. Gastaneau. Now, stand up slow, I've got you, just take it slow and easy." He steadied me and guided me to the bathroom, pulling the IV pole along with us.

After he'd tested the water in the shower, he untied the hospital gown I had on, and as it dropped to the floor, I remembered my saggy baby tummy and stitches. I hadn't even had a look at it yet, I'd just felt it under my gown. I certainly didn't want Banton to be the first to see it.

"Banton, wait, I…" I hesitated as he took my shoulders in his hands. I was so self-conscious and nervous.

"What's wrong, Chandler?" he asked, kissing my shoulder.

"I don't want you to see my stitches, and…everything," I muttered.

"Sweetheart, turn around," he urged as I slowly turned. He pulled my hands away, and looked down at me, and then looked back up at my face. "Sweetheart, you have nothing to worry about. Those stitches look mean, but Doc assures me, the swelling around them will go down, and the scars will shrink in no time. He called it a bikini cut. It will be well below your bikini line, so no scars at the beach." He smiled reassuringly as I looked down. The skin did sag a bit, but it was so much smaller than what I was used to, and I was almost back to a normal size.

"It's just…I thought it would be so flat. I've been dreaming about wearing belts again, and then when I tried to turn over last night, I had no feeling down there. I had to hold my stomach to turn over!" I teared up as Banton chuckled.

"It's not funny."

"Oh, Chandler. You are perfect. You just gave birth to two big babies, and half of the women in this country would kill to have your body just like it is right now. Would you please quit worrying? You'll get the feeling back in your abdomen, and you

164

will be swimsuit ready in no time. Now, come on, I've got you," he urged, kissing me. He guided me into the shower and helped me to wash my hair. He squeezed body wash out on a washrag, and washed my back as I let the water hit my face. I began to tremble and shake. I felt weak, and the pain in my abdomen was getting worse by the hour.

"Let's get you out and back to bed. You need to eat something." He turned the water off and wrapped me in a towel as he swung me up in his arms, soaking himself in the process. I leaned my head over on his shoulder while he limped back over to the bed. I removed the towel and handed it to him. After he sifted through the contents of the bag Everett had packed for me, he came up with a gown and robe and brought it back over to the bed.

"These look new. I bet Fruit-Loop went shopping, didn't he?" he asked, drawing the gown up over my head. It was white lace with wide lace halter straps, and a soft satin that draped down to mid-calf with a matching lace robe.

"That's beautiful, Chandler," he murmured, leaning over to kiss me. He slid his lips slowly back and forth across mine, making my pulse quicken. He pulled back as a slow grin spread across his face. "Plus, it has quick access!" He reached up and flipped a hidden snap, and the right panel fell down, exposing my breast.

"Banton Gastaneau, that's for nursing the babies." I slapped at his hand as I grinned up at him.

"So you say…" He smirked back as he helped me snap it back. The door opened without warning, and Everett stuck his head around.

"Can I come in, Bebe? I don't want to disturb."

"No, come in Ev. Where have you been?" I asked as he walked over and sat down on the bed next to me.

"Oh, I left late last night after I knew you were all right and checked on Mother and Grandmother. Then I went to check the shop. We lost our front windows, so I've been boarding them up and sweeping up glass."

"I'm sorry, Ev. Was anything damaged?"

"Not really, just some things close to the front of the store. We'll just have a hurricane sale next week. Now, where are our babies?" He looked around as Banton handed me my brush and comb.

"The Pediatrician is with them. They'll bring them back shortly."

I lay back into the pillows, exhausted already from just getting up and showering. Banton handed me my water, and then sat down in the chair beside the bed.

"You need to drink something, Chandler. I don't want you to get dehydrated," he urged as he watched me. "I know you are in pain. Let me get Doc to give you…"

"No, Banton. I'm fine, really. I'm just tired."

"You just had major surgery, darlin', and gave birth to two babies. It's going to take a day or two for you to get back to normal. You'll heal quickly, you little half-breed, you." He grinned, and picked up the brush. "Now, where is your hairdryer? Let Ev get you all fixed up." He retrieved my hairdryer from the suitcase, and then found a plug next to the bed.

"Just relax back into the pillows and let Uncle Ev work his magic." He had my hair dry in no time. Banton sat in the chair watching, chuckling as he watched Everett fuss over me. When he finished, the nurse came in with my tray.

"Here's your lunch, Chandler. I'm afraid it's only liquids, this time." She set the tray down on the table and then left.

"That's all right; I'm not hungry, anyway."

"Chandler Ann, eat something. You haven't had anything since yesterday," Banton urged as I took a couple of spoonfuls of soup. I ate some crackers and managed to drink half of the juice before I lay back into the pillows. Before I knew it, I was sleeping.

* * *

I woke to the sound of both babies crying at once.

"Boy, those babies sure have some lungs on them!" Everett picked Elly up and brought her over to me. I pushed up in the bed and took her from Ev as Banton picked up Matty. As they continued to shriek, I noticed the front of my gown was soaked, evidently a reaction to the babies' wails. And I felt huge!

166

"Please tell me I can nurse them?" I looked up at Dr. Lane as he came back into the room and he nodded.

"Do you need instruction?" he asked as I shook my head. "All right, well, if you need her, buzz the nurse." He left the room as Everett rose to leave.

"I'll just step out, and leave you two alone for this. Call me when they're done. I need to get some Unca Ebret rocker time in." He grinned and waved as he pulled the door closed.

"Sweetheart, how do you want to do this?" Banton asked. I unsnapped the panel under Elly's head.

"He's always so much hungrier than Elly. Switch with me, and I'll nurse him first. Maybe you can pacify her until he finishes." We switched babies, and he picked up a pacifier from her crib and offered it to her. She took it immediately and closed her little eyes as he rocked her back and forth. Banton sighed, and then watched me as I worked to get Matty to nurse. After several tries, he finally got the hang of it and I let my breath out, relieved.

"Are you all right?" Banton asked as he watched me.

"Yeah. That's better already, I feel like I'm about to pop." He grinned as he continued to watch Matty nurse, seeming to be fascinated by the process.

It took him forever, but Matty finally seemed to get full and drifted off to sleep. Banton rose and handed me Elly as he took Matty back and sat back down.

"Wow, I can feel his little tummy sloshing around...he's really full." He said as I worked to wake Elly up to nurse her. It took a lot longer to get her to nurse, and I was about to give up when she caught on. She nursed hungrily, and seemed to take as much as Matty did. Banton watched silently for several minutes, and then rose and sat down on the bed next to me, pulling me over against his shoulder. He placed his hand gently on her head and then stroked her cheek.

"Banton, you don't have to babysit us constantly. I know you probably want to go home, and change, shower...I'll be fine here."

"Are you kidding? I don't want to miss a minute of this. I could watch you with them all day. This is...it's so..." He didn't finish his thought. As I watched him, a tear slid down his cheek.

167

I reached up with my free hand and wiped it away. I was touched he was so emotional.

"I love you so much. My life began again, when I heard your voice on the phone day before yesterday," I whispered.

"And I love you. My life began the first time I kissed you. I didn't think it got any better than that, until you said you would marry me. Then my heart actually hurt...skipped a beat when I found out you were pregnant. It just got better when you told me we were having twins. But the sweetest moment of my life was when the doctor pulled them both from inside you, and wrapped them up and handed them to me. I held them both at the same time, and it was like a bright light came on in the room. Life just doesn't get any better than this." He caressed Elly's cheek again, and then slid his finger down beside her mouth, trailing along my breast as she continued to nurse. I lay my head back against his chest and watched his eyes, still brimming with tears. He drew his breath in sharply and shook his head, embarrassed by his emotional display. Then he grinned down at me and chuckled. "No, really...I'm just jealous. I want my turn." He leered at me, and as Elly finished and drifted off, I snapped the gown shut and grinned up at him.

"Oh, you are such a guy!" I leaned my head back as he lowered his mouth to mine and moved his lips slowly.

"Hey, hey now...that's how you got in this mess in the first place, remember?" John knocked softly on the door and pushed it open as he came into the room with Brie in tow.

Banton stiffened as he looked at John. My apprehension grew at his reaction to John's presence, and I knew he was still bothered about the kiss John and I had shared. I wondered if I should have stayed silent, but I knew that was never a choice for me. I had to tell him, even though John and I hadn't acted on our feelings beyond the kiss. The mood in the room shifted, and Banton rose and placed Matty back in my empty arm, and then turned to hug Brie. "Gabriella, it's really good to see you! You look wonderful!" He pulled back to look her over. "How are you? Are you adjusting all right?" he asked as he pulled her back into a warm hug.

"Yes, I'm better than I ever dreamed I'd be. John makes it easy for me. He's been wonderful."

"I'm so happy for both of you."

The awkwardness in the room was palpable, and as I watched John, I knew he sensed Banton knew about our closeness while he was gone. After a moment, Banton squared his shoulders and took a deep breath.

"I'm sorry, John, about knowing about Brie and not being able to tell you. It was one of the hardest things I've ever had to do."

John relaxed. "I know, brother. Chandler told me. And I need to apologize to you. I really let you down the night Chandler broke her promise to Everett and finally told me about Brie. It was one of the darkest days of her life, and I turned on her, cursed her, and left her alone. I'd give anything if I could take it back now. I was angry about being kept in the dark, and I took it out on her. I can't believe she forgave me for what I said to her, but she did."

Banton walked back over to the bed and sat down beside me, drawing me and the babies in to his side again. "But she told me you were there for her all the rest of the time. I owe you for holding everything together for me." He reached out and shook John's hand. I was so relieved he seemed to be at ease with John, even when he mentioned our closeness during his disappearance.

"Well, let me see those babies." John came over closer and watched them as they slept in my arms. "They're perfect, Chandler. Congratulations, guys. They're beautiful." He smiled as he stepped back over to Brie, who was keeping her distance. I knew certain situations still made her uncomfortable, and she was still extra cautious, putting space between herself and humans on occasion. She blew me a kiss, and then stepped out of the room.

"It's still hard for her sometimes. I'd better go and see about her."

"Certainly, John. Go and get her. We'll see you later," I urged as he followed her.

Banton took the babies and put them back in their bassinettes, and then pulled them over close to the bed so we could watch them sleep.

Later that day, Dr. Renault came in to check on us. I'd been napping, but the pain had worsened, and I was fighting tears as he came over to check me.

"Chandler, are you hurting?" he asked, pulling my gown up to check my incision.

169

"No, I'm good," I lied.

"She's not, Doc, but she won't ask for anything because she wants to nurse the babies," Banton said. I frowned at him for ratting me out.

"Chandler, there are things we can give you to help. It won't hurt the babies." He left the room, and then came back later with two pills.

"Take these, and the nurse has a heated pillow for you to hold over your abdomen. It helps when you need to cough or to walk. I also want you to get up and walk every two hours or so. If you continue to do well and the Pediatrician releases the babies, you can go home tomorrow afternoon if you would like." He patted me on the leg, and then turned to leave.

Banton rose and crossed over to the bed, and sat down gently on the edge. "Can I get you anything? Rub your back, maybe?" He asked, stroking my arm. I lay my head back on the pillow to gaze into his eyes.

"Nothing...but just stay near me. It seems I can't get close enough to you."

He leaned over to kiss me.

Everything was so new again. His kisses, like when we went on our first date. I felt like I needed to slow time, to take in every moment, every sound. I pulled away again to gaze into his eyes.

"What is it, Andie?"

"I...I'm just still so overwhelmed. I know what it is like to lose you. I don't want to take one moment for granted. I feel like I'm experiencing everything over for the first time."

Banton chuckled and pulled me in closer to his side, pulling the covers up over us both. "And we will. I want to re-acquaint you with everything," his eyes burned brightly with promise. "I can't wait to take you and the babies home for good."

We lay watching the twins sleep as he stroked my shoulders, leaning over every so often to place a kiss on my neck. I sighed and slid down lower in the bed beside him.

"You'd better get some more rest while you can, Chandler. The babies will be awake soon and they'll surely be hungry again." Banton urged me softly.

"'kay," I replied, glancing up apprehensively.

"I'm not going anywhere, I promise. I'll be right here beside you when you wake up," he promised.

Chapter Twelve

Banton's cell ringing woke me from a pleasant dream. I moaned as I stretched, feeling as though I'd been run over by a freight train.

I reached over to touch Banton and found the bed empty. Apprehension immediately took over, and I sat up in bed to search the room. He was nowhere to be seen. I seemed to have trouble focusing again on anything, much like looking through someone else's prescription glasses. I blinked hard, trying to focus. The problems I was having with my eyesight made me more unsettled. My heart began to pound as a strange anxiety took hold of me. It was the first time since Banton had come home he hadn't been in the room with me when I woke.

Get ahold of yourself, Andie. He can't stay in the same room with you forever, I thought. I knew my reaction to his absence was silly, but I couldn't control it just the same. I broke out into a cold sweat, flinging off the sheets as I pushed myself from the bed to rise. I spotted a glass of water on the nightstand, and decided I needed to drink something. As I reached for the glass, I realized my hands were shaking badly, almost like I'd lost part of my muscle control. I reached to grasp the glass and missed, knocking it clumsily to the floor. The shattering of the glass broke the extreme silence in the room.

I jumped and gasped as the sharp noise startled me. Both babies stirred in their cribs as the door to my room opened.

Banton rushed in, full weight on his booted leg, alarmed by the noise. "What happened?" he asked as he noticed the glass on the floor at my feet.

"Don't move, you'll cut yourself. Sit back down, and I'll get it," he commanded. I sank back on the bed in relief. As he knelt to pick up the pieces of glass, he looked up at me.

"Chandler! You're so pale. What's going on?"

"I...woke, and didn't see you..." my voice shook as I spoke. Banton placed the pieces of glass back on the nightstand, quickly wiping the water from the floor with a towel.

Reaching over to touch me, he exclaimed, "You're shaking like a leaf! I can hear your heartbeat," he checked my pulse and then eased me back into the pillows.

He continued to watch me intently as I offered, "It's silly. I guess I had a panic attack or something." I took a deep breath, and then looked past him to the babies, who had begun to whimper. "And I guess I woke the babies," I said.

"Sweetheart, I'm sorry. I just stepped out to answer the phone. You were sleeping so peacefully I didn't want to wake you. I know I promised I wouldn't leave your side," he frowned, wiping the sweat from my forehead. "I hate what my disappearance has done to you," he murmured.

"I'm just being over-emotional. I'm fine now, really," I assured him, grasping his hand. He watched me intently for several moments, and then moved to pick the babies up, first Elly, then Matty, and brought them over to me to nurse. After I'd finished feeding both of them, Banton helped me change them, and then he sat down to rock Ellyson while I continued to hold Matty.

"Banton, who was on the phone earlier?" I asked.

"Oh, it's a secret. You'll find out tomorrow," he replied with a mischievous look.

Both babies drifted off, dry and comfortable with their little tummies full. Banton rose to put them both in their bassinets, and then joined me back on the bed.

"So, I guess it's time I asked you for an update. Where do things stand, did you get the ringleader, Dante? Is it over?" I almost whispered.

Banton played with the lace on the front of my gown for several moments, and then reached up to stroke my cheek as he let out a sigh. "No, Chandler. We took out a compound where we knew he was operating. We killed twenty or so Orcos there, along with some Somali pirates, and then we followed their trail to another location. We thought we had them several times, and they were always able to elude us. We killed Grant," he paused as I studied him. "But we never caught up to Dante or Lucien. Damn, but I'd hoped we'd get both of them and end all of this. We've bought some time, and we've brought their operation to its knees.

173

But I know in my heart, you'll never be out of danger until those two are dead."

"You were able to rescue those hostages," I began.

"Yes, but I knew the whole thing was a ploy to get us over there. We were ambushed, Andie…several times. I still don't know how either one of us made it back. The Navy considers the whole operation a success, even with losing the ship. But they don't know Dante the way we do. They think we've taken him out of operation. Reed wouldn't listen to me; he blows off our warnings about what he's capable of with a wave of his hand."

"Banton, you almost sound like you want to go back," I surmised cautiously.

"I do. I want to end him and all the evil the Orcos represent."

I shook my head furiously.

"No! Banton, you can't! I won't lose you again! No!" My heart pounded as if it would jump from my chest as I pushed up in bed to challenge him.

"Andie, calm down…Shhh. I'm not going anywhere, not now, anyway. Shhh, I'm sorry, I shouldn't have brought it up. It's all right," he soothed. "I'm staying right here with you for a while, I promise. Calm down. I'm so sorry. I can't stand what this has done to you."

He continued to hold me, and then after several minutes, he pulled my face away to look down into my eyes.

"I'm on extended leave, to heal and spend time with you and the babies. With everything that has happened, Ty and I have both been told our service terms might be shortened, so my time as a SEAL might be shorter than we thought. I might be able to get out early," he offered as I smiled at him. "So get used to it, lady…you're stuck with me."

I wound my fingers in his hair and pulled him down toward my lips. "Forever, I hope," I whispered against his.

* * *

The next morning found me up before dawn, ready to get my family home. After the Doctors had both given us their blessings of good health, Banton loaded me and the twins in our new SUV.

I watched the babies nervously from the front seat, checking them every few minutes.

"Is everything all right?" Banton asked as I checked them again.

"It just bothers me I can't see their faces with them facing backwards. I should be back there with them," I sighed as he chuckled.

"You are going to wear yourself out before we even get home. Relax, Andie, they're fine," he assured me.

As we turned onto Rue Dauphine, it was as if a page had turned on a dark chapter of my life. I was returning to the house I loved with my family intact. Banton sensed my joy, and reached over to squeeze my hand. I searched the vehicles parked in front of our house.

"Hmm," I murmured as I shot a glance back at his amused face.

"Oh, Sweetheart, this won't be a quiet homecoming, I assure you," he grinned. "But I'll run everyone out the minute you give the signal," he joked. I shook my head and leaned over to kiss him.

"Well, that's good...because I think everyone we know is here," I remarked as he parked our SUV and jumped out.

Before I could even get out, John and Ty were bounding down the steps.

"Andie-girl, welcome home!" John greeted me as he kissed my cheek. "Here, let me get Matty out. I'll carry him in for you," he offered, lifting the car seat from behind me. Banton came around the side carrying Elly, who was promptly picked up by Ty. Both Ty and John bounded up the stairs and through the front door with our children, without as much as a backwards glance.

"Well, you see how we rate," I mumbled. Banton chuckled and leaned over to kiss me.

"We've got babies!" I heard John yell as the front door slammed behind him.

Banton laughed at John's announcement and then took my hand and hobbled up the stairs to the front porch.

"Bant-dweeb!" Julia's squeals met us in the foyer. In an instant, Julia jumped at Banton, and in spite of his boot-cast, caught her in mid-air and swung her around in a circle.

175

"Ju-bean, it sure is good to see you," Banton breathed into her hair as he hugged her tightly.

"I still can't believe you are home," she whispered, gazing over his shoulder at me.

I smiled at her as I asked, "Aunt Julia, did you see your new niece and nephew?"

"Oh, gosh…I almost forgot," she whirled as Banton put her down and rushed into the living room to see the babies.

"Chandler, they're so beautiful," Claudia came into the foyer to hug me with Will close behind her.

I nodded to her as we embraced. "They are, aren't they?"

"Beau! Come here, boy!" Banton exclaimed, patting his leg. Beau stood, wagging his tail silently in the hallway, waiting for Banton to notice him. He lurched into motion, flying at Banton and knocking him backward a step or two as he nudged against Banton's legs. Nothing would suffice but a complete hug and roll on the entry floor. I giggled at the way Beau's entire body seemed to wag in complete joy at being reunited with his best friend.

As we heard the patter of Ava's little feet, I turned and looked down at her. "An Andler, no one will wet me see my babies," she pouted, placing her little hands on her hips.

"Ma Petit, come here. Uncle Everett will let you see them," he called out from the sofa. Banton and I followed Claudia and Will into the living room.

Everyone was talking at once. Mrs. Elaine and Mr. Matt sat on the sofa, each of them with a baby in their lap. Everett walked over and took Ellyson from Mrs. Elaine, and then knelt down and sat down in the floor so Ava could sit on his lap. He then placed Elly in Ava's little arms as he continued to support her head and her tiny butt, allowing Ava to appear as though she were holding the baby herself.

"See, my little Ava, here is your little baby Elly," he cooed to her. Ava looked up excitedly at me and Banton.

"What do you think, Ava…should we keep them?" I asked her. She nodded furiously.

"Chandler, we have a little surprise for you," Banton whispered as he placed a kiss on my neck.

"What is it?" I asked as I turned back to look at him. I caught a movement over his shoulder as he chuckled and moved to the side.

"Laurilee! Dan...when did you get here?" I squealed when they both appeared around the corner by the staircase.

"We got here early this morning! We just had to come and see you and the babies and Banton!" Laurilee gushed as she hurried over to hug me.

"Banton, it sure is good to see you alive," Dan shook Banton's hand warmly. "I wish I had a video of Laurilee's reaction day before yesterday, when she realized she was talking to you on the phone. I don't know which hit the ground first, her jaw or the phone!" Dan said as he moved over to hug me. "Man, Chandler...you sure spit out some good-lookin' stock there!"

"Gee thanks, Dan...I think," I teased as I moved over to gaze down at Matty.

"Andie, do you need to go on up? " Banton moved close behind me and placed a kiss on the back of my neck.

"No, I'm good. I've had enough of hospital beds to last me a lifetime. I will sit a bit down here, though, and visit with everyone," I replied as John ushered me over to the sofa.

Everyone took their turns holding the babies and exchanging their own versions of just how exciting Banton's homecoming, the hurricane, and the babies' births had been. After a couple of hours, Matty and Elly finally tired of all the excitement and let everyone know how hungry they were.

"Crap, Chandler...those things come with an 'off' button?" Cade asked, his hands over his ears for effect.

"Very funny, Cade. Chandler, I'll help you and Banton get them fed and settled in upstairs," Aunt Sue offered as I rose.

"Let me carry him upstairs," Uncle Lon added, rising with Matty in his lap. Banton took Elly from Mrs. Elaine and followed us up the staircase. After I settled down in our bedroom, Banton and Aunt Sue brought the babies in to me.

"I've got a few things to do in the nursery, and I'll leave you to nurse them. Call me if you need me," Aunt Sue leaned over to kiss me and handed Elly to me. "Chandler, I don't want to alarm you, but have you noticed Elly's color?" Aunt Sue asked, straightening.

"What do you mean?"

"Well, her complexion has been a healthy pink until today. I just think she's a little pale, that's all," she murmured, brushing a lock of hair back behind my ear. "It's probably just the lights here at the house."

"I'm still a little worried about her appetite. It doesn't seem like she eats like Matty," Banton added.

"I know. I asked Dr. Renault about it, and he didn't seem too concerned yet," I replied. I watched her as we talked. It did seem her skin was more translucent and pale.

"Well, I'm sure she'll be fine. Most babies lose a few ounces when they first come home." Aunt Sue assured me as she left the room.

Banton sat down gently on his side of the bed, and then slid closer to me as he cuddled Matty to his chest. He watched me nurse Elly as he rocking and patting Matty to pacify him until she was finished. When he switched babies with me, he leaned over to kiss me.

"Andie, I don't know how you are going to keep this up, nursing both of them every two hours or so. One baby is exhausting. Did the Docs say anything about you supplementing with bottles?"

"I can do this. Everything I've read says it's so much better for the babies if you breast-feed. I want to give them the best start possible. Besides, this is the only chance I'll get to do this," I whispered, glancing up at him.

"Chandler, we don't know for sure," he murmured, sliding his thumb down my cheek. "I'll help you as much as I can. I'm just worried about how much sleep you can get."

I had to laugh. "Believe me, if I can catch a full two hours here and three hours there, it will be much more than I got the last month with them tumbling around inside," I replied.

Just as I finished nursing Matty, Aunt Sue returned to help Banton carry the babies back to the nursery. I snuggled down in my mother's comforter on my bed, the down enveloping me like a warm hug. Beau raised his head from his paws, yawned, and then

178

rolled over to his side to nap beside me on the rug. I watched the warm sunshine spread across the foot of the bed, and as Banton re-entered our bedroom, I smiled. We were finally a family in our house on Rue Dauphine.

* * *

Banton's wounds healed quickly, and his cast, boot and bandages came off soon after we arrived home. Sadly, I could tell he was far from back to normal. As the first couple of days passed, I sensed something was off. I could feel anger coming off of him like radiation. There didn't seem to be any particular trigger, and I couldn't pinpoint what was causing it. I knew Laurilee picked up on it too, and she and Dan had made plans away from the house to give us some alone time.

"Hey, Andie-girl! How are our babies?' John greeted me as he came through the front door.

"Good. They have their days and nights mixed up, I think. They're asleep right now. Banton just went up to check on them." I replied as I sat some laundry down on the bottom step of the staircase.

"And everything else? You seem a little on edge, darlin'," he murmured, placing his hand on my cheek.

"Oh, it's just a lack of sleep and the effects of chaos. I'm okay," I assured him.

We walked arm in arm into the living room and sat down on the sofa. When I picked up some baby things to fold, I sensed him watching me.

"So Brie would like to come down and see the babies. Would that be all right?"

"Sure, John. I'd love for her to. How is everything with her? I know she still has some trouble from time to time."

"Getting better all the time. She's great, thanks to everything you have done for her."

I smiled at him as tears gathered. "I'm so glad everything is good between you two. It makes me really happy," I assured him. He reached up to wipe a tear from under my eye.

179

"Is everything okay, Andie...with you and Banton?" John asked as he continued to gaze at me. He knew me too well and could tell something wasn't quite right.

"What the hell is going on here?" Banton's voice broke the silence from the doorway. I looked up, startled, as John removed his hand from my face and stood.

"I'm home now, John. I can take care of my own wife."

I stared at Banton in shocked silence. I'd never heard him use the sarcastic tone, and it disturbed me.

"Banton, what's wrong with you?" I asked, looking back and forth between the two of them.

"Calm down, brother. I just came down here to check on you and Chandler and the babies. I know new babies in the house can be stressful," John offered as he started to cross the room.

"You can stop with the 'brother' stuff. We're fine, and Chandler doesn't need you looking in on her. I'm home now. Go see to your own wife." Banton nodded toward John's house as John brushed by him in the doorway.

"I thought we were passed all this, I guess I was wrong," John murmured as I continued to stare at Banton. As John shut the front door, Banton broke his gaze and turned to mount the stairs.

I couldn't believe what I'd just seen. Banton had never acted out of jealousy before, and he'd never shown any distrust toward me or John. I rose and followed him silently up the staircase.

Our bedroom door was closed, and as I pushed it open, I found Banton pacing agitatedly back and forth in front of the window, grasping handfuls of hair in frustration. I walked silently over to the bed and stood in front of him.

"Are you all right?" I asked softly. I waited several moments, and got no response.

"Banton, what's wrong? What has gotten into you?" I asked cautiously.

He removed his hands from the sides of his head and sighed. "Nothing has gotten into me. He just needs to mind his own affairs. The Orco business is over, and we don't need his protection anymore. I think he's just still a little too involved, and too attached to you," he replied in a menacing tone.

I was really irritated with his bad mood and attitude toward John, but I was trying to keep my cool, to try to understand where this animosity was coming from.

"Sweetheart, that's ridiculous. I think you just misunderstood, that's all. John has been a good friend to us," I continued.

"Evidently a really good friend to you while I was away," he muttered, sliding his hands down his thighs in an agitated manner. "I've been meaning to ask you, just what the hell did you two share besides a kiss before you finally told him Brie was alive?"

I gasped at his accusation. His tone gutted me. "Banton, I thought you understood about all of that, nothing else happened. We were both just missing you and Brie, and…"

Anger was rolling off him in waves. I was scared of what I felt radiating from him. He barely contained a fierce hatred I could sense just below the surface. The muscle in his jaw worked hard. Finally shutting his eyes, he paused, and then spoke softly. "Chandler, not now. I just need to be alone," he murmured as he whirled and stood at the window with his back to me. I went cold inside. A large hole opened in my chest again, one that hurt much the same as when I thought I'd lost him. Something had changed.

I slipped from the room and made my way to the nursery. Finding Elly awake, I picked her up and sat down with her in one of the rockers. Tears gathered and threatened to spill over, but I was determined I wouldn't make more of this thing with Banton. *He's probably just exhausted like I am*, I reasoned. I rocked and hummed to Ellyson. After a bit, a noise at the doorway alerted me to Banton's presence. He was propped against the door, his arms folded. As my eyes rose to meet his, his gaze softened. He simply mouthed, "I'm sorry."

I nodded tearily at him as he crossed to Matty's crib and picked him up. He sat down in the rocker next to me, and placed Matty on his shoulder, kissing him on the forehead. As we sat and rocked together, Banton reached over and covered my hand with his. A jolt went through me, much like the day Brie and I had connected. Startled, I looked up at him. He was filled with such a longing, mixed with anger and frustration. I'd never felt anything like it.

181

I studied his eyes as he gazed at me. I hadn't seen him look that tortured since the day he watched me fight through the first bite at Dr. Lane's.

"Banton," I whispered.

"Hmm?"

"I can feel you, feel what you are feeling. I can feel your emotions, just like with Brie before. What is it? What can I do to help you?"

He shook his head, agitated. "It's nothing, it will pass. I just...I'm just having more of a reaction this time, that's all.

"Reaction to what?" I asked, rising to place Elly down in her crib. Banton put his lips softly on Matty's forehead and lingered there with his eyes shut. After several moments, he raised his head and met my gaze. He stared at me for several minutes as tears gathered in his eyes.

"Banton, what is it? You can tell me," I urged as I knelt in front of him. He rose and quickly crossed the room to lay Matty down in his crib beside Elly's. As he turned he seemed angry. I could feel it radiating toward me, and my heart beat faster.

"Chandler, I haven't told you everything about Somalia. It was a miracle any of us survived," he reminded me as I nodded. "While we were cleaning out the Orco camps, I was ambushed and captured for a few days. Ty and the two new guys were able to rescue me and get me back to the ship. That was right before we were hit," he murmured. I nodded silently. My heart began to ache just thinking about it.

"While the Orcos held me captive, I got a taste of what Sam went through when he was captured. They tortured me with their venom. Men, women...They would bite me, numerous times. Several at one time. Evidently, different venom affects us different ways. Having more than one Orco's venom in your system at a time has...lasting effects. I'm having a hard time shaking it," he admitted as his eyes rose again to meet mine.

"Oh, God...Banton, why didn't you tell me? Are you taking something for your nerves? Have you talked to Dr. Lane?"

"Yes. I'm taking the pills and the valium. But it's not helping much this time. I just thought I had a temper before. I'm..." he

182

trailed off as he watched out the window into the distance. My heart pounded, and I felt helpless. I knew he wasn't in control.

"Well, that explains a lot. Will you let me help you, like before?"

"That's why I haven't said anything. You have your hands full with the babies, you don't need to have to nursemaid your husband too!" he shouted as he threw his hand out.

I rose up and crossed the room and put my arms around him. "At least now I can understand better. Did you forget, no secrets between us?"

He nodded and bent to place a kiss on top of my head.

"We'll get through this together. We always have," I murmured into his chest as I wrapped my arms around his waist. At least now he was opening up.

Chapter Thirteen

We settled into a routine. The first three days Aunt Sue, Banton and Laurilee took turns helping me get up with the babies to nurse. Everett hovered, staying close and helping Aunt Sue and Constance. The extra help was wonderful, and I hardly got to change a diaper. But Banton was right; I was exhausted from the feedings.

"Sweetheart, I thought you were going to nap when the babies napped," Banton scolded as he came down the staircase. He found me folding laundry at the dining room table.

"I will. I just had a few things to do first."

"Chandler, I can do that. And Constance told you to leave chores for her. She wants to help more since her mother went back to Denham Springs. You need to sleep when the babies do."

"I can do this. I'm almost finished," I argued as he strode angrily across the entry hall and placed his hands on my shoulders.

"No arguments. Upstairs, now!" Banton grasped my shoulders and gently urged me up and toward the staircase.

"Everyone is waiting on me hand and foot. I'm healed, and I need to do my own housework," I complained. He shook his head.

"As long as you have those dark circles under your eyes, I'm not giving in. You either let me hire somebody to help with the house, or you let me and Constance help," he commanded in a rather irritated tone.

"All right," I gave in at his stern insistence. He seemed to be losing patience, and I knew he was tired too.

"I'll just check on the babies, and you lie down. I'll be in there in a minute," he called over his shoulder as I pushed the door open to our room.

As I sank down onto our bed, a sort of sadness descended on me. It seemed so irrational to feel this way. Ever since we'd arrived home with the babies, my emotions were worse than ever. I was all over the place, much like a bouncing ball.

"I'm supposed to be less emotional now, darn hormones..." I murmured as I heard a knock on our bedroom door.

184

"Bebe, what's that about hormones?" Everett called out as he smiled and shut the door behind him.

"Me. I thought once I wasn't pregnant anymore, the hormones would be under control. I'm worse than ever!" I exclaimed.

"Darlin', even though you've transformed, you are still a mother. Maybe you have a little post-partum stuff goin' on."

"Everett, that's ridiculous. I love being a mother, I can't get enough of the babies," I argued.

"That's not what I mean. I've heard some new mothers get the blues for absolutely no reason."

"It's not so much that, it's a feeling I get, especially around Banton. Everett, I'm afraid..."

He moved closer to the bed and sat down beside me as he pulled me into his side.

"Afraid of what? Is something wrong?"

"Yes. I know Banton is tired too, all of this is so new. And I know his experiences in Somalia are eating on him. I'm just afraid it's more than he expected, and that he is disappointed in me."

"You are kidding, Ma Petit? He adores you!"

"I just...sense his moods now. It's like I can feel what he's feeling. Like when I'm with Brie, or with you," I looked up at him.

"Oh, I see. Hmm. I think your senses are even sharper than I first thought. I talked to Dr. Renault a little bit a while back about your aura, and your connection with Brie and others. He seemed to think they would heighten with your pregnancy. And the fact you've been bitten again, different venom being introduced into your system...well, I think you might be affected more than we expected."

"Then that's bad! If I'm right about what I'm sensing from Banton," I began.

"Wait, has he said something?" he asked.

"No. He doesn't say anything at all. We are so busy with the babies, and he scolds me a lot, worrying about my sleep...he seems to be angry with me. And he hasn't touched me...since he's been home.

"What? What do you mean?" he drew back to look at me. As I paused, Banton pushed the door open.

185

"Hey, Banton-babe. I just had to check on our girl before I run downtown to the shop for a while." He stood and patted Banton on the shoulder. "I'll talk to you later, Sweet Bebe," he finished as he blew me a kiss.

Banton watched Everett leave, and then crossed the room to me.

"If I didn't know he was gay, I would be jealous," Banton commented, dropping down on the bed beside me.

I gave him a sideways glance as I commented, "Well, about that…I think there's something you should know."

Banton stretched, and then pulled me into his arms. It was the first time he'd really held me in a couple of days, and it sort of took me by surprise.

"What's that?" he asked, yawning.

"Um…as it turns out, our Everett is not gay."

"What?" He turned to me, curious.

"Everett isn't gay. He's just extremely eccentric, and I guess his mannerisms which have carried over from the last century make him seem gayer to us in this day and time, than just gentlemanly."

Banton pushed up a bit in the bed and peered down at me. "How do you know? Did he tell you?" he asked.

"Yes. He finally told me one day, when we thought we'd lost you. He said he understood how I was mourning, and told me what had happened to his true love. As it turns out, he was in love with Marie-Claire Johnson DeeLee, the owner of our house. She'd nursed him back to health when he was wounded on the battlefield, and he feel in love with her. He was away making arrangements to get her out of the countryside, away from the fighting, when she was attacked…by Lucien and a gang of Orcos. That is how she and the babies died," I finished, gazing back up at him.

"Holy…wow. That's…that's incredible. He waited all that time to tell you about his connection to our house? Why?"

I watched him curiously. He seemed a little agitated with Everett. I remembered, I had been too when he told me the story.

"Everett said until we went to the cemetery that day, he didn't know what her last name was. He put two and two together when we saw their graves," I finished.

186

"How could he not know her name? Did he not remember the house?" he asked. I leaned over and retrieved my laptop from the nightstand.

"Here. I've written those parts of the history of our house already. Read this, it will explain everything." I handed him the laptop. He appeared to be processing the new revelations as he studied the story on my laptop. As he read, my eyes became heavy and I drifted off to sleep.

* * *

Hungry wails woke me from my nap.

"Here, Mommy. I brought them to you." Banton smiled as he placed Matty on the bed beside me. "He's always the first one to wake up and demand some attention," he commented as he sat down beside us.

I automatically began to nurse Matty, and then looked up at Banton.

"Andie, I'm really impressed. You've done a great job with your writing." He watched me as I gazed back up at him. "But I have some more questions about Everett, this whole thing...it got me to thinking," he frowned, and I grinned wryly at him. I knew he was thinking about all the times Everett had stayed and slept beside me.

"He certainly spent a lot of intimate time with you. Chandler, he let us think he was gay...all that time, he never corrected us. I was okay with his close friendship with you, because of those assumptions."

"I know. But you have to know, he really never thought of me that way."

He turned and cocked a disbelieving eyebrow at me.

"He told me he thinks of me as a sister."

"Um, yeah. Right," he snorted.

I could tell he was still skeptical and suspicious of Everett's motives. We sat in silence as Banton watched in his usual fascinated manner as Matty nursed at my breast. When I sensed he was full, I tugged him away and pushed down on my nipple,

187

breaking the suction. My nipple was taught and hard. I looked down into Banton's eyes, and they darkened as he gazed up at me.

"Chandler, that's so hot," he murmured as he leaned up and placed a kiss on my shoulder. I shuddered, longing for his touch after such a long time. His comment caused my pulse to quicken. *Maybe he was ready to touch me now!* As Elly began to whimper in his arms, he broke his gaze and switched babies with me.

Banton sat watching Ellyson as she took her turn nursing, falling asleep almost immediately in my arms. After several moments he raised his gaze to mine.

"I think it's time to call Dr. Renault. She's not eating and doesn't seem to have any appetite," he murmured.

"I know. Their checkup is in two days, but I don't want to wait any longer. I'll call him this afternoon," I commented as I began to tear up. "I'm not feeding her right, or something…maybe my milk isn't right,"

"Chandler! Dammit, this isn't your fault! Just stop it! I want the Doctor to check her over. Maybe there is something going on with her, medically.

He almost shouted the words at me. It only made me get more emotional. He rose and placed Matty down on the bed next to me, and then carefully lifted Elly. He left the room with her, leaving me alone with my tears as I changed Matty's diaper and then rose to carry him back to the nursery. As I entered the nursery, Banton was leaning over Elly's crib.

"She's in a deep sleep." He placed her on her back, and then tucked her little blanket around her. "Do you want to try to feed her some more?"

"No, just let her sleep. She took more last feeding, and it hasn't been quite two hours yet," I replied as I watched her.

"Come on back in the bedroom and rest while the babies do," he murmured as he placed an arm around me and pulled me from the room. He caressed my arm as we walked, and my heart began to quicken. I lay back down on the bed, and Banton crawled in beside me and pulled me over to his chest. We lay for several minutes, and I silently hoped he was ready to be intimate and had been waiting for a time when the babies were down. After waiting for a bit, I decided to take matters into my own hands. I slid my knee across his thighs as I reached to unbutton his shirt.

"Chandler, wait…we're both tired. You need to rest," he protested as he buttoned his shirt.

"I'm not that tired, and I just woke from a nap," I began as I stretched to kiss his neck. He pulled away as he replied, "I've got a couple of things to do downstairs while they're sleeping. I'll be back in a little while," he retorted as he rose and left the room.

Never at any time in our relationship had he ever pulled away from me, or acted like he didn't want me. Just as when I'd felt his anger and frustration with John, I could feel disappointment now. I disappointed him. My heart sank as I ran over a dozen possibilities in my head. Now, since I had given birth, I no longer appealed to him. I had heard of men that reacted this way to having children, but I couldn't believe Banton could be one of those. It just didn't fit.

I had to pull things together. Maybe he was disappointed in the way our lives had changed. He had to help me so much, and he hadn't been out with the SEALs in days. I rose to find him and suggest that he go with Ty and the others to work out. As I walked out on the landing, I heard him talking to the babies, so I turned and went into the nursery. I found him leaning over Ellyson's crib.

"And baby-girl, you are so beautiful, just like your mother. Do you know how precious you are to me?" he murmured, placing his lips on her little forehead. "Oh, God…she's so pale! She's…she's not breathing!" he exclaimed as he grabbed her from her bassinette.

I crossed the room to Banton's side, my heart pounding. Banton immediately turned Elly over, and patted her tiny back and then turned her upright again. He pressed gently on her chest as he breathed into her mouth. Tears ran down my cheeks silently as I watched from beside him.

No sooner than he had drawn back from her little face, she began to squirm and cry out. I breathed a sigh of relief as he turned to me, still cradling her close to his chest.

"Let's get them to Dr. Lane's now!" he shouted as I grabbed Matty out of his bassinet and headed down the staircase behind

Banton. Dan and Laurilee heard the commotion and followed us out the front door and to the car.

"Chandler, what's wrong?" Laurilee asked breathlessly. "I heard Banton shouting."

"Elly quit breathing and turned blue. We're taking her to the clinic. Call Constance and Ev for me, please?" I sobbed out as I buckled Matty into his car seat.

"Sure, Chandler. Be careful, and call me…let us know if there is anything we can do," she called out as I crawled over Matty's car seat into the middle between the twins in the backseat.

"Chandler," Banton began.

"I'm riding back here so I can watch her, in case…" I breathed out as he nodded at me. We flew down the highway. I had no idea how fast Banton was going, for I never took my eyes from Elly's face. I kept holding her chest gently, making sure she was still moving. Her breathing seemed labored, and she was lethargic, only opening her eyes occasionally. Matty watched me silently as though he sensed the intensity of my emotions. He never cried out or made a fuss. Banton called ahead to the clinic to alert Dr. Lane. He was waiting for us with the doors open as we slid to a stop at the emergency entrance.

"Doc, she quit breathing, and her color isn't good," Banton exclaimed, jumping from the vehicle as he threw it in park.

"Just let me have her," Dr. Lane said calmly. He removed her from the backseat. Banton followed him into the clinic as I took Matty out of his carrier and rushed to follow them in.

"I've called Renault; he is bringing the Aldon Pediatrician with him. They should be here in about an hour," Dr. Lane commented as he hooked several monitors up to Elly. After he had the monitors on her, his nurse joined him and gently removed Elly's clothes while the Doctor started an IV.

"Banton, Chandler…I'm going to start her on an IV and take some blood, so I can have some results for Renault to look at. We'll know more about what we are dealing with when he gets here. But from the looks of her, kids, she needs a transfusion. It's common with Aldon children, and I think that is what we are dealing with. Has Matty had any symptoms like hers?" he asked as he looked up at me. I cradled Matty close to my chest as I shook my head.

"Why don't you take Chandler in the waiting room and tend to Matty. I'll come and get you in a bit," he urged Banton.

"Come on, Andie. We need to let him work," Banton murmured as he placed his arm around my shoulders.

I hesitated, not wanting to leave Elly's side for a second. Banton pulled me again as he whispered in my ear, "Please, sweetheart...she'll be all right, and we are only in the way."

I nodded at him, my eyes filling with tears. As we sank down into the cushions on the sofa, Banton's cell rang.

Banton retrieved it from his pocket and murmured, "It's John. Hey, John...yeah, we just got here....no, not yet. Doc's in with her now. Thanks, yeah, tell them we will call when we know something. Okay, brother, I will. Thanks, Bye."

Banton's tone surprised me. He talked to John as if he'd never been rude to him . The jealousy and bitterness seemed to have passed, and I was relieved. I patted Matty's behind rhythmically as I hummed to him, cradling him to my chest. As Banton watched silently, I held our son closer as he nuzzled in between my neck and collarbone, making little sucking noises while he napped. Banton reached over and touched his cheek gently as he murmured, "John said Laurilee called him after she called Constance and Ev. Mr. Lon and Mrs. Sue are on their way here, and John said he and Brie are coming too."

I nodded at him numbly.

"Chandler, she'll be okay," he tried to assure, pulling me into his shoulder. I began to sob, not able to cope with the thought we might lose her.

"Shhh." He stroked my hair as he held me.

"You saved her, Banton," I whispered. If you hadn't found her just then," I breathed out as he kissed my temple.

"Sweet Bebe, what on earth happened? Is Elly okay?" Everett rushed breathlessly through the front doors.

Banton rose and embraced him. "The Doctor is with her now. He's running some tests," he answered.

"Laurilee said she quit breathing," Ev continued as he took in my red-rimmed eyes. I nodded silently.

191

Everett crossed the room to me and sat down beside me. "Please, Bebe...let me have Matty."

As soon as I handed Matty to him, Banton pulled me around and into his arms. I held him tightly as he rested his cheek on top of my head.

Aunt Sue and Uncle Lon arrived soon after Everett, and just as Banton began to relay what had happened to Elly, Dr. Lane came to get us. I flew to him as he pulled me back into the room where he'd been examining Elly. I rushed to the bassinette and found her sleeping peacefully on her side.

"Banton, I've done some blood work, and she's extremely anemic. We'll start a transfusion, but there's a lot going on. She isn't processing your milk, Chandler. Although Matty doesn't seem to be having the same problem, I fear he soon will. I can't be positive, until I talk to Renault and the other Aldon doctor, but I think we need to start them on whole blood."

"What? I thought Aldon could live on human food, too," I began as Banton rubbed my arm.

"They do. But they have to have blood...whole mammal blood. Just your rich diet of raw meats isn't enough. We will get some animal blood to get her started. We'll blend it with a special mixture."

"I don't really understand. If the babies are Aldon, doesn't that make them immune to sickness like this?"

"Not until they're a little older, Chandler. Aldon children are as vulnerable to infant mortality as human children, maybe more. Their little bodies seem to fight between the two worlds, only wanting to process one food type or the other. Her little body is fighting itself right now. If I'm right, she'll get a lot better when we start her on the blood."

"Why didn't you start them on blood from the beginning?" I asked, not masking my irritation.

"I'm still not sure about the Aldon thing, and neither is Dr. Renault. The tests aren't showing us Aldon results. The blood could make them sick if they aren't fully transformed. We wanted to wait until we knew for sure," he said as Banton nodded to him. "All of the injections we were giving you were probably still built up in their systems, but now they need more. Her birth weight was

192

lower, and we've always been concerned about her gaining. This just confirms."

"Is there anything else we can do?" Banton asked as he continued to hold me.

"Yes, bring Matty in and let my nurse take some blood. I want to have something for the other two Doctors to look at when they get here, so they can compare the two. And Chandler," he began as I looked up at him. He walked closer to me and reached up and gently pulled my bottom lid down, checking my eye, "I think you are anemic too. I've got a feeling you need a transfusion. Your body is going through lots of changes too, and I want to run some tests on you. Elly isn't the only one I'm concerned about," he admitted as Banton turned back to look at him.

"What's wrong with Chandler?" he asked, alarmed.

"I'm not sure, but her color isn't good. Let's get you in a room, and I'll get my nurse."

I numbly followed him back to an empty room. Banton helped me get into a gown as the nurse came in and began to draw blood. After she'd left the room, Banton sat down on the edge of the bed.

"Chandler, maybe your body isn't bouncing back after the babies, because of the transformation," he murmured as he held the side of my face. I just nodded at him as I glanced up.

"I know you've probably bled a lot after the birth, and your body may not be making blood to replace it, like it should…since you've transformed. I'm so sorry that nothing is normal for you."

I murmured, "I haven't bled, since I left the hospital."

"What? What do you mean? Aren't women supposed to…" he began.

I nodded as the tears began again. "Normal women do, usually for several weeks. I stopped right after the birth. That's why I don't think I'll ever be able to get pregnant again. My transformation is complete, I guess," I whispered as I looked back up at him. I was beginning to feel defeated. It was just one more thing to add to the list of things that were wrong with me, things for Banton to be disappointed in.

"Chandler," Banton pulled me up into his arms. "You don't know that for sure. Don't worry about it, because I'm not."

193

I took a deep breath. "Just go out and get Matty for Dr. Lane. Stay with the babies, I'm all right here," I urged him.

He stood and then paused at the door. "I'll be back in a bit," he said as he closed the door.

I lay back on the pillows, feeling the most useless and helpless that I'd ever felt. My babies were both in danger, and there was nothing I could do. Once the nurse and Dr. Lane had the blood going for my transfusion, Aunt Sue and Uncle Lon arrived.

"Sweetheart, we came as soon as Constance called us. She and Ty are at your house with Laurilee and Dan. She filled us in. Do you know anything yet?" Aunt Sue asked as she sank down on the bed beside me. Uncle Lon sat down in the chair on the other side of the bed.

"No, Banton is in with the babies now. Dr. Lane is running tests on both of them, and on me too," I replied. She brushed the hair from my forehead and leaned over to kiss me

"Has he called that vampire doctor? I'll feel better if he's here to help him," Uncle Lon blurted out as I smiled.

"His name is Dr. Renault. Yes, he should be here any time, and he's bringing the *Aldon* pediatrician with him," I assured him as he relaxed.

"What's this they are doing with you?" Aunt Sue asked. She checked the machines they'd hooked up to me.

"Transfusion. Doc says I need blood, and he's running some more tests."

"You've let yourself get too run down, Chandler. You are doing too much, and you and Banton are both worn out."

"Well, I don't have to worry about nursing anymore. I think they're going to put Matty and Elly both on whole blood," I informed them as Uncle Lon made a horrible face. "I know, it sounds awful. But Dr. Lane thinks Elly's body is fighting itself, and she needs a pure Aldon diet," I tried to explain.

"Boy, this is one I never thought I'd deal with concerning my grandkids," Uncle Lon shook his head as Aunt Sue smiled. She patted my leg, and then she grasped my chin and turned it back toward her. "I know you, Chandler Ann. You somehow blame yourself for your milk not being enough for the babies. That is absurd, of course! Normal mothers have the same problems, and this is all anything but normal. Everything is going to be fine." She pulled me into a hug and whispered, "Grandmothers know these things."

I laughed through my tears and nodded at her. They waited with me until Banton returned about thirty minutes later. When Uncle Lon's cell rang for about the fourth time signaling yet another call from Constance, he rose and motioned for Aunt Sue to follow him.

Banton joined me on the bed. "The other Doctors are here. They're checking her out thoroughly. It's puzzling they still don't have conclusive results about the Aldon thing, but the other Doctors agree with Dr. Lane. They've already started her transfusion, and her color seems to be a bit better to me."

He watched my expressions intently as I processed. "Are they optimistic?" I asked hesitantly.

The muscles in his jaw clenched, the agitated twinge showing that always signaled his frustration. "I wouldn't go that far, but they seem to think they're on the right track. Matty seems good, but he's getting fussy. They have some of the new formula ready and were about to feed him, but I asked them if they would bring him to you. I knew you would want to do it if you feel up to it."

I nodded at him enthusiastically and smiled.

"God, Chandler. That's the first time I've seen you smile like that in days." His statement took me by surprise, because I felt the same way about him. He pulled me into his chest and murmured into my hair, "I've been so worried about you, and we've both been exhausted. I admit, I've been frustrated that I couldn't help you more, and it made me angry at myself. It didn't seem fair you had to get up with both of them every time to feed them all night long, and I couldn't relieve you. Now we can take turns, and you can sleep through some of the feedings." He sighed as he pulled back to look into my eyes.

"Oh, Banton...I'm so relieved!" I exclaimed as he shot me a puzzled expression. "I could sense your frustration and anger, and I thought it was me, that somehow you were disappointed about how hard everything was, and you were somehow unhappy with me..." I trailed off as he shook his head.

"Never. I could never be unhappy with you. I can't believe you even thought that," he murmured as he held my face in his hands. "I just felt inadequate and I hated myself for it," he stated. "And I hate to admit it," he began as he looked back and forth in to my eyes.

"What?"

"I miss touching you and I've been really, really impatient. I've been fighting the venom…the anger and adrenalin again, since I've been back. I'm a little selfish when it comes to being intimate with you." He slid his hand down to my shoulder as he gazed at it, and then glanced back to my eyes.

"I've been worrying about why you haven't tried to…haven't touched me like that since you've been home," I admitted, watching his reaction. "I was afraid somehow your feelings had changed."

He studied me intently for several moments, and then crushed his mouth to mine. I weaved my fingers in his hair, holding him there as I returned his kiss. It was like I was finally home. He kissed me with a desperation I felt down to my core. Breathless, he drew back and exclaimed, "Nothing could be further from the truth. I adore you, you know that. I was holding back, afraid of the anger again, and of my own strength. And I just thought we had to wait, thought that you would still be bleeding, and I didn't want to start something we couldn't finish, I'm so, so sorry," he finished as I pulled him back down to hold him close. The sound of the door opening interrupted the moment. Banton straightened, and touched my cheek as he turned to see who it was.

The Nurse carried Matty in to me, and then handed the strange-looking bottle of blood formula to Banton.

"See how much he takes, and then let me know. I'll be back to check in a bit," she instructed as she checked the machines hooked to me before she left. Banton moved to sit down on the bed beside me, and watched as I fed Matty. As usual, Matty latched on immediately and sucked the bottle dry, seeming to adjust to the taste of the formula as though it were nothing different.

"He's a Gastaneau, all right," Banton chuckled as I removed the empty bottle from his mouth. I switched him to my shoulder, and after several moments of gently patting him, the inevitable burp erupted.

"All Gastaneau," Banton repeated as he grinned at me and flashed his dimple. I reached up and circled it with my finger, like I'd done a million times.

Matty drifted off to sleep in my arms as I watched him.

"Do you want me to take him back and put him in his crib?" Banton asked. I shook my head.

Thinking of my tiny daughter in the next room, I replied, "No, I want him here with me. I need to feel his skin against mine."

Banton nodded silently and then pulled me in close to his side. After a bit, Dr. Lane and Dr. Renault stepped into my room.

"Chandler, Elly seems stable, but we have a ways to go. We should know more by morning. I have to tell you, it's been touch and go."

Banton held me tighter as he felt me take a deep breath.

"Touch and go? She's going to be all right, isn't she?" my voice rose.

"We are cautiously optimistic. Let's just get her through the night." Both doctors moved closer to the bed.

"We want to ask you some questions, Chandler. We are puzzled, and Dr. Renault says your tests aren't normal. Exactly how many times have you been bitten?" Dr. Lane asked.

I glanced at Banton as I answered, "Twice, once in the beginning, and then again when we were attacked at the house. Why?"

"Chandler, your blood has changed tremendously since we ran the first series of tests on you. It's even changed since the second bite." Dr. Lane replied.

Dr. Renault spoke up. "Everett tells us your sense of emotions seems to be getting sharper, that you are connecting with the emotions of those around you more and more. Is that right?"

"Yes, it seems to be. Even beings…things in our house…there are certain things going on there I seem to connect with," I offered as Banton looked down at me.

"Chandler, I need to ask you…are your cheekbones or mouth sore? Has anything happened with your teeth or your eyes?"

"Not my teeth, no. But my vision has been blurry at times like when I first wake up, since I had the twins. I thought it was just fatigue," I answered. "Why? What does that mean?"

Dr. Renault walked over and placed his hand on Banton's shoulder as he answered, "Well, we're just trying to form an opinion with a process of elimination. Chandler, like the twins, is sort of an unknown for us. I've always made a study of half-breeds like you and Banton, Aldon, and Orcos. We really know so little, and of course nothing is published in the mainstream. We thought there were no degrees of transformation, you either transform to an Orco when bitten, or you stop at a certain point like Banton. Only Chandler's transformation hasn't stopped. She's progressed past where she should have.

"I don't understand," I began, shaking my head. Banton looked worriedly back and forth between me and Dr. Renault.

"Chandler, your tests resemble that of an Aldon. I ran them twice. You test more Aldon than human. So do the babies."

"That's not…possible, is it?" I whispered.

"I didn't think so. Dr. Lane has a theory. The more you are bitten, and depending on whom it is…well, your transformation can progress further than first thought."

Banton and I sat in stunned silence, processing the possibilities. My heart began to pound, and a new kind of fear took hold.

"Am I…will I have to fight through changes like Brie did? Am I venomous? What will…" I trailed off as I looked worriedly up at Banton. He leaned down and kissed me on the forehead.

Dr. Renault gave me a sympathetic smile. "No, Chandler, I don't think so. I would like to check your vision, and we may need to address your diet if you continue to sway anemic. You don't have fangs, and don't seem to be developing any. Do we have your permission to run some more tests? You too, Banton, since you've been bitten more than once yourself."

I nodded as Banton replied, "Sure…anything to help your research for Chandler or the babies," Banton replied.

"Dr. Renault," I called to him as he started for the door. "May I stay with Elly tonight?"

"No, Chandler, I would like for you to stay in here tonight and rest. Dr. Lane or I will be with her the entire night, I promise. We'll get you if there is any change," he assured us before closing the door.

I gazed up at Banton with tear-rimmed eyes. "She just has to pull through," I murmured as he placed his lips in my hair.

Banton and I slept little that night. Dr. Renault came in at midnight and unhooked me from the transfusion, and then took me to see Elly for a few minutes. She was still so pale, her skin so soft, but chilly to the touch. Although her skin was a beautiful translucent powdery white, the veins in her arms took on a bluish cast, making her appear ghost-like. I leaned over to kiss her tiny cheek, and she opened her eyes and gazed at me as I whispered, "Get well, little girl...you are everything to us."

"Come on, Sweetheart. We'll come back in a little while," Banton murmured as he gently rubbed my back. After he helped me back to my room, he climbed into the bed beside me, and pulled Matty's crib over beside the bed next to us.

Aunt Sue and Uncle Lon napped on couches in the waiting room, along with John, Brie, and Everett.

I could hear the clock on the wall ticking away the minutes in my room. All I could think about was Elly. It was unthinkable that I could lose one of the babies, and as I turned over for the hundredth time, I found Banton watching Matty silently, his thumb making tiny circles on his back as he slept in his crib. Finding comfort in the fact the doctors watched Elly and Banton watched Matty, my eyelids finally closed.

My breathing became labored...my heart pounded as I walked toward the tiny bassinette that held my precious daughter. As I reached my hand out to pull the blanket away from her shoulders, I gasped. Her skin was ashen gray as cold as ice to the touch. I gently touched her to turn her over, and her little stiff body rolled to the side, her eyes fixed in a green, translucent stare.

"Nooo! Oh, no...God, please! Don't take her," I yelled out, frantically searching the room as I sat up in bed.

Banton hurried around the bassinette and sank down beside me, pulling me up into his arms. "Andie, Sweetheart, it was only a dream. Shhh….wake up, it's over," he comforted as Matty stirred in his crib.

Realizing I was only dreaming, I pulled back and asked Banton, "Have the doctors been back in here since midnight? What time is it," I demanded as I looked over his shoulder at the clock on the wall. It said 4:45 am.

"No. That's a good sign, Sweetheart. I'm sure of it. They would come and get us, if she were any worse," he assured me as he pulled me back into his arms. After several more moments he kissed my shoulder gently where my shirt had dropped lower, and then raised his eyes to mine.

"Do you want me to get you anything? You haven't had anything to eat in hours…or I could get you something to drink?" Banton offered. I shook my head.

"No, I'm good. I just…" I began as the door to my room opened. Dr. Lane stood silently as he watched the two of us.

"Oh, God, no," Banton whispered as I watched him shake his head. I looked frantically back and forth between him and Dr. Lane as Dr. Renault came up behind him.

"No, no…Elly's fine. We just heard you and knew you were awake, and it's time to try to feed her again. We thought you might want to do it. She seems much better than she was at midnight," Dr. Lane assured us as I let out a sigh of relief. I looked back up at Banton as a tear slid down his cheek. I noticed he was shaking. Evidently he'd been worrying as much about Elly as I had been, although he'd seemed like a tower of strength. I reached up and held his cheek in my hand, wiping the tear away with my thumb. He kissed my hand quickly and pulled the covers back for me.

I turned quickly back to Dr. Lane. "Of course I do!" I jumped from the bed and passed both of them as I flew into the emergency room where Ellyson still lay. She was napping on her tummy, making little sucking noises as she nursed on her tiny fist.

I picked her up gently, carefully avoiding the wires and leads that hooked her up to the many machines surrounding her crib.

Banton grabbed a rocker from across the room and pulled it next to the crib as I sat down in it. As Dr. Lane handed me the bottle of specially blended formula, she cried out healthily, letting us know she was hungry. Banton chuckled at the sound and firmly grasped my shoulder.

"That's the first time she's made that sound in days! It's the sweetest sound I've ever heard," he exclaimed as I began to rock her. She sucked at the nipple on the bottle noisily, eating faster than Matty had earlier in the evening.

The door across the room opened, and Uncle Lon stepped through cautiously.

"I thought I heard Banton's voice. Is everything all right?" he asked as he watched me feed Elly.

"Much better, Mr. LeBlance. Ellyson seems to have turned a corner, and I think we are on the right track with her. You can tell the others. I think we are out of danger," Dr. Renault replied.

Uncle Lon took a deep breath as I noticed large tears in his eyes. He nodded and turned to tell the others. A cry coming from the other door alerted us Matty was hungry as well.

"Banton, would you go and see about Matty?" I asked as he nodded. He took his hand from my shoulder and started for the door as it opened.

"Bebe, this little one is hungry too," Everett informed us as he carried him cradled in his arms.

"Here, give him this," Dr. Renault offered another bottle to Everett as Banton held his arms out for our son.

"No, please…may I? I would love to do it," Everett offered as Banton smiled and nodded. Everett took a chair on the far wall and proceeded to feed Matty.

I smiled as I watched Ellyson finishing off the rich blood mixture in the bottle. As I pulled the empty bottle back, she opened her eyes and gazed up at me, seeming more alert that I'd seen her since she was born. She began to squirm and fuss, and I raised her gently to my shoulder and patted her back rhythmically as I rocked her. Without warning, she burped loudly, sounding much like Cade and Drew after a large meal at Mrs. Anne's. Banton and Ev chuckled as I pulled her from my shoulder and placed her gently back down on my legs.

"That's a good sign. She's taking the rich mixture, and it seems to be agreeing with her. If she keeps it down and her little body processes, it means we're on the right track. Kids, you have yourselves twin Aldon babies," Dr. Renault stated as he patted Banton on the back.

I'd been secretly dreading the confirmation for months, but now that we'd almost lost Ellyson, it seemed like such a minor detail. As I gazed at my daughter, it occurred to me. They were my babies, a part of me and Banton, and I couldn't love them more. I didn't care if they were Aldon, Orco, half-breed, or Yankee vegetarian democrats. They were Gastaneau's.

Chapter Fourteen

On our way home, I insisted on riding between the twins in the backseat as I was hesitant to let either one of them out of my sight. Banton nodded indulgently as he well understood my over-protective state. When we drove up in the driveway of our old southern home, our relatives and friends poured out into the front yard to welcome us.

"Son, it sure is good to see you home!" Mr. Matt greeted Banton as he opened his door. Mrs. Elaine opened the back door to our SUV and unbuckled Ellyson from her car seat.

"My sweet little girl, how you had us all worried," Mrs. Elaine murmured as she kissed Ellyson's cheek. Banton removed Matty and his entire carrier from the other side, so I could climb out the door behind them. After he shut the car door behind me, he put his arm around me as he carried Matty into the house.

"Chandler! We are so glad you're home!" Laurilee greeted me at the front door as she took in my appearance. "You look so much better. You're color is back!"

"Did I look that bad before?" I cocked an eyebrow at her as Dan laughed behind her.

"You were lookin' a little pasty, Chirpy, that's all...Now you look like you've had some sun!" Dan exclaimed as he picked me up and whirled me around.

"I hope y'all are hungry, because Laurilee and Dan have been cookin' all mornin'," Claudia inserted as she pushed around the crowd and took me in her arms. "I've been so worried about all of you, and Will and I just had to come when Momma and Daddy called. I hope that's all right," she whispered.

"Of course! I love that everyone is here!" I assured them enthusiastically. Banton knelt down and removed Matty from his car seat, and then handed him off to Claudia who waited impatiently. Ava Grace tugged at Claudia's pants leg and exclaimed, "Pweese wet me see my babies, I need to feed my babies!"

"Come here, Doodle-Bug! Uncle Banton needs some Ava time," he declared as he swept our little niece up in his arms. She giggled as he covered her face in kisses. It had been quite a while since he'd been relaxed enough or had the time to shower her with some attention, and I could tell she was overjoyed as she giggled, her face lighting up like the dawn.

I turned to Laurilee. "What the heck is this about y'all cookin'? I thought you hated to cook," I added.

"Everyone here is always cooking all this wonderful Cajun cuisine, and I thought we'd treat y'all to a little taste of Texas! When we found out Elly was well and you were comin' home with her, Dan ran to the grocery store and bought a ton of ribs, beans, and all the fixin's. He fired Banton's grill up outside, and he's got a brisket on, and has been marinating ribs all mornin'. We're going to have a good-ole Texas picnic to celebrate!"

"Wow, this is a treat! Let me help you, and we need to have a little wedding talk," Everett took Laurilee and guided her back toward the kitchen.

"If you will watch the kids, I need to shower…clean up a bit," I said as I turned to Banton. He nodded, put Ava down, and then leaned over to kiss me before I mounted the stairs.

"I'll make sure Mother and Claudia watch them, and then I'll be right up behind you," he assured me.

Once I'd showered and dried my hair, I searched through my closet and found a red sundress, one of my favorites. Shaking my head, I was leery of trying it on. It had been a long time since my tummy had fit into a size six.

"Oh, what the heck…let's see how much I have to lose," I muttered as I dropped the hanger on the bed and then slid the soft rayon fabric down my body. It fit me like a glove. I smiled and then turned to take in my reflection in the floor length mirror on the back of the door. I couldn't believe it fit. It was a little tight across the bust, the halter straps needed to be let out a bit to accommodate my full bust line.

"Guess I'll lose those now that I'm not nursing," I sighed as I said the words.

I heard Banton chuckle as I raised my eyes to look at him. He shut the door gently as he crossed to me.

"You look beautiful. The muscles in your body are more defined now than they were before you got pregnant. And your curves," he shook his head as I glanced up into his eyes.

204

"What? Oh, I know. I've got some exercising to do," I muttered, knowing my butt and thighs were rounder since the pregnancy.

"Are you kidding? You are a knock-out, Chandler. You are all curves, like old Hollywood. So sexy," he murmured as he dropped a kiss on my shoulder. I wanted him so badly. I'd silently been doing the math in my head, we hadn't made love since before he'd left in May. It had been over three months, and I was on fire.

I pulled his head down to mine and kissed him passionately. He wound his arms around me, picking me up and then placing me on the bed as his body covered mine. Sliding his hand down my leg, he grabbed the dress and pulled it up, sliding the fabric up and exposing my hip as he wound his fingers in the fabric of the silk panties I'd donned. He worked his fingers up under the fabric, and then slid his hand over intimately between my thighs. I moaned, pushing into his cupped hand. The muscles in his neck rippled as I slid my lips down, tasting his skin. I pushed his shirt back, exposing his tanned chest.

"Andie, it's been so long. I want to make love to you, now…" he whispered, pulling my dress up my ribcage. A knock on the door startled us both back to reality. His head rose angrily to look at the door as I called out, "Who is it?"

"It's Aunt Sue, Dear…the babies are both getting a little fussy, and we thought they might be hungry, but we didn't know what we need to put in the formula," she called out as I looked longingly into Banton's eyes. He watched me intently as he called out, "Chandler will be right down."

"All right." I heard Aunt Sue's footsteps as she descended the stairs. I sighed as Banton looked back down at me.

"So we have a date…right here, about four hours from now? I'm going to ask Claudia and Momma to take the first shift with the babies tonight, and then we can get up with them at three," Banton insisted. I smiled up at him and nodded. He released his hold on me, and I stood and straightened my clothes as he chuckled. He continued to lie across the foot of our bed as he watched me brush my hair. I then pulled it to the side and fastened it with the diamond clip he'd given me for Valentine's Day.

205

I turned back to him as I opened the door. "You promise, four hours from now?"

"Or sooner, if I can get us back upstairs faster," he grinned and flashed me my favorite dimple. "I'll be right down as soon as I shower," he added, rolling off the bed and padding over to the bathroom door.

As I entered the kitchen, I found Everett already preparing the formula. He leaned over to me and whispered, "The doctors had this couriered over a little while ago. This is the blood we mix with the formula the pharmacy sent. And Dr. Renault told me to tell you that you need to drink at least sixteen ounces of this a day, too, until we see how your body is going to process," he added. I wrinkled my nose at him.

"Ev, eating rare meat is one thing, but this…I don't know if I can do this. I'm not completely Aldon," I whispered, glancing at Laurilee as she came in from the backyard.

"Ribs are almost ready. I've got the beans in the oven, and the coleslaw and potato salad are in the fridge, thanks to Everett," she commented as she watched us curiously. "What's going on?"

"Oh, nothing. Everett's just being a mother hen, that's all," I offered as Everett chuckled.

"What's in those jugs? Laurilee asked, moving toward the blood lined up on the kitchen table.

"Oh, those are for the special formula mixture we have to feed the babies. Don't use those, we'll save them for that," he said as he crossed the kitchen to place the jugs in the refrigerator. I could imagine her confusion if she poured the liquid from the white jugs, anticipating milk and getting blood.

After Everett had placed the blood in the refrigerator he placed notes on them stating "for the babies." I finished helping him fill the bottles, and then walked them into Mrs. Elaine and Aunt Sue.

"Just in time," Aunt Sue chimed. She and Mrs. Elaine took the bottles from me. They both sat on the sofa side-by-side with the babies cradled in their arms.

"Here, let me," I began as Constance came up behind me and placed her hand on my shoulder.

"Do you think either Mimi is going to give them up? Forget it, Chandler. Claudia and I are waiting our turns! You might not get to feed them again until they're ten," she quipped as Banton bounded back down the staircase and into the room. He looked gorgeous in a soft pink knit polo shirt and faded jeans.

"I was just going to ask if maybe the grandmothers would take the first shift from bedtime till three, and give me a chance to get little mama to rest?" Banton asked, pulling me back into his arms.

Ty chuckled as he rose to greet Banton. "Yeah, that's it. You want alone time to get Chandler to sleep," he repeated. Banton laughed at him.

"Yeah, good luck, brother…with that sleep thing," John teased from across the room.

I felt so warmed by all the friendship in the room. I hadn't heard the guys tease each other like that in months, and it felt so good. I missed Brie, and looked around. I spotted her in the dining room, sitting by herself, silently watching Aunt Sue and Mrs. Elaine as they fed the babies. I crossed the foyer and sat down in a chair beside her as she looked at me.

"Brie, are you all right? I know it's hard for you to be around so many humans…" I trailed off.

"No, not at all. It doesn't bother me anymore. I'm good," she assured me as she smiled at me. As I watched her it occurred to me, she had become more beautiful since the transformation. Her skin seemed so silky, almost airbrushed, and her hair was an even more beautiful russet. The green in her eyes was so deep and reflective, and even though she controlled the intensity, they seemed to sparkle.

"Then what is it?" I asked as she gazed back at me.

"The babies. Chandler, do you think maybe one day soon, you might let me hold them? I have control, I promise. You can trust me. I can't even smell a human blood scent on them," she whispered as I nodded.

"They're Aldon, Brie. You don't have to worry. Of course you can hold them! Right now, if you could pry them lose from their grandmothers," I sighed as she laughed.

"That might be the greatest battle I've fought yet as a vamp," she commented wryly as I giggled.

"Beef's ready. Come and get it," Dan called out from the kitchen.

"Can you stomach it, or do you need to pass?" I asked Brie. She nodded.

"Some rare brisket is the one thing I think I can stand," she assured me as I wound my arm in hers. We made our way back to the kitchen and filled our plates as everyone piled out onto the patio. Everett had worked some magic with the help of Mr. Philippe, stringing up lights across the patio and setting up patio tables and chairs.

"Crank up some music!" Ty suggested as he bounded down the back steps. The tables filled up quickly, and the SEALs and Cade and Drew lounged on the ground with their heaping plates of food. I cleaned my brisket up quickly, and then watched as everyone celebrated. Julia sat quietly in a chair by the greenhouse, wistfully watching the SEALs as they joked about and teased one another. I knew she was thinking about Ben.

Banton came up behind me and placed his hand around my ribcage, brushing my breast with his thumb. The familiar warm rush washed over me as I felt the deep ache in my stomach…the ache that told me it had been too long. He whispered, "Can I yell 'fire,' and clear everyone out yet?"

I turned to him and smiled. "I wish you would, but first, you might go and talk with Julia. She seems really lonely tonight," I whispered as he looked over my head at her. He looked back down at me, placing a kiss on my forehead before crossing the yard to her.

"Diva-Doll, you up for a little pool basketball?" John asked as Constance flopped down on the ground beside him.

"Thought you'd never ask, Cowboy! I feel the need to kick your ass at something tonight!" she shot back with a grin as she rose.

"For the love of good manners, please, Constance…Watch your language! There are children present!" Aunt Sue scolded her, holding her hands over Ava's little ears.

"Kick 'is ass! Kick 'is ass!" Ava squealed as she kicked her leg in the air. Aunt Sue looked at Constance with a horrified glare.

"Oh, no…Princess Ava, Princesses never say that word. She meant, 'kickin' class…we will learn to kick and fight!" Uncle Everett came to the rescue, diverting Ava's attention.

"Good save, Unca Ebret," Brie joked as she sat down in John's lap. John leaned over and kissed her on her shoulder, and then ran his thumb across her creamy white skin. She leaned her head back into his chest as he pressed his lips into her hair. Watching them filled me with such joy...they were so in love, and I could feel it radiating across the courtyard to me. I gazed across the tables and found Banton holding Julia quietly as she sobbed into his shoulder. My heart ached for her; I knew how she was grieving for Ben. She was experiencing such joy at Banton's homecoming, and it was bittersweet for her.

The music changed abruptly, from oldies rock to some forties Sinatra. After checking the babies for the hundredth time and finding them napping peacefully in a playpen we'd placed just inside the greenhouse, Banton grabbed my arm and pulled me down the stone path to the back of the structure. The streetlight in the alley cast an orange glow across the small patio, and as he turned me around in it he whispered, "May I have this dance?"

His eyes sparkled in the darkness. I nodded, melting into his arms as he crooned into my ear. His deep beautiful voice sent shivers down my spine. He whirled me around the patio, holding me so close to his body I could feel his passion through my thin sundress. I blushed in the moonlight...I couldn't believe I did. *He's your husband, for gripe's sake.* But it had been so long, everything was new again.

"I'm so sorry. I should have been stealing moments like this with you these past few weeks. I promise never to let stress, work, or kids come in between us again."

His voice, so deep and dreamy...almost raspy...was the sexiest thing I'd ever heard. I shivered as I nuzzled his neck.

"I'm sorry that I'm so insecure I need constant reassurance," I murmured as I gazed up into his eyes. He lowered his mouth to mine, moving his lips slowly, breathing in and out rhythmically. His breath tasted sweet like the wine we'd been drinking. He slid his hand down inside the back of my dress and caressed my bare skin between my shoulder blades.

"I have found the one whom my heart loves," Banton whispered into my ear as the song ended.

"Mmmm. Song of Solomon," I replied as he nodded. "I love those passages."

"All beautiful you are, my darling, there is no flaw in you," he murmured, sliding his thumb along my cheekbone. "...the beauty of the love given by God between a man and a woman. It expresses exactly how I feel," he continued as he pulled me back into his kiss.

"Chandler? Banton? We thought we'd get in the hot tub, if that's all right with you," Constance called out as she came around the corner of the greenhouse. "Oh, my. Holy crap, Chandler! Get a room," she announced as Ty came around behind her.

I pulled away and gazed up at Banton as I replied, "My house, my rules." Banton chuckled as he offered, "Y'all go ahead. That's what it's there for. I thought John challenged you to a basketball game in the pool."

"Well, we had second thoughts, thinking about the girls in their swimsuits and all, and the water might be chilly in the pool," Ty grinned as he kissed Constance on the neck.

"We'll be along," I called after them as they disappeared down the stone path back to the courtyard. I sighed, and then gazed back up into Banton's eyes.

"Why don't I help you carry the babies in, and get them down for the night. We can leave our guests to wrap things up out here," he suggested, running the back of his hand down my cheek.

I nodded and grabbed his hand, following Constance and Ty. We gathered the babies up from their playpen and carried them into the house. After I settled down into the rocker in the nursery, Banton handed me Elly, and then sat down beside me in the other rocker with Matty. We both rocked as we fed our babies, Banton singing along to the music we could hear wafting up from the backyard. I watched Banton silently. His hands were so tanned and strong against Matty's fair skin. He held Matty with one hand cupped under his head, stroking his cheek with his thumb as Matty sucked the bottle.

I laid my head back on the rocker and smiled at him. "This is just like in my dream. So perfect."

He looked up at me and smiled, flashing his dimple. His eyes twinkled, and I couldn't wait to go to our room. My heart pounded as it did the night he made love to me for the first time.

Rising from the rocker, he murmured, "He's asleep. I'm going to put him down, do you need anything?"

"No, I'm good. She's almost finished, and I need to change her before I put her down," I replied as he turned back to me.

"I have something to do, I won't be long," he whispered over his shoulder as he shut the door to the nursery.

I watched Ellyson silently as she finished sucking the last of the formula from the bottle. She was tired, having been passed around so much during the evening. After I worked to get her to burp, I rocked her a little longer, making sure she was fast asleep. She cooed in her sleep, making her little baby noises as she dreamed her little girl dreams. I placed a gentle kiss on her lips, tasting her sweet baby breath only newborns have. The time was passing so fast, I wanted to savor every moment. *I could sit here like this for hours*, I thought as I rocked her on my shoulder. Then I thought about Banton waiting for me in our room.

I rose and crossed over to her bassinette, and placed her on her back. She sighed and stretched, and then slipped back into the deep dream state that she'd been in on my shoulder. Matty lay on his side, sucking his fist in his sleep. "Always hungry," I murmured as I placed a kiss on his forehead. I slipped from the room, and then walked down the landing to our bedroom door. I opened it and gasped.

Banton stood beside the window in the candlelight, his white silk pajama bottoms hung provocatively low on his hips. He smiled at me as I took in the room. Candles spilled from the windowsill and the nightstands, and rose petals covered the bed and across the floor to the doorway. Crossing the space between us, Banton offered me a glass of wine.

"This is so romantic," I commented as I gazed around the room again.

"As I meant for it to be," he replied, handing me the glass and leaning to kiss me. I took a big sip, and then he took my glass from me and placed it on the dresser. His tone and manner were so serious. As he shifted back to me, he murmured, "Turn around."

211

He placed his hands on my shoulders, turning me as he unzipped my dress slowly, placing his lips at the base of my neck. I laid my head back on his bare chest as he untied the silk tie at my neck. My dress dropped to the floor at my ankles. Moaning, I raised my arms over my head and around his neck as he slid his hands around my ribcage and cupped my breasts in his hands.

"Banton, make love to me," I whispered as I tried to turn.

"Not yet, I have more for you," he answered as he slid his hands down my abdomen, trailing his thumb across the scar where my incision had been. He continued to kiss my neck as his hands slid lazily down the top of my thighs and around my hips. Swinging me up into his arms, he carried me toward the bathroom. Kicking the door to the room open with his foot, he whispered softly in my ear, "I'm not finished touching you yet," as he slid me down into the scented water in the tub. Rose petals floated on the water and tickled my legs as he ran his hands beside them in the water.

"Banton, I still have my panties on," I protested as he slid his hands back up to my thighs.

"Not for long," he whispered. He hooked his thumbs down inside the lace at my hips and slid my panties down my legs, leaving them floating in the water.

"We don't have room enough for two in this tub," I pouted, wondering why he'd set this up.

"Don't need it. Tonight, this is all about you," he replied as he took a bottle of scented massage oil off the side of the tub and flipped the top open. He poured it in his hand, and then sat down in the floor beside the tub. Lifting my foot out of the water, he began to caress my calf, sliding his hands to spread the oil into my skin. I shut my eyes as he kneaded the muscles in my leg. As he slid his hands higher, I opened my eyes and gazed at him. His eyes burned fiery amber and brown as he worked his hands slowly up my thighs, sliding his fingers across my skin and then bringing his thumbs together between my legs, moving in circles higher and higher. My breathing became shallow.

"Mr. Gastaneau, do you know what you are doing to me?" I asked breathlessly. He smiled slowly, flashing his famous dimple as his gaze met mine.

"I hope so, Mrs. Gastaneau. I hope I have your full attention," he whispered as he continued to grin. He continued his slow, tantalizing circles between my thighs, and then moved his upper body to gaze closely into my eyes as he moved his thumbs higher and across a very intimate spot.

I drew my breath in as he slid his hand lower and moved his fingers under the water. I instinctively closed my eyes as I moved rhythmically against his hand, silently giving my approval.

"Oh, Banton...please," I whispered.

"Shhh. Let me love you slowly," he replied as he moved over me and brushed his lips across my breastbone. He continued to explore with his fingers under the water. I lay my head back and moaned as I parted my thighs. His mouth made a trail back up my throat, tasting my skin and nipping with his teeth as he moved back toward my lips. His kiss was slow and sensual, his tongue matching the strokes that his fingers made inside me. Pulling away, he oiled my entire body, massaging my shoulders, my neck, and my arms. It was so sensual as I watched his eyes as he worked. The translucent brown seemed to come alive with the candlelight, sparkling as the flecks of gold reflected the light.

"You are driving me insane," I murmured. I caught the back of his neck and pulled him back down to my lips. He covered my lips with his, and drew me up out of the water and into his lap. As I slid my arms up around his neck, the oil from my bath rubbed off on his muscular chest. I rubbed the oil in his skin with the palms of my hand as he watched my expression intently. Slowly he lowered his mouth back to mine. Twining his fingers in my hair at the temples, he gulped in my kiss as if he were drinking water, pulling my tongue in slowly as he explored my mouth with his.

"The massage felt good," I murmured as he drew back to look at me. He smiled, and wrapped a towel around me. Rising up off the floor, he picked me up in his arms in one swift motion, and then carried me back into the bedroom.

"No fair, you have on pants," I whispered against his lips as he pulled the towel from under my arms.

"Here, drink your wine." He pulled away from the kiss, handed me my glass, and retrieved his own. I sank down into the covers on the bed and pulled them up over me, taking in the scent of the rose petals that slid down the sheets.

I watched silently as he stood in the flickering candle light. The silk pants he had on were wet from my body, and they molded to his muscular thighs and groin. My face grew hot as I gazed at him, his body was so tanned and hard, his passion straining against the wet fabric. He slowly slid out of his pants, and I caught my breath. He was even more toned than I remembered…his six-pack abs had hardened, tapering off down between his hipbones in a 'v', drawing my eyes downward.

As I looked back up into his eyes, he strode across the room as he downed his wine. Taking mine from me, he placed both glasses on the nightstand as he slowly pulled the sheet down my body.

"You won't need that," he murmured as he pulled me in under his hard body. I ran my hands up across his chest and over his shoulders, feeling his muscles ripple as he moved. The fire blazing in his eyes was the sexiest thing I'd ever seen.

"I've missed you so much. I've missed us. I've missed your touch, missed you inside me," I whispered as he positioned himself over me, cupping my hips in his hands.

"I'm so sorry. I've kept my distance, only because I was afraid of the venom. I was full of so much hate when I returned. I was afraid I would hurt you. I love you, Chandler," he whispered, sliding his hand down my leg and grasping my knee, drawing it up as he began to move against me. Fisting my hands in his hair, I gasped as he pushed to enter me. It had been so long since I'd felt him.   After a few moments, I relaxed enough to pull him in fully. His eyes burned as he made love to me. We savored every moment. I wrapped my legs around his hips, and as he filled the deep, hollow ache that had been with me for these long four months, I felt complete again. He watched me intently as I gasped, drawing him in completely as waves of fulfillment washed over both of us.

He withdrew slowly, and then pulled me into his chest and held me as our breathing calmed. He pressed his lips to my forehead and murmured, "Do you feel good?" I could hear the chuckle in his voice.

"Mmmm. Better than good. Amazing."

214

"Chandler," he whispered in the candlelight as he played with my hair. I lay with my face on his chest, my leg hitched intimately across his thighs.

"Mmm?"

"Would you marry me all over again?" he asked as I felt him move his arm toward the nightstand.

"Hmm. I'd have to think about that one," I teased as I turned to look up at him. He cocked an eyebrow at my response as he played with my hair, so I continued, "Of course. Every time you ask," I replied, sliding my hand across his chest.

"This is for you, sweetheart. I've wanted to give it to you since the babies' birth, but I haven't had the time to make it a special occasion until now." He pulled me up higher on his chest as he placed a tiffany-blue box on my shoulder.

I caught it before it toppled off and pushed up to remove the lid. Inside I found a diamond bracelet with three loosely braided rows of diamonds, and two large diamonds in the center.

"Oh, Banton," I breathed out in awe as he slid it across my wrist. "I've never seen anything more beautiful," I finished as I gazed down at him.

"Neither have I," he murmured, pulling me down to kiss me. "This is for changing my life in ways I never thought possible. You are my life," he finished as he slid his hand across my abdomen. "You went through so much for me, and I love you."

He fastened the clasp on my wrist, and then placed a kiss there before turning my hand back over. Reclining back on the pillows, he added, "I searched everywhere while you were in the hospital. I couldn't find anything that suited my purpose, so I had this made."

"I love it...it's perfect," I murmured as I glanced back up at his face.

"The three ropes are significant. In the bible… Ecclesiastes, I think, it says 'A chord of three strands is not quickly broken.'"

"Three?" I whispered in wonder.

"God, Husband and Wife. The diamonds are for the babies," he added. I gazed back up at him.

A tear slid down my face, my emotions finally catching up to the moment. Banton smiled and leaned up to kiss it away before it left my cheek.

"I always seem to make you cry," he observed.

"Yes, but they're such happy tears," I whispered as I circled his dimple with my finger.

He pulled me back down to his chest, and wrapped his arms securely around me, where I drifted peacefully to sleep.

*　*　*

At midnight, hungry little cries drifted across the upstairs landing and through our closed bedroom door.

"Don't get up, I'll make sure my mother has them," he whispered against my ear as he slid from bed. I nodded as I heard his footsteps cross to the doorway. After a few minutes, I felt him slip back into the bed.

"Are the babies okay?" I murmured sleepily.

"Well taken care of by Claudia and Momma," he replied as he chuckled in the darkness. He reached over and pulled me back into his side. Around three-thirty, their wails woke us again.

"I think this is our shift," I muttered sleepily, throwing the covers back.

"No, stay here, Chandler, and rest. I'll bring them in here," he offered. Stroking my arm, he kissed my forehead as he covered me back up and rose to get them. After a moment he pushed the door to our room open as I sat up in bed. He cradled Elly and Matty each in an arm as he crossed the room to me. Placing them one on either side of me, he kissed me and then made a trip down to the kitchen to get their formula. After helping me feed them, he returned them to the nursery and then climbed back into bed.

"Thank you. The next time is my turn," I offered sleepily as he snuggled down next to me.

Chapter Fifteen

The next afternoon, Laurilee stood in the center of Mr. Philippe's dressing room, waiting for Everett to come back with dress number ten.

"Why is this so hard for me, but it was so easy for you," Laurilee complained.

"Maybe it has something to do with the fact that we have too many opinions in the room," I offered as Constance rolled her eyes.

"I still think you need to go with the first dress," Julia suggested. Aunt Sue shook her head.

"Darlin', you need to tell them all to hush and keep their opinions to themselves until you've had time to react. When you try the right dress on, you'll know. It will be the one that makes you cry," Brie retorted as she stood and put her hands on her hips.

"She's right, you know," I agreed as I pulled Matty back up to my chest from a diaper change. "I've known you since we were ten years old. I haven't seen the dress yet that says 'Laurilee.'"

"But you will, sweetie, I swear. We'll stay all night if we have to," Mr. Philippe assured her as he and Everett re-appeared with a beautiful champagne lace gown.

"That looks like Mawmaw Ann's tablecloth," Constance began.

"Shush! No comments from the audience. Let Laurilee feel it as she tries it on," Everett reprimanded Constance as I smiled. Everett and Mr. Philippe helped Laurilee step into the dress, and then Mr. Philippe drew it up as Everett began hooking the loops over the tiny buttons in the back. As she turned, I got goose-bumps on my arms. The dress fit her like a glove. The long sleeves hugged her tiny arms, and the full A-line skirt puddled on the floor around her feet. The bodice was lined with satin, barely covering the top of her breasts. The lace up to the neckline was sheer like the sleeves, and the lace was sheer all the way down the back of the gown to right above her tailbone. The train in the back disappeared into shredded ruffles of antique lace in shades of cream and off white, giving the gown a vintage feel.

"I can definitely see cowboy boots with that one…it looks like a sexy version of a hundred and fifty year old dress," I commented as she turned to me. The sparkle I noted in her eyes was the most we would see of tears from Laurilee.

"This is the one," she nodded. Everyone applauded. I nodded my approval as I smiled and rose to hug her.

"It will be beautiful with the bridesmaids' dresses," Mr. Philippe clasped his hands and pressed them to his lips.

I was to have my fitting for my dress later, so we all scattered throughout the shop to browse as Mr. Philippe finished with Laurilee. After our girl's outing, we all returned to our house to find it empty.

"Guess they all went to work out, even Dan," Laurilee commented as she sat her bags down in the foyer.

Constance shot me a look, having the same thought I was having…that Dan would be more confused than ever if he witnessed the SEALs running or lifting weights. I took a deep breath, trying to calm the quickening of my heartbeat. I was having a full-blown panic attack once again because of Banton's absence. I felt silly, knowing Banton was only miles away and would return any time. I was determined to handle this and not let Banton know I was still having them, but they were getting worse, not better. I glanced around the foyer at everyone and then placed Matty down in the floor and took him from his carrier as Claudia did the same with Elly.

"Constance, could you take him for just a minute, I need to run upstairs," I asked as I handed him to her.

"Sure, are you all right?" she asked, cocking an eyebrow at me.

"Yeah, I'll be right back," I murmured as I hurried up the staircase. When I had my bedroom door closed, I sat down on the bed and put my head between my legs, taking deep, slow breaths. My chest hurt like I'd swallowed a large balloon of air. As I sat back up slowly, I pushed my hair back and noticed my hands shaking uncontrollably. My eyes filled with tears of frustration. I hated being the weak female, terrified of losing Banton. But that's what it was. I had to remind myself daily that he was home, and he was alive.

I heard a soft knock on the door. I straightened and cleared my throat as I answered, "Come in."

Brie opened the door cautiously and then entered, closing the door silently behind her.

"Chandler, what can I do?" she asked, sitting on the bed beside me.

"What do you mean?" I asked. She covered my hands with hers and I immediately felt such a warmth and love.

"Come on, Chandler. We have a connection, remember? I can feel what you feel as much as you can feel me. You're having some sort of anxiety attack, like nothing I've ever felt before. What is it? Is it the babies? Are you still anxious about Ellyson?"

I shook my head, and then raised my eyes to her. "No, it's silly, really. I feel so stupid," I began.

"Chandler, nothing is silly if it affects you like that! I've never felt anything like it, except maybe while I was fighting the venom."

"It's Banton. I do this, when he's not here. It's like I know he's coming back, but until I see him, I can't convince my heart, or something. I can't control it, and I hate it!"

"Does he know his absence affects you like this?"

"He knows I've had a couple of panic attacks, one in the hospital. But I don't want him to know I'm still having them. He can't stay with me all the time, Brie."

"Well, I think you need to be honest with him and tell him. His disappearance did something to you, Chandler. You might need to see someone," she suggested as my head snapped up.

"I can get through this on my own, I promise. I'll be fine, just give me a few minutes," I argued as she nodded reluctantly. She rose, and then pushed the door open and returned down the staircase.

I refused to be that female. Since Elly had recovered and we brought the babies home, everything had been so perfect. I didn't want anything to mar our happiness. I knew as time passed, I would be able to work through these panic attacks.

After I had my heart in a more even rhythm, I rose to make my way back downstairs. Voices in the nursery halted me.

219

"Banton, she isn't being honest with you, and I'm worried about her," Brie's voice drifted out the door.

"What's going on?" Banton's voice answered, thick with concern.

"When we got home a little while ago, I could feel it. I felt what Chandler was feeling...and it was awful! It was so intense."

"What was?" he demanded.

"She's having panic attacks. She admitted it to me, whenever you are gone. She says she knows you are coming back, but she can't convince herself. Banton, it made me physically ill. I've never felt anything like it, except maybe when I thought I wasn't going to be able to see John again. Chandler is fighting through something, something emotional because of your disappearance. It's done something to her."

My heart began to pound again, angry Brie had told him. Several seconds of silence passed as I pondered what to do. I finally stepped back into our bedroom and pulled the door partially to.

"I'm sorry, maybe I shouldn't have said anything," Brie began. Banton interrupted her.

"No, Brie...Thank you. I needed to know. Chandler is determined to make everything normal for us right now, and I knew she'd had a panic attack or two. I just didn't know she was still continuing to have them. I'll take care of her," he assured her as their voices got louder moving toward the stairs.

I waited until I knew they were back downstairs, and then I followed them. I found everyone in the living room playing with the babies.

"I swear he just smiled at me," Dan argued.

"Mrs. Elaine says it's just gas. Babies don't really smile until they're older," Constance informed them as John snickered.

"Then Cade and Drew should be grinning all the time!" Ty exclaimed as everyone laughed, my dear cousins included. I grinned at them as I came into the room.

"That's great, boys. I'm so proud that you are so famous for such dignified behavior," Aunt Sue rolled her eyes as Cade punched Drew in the arm.

"Well, I happen to know they are smiling. Elly smiles at her daddy all the time, isn't that right?" Banton kissed Ellyson on the cheek right on her dimple, and then turned her so everyone could see her.

"Come here, sweet little Ellyson Marie. It's time Uncle Everett had some one-on-one time with you," Everett declared, taking her from Banton and cradling her to his chest. He sat down in a rocker that we'd added to the room.

Banton came up behind me and placed his arms around me. "How was your day?" he murmured in my ear, placing a kiss there. I turned in his arms and gave him the biggest smile I could produce.

"Great, now that everyone is here."

"She's lying, we wore her out so badly, she had to go up and rest for a few minutes when we got back," Laurilee added. "I know you'll be glad when Dan and I go back tomorrow. It will be the first time since you've been married you have the house all to yourselves," she finished as Dan put his arms around her from behind.

Banton continued to gaze at me, and I knew he was thinking about the panic thing. I rose on my toes to kiss him, and then hurried to the kitchen to start supper like nothing was out of the ordinary.

I cooked a big Southern-fried dinner, with the help of Constance, Brie and Laurilee. I caught Brie making faces several times as she smelled the food cooking, and once or twice I thought she was going to hurl. I finally pulled her to the side.

"Brie, you don't have to do this. We can handle it," I whispered, not wanting Laurilee to hear us.

"No, I need to practice. You won't believe this, but it's really hard to cook now, now that everything tastes different to me. It's like trying to prepare something for John and make it taste good to him, while it's revolting to me."

"Have you told Everett? Maybe he might have some pointers," I suggested as she cocked an eyebrow at me.

"And what about the pure blood thing? I know you haven't tried it yet, and I can tell you are getting pale again. Chandler, Dr.

Renault says we have to have it. You will get sick again," she cautioned as I nodded reluctantly.

"I just can't stand the thought," I began.

"It's no different than eating raw steak. Try holding your nose," she suggested.

We went back into the kitchen, and when Laurilee went out the backdoor with Dan, Brie got a plastic cup from the cabinet and Constance helped her fill it from one of the jugs.

"Here. Hold your nose," Brie urged as I stood over the sink. I raised the cup and made the mistake of looking at it. It wasn't so much the color or odor, but the consistency. And it felt slimy.

I downed it all at once, holding my nose. I stood for several seconds, trying to concentrate on not getting sick…anything but what I'd just ingested.

"Sweetheart, I'm proud of you," Banton startled me as he came up from behind me. I rinsed the cup out in the sink, and then took a big drink of water to rinse my mouth out. As soon as the water entered my mouth, it was like it brought the salty rusty iron taste of the blood out. The taste and smell ran though my sinuses and nasal passages, and my stomach started to turn over. I placed my hand over my mouth as I searched wildly around the room. Pushing past Banton, I flew down the hallway and around the corner in to the bathroom. Throwing the lid back on the toilet, I heaved and all of the blood I'd just drank flooded back up my throat. I continued to heave uncontrollably, the spasms racking my body. The more I heaved, the sicker I got. The smell was awful.

Banton was in the floor beside me at once, rubbing my back as I continued to lose it. He held my hair back and wiped the sweat from my forehead.

I finally relaxed and sat back in the floor, exhausted from the ordeal. Banton pulled me up into his arms and picked me up from the floor.

"I can't do this, Banton…I just can't! Can't he give me transfusions whenever the meat isn't enough?" I begged as I buried my face in his neck. "Can't he just give me a shot, or something?"

"I don't know, Chandler. We'll call him and see if there isn't something he can do to help you," he whispered as he kissed my forehead. He continued to climb the steps with me, and then pushed the door open to our room and deposited me on the bed.

"You stay put, I'll bring something up to you," he murmured, reaching down and stroking my cheek with his thumb. I heard Everett's voice in the hallway as Banton passed.

"Is she all right? I've been worrying about her following the doctors' orders," he commented as he pushed the door open.

"Bebe, there are easier ways to start that. I thought you'd already started the feedings," he scolded as he sat down on the bed beside me.

"No, I can't stand the thought. I got my courage up tonight, and Brie tried to help, but," I protested as he shook his head.

"You need to mix it with something. Brie can stand pure blood, she craves. True Aldon and the fully transformed crave. You do not, so it won't appeal to you. Have you tried drinking the babies' formula? It doesn't bother you to feed it to them, does it?

"No, mixed with the proteins and dairy, it smells more like vitamins, and the slimy, oily consistency is hidden. It just looks like reddish-brown milk."

"Well, then. Maybe not tonight, but we'll try again in the morning, okay? If that doesn't work, we'll make an 'au jus' to pour over bread or something," he offered flamboyantly as he kissed his fingers and flung them in the air like a French chef. I had to giggle.

"Here. I brought something to settle your stomach --some good old-fashioned sprite and crackers," Banton offered when he came back into the room.

"No, I'm fine now. I need to go and finish supper."

I tried to rise, but Banton pulled me back down on the bed.

"Nope, Constance and the girls already have everything on the table, and everyone is filling their plates. The babies are sleeping, so just lay back for a little while," Banton ordered as Everett nodded.

"Well, I think I'll just go down and make sure everyone is taken care of," Everett commented as he stepped back out the door. "I'll see you later, Bebe."

"Thanks, Ev," I replied.

Banton watched me for several moments as I nibbled on the crackers and drank some Sprite. I could tell he wanted to talk to me, and I patiently waited until he was ready.

"Sweetheart, why haven't you told me about the panic attacks?"

"I know Brie said something to you," I began.

"Yes she did, and she also said they're pretty intense. She's worried about you, and so am I." He reached out to stroke my cheek.

"I'm fine…I just need to get used to a routine. I don't want to make more of this than it is, and you can't stay with me twenty-four seven."

"Chandler, that's not the point. I think maybe you need to talk to someone. Have you mentioned the attacks to Dr. Lane? Maybe when you talk to him about the blood diet thing, you could mention it. He might be able to help you."

I teared up as I nodded. "I hate being the weak female! I want to be strong, to be a wife you can be proud of, not some wimpy female…" I began.

"Chandler Gastaneau! There is nothing wimpy about you!" Banton exclaimed, his tone taking me by surprise. "I am so proud of you. You endured so much pain and heartache while I was away! I hate what my disappearance did to you, and if you need help dealing with it, it is perfectly understandable. God knows I've gone through a bit of a transition myself. "

"What do you mean?" I asked as he rubbed my arm. He glanced back up at me sheepishly.

"I fight with myself every day. I fight the jealousy inside. I'm jealous of what you and John shared while I was missing. I'm jealous of Everett and the time he spent with you, helping you through the end of the pregnancy. I'm even jealous of my own sister! I know it's crazy, but I still have to stop myself from being harsh with John sometimes. I know nothing happened between you, but I can't help myself. I feel like I was cheated out of the most important months of your pregnancy," he declared, baring his deepest feelings to me.

"I had no idea that still bothered you," I whispered as I touched his cheek.

"I'm just human, after all. I just wanted you to understand we all have weaknesses, and maybe talking to someone isn't the end of the world." He took my hand and pulled me up into his arms. "I love you so much. Until this gets easier for you, I'll take you with me, if I have to. When I go to N'awlins to base next week, I'll take you and the babies with me. We can spend the night at Claudia's. She's been dying for us to come and stay with them," he whispered in my ear.

I pulled back and looked at him. "That would be great. Don't worry; I'll talk to Dr. Lane. We'll get through this."

* * *

The next morning, I sat watching the babies in their playpen, having moved them to the patio so we could watch Banton mow the grass. Glancing over my laptop, I watched the twins as they lay quietly on their backs, watching the leaves blowing in the trees overhead. They seemed very happy and content for the most part and already curious about their surroundings.

I returned my attention to my laptop and the writing at hand. Going through my notes, it occurred to me I hadn't checked my facts against the inscriptions on the headstones in the cemetery. As I scanned my photos, the latest pictures popped up, ones I had taken every day since the babies had been born. I hurriedly flipped through them, and then finding the pictures Laurilee had sent to me from Texas, I stopped. "I've never shown these to Aunt Sue," I murmured out loud, tagging some to print out.

"What is it?" Everett asked as he walked up behind me.

"Pictures Laurilee took of my parents' grave in Texas. I knew Aunt Sue would want to see the headstone. It turned out really beautiful."

"Let me see those, Bebe," Everett asked as I turned my laptop around and handed it to him.

"What is this?" Everett asked, flipping my laptop around so I could see.

"Oh, the symbols. Those were on my parents' headstone. Dad's lawyer friend back home took care of all of those details. I've been meaning to call him and ask him what it meant. I know

225

the horses were for my Daddy, and the gardenias were for Momma. Momma loved 'fleur-dis-lis,' but I don't know what that other symbol wrapped around it means.

"Would you e-mail this picture to me? I've seen it somewhere before," he murmured, studying the picture.

"Sure, no problem."

He handed the laptop back and then sat down beside me as I finished the e-mail and hit "send." When the babies began to fuss, Everett stood and picked Elly up to hand her to me, and then bent over to retrieve Matty.

"Little man, you sure can make a fuss," he cooed at Matty.

"He has an appetite, that's for sure. Thank goodness we're bottle feeding now, and I don't have to get up with them every time they wake."

"I told you I would stay over and help, now that Mrs. Sue and Mrs. Elaine have gone home," Everett offered as I shook my head.

"It's all good, Ev. They're just getting up once a night now that they're eating more. Constance helps some, so Banton and I are both more rested," I replied as we rose to carry them in the house. I retrieved two bottles from the fridge and warmed them, and then followed Everett into the living room.

"You are so much more relaxed...and content, I might add," Everett threw over his shoulder as he turned and sat down in the rocker by the fireplace.

I handed him Matty's bottle, and then sat down in the other rocker.

"And how do you know?" I raised an eyebrow at him.

"The relaxed part is easy to see, and the content part...well, you and I, we have that connection," his eyes twinkled as he teased me.

"Yes, that too. Banton came around."

A couple moments of silence, and then I looked up at Everett's big grin.

"No, you don't get details. It's time you stopped living vicariously through me. Now, let's talk about your love life," I began.

"You never give up, do you, Sister? Just who in the world do you think you would fix a one-hundred and fifty year old vampire boutique owner up with?"

"Are you saying I can start thinking about it?" I teased excitedly.

"Just come up with a short list, and be creative. I'd love to see who you would consider!" he teased back as we heard the front door slam.

"Look who I found wandering down the sidewalk!" Banton announced as he ushered John and Brie into the living room. "Hey, beautiful lady," Banton greeted Brie with a kiss on her cheek.

"Are Laurilee and Dan gone already? I wanted to tell them goodbye," John commented, looking around.

I placed Elly's empty bottle down on the table, and then cuddled her on my shoulder as I rocked. "Oh, I'm sorry, John. They left this morning. They really want you, Brie, Ty and Constance to come with us when we go to the wedding."

Brie's eyes sparkled. "We'd love to, if we can manage it. Ev, are you going too?" she asked as she knelt down beside me to see Elly's face.

"Of course. I'm the wedding planner! It seems I have a new career, with this one next month, and Constance and Ty's still to plan."

"Wow, this ought to be pure entertainment, with Diva-Doll and the Fruit-Loop on the same trip. Maybe we ought to rent one of those big motor homes to travel in together, and make it a trip we'll never forget," John suggested.

Then Banton spoke up. "Oh, and speaking of trips…Chandler, I talked to Claudia this morning. She and Will want us to stay with them while we have our meetings in N'awlins. The night we finish, probably Thursday, she and Will would like for all of you to come over for a dinner party."

"Sounds great. I'll tell Constance and Ty," I said, watching Brie gaze at Elly. It occurred to me, she still hadn't held the babies. "Brie, would you like to rock her?" I sensed Banton tense up across the room. His apprehension at having Brie so close to the babies was apparent to me, but as I glanced around the room, I could see no one else picked up on it.

227

Brie's eyes sparkled, her face lighting up. She nodded silently. I rose and handed Elly to her. Sitting down slowly, she cradled Elly's head in her hand as she settled down in the rocker. She began to talk to her, cooing at her expressions, and Elly's face lit up with the most precious little grin.

"You have the touch, Aunt Brie. See, she adores you already," I assured her as she looked up at me with tears in her eyes. I met John's gaze, full of gratitude at my offer of trust to Brie. It wasn't a sacrifice or gamble on my part, for I could feel everything Brie was feeling, and her feelings of love and protection were overwhelming. I knew she would protect the twins as fiercely as Banton or I would, and she was in full control.

The babies went down for the night earlier than usual, so while Banton showered upstairs, I tried the blood again at the insistence of Everett. Instead of downing it all at once, I decided to try half at night, and then the other half in the morning. Mixing it with the baby formula, I then added more milk, and sipped it slowly while I watched out the back window. Lost in thought, I forgot about the rusty taste to the milk while three birds entertained me as they splashed about in the birdbath in the courtyard. Motion in the alleyway drew my attention, and as I drained the glass, I strained to see what moved beyond the gate to the yard. After a few moments, I decided there was nothing there. *Old habits are hard to break*, I thought. We hadn't seen anything of an Orco since Banton had been home, and I was reluctant to let my guard down.

I climbed the stairs hurriedly, hoping to brush my teeth and get my mind off the blood shake I'd just consumed before it came back up on me. Pushing the door open to our bedroom, I thought, *Problem solved!* Banton stood with his back to me, watching out the bedroom window with nothing on but his boxer-briefs. Seeing him in a half-dressed state was always good for distraction. I hurried over to the bathroom to brush my teeth and get ready for bed.

"Sweetheart, are you coming to bed," Banton asked as he pushed the bathroom door open.

"In just a minute," I answered as I finished putting lotion on my arms. I'd donned a new black satin gown that Claudia had given me after the babies were born.

"Wow. That's too beautiful to just wear to sleep in," Banton murmured, placing his hand on my waist and sliding it down around my hip. The satin hugged my body and fell to the floor, but with a slit up the side to just under the hip. I turned in his arms, and he took in the front, a halter-style solid lace bodice with no lining.

"Claudia gave it to me. She must have been afraid you might get bored after the babies were born," I commented as he shook his head.

"I really wanted to talk to you, but you are kind of distracting me," he teased, bending to kiss me. I wound my hands around his neck as he picked me up and carried me to the bed.

A small cry from the nursery interrupted the moment.

Banton chuckled, pulling away first. "I'll go see which one is hungry."

I rose and pulled the comforter back on the bed and climbed in just as Banton reappeared.

"False alarm. Matty is just crying out in his sleep. Now I think he dreams about being hungry," He mumbled.

Snuggling down into his arms, I remembered his earlier comment. "So, what did you want to talk to me about?"

"Oh, nothing, really. I was just a little concerned when you handed Ellyson so readily to Brie tonight. Do you think she's got control enough to be so close to the babies? I love her and want to trust her, Andie, but..."

"I promise you, she is in full control. You know I can feel what she feels, when we are close like that," I began.

He shot me a skeptical glance, raising one eyebrow.

"I could feel it, Banton. It was overpowering, the love and the protective waves that seemed to radiate from her. She would protect the babies just like you or I would."

"I know that, but this is all still so new to her. What if she's tempted, if their scent..." he trailed off as I shook my head.

"That's the thing. The babies are Aldon, and she can't smell a human blood smell. The babies won't be a temptation."

He seemed to relax, and then pulled me closer to his side. "I forget about how you can feel what she feels. Hey, are you having that connection with anyone else?" he asked as he played with the lace on my gown.

I turned in his arms as I gazed up into his eyes. "Well, I'm picking up on your moods more and more, although I guess I'm too close to your emotions not to be biased. I got your moodiness and agitation all wrong before we brought the babies home the second time." I raised an eyebrow at him, giving him a crooked grin.

"But you can really sense my moods?" Banton asked curiously. I turned in his arms and studied him as he stared into my eyes. Without warning, my heart began to quicken, and a deep ache began deep in my abdomen. I'd never wanted him so much before, not even the night he gave me the massage. Warmth spread over my entire body...down the inside of my legs. As I opened my mouth and drew my breath in, his lips came down on mine. He silently caressed my lips as he slid his hands down my arms and around my shoulders.

"Could you feel that?" he murmured,

I nodded, gazing up into is eyes. "Intensely. It kind of freaks me out, actually," I added as I dropped my eyes.

He chuckled. "Just as long as you can't feel anyone else do that. You don't connect with anyone else, do you?"

"Sometimes. I can feel Constance's moods, and I'm beginning to feel the babies. Just simple things, like fear or hunger. Oh, and I am definitely tuned in to Everett!" I exclaimed. He snapped his head down to look at me.

"And just how do his emotions run? I've been meaning to ask you about that. The bombshell you dropped on me when I got back --that Ev is straight," he began.

"I know," I sighed. "It's still hard for me not to think of him as gay, we've been doing it for so long. He says he's not anything, really. It's been so long since he's let himself feel anything."

"Chandler Ann, he's a guy. I'm not stupid...and when I think of all the times he slept in your room, watching over you as you slept...you can't tell me he's not attracted to you," he argued.

"No, he's not. He told me jokingly when I asked him about it, that he might have been drawn to me in the beginning, but he always felt like I was more of a sister, really. He said he sensed that was what I needed from him was a friend and a protector.

Then he laughed and said he probably could have fallen for Constance, but she's just too much woman for him.

Banton chuckled. "No truer statement was ever spoken."

"Then he told me that he has fallen for someone but it was unrequited love, and he'd probably scare her to death, and that he would take it to the grave. He probably just told me that so I wouldn't try to match make," I said as Banton contemplated the ceiling. "Everett is just eccentric, from another century. He's a gentleman."

"Yes, he is," Banton agreed, rolling over and covered me with his body. "But I'm not, not right now, anyway."

Giggles erupted, but Banton immediately smothered them.

Chapter Sixteen

For the first time in our marriage, everything was normal. Well, as normal as it could be with blood-drinking twin babies and a mother who could feel other people's emotions. But this normal and happy was something I could get used to.

It was for this reason that I was a bit annoyed when Banton informed me he and the SEALs had to go to N'awlins. I knew Banton would have to go back sometime, but I wasn't ready yet. I was nowhere near ready.

I decided to catch up on laundry and to lay some things out in anticipation of our N'awlins trip. My cell rang, interrupting my thoughts.

"Hey…Everett, what's up?" I greeted him as I folded a pair of Banton's pants.

"Bebe, start getting packed now, because I have a week planned for us!" Everett gushed.

"Well, I am actually doing that now, but what's with the excitement?" I asked, amused at his flamboyance as always. I finished the last of the jeans and then turned and sat down on the bed beside the stacks of laundry. I gave Ev my full attention.

"Grandmother Wellington and Mother insist I bring you over to see them while you are in N'awlins. They want to see the babies. I think they have sort of a baby-shower thing planned."

"Oh, Everett, they shouldn't have done that, but I will be happy to go and see them. In fact, I'm really looking forward to it," I assured him.

"They can't wait to see the babies, and they want Constance, Brie, Claudia and Mrs. Elaine to come as well. I think they're sending out invitations or something."

"Well, remember you are invited to Claudia and Will's on Thursday night for a dinner party…it will be sort of a house-warming, I think."

"I wouldn't miss it. Do you need help with getting the babies packed up?" he asked.

"No, I think I've got it covered. Constance went shopping with us this morning, and their little bags are almost ready to go."

232

"And are you drinking like you are supposed to? How is that going, Bebe?" he nagged as I smiled.

"Yes, Mother. I'm drinking it twice a day."

"And the panic attacks..." he began.

"Everett, I'm fine. I talked to Dr. Lane when I went in for a blood checkup last week. He's started me on some anti-anxiety medicine."

"Is that helping?" he continued with his barrage of questions.

"Well, I haven't had the chance to try it out yet, because Banton never leaves me. I feel guilty. I know he needs to do things, but he's been staying around here ever since he found out I'm still having the attacks. I'm going to urge him to go with John this afternoon. We'll see how I do."

"If you need me..."

"I know, Ev. I love you," I stated.

"I love you too, Ma Petit. I'll see you later."

I sighed as I hung the phone up. Everett, like Banton, was another love in my life who I almost didn't feel worthy of.

"Who was that on the phone?" Banton asked as I glanced up at him. He flopped down on the bed beside me and leaned in to kiss me.

"Mother Everett. He was making sure I'm taking my medicine, that I'm drinking the blood... that I'm preparing for our trip," I sighed.

Banton chuckled. "I bet he's planning our whole trip again."

"Yep."

"John and I need to go work out this afternoon, do you and the babies want to come?" he asked.

I shook my head "No, you go on. I'm going to spend a little quiet time with the twins, and then when I get them down for their nap, I'm going to write a little."

"I don't have to go, Andie. I can lift weights here," he argued.

"I'm fine. Dr. Lane has me on medicine, and I have to do this. I promise, if it gets too bad, I'll call Brie or Everett. Now, go!" I urged him.

"I don't know. Are you sure?"

"Yes. Please Banton, I need to do this."

He pulled me in for a kiss, sliding his fingers into my hair as he held me there. After a few moments, he pulled away and smiled at me.

"If you don't get out of here, I might change my mind. I can give you a workout," I cocked an eyebrow as he grinned at me. He rose, playfully slapped my behind, and then stopped at the door to give me a dark, inviting stare. It took every ounce of willpower I could muster not to call him back.

* * *

Ellyson went down first for her afternoon nap, but Matty was a little fussy so I decided rocker time would do us both some good.

"I love you, yes I do,
   …the moon and the stars
  And the clouds do too,"

I smiled, singing the song I remembered my mother and Mamaw Irene singing the most to me when I was a child. As I rocked, I watched his little eyes drooping as he drifted to sleep. I could feel his heartbeat next to mine, and the emotional connection that followed as we both relaxed was one of sweet, innocent contentment.

"This is what I need to do for therapy for my panic attacks," I muttered as I finally rose and placed him in his crib. After I found my laptop in our room, I returned to the nursery to watch the babies as I worked. Ellyson's little incident was always in the back of my mind, and I checked on her often when she napped.

I read through some of my notes from the last conversations I had with Mr. Jackson, and teared up as I thought about my dear friend. After I finished the draft I was working on, I returned to our bedroom and dug through the dresser to find some notecards, and penned a quick note to Aunt Chloe to let her know about the twins birth, and to ask her for her phone number to see if I could visit her. As I addressed the note, Elly's shrill little cries startled me from my thoughts. I retraced my steps back to the nursery, thinking I'd made it almost three hours with Banton absent, and not one hint of a panic attack. Not one hint, that is, until I reached her crib. Her eyes were closed as she squeezed out her little tears, letting me know she woke wet and hungry.

I leaned over and kissed her forehead. "Oh, sweet girl, what's all the fuss about?" I cooed, reaching down to pick her up. As it registered with her that she heard her mother's voice, her little eyes snapped open, glowing through the brown with flecks of sparkling turquoise. I gasped as I drew her in to my chest. I continued to meet her gaze as my heart began to pound.

I should have been ready for this. I knew that Dr. Renault had pronounced them Aldon children when he'd put them on the blood formula. I was relieved at the time, just to have them healthy. I hadn't thought everything through to the obvious conclusions. What would we do with them in public? How would we answer questions about their eyes…what about the fangs? What if they were venomous? *Oh, God…what if one of them accidentally bit Uncle Lon, or Ava Grace or Mrs. Elaine!*

I reached over to the table beside the rocker and grabbed my cell phone. My first thought was to call Everett.

"What's wrong?" Everett answered on the first ring.

"Ev, it's Elly," my voice shook. "Her eyes, she's…her eyes are glowing!" I exclaimed as he sighed.

"Bebe, calm down. I'll be right there," he assured me as he hung up.

His sigh sort of irritated me. I was in full-blown panic mode. Elly continued to fuss, her eyes dimming a bit when I held her close to me. I cuddled her and kissed her forehead, hurrying down the staircase. I opened the fridge and took out a jug to mix with the formula we had ready. After preparing two bottles, I carried her and the bottles back upstairs to find Matty awake. As soon as Matty sensed Elly's mood, he began to fuss as well. I sat down with Elly and began to rock her as she took her bottle.

My hormones kicked in, and the overwhelming instinct a mother has to quiet her babies. Try as I might, I couldn't fight the tears that threatened to spill at my frustration of not being able to take care of both of them at once. Elly's eyes began to dim, and then fade back to normal as she quieted down and gazed at me. Raising her little hand, she seemed to want to touch my face as she looked at me intently, almost knowingly. It was amazing; it seemed she was still too young to be reaching for things like she knew what she wanted.

I heard a thud in Matty's crib, and then a break of silence in his fussy half-wail as if something had captured his attention. I rose still feeding Elly, and peered over the end of his crib.

"Oh, my gosh," I murmured. I walked around to the side. He lay on his stomach, his little arms pushing his upper body up to gaze at me. He'd rolled over on his own.

The tears I'd been fighting spilled over. My babies were growing...and changing...right before my eyes. I wiped my eyes with my shoulder as I heard keys in the front door downstairs.

"Bebe, I'm here," Everett called out.

"Upstairs, in the nursery."

I could hear Everett taking the stairs two at a time. He entered the nursery and hurried to embrace me, kissing me on the cheek and then Ellyson on the forehead.

"What's this about you scaring your mother, Miss priss?" Everett cooed at her as she smiled at him, temporarily letting the nipple to the bottle go, her little dimple appearing.

"Well, they've calmed now, haven't they," he stated, looking up at me.

"Of course, now that you're here," I retorted as he chuckled. "She was screaming when she woke, hungry as usual. Her eyes dimmed and then stopped when she calmed and got full."

"As they should. It's a natural reaction to hunger, to anger...or to fear. We knew this would happen," he reminded me, rubbing my back.

"I guess I hadn't really thought about it much. So what do I do?"

"Well, we have to consider the people around you who don't know the situation. It's just out in public you will have to worry. Banton's family, your family...the SEALs...they all know. Your Texas friends have returned home for now, so it should be fairly easy. You will just have to keep the babies at home."

"How old will they be when they can learn to control it?" I asked hesitantly.

"Well, I haven't been around Aldon children in a long time, but I think around three or four. I would imagine, knowing you and

236

Banton, the children will be above average in intelligence. And Aldon children develop and learn much faster than human children. Their motor skills and strength will overwhelm you at times, I'm sure. I see our little Matty is already pushing up and turning over on his own," he noticed as I nodded.

"Yes, he just had one of his 'firsts,' and Banton missed it!"

"Oh, Bebe…there will be many, many more, I assure you! Have Matty's little eyes given him away yet?"

"No, just Elly so far. Ev, what about the fangs?"

"You need to ask Dr. Renault and the Pediatrician, but if my memory serves me, they will cut their normal teeth first. Then their fangs, if they cut them, will come after --about the age of six or seven. They will be old enough to learn to control them, much like knowing not to throw a temper tantrum."

"Oh, you make it sound so simple!" I frowned at him.

"They may not even cut them. We just don't know."

I looked down at Ellyson as she finished her bottle, and handed her to Everett so I could pick Matty up.

"So if they do, will they be venomous?" I asked.

"Their fangs are for feeding only, at first. They will crave more if they cut them. Then with puberty comes venom."

"Oh. I don't know whether to be relieved at that or worried," I mused as he laughed.

"You won't have to worry about them infecting anyone while they're little. Like I said, take it one thing at a time. You may have to home school them until you see their level of control. Even then, I can help you place them. We very discretely know Aldon teachers on all levels, and can help place them where they can be watched and separated or sheltered if necessary," he offered as I shook my head.

"Wow, I would have never thought of it," I replied, sighing.

Elly began to squirm in his arms, making her little girl gurgle noises. As Everett looked down at her he observed, "Oh, here she goes."

"What?" I rose from the rocker to see what he was talking about. Her eyes were faintly glowing again.

"I'll bet she's wet and she is showing her displeasure," he surmised, placing her in her crib to change her. Noises in the foyer downstairs alerted us to someone's arrival.

"Andie, I'm home…where are you? Ev's car is out front, is something wrong?" Banton called out.

"Upstairs with the babies," I called out as I heard him on the staircase. He hurried breathlessly across the landing and into the nursery.

"Well, I almost made it this time without a panic attack. This time, it wasn't over your absence, but the babies," I murmured as he leaned over to kiss me.

"What? Are they all right?" he asked, alarmed. "What happened?"

"They're fine. I was just a little shaken when I saw Elly's eyes," I replied as I nodded in Everett's direction. Banton peered over the crib.

"Oh, wow…Ellyson Marie," Banton breathed as he took in her eyes for the first time. "Is this…is this normal, I mean…is she the right age for this to happen?" he asked hesitantly.

"Yes, I told Chandler that this is perfectly normal. It will happen with hunger or anger. She will learn to control it. You will just have to keep the twins sheltered here at home and with family and close friends."

"Has Matty," he began as he peered back at him in my arms.

"No, but you missed one of his firsts. He rolled over by himself and pushed up on his arms to look at me," I said proudly, like he's just ridden a bicycle for the first time.

"You're kidding. Isn't that a little early?"

"Yes, for a human, but not for an Aldon," Everett said proudly as he finished changing Ellyson's diaper and picked her up. "She's already holding her head up and reaching like a five or six-month old."

"Guess we'd better start baby-proofing the house," Banton surmised, taking Elly from Everett.

"Well, I'm off. I have some things to do this week at Vintage, but I will call you before the weekend so we can make plans about our upcoming trip." He leaned over and kissed me gently on the forehead. "And Bebe," he added, gazing into my eyes, "The babies

238

will be fine. We are all here to help you." Then he waved as he left the room.

"Thanks, Everett," Banton called after him. He crossed the room and kissed me on the forehead, and then took the rocker beside me.

"So, you had a panic attack?" he asked after a few moments.

"No, not really. I was doing fine until I found Elly's eyes glowing. I panicked, but not like an attack. I just realized there are all kinds of things to consider...whether they have fangs, what we will tell people about their eyes..."

Banton laid his head back on the rocker, gazing at me as I continued, "I guess I was just being silly, worrying too much. But I don't know if we can take them to Texas to the wedding. How do we explain it?"

He reached over and touched my cheek. "It's really kind of subtle so far. Maybe we can figure out a way to explain...to Laurilee and Dan, anyway. We'll work it out, or I will just hire a nanny to keep them at the hotel," he assured me. "Whatever you want."

Voices in the downstairs foyer drifted up to us when the front door slammed.

"Would you quit trying to pacify my mother? The suck-up thing is getting a little old, Ty. Mother and Daddy are on board for us getting married, so stop already," Constance's voice carried up to us as they searched downstairs.

"Banton, Andie...Y'all here?" Ty's voice interrupted her.

"In the nursery," I called out as Banton rose with Matty.

"We're coming down," he called out, reaching to help me to my feet.

When we reached the living room, we found Ty seated on the sofa, watching Constance as she paced back and forth in front of the fireplace.

"So what is it this time?" I asked. Ty rose and took Matty from me. I'd observed that Ty rarely came into the room that he didn't pick one of the twins up to play with them. I could tell he loved kids.

"Ty just agreed with Momma about every little plan she's already come up with about our wedding. She thinks she can just plan the whole thing and Ty just rubber stamps everything before I can object!" Constance threw her arm out accusingly.

"Constance, your momma is just excited, and I can tell she loves this wedding stuff."

"Ty, we talked about this. I don't want a big wedding!"

Banton sat down in the chair by the fireplace with Elly, and I joined him on the arm of the chair.

"Have you told her?" I asked hesitantly.

"I brought it up, and told her I would much rather get married on the beach --just family and close friends. She just waived it away with a swish of her hand, and said I was being hasty."

"Maybe you should talk to her again and let her know you are serious," Banton suggested.

She whirled and glared at Ty accusingly. "That is what I was trying to do this afternoon when we met her and Daddy for lunch. Every time I tried, Ty just agreed with her about her plans," she said exasperatedly.

"Constance, I just think you should humor your mother a little," Ty countered as she shook her head and exited the room up the staircase in a huff.

"Ty, brother...not backing your fiancée up is really not the way to go in starting out your relationship," Banton warned as I chuckled. "And the look on her face...I'd be a little scared, brother!"

"I know. I just hate to disappoint Mrs. Sue; she has been so great about our decision to get married."

I grinned down at Banton as he sat Elly up on his lap to watch her reach for her toes. "Ty, if you and Constance are in agreement about what you want, then back her up. Aunt Sue would rather you do that in the long run. She might be a little disappointed she doesn't get to do the big affair like all of Constance's friends will, but she'll get over it quickly, I promise. And I really think you might score some points with Uncle Lon. He might be relieved you all want something simple," I offered as Ty grinned and nodded.

"I think I'll go up and talk to her," he said, rising and handing Matty to me and then turning to follow Constance.

"Never a dull moment," Banton grinned as I shook my head.

240

I leaned over and placed my head on his shoulder as he wrapped his arm around me.

"At least now the drama in our lives is a little more normal."

Chapter Seventeen

Normal. I wrapped my arms around my shoulders, giving myself a hug. My happy normal. My ecstatically ever-after piece of heavenly normal. I sighed and glanced toward the staircase. The babies had been down for a nap for a couple of hours, and should wake soon. Banton was downtown taking care of some banking business, and then he was going to meet his father for a business lunch. I leaned my head back on the sofa and smiled. Peace and quiet was nice…the only worry I had today was what to cook for supper.

The doorbell broke into the silence.

As I opened the door, my first thought was that this woman must have the wrong house. Appearing to be around my age, she was average height, slender…beautiful long blond hair with highlights and beach curls, and dressed in a revealing orange sundress. She smiled at me…the kind of smile that blinds, but never reaches the eyes.

"Can I help you?" I asked, gazing behind her at the sports car parked in our driveway.

"Yes, I hope so. I'm looking for Banton Gastaneau," she purred. "Is he home?"

The hackles automatically went up on the back of my neck. "No, I'm sorry. He's out at the moment. I'm his wife, can I help you?"

She stared at me --the comic strip stare, where the mouth hits the ground. After a pause, she recovered and her eyes narrowed, taking me in from head to toe.

"Wife?" she spat it out like it tasted bad. "I wasn't aware Banton was married. Hmm, well…I need to speak to him. Will he be back soon?"

Apprehension crept up my spine, alerting me I should be wary of this woman. My inner southern belle shouted at me, *guns up, buttercup!*

"I'll be glad to tell him you stopped by, Miss…?"

"Rhoades. Alexandra Rhoades. He'll want to speak to me, believe me," she added. I detected moisture gathering in her eyes.

242

"Please just tell him I stopped by. I need to see him. Just give him this number. I'm staying at the Embassy Suites." She handed me a card with her number written on it, with the address of the hotel on the back.

"I will," I answered hesitantly as she smiled her fake smile at me again, then turned swiftly and sauntered back down the steps to her little sports car.

I closed the door slowly, and then moved to watch her through the side windows. She looked back at the house for a moment as she fitted her keys back into the ignition, started her car, and then zoomed down the street out of sight.

Who on earth was this woman? She obviously knew Banton, but I'd never heard of her. I'd barely had time to process our conversation when Banton returned from his trip downtown with John following.

"...just finished talking with Dad. He drew a contract up, and you can look it over," Banton was saying to John as he opened the front door. He dropped his laptop case and small duffel bag on the table in the foyer, and then crossed the living room to greet me.

"Hey, beautiful, how are my babies today?" he gushed as he lowered his lips down to my hair, kissing me on top of the head while he kneaded my shoulder with his thumbs and forefingers.

"Great. They're still napping upstairs. Hey, John," I greeted John as he came around the sofa and sat down in a rocker by the fireplace, first stopping to kiss me on the cheek.

Banton sat down beside me and placed his arm around me. "John, Dad had his accountant draft three or four plans for you to look at...you can set the payments up however you'd like. I think he figured it at fifteen, twenty and twenty-five years."

John looked over some papers in his hand. "Banton, these interest rates are about half of what a bank would charge," he seemed defensive.

"I've told you before. You and Brie are doing us a favor. With your remodel, you just boosted the value of every house on the block. I intend to buy every property that comes on the market in a two-block radius, to flip or control. If I'm staying here, I want to control who lives here. I can't think of anyone else I'd rather have as neighbors, brother. I mean that."

243

John shook his head as he skimmed over the papers. After several moments, he looked back at Banton. "I'd feel better if you were charging us normal interest rates."

"I don't want to make money off you. It's not charity. You're paying me for it. You are doing more for me, believe me. Besides, I like that you and Brie are so close. That kind of thing is important to us with the babies and all."

"All right. I'll go home and discuss it with her and get back with you. By the way, I came down here to invite you to dinner. Brie wants to have you over tonight...you know, our first dinner party in our new house." He raised his eyebrow as he turned to me.

"Sure, John. We'd love to. But I know she has trouble cooking sometimes. Is she up for this?" I asked.

"Absolutely. She's been practicing on me and she's got that hurdle licked."

I looked up at Banton to find him frowning, his brows drawn together as he leaned over to the coffee table.

"What's this?" He picked up the card that the woman left.

"Oh. A woman came by right before you got home. She wanted to talk to you. She left her number, and the name of the hotel where she's staying. Her name was Alexandra. Alexandra Rhoades?" I offered, studying his expression. His eyes narrowed as he glanced back up at me.

"Do you know her?" I asked as I glanced over at John. John had an eyebrow raised to alert me he knew who she was.

"Yeah, I *knew* her," he answered curtly. After an awkward moment of silence he asked, "Did she say anything else?"

"She just said you would want to talk to her, and she seemed surprised you were married," I added.

"I'll bet," he snorted. Then he raised his eyes to meet mine. "We went out a couple of times, right after I broke it off with Hillary. It was a blind date," he murmured absentmindedly as he fingered the card.

"Why would she pop up after all this time, brother?" John asked. *I knew it, he knew her too.*

"I have no idea. I haven't talked to or seen her in three years," Banton admitted as he caressed the back of my neck with his thumb.

244

"I guess you could call her and find out," I suggested with a hint of irony in my voice.

"Well, I'll go down and see if I can help Brie with anything. We'll see you guys around six. Is that all right?"

"Sure. We'll be there," I answered. Banton seemed lost in thought.

"Oh, and Constance and Ty are invited too. Bring them along with the babies."

"Sure, we'll see you then," Banton muttered as John shut the door.

"Banton, is something wrong?" I asked. He continued to stare at the card in his hand. Shaking his head, he met my gaze.

"No, I don't think so. I just can't imagine what she would want after all this time. I barely knew her."

The apprehension was back as chill bumps formed on my neck. "Banton, is there anything I need to know?" I asked, dreading the answer. I'd never even heard him talk about ex-girlfriends except Hillary. It occurred to me, I'd never really asked him about anyone else. My post-partum Sange-Mele hormones kicked into overdrive, killing any effect my anti-anxiety medicine might have had on me and my confidence.

"Banton, now might not be the time to ask this question, but…"

He finally joined me in the present. "What, sweetheart? What question?"

"Well, I told you when we started dating, that first weekend in N'awlins, I'd never been with anyone. And I told you about the only real boyfriend I've ever had. But aside from Hillary, you've never mentioned anyone else. Have there been…others?"

"Hmm. I think this is one of those questions a guy better think about carefully before answering," he countered warily as he pulled me closer to his side.

"I'm serious. I assume…I mean, I know you must have been intimate with Hillary?"

He regarded me intently. After several tense moments, he replied softly, "Yes."

"How long did you date her?"

"About six months."

245

"And you broke it off?" I asked, seeming to have to pull every answer from him.

"Yes."

"Why?"

"I would think it was obvious. She was beautiful, sexy…but 'bitch' trumped everything else. I broke it off with her when I realized I really didn't like spending time with her, and I certainly didn't want to take it to the next level with her."

"Oh. What about this other woman…Alexandra."

"She was a blind date. Another guy John and I used to serve with fixed us up. I got the sense she was really too young for me, so I didn't pursue her. Then she started stalking me when I didn't ask her out again."

"I thought you said you went out with her a couple of times."

Banton rose and crossed the room to the fireplace, then turned back to me. "She showed up at a SEAL party a month or so after the blind date. I was drunk, and she was very persuasive."

"Persuasive, how?" I urged him to continue.

"Chandler, it was a long time ago. I'd forgotten about her, until today. I don't want all of this to upset you." He ran his hand through his hair in exasperation.

"Banton, did you sleep with her?" My stomach was tied in knots as I waited for his answer.

"I think so."

"What? What do you mean, you think so. Don't you know?" I asked, incredulous.

"Chandler, I was drunk, and she drove me back to her place. I woke up in her bed, and it was mortifying. I didn't even remember how I got there," he explained in a rush as he threw his hand out dramatically, pacing back toward the fireplace.

I couldn't believe what I was hearing. This didn't sound like the Banton I knew. He turned and looked at me with the tortured expression I'd only seen a few times since I'd known him.

"Have there been others…how many women were you with, before me?" I asked softly.

"Oh, Chandler." Banton walked back over to the sofa and sat down beside me, taking me in his arms. "You don't really want to know that," he murmured as he kissed my forehead.

246

I pulled away quickly. I didn't like the condescending tone that my thirty-year old husband was using on his twenty- two year old wife.

"Um, yes. I would like to know. I think I should have asked before now," I countered, my back up.

He sighed and studied my eyes. "I dated four women between the time I graduated from high school and when I met you. That's only four women during college and Navy. The first was a girl named Courtney, the second, Beth. Hillary was the third, and you met number four today. I slept with all of them, but I never felt about any of them the way I feel about you," he paused as he studied my eyes, his expression intent. "I knew from the moment I met you that I loved you, and I wanted things to be different between us. That's why I waited so long."

"Oh." I looked down at my hands. I had no idea what to say to him. I couldn't believe it had never occurred to me he'd been intimate with anyone else besides Hillary, and I was having trouble processing the information.

"Chandler, look at me." He placed his finger under my chin and tilted it up. "I'm sorry. I didn't mean to hurt you. All of this was before you. The only reason I'm bothered is that I feel guilty to this day about that night with Alexandra. I'd never been that drunk in my life…so drunk I didn't remember anything. And I've never done it since. I feel bad about it because I would have never slept with someone after just two dates, and I certainly would have never…" his voice faltered as I searched his eyes.

"Would have never what?" I asked warily as I touched his cheek.

"Would have never been with her if I'd known she was just eighteen."

I felt like someone had punched me in the stomach. I swallowed hard.

"Eight…eighteen?" I whispered.

"Yes. I was horrified when I found out. She was so young and immature. I had a hard time breaking it off with her; she had delusions about us being serious right away. I tried to let her down easy, and then she disappeared. I heard her family moved, and I

247

quit hearing from her." He shrugged and then glanced back down at me.

I reached up and placed my hand on his cheek. "Is that one of the reasons you held back for so long with me...because of my age?"

"Maybe, I don't know. It wouldn't have mattered, I was so in love with you," he breathed out, lowering his lips down to mine. I believed him. I had no reason not to. His kiss was hungry, seeking my forgiveness. I rose up on my knees, threading my fingers into his hair as I answered his kisses, pushing against him as my tongue met his.

As I pulled away, I could see relief on his face. He raised the card again and read the numbers on the front.

"She didn't tell you how old she was, did she?"

"She lied and told me she was twenty-two. I believed her at first," he admitted. "Then after that night...she dropped the bomb that she was only eighteen."

That night...what was different about that night? Something that made him want to get drunk?

"Banton, you never drink too much. Why that night?" I asked softly. *Three years ago...* I already knew the answer.

"That was the first night back after...when Sam went missing," he said sadly.

And just like that, the pieces of the puzzle fit back together. I knew my Banton...the Banton I loved with all my heart, would not have just had a random night of drunken sex.

"John and I...the whole team...we weren't in such good shape the next day. It doesn't excuse our actions, just puts it in perspective I guess," he muttered as he ran his hand back through his hair.

I pulled myself back up, deciding it was time I acted like a grown up instead of a jealous teenager.

"So are you going to call her and put this to rest?" I asked as I turned his head back toward me.

"Do you want me to call her?" he asked, slightly amused.

"Yes, out of courtesy. I'll give you some privacy; I hear the babies." I rose and kissed his lips softly, then jogged up the

248

staircase, pleased with myself. *I trust him completely*, I thought. I'll let him handle this, whatever it is.

After changing both wet and fussy babies, I dressed them in more appropriate clothes in anticipation of our dinner at John and Brie's. As I gathered some things to take in a diaper bag, I heard Ty and Constance arrive downstairs. I glanced at my watch. I had just enough time to change and throw a little makeup on. Grabbing both babies, I carried them into our bedroom and placed them on the bed while I thumbed through our closet. I finally found an ecru lace maxi-skirt and tank top that I'd forgotten I had. I slipped it on hurriedly, and then located a pair of sandals. A wide leather belt that dipped down low in front completed the look. I stood back to look at myself in the floor-length mirror on our closet door. "Not bad for the little wifey," I thought snidely. I was comparing myself to the gorgeous blonde I'd met only an hour earlier.

After stopping to talk to both babies on the bed, I turned back to the dresser to freshen my makeup.

"Chandler...hey! I understand we're going to John's for dinner?" Constance commented, crossing to the bed. "And how are Aunt Constance's babies today? Hey, big man...where are you going'?" Constance grabbed Matty's ankle and pulled him back over to the middle of the bed as he tried to roll away from her. He giggled, causing Elly to giggle too. She plopped down on the bed, causing both of them to giggle harder.

"I swear, Chandler...I don't know how you get anything done. I have a hard time; I just want to play with them all the time. Hey, do you need for me to do anything to get them ready?"

"Nope, their bag is ready."

She rose, and picked Elly up. "I'll take her down for you. You almost ready?"

I turned to her as I swiped some pale pink lipstick on my lips. "All done, let's go," I said, turning to pick Matty up and following her. As we made our way down the staircase, I heard Banton talking on his cell in the dining room. Constance continued to the living room, but I paused at the bottom of the stairs.

"What is it, Alexandra, that you want to see me in person?" Banton's voice sounded strained. "Don't you think that's a little melodramatic? Alexandra, I'm married now. I don't know what you could possibly need to talk to me about, but whatever it is, my wife can certainly be here. I don't keep secrets from her," he said with exasperation.

I hurried on into the living room with Constance. I didn't want Banton to know I'd been listening to his conversation.

As I entered the dining room, Constance watched me curiously.

"Chandler, is everything okay?"

"Yes. Why do you ask?" I replied, placing Matty in his carry-seat. After I strapped him in, I picked him up just as Banton joined me.

"Here, let me carry him," he offered as he kissed me on the forehead.

Constance stood and walked toward us with Elly, having already strapped her in her carrier. Ty held his arm out to take Elly from her.

"I don't know. You both just seem preoccupied," Constance replied as she regarded Banton.

"We just had a strange visitor today, that's all," I commented, glancing up at Banton. "Are you ready to go?"

He nodded. After we'd locked the front door, Constance and Ty walked ahead of us a few feet, talking to Elly as they strolled down the sidewalk. I gave Banton a sideways glance. The air seemed cooler tonight, so I leaned over and drew Matty's receiving blanket up over him.

"So, what did Alexandra want?" I asked off-handedly.

"I don't know. She wanted to meet me somewhere tomorrow to talk to me. She said she had something she wants to tell me."

"Are you going to meet her?" My heart stopped.

"I told her if she needed to talk to me, she could come back here." He frowned as he said the words.

"And?" I waited for him to finish.

"She said she wanted to see me alone. I told her that I'm married, and I don't keep secrets from you…if she wants to see me, she'll have to come here to our home."

"So is she coming?"

He paused on the sidewalk and I turned to study him.

"I don't know. She hasn't changed. She's still a drama queen. She hung up on me."

"And you have no idea what she wants?" I asked exasperatedly.

"Andie, I really don't. I assume she's in town for some reason and decided to look me up. Maybe she wants to meet me, to see if I'm really married, or if she still has a chance with me. Who knows? She was really a spoiled, messed-up girl. She doesn't seem to have changed."

He frowned, the lines between his brows deepening. I reached up and touched my thumb there, attempting to erase his worry. I smiled at him, forcing my own apprehension down.

"Well, then we won't worry about her. If she shows in the morning, she shows. Maybe when she sees that you are happily married with twins, she'll leave you alone," I tried to reassure him.

"You're right as always, Mrs. Gastaneau," he smiled finally, flashing my favorite dimple.

"Are y'all coming or what?" Constance called from John and Brie's front porch. I turned back to Banton just as his mouth found mine. Tugging at my bottom lip with his teeth, he murmured, "Let's have dessert back at our place."

I nodded enthusiastically as Constance exclaimed, "Oh, for Pete's sake!" and slammed John's screen door for effect.

Chapter Eighteen

"Wow, Brie...you're giving Chandler some stiff competition in the cooking department!" Ty exclaimed as he wiped his mouth with his napkin.

"Well, I learned everything I know from her," she smiled, leaning over to kiss me on my cheek as I hugged her.

We'd just finished pork tenderloin with dill sauce, buttered new potatoes and homemade herb bread. The candles on the dining table flickered, bouncing light off the antique mottled glass in the dining room windows, making everything sparkle. John had built a fire in the fireplace, and their house was truly a showplace of fine mission-style craftsmanship. I admired the wide, dental molding around the built-ins and crown molding at the ceilings.

"John, you did a superb job as always," Banton complemented. I nodded in agreement.

"The house has good bones. I just polished them up...with a little help from Sister Everett, of course," he grinned as he raised his glass in a toast.

"Well, about that," Banton grinned at me as I shook my head at him.

"What? It's not like we wouldn't talk about him, if he was right here," Banton countered. I sighed and picked our plates up to help Brie clear the table.

"What's up with Everett?" Constance picked up immediately on Banton's remark.

"Never mind. Chandler doesn't want me to say anything," he muttered.

"Come on, brother...spill! You can't say something and just stop. Not with this crowd," John teased as he took another big swig of wine.

"Everett's sexual orientation shouldn't concern us." I stated firmly as I strolled back into the dining room and took my chair.

"Well, that's old news. Tell us something we don't know, brother," John countered. Banton cocked an eyebrow at him.

"Oh, for heaven's sake. I found out while Everett was staying with me that he's not gay after all."

"What?" Constance, Ty and John all called out together in unison.

"Y'all are the ones who are behind. And by the way, did any of y'all ask him, or did you all just assume he was gay? Because I did," I retorted as I took a big drink of my wine.

"Andie, you asked him plenty of times. He just always blew you off and made some vague comment," Constance replied.

"Well, he finally got around to telling me. He's extremely private and had his heart broken a long, long time ago. He hasn't been in a relationship since."

"How long ago?" Constance continued to probe.

"When he was nineteen or twenty," I replied softly. "And he absolutely does not like to talk about it, so please don't say anything."

"No, of course not," John replied softly.

"I don't even know how old he is," Ty muttered as Brie laughed.

"Brie, did you know about this?" John asked her incredulously.

"Well, yes, but only because he let something slip once. He said something about loving someone who doesn't know – an unrequited love. I always assumed it was Chandler," she offered as I choked on my wine.

Banton was quick to rub my back as he murmured, "Are you all right?"

"Yes. I'm fine," I managed to choke out after I caught my breath. "He is absolutely not in love with me. He thinks of me as a sister, that's all," I assured them. Banton snorted.

"Well, who isn't in love with Chandler," Ty joked, passing by me to refill his wine glass at the buffet. After filling it, he turned and kissed me on top of the head, leaving me to blush profusely.

"Hey…watch it," Constance called out good-naturedly.

"Seriously, Chandler…you can connect with the feelings thing, kind of like a 'super Aldon.' Have you ever gotten the love or lust vibe when he was around someone?" Brie asked.

Constance's mouth dropped open. "Andie, what the hell is she talking about?"

I glared at Brie, much like I had glared at Banton earlier.

"Chandler has many talents as you all know. But since she's been bitten numerous times, and going through the pregnancy...her ability to sense other people's moods and feelings, especially ones she is close to, has been dramatically heightened." Banton explained as he placed his arm around my chair.

"What? Whose feelings can you read?" Constance demanded.

"No, it's not like that," I retorted. I paused and glanced at Brie as she smiled softly at me, nodding her head to encourage me to continue. "The first time I felt it, it was with Brie. I could feel what she was feeling, when I was working with her to get through her transformation issues. Then there are the spirits in our house," I paused and took in the many curious glances around the table, Banton's included.

"I've been meaning to ask you about that comment at the hospital when Elly was sick. What things in our house are you able to connect with?"

"Well, I can feel my mom," I paused and glanced at Constance as her eyes misted. "It's mostly a calm feeling, like a warm hug when I'm anxious or frightened. Then there's the soldier, DeLee..."

"Who?" Ty and John chimed out in unison.

"Banton, Ev and I have seen him on more than one occasion in our house and at the cemetery down the road. He's the famous soldier...the one in the papers from time to time."

"I've read about him. People think they see a bleeding soldier walking down the road by the cemetery," Ty commented.

"Chandler thinks he is Marie-Claire's dead husband, killed during the war while she was pregnant." Banton added as he rubbed my back gently.

"Who's Marie-Claire?" Ty asked innocently.

"She was Judge Johnson's daughter. I told you the story about Chandler's house," Constance reminded him as he nodded. "So, you can feel his spirit...sense his emotions?" Constance urged me to continue.

"Yes. He's filled with such a deep longing. He's also very protective. I feel it strongly. Whoever he is, he isn't there to harm anyone. He's there to protect, and I think he's looking for his family."

Constance shuddered, wrapping her arms around herself. Ty placed his arm around her shoulders, and then looked up at me. "I've never seen anything except the mist."

"That's Aunt Kelly. That's Chandler's mom," Constance said softly.

"Anyway, I can feel Banton's moods, although I don't decipher them accurately. I guess I'm too close to him to feel them clearly," I stated as he grinned down at me. "I can feel Constance's moods sometimes…and I realized recently I always have, even before I was bitten."

Constance's head snapped up. "Really?"

I nodded at her as I smiled. "Even when we were little. I sensed when you were jealous, happy…frustrated."

"I just always thought you were super easy to get along with, and all along, you were one step ahead of my moods." She smiled and placed her hand over mine at the table.

"So why can't you use those super powers to figure Everett out," Ty asked as Constance elbowed him.

"I'm not sure I'd ever tell any of you specifics about what I feel. It seems like a breach of your trust, somehow. But I do know that all I've ever felt around Everett is extreme love and devotion. He's extremely protective of all of us. But I've never gotten that sense of physical love or longing toward anyone. Not like Constance and Ty put off, anyway," I joked as Ty leered at Constance.

"Oh, stow it, Preston…you're not gettin' any tonight," she joked as he pulled her into a hug.

John was strangely quiet throughout the entire monologue, and when I glanced at Banton, I realized he'd gotten quiet too. When John sensed that there was a break in the camaraderie, he looked up at me and his discomfort was apparent. Brie moved her hand and silently clasped his on top of the table. I knew John was wondering if I had ever felt his feelings while Banton was missing, and Banton was wondering the same thing. *Would we ever get passed this emotional hurdle?*

"Well, I don't know about you, Banton, but this raises a lot of questions about when he was staying with the girls. He was sleeping in the same room with Andie, for Christ's sake," John blurted out. I noted an undertone of jealousy, and anxiously wondered if Banton picked up on it.

"Yeah, I've had that same thought." The muscle in his jaw flexed with agitation, and I realized I was holding my breath as he continued. "Chandler assures me he's never felt anything for any of them except like a brother," Banton finished distractedly. I was so proud of Banton. I knew he still struggled with jealousy toward John, and we'd skirted the issue tonight. But he was hiding it well, and treating John almost normally. I placed my hand intimately on his thigh, and I felt him relax.

"Well, I hear little gurgling sounds from over here. It's time to get some Aunt Brie kisses," Brie announced, standing and moving toward the twins. We'd placed them in the corner on a small sofa, and they'd been napping throughout dinner. Matty and Elly were awake, and it soon became apparent they would be the entertainment portion of the evening.

After we'd cleared the dishes and helped Brie clean the kitchen, we visited for a while in the living room. Ty and Banton joined John in a short tour of the unfinished attic space, and left us girls to talk and enjoy our wine.

"So, Brie…what's the sex like now that you're a super- human Aldon?" Constance blurted out as I choked on my wine for the second time that evening.

"Not bad at all. That's one transformation I've enjoyed," she offered. I glared at both of them.

"Oh, come on, Andie. Don't be a prude! I know you are wondering too." Constance could always be counted on to shock everyone and liven up the conversation.

"The question is, does John enjoy it too?" Constance asked as I drained my glass on purpose.

"That's a definite yes," Brie grinned over at me and winked. "I never knew it could be so…hot."

256

"I think I need more alcohol for this conversation," I said wryly as I held up my empty wine glass.

"Here, let me get everyone a refill," Brie offered, grinning as she took the wine glasses and retreated to the kitchen.

Elly began to fuss, so I picked her up from the pallet we'd made them in the floor and then searched in the diaper bag for their bottles. Constance automatically picked Matty up. She was so used to helping me that we worked in unison where the twins were concerned.

After we had them both nursing contentedly, Constance started in on me.

"Okay, Andie...dish. What's wrong with Banton?"

"What do you mean?"

"Who was the awkward visitor? You've both been on edge this evening."

"Someone from Banton's past. An old fling," I added.

She raised a perfectly manicured eyebrow at me. "What did she want?"

I sighed. "I wish I knew. She left a card with her number and said she needed for Banton to call her. He called her back before we came over here, and she wanted to meet with him. In private," I added.

"Whoa, sister. He didn't say yes, did he?" she asked as she pulled the empty bottle from Matty's mouth and then lifted him to her shoulder to burp him.

"No, of course not. He told her if she needed to talk to him, she could come to the house. He told her he didn't keep secrets from me. Whatever it was, she could talk to both of us."

"Well, that's a relief. Does he have any idea what it is that she wants?"

"Not a clue. I guess we'll find out tomorrow if she shows."

I watched Elly as she worked to finish her bottle. She held up her tiny hand to touch my face as she did every night. I smiled and leaned my face down to let her touch me. She grinned, letting go of the nipple and drawing her breath in to cackle out loud.

"Is my baby girl still awake?" Banton asked, returning with John and Ty.

"Here, see if you can get her to take the rest of this," I urged as I handed her over to Banton. He grinned down at her as he took her in the crook of his arm, readjusting the blanket around her and balancing the bottle against his chin.

"They're growing so fast, Chandler!" John exclaimed as he took Matty from Constance. He settled down in his recliner, and sat Matty down in his lap to play with him.

"Uh-oh, I think somebody's diaper's full," John announced, wrinkling his nose. "It's a little warm down there, and he's gettin' squirmy."

"Time to give him back, man! That's the one thing I can't do," Ty joked as Constance rolled her eyes.

"Holy mother," John gasped out as his eyes widened. "Look at his eyes!" His eyes darted to Banton. Banton rose and walked over to see. I already knew what it was. Matty's eyes were glowing like Elly's.

"There he goes, Mommy," Banton murmured, glancing at me. John looked up at Banton as Banton added, "Elly's have been glowing like that a few days. Matty's just now catching up."

"Wow, do they have fangs?" John asked excitedly, lifting Matty's little lip. Brie reached over and slapped his hand away. "No, of course not! Don't be an idiot," she scolded John.

"Chandler, what do the doctors say? Will they have fangs like Everett? Will they be venomous? How will they be able to go to school?" All of the questions that had been on my mind when I first saw Elly's eyes occurred to Constance.

I rose and picked Matty up out of John's lap and took him back to the pallet to change him. "They will be fine, and we'll home school them if we have to," I said a little too forcefully as tears gathered in my eyes. I gazed down lovingly at my son, choking back the lump in my throat. His eyes were glowing with the little flecks of turquoise mixed with the beautiful brown like Elly's. I knew we would have challenges with the twins, but I didn't want anyone else pointing it out.

Banton was immediately at my side, sensing that my feelings were hurt. He sat down beside me and placed his arm around me, nuzzling my hair.

"Andie, she didn't mean anything by it," he murmured.

"Oh, gosh, Chandler...I didn't mean...I just worry about them, you know. I love them so much," Constance declared as I nodded.

"All of this is just a little much to take in, and there's a lot to consider. They may cut their fangs around five or six, and the venom may come with puberty. We just don't know for sure. Ev says there are Aldon teachers planted in the public schools, and they can be placed where they can be protected," Banton informed them. I looked up to find they were all listening intently.

"You know, Chandler...your babies may be the only children who any of us get to help raise," Constance said softly as she gazed at Brie. John placed his arm around Brie, pulling her down into his lap.

The room was silent while everyone considered what challenges each one of us faced.

"Well, we certainly have more interesting things to talk about than most couples our age," Ty joked as everyone chuckled.

"And on that note, I think it's time we called it a night," Banton urged as he helped me get the babies back into their baby seats. After the goodbyes and kisses were exchanged, Ty and Constance walked back with us to our house.

Chapter Nineteen

I sat silently brushing my hair out, watching the soft rain falling outside the bay window in our bedroom. I was mesmerized by the dancing patterns that the moisture made as the wind swirled it around under the soft light in the alley. I placed my chin on my knee and thought about the many nights I'd sat here waiting for attacks from the Orcos. Fear had become so common place that it felt as though I was missing something. It was hard to grasp that we didn't have to look over our shoulders constantly. Since Banton and Ty had returned home, there had been no reports of any Orco activity, and the Aldon had finally stopped their scheduled watches. Everett told us they still patrolled our neighborhood from time to time, and there was an organized effort to keep track of any Orcos in Baton Rouge.

I still had a feeling of unease. I wondered if I would always feel this way. As the stairs creaked outside the door, I knew Banton was returning from checking the doors downstairs and letting Beau back into the house from his nightly romp. I stood quickly and checked my reflection in the mirror. While dressing for bed, the urge hit me to feel sexy and alluring, so I'd searched through the dresser until I found the white satin gown I'd worn the night Banton proposed to me.

The blond bombshell ex-fling with the sports car had nothing to do with it, I thought as Banton opened the bedroom door. He paused and slowly raked my body with his eyes.

"Oh, baby," Banton breathed, crossing the room to me. He looked so sexy with only his pajama bottoms on, the white ones that hung provocatively low on his hips. As he moved to touch me I was still staring, fascinated with his muscled abs. I reached out and traced the pattern of his muscles with my fingers as he wound his fingers in my hair.

"Your hair is getting so long, Chandler." He breathed in, taking in the scent as he buried his face into it. I wound my arms around his waist and slid my fingers into his waistband, caressing his bare skin.

"The twins down for the night?" he asked, pulling away to look down into my eyes. He touched the hair on my forehead, sweeping it back and around behind my ear. I nodded.

"They're out. It was late and they were so tired when we put them down, I don't think they'll be up till five or so," I answered, tracing my lips down his throat.

"Good. Because I might not be through with you until then." He brushed his lips back and forth across mine. I caught his bottom lip with my teeth and tugged gently as he moaned.

"Do you have any idea what you do to me?" he rasped out, his voice ragged. He tangled his hands in my hair once more and pulled gently, pulling my face up to look at him. I shook my head.

"You paralyze me. Sometimes I think I'll go mad if I don't have you, right at that moment. Like tonight, when you blushed as Ty teased you. You were so beautiful in the candlelight. I just wanted to whisk you around the corner and push you against the wall," he said forcefully. "All of a sudden, all I could think about were your legs wrapped around me, my hands on your body, sliding your dress up, sinking into you and losing myself," he said huskily.

"Banton!" I scolded him, mortified. *Well, maybe not mortified...maybe a little flattered.*

"I can't help it, baby, you get me so hot. Just one touch, one glance..."

I pulled back to look up at him through my lashes. "What's stopping you now, stud?" I asked huskily, emboldened by his declarations of lust.

His nostrils flared as his eyes narrowed. Picking me up, he moved me across the room, pressing me up against the wall beside the window. As he slowly slid his lips down my throat, I threw my head back and moaned. He jerked my gown up, cupping my hips in his hands and lifting me up. I wrapped my legs around his waist. I tugged at his waistband, and in a moment there was nothing between us. His mouth trailed down across the thin lace on the bodice of my gown, and my breath became shallow as his mouth found a tender peak. Readjusting my hips once more, he slowly entered me, moving slowly. As I held on to his massive shoulders, I wondered at how much bigger his shoulders and chest seemed to

261

be. He was solid muscle, rippling as he moved against and inside me.

"Chandler, oh…baby, you feel so good," he moaned as we both found our release, reveling at our connection, our bodies once more melded into one. When our breathing slowed, he rested his forehead against mine.

"Chandler, I love you, from the very depths of my soul," he whispered breathlessly.

"I love you too, Banton. So much that it scares me sometimes."

He gently lowered me until my feet touched the floor, and then he picked me up in his arms. Turning back toward the bed, he kissed me softly as he sank down into the covers with me still in his arms. My eyelids were so heavy I couldn't keep them open.

"Sleep, Andie," he murmured, kissing me on the forehead. I snuggled into his chest, with his arms firmly wrapped around me, drifting off into a peaceful sleep.

* * *

Elly gurgled baby noises at me as I finished her bath. I could hear Banton blowing kisses on Matty's tummy in the bedroom as I wrapped her in a towel. I smiled, enjoying the moment. The happy baby noises that surrounded us were the most precious sounds I could imagine, and I found myself waking up before the twins every morning in anticipation of what wondrous thing they would do next.

Banton was stretched out on the bed with his head propped on his hand, watching Matty play with his toes.

"Chandler, watch this," Banton said excitedly, turning Matty over on his tummy. He scooted back away from Matty, and I watched in awe as Matty pushed up on his hands and knees and then proceeded to flop forward toward Banton in a sort of crawl.

"Oh gosh…they're mobile," I breathed. Banton chuckled at my reaction. He pulled Matty over to his chest and kissed the back of his head softly as Matty resumed reaching for his toes.

I shook my head. "It's too soon…they're barely two months old!"

262

"I'm glad I got to see *this* first," he smiled up at me as I knelt on the bed with Elly. I finished dressing her, and then picked her up in my arms. Banton gazed at me over Matty's head, and his eyes were so full of love…my heart melted.

Our moment was interrupted by the doorbell. Banton glanced down at his watch.

"Hmmm. Ten o'clock. I guess she decided to come after all," Banton muttered, rising to go downstairs.

"Do you want me to come down?" I asked warily.

"Of course." He smiled over his shoulder as he left the room.

I could hear Banton greet our visitor when I started down the staircase with the twins.

"Hi, Alex. How are you," he greeted her. She stared at him.

"Hello, Banton. It's been a long time."

"Would you like to come in?"

"Yes," she almost whispered, catching sight of me. She was dressed in another short, wispy skirt that showed off her tan, long legs. I was achingly aware of her blonde locks and dark tan this morning. She took only one step forward, just inside the doorway. She was staring at the babies in my arms.

Banton walked over hurriedly and took Ellyson from me as he turned back to her. Placing his arm around me, he introduced us.

"Alexandra, this is my wife, Chandler. And these are our babies, Matty and Elly."

She stood there staring much like she had the day before. I couldn't tell if she was stunned by the babies, or if she still couldn't believe Banton was married.

Her eyes narrowed as she studied me and Matty, and then she jerked her head back up at Banton.

"I can see you are still determined to talk to me with your wife present, so I might as well come out with it," she said, backing out a step onto the front porch. She reached down to her side, and then urged a small child, not more than two years old or so, into view.

"Banton, this is your son, Reece."

The air was sucked from the room.

* * *

263

I closed my eyes. A hundred thoughts ran through my mind at once, but the one I zeroed in on was *she has to be lying.*

"My son?' Banton's voice was incredulous. "Alexandra, we both know that's not true." I opened my eyes to stare at him.

"I came here today because I felt like after all this time you needed to know he existed. He needs a father," she answered huskily as she picked the child up in her arms.

I was already in defense mode. I searched the boy's features. He had blue eyes like his mother, a round face, and black, thick slightly curly hair. I looked down at Matty's black hair and my heart sank.

Could this be Banton's son? Banton had a child with someone else? The pain that tore through my heart was unimaginable.

Banton turned to look at me warily. I kept my face cool, trying not to let my inner hurt show.

After several awkward moments, I found my voice.

"Let's not stand here in the doorway. Please go into the living room and sit," I suggested as I turned to lead them in. I heard Banton shut the door behind me.

Motioning for Alexandra to take a seat by the fireplace, I sat across from her on the sofa with Matty on my lap. Banton predictably sat down beside me with Elly.

"Alex, if he is my son, why are you waiting until now to tell me," Banton asked wryly.

If he is? My heart rose into my throat. No!

"When my father found out I was pregnant, he took a transfer to Virginia. He wanted me to get an abortion, but I refused. When I convinced them that I was going to have the baby, my mom and dad sent me away. I wanted to contact you, but you had been deployed. I of course was busy after I gave birth to him and I've been planning to come and see you, but my Dad didn't want me too. But now they've turned their back on me," she murmured as she placed her lips on her son's head. She then looked back up at me. "I have nowhere else to go."

"Alexandra, I'm sorry you aren't on good terms with your family, but that doesn't explain why you would come here now after all this time," Banton said forcefully as he placed his arm around me protectively.

"I can't believe you are being so cold about this. I thought you would be more…I thought you loved me," she whispered as a tear slipped down her cheek.

I felt like someone had punched me hard in the chest.

She looked desperate. I found myself feeling sorry for her…feeling sorry for the small boy with the curls that looked like Matty's. This beautiful, wounded woman wanted my husband. She loved him and wanted him to be a father to her son. My world turned upside down. I felt like an intruder in my own home.

I couldn't look at Banton. I knew if I did, the tight reins which held my emotions in check would break.

Banton's voice sounded like a parent reasoning with a small child.

"Alex, you appear to need someone to help you. But he's not mine. We only went out once."

"Twice. And it only takes once," she murmured as she looked back up at him through her thick, model-like lashes.

"And I'm not completely sure we were ever together that way."

She exploded. "Banton! How can you say that after the night we spent together? You were so loving! You said such sweet things to me," she cried out as the little boy jumped in her lap and watched her warily.

I had to leave the room, and quickly. I was sick, angry and jealous, all rolled into a quivering mess. I had to escape, to think. I couldn't take anymore.

Rising quickly, I startled Banton. "Alexandra, why don't you let me take…Reece, isn't it…into the other room with the twins, so you can talk about this in private. I don't think the kids need to be here," I reasoned, watching the little boy's wide eyes. I felt sorry for him.

Not waiting for her approval, I rose with Matty and took Elly from Banton, and then hugged them both to my chest with my left arm. I walked over to her and smiled as warmly as I could manage at her little boy. He smiled back and took my hand, following me into the dining room. I could still hear their voices from the living room. My Aldon hearing was sharper than ever.

"She's a lot nicer than I would be, if my husband's ex showed up with his love-child," she said snidely as I sank down into one of the dining chairs, placing the twins in the floor.

"You aren't my ex, Alexandra. You are over-dramatizing our involvement. And Chandler is a kind, loving person. She is amazing." His voice was forceful and resolute.

"Banton, I understand you are married. But you didn't know about your son. That might change things a bit," she said softly, changing her attitude.

"Alex, stop this. We never had a relationship. I was drunk the one night we could have possibly been together, and I remember none of it. I'm sorry. I know that you wanted more from me after we went out but I just didn't feel that way about you. You lied to me about your age," he started as she tried to interrupt him, "and I would have never gone out with you in the first place if I'd known how young you were."

"I know, you have always been such a sweet, caring man," she murmured as I heard her chair creak. I knew she had risen, probably walking over to him. I glanced down at the little boy in front of me. He watched me warily, not knowing what to do. I absentmindedly handed him some baby toys from the tabletop, and he sat down with them in the floor beside the twins.

"No, Alex…stop. This is awkward."

There was a long pause. *What did she do? Did she make an advance toward him?* I was irate, wanting to fly back to him. I waited, holding my breath.

"If you need money, I will help you. I'm only helping you out because I would help anyone out in your situation."

"Banton, you do still care. You do still want me," her voice was soft and silky.

"Alexandra, please. Stop looking at me like that. Don't read anything into my helping you," he said forcefully.

If there was a chance this little boy could be his…how could he treat her so callously? Part of me was relieved he was being firm with her. The Banton I knew --my Banton would never treat her this way if he thought the boy was his. *Hadn't he told me he wasn't sure about that night? That he might have had sex with her?* I thought I was going to be sick.

266

I swallowed the huge knot rising in my throat.

"I can see the fact you have a son...that *we* have a son, is going to take a while to sink in. I'll go and let you break all of this to your wife. When you are ready to see me, you can call me on this number. Your son and I will be waiting," she purred as I wrapped my arms around myself.

I glanced down at the child in question. He handed the toys, one by one, to the babies. Elly laughed at him, and he grinned back at her. I studied his smile. There was no trace of the dimple that marked my children.

"There is nothing to break to my wife. If you are going to keep pushing this on me, I have to insist we all do blood tests and clear this up once and for all," Banton said forcefully, his tone indicating he'd reached his limit.

"I can't believe you are throwing us out," she declared as I heard her sob.

"I'm not throwing you out, Alexandra. I told you I will help you. But I'm not taking your word that Reece is my son. I'll discuss this further after we've gotten the results of the tests," he stated plainly. I heard their footsteps coming across the foyer. I glanced up into her tear-stained face.

"Come, Reece! Come here," she choked out, grabbing his hand roughly and pulling him up from his perch between the twins. He winced in protest when she pulled him toward the front door.

"Mommy, pway. Weece wants to pway wif babies," he sniffed. She swung him up unceremoniously on her hip.

"Alexandra, don't be so rough with him, you are angry with me," Banton said softly, his concern for the child evident.

"Oh, so now you sound like his father," she said in a pouting manner.

"No, I can't stand to see anyone handle a child roughly. I will call you to let you know when I have our appointments set up," Banton said as she slammed the front door.

I sat in silence, staring at the fireplace. Matty flipped himself over on the rug and pushed up, reaching his hand out and touching my leg. I instinctively reached down and picked him up and sat him in my lap. As I placed my lips against the back of his head, Banton crossed quietly beside me and bent over to pick up Elly. He turned and faced me. I couldn't look up at him. I closed my eyes, my lips still pressed into Matty's hair.

"Chandler," Banton called to me softly. "Are you all right?"

I opened my eyes and looked up at him. My eyes stung with the sudden rush of moisture as the tears pooled.

"Oh, Chandler. You have to know," he began as I shook my head. I looked up at the tortured expression on my husband's face.

"No, I don't know. I don't know anything right now," I whispered. "I think I need to be alone," I muttered as I rose.

I walked silently down the hallway into the kitchen. Methodically I opened the refrigerator and removed two of the pre-mixed bottles for the babies. After I'd warmed them in the microwave, I turned to find Banton standing in the doorway with Elly.

"I need to feed them and get them down for their nap," I said without raising my eyes.

"Chandler, let me help you," he offered.

"No, I've got them," I replied as I took Elly from him. I could sense him following me when I climbed the stairs with the twins and entered the nursery. I sat down in one of our rockers, and carefully positioned each twin against me, and then rolled a bottle over on Matty's chest. He'd already begun to hold his own bottle, and he took it in his hands and raised it to his mouth. I then turned to Elly, clutching her to me as I worked her bottle around with my chin and then crooked my wrist around her head to hold the edge of the bottle. She placed her little hands on her bottle as well, but I still had to support hers. They both watched me intently as they nursed. It was as if they sensed I needed them near me.

I could feel Banton watching me from the doorway. After several moments he crossed the room quietly and leaned over, placing a kiss in my hair.

"Chandler, please talk to me. I know this has to be upsetting to you," he said. I shook my head furiously.

"God, Banton...please. I can't talk about this right now. Please, just leave me alone for a while. We'll talk, later," I whispered, choking back sobs.

He stood, and then hesitantly walked out of the nursery and down the stairs. After the babies had finished their bottles, both of their eyes were drooping, so I placed them in their cribs. When I decided that they were both down for a nap, I made my way around the landing to our bedroom. After I had our door closed, the dam broke.

I drew myself up against the pillows, wrapping my arms around my knees. My mind whirled around all the hurt. So many feelings...I couldn't possibly sort them all out. *Alexandra was lying.* She knew Banton wasn't the father of her baby. *Who was, then?*

Reece was certainly the right age to be Banton's, if the night in question did happen. *If it did happen.* Banton...my beautiful, dark, dimpled...sweet, sexy husband...didn't belong only to me. The special birth of our babies, the only babies I'd be able to give him, was second. *Banton has a child with someone else.*

I couldn't wrap my head around the shocking accusation. I curled up in a ball in the center of the bed and sobbed. The image of Banton holding *her* son, embracing someone else's child as his own, haunted me. The thought of him sharing that bond with another woman shredded me. The unwanted thought pushed through to the forefront...*This other woman, from his past...This attractive woman from his past, who he'd been intimate with, could have more children.*

I closed my eyes tightly against the images...Banton, his naked body, wrapped in sheets in her bed... *You were so loving, you said such sweet things to me...Banton, I thought you loved me...call me, your son and I will be waiting...*

"No! Banton, no," I sobbed out loud. Then after several minutes of crying it out, I had to calm myself. I had to begin to think rationally, to get a grip on the hurt.

If the blood tests came back positive, could I accept this child? Could I swallow my jealousy and hurt, and accept him as a sibling to my children? I hated myself for being so selfish. *This wasn't about me!* I thought about him, about Reece...sweet, innocent, playing with my babies in the floor as his mother wormed her way back into Banton's life. He was an innocent child, possibly Banton's son. I rolled over and stared out the window.

If he was Banton's child, I would love him with all my heart. Because no matter what, I loved my husband with all my heart.

269

Part of the bitter ache eased as I considered my feelings. That was at the root of my distress, that I might have to share my husband, and I wouldn't be a strong enough person to handle it. If I was ever going to be worthy of Banton's love, I had to be strong. I would have to love this child unconditionally. I finally drifted, exhausted with the overwhelming emotions of the events of the morning.

I woke to warmth that enveloped me. I gazed toward the open doorway. Someone had opened the bedroom door. As I slept, someone had drawn the comforter over me. And that someone stroked my hair, his breath, warm and sweet, blowing into my hair as he breathed. I turned over to find Banton watching me, his head resting on the pillows above my head.

"Hey," he murmured as he stroked the side of my face. "You've been asleep for quite a while."

"I didn't plan on falling asleep. Are the babies awake?" I asked, pushing up on the pillows.

"Yes. Constance came home after you fell asleep, and I told her what transpired this morning. She helped me feed them and change them when they woke earlier, and then Ty suggested they take them to Denham Springs so we could have some alone time."

"What? To Denham Springs? Banton, I…"

"Shh. They'll be back later tonight. She packed formula and took their diaper bags. They're going to eat with Mrs. Sue and Mr. Lon. She said they will be back around ten-thirty or eleven."

"But their car seats! Banton," I protested.

"Andie, I gave them your car keys. They took the Lincoln so the babies would have their safety seats," he assured me.

"I've never been away from them," I whispered, tears gathering. I knew I was being silly, and I angrily wiped the tears away.

Banton pulled me into his chest as he placed his lips in my hair.

"Are we okay?" his voice sounded desperate.

I pulled away to look up into his eyes. As he searched my gaze I read the anxiety in his face.

"Yes, Banton. We're going to be fine, no matter what the outcome. I'm sorry, it's just hard. I hate the thought that you…that

270

someone else…that she carried your child before I did. That she might have had a part of you inside her. I wanted to be the only one. This never occurred to me," I whispered as I began to cry again.

"Oh, Sweetheart, don't. Don't do that to yourself," he said. He placed both his hands around my face and held it as he gazed at me. "You have every right to be upset. I'm upset. So I already called Dr. Lane and set an appointment up for her tomorrow morning."

"And Alexandra agreed?"

"Yes. I called her and told her I wouldn't see her again, or help her financially until she took the test. She protested at first, wanting us to use another doctor. I told her it had to be my doctor or the deal was off. I can't have an outside doctor looking at my blood, or our babies."

I shook my head. "No. I know," I murmured as he continued.

"After you told me you wanted some time to think, I went downstairs and started making phone calls. I got the blood test squared away, and I called my Dad."

"You told him?" I asked, disbelievingly.

"Yes. I needed his advice, and possibly his support, if…" he trailed off.

"If? You don't really know, do you? You think Reece could be your son?"

"God, Chandler…I don't know anymore." He ran his hand through his hair in agitation. "No, I don't think so. I just can't stop thinking if we'd really been together that night, I would remember something. I don't!" he said, becoming really upset. "But if these tests are positive, then…"

I searched his tortured eyes. They burned with emotion, the gold flecks glittering in the late afternoon sunlight. The muscle in his jaw twitched, an involuntary reflex that I knew only meant one thing. He was worried about me. I loved him so much. My heart ached at his anxiety. I slipped my arms around his chest and pulled him to me.

"If these tests are positive, then we will deal with it. I made myself a promise earlier that I will love Reece just like our other two children and accept him unconditionally. I have to, to be

271

worthy of your love. If he is a part of you, then I will love him." The tears slid down my cheeks as he tried to wipe them away with his thumbs. As I said the words, my heart ached with a new hole in it.

"Oh, Chandler. I don't deserve you," he whispered as he pulled my lips up to his, covering my mouth with his as he held my head firmly with his hands knotted in my hair.

"And in view of the fact that the twins might be your only children," I whispered against his lips, and then stopped. The thought hurt too much, and the tears gathered again.

"Andie...stop it. I want you to stop agonizing about conceiving again! You seem so tortured by it, and you shouldn't be! I don't worry about it. You have given me two, beautiful healthy miracle babies, and you and those babies are my whole world. You have to promise me you will stop beating yourself up about the possibility you can't carry another baby. Promise me!" He shook me gently as he held me. I nodded. He pulled me against his chest and wrapped his arms around me. After several moments he pulled away and looked down at me.

"Sweetheart, I hope you won't be upset with us, but I also called Mr. Lon, at Constance's insistence. She's right. We may need his help no matter the outcome of the test."

"Oh, Banton, no! You didn't. He's so quick to judge you, he'll go nuts with this one," I protested as my guts twisted thinking about discussing all of this with Aunt Sue and Uncle Lon.

"Chandler, he's fine. He is already bracing for anything legally, and if Alex is the type of mother I suspect she is, we could be in for a fight. I really respect the way Mr. Lon's mind works. He was great. His reaction and response made me feel like he thinks of me as one of his kids," he murmured, his eyes filled with wonder. "And he said he wouldn't say anything to Mrs. Sue until you were ready."

"Why did you tell Constance so quickly," I looked back up at him.

"Because I felt so helpless after I left you up here alone, and I knew you were hurting. She's so close to us, I knew she would help you. And I respect her opinion."

272

"What did she say?" I asked after a pause, folding the comforter back and smoothing it back across my tummy.

"That I needed to give you a little space --that she knew you would be hurt, but you would put the needs of Reece above anyone else's, because that's the kind of person you are," he murmured into my hair, kissing the back of my head.

"You both are giving me too much credit," I shook my head.

Banton's cell ring broke the silence. Pulling it out of his pocket, he touched the screen.

"This is Banton," he answered it on the second ring. After a pause, he replied, "Yes, I'm the one who called...No, I'm not staying there. I want to make arrangements to pay Miss Rhoades' bill there. Yes, it's the card number I left, hang on..." He pulled away from me, working his billfold from the pocket of his jeans. Sliding a credit card out, he flipped it over on the back. "The three digit number is 925."

He paused a moment, obviously for them to run the credit card.

"Yes, that would be fine. Leave instructions to call me whenever the charges are made."

So, he'd already made arrangements to take care of her hotel bill. He wasn't waiting on the outcome of the tests. *That's the Banton I know and love,* I thought.

He hung up and slid his phone back into his pocket.

"Chandler, there is a lot to consider if these tests..." he trailed off.

I nodded quickly in agreement. He grasped my shoulders and turned me over to face him.

"If he is mine, I've passed on the gene. He could be in danger from Orcos," he admitted out loud.

I hadn't even thought that far ahead, that far beyond my own insecurity. Banton was already worried about Reece's safety.

"Banton, that hadn't even occurred to me. If he is yours, how will we be able to keep him safe? What will we tell his mother, if he..."

"I honestly don't know. But I get the feeling that money might trump everything else with her."

"Hmmm. So you think she might let us have him, if we buy her off?" I asked disbelievingly.

"It wouldn't surprise me. We're jumping way ahead of ourselves. Do you feel okay?" he switched gears.

"I'm fine, Banton."

"No, I know you're not. But what I mean is do you feel like going out to dinner? I'd like to take you out, just the two of us, since Ty and Constance have the kids tonight."

"I'm really not that hungry," I murmured as he pulled me into his chest. He placed his cheek on top of my head.

"I still want to take you out. You need to get out of the house while you have the chance."

I nodded and rose to start the shower.

* * *

Banton watched me intently as I picked at the rare prime rib on my plate.

"Chandler, please. At least eat the beef. You look pale, are you drinking the blood mixture like Dr. Renault ordered?"

"Yes." I snapped back a little too quickly. Banton became silent as I glanced up at him through my lashes. He'd ordered a second bottle of wine after I'd uncharacteristically finished the first bottle off. I reached for my glass again and drained it. The warm flush I was feeling was welcome - the ache in my chest had temporarily ceased. I understood addiction better. It was a form of self-medication, and at the moment it would be easy to join the alcoholics. Jess, Ava Grace's mother, came to mind. She'd been mourning the death of Ava's father when I met her. I'd shown little sympathy for her plight when I'd considered Ava Grace's lack of supervision and care. One more drink, and I wouldn't be able to care for my own babies tonight. I pushed the wine glass back in disgust.

"Chandler, what is it?" Banton reached across the table and covered my hand.

"I've just had more than I should," I admitted as he continued to study me. He raised his hand and motioned to our waiter.

"Sir?" the young man was quickly at the table.

274

"Please bring each of us a glass of sparkling water and our check."

"Of course. Very good, sir," he responded as he hurried back to the kitchen.

I watched the votive candles on our table, floating in a crystal vase filled with limes and rose petals. As they flickered, I noticed the flecks of gold mixed in the deep brown of Banton's eyes. My gaze softened. He had so much on his shoulders right now, and I needed to stop wallowing and giving him more to worry about.

The music coursing through the arched doorway to the dance floor changed, and a singer began to sing. The strains of *Unchained Melody* drifted around us.

"Dance with me?" Banton asked softly. I glanced up through my lashes into his beautiful eyes and nodded silently.

Taking his hand, I stood shakily. I realized at that moment as I wobbled on my heels that I'd definitely had too much wine. When the room continued to list, Banton pulled me close to his side and steadied me as he led me to the dance floor.

"Chandler, you are beautiful tonight. Pink is definitely your color," he whispered into my ear, closing his arms around me. His beautiful deep voice sent shivers down my bare back.

When I'd contemplated what to wear to dinner, I'd stood in our closet glancing disinterestedly around. Banton had said, *semi-formal* when I'd asked him what to wear, so when the pale pink cloud of a skirt had swirled on the hanger when I'd passed it, I grabbed it. It was a strapless dress, the bodice covered in tiny pale pink and clear crystal beads that shimmered in the light. The skirt was cloud-like chiffon that rippled when I walked, brushing my legs just above my knees. I had a pair of pale pink Manolo Blahniks to match, the only pair I owned. Everett had insisted on them...he said every woman needed at least one pair of shoes that cost more than her first car to feel confident and sexy in.

Banton held my neck in his firm grasp as he softly brushed his other hand on my bare back. If he'd held me any looser, I might have fallen to the floor in my inebriated state.

"Your legs look long and sexy in that dress," he whispered into my hair. "You definitely don't look like you gave birth to twins less than three months ago."

275

"Mmmm." It was the only response I could manage. I didn't trust my thick tongue to enunciate anything else.

He chuckled, the first time since this morning before *SHE* rang the doorbell, that I'd heard the sound. It was such a beautiful sound.

"I'm at a loss, Chandler. I don't know what to do…how to ease the pain for you," he stated softly. I pulled away enough to gaze up at him as I managed to cock an eyebrow.

"I want to make sure you know that no matter what happens, you are still the center of my universe. I wanted to take you out on a date tonight. I had this planned, long before Miss Rhoades interrupted our lives yesterday. Do you know what tonight is?"

I shook my head, perplexed.

"It's the anniversary of the day we moved into your house. It's been a year since you turned my life upside down, and I fell hopelessly in love with you. I wanted you to know you are everything to me, and I'll never stop wooing you, Mrs. Gastaneau."

I fought through the cloudy thickness in my brain and mouth.

"Wwooing? Thath's some word. You've been hangin' around Ev and the nineteenthth century too long, Lieutenanttt Gastaneauwww," I slurred as he chuckled again.

"Come, let's get some water down you to dilute that wine a little, and then get you home."

"Kay," I mumbled against his neck, the wine numbing my senses. I somehow managed to float with him across the dance floor and back to our table without stumbling, due to Banton's strong arms around me, taking on most of my weight as we walked. He helped me gently into my seat and offered my glass to me. I drank most of it, watching him pull his wallet out of his jacket. He dropped two one-hundred dollar bills on the table with the check, and then helped me from my chair.

I woke as Banton carried me up the stairs to our bedroom.

"Hey," he said softly, gazing down at me. "You okay?"

"Mmmm. I closed my eyes again, the room spinning when he placed me on the bed. I was vaguely aware of him sliding first one shoe off my foot, then the other. My dress was next as he pulled me gently against his chest to slide the zipper down the back. He

276

laid me back into the pillows as he pulled the dress down under my hips and down my legs. My stockings were next. I was aware of him as he slipped his thumb inside each thin band at the top of my leg and slowly slid them down my thighs, first my left…then right. I shivered; the only remaining garment was my panties. As I watched him, aware of his closeness, he bent over and placed a kiss on my abdomen. I sighed, closing my eyes and winding my fingers in his hair. I moaned, for even in this half-conscious state, he had me. I ached for him to touch me.

He sat back up and drew the comforter back over me, tucking it in around me.

"Aren't you coming to bed," I murmured without opening my eyes.

"In a bit," he answered, placing a kiss on my forehead. "I have some things to do, and I wanted to wait up for the twins. I'll come to bed after they're tucked in," he replied.

The twins! I forced my eyes open. I needed to take care of my babies when they got home.

"No, baby… sleep. I'll get them to bed; you go to sleep," he urged in a firm tone. My eyelids obeyed his command, rebelling against my brain as sleep took over.

Chapter Twenty

"Okay, *Prom-Queen*, time to get up and fill me in."

Constance's voice mixed with the dull thudding in my head. I stretched, aware of the sweet smell of the twin's hair under my nose. I opened my eyes, and Matty and Elly both grinned up at me. I vaguely remembered Banton putting both of them in bed with me when he insisted on getting up with them at dawn.

I pushed up on my pillows as I focused on Constance. She bent over and picked my shoes up out of the middle of the bedroom floor, and then raised an eyebrow at me.

"What?" I asked as she shook her head. She crossed over to the chair by the dresser and placed the shoes on top of my stockings. She then turned and picked my dress up from the floor.

"Some night, huh?" she asked, crossing over to me and sitting down beside me on the bed.

"Mmm. Yeah, you could say that," I mumbled as I picked Elly up and placed her on my chest. Matty turned over and then scooted closer to me, reaching out with his hand and placing it on my face. I turned and smooched his cheek loudly, causing him to giggle.

"Thank you for taking them yesterday. The alone time with Banton was good."

"Well, Momma and Daddy were tickled we brought them. Cade and Drew wore them out playing. They were no trouble at all. So, are you all right? Banton is really worried about you," Constance said as she reached over me to pick Matty up. He grinned at her as she sat him down in her lap, causing her to lean over and cover his face in kisses as he tried to hide his face in her chest.

"I'm fine. It's Banton I'm worried about. He's got so much on his shoulders already, and now it seems he has more responsibility to worry about," I sighed as she made a face.

"What?" I asked her.

"Some things are better left unsaid...but you can bet your sweet ass I'm gonna say them anyway," she asserted, classic Constance style. "Y'all don't know anything yet, and this little gold-digging bitch from Banton's past is stirring up a whole lot of trouble. We don't even know if that little boy is his...he doesn't even remember if he screwed her! I wouldn't let her step foot in this house again, or come near my family until she proves it. And I don't want to see you shed one more tear. Not one!"

"I know, Constance. This isn't about me, and I've been a little selfish," I began.

"That's not what I meant, sweetie. You have every right to be upset! And for the record, you are one of the most unselfish people on the planet. I'm talking about Banton. He absolutely adores you, and I don't want some little 'ho' from his past upsetting your little family. Since the babies were born, you and Banton are the the happiest I've ever seen you. Everything finally calms down with all the Orco crap, Banton and Ty come home alive, and you two finally get to be happily married. Then in comes this bitch and tries to ruin everything."

"I know he loves me. This just all hit me so hard. The thought that someone else might have had his baby…"

"I know. It would tear me up too if someone came out of Ty's past with a bombshell like that. I wouldn't be as tolerant as you are. I can't believe he's paying her bills for her before he even knows," she said angrily.

"He feels sorry for her since her family evidently cut her off," I cut in.

"And that's why she showed up. She's looking for a paycheck, and her gorgeous ex-fantasy just happens to go with the package," she finished adamantly.

I flung the covers back to stand, still dressed in the lacy pink panties I'd worn the night before, and nothing else.

"Whoa, hello sexy mamma," Constance teased as she reached over and flung my satin robe at me. I giggled as I caught it. Turning around to place Elly down on the bed, I then shrugged it on and turned at the sound of Banton's voice.

"That's my favorite giggle. Hey, beautiful, how do you feel this morning?" He popped his head around the door and then opened it wide as he entered. "Morning, Constance."

"Good morning, Stud. Like the way you dressed her for bed last night," Constance quipped as she cocked her eyebrow at Banton.

"When your wife's this beautiful, you don't cover it up," he murmured, placing his lips against my neck. He pulled away to look down at me, and I smiled at him. "Feel all right this morning?"

I picked Elly up from the bed and turned back to his waiting arms. "A little fuzzy. But I'm fine," I sighed, leaning into him.

"Well, I'm going to take the babies down with me, and see if Ty wants to help me give them a bath. We'll see y'all downstairs." Constance crossed the room to me and took Elly in her other arm as she kissed my cheek.

"Thanks, Constance. You're a doll," I called after her.

"Yeah, yeah...you owe me!" she called as she descended the staircase.

Banton turned and sat down on the bed, pulling me down into his lap. He placed his hand on the back of my head, and pulled me into his lips. I was mortified. I had stale wine breath from the night before. I soon forgot my mortification when his kiss deepened. I wound my arms around his neck as his tongue softly worked its magic. When he had me breathless, he pulled away to gaze down at me.

"I'm leaving in an hour to meet Alexandra at Doc Lane's. Do you want to come with me?" he asked, cocking an eyebrow at me.

"Hmmm. I'd rather not. I'm not feeling entirely together, and I don't want to break down in front of her. I don't think that would do you any good," I muttered as he placed a finger under my chin.

"It's up to you, Sweetheart. I'd rather you never have to deal with her again. I just wanted you to know you had the option."

I nodded silently, holding in the tears.

"I'll call you as soon as we are done. Since you don't want to go, I'll run a couple of errands first."

"All right."

He rose, and then turned back to me hesitantly.

"I love you, Banton. I'm here, no matter what the outcome. We'll handle it together."

He smiled at me, the warmth reaching his eyes, making the lines there crease as both his dimples popped. My heart melted as always.

280

After I heard the front door close, I rose and drew myself a hot bath. I searched in the medicine cabinet for some Tylenol, and after taking two, I soaked a cold rag in the sink. When it was good and cold, I stepped into the tub and sank down into the bubbles, placing the rag across my eyes.

I tried not to dwell on what was going on this morning. I let my mind drift. I could hear Constance and Ty laughing in the bathroom downstairs and water splashing. The babies' belly laughs and giggles made me smile under the cloth. I loved them so much that it scared me sometimes. My mother had told me once you couldn't understand a mother's love for a child until you had one of your own…that there was no other feeling like it. It was a love like no other, an unconditional love and bond that could not be broken. She'd gone on to say that there was also no other hurt in the world that you could possibly feel like the hurt in your own heart when someone else tried to hurt your child or your family. Once again, my mother was right. I just wished she was here for me to tell her. The tears gathered under the rag. There were so many things I wished I could talk to her about. I took the rag off my forehead and finished bathing, then rose to dry off and get dressed. I was lucky. I had Aunt Sue and Constance to fill in for my mom. And right now, Constance was filling in nicely downstairs. It was time to go and relieve her.

After the babies were dry and dressed, Constance and I carried them into the living room. I placed a pallet in the floor, and then proceeded to spend our morning playing and lounging on the pallet with them. When I heard the front door open, I sat up apprehensively, only to find Everett breezing in with sacks under his arms.

"Bebe…hello," he called out.

"In the living room, Ev," I called out. Beau bounded in, having entered with Everett. He circled the pallet three or four times, and then plopped down beside the babies.

"I just had to come over this morning and check on my favorite girls," he gushed as he sat the sacks down on the sofa. "And how are my sweet babies today?" He leaned down and kissed both Constance and me on our cheeks, and then sat down cross-legged in the floor beside the babies.

"Hey, fruit-loop," Ty called out as he came through the foyer.

"Ty, my boy, how are you? I feel like I'm no longer in the circle, now that I'm not living with you all."

"Yeah, I kind of miss seeing you every morning, Ev," Constance said, Everett lounged beside Matty, letting him play with his nose and mo

"Hum. That's the kind of comment that might make a fiancée jealous," Ty joked, glancing at Constance.

"Well, watch it, baby. A girl could sure learn to love a guy who can cook, decorate, coordinate weddings and parties, and tucks you in with a kiss every night," Constance shot back as Ev chuckled.

"Sorry, darlin'. I've tried to get these cretins to get in touch with their feminine side but they won't cooperate," Everett retorted.

"I thought you had to bat for the other side to truly embrace those qualities, but I guess I'll have to rethink that one."

Everyone became silent at Ty's inference as Constance shot a glance at me, and then glared at Ty.

"Things aren't always what they appear, my boy. Did I miss something?" Everett sat upright as he picked Elly up and cuddled her to his chest.

I shrugged my shoulders. Constance tried to change the subject. "Ev, what's in the sacks?"

"Oh, I just got off the phone with Laurilee this morning, and I remembered that I have all of Chandler's things for the wedding. I hadn't heard back from you, sister, so I went ahead and picked a dress out for you to wear. You are still going to Texas with us?" he asked Constance.

"I'm planning on it. If we don't have any more drama or the creek don't rise," she said in her best attempt at my Texas drawl, glancing at me.

"Did I miss some drama?" Everett asked innocently. "I thought I picked up on some tension in the air."

"Mmm. You could say that," Constance said as she rose to look through the sacks on the sofa.

"Well, are you going to fill me in? What have I missed?" Everett urged as he sat up and scooted closer to me.

I sighed, and then decided he might as well know. "A lot, actually. Banton had an old girlfriend show up here day before yesterday, wanting to see him. He called her and invited her over to find out what she wanted, and she showed up with a little boy, about two and a half years old or so. A little boy with curly black hair," I almost whispered, the tears gathering once more in my eyes.

"Oh sweet Jesus," Everett exclaimed as Constance nodded.

My cell phone rang, interrupting my explanation. I scrambled to retrieve it from the coffee table. Banton's name and number lit up.

"Banton," I breathed out in relief. Everett had risen and was seated beside Constance on the sofa. Evidently she was finishing the story, explaining where Banton was.

"Hey, sweetheart. I told you I'd call when I was finished. Dr. Lane just finished with the buccal swabs, and he said he would call me later tonight, tomorrow at the latest, with the results."

"Buccal swabs?"

Constance and Everett both watched me silently.

"Yes, a cheek swab. Evidently they're just as accurate as blood tests."

"And did Alexandra cooperate? How was Reece about the test?"

"Yes, at first she balked. She seemed to be stalling, and she pulled the "tug on my heartstrings" thing, but I reminded her I wouldn't do anything else without the tests. She cooperated in a huff and then took off."

"Oh. Did you make arrangements to meet with her about the results?" I asked, dreading the answer.

"No, surprisingly she left before I could talk to her about it. I was going to ask her if Reece needed anything…clothes, medicine…but when Doc had swabbed her cheek and Reece's, she gathered him up and left. When I realized she'd left out the front door, I ran out into the parking lot but she was already gone."

"And Doc said he'd have the results tonight?" I'd already looked it up on my I-phone, and most websites had said three to five days, depending on the laboratory.

"He's got the inside track on the lab, and he said he'd oversee this personally. Chandler, I'm on my way home, almost there. I'll see you in ten."

"Good. Okay, bye." I hung up and looked up at Ev and Constance. Ty stood silently in the corner, having listened to our conversation.

"Well?" Constance asked, glancing at Everett.

"Tests are done, we'll know something tonight or tomorrow," I answered.

"And the ho?"

Everett laughed as I shook my head.

"*Alexandra* took off right after the test. She didn't even stick around to make arrangements to meet Banton, if…" I trailed off.

Constance crossed her arms smugly. "Of course not, because she already knows the results!"

"Bebe, you are certainly calm about all of this. Are you all right?" he asked. He rose and crossed the room toward me.

"Yes, I am. Or I'm gonna be, anyway," I murmured. I sat my phone down on the coffee table, and then turned to lie back down on the pallet between the twins. Everett sank down beside me and pulled me over into his arms. He hugged me tightly, and then I rested my head in his lap. Everett absent-mindedly began to braid my hair as I patted Elly's back. She was tired, and her little eyelids almost drooped completely shut.

The house phone ringing in the foyer startled me. I sat up as Everett and I glanced at each other…no one called on that number unless I'd let my cell die. I rose and went around the staircase to answer it.

"Hello?'

"This is a representative with Navy family services. I'm calling on behalf of Commander Reed's office. Is Lieutenant Gastaneau there?"

"No, I'm sorry. I'm his wife, Chandler. Did you try his cell?"

"No Ma'am. It is our policy to try a home number first. We have received notice of a situation with Lieutenant Gastaneau. A formal complaint has been filed with us by a Miss Rhoades. Our office has been asked to set up medical tests to be run here at the medical facility on your family."

284

Alexandra Rhoades is up to more than we know, I thought. "You will need to speak with my husband. I can't speak for him. He will be home shortly, and I will have him contact you immediately." I was furious. This wasn't going to be as easy as a private genetic test. *Now she wants tests on my children!*

I slammed the phone down, and then turned toward the front door to find Banton's stunned gaze on me.

"You might want to return that call to Commander Reed. Your …whatever she is to you…has filed a formal complaint with the Navy against you, and they're demanding testing on us now," I managed to choke out as I flew up the staircase.

"Chandler, wait," he called out. The bedroom door slammed behind me. I'd reached my limit. That limit where understanding wife meets bat-shit crazy. Flinging myself on the window seat, I pulled my knees up to my chest. *What was this woman up to?* Oh, Reed would have a field day with this. He and Banton weren't exactly on good terms, and Banton and Ty had managed to push for an investigation into the way that their last mission had been handled.

It hadn't occurred to me that Alexandra could make trouble for Banton with the Navy. The SEALs were held to all kinds of moral codes…but surely an unmarried fling from his past wouldn't be the first the Navy had ever seen. Maybe she's after garnishment, benefits? Why would she want me and the babies to be tested? The fact that she was involving my children made me furious! And the fact that they called the house…that they talked to me at all…it didn't make sense. It certainly didn't seem professional.

"Chandler, hey." Banton was standing in the doorway watching me. "I'm sorry you took that phone call. It never should have happened," he murmured, crossing the room to me and reaching out to pull me into his arms.

"Why are they involved all of a sudden?" I relaxed with his arms around me. He always had that effect on me.

"They shouldn't be. That phone call wasn't even protocol, even Ty said so," he replied. "I'm so sorry. I'm going down right now to straighten this out. Just stay up here and rest. Ev and Constance just put the babies down and they're asleep. I'll be back in a few minutes." He kissed me on the forehead and then left the room.

I couldn't shake the feelings of anxiety. Why did this woman have to show up now? And why involve the military? One complication after another seemed to threaten my happiness. I sighed…maybe our lives would always be like this.

I decided to take Banton's advice and rest. As I pulled the comforter back and curled up on the bed, I noticed a dull ache in my lower back. I'd been running with Constance in the early mornings a few days a week, but most of the soreness from that was gone. After a few minutes, my abdomen began to cramp. Worried, I rose and crossed to the bathroom. When I pulled my sweats down, I realized I'd started my period. I stood there, shocked. It had been so long, I wasn't even keeping up with when I should start. I'd even accepted the fact I probably would never have another normal cycle again, since I'd transformed. I stripped down, and started the shower. *Wow, that's a lot of blood*, I thought as I picked my panties up and placed them in the sink to wash them out. After I'd stepped into the shower, I mentally counted back. The babies were three months old…and I'd stopped bleeding immediately after I'd given birth. Three months was a long time to go…it certainly explained the amount of blood. The tears started when I clipped my braided hair up on my head, gazing at myself in the mirror. I'd been depressed thinking I couldn't conceive again, but I hadn't really realized how important this phase of my life was to me. Then it occurred to me… *maybe I could get pregnant again after all*. Just the fact that I had my cycle again somehow made me feel more normal…more like a normal newly-married bride. I smiled …I hadn't realized how much I'd let the whole thing affect the way I felt about myself.

A knock at the bathroom door brought me out of my musings.

"Chandler, baby…can I come in," Banton called through the door.

"Sure…I'm in the shower."

I heard the door open, and then close.

"Andie, are you okay? Banton asked. I could see his outline by the shower door.

286

"I'm fine. I'll be right out," I called out. I finished rinsing the soap off my skin, and then as I started to open the shower, a towel appeared over the top.

"Mmm…Wow, thanks!" I called out, drying off. Opening the door, I spied Banton sitting on the corner of the tub. Embarrassed, I remembered the panties I'd left in the sink. I glanced over at the sink and then blushed when I met Banton's eyes. He gave me a soft, hesitant smile, and pulled me into his arms.

"So, you've started bleeding again?" he asked as he studied my expression. I just nodded. It occurred to me, this was the first time I'd had a cycle since we'd been intimate.

"Does this mean that we might be able to get pregnant again?" he asked, still serious.

"I don't know. I'll have to talk to Dr. Lane. I guess there is always that possibility. I'm just shocked…I didn't think I could."

"Are you upset?" he asked softly, pulling me down into his lap.

I shook my head. "Actually, I'm happy. I'm relieved…I feel normal again."

"Oh, baby," he murmured as he pulled my head into his chest. "I know this has been worrying you. I'm glad you feel things are normal. But I have to ask, do you want me to start using something now?"

"No! If there is the slightest chance I can have another baby, I don't want to miss the opportunity! What if I'm bitten again, and the next time it stops my cycles completely?" I realized my outburst took Banton by surprise. I couldn't tell by his expression how he felt.

I stood, finished drying off, and then shrugged into my bathrobe. Banton remained silent as he watched me. After I'd had time to process, I turned to him.

"Banton, I'm sorry. You probably don't want to think about another baby this soon after the twins. I just want the option. I don't want the twins to be it…for it to be so final."

Banton rose and walked over to me and pulled me up into his arms. "Chandler, I want nothing more than to make you happy. But we have all we can handle right now, and what you had to go through with the twins and all the attacks…I don't think I could

287

stand to put you through that right now. I forget sometimes how young you are. You haven't even finished college yet. Let's just see what happens. Your body has been through so much. I would feel better if we used something. I think you should make an appointment and talk with Dr. Lane about our options."

I busied myself with washing my lingerie out in the sink, avoiding his eyes. He finally walked over behind me and pulled me around, placing his finger under my chin.

"Chandler, please don't cry. Talk to me," he murmured as he kissed a tear that rolled down my cheek.

"I'm sorry, I just got so emotional when I finally started my period. I haven't had time to process yet. I know you are right. I'm just not sure I want to take any precautions. It's almost like we might be passing up our only opportunity," I whispered as he looked back and forth into my eyes. "It's probably a moot point anyway, this is probably a fluke, and I still won't be able to get pregnant," I murmured, wringing the lingerie out and placing it in the hamper.

Banton walked back into the bedroom as I rummaged through the drawers in the bathroom, finally locating my nightgown. My cramps were getting worse by the minute, much worse than before I'd had the babies. After I'd pulled my gown on, I entered the bedroom. Banton had the comforter pulled back on the bed, waiting on me.

"You don't look like you feel well, I thought you might want to lie down," he said as I crossed the room. I nodded and crawled into the bed as he pulled the comforter up over me. He kissed me on the forehead. "Andie, are you cramping?" he asked softly, leaning his forehead against mine.

"Yes, pretty bad. I've never had them this bad before."

He pulled back and nodded. "What helps? What can I get for you?"

"There is a heating pad in the hall closet, and some Ibuprofen might help," I murmured as he nodded. No sooner than he'd left the room, he was back with both items, plus a cup of hot tea. After he had the heating pad plugged in and pressed to my tummy, he urged me to take the medicine and some of the tea.

"Now, how about some company? Will it bother you if I lay with you, maybe rub your back, or would you rather I leave you alone?" he asked sweetly.

"Wow. Just when I thought you couldn't be any more romantic…of course I want you here. Spoon with me?" I asked, smiling up at him.

He grinned back as he pulled his boots off and then climbed under the covers with me. He pulled me into his body, and then placed his hands across the heating pad, cradling it to my tummy.

"So the babies are down for their afternoon nap?" I asked after a few moments.

"Yes. I left our door cracked, so we could hear them when they wake."

"Did you call Commander Reed's office back?" I asked, dreading what he'd found out.

"Yes. Evidently Alexandra has made a formal complaint asking for paternity tests, full benefits, and the works. I think she was hoping that by going to my superiors, I would offer to buy her off and make her go away quietly. She doesn't know that I don't intimidate easily.

"She obviously went to them before the tests today," I reasoned.

"I got nowhere when I called them back. I'm going to meet with Reed as soon as we get to N'awlins for our trip. He mentioned testing you and the twins again, which is crazy, there is no point. He has an ulterior motive. I think she's trying to hedge her bets with involving the military, and Reed jumped on this as an opportunity. Don't worry, I'll handle this. You don't have to talk to them again," he assured me.

"Banton, I don't want the Navy testing one hair on the babies' heads," I whispered as he placed his lips in my hair.

"No, of course not. There is a lot more to this than a simple complaint and paternity test. I'll get to the bottom of this," he swore as I turned my gaze to meet his. I was frightened at the implications.

"Andie, please don't worry about this. I will handle it," he assured me, his gaze never wavering. I nodded, giving my best try at being positive. He broke into a smile immediately, and changed the course of the day 360 degrees.

"What did you do to your hair?" he asked, flipping the braid around my shoulder.

I laughed at his sudden change. "Ev braided my hair while we were talking, lying in the floor with the twins."

He chuckled, raising an eyebrow. "Y'all just have this 'girly-talk slumber party' thing going all the time – what is it with Everett?"

I giggled and smiled a sly smile. "Ty already knows, you cretins might want to get in touch with your feminine side, if you don't want some stiff competition," I teased as he teasingly nipped at my neck with his lips, sliding his tongue along as he went.

"But can he do this to you?" he demanded in a low, sexy voice as he ran his nose up my neck. My heart rate quickened as his hands slid down the back of my waistband, caressing my skin under the lace of my panties. As my breathing became shallow, he slowly kissed along my jaw and turned me in his arms, covering my lips with his. He breathed into my mouth. I moaned, the sound vibrating into him as his fingers slowly slid under my gown and around my ribcage, his thumbs teasingly caressing under my breasts.

"Banton," I gasped. "I...we can't..."

He sighed, and then moved his hands to a more modest position, quickly adjusting my gown as he settled his hands back across the heating pad.

"Sorry. Your braid just turned me on," he shrugged his shoulders and then playfully slapped my rump.

"What has gotten into you?" I asked, amazed.

"I just realized I'm married to one hot, twenty-three year old," he shot back as I murmured, "twenty three?" *Oh, gosh...I'd forgotten!* It was October 15th. Today was my birthday.

"Happy Birthday, Chandler Ann." His eyes gave him away, sparkling brightly with some delicious secret.

"I can't believe I didn't remember my own birthday," I said disbelievingly.

"Well, you have been a little preoccupied."

290

He pulled me into his arms, his hands loosely clasped behind my waist.

"I wish there was something I could do to make you forget everything that's going on right now," he whispered as he pushed a lose strand of hair behind my ear.

"Well, two bottles of wine last night didn't do it, so I think it's probably impossible," I answered him. "By the way, I'm sorry I did that, and you had to carry me in, undress me…"

"You were fine, sweetheart. I don't ever mind undressing you," he murmured as he pressed his lips against my throat. "I just wish you had been something other than comatose when I finished."

"Oh, Banton, I am sorry."

I felt him grin against my neck. "Well, you can make it up to me… I was hoping for tonight, but I guess it will be a couple of days, now. I've been thinking about those pink lace panties you had on, those pale pink stockings…all day long today."

I placed both my hands on either side of his head, bringing his eyes back up to mine. "I promise, I'll more than make it up to you soon."

His eyes sparkled down into mine and I read the love there. As he smiled and flashed his dimple, he kissed the end of my nose. "Now rest. I want you to feel better," he stated, turning my shoulders back so he could spoon me. As his fingers kneaded my shoulders, I began to relax and to drift.

Chapter Twenty-One

After a long nap, I woke to those same, strong hands massaging my lower back. I stretched as I felt Banton's breath on my neck.

"How do you feel?" he murmured as I turned to look at him.

"Better. The cramps are easing up a bit," I replied. "Are the babies awake yet?"

"No, I haven't heard them yet. I know Constance checked on them a few minutes ago. I saw her go into the nursery. I guess y'all wore them out playing with them this morning."

"Have you heard anything from Dr. Lane yet?" I asked, searching his eyes. He shook his head.

"No. Don't really think we'll hear from him until in the morning sometime."

"Hmm. Well, I guess I should go downstairs and start something for supper."

He pulled back to look at me. "Chandler Ann Gastaneau, do you really think we'd let you cook on your birthday?"

"Well, I hadn't really thought about it."

"Don't worry. It's all taken care of. By the way, I have a compromise for you," he murmured, placing his lips against my neck.

"Mmm. What's that?"

"Well, if you will accept one of my birthday gifts without a fuss, then I will concede your point."

"What point?" I asked warily.

"I'll agree not to use any protection and let nature take its course. If God means for us to conceive again, then we will. IF," he began.

"If what?"

"If you will be a good girl, and let me hire a housekeeper and part-time nanny. Let me hire someone to help you with the housework and the babies."

"But Banton," I began.

"Chandler, you have proven many times over you are supermom! You've given up school this semester, and you're worn

292

out. Just let me bring someone we trust in to help. If you want her to cook and clean, and you take complete care of the babies, then do it. Or if you just want her help a little here or a little there…you are in complete control. Just please, do this for me. If nothing else, do it so I can get my mom and Claudia off my back!" he said with a slight grin.

"Your momma said something?" I asked. It had never occurred to me.

"Chandler, she's been on me since day one. They both think you work too hard," he said as he traced my jaw with his finger.

"Okay, I'll think about it. If you want me to," I added as he flashed me the dimple.

"Good, because she's part of your birthday surprise downstairs." He rose and pulled me from the bed.

"What? Who's downstairs?" I asked as his eyes sparkled.

"Just a few members of our family and some friends. Feel like getting dressed?" he asked, kneeling to kiss my forehead.

"Sure, just give me a minute."

I flung the covers back, crossed the room, and dug through my closet. Excited, I flipped through my clothes, finally deciding on a pink sweater dress that softly hugged my body. It had crisscross cut outs across the chest and bared my shoulders. I stood back and checked myself in the floor length mirror. I looked rather sexy in it. My hair was still in the loose braid that Everett knotted it in earlier, and even mussed-up, I decided it looked quaint. It was warmer today, so I opted to go bare and lose the leggings. I pulled on a knee-high pair of soft pink suede boots with fringe around them. As I sat down on the edge of the bed to pull the boots on, Banton stepped back out of the closet wearing a pair of ripped Levi's and a white linen shirt, opened down the front. The shirt framed his chest perfectly, showing off his tanned, finely chiseled six-pack.

"Wow…" I breathed, watching him button his shirt.

"What?" he asked innocently.

"You are lucky I'm indisposed at the moment, or we would never make it downstairs," I murmured truthfully as I stared at him. He chuckled low in his throat, and walked slowly over to the bed as he kept his eyes on mine. He hadn't shaved today, and he had the sexy dark stubble thing going on. I drew my breath in.

"If you weren't indisposed, we wouldn't be going downstairs," he answered, his lips covering mine. His kiss was so soft, so sensual that I lost myself in it. As he pulled away, I leaned into him and had to catch myself. He grinned at me cockily.

"Come on, everyone is waiting," he urged, pulling me up from the bed. As I stood, he swept his heated gaze down my body.

"I told you last night that pink is definitely your color," he murmured, tracing the outline of the cutouts on the sweater.

"You like?" I asked, twirling.

"Oh, yeah. I like, a lot. He grinned and tipped my chin up to give me a chaste kiss.

As we made our way down the staircase, Banton pressed his lips against my neck, "And leave your hair in the braid tonight. I love it like that."

I turned to stare at him, just as I heard a chorus of voices downstairs, "Surprise! Happy Birthday!"

Everyone I could think of was in my living room and foyer. Aunt Sue, Uncle Lon, Cade and Drew…the SEALS, Olivia and Patrick, Banton's Mom and Dad, Everett and Mr. Philippe…even Stephen stood silently in the background. Brie and Constance came forward and both kissed me on the cheeks.

"No one was going to let this birthday slide like last year, baby-girl," Uncle Lon exclaimed as he hugged me.

"Did you suspect anything?' Julia bounced through the crowd to hug me.

"No! I didn't even remember today was my birthday until Banton reminded me upstairs," I answered truthfully.

"Well, I just had to make sure everything was done just right for my best friend in the whole world!" Everett gushed, taking me in his arms and swinging me around. "So I called Miss Astrid, and told her we needed another little-ole southern celebration, complete with the most beautiful birthday cake she could come up with."

I turned to Banton with tears threatening. "You weren't here this summer to celebrate yours…I feel so guilty," I began.

Banton kissed me on top of the head. "We'll make up for it tonight. I have so much to celebrate with you," he murmured.

"Well, shall we get this party started? I have food ready in the kitchen, just make your way through buffet-style," Miss Astrid instructed. Everyone formed a line down the hallway.

"Miss Astrid, thank you. It smells wonderful."

"Everett and Banton instructed me to make all your favorite dishes, so maybe you would eat something. You are wasting away to nothing." She pinched my shoulder. "Maybe after I'm working here, I can get some meat on those bones," she admonished. I glanced at Banton. He nodded slowly.

"Miss Astrid is who you have hired to help me?' I asked disbelievingly.

"Well, Everett suggested it, when I mentioned it to him. He reminded me we would have to have an Aldon or Sange-Mele, because of the babies. And she would be extra protection at the house, if we should ever need it again," he added.

"But do you really want to do this?" I turned back to Miss Astrid, thinking that working for us might be beneath her.

"Oh, Chandler, nothing would give me greater pleasure! I just work to stay busy, and catering is something I like to do. But like Everett, working is something to pass my time. I would love to come and help you with your house and your babies! It would be a welcome distraction from what I've been doing these last few years. And I can still take the occasional catering job, now and then," she winked at me as she started back down the hallway.

"Bebe, Miss Astrid told me a while back when we were still battling the Orcos, if we needed her she would be more than willing to help. She tells me she used to be 'in the middle of the fray,' so to speak, many years ago. She is like me. She sees herself as the protector of humans. She wants to do this."

"I think it would be a good move, and I think it will be a good move for the babies when they're older," Banton added.

"Well, I guess we have a housekeeper, then," I said apprehensively. Banton hugged me close.

"That's great, Bebe! Now, let's go and eat." Everett and Banton both urged me into the kitchen.

295

After we sat down in the living room with our plates, Banton's cell rang. He rose to answer it. Remembering Dr. Lane, I looked up at him. His back to the door, he was nodding his head as he talked. After a few moments, I heard him say "Thank you, I'll be in touch," and then he hung up. He stood with his back to me for several minutes, gazing out the window on the front door. I realized I hadn't taken a breath since he'd left the room. I put my fork back down on my plate as he slowly turned back to look at me. I couldn't read his expression.

Trembling, I placed my plate on the coffee table, and as everyone continued to chatter around us, I made my way to him. As I reached him, I placed my arms around his waist.

"Was that Dr. Lane?" I asked softly. He nodded.

"Did he give you the results?"

Banton nodded and pulled my hands from around his waist, and then pulled me back into the dining room. After he had me around the corner, he took a deep breath. "Chandler, Sweetheart, they had to send the swabs to another lab, some complication or something. It's going to be a few days before we know anything."

I sighed and nodded.

"Chandler, I'm sorry. I was hoping I could tell you this was all over with tonight."

"No, Banton…it's all right. I know you are still worrying. I know you. You had already started making plans for him…now you feel helpless," I said as he nodded at me. I placed my hand on his cheek, so full of love for this man.

"Part of me will be relieved if the tests come back negative. But if they do, part of me will worry about Reece," I whispered truthfully, gazing into his eyes,

"God, Chandler…that's one of the million reasons why I love you so much," he said, pulling me in tightly.

Cries from the nursery broke in on our intimate moment.

"Well, the two who *are* mine are demanding some attention. What do you say we go up and get them, Mommy?" he asked as he wiped a tear from under my eye.

I nodded at him as he wrapped an arm around my waist.

No sooner than we had the twins downstairs, they were swept up into the waiting arms of grandparents. I was overwhelmed with all the love in the room as I made my way through the crowd of our close friends and family. Brie cuddled Elly close to her as John played with her over Brie's shoulder. I smiled as I watched them.

"Well, Bebe, are you all packed for our little trip day after tomorrow?" Ev asked as he came up behind me.

"I will be, I just have a few more things to do tonight," I said, shaking a finger at me.

"Oh, noooo, Bebe…there will be no time for that tonight."

"What do you mean," I asked. Banton picked me up and swung me around.

"Everyone, may I have your attention?" Banton announced as everyone quieted down.

"To celebrate my beautiful wife's birthday, I wanted to surprise her with a trip. Those plans fell through, so I've improvised. I'm sure you will excuse us because I need to whisk her away to her second surprise." His eyes twinkled as he looked down at me. "We have babysitters for the night, so if you will step this way and wish everyone here goodnight," he said grandly, sweeping his hand toward everyone in the living room. Everyone chimed out, "Happy Birthday," and "Goodbye, Chandler," as Banton pulled me down the hallway and into the kitchen.

Miss Astrid turned and grinned at Banton as he raised an eyebrow at her.

"Everything is as you ordered," she said conspiratorially.

"Okay, Mrs. Gastaneau, for the rest of your surprise, no peeking," he said as he pulled a handkerchief from his pocket and wrapped it around my eyes, securing it in the back. I couldn't help myself. I grinned like a fool when he led me out the back door.

"Watch your step, just hold on to me," he whispered into my ear. Music wafted across the yard, becoming louder the further we walked. I could feel a soft breeze blowing on my face, and then a soft fabric brush softly across my cheek. The smell of fresh flowers overwhelmed my senses.

"Banton, where are we going?" I asked as he turned me around.

"Since I couldn't take you to an oasis, I brought the oasis to you," he said, removing the blindfold.

I blinked in disbelief. We stood in the open French doors to the greenhouse, which had been totally transformed. Gossamer and twinkle lights were draped from the ceiling and every corner, and a beautiful four-poster canopy iron bed sat toward the back in the center of the room, adorned in white gossamer and silks. The bed was piled with thick comforters and pillows in shades of white. A white limestone fireplace stood just outside the open French doors, and a fire blazed inside, the wood popping and crackling, inviting us into our own little piece of heaven. Soft piano music played in the background, and candles were lit around the room, sparkling and bouncing off the wavy thick glass of the windows. Every available surface was covered with white roses and gardenias. I turned back to the fireplace and noticed our fur rug had been placed in front of it on the stone patio. Everything seemed to twinkle and sparkle in the darkness.

"Banton, did you do all this?" I whispered, barely believing my eyes.

"With a little help from Everett. He's trying to get me in touch with my feminine side," he said, rolling his eyes. I threw my arms around his neck as he buried his face in my hair.

"It's perfect," I murmured as he breathed into my hair.

"Well, the trip I'd planned would have been perfect, if not for all the drama the last couple of days," he sighed.

"So, where were you going to take me?" I asked.

"Well, that's the other part of the surprise. Here." He handed me an envelope with my name on it. I looked up at him curiously as he scooped me up and carried me over to the bed, placing me in the center. He sank down beside me as I crossed my legs and opened the envelope.

"What is this?" I asked, skimming the page. It appeared to be a lease/purchase agreement from a real estate corporation in the name of Banton and Chandler Gastaneau.

"Florida? You bought a condo in Florida?" I asked incredulously.

"Yes, I did. For us. We can go anytime you want to. It has four bedrooms and three bathrooms, secluded, right on the beach. We can take our friends, our family…it's a vacation home for us and the twins."

I looked back at him, stunned. I was used to the occasional diamond, or hot tub...the new car. But a vacation home? I was speechless.

"What's wrong, Chandler? You don't like it? Constance said you liked the beach," he began; the disappointment in his voice was palpable.

I held a finger up to silence him. I sat studying the papers, and then looked up at him. "I can't believe you bought me a vacation home. A place where we can make memories...where we can just be...Banton, I love it," I whispered.

He seemed to sigh in relief.

"I love it so much! And I love you," I cried as I launched myself at him. He caught me and laid me down into the pillows.

"I just want us to have the same wonderful memories when the kids are little that I had...taking them down on the beach, watching the turtles hatch and then helping them back to the water...chasing crabs with flashlights after dark...teaching the twins to ride boogie boards..." he went on and on, excitedly, almost like a small boy. At that moment, he was my boy. I circled his dimple with my finger.

"It all sounds wonderful. I can't wait to go," I said as I watched his eyes. "And the twins will learn to swim while they're young. I don't want them to ever be afraid of the water like I was," I began as Banton's eyes widened.

"Chandler, I didn't think of your fear of the water! I'm sorry, we can buy property somewhere else," he began.

"Absolutely not. I'm past that fear, Banton. I don't want the kids to have it. I want them to grow up fearless! And I know they will with you as their dad," I whispered, looking back and forth into his eyes.

"What?" he asked as he stroked my cheek.

"I was just thinking, how close we came to losing you --how close the twins came to never knowing you," I whispered as I began to choke up.

"None of that, Chandler Ann. I'm here, and I'm not going anywhere. Now, let's get your special night started." He took the envelope from me and placed it on the table. Crossing behind the bed, he walked over to the kitchenette that John had built months before. As he came back into view around the bed, he carried two glasses of red wine.

"Here you go, Tuscany's finest," he said, handing me a glass. He touched his glass to mine, and then raised it as I sipped. It was the most delicious wine I'd ever tasted, not sweet, but not too dry. So smooth, in fact, that I'd downed the entire glass before I realized it.

"Would you like some more," he asked, producing the bottle from behind the bed.

"I'd better wait a bit. We don't need a repeat of last night," I said as he laughed.

"I'm not worried. I don't think another glass will hurt. Besides, it's delicious. Here," he filled my glass again, and then touched his to mine.

"Well, I guess it kind of ruins the mood, with me in my condition," I blushed, referring to the sudden reappearance of my cycle.

"You know I don't care about that," Banton replied. "Well, I do, but I...well you know what I mean," he stammered. "Here. I have something else for you."

He brought out a box wrapped with turquoise blue ribbons. Curiously, I un-wrapped the bow and removed the lid. Inside were beautiful intricate antique lace gown and robe, camisole and panties.

"Banton, these are so beautiful," I gasped as I pulled them from the box. "Everett?" I asked.

"Um, *No*. I wasn't about to ask Everett for help on this one, now I know he's straight. I asked Constance to find something special for tonight, and described what Everett was going to do to the pool house. I told her I wanted something vintage and classic...just like you," he said, leaning in and kissing me on the forehead.

"So, just what do you have in mind, Mr. Gastaneau?" I asked as I fingered the lace on the bodice. It was all hand-crocheted and extremely revealing.

"Just to spend the night in heaven, wrapped around you," he answered, walking over and taking the garments out of the box. He turned around, and pulled the gossamer and silk fabrics across the

300

open doorway, hiding us from the view of the house. All of the windows were layered in white fabrics, and we were enveloped in our own little tent of soft glowing lights. He moved back over to the bed and pulled my sweater dress over my head, then methodically reached around and unsnapped my bra, dropping it to the floor. He knelt to the floor, dropping first one boot to the floor, then the other as he slid his hands up my legs and grasped my thighs.

"Your bare legs under this sweater were so sexy tonight," he said huskily, his thumbs rubbing across my skin. He then rose over me and smiled devilishly, gathering the camisole up and then sliding it down over my head as I worked my arms under the straps. He pulled it down into place as he ran his hands slowly down my ribcage, sending shivers down my spine. The lace was so open, I felt naked, and sexy.

"Damn, but you are so beautiful, Chandler. Sometimes I can't believe how lucky I am," he murmured, pulling me up to his lips. He moved them softly over mine, grasping my camisole in the back. His tongue explored, softly grazing my lips and my teeth as he moved slowly into my mouth. I moaned when his kiss deepened.

"How can you do this to me, knowing that we can't do anything tonight?" I murmured as I pouted against his lips.

He sighed, and then pulled away. "Well, Mrs. Gastaneau, tonight, this is all about you. I have some things here that I think you will like, so since you are feeling a little under the weather, we'll see what we can do about that," he said, flashing the dimple. He rose and then unbuttoned his shirt, and then shrugged out of his jeans until all that remained were his boxer-briefs. He returned to the side of the bed as I watched him move. His muscles rippled in that sexy way with every move he made. The muscles tightened in my abdomen, making me acutely aware of the dull ache that still accompanied my cramps. He leaned over, opened a drawer beside the bed, and brought out a crystal decanter set filled with lotions and oils. As he removed the top, I recognized the scent...the insanely expensive lotion he'd bought for me on the trip to N'awlins before Mardi Gras.

"Come here," he motioned. I moved closer to the side of the bed. "Lie face down." I smiled and did as he asked. He pushed the camisole up under my arms, brushing my breast with his thumbs. I shuddered, wanting him so badly. I shook my head...this was going to be torture. *Why did I have to start my period today?*

I could hear him remove the stopper from the bottle, and then replace it as he rubbed his hands together. I felt the bed give way as he settled down on the bed beside me.

"Now, relax, and let me love you all over," he murmured in my ear, his hands beginning to move. I melted into the mattress. He ran his hands up and down my back, kneading the muscles as he worked the heavenly smelling oil into my skin. Working in circles, he kneaded the muscles of my lower back, and then worked around, under my ribcage until he was caressing the sides of my breasts. I couldn't stand it any longer, so I turned over.

"Mmmm, you want me to work on this side?" he grinned as I nodded wickedly. I watched his eyes grow warm as he gazed down at me. Slowly sliding his hands up over my breasts, he rubbed the oil into my skin, moving his hands over my chest and around on my shoulders. He was so serious as he removed the stopper to the bottle and re-oiled his hands. Rubbing them together again, he pulled the lace of my panties low as he rubbed his hands gently over my abdomen, massaging the muscles there, up and around my hip bones. I closed my eyes, the warmth of the oil and the friction of his hands warming me, easing the dull ache somewhat.

He leaned up over me and whispered in my ear, "Does this help?"

"Mmm. Yes, it does. Don't stop," I replied. I felt him grin against my neck.

"Do you want me to continue, Mrs. Gastaneau," he asked dreamily. "I will take you as far as you want to go."

My eyes snapped open, gazing up into his. What did he mean? Surely he didn't want to...

As if he were reading my thoughts, he murmured, "Remember when you were first pregnant? There are all kinds of ways for me to love you, baby," he murmured softly, sliding his lips down. He leaned back up and continued his slow, mesmerizing circles with his fingers across my abdomen, up over my hipbones. Each time, his thumbs worked lower, until they reached my bikini line scar. He shifted and placed his lips there as if to kiss it away.

My breath caught in my throat. His mouth was so close to…when I was…my eyes flew open and I stared down at him.

"How do you feel?" he said softly, gazing up at me.

I cleared my throat. "Mmm, good…relaxed…hot."

He gazed down at my panties, and pulled them slowly off as he looked back up at me cautiously. He'd already explored enough to know there were no pads involved, and I must have a tampon in. I blushed bright crimson at the thought.

He discarded the panties behind him, and then slowly and methodically re-oiled his hands again. As he continued to oscillate, he let his thumbs knead all the way down, across and between my legs. Oh, it felt so good…relaxing the cramps, the day's anxiety…and slowly building my need. I unconsciously pushed against his hand as he slowly worked his thumbs, his mouth on my abdomen, up to my chest…his teeth trailed small bites up my neck, and then his lips covered mine. My breathing hitched, and he increased his pressure and speed. I drew my breath in. It was torture. I needed release, but had no idea how I was going to find it in my condition.

Banton instinctively knew what I needed. He pushed his leg between mine, his own passion against me. I pressed to meet him. Moaning as everything contracted, I spiraled out of control.

"Banton," I cried out involuntarily. He covered my mouth with his, smothering my cry.

"Shh. You'll have the whole party out here to rescue you," he chuckled against my neck as I tried to get my breathing under control.

"What you can do to me with just your thumbs," I muttered. He grinned down at me. He still lay on top of me, his elbows on either side of my head, pinning my hands down to the mattress.

We stared at each other. He released my hand, so I could slide my hand down the side of his face, tracing his hair line around his ear lobe. I smiled and touched my thumb gently to the skin between his eyebrows, brushing it softly to and fro.

"The lines are gone. You're finally relaxed," I breathed out as he smiled.

"You do that to me, Chandler. You relax me, excite me, intimidate me, and inspire me. I told you a long time ago, you are everything."

"But I didn't excite you tonight," I murmured, sad that I couldn't give him what he'd given me. *Or could I?* I'd learned from conversations between Constance and Brie lately that most men, evidently, expected something other than just plain intercourse. Banton had never asked, but I'd wondered.

"Oh, you excited me plenty, Andie." He stroked my cheek with his fingers, and then tucked a stray strand of hair behind my ear.

"But," I began.

"Hey. It's your birthday. I can wait a day or two," he sighed, kissing me on the forehead.

I was so in love with him. And I was suddenly, uncharacteristically brave. I grinned up at him slowly as I grabbed the back of his briefs, pulling them down when I cupped his buttocks. I felt the muscles tighten as his passion flexed against me.

"Chandler, what are you doing?"

"Isn't it obvious," I whispered against his chest. I squirmed under him, working my way down his abs.

He moved to the side, taking most of his body weight off me as he grasped my head in his hands, pulling me back up to his face.

"Chandler, no. You don't have to do this," he murmured, shaking his head at me. "Just because I…"

"But what if I want to?" I asked huskily. *Could I do this?* My heart pounded in my chest so loudly, I was sure he could hear it.

His eyes widened at my question. He considered me for a moment, and then shook his head slowly.

My heart sank. He didn't want me to. I felt ashamed, my face immediately heating back to crimson in point two seconds.

"Chandler, please…I hadn't even considered you would. I…you have to know I want you to. I'd have to be crazy not to. But I'm not sure you are ready for that. Are you? You don't know do you?" he asked softly, searching my eyes.

"Yes, I think I do," I whispered as I glanced shyly back up at him.

304

"No, Chandler. When I know you are ready, then fine. Not until then. I don't want you to do anything you aren't ready for."

"Why? What are you worried about?' I asked. "Is it still my age? Because I just turned another year older, mister!" I exclaimed.

"No, sweetheart." He shook his head, and he was serious. He reached up, and cupped my cheek. "Sometimes, when I undress you, when there is too much light in the room, I see something in your eyes. It reminds me of the night we chased the peeping tom off. It was months before I stopped seeing that look in your eyes. Then when you were in the hospital, after the attack in the tunnels, I saw it again...a tortured, scared look that told me you felt vulnerable and violated. I will do anything in my power to keep that look out of your eyes. No, until I know you feel totally secure with yourself, with me...No."

I studied his face for several moments, and then lifted my lips to kiss him. He answered my lips, warm and soft, inviting me slowly as his tongue traced slowly along my lips, his breath mingling with mine.

My hands were still on his buttocks, and I slowly brought them around as my thumbs traced the V downward to his passionate response. His breath hitched as he pulled back to look down at me.

"Can I touch you?" I asked, amazed that it had never occurred to me. He nodded slowly, and I grasped him firmly as he flexed in my hand. I watched his eyes, and I could tell this was something both of us could handle. I began to massage him slowly, pulling...kneading...as he closed his eyes, his breath becoming shallow, more rapid. He pressed his hips into my hands, in rhythm with my palm and fingers as I stroked him.

I felt the muscles around his groin contract as he stiffened in my hands. Moaning softly, he buried his face in my hair.

"You are amazing," he whispered against my hair.

I giggled, pleased with myself. I felt so much better knowing I'd made him as happy as he'd made me.

"And you have totally distracted me from my job," he reprimanded me sternly. I looked up at him with a cocked eyebrow.

"Your job? Oh, you finished that quite satisfactorily," I replied playfully, slapping his bare behind.

"No, not that job." He laughed, and the sound was so carefree, I smiled at him. A totally ear-splitting smile that lit his world. I was so happy. I'd never felt closer to him, more intimate, than in this moment.

"No, I'm talking about your massage. I have two more products to go," he motioned to the tray beside the bed, and the unopened bottles there. "And my intention was to massage your body until you fell asleep under my hands. I see, to my distress, that you are wide awake, Mrs. Gastaneau."

I tried a full-blown pout, and failed miserably as he smirked at me.

"Okay, you win. No one is stopping you," I taunted him as I opened my arms wide. He looked down at my stomach, where the remains of my escapade were apparent.

"Oh," I pursed my lips as he reached for one of the towels stacked on the nightstand. He gently cleaned me up and then threw the towel in the corner.

"Now as I was saying, I have a job to finish. Turn please," he ordered, twisting his index finger in the air indicating that he wanted me to lie face down. I complied with a sigh. He leaned over me and selected another bottle from the table. He continued his slow, gentle massage until I was almost asleep. Then I felt his hands, suddenly cool, kneading and working the lotion into my skin. As I continued to drift, lost in the beautiful music and the heavenly scent of the lotion mixed with Banton's cologne, I felt the bed dip with his weight. His breath on my neck was warm as he nuzzled close to me.

"Do you need the heating pad?"

"No, just you," I whispered as he pulled me in close to his body, his hands pulling my abdomen close as he continued to rub it gently. I fell asleep, completely relaxed, and completely and hopelessly in love with this beautiful man beside me.

Chapter Twenty-Two

I woke with a gasp of air. I turned to find Banton asleep. The moonlight highlighted his beautiful face as he lay peacefully dreaming. Something woke me. I listened intently for the babies, thinking maybe they were crying in the house. The only sounds intruding into our little piece of heaven were the dying embers in the fireplace just outside the open French doors, and the whispering of the Spanish moss swaying in the trees overhead.

I relaxed, easing back into the mountain of pillows around us. I must have been dreaming. As I took a deep breath, my nerves sprang into action. I could smell the rotting smell of Orcos.

"Banton…Banton, wake up," I pushed against his bare chest as his eyes sprang open. "Banton, can you smell it?"

He sat up, concerned as he studied me in the darkness.

"What is it, Chandler?"

"I could smell them. Do you?" I took in another deep breath, but I couldn't smell them now.

"What, Chandler? What is it…did you have a nightmare?" he asked as he stroked my cheek with the back of his hand.

"No, something woke me. I smelled Orcos," I said, looking around.

Banton bolted from the bed and grabbed his jeans. Sliding them on hurriedly, he flung my robe at me. "Get dressed, I'm going to check outside," he whispered, moving toward the curtains across the French doors.

I scrambled to put the gown and robe on, and then tied the ties on the belt as I dashed across the stone floor to follow him. Once outside we searched the yard, stopping to smell the breeze blowing gently from the south.

He turned to me and pulled me into his arms.

"I'm sorry, Banton. I guess my imagination is running away with me. It's an old habit," I murmured. He pulled me away and shook his head.

"No, Andie. I caught a scent too, but only for a brief moment and then it was gone. Maybe a rogue, out for a nightly run…a coincidence, I'm sure." He looked down at me, rubbing my arms for reassurance. He glanced down at his watch.

"It's five forty-five. The sun will be up soon," he whispered as he leaned over to place a kiss on top of my head.

"Last night was wonderful, Banton. It was magical," I said as I gazed up at him. "Thank you for my birthday present."

"You are entirely welcome. I just wish I could have finished that massage completely," he teased with a twinkle in his eye.

"Rain check, then? We'll be back from N'awlins in a little over five days," I grinned up at him.

"Oh, yes. Definitely. Let's go out and make sure all the candles are out, and I'll lock up the pool house. The babies should be up soon," he said, pulling me toward the greenhouse.

After we'd secured everything and I'd gathered our clothes up from the previous evening, we headed back into the house. As we started up the back steps, Banton swept me up into his arms and carried me through the back door.

"Well, if it isn't the lovebirds," Everett chirped. Miss Astrid turned to gawk at us.

Banton chuckled. "Ev, you're up awfully early. What gives?"

"What do you mean, up early? I never go to bed, remember? I just thought I'd stay and help Constance and Ty out, if they needed me. Miss Astrid and I were just getting the bottles ready for our sweet little Matty and Elly."

As if on cue, the sound of both babies' wails rang out from upstairs.

"Come on, let's get them before they wake Constance and Ty," Banton said as he dashed for the stairs. I hurried after him, racing up the staircase right behind him. As we burst into the nursery, we both stopped dead in our tracks. Both babies stood at the foot of each crib, clutching the edge as they teetered on their feet.

"They're standing! Banton, they're too young for this!" I exclaimed. He turned and gave me an incredulous look.

Banton moved to pick up Matty as I turned to get Elly. When I approached her crib, she turned loose and held both arms up to me. I grabbed her up in my arms, and watched as her little eyes glowed with the turquoise flecks that I'd come to expect whenever she was hungry. I turned back to Banton and exclaimed, "Turquoise is now my favorite color in the whole world."

He nodded at me with moisture brimming in his eyes. "Yes, next to velvety brown," he murmured as he placed his forehead against mine, "Turquoise would definitely be my next favorite."

We both took a rocker, settling down with the twins and giving them their morning bottles. As we rocked, I savored the moment…breathing deeply, taking in their sweet baby scents mixed with my lotion and Banton's clean, earthy smell…I was making a memory. Both babies held their hands up, touching our faces as we talked baby-talk to them. I became aware that we had an audience.

"Wow, this is a Norman Rockwell painting," Constance giggled, leaning against the door facing. "Good, you're up. Now I can go back to sleep and catch another two hours," she yawned as she turned to go back to her and Ty's room.

"Oh, no you don't, we're going running in exactly forty-five minutes, then time to pack for our trip to Claudia's," I corrected her as she rolled her eyes at me.

"I'm going back to bed. If you want to run, come and roll me out then," she called out in a big yawn.

"Chandler, I bet Ev will watch the babies if you want me to run with you?" Banton offered.

"Well, I don't know. Constance and I run a pretty consistent pace. You might not be able to keep up," I teased. He narrowed his eyes.

"You're on, Miss Collins," he challenged as I glared at him.

"Miss Collins? Did I get demoted?"

"Only until you prove you can run like a Gastaneau," he mocked me as I looked back down at Elly. She must have sensed my mood. She dropped the nearly empty nipple from the corner of her mouth and grinned at me, drawing her breath in and cackling.

"See, even your daughter is on my side," he challenged further, his eyes sparkling.

"Okay, hot-shot…you're on. I'll change her diaper and take her down to Ev. You'd better hurry. I'll meet you on the front porch in fifteen."

"You're on Miss Collins," he took the challenge, removing the empty bottle from Matty's mouth.

He battled to get Matty to burp as I quickly changed Ellyson's diaper. I dashed in the bedroom with Elly and placed her in the center of the bed as I dug out a pair of spandex running pants and sports bra. After I located my running shoes, I found Ellyson playing with her toes in the air, giggling as she caught her feet. I scooped her up in a hug, and silently wished we had some of those strollers you could run with. I hurried down the staircase and called breathlessly out to Everett.

"Bebe, what are you doing?' he called out as he came down the hallway from the kitchen.

"Banton has challenged me to a little run this morning…will you watch the twins for me?"

"Mais oui, Ma Cherie! This is my favorite time of day with them; they're so playful after their morning bottle. Just be sure you're back before doody-time, or I might have to wake poor Constance and Ty. I don't do diapers," he wrinkled his nose as I laughed.

I handed him Elly, and he immediately smothered her face in kisses as she collapsed into a fit of baby giggles. I smiled watching him. I couldn't believe I so readily handed my precious daughter to a vampire. A vampire who I couldn't imagine my life without…my best friend.

As I heard Banton start down the stairs, I flashed a grin at Everett and dashed out the front door. Just as I finished stretching the right side of my body, Banton flung the front screen door open.

"Ready?" he asked excitedly.

I didn't answer. I just streaked toward the road. I could hear Banton's feet as he followed closely behind me, so I picked up the pace. I had no idea how fast we were running; I just knew that once daylight was upon us, we would have to slow down or we would draw a news crew to see the couple speeding like a locomotive down Rue Dauphine. After a few miles, I turned to find Banton struggling to keep up.

I slowed, allowing him to draw along beside me.

"Too much for you," I asked as he glared at me.

"Chandler, you've got to be kidding. There is no way you are that much faster than me," he exclaimed as we reached the end of the road, turning on a wider avenue that had wide sidewalks. We took to the bicycle path along the sidewalk and slowed our pace.

"How about a race?" he challenged.

"Banton, this isn't about winning," I said, trying to catch my breath. I had to admit, the running was exhilarating. This is what I'd needed for my nerves and the post-pregnant hormone changes.

"Stop here. Rest a minute," he urged as he placed his hands on his hips, taking in big gulps of air. "Do you see the four-way stop ahead, about one and a quarter miles up the road, with the flashing light? Race me to that corner. Give it all you have, don't hold back."

I nodded and grinned at him.

"Okay, now...on three. One, two...three!" he yelled when we both bolted forward.

I streaked along as fast as my legs would carry me. Never looking back, I pushed on, pumping my arms in rhythm just as my track coach in high school had taught me. I was amazed...my breathing wasn't even shallow. Soon, it seemed as though if I thought about my legs, they would tangle up. I just focused on the stop sign, and found myself there in record time. I paused, shaking my legs out, and then turned to find Banton about a half block behind me. I smiled at him smugly as he pulled up beside me, winded.

"Chandler Ann, how did you do that?" he asked breathlessly.

"I...I really don't know. It's just easy. I could never do that in high school. I was never fast. It's like I don't even have to will my legs to move, they just do," I explained. He shook his head.

"Why were you holding back?" I asked.

"Chandler, I wasn't. I gave it my all. I couldn't catch you. That's amazing," he whispered as he pulled me in to his sweaty torso and kissed me deeply. My heart raced right there on the street corner.

"Come on, let's jog back. I don't want to stay gone too long, with the smell we noticed this morning," he urged as I nodded.

311

We jogged back at a leisurely pace for a couple of Sange-Mele. I was sure it was quite fast to the casual observer. In less than ten minutes, we were back in our yard.

Constance and Ty were waiting for us on the front porch swing.

"I thought we were going running," she pouted as we bounded up the stairs.

"Come on, babe. Race me for a change," Ty challenged. She grabbed his hand and they were off.

I took Constance's place on the porch swing, suddenly tired. Banton sat down beside me and pulled my feet over into his lap, unlacing my tennis shoes.

"Feel okay?" he asked, massaging my foot.

"I feel fine. Why?"

"No cramping today?" he asked as he looked up at me.

"A little, but exercise helps. I'll be fine after today."

"Well, why don't we go and take a shower and then I'll treat you to a little rubdown, if you'll return the favor," he grinned impishly. "Then we'll finish packing. I thought we'd go on to Claudia's tonight, if you'd like."

"Banton, I'd love to. You read my mind." He pulled me over into his lap. Sweeping me up in his arms, he whisked me into the house and up the staircase as I heard Everett chuckling from the living room.

* * *

After our shower and rub-downs, we returned downstairs to find Everett, Constance and Ty totally enthralled by the twins.

"Chandler, did you know they're pulling up already? Watch Ellyson," she exclaimed, placing her beside the coffee table. Elly immediately reached out and grasped the edge of the table and pulled one knee under her. She then moved her wobbly other knee up, then one foot, then the other. As soon as she was standing, she looked around the room for approval. Everyone burst into applause, and she let go, plopping down on her padded backside and giggling.

312

"I could watch them all morning, Bebe! Whatever did we do for entertainment before you brought these two darlings into the world?" Ev declared. Miss Astrid smiled at him.

"We watched you, Fruit-Loop," Ty teased as everyone laughed.

"Well, I think I'll take them upstairs and give them their bath," I said as I scooped both of them up and started up the stairs. Banton soon followed and took Elly from me as he kissed my neck.

"Let me help, I'm never here when you do this," he said, grinning at me.

I ran our tub about a third of the way full of water, and then Banton stripped the twins naked while I placed both of them in the tub. They sat and splashed as Banton added bubbles to the water. We both took a small washcloth and soaped them while they played together in the water, giggling as they splashed each other and then Banton and me. Beau nudged the door to the bathroom open, not wanting to be left out of the fun. He hung his head over the side of the tub and lapped at the water as the babies giggled. I scolded him as he tried to lick the water from their faces. I glanced up at Banton, and he was serious, staring at me as I rinsed the soap from Elly's hair.

"What is it?"

He shook his head, leaned over and placed a soft kiss on my lips. Pulling back, he murmured, "I just love them so much. I can't imagine my life without them. To think only a year ago, I was just falling in love with you, and now I have all three of you," he said in amazement.

I just nodded, choked up. We finished their bath, and then wrapped them in towels as we carried them back into the bedroom. By the time we had both of them dressed for the day, they'd fallen fast asleep on the bed. Banton carried them back into the nursery and placed them in their cribs as I finished packing for our trip to Claudia's.

* * *

"Man, it sure is more of a production to load the car for a trip

313

than when it was just you and me," Banton stated, turning to look at the babies. Beau answered him with a big slobbering kiss right across his mouth. Beau had positioned himself in the seat right between the babies where he could watch over them. He'd proven to be protective of the babies, just as I'd known he would be.

After wiping Beau's slobber off his face, Banton got us on the road. As always, the miles seemed to fly by. We talked the entire way to Claudia and Will's.

"Everything has been so quiet since you've been back. Do you think Dante and Lucien have given up?"

He sighed as he checked the rear-view mirror, and then turned back to study my reaction.

"I think we hit them hard enough here, and then in Somalia, that they're having trouble regrouping. But make no mistake, they will regroup. They won't give up. I just wish I knew why."

"I know why, at least why Lucien is so obsessed."

He snapped his head toward me. "What do you know, Chandler?"

"Everett told me a story while you were missing. It has to do with his past," I began as he drew his brows together in a frown.

"It has to do with Everett?"

"Actually, Everett's father. He was a human and was bitten and transformed before he and Everett's mother were married. You remember Mr. George, Grandmother Wellington's butler?"

"Yes, Ev told us he raised him."

"Well, he is an Aldon, and he and a group of Sange-Mele found Everett's father in the swamp after he transformed and helped him gain control. He and Everett's mother were married, and they had Ev's sister and Everett. Then one day, two boys broke in on Everett's family. They raped his mother and sister. Everett saw part of it. He was only about seven. He blamed himself for not fighting them."

"He was a little boy. There's nothing he could have done."

"His father went on a rampage and attacked the boys and their family and left them for dead. Only the two boys didn't die, they transformed. One of those boys was Lucien," I finished as Banton's eyes widened.

314

"So Lucien has this vendetta against Everett because Everett's father is the one who transformed them?"

"Yes, and then years later Lucien and his brother killed Marie-Claire. Everett chased them and killed Lucien's brother. He said the brother was the only one that Lucien cared about. He vowed to hurt anyone close to Everett," I finished.

"But that still doesn't explain Dante's obsession." Banton said as he took my hand in his.

"Banton, do you think the scent we picked up last night means more trouble?" I asked.

"It was faint, Chandler. It was most probably random. We'll just have to keep our guard up."

I nodded. I'd been feeling for weeks like we were being watched, but had decided I was just paranoid.

As we drove into their driveway for the first time, I decided the only word that described Claudia and Will's new home was elegant. It was new construction, built on a site in an older district which had been cleared of old structures, keeping the trees intact. The house was Greek revival, with massive columns across the front porch, and floor to ceiling windows across the entire front that opened like French doors. The wide front porch was dripping with enormous baskets of southern ferns. Ava Grace was the first out the front door when she spotted our SUV in the driveway.

"An Andler! Unca Banin! Where's Aba's babies?" she babbled, meeting us at the car.

"Come here Doodle-Bug and let Uncle Banton get a look at you! I thought I told you to quit growin'," he teased her as he picked her up and swung her around.

"How do you wike my haw-ouse" she asked in her little southern-girl drawl.

"It's beautiful, Doodle-Bug, just like you!" he exclaimed as he tickled her, causing her to collapse into a fit of giggles.

Claudia and Will hurried down the steps to greet us.

"Chandler, you look great! I swear you are smaller than you were before you got pregnant! How did you lose so much weight so quickly?" Claudia asked, hugging me.

"I really didn't even have to try. I guess it's trying to keep up with both of them," I motioned to the back as Banton and Will took the babies out of the backseat. Finally having been unblocked from unloading, Beau bounded out and ran around to greet Ava. She giggled as he licked her face in his usual greeting.

"Ava, you are going to have to give Beau a little attention! He needs some serious fetch time," Banton assured her. She ran inside to find a ball for him. After we were seated in the living room, Banton and Will unloaded the car as Claudia and I took the babies out of their car seats.

"I can't wait for you to see the babies' room! I have it all ready, and I have two cribs already set up for you," she gushed, cradling Elly and cooing to her.

"You didn't have to go to all that trouble. We brought their pack-n-plays," I offered.

"Don't be silly. I loved doing it, and Ava and I had so much fun decorating it! I just hope we will be able to use it for something more than a guest nursery for these two," she lamented, kissing Elly on the forehead.

I knew even though they had been lucky enough to adopt Ava, she still longed for another baby. As I watched her, I could see the pure joy in her eyes as she cradled Ellyson to her. I spread a blanket out on the floor and placed Matty down on his back. He immediately threw one little leg in the air, and twisted his little body until he rolled over and pushed up to look at his Aunt Claudia.

"Chandler! When did he start doing that! Isn't it a little too early?" I nodded as Banton and Will came back into the room.

"They just started a few days ago, and they both started pulling up this morning. Everett says it's normal for Aldon babies to develop their motor skills faster than humans," I stated as Banton sat down beside me. "And I will warn you, Ellyson and Matty have started the glow thing with her eyes."

"Already? Well, they're growing much too fast! You are just going to have to come and stay with us more often!" she exclaimed as Will sat down beside her on the other sofa.

"So where are the others?" Will asked.

"Ty and Constance are riding down with John and Brie, and they should be here any time," Banton replied.

"Everett is already in N'awlins. He came by earlier this afternoon, and he's called me twice! I'm supposed to deliver you, Constance and Brie to his grandmother's house about three o'clock tomorrow afternoon for tea and baby celebration," Claudia informed me as Banton chuckled.

"This should be the baby shower of the century," he said "My mother called me to see if we'd left this morning, and said she and Julia are meeting y'all there tomorrow afternoon," Banton added.

"Well, we have dinner all planned tonight. I have a friend who just opened a steakhouse in the quarter, and he is sending over some catered food for us tonight. I invited Everett, Mrs. Elaine, Mr. Matt and Julia. I hope y'all don't mind," Will said. I shook my head.

"William, I miss my family so much. I love being around yours. I could never get enough," I assured him as Banton put his arm around me.

"Chandler Ann, you are family. Don't ever forget that," Claudia said as there was a knock at the door.

"I wiwl get it, Mommy! Wet me," Ava Grace called out as she raced down the hallway, Beau close on her heels. We all laughed as she swung the door open to find Constance, Ty, John and Brie.

Ava never opened the screen door; she just bounced into the living room, announcing, "An 'Stance and An Briew awre hewe! They awre hewe, Mommy!"

Will moved to let them in. "She gets so excited, she forgets to open the door," he explained as Constance laughed.

"Come here, Doodle-Bug, and let me see you! I swear you've grown a foot!"

Ava comically sat down in the floor, raising both her feet in the air at Constance. "An Stance, I jus hab two...see, one...two," she counted, flipped them up in the air at Constance. Constance giggled and pulled her up out of the floor into her arms.

"I just meant you are growing so tall," she corrected as they came into the living room with us.

"An Stance, I hab a twampoween in the yard...wiwl you jump wif Aba?" she asked.

"I'd love to, Ava! Come, show me your trampoline!" she exclaimed, taking Ty by the hand. They switched Ava between

317

them and swung her back and forth in the air as they made their way through the house.

"So how was your trip?" Claudia asked. Brie sat down beside her.

"Exhausting! Those two never stop fighting. I swear Diva-doll is going to implode before this wedding ever gets off the ground," John exclaimed.

"It's funny, I had Diva pegged as the over-the-top twenty-thousand dollar gown type of girl, not the get married barefoot on the beach type," he commented as he shook his head.

"She's changed. I think she's tired of all the drama and all we've been through. She's just in love and wants to be married," I said as Elly crawled away from me toward Matty.

"So, what's our plan for tonight?" John asked, sinking down in a chair across from us.

"Just relax, and play with the kids. Will is having dinner brought in. Since you all have a meeting at the base in the morning, we'll hang out here, and then go to the baby shower. We'll all meet up here afterward. Will has tomorrow night's meal covered too," Claudia commented as she slid off in the floor and crawled around the coffee table to chase Matty. Matty sat up, and then peeked around the table leg at Elly. Elly cackled, seeming to catch on to his game of "hide and seek." I jumped up and hid behind the other side of the chair, and then popped out at her as I called "peek-a-boo!"

Ellyson cackled again, and as I watched her, everyone gasped. Her skin became translucent, almost see-through…as if she were fading!"

"Holy shit! What is going on?' John exclaimed. Banton turned to look, and he blanched as he looked quickly at me.

"Chandler?"

"I don't…I don't know! I've never seen her do it before. She almost looks like she did in the hospital when they were giving her transfusions."

As we watched her, she grinned at us, and then became so translucent she almost disappeared. I watched, horrified as her color faded. No one said anything for several moments, and then

Matty laughed at her. She turned, her color fading back to normal as she mumbled in a sort of baby garble, "Boo!"

I grabbed my purse and dug my phone out. Everyone else in the room sat motionless, not believing what they'd just seen. I dialed Everett's number, and he answered on the first ring.

"Bebe, what is it? What's happened?"

"Ev, it's Elly. Where are you?' I asked frantically.

"I'm at Grandmother Wellington's."

"Are you coming over here?" I asked.

"Just about to leave. Bebe, what is wrong?" he asked intuitively.

"Ellyson. Everett, if I didn't know any better…I'd say she just faded like an Orco," I whispered as Banton snapped his head up to look at me.

"I'll be right there," Ev answered before hanging up.

Banton stood and scooped Ellyson up, cuddling her close to his chest as he searched my eyes.

"Everett is on his way over," I whispered.

Brie leaned forward and said softly, "Chandler, many times when Patrick and Olivia would come to the safe house to work with me, they called you a fader. Do you think that is what they meant?"

"I…I don't know," I answered shakily, looking down at Matty. He pulled up on my pants leg and I leaned down to pick him up.

"What's going on? You all look like you've just seen a ghost," Constance joked as she and Ty came back in with Ava Grace.

"We did. You just missed the show," John said. Constance cocked an eyebrow at him. He proceeded to explain what had just happened with Elly as Banton came over and knelt in front of me.

"Chandler, baby, everything is going to be okay. I'm sure there is a simple explanation for this. Do you want me to call Renault?" Banton asked softly. Everyone began talking at once in the background.

I nodded at him as I placed a kiss on Matty's head. Banton handed Elly down to Claudia and then pulled his cell out and walked into the other room to call Dr. Renault.

Amid all the confusion, Will's friend arrived with our dinner, so he and John left the room to go and place everything out in the kitchen. As everyone calmed down, they all left the living room and wandered back to the kitchen to eat. Banton came back to the living room and sat down with me on the sofa.

I changed Matty's diaper methodically, going over the earlier events in my head. Elly lay beside Matty on the couch, smiling at him and playing with her toes like a normal three month old. As I watched them, my heart was beating so hard I was sure it was about to launch itself out of my chest.

"Chandler, I can hear your heartbeat. Everything is going to be all right, calm down," Banton said softly, bending over to pick Elly up from Claudia and then sitting down next to me. I finished dressing Matty and then pulled him to my chest. As we watched them, Matty held his hand out to Elly, and Elly leaned her face out to him, almost in a sort of silent communication. Banton and I watched them, mesmerized.

"I'm terrified, Banton. My children have issues I can't even begin to understand. They're not even three months old, and they already silently communicate with each other. Now one of them can fade. How am I supposed to…what if she…Banton, I can't do this!" I broke down in sobs.

"God, Chandler…come here." He pulled me into the safety of his arms, holding me and the babies. He stroked my hair as he murmured, "Don't think for one minute you are alone in this. I'm here, and we'll handle this. You and me…and Everett, and Constance, and Claudia, and Brie…thank God we've got the support system that we do. Everything is going to be fine," he continued to assure me as the doorbell rang.

I wiped my eyes, glancing up at him. "That will be Everett."

As Banton pulled away, Will moved into the entry to open the front door.

"Hey, Everett. We're sure glad to see you," Will welcomed him with a warm hug.

"Whatever is going on now?" Everett came into the living room and hurried over to kneel in front of me. He reached up and wiped a tear from under my eye.

"Everett, I don't even think I can describe it to you. You have to see it for yourself," I shook my head as he studied me.

"Ev, can all Aldon babies fade?" Banton asked. Everett looked back and forth at us, and then down at Elly.

"Fade? You mean like those Orcos we fought in your house?" I nodded.

"No. I don't know any Aldon who can fade. That's why Dr. Renault was doing all the research on the Orcos the Seals killed here when they were on that first mission. We'd never seen it before."

I had a sick feeling, the bile beginning to rise in my throat. "Do you think Elly can fade because one of them bit me while I was pregnant?" I almost choked on the words.

"Oh, Bebe. I don't know. Have you called Dr. Renault?"

"I just got off the phone with him. He's on his way over here now," Banton replied.

Everett reached up and rubbed my leg, sensing how upset I was. "Bebe, how exactly did she do it? Did she fade completely, or was it subtle?"

"I would say completely," Banton answered.

"Put them back in the floor like before," I suggested to Banton. We placed the twins in the floor again, and I hid behind the chair and popped my head out at Matty like I'd done when Elly faded. Matty immediately giggled, crawling toward me. Elly sat watching quietly. I popped out a couple more times, Matty giggling louder each time. He then crawled back toward Elly, reaching out to her. She leaned over and lay down in the floor, her face flat on the carpet as she watched him. Just when I thought she wasn't going to play, she began to fade again. Only this time, she faded completely, blending in with the rug. All you could see was her outline.

"Sweet Jesus!" Everett breathed out as he shot a worried glance at me. Banton called out softly, "Ellyson Marie…where are you?"

She giggled, but didn't fade back in. I began to cry silently.

"Ellyson Marie, Daddy can't see you. Where are you," Banton said in a sterner voice. The outline of Elly's form pushed up, and then began to fade back into form. I took a deep breath as I looked over at Banton.

"What are we going to do?" I said, the tears threatening again.

Everett sat down beside me as Banton picked Elly up out of the floor. Elly looked at Banton warily, pulling away from him slightly. It occurred to me he'd never talked sternly to either one of the twins before. He must have realized her reaction was from his tone, too. He pulled her into his chest and kissed the top of her head.

"You're okay, baby girl. Daddy's not mad at you, sweetheart. Daddy loves you so much," he cuddled her.

"Oh, sweet Bebe…everything is going to be okay. Please, don't cry. Everything will be fine, yeah." Everett said, hugging me close.

"Banton, the food is out in the kitchen, and everyone else is almost finished. Why don't you and Chandler go in and eat, and Brie and I will stay here with the twins," John offered softly as I shook my head.

"Not right now, John. I'm not hungry."

"Chandler, come on. You need to eat, and the twins are fine," Banton urged. I looked up at him and shook my head again. I was so upset and nauseated that there was no way I could eat.

"It's time to feed the babies and get them down. I think I'll take them up," I said, rising.

"Chandler, let me help you," Brie offered as she came around John. When she picked Matty up I took Elly and started for the stairs.

"Sweetheart, I'll fix their formula, and I'll bring it up to you," Banton offered, kissing me on the forehead when I passed him.

Claudia came through the foyer from the back of the house. "Chandler, I'll show you to the nursery," she offered, taking the stairs in front of us.

After we had everything laid out, Brie helped me undress the twins and put them in the tub. Even in my state of distress, I wondered at the beautiful nursery suite that Will and Claudia had built. It had an en suite Jack and Jill bathroom, with a tiny, half-size tub that had an indention with a small seat, so an adult could sit against the tub and easily lean over to wash the babies. Each

322

end of the tub was reclined much like a baby bath-tub, and was covered with a removable pad sort of like Velcro fabric.

As we watched the twins play and splash, Brie took me in her arms.

"Andie, it's going to be okay."

I nodded at her. "Thanks, Brie. I know. It's just hard. I find myself wishing we could have a normal life and that all I had to worry about was ear infections and chicken-pox. I catch myself feeling sorry for myself and for them. They will never have normal, will they?"

She nodded as she touched my cheek. "I don't even know what normal is anymore. I just try to look at my life, and thank God every morning for John…and for you and Everett," she whispered. I smiled at her.

"You do know how I feel, thank you," I murmured as Banton cleared his throat behind us.

"Andie, Dr. Renault is here, if you are ready to get them out," he said.

Brie helped me dry the twins off and dress them on the elaborate changing tables built into the bathroom. When we had them dressed, we took them back into the nursery where Dr. Renault and Everett waited with Banton.

"Well, I must say this is the most beautiful nursery I've ever been in," Dr. Renault commented as I nodded. "Now, let's see about these two little ones," he said as he examined Elly first, then Matty. He checked their vital signs, examined them physically, drew blood, and made notes on his laptop. After he'd done everything he could without more equipment, he turned to me.

"Chandler, can you describe exactly what happened when she faded?"

I relayed the events as best as I could, with Banton and Everett joining in. After we'd explained everything, Dr. Renault considered Elly for a moment.

"Do you think you could get her to do it again?" he asked.

"We can try," I replied, lifting her from her crib. Banton picked Matty up, and we placed both of them in the floor. Banton got on his hands and knees and I did the same. We tried several times, but even as Matty immediately joined in our game of hide-

and-seek, Elly just watched silently, eventually laying her head over on the carpet and placing her thumb in her mouth. Banton tried to engage her, but her eyes widened and she shook her head at him, telling him she didn't want to play.

"I think Banton's reaction earlier when he talked to her sternly made her think he was angry with her. She sensed she might be in trouble for fading, and now she is reluctant to," Everett observed as I nodded.

"Yes, I think that might be it," I agreed as Banton looked at me curiously.

"Well, I can take your word for what happened. I believe you. I'm at a loss, kids, so I'm going to confer with some of my colleagues and with the pediatrician who helped me with them before. In light of this newest development, I'm sure you are more apprehensive than ever about their development. You will need to keep them sheltered until we get a handle on this."

I nodded. I'd already been thinking about having to keep them from public view.

"There is one more thing," he began as he looked over at Everett. "I know your circle of acquaintances in the Aldon world is small, but you need to keep this latest development to yourselves. Your children put our privacy in great jeopardy, and this is new territory. We don't want to raise any alarms that might cause a stir with the Aldon, Orcos, or the Navy. Let's keep this quiet, and keep the twins low-key," he warned as a new fear gripped my heart.

"We will, Doc. Thank you for coming out."

"You're welcome, son. Take care of them. I've grown quite fond of your little family. I'll be in touch," Dr. Renault said, placing his hand on my shoulder as he left the room.

Voices drifted up the staircase as Banton's parents and Julia arrived. I looked at Banton. I was exhausted and emotionally drained from the events of the last two hours.

He sensed my thoughts as usual. "Why don't I go down and explain things to Mother and Daddy, while you and Brie feed the babies. Mother will want to see them, so she can come up and kiss them goodnight. You don't have to come down tonight. Everyone will understand," he said as he kissed me on the forehead. He

324

handed me their bottles, and then closed the nursery door behind him.

"Brie, do you mind helping me feed them?' I asked her. She shot me an incredulous look.

"Are you kidding? Some nights, I want to walk down to your house and offer to help. I love this so much. I just don't want to intrude all the time," she said, a sparkle in her eye. I nodded at her as I picked Elly up out of the floor, and then took a rocker as Brie settled into the other with Matty. After we'd fed them, they drifted off so we placed them gently in their cribs.

"I'm going to go back downstairs with John. Andie, please call down if you need me. I love you, darlin'," she whispered as she hugged me close.

"Thank you so much, Brie. I love you too. Remember when I said I'd be calling in all those favors?" I reminded her of our conversations after she'd transformed.

"Yeah, and I'll even change dirty diapers," she called back as she left the nursery. I looked down at my sleeping babies, both of them on their backs, Elly with her thumb in her mouth, Matty making sucking noises in his sleep. I was so unhinged by Elly's episode I was hesitant to leave them. I wanted so badly to take them in our room and let them sleep with us, but then I thought, *it's you who's upset, not the babies.* I looked up, realizing for the first time that there was a door between the nursery and our room, connecting the two. I went over and opened it and sighed. I got ready for bed, taking my makeup off and then donning my nightgown. As I climbed into bed, there was a soft knock at the door.

"Chandler, dear, are you awake?' Mrs. Elaine whispered.

"Yes, I'm still up. Come in, please," I answered, grabbing my robe from the foot of the bed.

She slipped in and crossed the room to hug me.

"Banton explained to us what happened with Ellyson tonight. I didn't want to bother you. I know you are tired. I just wanted to kiss you and the babies goodnight," she said hopefully.

"Of course. I hope everyone's not upset with me. I just needed some alone time with them, to get them down."

"No need for explanations. You have been through so much, sweetheart. I'll just go take a quick peek," she said. I nodded and motioned for her to go into the nursery. She tiptoed in and looked down lovingly at Elly.

"Go ahead, they won't wake. They're such good sleepers," I said as she nodded. She bent over the side of the crib, placing a kiss on Elly's forehead and then moving to Matty. After she tucked his little blanket around his shoulders, she made her way back over to me.

"Get some sleep. We'll see you at the shower tomorrow afternoon and catch up then," she said as she kissed my cheek. After she left, I crawled into the bed and snuggled down in the covers. My mind whirled with all that had transpired. I couldn't get a handle on what complications this new development with the twins would bring. It made my head hurt just trying to sort it all out.

*   *   *

The twins woke up around three a.m. and I managed to feed them and get them back down without waking Banton. I knew he needed to be rested for his meetings. He was up and dressed for the day before I even stirred. Before he left, he leaned over and woke me with a kiss.

"Mmm. My favorite wake-up call," I murmured as I turned over fully to look at him.

"You were sleeping so soundly I hated to wake you, but we're on our way to the base. We'll be there until around four or so, so we'll meet you girls back here this afternoon."

I smiled at him as I played with his collar, pulling him back down for another kiss. After thoroughly satisfying me, he pulled back with a grin.

"Are you still taking your medicine? Will you be all right, with me gone today?"

I nodded at him. "I'll be fine, Banton. You go ahead," I urged him.

326

"You can call me if you need me…if anything else happens with the twins," he added as I nodded. "I'm only thirty minutes away. And Ev promised he'll be with you all day," he finished as I pushed at his chest.

"You'd better go, before I pull you back in," I teased, batting my eyelashes at him.

Okay, okay…see you later, beautiful," he said as he left out the door.

Chapter Twenty-Three

Everett rang the doorbell to his Grandmother's grand entrance, proudly holding a twin in each arm. Claudia winked at me behind him as Mr. George opened the door and greeted us.

"Good afternoon, Mr. Everett. And who are these beautiful children you have here?"

"Mr. George, these little ones are the absolute loves of my life, Ellyson and Matthew Gastaneau."

"Well, they're surely the most beautiful children I've ever had the privilege to meet. Hello Mrs. Gastaneau, it is wonderful to see you again," he greeted me in his deep, elegant voice. He closed the door behind us.

"Mr. George, this is Banton's sister Claudia. She didn't get to come last time we were here," he introduced Claudia as Mr. George continued, "Your mother and grandmother are in the living room, and the rest of your guests have arrived," he ushered us in.

"And there they are…my precious babies! Come, come and let Grandmother Wellington see those darlings," she gushed as she held her hands out to Everett. He obediently handed Matty to Mrs. Wilhelmina, and then Elly to Mrs. Henrietta. Constance and Brie were seated on a sofa across from the older ladies, and Mrs. Elaine and Aunt Sue were seated on a loveseat by the massive fireplace. A low coffee table was placed in the center of the room, covered with gifts.

I walked over and kissed both ladies on the cheek. "Thank you so much for throwing this shower for the babies! It was so sweet of you." Everett ushered me over to a chair by the table.

"It is our pleasure, dear. We couldn't pass up an opportunity to visit with all of you. You are such a delight to have in our home. And these babies! I'm so in love!" Mrs. Henrietta hugged Elly to her as Elly smiled at her.

After the rest of the introductions were made and old acquaintances were renewed, Everett's grandmother got everyone's attention.

"Well, why don't we dispense with the formalities, let's just enjoy the afternoon. Mr. George, if you will just have them bring cake and refreshments to everyone in here, we'll let Chandler open her presents while we visit," she suggested as Mr. George left us. The twins were particularly active, so Constance and Julia placed them on a pallet on the floor so they could crawl around and play. After a few moments, Everett's grandmother could stand it no longer. She rose, hiked her skirt up, and crawled onto the pallet with the twins, much to the shock of Aunt Sue and Mrs. Elaine.

"I've just got to play with these babies. They just light up the house," she exclaimed. Everett rolled his eyes.

"And this one …he looks just like his tall, dark and dimpled daddy! Where is Mr. Gorgeous, by the way?" She winked at me as Mrs. Elaine choked on her wine.

I giggled at her, remembering the way she'd flirted with all the SEALs during our last visit.

"They are all at the base today at a meeting."

"Oh, that's a shame. I was hoping for another glimpse of all that muscle," she flipped her hand in the air and turned back to the twins. She made a face at Elly, and Elly giggled at her.

Mr. George came back into the room with a cart laden with assorted meats, cheeses and desserts. After everyone settled down with a plate, Mrs. Henrietta suggested that I open presents.

Julia sat down in the floor at my feet, and helped me list the baby gifts in a book that Everett presented. As the last of the gifts were opened, everyone relaxed with glasses of wine as the babies fell asleep on the pallet in the floor.

Everett sat next to me, studying his mother intently.

"Mother, what is that necklace you are wearing?" he asked as I turned to her.

"Oh…This is a family heirloom, something your father gave me. I'd forgotten I had it until recently. I found it when I was cleaning some things out, and I started wearing it again. I wore it often when you were a little boy, remember?"

"Yes, yes I do," he said as he rose and picked it up from where it rested on her neck. "Finally, the piece to the puzzle. Bebe, do you remember this?"

"What?" I swallowed the drink of wine I'd just taken, and looked around him to see the necklace in question. It was silver and gold mixed delicately with a Victorian flair…the symbol was hard to make out. On closer inspection, I gasped.

"Yes, I was wondering how long it was going to take you to notice," he commented wryly.

"Ev, that's the symbol from Mamma and Daddy's headstone," I exclaimed as Aunt Sue looked up.

"Everett, what are you talking about?" Everett's mother demanded.

"Mother, what is this symbol? What do you know about it?"

Mrs. Henrietta had an uncomfortable look on her face as she glanced at Everett's grandmother.

"Henri, I thought you'd put that thing away," Everett's grandmother admonished her.

"Mother, I've just been a bit nostalgic, that's all. It once symbolized a great sense of pride for our family," she began.

"That was soon tarnished by one we shall not speak of," Grandmother Wellington finished adamantly. As Constance engaged Ev's grandmother in a discussion about the artwork in the room, Ev turned back to his mother.

"Why don't we take Chandler out to shoot some pictures of the trees in the courtyard? She brought her camera for that purpose," Ev lied and gave me a sideways glance.

Catching on a little belatedly, I chimed in. "Oh, yes…please, if you don't mind."

I grabbed my camera out of the diaper bag, and then the three of us made our way through the grand house and out to the courtyard. Everett's mother took a place on a bench, and then pulled a throw that had been placed there around her shoulders, seeming chilled.

"Mother, I need to know about that symbol. What can you tell me about it? What does it have to do with my father?" he demanded as he sat down beside her and placed his hand in hers.

"It's been so long, Everett. I want to begin by saying I loved your father with all my heart and soul. He was a good man, even after he turned. It was one unfortunate circumstance which banished him from our lives forever."

"Mother, Chandler knows the story. I hope that you don't mind," he said as he stroked her cheek. She nodded at me and I smiled at her.

"It was a very long time ago, and time will heal wounds. But not a broken heart," she murmured as she placed her hand on Everett's cheek.

"Mother, what is the symbol?"

"It is the symbol of The Protectors."

"The Aldon?" Ev asked curiously.

"No, older than that. The first ones to fight the Orcos were humans…Sange-Mele. They banded together to fight the plagues of Orcos that came to the new world. As the Revolutionary War raged on, Aldon soon had to band with them. There were as many deaths around the battlefields from Orco attacks as there were casualties from battle. The Aldon were moved to action to help the Sange- Mele at the time. The movement continued after the war, and Aldon began to take a greater role in protecting humans. This symbol that I wear is from before the Revolutionary War…to identify one Sange-Mele to another.

"But my father was an Orco who fought to become an Aldon," Everett interrupted her.

"That's not entirely true. Your father was a Sange-Mele, and the first time he was bitten, he was bitten by an entire coven of Orcos. He almost died, and the venom was such that it almost completely transformed him. He began a crusade or sorts, after we were married, going out at night and fighting the Orcos that roamed the streets of N'awlins. In those days, there were many. The plagues that ravaged the countryside made humans easy targets. Your father, along with ten or so other Sange-Mele fighters and Aldon, cleaned up this city for a time. Your father was bitten so many times during his crusades that he eventually fully transformed. At first it was just the eyes…then came his fangs, and then finally, the venom."

I listened, fascinated. "So Dr. Renault and Dr. Lane were right. I have transformed more each time I've been bitten," I remarked as Ev studied me warily.

"Yes, I'm afraid that it is possible, my dear. Dr. Renault should know this, he knew your father at the time, although he

331

might not have known at the time that he was a Sange-Mele in the beginning," she offered.

"Mother, why would Chandler's parents have this mark on their headstone?" Everett asked as his mother shook her head.

"I don't know, but it isn't used lightly. And there are few beings left that would even know what it meant. If your parents left instructions to put it there, they must have wanted someone to ask questions about it."

"Chandler, your mother was Sange-Mele as is your Aunt Sue. Do you think she might have some family history?"

I shook my head. "She knew nothing about all of this until the night we told her. You revealed yourself to them, remember?"

"What about your father?"

I stared at him. It had never occurred to me that he might be Sange-Mele too.

"Do you have any relatives on that side of the family that might be able to shed some light on this?" Everett asked as Mrs. Henrietta patted my leg.

"No one I can think of. My father was an only child, and my grandparents passed years ago."

"Well, it sounds like we might have some genealogy research to do, Bebe, to satisfy your curiosity."

Everett's mother rose, and then embraced me. "My dear, please be careful. Everett has told me of your heightened abilities, and the fact that the babies seem to be fully transformed as well as faders. Everett's father spoke of faders, but I've never seen one. There seems to be a lot of buried history coming to light, and there might be complications to finding out too much," she cautioned.

"Oh, Mother...don't be so melodramatic," Everett scolded, embracing her.

"Everett, you've never taken any of this seriously. We've buried our heads in the sand far too long, and we might have to pay a price if too much comes to light," she said as she took my arm in hers.

"I'm so sorry, my dear, that you've become entangled in our world. But you are now a part of it, and you need to be careful. Find out what you can about your own family history, but be discrete about it," she warned.

We walked back into the house in silence. I was dying to know what was in all of the boxes in my dining room that I had yet to unpack. I knew that there were albums full of black and white photographs from my father's side of the family that I'd never even opened.

"Andie, where have you been?" Constance called out as giggles erupted from the living room. We walked back in to find Everett's Grandmother with a diaper on her head and pacifiers hanging from her ears. The babies crawled around the large round table in front of the sofas, seeming to chase her, first one way and then the other.

Julia grabbed Elly up in a hug as she teetered at the table, trying to stand up.

"Phew, somebody needs changing," she complained, holding her nose. Brie laughed and took her as I picked Matty up. After changing the babies in the powder room, we returned to find everyone loading the presents for us.

"My dears, I have enjoyed this afternoon immensely! Please, when you visit N'awlins again, bring these dear little ones to see me! They are such a joy," Mrs. Wilhelmina gushed as Mrs. Henrietta nodded.

"I will, I promise. Thank you so much for the party and for your lovely gifts! I can't wait to show Banton," I assured them as we walked out onto the lawn.

"And bring those dear, handsome SEALs next time. I missed seeing them."

"Okay, Grandmother, we will," Everett rolled his eyes as he kissed her on her cheek.

*　*　*

"Well, I have to say that was the most interesting baby shower I've ever been too! And I absolutely love Everett's mother and grandmother!" Claudia exclaimed as she checked her mirrors. I'd opted to take the twins and ride back with Claudia and Julia to Claudia's house.

"I'd forgotten that you didn't go with us when we came for Mardi Gras," I replied, turning to check the babies. Julia and Ava

Grace sat between them in the back seat, singing to them and laughing at their reactions.

"Chandler, I don't know how you get anything done with them around all day. I'd never be able to tear myself away from playing with them!" Julia exclaimed as Elly laughed at her – a long cackle followed by a squealing intake of air.

"An Andler, Ewwy waughs when she screams!" Ava Grace cackled, clapping her hands.

"She has the funniest little laugh. It amazes me how much they've changed in just a few weeks and how their little personalities are so developed!" Claudia added.

Upon entering the long driveway, we found none of the SEALs SUV's had returned.

"Mmmm…I'd hoped they would be back by now. I can't wait to show Banton all the things that everyone gave the twins," I observed. The familiar pangs of panic began to rear their ugly head. I took a deep breath. The anxiety medicine that Dr. Lane had prescribed for me was definitely wearing off after seven hours.

"It shouldn't be too long. Will texted me before we left Mrs. Wilhelmina's to let me know he was stopping for crawfish etouffee at our favorite restaurant, and that he would be right behind us. I've got some homemade bread rising. I love cooking in my new kitchen!"

"You should with the gourmet stove and sub-zero refrigerator," Julia teased as Claudia shot her a look.

"I'm having some fun. This is the first time that we've lived in the same city with our family, and Will is home most nights. I've found that I really do like the little wifey, Betty Crocker thing!" she retorted, putting the vehicle in park.

After we unloaded the twins, Julia and I carried them in their carriers into Claudia's sunny kitchen and breakfast nook off the large covered patio. We sat them down in the floor beside the window, and Ava Grace immediately settled down between them, continuing to sing the songs that she and Aunt Julia were singing in the car.

"Julia, would you watch the twins and Ava for a few minutes? I'd like to unload the gifts out of Claudia's car," I asked as she grinned and nodded.

"Of course…I'd love to."

As I stepped out the doorway onto the patio, the breeze shifted, and the rotting smell of Orco alerted me to danger. I froze. It had been months since I'd smelled the odor so strongly. The hair stood up on the back of my neck as I frantically searched the yard and drive for the creatures. As Claudia rounded the back of her SUV, a man appeared directly behind her. Before I could caution her, he had her firmly grasped around her chest, his teeth gleaming in the late afternoon sun.

I quickly came to my senses, my adrenalin beginning to pump. "Julia, grab the kids and lock your selves in an interior bathroom. Now! Call Banton on your cell," I commanded as I streaked across the yard. I could hear Ava's protests and the twins cry out when she did as she was told. The Orco holding Claudia smirked at me as I reached him, and as I pulled up to stop in front of them, he shifted his eyes over my shoulder.

I wasn't alone.

My skin prickled with apprehension when I felt hot breath blow on my shoulder. Claudia's eyes held a look of sheer terror, and as I searched frantically in my brain for some recourse, I swallowed the sick feeling that rose up inside. Every hair on my body was standing on end. Not only did the Orcos pose the immediate danger to Claudia and me, I knew that their ultimate goal might be the twins.

"Ah, the first touch of tender flesh after such a long separation," the voice I knew from the past sent revulsion through me. Lucien sucked his breath in as he raked his teeth down my bare shoulder.

"It's me you want, just take me and let her go," I whispered, not taking my eyes from Claudia.

Lucien laughed the deep, bone-chilling laugh that I hated. "No, not just you…and we've tried that bargain before. All I will promise is that if you cooperate, it might be painless for her and the others in the house," he offered as Claudia shook her head furiously at me.

Time stood still. I checked my peripheral vision to find two more Orcos creeping in on my right beside the vehicle, and one on my left beside the house…all of them slowly closing in on us. I was sadly outnumbered by two of them, much more so by five. It seemed hopeless. As badly as I wanted to help Claudia, my heart was torn into pieces wanting to retreat back to my children.

Oh, God...help me! What can I do? I was paralyzed with fear and indecision. Without warning, tires screeching in the driveway alerted the Orcos to the arrival of more of our party, and as they reacted, I had just enough time to lunge at the Orco holding Claudia. Adrenalin pumped into every part of my body and I hit him hard in his face with my fist, loosening his grip enough on Claudia that she pulled away from him for a split second. I dove at him, knocking us both into the driveway as I heard Constance's voice.

"Chandler, wait!"

A flash of turquoise fabric and red hair alerted me to Brie's presence as well. As I continued to fight the Orco in the driveway, Brie and Constance took on the other two. Claudia dove into the back of her SUV and slammed the door, just as Lucien rammed the back, caving it in toward her as we heard her scream.

As I listened to the melee around me, I could do nothing but strain against the Orco that held me down. His forearm crushed my throat as his teeth seemed to elongate, almost pulsing while they struggled to find my throat. Just when I thought he would cut my air supply, I managed to work my leg loose to knee him in the groin, buying enough time to push him off of me. I rammed his chin back with my hand, and as I heard it pop, another set of hands grabbed his arms and dragged him back away from me. Constance had managed to incapacitate the Orco that she'd been fighting, and had come to my aid. Evidently her working out with Ty had paid off, and I was wishing that I'd had a little more training. As I flipped over and held him down, she grabbed his arm and twisted, totally severing it at the shoulder and twisting the muscles and bone like a chicken leg. When he lay limp and lifeless, I realized that we'd snapped his neck. While I watched in horror and revulsion, the Orco's eyes continued to glow intensely as he unremittingly jerked his head to the side, trying to bite me much like a snake's head tries to bite after being severed.

"He's not dead, but he's not going anywhere," Constance breathed as she stood. We raced to the SUV where Claudia still huddled inside. Lucien had Brie pinned against the side of the garage, and just when we reached her to help, two more Orcos appeared and circled us and a third smashed the windshield out of Claudia's car, gaining access to her.

"Claudia!" Will screamed across the courtyard, running out the back door.

"Will, don't…NO!" I screamed in warning as he flew toward us. Before he could reach the car, the Orco pulled Claudia from the back like a ragdoll, dragging her out the window. Will flew at him when the Orco prepared to sink his teeth into Claudia's neck. I could hear her desperate screams as William shrieked and clawed at her attacker.

The hopelessness of the situation sank in. Although Constance and I managed to take two of them out, we were still sadly outnumbered. Constance dove head first into the two Orcos challenging us, and as I reached Brie to try and free her, I heard Julia's screams inside the house.

"Chandler, the kids!" Constance gasped in warning. I turned to run to the house. Bursting through the back door, I searched frantically through the main floor. Julia screamed again, alerting me to their location somewhere upstairs. I took the stairs two at a time, and then stopped cold. Julia sat against the wall at the end of the hallway with Matty clutched to her chest. Ava Grace lay at her feet in a ball, her hands covering her face as if she were trying to hide. My gaze rose to the Orco standing over them, his teeth hovering over Elly's neck as she whimpered.

"Oh, please, don't…no," I whispered, my heart beating out of my chest. "You can't take her from me," I shook my head frantically. He smiled at me, flashing his sharp fangs and preparing to drain the life from my daughter.

My prayers were answered. Banton flew past me, ramming himself into the Orco just as the creature moved to bite. He released Elly, her little limp form rolling down his body to the floor, hitting the carpet when I sprang to catch her. I managed to cradle her head before it hit. I swept her under me as Banton and the Orco rolled over the top of us and down the staircase. No sooner than they'd reached the floor, John bounded into the hallway downstairs, followed closely by Brie. The three of them made short work of the Orco who had threatened Elly.

Everything was eerily quiet. I took a deep breath and exhaled as Julia reached out to touch my shoulder. As I drew her into my side, Ava raised her little head. Upon seeing me, she ran and threw her arms around me, clinging as if her life depended on it. Julia sobbed into my shoulder as I checked both the twins for injuries.

"Julia, are you all right?" I asked, taking her chin in my hand to look at her face. She nodded as I sensed Banton coming up the stairs behind me.

"Chandler... are you hurt? Are the kids," he asked breathlessly.

"We're all okay up here. What about Claudia and the others?" I asked.

"Claudia is in shock. You stay here with Julia and the kids. We've got a mess outside. I'll be back," he cautioned as he kissed me on the forehead. He pulled away and studied my eyes before he rose. Hurriedly checking all the rooms upstairs, he then ran back down the staircase.

I could hear low voices attempting comfort as Claudia sobbed. After checking all the rooms upstairs as Banton had, I determined there were no other Orcos lurking in the house. I pulled Julia into the first bedroom by the top of the stairs and sat her down on the bed, placing the twins beside her.

"Ava, Sweetheart, you've been a brave little girl. Can you do Aunt Chandler a favor, and watch the babies for me?" I asked as she jumped up on the bed beside them. She wiped her chubby little arm across her eyes and nodded furiously. I kissed her forehead and then descended the staircase.

I found Claudia crumpled on the kitchen floor in Brie's arms. I shot Brie a questioning look. She shifted her eyes toward the window, warning me of the reason for Claudia's distress. Everett rose from the ground with William's lifeless form in his arms. He walked slowly toward the patio and placed Will's limp, broken body on a chaise lounge. Several Aldon were present, I assumed called there by Everett. As I watched, two of them twisted the head of one of the disabled Orcos to still him, and then hoisted his body into the back of a black SUV.

338

As swiftly as it had begun, it was over, and all that remained in the yard was Orco blood. Banton crossed the yard with Ty and Constance, placing his hand on Everett's shoulder as they reached him. Everett turned and looked at Banton and shook his head. Banton pushed around him to kneel beside Will, taking his limp hand in his as he touched his fingers to Will's neck, checking for a pulse.

I felt weak, shaking from the extreme adrenalin flow I'd experienced. I pushed the back door open silently, and moved toward Banton.

"It's no use, Banton. I've done CPR on him for over ten minutes. There isn't any blood left in his system," Everett whispered, his voice quivering. I'd never heard Everett like that. He sounded like a stranger. He raised his tear-filled eyes, burning with the fiery green rage of an Aldon in battle. His gaze was one of tormented remorse.

"I tried, Bebe...I promise, I tried," he ground desperately through his teeth. My heart broke for him. I could tell he blamed himself for not getting to Will sooner.

I pulled him into my arms. "Shhh. I know you did, Everett. Shhh," I tried to soothe him as he sobbed into my shoulder.

Banton rose after a few minutes and grasped Everett by the shoulders.

"Ev, who do we call? How do we handle this?" He released a deep breath as he grudgingly tried to take charge of the impossible situation.

Ev finally managed to gain some control. "We have our Aldon friends with the NOPD. I'll give them a call," he whispered in a resigned voice as he pulled his cell out.

Banton nodded and pulled me back into the house. He gave my hand a quick squeeze before he released it.

"Claudia, Sweetheart, come here," Banton urged as he pulled her up from the floor into his arms. As he slid his arm up under her legs and pulled her into his chest, she broke into loud sobs.

"Banton, please...do something for him! You can't just leave him! You can't let him die! Will...William!" she screamed, pushing against Banton's chest. "Please, Banton, don't let them take him," she begged. My shoulders shook and my chest heaved

339

as I tried to swallow a sob. I relived the moment in my own foyer, when I'd begged Banton not to leave me after the Navy had brought me the awful news that day in July.

Ty and John helped Constance into the house. She had multiple wounds on her arms and face. Ty pulled her over to the kitchen sink and wet a rag to start cleaning her up.

"Here, Ty...let me take her upstairs to the bathroom," Brie urged.

"Brie, baby, are you in control? Can you handle the blood?" John asked softly from the doorway.

"I've got this. I'm fine. It doesn't bother me I promise."

I followed them up the staircase, and as I entered the bedroom to check on the kids, Ava met me at the door.

"An Andler, what's wrong wif my Mommy?"

My heart sank. *How do I tell her?* She lost her birth mommy – Mommy Jess. She settled with us, transferred to Claudia and Will, and then thought she'd lost her beloved Uncle Banton. Now she'd lost her daddy Will. I struggled to swallow the lump in my throat and still my aching heart.

I sank down into the floor beside her, drawing her up into my lap as I stilled my voice.

"Oh, sweet girl, Mommy Claudia is so scared and tired from the attack, but Uncle Banton is taking care of her. She will be fine, but right now Aunt Julia and I need for you to be our big, brave little girl. You can help me feed the twins, and then you and I will lay down with them for a nap."

Ava smiled her wide, little girl smile and nodded enthusiastically at me. I fought the tears again. I had no idea how we would tell her Daddy Will was dead and wasn't coming back. I didn't want to do it right now. I wanted to wait for Claudia to make that decision. I kissed her hair and pulled her in tighter to my body as I heard Claudia's weeping down the hallway.

Meeting Julia's eyes over the top of Ava's head, I could tell Julia suspected the worst. As her own eyes filled with tears, she rose and offered, "Why don't I go down and fix the babies' bottles? I know how," she whispered I rose from the floor with Ava clinging to me and placed her on the bed beside the babies,

340

drawing them in to me. Ava mimicked my actions with Elly as I played with Matty's dark curls.

A few minutes later, Julia returned with red-rimmed eyes, clutching the babies' bottles and two blankets. I pushed up on the pillows and took a bottle from her for Matty as she helped Ava Grace pull Elly up between them. After Matty was nursing contentedly, I glanced over and met Julia's eyes. Tears slid silently down her cheeks as she confirmed that she knew about William.

"Are we going to tell her?" she mouthed silently to me. I shook my head and we both turned toward the doorway. Banton stood watching us silently, and when my eyes met his, new tears threatened. I knew he'd been just down the hallway with Claudia, but such a sense of relief enveloped me at the sight of him. He crossed the bedroom in two steps and sank down on the bed beside me to pull me into his arms.

"You are all safe now, shhhh." His breath blew into my hair as he held me close, stroking my shoulders and arms as I shuddered. He leaned over and placed a gentle kiss on Matty's head and reached over to touch Elly's cheek. Elly continued to nurse contentedly in Ava's arms, oblivious to the danger from which we'd all just escaped.

Ava looked inquiringly at Banton, and then released her hold on Elly when Julia moved the baby completely into her lap. Ava scrambled over my legs onto Banton's lap as he released his hold on me. As she gazed up at him, she asked, "Unca Banin, why is my Mommy Cwadia cwying? Where is my Daddy Will?"

Banton closed his eyes to mask the pain I saw there. Placing his lips on top of her head, he paused, took a deep breath, and then opened his eyes as he looked to me for strength. I felt Claudia would want Banton to tell her, so I nodded at him.

"Oh, Doodle-Bug…come with Uncle Banton, I need to talk with you, sweetheart."

He rose, cradling her on his hip as he left the room to talk quietly with her. The minute they were out of range, Julia sobbed out loud.

"Come here," I murmured as I pulled her over to my shoulder. We lay for what seemed like hours, the babies sleeping, curled up in their little baby balls on our shoulders. She cried as we both relived the awful scene in our heads.

"God, Chandler. Will was like my own brother," she whispered, her voice faltering. "I don't have a single childhood memory without him in it!" She sobbed as I stroked her hair. "Did you know he taught me to ride a bicycle? He drove me to my first high school dance! The first time I had to pull a tooth, he tricked me and tied my tooth to my Barbie car, and then hit the remote," she smiled through her tears, remembering the sweet moments she'd shared with him. "I didn't realize he'd pulled it until it raced back in front of me, dragging my bloody tooth on the string behind it." She laughed through her tears, and then broke into sobs again. "Oh, Will…"

Wails reached us from down the hallway. "No Unca Banin, pweese? Wet me see my Daddy Will! No! DaddyWill will come back 'cause my Uncle Bannin came back! Daddy Will will come back too," she insisted in a high pitched wail. It was almost more than my heart could take. I heard hushed voices, and then Mrs. Elaine's voice rose above the others. Banton's parents had arrived, and I could tell by the tone of their voices that Mrs. Elaine had taken charge and was carrying Ava down to Claudia's room.

Banton strode back into the bedroom and took Elly from Julia.

"Ju-Bean, I'll take her. Chandler, let's get them down," he murmured, motioning to me. I rose with Matty, already stiff from my fight earlier with the Orcos. My side and hip had stiffened and ached terribly. I frowned as I followed Banton down the hallway to the nursery; I didn't remember being injured that badly.

As soon as we placed the twins in their cribs, they were fast asleep. Banton turned to me.

"Chandler, let's get you in the tub," he urged, placing his lips in my hair.

"Banton, I need to see about Claudia and see how Constance is doing," I protested.

He shook his head sternly at me. "Brie has Constance all fixed up, and Ty is taking good care of her. Claudia is with Momma and Daddy; they're helping her with Ava. We need to see about you."

"I'm fine," I argued. He shook his head. We entered our bedroom and he pointed to my face as we stepped in front of the floor length mirror.

"Oh, gosh," I whispered as I took in the bruise that was beginning to darken on my cheek.

"And I noticed you wincing when you rose with Matty just now," he continued, reaching out and slipping my blouse up. Another bruise was darkening on my ribs.

"Andie, you're hurt. Come in here."

He pulled me into the bathroom. As he leaned over to start the water flowing in the tub, I slid out of my pants and realized my injuries were more extensive than I'd first thought.

Banton drew his breath in sharply when he turned back to me.

"Damn," he growled, reaching out to touch my hip. There was another large purplish-gray bruise forming up my thigh and around my hip.

"I'm so, so sorry," he murmured as he ran his thumb over the spot. And like a cold blast of air into the room, his mood shifted before my eyes. Raising his eyes back to meet my gaze, his eyes grew dark with rage as he scolded me.

"Why the hell didn't you lock yourself in the house with the twins and Julia? What were you thinking?"

His rant took me by surprise. "Banton, please don't. I had to go back out there. Claudia was by herself. I had to try to do something, and I knew Julia would lock herself away with the twins and Ava. I didn't have a choice."

"You always have a choice. By your going out there, you could have been killed ..."

I pulled away from him and shook my head. "Stop it, Banton. I've been bitten. Claudia hasn't. I knew I could at least hold one of them off her. I had to try!"

"Chandler, don't you understand? It's not about just being bitten. Just because you've transformed doesn't mean one of them can't drink enough of your blood to kill you in a few minutes. You aren't immune to death!" He bellowed, and I was sure everyone downstairs could hear him.

I shook my head at him again in disbelief. He was yelling at me for trying to protect his sister.

343

As I slipped the straps down to my bra, Banton reached up silently and unhooked it for me. I dropped it to the floor as he traced the outline of another sore spot on my shoulder.

"They weren't trying to kill me. They want me alive. But that's not the case with everyone around me. We found out the hard way with Brie, and now Will," I whispered, my voice breaking on the words. "I had to protect your sister," I repeated as he shook his head stubbornly.

This argument wasn't going anywhere, so I stepped over into the tub and sank down into the water. Now every bone in my body hurt. I felt I'd been unhinged at all my joints and reassembled the wrong way.

Banton turned and strode out of the room silently, leaving me to brood in silence.

On a deep breath, I began to shake as I tried to relax in the warm water. The Adrenalin rush I'd experienced when I fought the Orcos outside was incredible, and that kind of physical exertion was completely foreign to me. Tears threatened once more at the images…Will running to save Claudia…Claudia crumpled on the kitchen floor watching in horror…Everett carrying Will's limp body across the yard.

"Banton, please…do something for him! You can't just leave him, you can't…"

"Please, Banton…don't let them take him,"

I wiped my eyes angrily. I'd tried to be strong. In my mind, I did the only thing I could do.

"NOOOOOO! He can't leave me like this, he promised me…"

I began to shiver uncontrollably as a sob escaped. The memories came flooding back as I relived the moments after the Navy visited in July, informing me of Banton's disappearance.

"He can't leave me with these babies! He has to come back! I can't live without him!"

And the dam broke. I lay my head back against the tile surrounding the tub as I cried out my frustration. The Orcos were back. The past couple of months had only been an interlude. And now, because of their relentless pursuit of me and Constance, Will was dead.

"Shhh. I'm so, so sorry, Chandler. I'm angry with myself, not you."

Banton's deep, beautiful smooth voice whispered close to my ear. I opened my eyes to find him staring down at me as he sat down beside the tub. The expression on his face startled me. His eyes were red-rimmed, and he looked as if he'd aged ten years. He placed his hand on my shoulder and rubbed his thumb back and forth across a bruise as he gazed down at me. My tears spilled over.

"Damn. Baby, come here," he breathed out, pulling me over against his strong chest. He held my head in his hand, stroking my hair with his other hand as he laid his cheek on top of my head.

"Sweetheart, it's okay. I'm an ass. My anger is still an issue, and I lost it when I thought about what could have happened to you and the babies. We never should have let our guard down. I'm angry we weren't here when they attacked. I'm angry at Will for trying to fight them. I'm angry my involvement in all of this has endangered both our families."

I was so emotional since I'd replayed the last two hours in my head. I couldn't reply so I just nodded. Banton pulled my face up between his hands and kissed me softly.

"Are you really okay? Some of those bruises look pretty bad. Dad called Doctor Renault to come and help with Claudia, and Ty wants him to check Constance over. I think he should see you too."

"Okay," I whispered as I nodded up at him.

"Here, I brought you some tea."

He reached over and picked a glass up off the floor and handed it to me. I took a couple of swallows. I didn't realize how thirsty I was. I took several more swallows as Banton pushed a strand of my hair back behind my ear.

"Constance told me just now how hard you fought out there. She said you took one of them down by yourself," his eyes darkened.

"Well, she's exaggerating just a bit. She had to help me. She's the one who's been training like a SEAL. I think Claudia and I would be dead or kidnapped by the time you got here, if it hadn't been for her and Brie," I whispered, my voice shaking badly. "Banton, I want you to teach me how to fight like Ty has been

345

teaching Constance," I turned to him. His eyes narrowed, and he shook his head at me.

"Banton, please! I don't want to be a victim anymore. I need to know I can at least try to protect the babies, if I have to..." I trailed off under his thunderous gaze.

"That's not necessary. If you want to work out with me, fine. I would welcome that. To gain your strength back, since the babies...but you don't need to know how to fight. I won't let anything like today happen again," he vowed as he pulled me up closer against his chest. After a moment, he relaxed his hold on me.

"Let's get you washed and out of the water."

He reached over and grabbed the body wash from the side of the tub and squeezed some out on a sponge. Leaning me forward, he held me, his arm across my chest as he washed my back, moving the sponge in soft circles. I lay my head over against his hand, grasping his arm as I closed my eyes, still in shock from the attack. I was barely aware of him as he gently soaped my stomach, under my arms and over my breasts...between my legs. He dipped the sponge back in the water, and squeezed the warm water slowly down my back and shoulders, rinsing the suds away.

"Come here, baby," he murmured, wrapping a towel around me and pulling me up and over into his lap. He was drenched, his own clothes soaked from bathing me and pulling me from the tub.

Banton hugged me tightly, snugly wrapped in the large bath towel.

"Um, I think I'd better go and check on the babies. They need their baths and it's probably time for them to eat again," I said, my voice sounding hoarse from all of the yelling and screaming this afternoon.

"They're fine, Andie. Ty just checked on them. I think they're down for the night."

I pushed up against his chest and looked up into his soft brown eyes. He leaned down and kissed me.

"Let's get you in bed," he urged, standing up with me in his arms. After he sat me down on the wide ledge of the tub, he left in search of something for me to wear. I tucked the towel in that he'd wrapped around me, and then searched in the drawers for a brush.

As I brushed the tangles out of my hair, Banton re-appeared with my gown and robe. I dropped the towel around my ankles as he slipped my gown over my head. I worked my arms through as he handed me my robe.

"I'm going to take a shower. I'll only be a minute," he murmured, placing a kiss on my forehead.

Banton leaned into the large shower, and turned the water on as he unbuttoned his wet shirt. I gazed at him lovingly. His outburst earlier was a result of his fear for me and the babies. I understood that now. I opened the door and headed to the nursery. As I moved toward the cribs, I could hear the babies both breathing in and out, the slow, deep rhythm indicating how soundly they slept. Ty was probably right. They seemed to be down for the night. I leaned over and kissed them both, placing my lips lightly on their chubby cheeks. Nausea rose and I swallowed, thinking about how closely that Orco had held Elly, his teeth grazing her neck. I swayed a bit, grabbing hold of the side of the crib.

"Chandler...finally. I was beginning to think you and Banton were never coming out of that bathroom," Ty broke the silence as he entered the room behind me. "Are you all right?"

I turned, steadying myself. "Yes, I'm just still a little shaken up."

"I don't know who looks worse, you or Constance. She sent me to check on you. Dr. Renault is with her now, checking her injuries."

"And Claudia? How is she?"

"Doc gave her medicine for her nerves and some strong pain medicine. She's out. He said he was going to keep her medicated for the next twenty-four hours or so. She's taking things pretty hard and that's understandable."

He walked over to Elly's crib and gazed down at her. "Constance had me go down and fix their formula for them, to have it ready in case they woke up. It's on the dresser over there. I can get up with them, if you want me to, Andie," he offered sweetly.

"No, Ty...we're good. Thank you for fixing their formula."

"Sure, no problem. If you need anything, just call. Dr. Renault will be ready to see you in a few minutes."

"Thanks, Ty. Thank you for taking such good care of Constance," I added as he grinned at me.

"She's my girl. I love her, Chandler."

"I know you do, Ty. Goodnight."

As I walked back to our bedroom, I could hear muffled voices, and Banton's mother talking soothingly as Julia cried. Mrs. Elaine was a tower of strength for her children. I wondered silently, *does she ever break down behind closed doors? Has Banton's father ever had to hold her in the shower, lift her from the tub?*

Back in our room, I switched the bedside lamp on, pulled the duvet back on the massive bed and crawled in. No sooner than I'd snuggled down, there was a knock on the door.

"Banton?" Dr. Renault voice carried through the closed door.

"It's Chandler. You can come in," I replied as I pushed up in the bed.

Dr. Renault pushed the door open and strode into the room, looking rather agitated and weary.

"Let's see how badly you're injured." He pulled the covers back and raised my gown. "You have a lot of bruises, but nothing seems to be broken," he murmured, pressing against my ribs. I cried out. He looked intently into my eyes as he continued to probe with his fingers.

"I think you have a couple of cracked ribs, Chandler…possibly a hairline fracture on this hip, but you should heal fairly quickly. You can take pain medicine now, so I'll leave something with you. You can also wrap those ribs. It will help with the pain."

As he placed the pills on the nightstand, Banton entered the room and stood behind Dr. Renault.

"Doc, how is she?"

"Cracked ribs, bruising…but she will heal quickly. I left her some pain medicine. I'll be back to check on Claudia in the morning," he said as he touched Banton on the shoulder and left the room.

Banton walked over and sat down on the side of the bed. "Everett and several of the Aldon are downstairs, watching the perimeter of the house. They've got some more information. This thing isn't over. We don't want to be caught unprepared again.

348

Sam is on his way with Patrick, so I think we'll be fairly safe tonight. We'll decide what our next move is tomorrow." I nodded. I was too tired, emotionally and physically, to think.

"Mother and Daddy are taking care of arrangements for Will. His mother is in the nursing home, and he has been estranged from his brother for some time. We don't even know how to contact him," he said as I stared out the window. After a few moments, he pulled me into his chest.

"Chandler, I'm so sorry about earlier. I never should have yelled at you. Please don't be upset with me," he said, sounding as though he were pleading with me. I looked up at him.

"That's over. I know why you reacted that way. We're good," I assured him as I kissed his lips. I pulled back to look into his eyes. "I'm just so...I feel so guilty. Will is dead because of the Orco's obsession over me and the twins."

"Don't. Not you too. I have my hands full with Everett," Banton sighed, kissing my hair.

"What do you mean, Everett?"

"He's torn up, Chandler. I've never seen him like this. He blames himself for not getting to Will in time. He keeps saying over and over he could have at least saved him from death, if he'd just gotten to him before his heart stopped. He could have just turned, like Brie."

"I guess he feels responsible for all of us," I murmured.

"No, it's more than that. Sweetheart, I'm going downstairs to meet with Ev and the others, I won't be too long," he said as I nodded. "Baby, come here," he murmured as he pulled me into his chest. He held me so tightly it scared me. He was trembling. The unexpected attack today that had taken Will's life had shaken everyone into the realization it was only a matter of time before Dante and Lucien attained their goal...to capture me, Constance, and the twins.

After Banton went downstairs, I finally drifted off, knowing the Aldon were watching over us. I dozed fitfully with Banton's side of the bed empty. Finally Banton's arms circled my waist as he buried his face in my hair.

"Mmm. Everything okay?' I asked as I turned in his arms.

"Yes, for now, sorry I woke you," he murmured.

349

"What time is it?"

"A little after two o'clock."

I turned over and rose up. "Did you check on the…" and then I stopped. Banton had pulled one of the cribs through the door into our room, placing it at the foot of the bed. Both twins were inside, sleeping peacefully. I looked down at Banton. He was gazing up at me in the moonlight.

"I just needed to feel them near us," he murmured as he pulled me back down into his arms.

* * *

When I woke at six to feed the babies, Banton was already up, visiting with Everett in the hallway. As I dressed the twins, Banton came back into our room. I turned to find him watching me.

"Ty, John, Sam and I are going back to the base this morning for a meeting with Command. Some of the Aldon are staying to watch over the family here, but I want you and the babies to come with us. You can wait on base until we're through. I'm sorry, but I don't feel good about leaving you right now," he stated, picking Matty up. I turned to stare at him. It was the first time he'd ever taken me to the base.

"What about the twins, if someone sees them, their eyes?"

"I'll arrange for an office or room somewhere away from everyone. Everett and Constance are coming too. The meetings shouldn't take long. Then we'll come back here until we decide what we're going to do," he said as I picked Elly up.

"Do they know about the attack here yesterday?"

"Yes, and our agenda's been altered. We'll find out more this morning.

My heart skipped a beat. One way or another, the peace that had surrounded my home and family had shattered.

Once Banton had us on the base, he seemed to relax. After arranging for a conference room for us to wait in, he rushed off to his meetings. When we settled the babies on a pallet to play, my cell rang. I didn't immediately recognize the number.

"Chandler! Finally, I've been calling and calling! Don't you ever check your missed calls?"

350

"Laurilee. I'm sorry, there's been a lot going on here," I sighed as I glanced up at Everett.

"Well, in case you've forgotten, there's a lot going on here!"

"I know, I'm sorry," I answered, knowing she must be irritated.

"So when are you and Banton driving in? The rehearsal dinner is all set, and the girls want to have my bachelorette party the night before," she chattered on as I pondered how I was going to handle this.

"Laurilee, we've had some more trouble here," I began.

"Not again! Chandler, you have to be here for all these events, you're my matron of honor!"

"I know, Laurilee. I promise you, I will be there for the wedding. I just haven't had time to talk to Banton yet. We're on base now waiting for him."

"What's wrong?' she finally sensed my distress.

"There was an incident at Claudia and Will's last night. Will was killed."

"What? Chandler, No! Was anyone else hurt?"

"Yes, but not seriously. Banton's parents are making arrangements for Will, but since all this has happened, I don't know when we'll be able to get away. And I don't want to bring trouble to you," I warned her, not being able to elaborate. "Laurilee, I'm so sorry. None of this should affect you. It's your big day. Let me talk to Banton, and I'll get back to you as soon as I know something."

"I'm sorry I went off on you about being here, when your family is grieving! Is there anything we can do?"

"No, just pray for us."

"Well, tell Everett I got the package and the other things he sent. Everything is beautiful. Chandler?"

"Yes?"

"Be careful. I still don't understand all of this, why you have to be involved."

"I know. I'll call you back when things calm down. I love you Laurilee."

"I love you too, Chandler."

351

I turned my cell off, and then turned to Everett. He was staring out the window.

"Bebe, who is that man?" Everett pointed out the office window.

"That's Commander Reed, the one who took Singleton's place in charge of Banton's SEAL team," I replied, his eyes narrowing.

"Bebe, did you know he's an Aldon?"

My skin crawled, up my neck and across the top of my scalp. "What do you mean?"

"I mean, he's an Aldon," he stated emphatically as he turned back to look at me. I stood, my mouth open.

"Why in the hell would he be…" I couldn't finish, my mind whirled around all the possibilities. Why would an Aldon be in the military? Why wouldn't he disclose this information to the other SEALs? What possible reason…and then it dawned on me. My eyes snapped back up at Everett.

"They've been using him to recruit Sange-Mele SEALs. That's how they knew to recruit Banton, Ty…John, the rest of the team."

"Quite possibly. Now it makes me wonder, even more than before, why he was so adamant about testing you and the twins over this paternity mess," Everett mused aloud as Constance and I stared at each other. I gazed down at the twins, apprehensive about having them on base at all.

"I have to tell Banton," I murmured, looking back up at Everett.

"Chandler, I don't like this," Constance stated. I nodded in agreement.

"I know. I feel like Banton and the others are being played somehow."

Everett stood silently, watching Reed as he strode across the lawn and into another building.

"Bebe, I'm going to make a call. I'll be right back," Everett said, stepping into the hallway.

Constance and I settled down in the floor to play with the twins. Matty and Elly played and giggled as always, crawling around and silently communicating with each other. As Constance

352

chased Matty under a chair to pull him back onto the pallet, he faded.

"Chandler, look!" Constance exclaimed as I blanched. I knew it was only a matter of time before he tried it too. Elly sat motionless, watching him. She giggled slightly, and then looked up at me apprehensively. I could tell she was trying to see if I was going to be angry with Matty.

I took a deep breath. "Matty…where's Matty?" I called. I could see his outline pause and turn to look at me.

"Matty, come back to Mommy, Mommy can't see you," I said firmly. He giggled and flopped his face down on the floor. But he still didn't fade back in. Elly crawled closer to me, and then turned back to him, seeming to sense my apprehension.

"Chandler, what do we do if he doesn't fade back?" Constance whispered as I looked at her.

"Matthew Gastaneau, come back to Mommy!" I said sternly. He giggled again, and crawled toward Constance, placing his hand in her lap. Finally, he faded back.

I breathed a sigh of relief. Elly had begun to whine, sensing that Matty might be in trouble. I picked her up and hugged her to me and smiled down at her. She buried her face in my chest, placing her thumb in her mouth.

"Chandler, you might have to give them a swat or something when they do that."

I shook my head. "No. It occurred to me when Banton was stern with Elly the other night. At some point, their fading might be useful, and they might need to do it. I have to figure out a way to teach them it's okay. I don't want to discourage them too much," I replied.

"Well, good luck with this one. I can already tell he's going to be a handful," she said as she picked Matty up and kissed his cheek. "Elly on the other hand, is just like you. All you have to do is look at her sternly, and she cries."

"I know." I hugged her to me closely and kissed her soft forehead.

The babies soon tired and fell asleep playing. After about an hour or so, Everett finally came back into the room.

"Here, sweeties, I brought you some coffee."

"Oh, Ev, I love you. Will you marry me?" Constance purred as she took her cup from him.

"Sorry, Constance, my beauty. I've fought in two wars, battled Orcos, lived through reconstruction, a depression, and Grandmother Wellington's menopause. But I just don't have the strength to tackle the entire woman that makes up Constance LeBlance."

I laughed, the heaviness of the morning lightened by their banter.

"Ev, where have you been all this time?" I asked as I took a sip of my coffee.

"I just had to communicate with some of the other Aldon. I need to take a trip, but I don't want to leave you two and Claudia right now."

"Did you visit with Mrs. Elaine before we left? How was Claudia this morning?"

Everett's eyes became dark, glowing with raw emotion. "I checked in on her before we left. She was resting, still drugged from the medication Dr. Renault gave her."

"Banton told me last night what a hard time you are having. You can't blame yourself for Will's death. We were all overwhelmed. You are no more to blame than any of the rest of us," I tried to reason.

"Bebe, you don't understand," he began, turning away to look out the window.

"What don't I understand?" I placed my hand on his arm. He turned back and quickly embraced me. "Everett, you have to let this go. You couldn't have done anything more," I began.

"Couldn't I" he said sarcastically, full of self-loathing. I couldn't understand where all this was coming from.

Banton barreled in followed by Ty and John.

"Banton!" I ran to him and wrapped my arms around his waist.

"Hey, is everything all right?" he glanced down at me with concern.

I lowered my voice as I watched Everett and Constance pick Elly and Matty up to place them in their baby seats.

354

"Oh, just Matty fading like Elly. And there's something you need to know. Everett saw Commander Reed walking outside, and he asked me if we knew he is an Aldon."

"An Aldon? Are you sure?"

Banton looked quickly to Everett, who nodded silently in agreement. I watched as a myriad of emotions crossed Banton's face, none of them good. He stared at me for a moment, and then finally spoke.

"Don't worry. I'll talk to Singleton," he murmured, lost in thought.

"So you didn't know, did you?' I asked.

"Chandler, don't worry. I'll handle this," he assured me, helping me gather the twins' things.

Banton was silent on the way back to Claudia's. I finally clasped his right hand in mine.

"Banton, I know now is not the time, but Laurilee called this morning," I began.

"Oh, no. The wedding. I'd forgotten," he breathed almost in a whisper.

"What can we do?"

"I don't know. Let's just get back to Claudia's, and see what arrangements Momma and Daddy have made. I have to think about this."

"Banton, I can skip the pre-wedding stuff, and just go for the ceremony. We can fly…"

"I don't think that's possible. I can't risk taking you away," he argued.

"I *have* to go. I can't do this to Laurilee."

"We'll discuss this tonight," he admonished, more anger in his voice than I'd ever heard before. I glanced at Everett in the rear-view mirror. He shook his head. I knew he was agreeing with Banton. I dropped the argument, knowing Banton was right. I just didn't know how I was going to break it to Laurilee that I wouldn't be there for the most important moment in her life.

We arrived at Claudia's to find Miss Astrid waiting on us to help with the babies.

"Everett called me. I can help with the kids, and I'm extra protection," she assured me as she gave me a brief hug.

"Unca Banin!" Ava ran down the staircase, her big brown eyes large with fear.

"What's wrong, Doodle-Bug?" He knelt to pick her up. She threw her little arms around his neck and buried her face in his shoulder.

Mrs. Elaine followed her down the staircase.

"She's been pacing and worrying herself sick, thinking you wouldn't come back. She's been asking if you were going on your ship again," she said softly. Banton nodded, understanding her meaning. He carried her into the living room and sat down on the sofa with her.

"Separation anxiety?" I asked. Mrs. Elaine nodded.

"I understand that emotion," I replied as I hugged her.

"I know you do, dear."

Everett helped me unstrap the twins from their seats, and then handed Matty to Mrs. Elaine. As we walked into the living room with them, he asked, "Is Claudia awake yet?"

"Yes. Matt is up there with her. She's calmer now."

"Good. I don't want her left alone," Everett commented, glancing up the staircase.

"Everett, why don't you go up and see her," Mrs. Elaine urged him.

"No, I will later. I have some matters to attend to now." He crossed the foyer to the back part of the house. I assumed he was going to talk with the other Aldon who were keeping watch.

Constance followed us, having ridden with Ty and John back to the house. After everyone was back, Banton rose with Ava asleep on his shoulder.

"I'm going to take her up and talk with Claudia, and then I'll help you get the twins down for their afternoon nap," he offered. I nodded, knowing he wanted to talk some more about the Texas trip.

Miss Astrid helped me get the twins upstairs, and then went in search of Mrs. Elaine to offer to prepare dinner for everyone. The twins were tired after their morning on base, and Elly fell asleep before she'd even finished her bottle. Matty finished his, and I rocked him a little to get him down. I was just placing him in his crib when Banton entered. He slipped up behind me and slid his

356

arms around my waist. I smelled the earthy, clean scent of his cologne before he even touched me. He smelled so good…like Banton. As I turned in his arms, he pulled me through the nursery door and pulled it partially closed.

Placing his mouth behind my ear, he whispered, "Are you still bleeding, Chandler?"

I shook my head. "No, I stopped yesterday. It didn't last long," I answered as he pulled me into his chest. He trailed his mouth along my neck as he reached under my sweater, his hands hot against my skin.

"Banton, the door," I protested breathlessly. He turned me around and covered my lips with his. His kiss was bruising as his hands cupped my buttocks. As he backed me up against the bed, I fell back as he worked his hands up under my sweater, and then slid my tights down my legs in one swift motion.

"Oh Chandler…baby, I want you," he breathed into my ear. He pushed me back into the pillows, unbuttoning his jeans as he moved against me. He slid his thumbs under the thin fabric of my panties and then grasped them in his hands. In one motion he shredded them as he pushed to enter me.

"Oh…please," I was begging him. I needed him, needed to feel him wrap himself around me. He began to move inside me as his lips continued their assault on mine. His strong hands grasped my ribcage as he moved over me, bringing me to the brink. There was a desperation like the night he'd come home from his first deployment. It felt as if we were living on the edge, neither one of us knowing whether we'd see each other the next time we woke. I gasped as we found our release together, his forehead pressed to mine. Our breathing slowed to an even tempo as he pulled away and gazed down at me. I rolled over on my front, hugging a pillow to me.

"Andie, I'm sorry. I just needed you; I needed to feel you," he whispered, easing down beside me. He grasped the bottom of my sweater and pulled it up over my head, covering my body partially with his as he placed kisses on my shoulders. Slowly moving down my back, he reached my lower back and pulled the bedspread up over me.

"I needed you too," I whispered, our breath mingling together as he tangled his legs around mine.

We lay, looking into each other's eyes, silently communicating how deeply we felt for one another. When my breathing was finally back to normal I murmured, "I'm safe, when you are inside me. I'm home. Nothing else matters but you."

"God, I love you, Chandler," he replied as he pulled my face into his chest. He slid his thumb methodically back and forth across my cheek and then said, "I hope you understand why you can't go to Texas."

"Banton, I understand. I just don't know how I will break it to Laurilee. Couldn't you and Everett just fly there with me early that morning, and then we could fly straight back after the ceremony?"

Banton turned over on his back, and ran his fingers through his hair. "It would take more than me and Everett to protect you. We would have to take at least two others, and I don't want to split our forces. That's when we are at our weakest and the Orcos know it. Besides, you don't want to lead this danger to Laurilee and Dan."

I began to cry tears of anger and frustration. "How am I going to tell her I'm going to screw up her big day? Banton, she'll be devastated," I argued.

"Chandler, it's only one day. She will get over it. This is not worth risking your life, or the babies' lives."

I knew he was right, so I dropped it. He was a man; he just didn't understand how big a deal this was going to be to Laurilee.

"I'll call her tonight," I said as he leaned over me and placed his lips in my hair. After several minutes, I rose and shrugged into my robe. I pushed the door open to the nursery to find Miss Astrid checking on the twins.

She looked at me apologetically. "I'm sorry. I just came up to check on them. I didn't mean to eavesdrop," she offered as I shook my head.

"There won't be many secrets between us with you living under the same roof," I replied. She placed a hand on my shoulder, leaving the room quietly. I kissed both sleeping babies on their cheeks, and then stepped into the bathroom to shower.

I stood several moments, just letting the hot water massage my face. It occurred to me, *I hope she meant she was eavesdropping on our conversation about not going to Texas, not our moments of passion beforehand!*

After I'd showered and dressed, I hurried downstairs to find Banton and the rest of the boys gone with Everett. Constance and Julia were resting on the sofas in the living room.

"Where did the guys go?" I asked, sinking down next to Julia. It was unlike Banton to leave without telling me goodbye. She immediately placed her head on my shoulder.

"Ev said something about going with Banton and the SEALs to straighten this thing out," Constance said as she gave me a sideways glance.

"Everett is going with them? Oh, surely they're not going to confront Reed," I said out loud as Julia pulled away to look at me.

"They're not in danger, are they?"

I realized Ava and I weren't the only ones with separation anxiety since the latest attack. "No, I don't think so, Julia. Don't worry, they will be back soon," I assured her.

"Claudia!" Constance exclaimed as I turned to look at the staircase. Claudia stepped off the last stair into the foyer and crossed to the living room. She looked so small, her hair pulled up in a loose bun on top of her head. I was used to seeing her hair always down and full around her face. Her face was pale, and the tell-tale signs of weight loss were already beginning to show…dark circles under her eyes, her cheekbones too prominent. She smiled bravely at us as she circled the grouping of furniture and came to rest beside Constance.

"Darlin', how are you?" Constance whispered, pulling Claudia into her arms.

"I'm dealin'. I can't stay in that room another minute. I had to get out. Too much sleep isn't good for your grief. It just makes you not want to wake up," she said, almost as if she were in a trance. My heart ached for her, having just gone through the same emotions only months before.

"Claudia, what can we do?' I asked, tears gathering in my eyes.

"There's nothin' you can do, sweet girl. Just be here with me. Just be here for Ava Grace. Besides me, it's you and Banton she cries for. She's so afraid something is going to happen to one of us, now. I don't know how to help her," she worried as Miss Astrid came in with some tea.

Julia cried silently beside me. I pulled her into my arms once again, at a loss as to how to help anyone.

"Well, why don't I see if I can make us a fire…it seems a little cold up in here, and my tidbits are nipply," Constance exclaimed, rubbing her breasts when she crossed over to the fireplace. Claudia burst out laughing.

"What?" Constance asked in her classic bossy, hoarse voice as Julia's laughter bubbled over to match Claudia's.

"You just never fail to lighten the mood, no matter what is going on. I needed to laugh," Claudia said as she wiped her eyes.

I kissed Julia on top of the head as we watched Constance turn the gas on to the fireplace. The four of us sat quietly, watching the flames.

"The fire is peaceful, calming somehow," Claudia mused as she laid her head on her arm draped across the back of the sofa.

A mewling cry, slowly morphing into a wail alerted us Ava was awake. Julia patted Claudia's leg and jogged upstairs to get her. No sooner than she'd topped the staircase, I heard the other two little cries join her.

"Oh, Ava woke the twins," Claudia remarked as I rose to get them.

"No, it was time for them to wake. I'll be right back."

I found both babies standing at the foot of their cribs. In the span of two weeks, the babies had gone from turning over to crawling and pulling up. I still couldn't believe they were developing so fast, even though Everett had told me they would. After Matty was dry, I placed him in Elly's crib while I changed her.

As I was snapping the legs on her little footed pj's, Matty uttered, "Mommy."

My eyes snapped up at him, shocked. He'd barely even been attempting garbled baby jabber, like Elly did. He grinned at my startled expression.

360

Tears gathered when I urged him again. "Say 'Mommy,' Matty."

"Mommy," he said plainly, without hesitation. I picked him up and hugged him to me, kissing the top of his head. Elly held her hands out to me, wanting to be picked up as well.

I carried them down, one on each hip as I sniffed back tears.

"Sister, what's wrong now?" Constance asked as I entered the room with them.

"Oh, you know me. Every first gets me," I said, placing them on the plush rug in the floor.

"What's new today? Did Elly recite the preamble to the constitution?" Julia asked, picking her up.

"No, but Matty just said his first word. He said, "Mommy."

"Hey, little man…that was supposed to be 'Aunt Constance.' Can you say Aunt Con-stan-ce?" she enunciated grandly as he grinned and crawled away from her.

Ava Grace sat quietly beside Claudia, buried into her side, watching everyone interact. I held my hands out to her, and she hesitantly made her way over to me and crawled up in my lap.

"Ava, you know the babies haven't been able to play with you in a while. They love it when you play with them. Would you like to get their toys out of their bag?" I asked. She shook her head furiously.

"It's okay. You don't have to, Doodle-Bug. Just sit here and keep me warm," I hugged her closer to me.

"Where's my Unca Banin?" she muttered, her face in my chest.

"He'll be back in a few minutes, sweetie. He just went with Uncle Everett on an errand."

Mrs. Elaine and Mr. Matt entered from the back of the house and came into the living room together.

"Claudia, sweetheart…it's good to see you up. We've just come from the funeral home. Would you like to talk with us a bit and tell us what you've decided for the service?" Mr. Matt asked her softly. She slowly met his gaze. After a brief pause, she nodded and rose to follow them into the dining room. Julia got up a moment later and handed Elly to Constance so she could join them.

"Chandler, where's Brie been today?" Constance asked.

361

"She's been with the other Aldon, Patrick and Olivia," I replied as I watched the fire. "I think she's sort of training since the fight the other day."

Matty grasped my jeans, pulling himself up as he tried to get Ava's attention.

"Mommy," he mumbled. Ava raised her head to look at him as he grinned at her.

"An Andler, Matty's talking," she whispered up at me.

"Yes, he is. I wonder if we can get him to say 'Ava'?" I asked her as she looked up at me. She scrambled down into the floor and pulled him down to sit in front of her.

"Say Aba, Matty," Ava challenged him. He grinned at her and cackled. Elly squealed at him from Constance's lap, trying to get their attention.

Constance grinned at her, and then looked up at me. "They're good therapy for her," she whispered over Elly's head as I nodded.

Banton, Everett, Ty and John returned. As they filed into the foyer, Ava jumped up from her spot on the floor and flew to Banton.

"Unca Banin! Unca Banin, hold Aba," she cried as she pulled at his jacket. He shrugged out of it hurriedly, and then picked her up and cradled her to his chest.

"Ava, it's okay. I'm home now," he consoled her as he glanced up at me. I smiled at him as I tried to corral Matty, who seemed to want to crawl in seven different directions.

Everett and the others wore grim expressions.

"Bebe, where is everyone?"

"Well, Mrs. Elaine and Mr. Matt just came back from the funeral home, and Claudia and Julia are in the dining room with them, talking about arrangements," I answered.

"Claudia is up?" he asked, concerned.

"Yes. She said she couldn't stay up in that room another minute. She's doing amazingly well, Everett," Constance answered.

Banton walked over and sat down beside me and reached to touch my cheek. "I'm sorry we left in such a rush. There have been some developments," he began as he glanced down at Ava. She watched him intently, her eyes wide.

"Doodle-Bug, Uncle Banton's home for the night. He's not going anywhere else," I assured her as she shrunk closer to him. "Banton, you might want to go in and sit with your family while they talk about arrangements," I suggested. He rose and kept Ava in his arms as he leaned over and kissed me.

Ty sat down next to Constance and took Elly in his lap. John sat down next to me and picked Matty up.

"So, fill us in. What developments?" I asked.

"Bebe, I'm afraid I set in motion a chain of events that we can't stop," Everett answered as he took a chair by the fireplace.

"Ev, don't jump to conclusions. I still say this was a good thing," John retorted.

"Would somebody fill me in?" I asked, slightly irritated they were talking over my and Constance's heads.

"Reed's dead," Ty responded as I gasped. Constance's eyes widened.

"How?"

"He was found in his office, his body mutilated, his blood had been drained. They found him right before we arrived back at base. We went to confront him about being an Aldon," Everett explained. "I'd called Renault earlier to inform our inner circle there was an Aldon who had been recruiting the Sange-Mele unit."

"Wait, you think the Aldon had him killed?" I asked disbelievingly.

"I don't know. I do know there are many in the Aldon ranks who have been suspicious of the Navy and their handling of recent events. They specifically were upset about their reluctance to help out when you were attacked at your house, and the way they treated Singleton, replacing him after the N'awlins incident," he explained. "When I called today, I assumed they would already know about Reed. They were as surprised as I was," he admitted.

"Well, obviously it had to be an Aldon or an Orco," Ty added as John nodded.

"And this happened right there on base...right after we left," Constance said as she shuddered. Ty pulled her in closer and kissed her on the forehead.

"Aldon or Orco aside, Reed's just as dead. Now Singleton is back in charge. I feel better already," John asserted as Ty nodded.

"Be careful, my boys. Keep those opinions to yourselves and stay vigilant. I trust no one," Everett cautioned as Miss Astrid came into the room.

"I have dinner ready, if anyone would like to eat," she urged as Ty and John rose.

"Chandler, I have their bottles, if you want to feed them now," Miss Astrid said softly as I nodded. The boys handed the babies back to Constance and me as Miss Astrid handed us their bottles. As we fed the babies, my mind whirled. It seemed too crude for the Aldon to kill Reed and just leave him there like an Orco attack. Something just didn't make sense.

"Chandler, what is it?' Constance asked, snapping me back to the present.

"The murder. This is all so surreal."

"I know. Do you realize, a year ago, my biggest concern was transferring to LSU and finding an apartment?" she said bitterly. Elly finished her bottle, and Constance placed her on her shoulder, placing her lips to her forehead.

Everett came back into the room and sat down on the sofa beside me.

"I think I'll go and fix a plate. Ev, would you take Elly?" she asked as Everett held his hands out.

"Come here, Ma Petit. Uncle Everett needs you near," he said, cuddling Ellyson to his chest. She curled up immediately, nuzzling into his chest as he pressed his lips to her hair.

I leaned my head back on the sofa and watched Everett. "You know, you are the only one who has that much of a calming effect on them," I observed. Matty finished and pushed up in my lap.

"They calm me, Bebe. I love them so much," he murmured, pressing his lips into her hair again.

"Everett, are you all right? We haven't had the chance to really talk, since…" I trailed off as he turned his head to rest his cheek on Ellyson's head. I glanced into the dining room, and Banton stood beside Claudia's chair, gently rubbing her back as she looked over some papers. I looked back at Everett, and his eyes glowed with the intensity that I'd seen in them after William was killed as Banton tried to console Claudia. I'd seen that same

364

intensity one other time, when Everett had read Marie-Claire's mother's entries in the diary.

It hit me like a bolt of lightning, startling me to my core. I hadn't even considered it. Everett was in love with Claudia.

My heart clenched, almost ached. As I continued to watch him, I realized he'd been in love with her for months. Memories flooded in as far back as the day we'd stood in my foyer decorating my Christmas tree, the dress fittings when I'd caught him almost worshipping Claudia during Mardi Gras, modeling as they fitted the dress to her. Besides Banton and Julia, Everett had seemed to grieve William's death harder than anyone. It was a revelation as I watched him continue to hug Ellyson to him, his eyes never leaving Claudia. He blamed himself for Will's death and wondered if his love for her had kept him from doing more.

"Ev, come upstairs with me, please?" I whispered.

He looked inquiringly at me.

"Help me with the babies?'

He nodded and rose. When we entered the nursery, I turned and shut the nursery door.

"Bebe, what is it?"

"I know you better than anyone. Better than your own mother, I think. Will you please be honest with me?"

"Mon chere, you know I will," he answered, sitting down in the rocker beside me.

"I know your secret. You've hidden it well and fooled us all a long time."

He raised an eyebrow at me, managing at the same time to keep his eyes guarded. I studied him, his beautiful dish-water blonde hair mussed a bit, clean starched pale linen shirt opened slightly at the neck, polo khakis. He was muscular, extremely handsome in a "Ralph Lauren Polo ad" sort of way. He pursed his sensual, full lips at me as he waited.

"You're in love with Claudia," I whispered.

He tensed, his forthcoming mood dissipating.

"What brings you to that conclusion, Bebe?" he tried to sound nonchalant.

I rose and placed Matty in his crib and placed a kiss on the corner of his mouth. He grabbed a toy and began to entertain himself as I turned to face Everett.

"I've watched you for months, worshipping her from afar. You told me you were in love with someone, but it was unrequited love. Then just now, I saw the impassioned plea in your eyes as you watched her with Banton. I've only seen that much emotion in your eyes twice, when you read Marie-Claire's mother's diary, and the day William was killed. You love her," I whispered simply as tears gathered in his eyes.

He rose and crossed the space between us to place Elly in the crib with Matty. They immediately began to tumble and play. Everett watched them for a moment and then turned back to me. He nodded.

" love her with all my heart. She's everything to me. I so desperately want to make this go away…this awful thing she's going through. If I could have only been quicker, if I'd been here when they attacked," his voice broke as his eyes began to glow again.

"Oh, Everett! You don't doubt yourself for one minute that you didn't do everything in your power to save William! Please, for me…stop this! Claudia is mourning, but she needs you. She needs all of us. I don't know where this thing will go between the two of you, but when the time is right you will know. In the meantime, please forgive yourself and just be there for her."

I placed my hand on his arm and he pulled me into his chest, burying his face in my hair.

"Oh, Bebe…I love you so much. You are right, and I will do anything in my power to make her happy. She and Ava, they mean as much to me as you and your children do."

Banton pushed the door open and stepped silently into the room. I pulled away from Everett, both of us wiping tears from our eyes as we met his inquiring gaze with a smile.

"Um, do I need to be worried?" Banton asked as he glanced back and forth at us.

"No, dear boy, I promise you have nothing to worry about. Our sweet Bebe here is just being her usual, loving self. You do know how absolutely lucky you are?" He turned to Banton and raised an eyebrow at him.

Banton chuckled and placed his arm intimately around my waist.

"Believe me, Everett, that is one thing I know. I'm the luckiest man in the universe," he stated, placing a kiss in my hair.

Everett looked back and forth at us, and then stated plainly, "Discretion, Chere. Discretion at all costs. Now is not the time."

"I know, Ev. I love you," I whispered as I glanced sideways at Banton.

"I love you too. Both of you," he answered as he left the room.

Banton turned me around in his arms. "So, what was all that about?"

I sighed. This was another secret Everett was asking me to keep from Banton. I'd sworn I'd never do that again.

"You're off the hook. I already know, I've known since the attack," Banton muttered as he played with my collar.

"What?'

"That Everett is in love with my sister.

"You know? Why didn't you say anything to me?"

He turned and gave me an incredulous look. "We really haven't had a lot of quiet gossip time now have we?"

I sighed and shook my head. "No, I guess you're right. Now, come and tell me about Commander Reed! Banton, what's going on?"

Banton pulled away and took my hand, leading me through the connecting doorway to our bedroom. Settling down on two overstuffed chairs beside the window, he ran his fingers through his hair as I waited for him to begin.

"I don't know what to make of all of this. I don't think the Aldon had anything to do with Reed's murder. The Aldon would have taken him out, and he would have just disappeared. This was done as a warning to the Navy...to us, to the Aldon maybe. I think the Orcos took him out," he said as he glanced back over at me.

"Ev is afraid he had something to do with Reed's murder because he alerted the Aldon.

"I think the Orcos took Reed out because the Aldon found out."

"Um, you've lost me."

"Andie, I get the feeling Reed was playing both sides. I talked to Singleton earlier, and there will be an investigation, more than likely I will be involved. But right now, we've just got to regroup and let Singleton sort out the immediate situation with the Orcos on the move again."

I nodded. "Thank you for telling me," I said softly, squeezing his hand.

"Well, none of it is classified, at least not yet, anyway. And you are as involved as I am in all of this."

We sat in silence for several minutes, Banton taking my hand in his and tracing his thumb over the back of it as he lost himself, thinking about the events of the day.

"What did you and your parents discuss?"

"We just want to make sure everything is as Claudia wants it. All the arrangements are in place. There will be a public service at their Church day after tomorrow at 10:00 a.m."

I took a deep breath. "How do you want to handle the twins? I've been thinking about this…" I began.

"I know, baby. We can't take them out in public with their eyes and their fading, and I really don't want to take them from the house right now anyway. Everett didn't want to alarm us, but he said that information the Aldon have about the attack the other day indicated the goal of their mission was to kidnap you and the twins."

My heart chilled. I'd feared all along the twins were the ultimate goal.

"I don't want to leave them here alone with anyone," I began.

"I know, Chandler. I don't either. I don't want to leave you, but I have to go and be there for my sister. I'm going to talk to Everett, and see who we can get to stay and guard you and the twins here at the house, while I go with the family to the funeral service. Are you okay with that?'

"Yes, Banton…of course. Whatever you think is best."

"We'll need Everett and the SEALs with us, there will be such a crowd there. I hate splitting our forces," he said, rubbing his finger across his bottom lip.

"Banton, I have Miss Astrid now to help protect the twins. Maybe she and Everett could recruit a few more Aldon, just to watch the house until you return. It will just be for three hours or so."

"Yes, that sounds good. I'll talk to Everett after dinner. Chandler, are you going to eat? Come downstairs with me," Banton urged, kissing the back of my hand.

"I think I'll just lay down with the twins for a bit, I'm really beat," I replied as he raised an eyebrow at me.

"I promise, I've had my blood shake today. I'm just a little nauseated, that's all. It's bath time, and I think I'll just put them in the tub with me, and then I'll lie down with them. Besides, I have to make that call to Laurilee. I need quiet time to break this to her gently."

Banton nodded and rose. He stood in front of me and then pulled me up into his arms.

"Wish I could change things for you. I'm so sorry. I just won't risk the Texas trip or splitting us up. Please tell Laurilee and Dan I am so sorry, and I plan to make it up to them in a big way."

I nodded as the tears threatened. I'd had an emotional day and hated to end it with letting my best childhood friend down in such a way.

"And how are you planning to do that?' I mumbled, nuzzling against his chest.

"There is a box, ready to be delivered to the wedding, for them to open at the reception. I've arranged for them to have five days in the Florida Keys, all expenses paid, first class room service…the works. I'm giving them their honeymoon, from us."

"Banton, that's really extravagant. That is a wonderful thing for you to do," I said as the tears threatened as I thought about this being his way of making it up to me.

"It's the least I can do. I just hope she'll forgive me," Banton said as he kissed my hair.

* * *

I woke when Banton slipped into the bed at midnight. He wrapped his arms around me, placing his leg between mine. I'd hoped once I was wrapped around him I could sleep, but my conversation with Laurilee weighed heavy in my thoughts, keeping sleep at bay. After I heard his breathing slow and get into a rhythm, I slipped from the bed. Slipping my robe on, I decided to check the twins. I turned and found them both in the same crib at the foot of our bed as I'd found them the night before. I smiled over at Banton. He'd moved them in with us again. I loved this man so much --this man who wanted to protect me and our babies. My heart clenched at the sudden thought that he might have another child out there. The subject of Reece was lost in the events of the last few days. I wondered if Banton had heard anything yet. I quickly pushed the troubling thoughts from my head as I descended the staircase. I paused at the bottom. Claudia sat on the sofa, sobbing softly as Everett held her in his arms. They both stared into the fireplace. After quietly talking to her for a few moments, he placed his cheek on top of her head. I knew it was too soon for anything romantically to develop between them, but Everett would take care of her, protect her, and be what she needed no matter what.

I padded carefully and silently back to the kitchen and poured myself a glass of milk. As I sat at the breakfast bar, tears threatened as I went over my conversation with Laurilee. She was absolutely heartbroken at my news that I couldn't risk coming to the wedding. She'd tearfully replied she understood and pleaded with me to stay safe, and convey to Banton's family her sadness at their loss. But I could hear the disappointment in her voice. I'd ruined her perfect plans for her perfect day. She assured me she would ask one of our friends to stand in for me, and I promised her Banton and I would make everything up to her, but it wasn't the same.

The tears spilled as I rolled the glass tumbler that held my milk between my hands. She was there at my wedding, shared our first Christmas together, and she and Dan had made the trip to Louisiana when the twins were born. I felt as though I was letting the world revolve around me, and only friending her when she was needed. I hated this!

"Chandler, what's up?" Constance had slipped into the kitchen unnoticed.

370

I wiped the tears from my cheeks with the backs of my hands as I cleared my throat.

"Guilt. I can't stand letting Laurilee down. She's devastated that we won't be there."

"I understand the protection thing with everything that has happened. But Banton can't give you a day? Just fly there and back, the four of us and Everett?"

I sighed and finished my milk. "I suggested that, but with everything that has happened he doesn't want to split forces. And to be honest, I don't think I could leave the babies behind. We know Lucien's ultimate goal was to kidnap me and the twins."

Constance sat back on the barstool with her knees clasped to her chest. "Ty wants to set a date. He is so anxious to get married all of a sudden with everything that has happened. Now, I'm not so sure," she sighed. I cocked an eyebrow in her direction.

"You can't be serious! Now you're the one putting on the brakes?"

"He loves kids, Chandler. You've seen how he is with the twins. He's made the comment before he can't wait to have kids of his own, and he always wanted a big family."

"Olivia and Patrick seem to think you and I are different."

"But Dr. Renault and Dr. Lane don't. I don't know if I can do that to him. You of all people should know how I feel. I know… I overheard you talking to Banton. You're afraid you won't be able to get pregnant again, and you want to give him more kids. That's a heartbreaking feeling, to know you can't," she said as tears threatened. It was so unlike Constance, and very sobering.

"Constance, you and Ty love each other. He is crazy in love with you. You can adopt," I began.

"It's not the same thing; you know that. I think it will be more important to Ty down the road than he realizes. It would kill me to know he wants something from me that I'm not equipped to give him. It would make me feel less…" she struggled for the right word.

"Normal. Like a young bride…a young woman. I know," I sighed and placed my hand over hers.

"Hey, there you are."

371

We both turned to find Ty standing in the side doorway to the kitchen, having come down the back staircase.

"Hey. We were just having some milk," Constance answered him as she wiped her eyes.

"Come back to bed. I can't sleep without you," Ty urged as he crossed the kitchen to her.

"I'm finished. I think I can sleep now. Goodnight, Constance...Ty." I rushed out of the kitchen, giving them some privacy.

"I heard part of what you said, baby. You are all I want...you are everything I want..." Ty began as I hurried back up the staircase. I didn't want to eavesdrop on their intimate moment. I sighed, understanding Constance so well, feeling exactly as she felt. Those feelings were still raw as I thought again about Reece, and the fact that Alexandra could still have more children. As I crawled back into bed with Banton, my heart seemed heavier than when I'd left, and I knew I'd never rest tonight.

Chapter Twenty-Four

The morning of William's funeral dawned gray and rainy. I rose early, wanting to fix breakfast for everyone and be on hand if Claudia needed anything. I knew I had to stay behind for the twins, but I felt a little guilty not going with the entire family to the service.

"My dear, what are you doing up so early?" Mrs. Elaine descended the back staircase in her robe.

"I couldn't sleep, and after I got the babies back down at five, I decided to stay up and fix breakfast. Would you like some coffee?"

"That would be wonderful, thank you." She smiled, taking her cup from me.

"How is Claudia this morning?"

"Still sleeping. I just checked on her, and Everett was asleep in the chair beside her bed. He hasn't left her side in two days. He is so precious, Chandler. He is a God-send," she said as she hugged me. I pulled a pan of blueberry muffins from the oven and flipped them out into a basket on the breakfast bar.

"Can I do anything to help you?" Mrs. Elaine asked.

"No, Ma'am. I almost have everything ready. I have a breakfast casserole in the oven, and I've already fixed some fruit in the fridge. Miss Astrid should be down any minute, and she will be upset with me if I don't leave something for her to do," I said as she smiled at me.

"Well, I think I'll take a cup of this delicious coffee up to Matt, then." She poured another cup, and then returned to the back staircase.

After I had everything ready and waiting on the stove, I sat down in a large chair facing the back windows, overlooking the patio. The scene replayed again and again in my head. Claudia being jerked from the back of her SUV, Brie crushed against the garage wall, Constance battling two of the Orcos. If I'd just stopped and helped Claudia…If I'd just stopped William. I shut my eyes, blocking out the images.

I sensed his presence before I felt his arms go around me from behind. Banton placed a kiss on my neck as I leaned my head over to give him better access.

"Hey," he murmured against my neck. "I could smell the blueberry muffins and coffee from upstairs. I woke, and your side of the bed was cold. I don't like waking up without you beside me."

"The babies went back down at five, and I couldn't sleep, so I decided to come down and make myself useful. I feel bad about not going with the family today."

"Sweetheart, everyone understands. We have to keep the babies here. Is that what's had you so preoccupied?"

He slowly made his way around the chair, and squatted in front of me, his coffee cup in his hands. Leaning over, he kissed my hand as I held it out to run it through his hair.

"You need a haircut," I whispered.

"And you are changing the subject," he retorted, sinking back in the floor, Indian-style.

"I'm just still upset about what I had to do to Laurilee and Dan," I sighed as tears threatened again. "She never answered when I called her back last night. I feel like I should be packing to leave for Texas in the morning."

Banton studied his coffee for a moment, and then looked up at me, seeming a bit irritated I'd brought it up again. The nerve ticked in his jaw, the muscles tense. He narrowed his eyes in an angry glare as he spoke.

"We've been through this, Chandler. I can't risk it, end of subject. I'm sorry Laurilee is disappointed, but she'll just have to understand.

"Disappointed? Banton, I know this isn't as big a deal to you guys as it us to us girls, but disappointed? That doesn't even begin to cover what she's feeling right now. She's devastated. She's inconsolable…distraught…her wedding day ruined! That's what she's feeling! It's horrible for me to stand her up, when she was here for mine. She was here for my first Christmas without my mother. She was here after the babies came! She was here for me!" I was shouting now, my emotions getting the best of me. I was angry at myself, not Banton. But his eyes indicated he thought

374

otherwise. They burned with anger as he considered what I'd just said.

When he finally spoke, his voice was truncated, barely controlling his anger. I'd never heard him talk to me like that, even after the attack.

"Chandler, I can't deal with this right now. We've got a funeral to get ready for, and I can hear the babies. I'm going up to see about them," he said angrily, rising and heading for the back staircase. After he was out of earshot, I let go and sobbed into my hands. I felt thoroughly rebuked, like a petulant child. Of course he had other things to deal with, his grieving sister for one. I shook my head, realizing my outburst was childish and selfish.

"Bebe, are you all right?" Everett had entered the kitchen without my hearing him. I rose and hurriedly wiped my eyes. Miss Astrid stood just inside the doorway behind him.

"Chandler, what can I do to help with breakfast? That's what I'm here for," she scolded as I shook my head.

"If you could just get some bottles ready for the babies. They may be hungry already. Banton just went to see about them," I replied softly as she nodded. I rose and crossed the kitchen meeting Everett half-way. He took me in his arms.

"I overheard…it's that darn Aldon hearing, you know," he tugged at an ear as I laughed through my tears. "Banton's not mad at you, Bebe, he's mad because he had to make a decision that is upsetting you. Maybe you two can have sweet Laurilee and Dan come to Louisiana after everything calms down, to do their vows here…as a sort of a second ceremony? I can throw a really impressive party, you know," Everett said with flair, his hand in the air.

I smiled. Everett could always make me smile. "All right, Ev. That does sound good. I'm going to go up and dress the babies for the day and make myself presentable," I murmured as he patted me on the shoulder. I took the stairs two at a time and pushed our bedroom door open. The babies were playing with each other, jabbering away in their baby jargon only the two of them understood. The bathroom door was closed, and I could hear the shower running. I used the opportunity to go ahead and dress the twins, and then I dressed in some soft jeans and a sweater. I'd just

375

picked both babies up when Banton opened the bathroom door, a towel wrapped around his waist. I took a deep breath and shook my head. Would my heart always quicken at the sight of his naked torso?

As I watched him move around the bedroom, my heart sank. He never glanced my way as he took his clothes out of the closet and began to dress. I left the room silently, descending the stairs and then settling down on the sofa in front of the fireplace. This was the first time I could truly feel a rift between us. I needed to apologize for my outburst this morning.

I placed the twins in the floor on the rug, and then pulled a bag of their toys around from the side of the sofa. I took out a couple of their favorites and placed them in the floor. As the family began to drift downstairs, the doorbell rang. Everyone else was either still upstairs dressing, or they were eating in the breakfast room. Thinking it was probably more flowers or food, I opened the front door.

Alexandra's stare greeted me.

My shock at seeing her got the best of me. "What are you doing here?" I blurted out in anger. *How dare she come to Banton's family, at a time like this!*

"Well…you certainly changed your little act from the other day. I thought you were the kind, caring little wife. I guess that's only for Banton's benefit. I should have known. Please, get Banton for me. I need to see him," she demanded as she smiled coyly at me. I glanced behind her, and Reece peered out the window of her car, strapped in a car seat.

"Banton's getting ready upstairs. How did you find us?" I asked, outraged.

"They told me at the base where I could find you. Are you going to get Banton for me, or do I have to force my way in? One mousy little wife isn't going to stop me from seeing Banton."

"Alexandra! What the hell," Banton's voice boomed from the staircase behind me. I turned, and found Everett, Julia and Constance staring from the hallway. I blushed, embarrassed our family witnessed any of this.

"I don't know how you got this address, Alex, but now is not the time for this," Banton's voice carried to the living room where

I'd escaped. I pulled the babies up on the couch with me, aware Constance followed me.

"Banton, I had to come. I know some of what has been going on, and I know your family is in danger. Reece is in danger too, if that is the case," she pleaded. "I thought maybe you might need to see us, and for us to make some plans…"

Banton pulled the door closed as he stood outside talking to Alex. I thought I'd worked this entire thing about Reece out in my own head, but the empty hole opened in my chest again when I thought about him having been with her, about Reece possibly being his son. As Constance corralled the babies, I stood, my arms wrapped around my waist. I crossed over to the windows and looked out. Alex stood facing Banton, sobbing, her shoulders shaking. Banton reached out, and held his hand out to her as he spoke. She launched herself at him, and he awkwardly held her for a moment. As I watched them, I shuddered. I recognized the ache I was feeling. It was the same ache I'd felt when I'd seen Cody's naked body wrapped around the rodeo 'ho" in his pickup. It was the same hurt I'd felt the night I thought Banton was in a relationship with someone else, the night Beau was bitten by snakes. It was that sorry for yourself feeling you get when you are jealous, and you feel like you've been wronged. The same feeling you get when doubt creeps in, making you think maybe you aren't good enough for him, that there might be someone else. I shook my head and watched as rain began to fall softly outside, slowly wetting their heads as they continued to embrace. I hated myself for feeling this way.

"Holy shit, Chandler," Constance exclaimed, peering at them over my shoulder. "What is going on?"

I looked back at her and shook my head as my eyes filled with tears. I refused to break down in front of the family, right before Will's funeral. I looked over at Julia and Everett, who still hovered close by as they played with the babies in the floor. Laughter bubbled up…I was thinking it resembled a page of a story book called, "White trash scenes from hell."

"Chandler?" Everett called softly, knowing my laughter was one step away from a breakdown.

377

I looked back at Constance, and then back at Everett. I shook my head, and then held my hand up as I passed him. He wisely remained silent. I made my way into the kitchen, and busied myself with a cup of coffee, and preparing bottles for the babies' next meal.

"Chandler, dear…who was that at the front door just now?" Mrs. Elaine asked.

"Just someone to see Banton," I murmured, placing the babies bottles back into the refrigerator. Taking a deep breath, I decided my hysteria had passed. In view of the awkwardness in the living room, I decided to retreat upstairs until the family left for the service.

I stopped in the hallway as I heard Everett's voice.

"I don't think I would right now, Banton-babe. You don't have enough time; we need to leave for the church in five minutes. Let her be. You can talk to her after the service. I think she might need a little space, and a good 'ole-fashioned southern belle crazy-bitch parade might be just around the corner waiting on you if you say the wrong thing now," he cautioned.

"It would have helped matters if Chandler hadn't watched you holding the 'ho' in your arms out on the front porch!" Constance snapped as Banton moaned. "What was that about, anyway? What the hell, Banton?"

"It's not what you think…what she thought…oh, hell!" Banton's voice sounded exasperated.

I turned, hurrying back around the kitchen and up the back staircase. I was on the verge of tears, and I didn't want a scene before they all left. Once in our room, I rummaged through our bags, and found the babies blankies, and then took a blanket off the bed so I could make them a pallet in the floor in front of the fireplace. I decided I would camp out there with them, and visit with Miss Astrid while we waited for the family to come home. I waited a few moments, and then descended the staircase when I knew they were all about to leave for the church. When I reached the bottom of the staircase, I could see Banton sitting on the sofa in front of the fireplace, with the twins cuddled against his chest.

"Banton, we're ready to leave." Mrs. Elaine called out from the foyer.

"Okay, Momma, I'll be right there," he answered, placing a kiss on each of the twins' foreheads. I rounded the large stone pillar that separated the living room from the foyer, and reached to take the babies from him. He searched my eyes as I stepped back for him to pass. He reached over and picked up his jacket, and as he straightened, opened his mouth to say something, and then closed it again. Tears pooled in my eyes as I realized he must still be mad from our quarrel earlier, and he didn't want to get into anything before he left. I smiled up at him and nodded. His gaze softened, and he reached out and cupped my cheek in his hand. I shut my eyes and kept them shut until I heard the family leave.

I sat down on the couch and released the tears. I cried about not being at Laurilee's wedding. I cried for Will and Claudia, and about not going to Will's service. I cried about my jealousy toward Alexandra and poor Reece. I cried because I'd burned the blueberry muffins a bit when I'd cooked breakfast this morning.

"Okay, Miss Chandler...enough. Let me have those babies, and we're going to go and have a little apple juice and a stroll out on the back patio. You lay down here on this couch and rest. Have a good little cry and work it all out. I'll put the babies down in the nursery for their nap after a bit," Miss Astrid said, picking the babies up out of my lap. Elly squealed at her and then giggled as she scooped them up, and then swooped down the hallway with them. I smiled at that. Elly seemed to love Miss Astrid.

I snuggled down into the soft cushions and stared into the fire. I was exhausted, having gotten up before five with the babies. I thought if I just closed my eyes for a few minutes…

* * *

I woke and sat up in semi-darkness. The fireplace was out, and the air in the room seemed a bit chilly. My eyes watered as I rubbed them. It was still raining outside, the water running down the window panes in rivulets. Shuddering as it thundered, my heart rate quickened as chills ran up my arms, the hairs standing up like antennae. I felt the need to check on the twins. My footsteps sounded hollow as I crossed the large living room, and with the family gone the house seemed cavernous. I took the steps two at a time, and then ran down the hallway to the nursery. Not wanting to startle the babies and wake them from their nap, I slowed my steps as I neared their door, and then pushed the door open slowly. My heart beat pulsed in my ears as I neared Matty's crib. I found it empty. I drew in a ragged breath as I whirled to check Elly's…again, empty.

"Miss Astrid, where are you?" I called frantically, already in an alarmed state. Surely she'd moved them or had them downstairs. I ran back down the hallway, and met Miss Astrid's stare at the top of the staircase. I stilled. There was no question in her eyes, no expression of wonder as to why I was frantically calling her. A sick feeling crept through me.

"Miss Astrid, where are the twins?"

"They've been taken somewhere secure," she said as her eyes began to glow. *Holy shit!* I'd never seen her eyes glow, and the irises around her pupils seemed to radiate with three or four shades of green.

"What do you mean? Has Banton moved them," I began.

"No. There is no time for talk. Shut up and listen," she hissed. I felt the color drain from my face. A thousand different scenarios ran through my mind, none of them pleasant.

"You are going to write a note for me, which we will leave for your family downstairs. Then I am to deliver you to Lucien at a pre-determined place in exactly forty-five minutes, or both the babies will die. Do you understand?

I shut my eyes as a sob escaped. My body was pure static…much like the day the Navy paid their visit. I had no way to get in touch with Banton, no way to let anyone know what happened to us. *My babies…oh, God…Lucien has my babies.*

She crossed the space between us in a split second, so fast her movements were a blur. Grabbing me by my hair, she fisted her hand around it, pulling me to her painfully as she hissed in my ear.

"I asked you a question, you little whining rich-bitch! Do you understand? Lucien will sink his fangs in them and drain them quickly, and give their bodies to the others for dessert! DO YOU UNDERSTAND?"

"Yes!" I screamed out as she slapped me hard, so hard I would have flown across the hallway had she not held a tight fist around my hair.

"Good."

Although small-framed and wiry, she managed to drag me down the staircase effortlessly and then across the great room into the foyer. She turned my hair loose and thrust me forward in one swift motion, slamming me into an antique Bombay chest sitting just inside the entrance. She'd already placed a pen and paper on the desk.

"Now, write. You will tell your husband you've decided to go to your friend Laurilee's wedding, and you are on Delta flight 455 to Dallas. You've taken the twins, so they are not to worry. You will call as soon as you get to Dallas. Write!" she screamed as I tried to write through my tears.

"He'll never believe this. He'll check, and there won't be anyone on the plane," I began.

"Oh, plane tickets have been purchased with your credit card, and there is a cast of characters posing on your behalf. It will be late tonight before he can confirm with your friends that you weren't on that flight. We'll be long gone in another direction by then."

My mind was whirling as I wrote. She was standing over me, so I had to be careful. After I finished writing, she grabbed the letter and folded it neatly, placing it in an envelope.

"Write his name on the front," she barked at me coldly.

I penned his name slowly, "Banton"

I never wrote his name in cursive. I always printed it as I had the entire note. I hoped he would catch the difference and consider it strange. Then a thought hit me. As she straightened she threw a jacket at me, and then picked a duffle bag that I hadn't noticed up from the floor beside the front door. As she focused her attention on the door, she glanced out the side windows, making sure that the family hadn't returned yet. I used the opportunity and slipped my diamond bracelet and wedding ring off, dropping them on the rug by the chest. She pulled me roughly out the front door, down the brick steps to a black SUV parked in the driveway. I looked up expectantly, remembering the security cameras Banton installed

381

only the day before. There was a dark disk covering the lens on the camera on the porch. My insides sank.

"We've thought of everything, believe me," she hissed, flinging the back doors open. "Get in!" she screamed at me as I shakily complied.

"Why are you doing this? How can you be one of them," I pleaded as her eyes narrowed.

"I've always been one of them. Your dear, sweet Everett isn't as good as he thinks he is at feeling someone's emotions."

"Maybe it's because you are dead inside," I challenged. She back-handed me in reply. The force bounced my head off the wheel-well inside the vehicle, and the blow caused my vision to darken and form a long tunnel. As I watched her as if from a distance, she pulled my hands together and secured them with thick metal bands, and then the same with my feet. She then secured them together, forcing me into a ball. For a finale, she placed a large piece of duct tape across my mouth as I used every last ounce of strength I had to fight her.

"Hmm. Only thirty minutes left...maybe it will be feeding time when we arrive," she hissed into my ear as my world went black.

Chapter Twenty-Five

Banton

I glanced in the rear-view mirror every few seconds. Dad held Claudia close, his soothing voice murmuring to her. She was doing amazingly well, and seemed in control during the funeral. My eyes shifted to Ava, who clutched Julia tightly and watched me warily. Chandler and I both were worried about her. I intended to talk to Chandler this morning about staying on with Claudia for a time. Instead, we had to argue.

Chandler...she'd looked so hurt this morning. *Why do I have to explode like that! She just doesn't understand how I feel about her safety.* My insides twisted every time I thought about being separated from her or taking her anywhere unprotected. I knew Laurilee's wedding was the only thing she would argue with me about. She never asked me for anything. I smiled --sometimes I wished she would. For the hundredth time, I wondered if I was being too over-protective.

No, I shook my head

Maybe I'd been hasty. She was so upset about missing the wedding and disappointing Laurilee. *Could I risk it?* It would take Everett and a SEAL or two to make me feel she was protected. John and Brie could go. That would be four of us to protect her, and we could leave the twins with Momma and Daddy and the rest of the Aldon. *I'll talk to her again.* Maybe we could charter a plane and come back the same day. *Shit! That scene with Alexandra before we left!* I couldn't believe I'd weakened and fallen for Alex's crap. I'd hugged her and tried to talk some sense into her. Chandler watched the whole thing. I knew she took it the wrong way. *When will she ever see she has nothing to worry about? She is my whole world!*

I couldn't wait to get back to the house. I shook my head. Chandler had that effect on me. Anytime I could make her smile...make her happy...those were the best moments of my life.

"What the hell," I muttered as I pulled into the driveway. The three Aldon Miss Astrid called in to help for the funeral were nowhere to be seen. They'd been stationed on the porch when we'd left this morning.

"Where are the Aldon?" Brie muttered as John glanced up.

"Maybe they're inside or out back," John replied as he unbuckled his seatbelt.

"Chandler, we're home!" I called out as I ran up the staircase. I was eager to hold her, and I felt an urgent need to make sure all was well between us. I didn't kiss her before we'd left for the services. Finding our bedroom empty, I drew my brows together. The bed was still unmade, and our suitcases were out across the foot of the bed. It was unlike Chandler not to tidy the room. Chandler couldn't stand an unmade bed, especially if we were staying with someone else. *Maybe she's ill?*

I pushed the door open to the nursery, and finding the cribs empty, returned to the hallway.

"Banton, down here…there is a note for you," Constance called out as I hurried back down the staircase.

"Where's Miss Astrid? Have you seen her," I asked breathlessly as Ty shook his head.

"There's no one in the back part of the house," he answered, alarmed.

Constance handed me the note.

"This doesn't look like Chandler's handwriting," I murmured, puzzled as I looked at the envelope. I unfolded the note hurriedly.

> *Banton,*
>
> *I know we discussed this, but I can't let Lauri down. I'll be just fine. I'm taking Miss Astrid with me, and she can keep the twins at the hotel during the ceremony, and she will be extra protection for me. We're on Delta flight 455, and I will call you when we get to Dallas tonight. I'll arrange for Daniel to pick us up at the airport. Don't worry, we'll be fine.*
>
> > *I love you with all my heart,*
> > *Chandler Ann.*

"What the hell," I said under my breath. Everett was immediately at my side, scanning the note over my shoulder. "She

384

wouldn't go to Texas, not after we talked. And she'd never take the twins."

"Banton, she didn't write that note," he said, alarmed.

"I think it's her handwriting all right, but," I frowned, rereading the note again. Something didn't fit. *Chandler! What the hell are you thinking! You know you need two or three people to protect you and the babies...*

It hit me. "Look at this, she never calls Laurilee 'Lauri,' and she wasn't going to stay at a hotel...it's a bed and breakfast." I had a sinking feeling.

Everett chimed in, "She never calls Dan 'Daniel' either."

My stomach turned over. "And she's told me more than once, when she's 'Chandler Ann,' she's in trouble."

"And that's what she's telling you, my dear boy," Everett said as he pulled the note out of my hands.

I looked up into my father's eyes. He'd been silently listening to us from the doorway.

"Son, I hate to tell you this, but we just noticed the lens to the security camera out front has been covered."

"Shit! Ty, John...get on the phone to Singleton! Tell him Chandler and the twins have been taken. Ev, call your friends with the NOPD and have them alerted. Do you have any idea what kind of vehicle Miss Astrid would be driving?"

"You think Astrid had something to do with this?"

"She had too! Or she's being forced to. Either way, we have to follow that lead."

Everett nodded, pulling his cell from his back pocket.

"Dad, I need traveling money. We have our passports, but I might need for you to pull some strings. Everett, get in touch with Renault, and whoever the hell is in charge of the Aldon! I need their full cooperation, and now!"

Everett's eyes widened, but he nodded in agreement.

"Banton, what can we do?" Claudia stood ghostly silent beside me, her arms around Constance.

"Run upstairs and go through our bedroom and the nursery. See if you can find anything that makes sense."

They both nodded, both of them beginning to cry. I couldn't let those emotions through. I had to stay calm and focused. My instincts warned me I had minutes to find something to give me a direction, or their trail would go cold. I had a gut suspicion my beautiful wife and my babies were on a boat headed for Somalia.

"Banton, I just called a friend of mine at the State Capitol. He's going to pull some strings and talk with the Board of Commissioners and Port Authority Harbor Police. They're going to try to halt anything leaving N'awlins; maybe we can delay their departure." My dad was dialing his cell as he spoke.

"We're assuming they're traveling by ship. What if they're flying?" John said, hanging his phone up.

"I'll get on the computer and check all the flights leaving the airport this afternoon," Brie offered.

"No good. You wouldn't be able to access all the cargo flights, and that's what they would use."

"I can still have the NOPD Aldon to check the airport, see if they can get any leads," Everett interrupted, dialing his phone again.

My insides tightened as I thought about our argument before we'd left for the funeral. I closed my eyes. For the first time I could remember, I didn't kiss her goodbye. It hadn't been intentional. *Think! Think, Banton...there has to be something you aren't thinking of!*

Constance ran back down the staircase with Claudia trailing behind her. "Banton, her small traveling bag is missing and a few of her clothes. But she left her bridesmaid dress, and the presents for Laurilee...her laptop. She also left the babies' blankies in the living room on the sofa," she added as her voice broke. "She'd never take Matty and Elly somewhere without them."

A tug at my pants leg startled me from my thoughts. Ava looked up at me, her big round eyes full of tears.

"Doodle- Bug, not now. I'm busy."

"Unca Banin, An Andler's bwacelet. Her dropped it," she said softly as she held it up to me.

I grabbed it out of her hand. "Sweetheart, where did you find this? Hurry, tell Uncle Banton."

"Ober dere," she replied, pointing over to the floor by the desk in the entry hall. I walked over to look, and something sparkled on the floor where she was pointing. I bent over, and picked up Chandler's wedding ring.

Constance gasped and placed her hand over her mouth as my eyes met hers.

"She told me the other day the only way that ring would ever come off her finger was at gunpoint. It was a joke at the time," I whispered as I closed my hand over it. My insides were on fire. Chandler...Oh, God. For the third time in my life, someone took by force my reason for living. Only this time, I had no clue where they'd gone or how to follow them. And my babies were helpless. Knowing the Orcos used them to lure Chandler away, I was filled with a rage that I'd never felt before. I began to picture her like I'd found her in the tunnels, chained to the wall, dehydrated, beaten beyond recognition. I shook with fury, my hands fisted at my sides.

"Banton, what do you want to do?" John asked as he pocketed his cell phone.

"Let's move. Take the gear we have in my SUV. Let's split up in two vehicles. Head to the Port of N'awlins. My gut tells me that's where they're headed. Ty, you and John take your car, Everett and I will take mine. Call Sam, tell him to get Patrick and meet us as soon as they can."

"I'm coming with you," Brie offered.

"No, baby...stay here at the house with Banton's family. You and Constance are their only protection until we can get someone else out here," John called over his shoulder to her.

"John, I don't want to contradict you, but consider this. Brie has Aldon senses, can smell other Orcos and she has a connection to Chandler. It might be helpful. I can have security around this place in no time. I'll call Lane and another friend at the Capitol. I'll get state troopers if I have to. Just go, please." My Dad pleaded with John, and John finally relented. I nodded to him, and then jumped into the SUV as Everett jumped into the other side. As I glanced in my rear-view mirror, my entire family stood on the front porch, watching silently and helplessly.

As we sped toward the Interstate, Everett's cell rang.

"Yes, we are on our way to the shipyard now." He snapped his fingers to get my attention, seeming to read a list off to me to commit to memory. I nodded as he repeated.

387

"A large grey and black ship, cargo ship, bearing shipping containers. One of four, due to leave in the next twenty-four hours. The names?"

He was writing on his jacket, not having found any paper in the glove box.

"Anything else?"

"Yes, I'll call you back if we don't find anything. How should we travel? Yes, four Aldon should be sufficient, with our team in place. We don't need to be too conspicuous until we know what we are dealing with. Go ahead and make the arrangements, and notify the Coast Guard. Yes, all the gear the SEALs might need for a stealth mission. We'll board her at sea if we have to."

"Good. Thank you for your cooperation, but with all due respect, you should have done this a long time ago."

Everett touched his phone, ending the call. "That was Aldon leadership. They're making the arrangements and providing us with an escort to Somalia, with or without the Navy's help, if we don't stop Lucien here," he said, his voice deadly grim. I glanced over at him, and his eyes glowed with intensity I'd never witnessed, full of tears and emotion. I put my hand up as if to stop his gaze. I couldn't go there, and neither could Everett. Not when our girl and our babies were counting on us. I knew I had the one person in the world who cared as deeply for them as I did, and I found some comfort in knowing that just like me, he'd die for their safety.

Chapter Twenty-Six

Chandler

My head throbbed. The throbbing consumed every thought, in time with the hum and thrum of engines. I could feel the vibration against my cheek. The dirty smells of diesel, grease, and something rotten filled my nostrils. I coughed, trying to clear the fog in my brain.

Opening my eyes, I took in my surroundings. I was in some sort of cargo bay. I detected a faint pitch, which caused my nausea to return with a vengeance.

The twins! Miss Astrid...Astrid said Lucien had the twins! I pushed up, willing myself to get control of my careening world. Faint light filtered from overhead through metal grating. I pushed to sit against a large shipping crate. My feet were no longer bound, just my hands, having been bound behind my back this time.

The sharp pains in my side let me know my ribs had been re-injured, possibly broken. I couldn't take a deep breath. None of that mattered now. Nothing mattered to me except getting to the twins. *Where were my babies?* I was so worried about Elly. Without the formula, she would get sick again. *What were they feeding them?* The thought sickened me.

"Hello? Someone, answer me! Astrid?" I called out hoarsely in hopes that one of them would come to investigate. I had to know where my babies were.

I couldn't believe Astrid was a part of this. She'd fooled us all...even Everett. She'd been so sweet at Christmas, taking me under her wing, going all out for the wedding. *Weren't she and Everett old friends? How could he not have known?*

As my anxiety level spiked, I wondered what time it was. *How much time had passed since we left this morning? Had Banton found my note?* I pictured him, reading it and frowning. Surely he wouldn't believe for a second I'd decided to go against his wishes and endanger the babies. Thoughts of how angry he'd been when I fought the Orcos at Claudia's house flashed in my head, and I moaned, placing my head back against the crate. My greatest fear was he would think this was another foolish attempt by me to be brave, like I had when I'd gone out to help Claudia instead of locking myself in the house. That was only to help his sister and keep the Orcos outside away from the twins. I wouldn't take the twins to Texas without protection. And I would never go without Banton. Never.

I hoped someone had found my jewelry by now. Constance and Banton both knew I wouldn't leave it behind. I never took my wedding ring off...even to wash my hands. That was the best clue I could think of to leave for them.

But unlike the kidnapping before Mardi Gras, I had no way to communicate my location. I had no cell phone. I recalled someone pulling it from my pocket and dumping it as I was removed from the SUV.

"You stupid bitch, they can track this! We told you to search her," a man had growled as I heard him slap Astrid hard. She'd hissed back at him, and there had been some sort of scuffle before I lost consciousness again.

The twins! I began to cry. I was so angry, so helpless. I needed to get to my babies. I could imagine how scared they were. Elly would suck her thumb and cling to Matty. I hoped they hadn't faded in front of the Orcos.

A door swung open at the far end of the hold. I couldn't turn my head enough to see who was approaching. As the footsteps neared, I could smell her.

"I heard your pitiful cries. Shut the hell up. They're bringing those half-breed brats to you, not for you, but so we don't have to deal with them," Astrid hissed, grabbing me by the collar. As I focused on her face, chills erupted at the base of my neck and traveling down my spine. She licked her lips as she studied my neck. I'd never seen her with her hair down. It fell in an array around her face, making her appear much younger.

"I've never tasted someone after they've transformed. Not a Sange-Mele, anyway. I hear it's sweet," she whispered into my ear. "I haven't tasted human blood in years." I could feel her breath on my neck. I was so repulsed; the bile began to rise in my throat.

"No, please," I begged.

"Oh, that was the wrong thing to do, bitch. That whine just made me want to taste you more," she breathed against my neck. A sharp pain, followed by intense pressure seemed to pull me to the floor as my world began to swirl out of focus. Her bite was intense. She moaned as she drank. I wanted to throw up on her.

"Stop! What the hell do you think you are doing, you Orco whore!" Lucien strode into the room, and struck her hard. As her head jerked back her sharp fangs tore at the flesh on my neck. Blood ran freely down my neck as I watched Lucien in horror. His fangs extended, throbbing with his thirst.

He leaned over me, and I could feel his fangs as they pierced the spot where Astrid had just bitten me.

"No, please...stop," I whispered, afraid I was about to die. I was weak, barely able to hold my head up.

After consuming what blood had already flowed down my neck, I felt the sting of venom as he injected it. My legs jerked involuntarily as I fought against the restraints on my wrists.

He pulled away, his eyes wild as he licked his lips. He pushed me back violently on the floor as his head dipped toward my chest. He licked the blood from my chest as I whimpered. I then heaved, throwing up beside me.

"Are you that revolted by me? You are lucky I injected my venom to heal your wound. After Dante is through with you, you are mine. You will get used to it and learn to like it. I will fully transform you, and you will pant like the dog you were born to be. Is that what you were? Everett's little bitch?"

Visions of what they had planned for me burned into my brain. Death would be better than this. I shuddered uncontrollably, the venom from his bite already working its way through my system.

The door opened again, and a young male Orco carried both babies around their waists as they wailed. He dropped them unceremoniously into my lap. Elly squirmed around and crawled up to my breast, laying her head there and placing her thumb in her mouth. Matty pushed up and sat against me, watching Lucien warily.

"You're lucky Dante has such grand plans for them when we reach shore, or they would be dead already. I've had to fight the crew off them twice."

I found my voice. "Please, uncuff me, so I can take care of them," I whispered.

Lucien grabbed my arm and jerked me around. With one swift motion, he tore the metal cuffs open, the jagged edges cutting my skin around my wrists. I cried out as I brought them around. My skin was crawling and burning from the two bites I'd received, and my nerves were on fire already.

"I'd stay quiet and keep them quiet. You don't want the crew fighting to get down here to you. The sounds of your wounded voices bring their appetites out, much like a wounded rabbit to a bear." He laughed as he strode from the room. Passing Astrid, he lunged at her, picking her up and striking her across the face as he strode to the door.

"You are not to come back here. Dante will deal with you," Lucien growled as she whimpered. He slammed the door, and I was enveloped in silence once again, the only noise the humming from deep inside the ship. I wept silently as I cuddled my babies closely.

I took a deep breath, my nose buried in their hair. They smelled so good, like their baby wash and Banton's cologne. I remembered how he'd held them both on the couch before the family all left for William's service.

The babies were calm. Elly held her thumb in her mouth. Matty curled up on my shoulder. As I rocked them to and fro, Matty's little hand patted me on my shoulder in rhythm as though he was comforting me.

"Oh, babies…Mommy's here. Shhh, Mommy's here, I've got you," I assured them as I began to cry.

"Mommy," Matty muttered as he continued to pat my shoulder.

"That's right, Mommy." I smiled. Just their heartbeats calmed my racing heart. I remembered the afternoon after the second time I'd been bitten, when Banton had held me and rocked me until I was calm. Banton. *What was he doing right now? Had he figured everything out? Was he making plans, following us somehow?*

392

I hadn't heard anyone say where we were headed, but I had my suspicions. Lucien had said it was lucky Dante had such grand plans for the babies once we were on shore. I shut my eyes and clutched the babies tighter. Visions of the story Olivia had told me while I was pregnant haunted me. *A tribal priest of some sort, a ceremony, twin babies...a machete...*

A sob escaped my lips as I continued to rock them back and forth. I would die protecting them. I had to bribe someone somehow to sneak them away. I would have to find an opportunity to escape with them. There had to be a way to get them out of this.

The babies dozed peacefully, one on each shoulder. I shut my eyes and began to drift, exhaustion setting in and taking its toll. Dreams flitted quickly through my head as I dozed...*visions of Banton, our dreamy night in the greenhouse, surrounded by a gauzy tent...the babies giggling as Banton and I bathed them...running in exhilaration down our street as Banton playfully tried to catch up. In a flash, it wasn't Banton, but a large, grimy hand clutching my shoulder, dragging me back into his filthy chest...*

"No!" I gasped out, waking suddenly. The babies jumped, but quickly settled back in slumber. My arms ached with their weight, but I had nowhere to lay them down.

Voices echoed from somewhere in the ship, increasing in volume as they neared, and as I strained, I could hear them.

"She was not to be harmed or touched in any way. You struck her repeatedly, and then you drank her blood to the point of rendering her unconscious," the eerie deep accented voice from my past berated Astrid as she whimpered in protest.

"Kill her and dump her for the sharks," Dante said coldly. I could hear screaming and grunts of pain as the faint sounds of limbs being torn passed through the metal walls of the ship. I wanted to hold my hands to my ears, but I clutched my babies instead. There was nothing to drown out the awful sounds of Astrid dying a slow, painful death. As much as I hated her for what she'd done, my stomach turned over at the thought of what they'd just done to her.

My babies and I were a heartbeat away from meeting the same fate. I shut my eyes and struggled to control my thoughts. As the babies woke from their nap, my immediate worry was feeding them. Surely Lucien would know I had to feed them. Or did he? The Orcos didn't know how far the babies had transformed, unless Astrid had told them. They might assume I could still nurse them.

I wanted to call out again. Wouldn't it be better for them to hear my voice than to hear the babies crying? I shuddered at the thought that any noise might arouse the other Orcos on the ship.

"Hello?" I called out. "Can anyone hear me? I have to feed the babies, please?"

I listened, but heard no one coming. I could still hear faint sounds, like conversation and arguments from somewhere inside the ship. I decided to explore my surroundings, now that my feet were no longer bound. Clutching both babies to me, I pushed against the crate and rose to my feet. My legs were like jelly, surely the after-effects of adrenaline and venom. I walked around the large crate, only to find ten or fifteen more of the same. They were all stamped with letters, all foreign to me. I peered through the slats of one crate and found the contents wrapped with foam rubber. At least it looked clean. Searching around, I found a reasonably clean spot on the floor. I placed both babies on the foam mat against the wall.

"Stay right here, Matty...Elly, stay for Mommy. Don't move," I held my finger up as they watched me, seeming to understand me. I turned quickly and placed my hands through the slats, tugging the foam out. A large piece loosened, and then came free as I jerked backwards. It was large enough to curl up on, and I could lay the babies down on it. I took it around beside the crate where we'd been, moving down a few feet away from where I'd thrown up. The floor was cleaner here, and there was more light, the air seeming fresher as I smelled the salt water of the ocean. I ran back and retrieved the babies, and then placed them on the foam as I sank down beside them.

At least I had a large space to roam around in. The thought occurred to me if I had to relieve myself like I did in the tunnels, I could at least find a far corner to use. I smirked disgustedly. I was finding my silver lining. I shook my head --some silver lining

I watched the twins as they played together, crawling around me, rolling over each other. Elly giggled every time that Matty made a sound. They were so precious to watch. After a while, Elly became silent and laid her head down, sucking her thumb hard. I knew they were both hungry. Matty reached up to me as he began to whine.

"Shhh. Little man, I know you are hungry. We'll figure something out."

As he continued to whimper, the tears rolled down my cheeks. Watching my children go hungry, their tummies rumbling, was one of the most heart-wrenching experiences I'd had so far.

"Please, someone...I have to feed my babies! Please, help me!" I didn't care anymore, I was sobbing. I knew it had been hours since they'd eaten, and the light was fading. It had to be eight thirty or so at night. They hadn't eaten since ten o'clock this morning.

"Orco bastards, you have to feed them!" I screamed as the babies began to wail now, their tummies grumbling so loudly it was echoing in the large chamber.

Without warning, the steel door swung open and Lucien entered, striding toward me with the duffel bag I'd seen in the entry this morning. As my eyes widened, he stood beside me and dropped the bag. I jumped at the noise.

A noise behind him startled me again. I peered around him and gasped. Olivia and Patrick's brother Noah stood, his eyes wide, with two bottles in his hands. I started to call his name in recognition, and then stopped myself. If Lucien didn't know I knew Noah, he might be able to help me. I stayed silent, watching him warily as he crossed the space between us and handed the bottles to me.

I sniffed one of the bottles, and the familiar smell of milk and blood greeted me. I wondered fleetingly where the blood came from, but pushed the thought from my head. The babies were hungry, and I couldn't question the food source. Matty grabbed his and sucked it hungrily. I left him to nurse on his own as I turned to Elly. She weakly held the bottle between her hands as I cradled her to my breast.

"Keep them quiet. Someone will be here in the morning to collect them," Lucien said icily as my heart constricted.

"What do you mean?" My voice rose in panic.

"For a time. Dante wants a few moments alone with you," he said menacingly as I grew chilled. "I'm leaving him here with you tonight," Lucien pointed to Noah. "He has instructions and knows what to do. Don't give him any trouble," Lucien hissed as he leaned down close to my ear. I pulled away instinctively as I shut my eyes.

Lucien growled at me and rose. Before he turned to walk away, he kicked me in the ribs, narrowly missing Ellyson's head. I cried out in pain as he back-handed me swiftly across the face.

"You will get this every time you pull away from me, you little bitch. You and your Aldon friends think you are better than we are. Everett has made this a most interesting game," he snarled as he turned swiftly and left the cargo hold. The steel door swung shut with a loud groan and a slam, and I jumped again. I cried out as my ribs protested the motion. I began to sob out in frustration.

"Banton," I whispered as I laid my cheek over on top of Elly's head.

"Chandler, isn't it? Do you remember me? I am Noah," Olivia's little brother came forward from the shadows. I'd almost forgotten him. My tears turned to tears of relief as he knelt in front of me.

"Noah, I'm so glad you're here," I whispered.

"Olivia and Patrick? Do you know what happened to them?" he asked, large tears pooling in his eyes.

"Yes. Your Olivia and Patrick are safe and well, and living with my friends in Baton Rouge. Olivia has been so worried about you, and the SEALs searched for you for days. A new life waits for you there."

His shoulders sank in relief at my words. He finally looked up at me and smiled.

"Do you know where we are going?" I asked the question to which I hoped I didn't already know the answer.

"Home. To Somalia," he answered sadly. As he confirmed my deepest fears, I sighed and lay my head back against the wall.

"There are things in the bag for you and the babies. Dante is being unusually generous in his instructions for you," he offered, moving around me and zipping the bag open.

"Lucien said you knew what to do. What did he mean?"

"You will find a large tub of water behind that crate. You are to bathe, and also bathe the babies, and change your clothes. There are other things there too for you to use. A woman will come and get me and the babies in the morning. I am afraid for you," he whispered.

I steeled myself against my imagination running away with me. *Take this one hour at a time, Andie. One hour at a time.*

I smiled a shaky smile at him. "Just keep my babies safe for me, okay Noah?"

"I will, I promise. We all have instructions to keep them healthy and safe until we reach land," he said softly as my heart clenched again.

Until Lucien gets them ready for his little ceremony, my thoughts snapped back. *NO!* I couldn't go there. I shook my head as Noah watched me, sympathy etched on his face.

Trying to change the subject, Noah motioned again across the room.

"We have food for you. Are you hungry? I will get it for you," he offered as he crossed the space and disappeared behind one of the crates I hadn't explored.

I took a deep breath and glanced down at Matty. He'd finished his bottle, and his cheek was pressed against my lap as he'd fallen fast asleep. Elly's eyes threatened to close as she sucked the remaining substance from the bottle. Before long, both of them were in a deep sleep.

I placed Elly down beside Matty, and then curled beside them. The cooler air of the evening blew softly through the grating above, chilling me slightly.

Noah appeared with a blanket and a tray of food. I sat up, ravenous.

"I don't know what all of this is, but here," he offered awkwardly. I remembered his sister's aversion to human food when she'd first stayed with us after Christmas, and I smiled. Taking the tray from him, I found pudding cups, Vienna sausages, and crackers. I popped the top on the sausages and ate hungrily. My stomach contracted as the food entered my system. I realized I hadn't eaten since yesterday at lunch.

397

I eyed Noah warily between bites. I knew I could trust him from my experience in the tunnels. He had a kind heart, just like his siblings. I silently thanked God that he was here…my one bright spot, my one hope.

"Noah, can you help me find a way to get the twins to safety? I know what Dante has planned for them. Your sister told me the story of the twins from a neighboring village."

Noah paled and swallowed hard. "I am afraid for them too, and for you. I will try to think of something," he said, settling back against a crate.

"What is he going to do to me, Noah? What is happening in the morning?" I whispered as I put the tray down. Now that I had something in my system, my appetite left me.

He shook his head and looked up at me, his beautiful green eyes wide. "I am not sure," he said quietly. "But I know what he has done to other Sange-Mele women. I do not want that for you." He looked up at me. "Please, do everything he says. Don't fight him. He will kill you quickly if you do," he warned as my heart constricted so hard I thought it had stopped beating. He continued to gaze at me pleadingly.

"You must stay alive, Miss. You must stay alive, for your little ones, and for me. You will get me back to my Olivia. Please," he pleaded as I nodded bravely. This poor boy needed me as much as I needed him. I held my arms out to him, and he surprised me by flying into them as he buried his head in my shoulder.

After a moment, he pulled away and murmured, "I will go now and find more of this." He tugged on the foam that we sat on. I nodded to him as he rose and left us. Noah looked like he'd aged ten years since I saw him last. His black hair was longer, curling around his face and down his neck. His eyes still glowed with the deep emerald green of the untrained Aldon, but the hard life he was living was chiseled into his young face. My heart ached for him, knowing he'd been surrounded by all these monsters for months without his sister or Patrick to help him.

I curled up again, pulling the twins against me. They both shuddered in their sleep, for the air was becoming quite chilly now that darkness was upon us. There were several bulb-like lights scattered around the top of the bay, casting eerie triangular shaped light across sections of the large space. It was just enough to see by. I reached over and grasped the blanket that they'd brought, and pulled it up around the twins.

Noah returned with a larger piece of the foam, and placed it next to me. Gratefully, I stretched my legs across it.

"Miss, you need to bathe now. Dante will be angry with me if all of his instructions are not obeyed," he whispered, his eyes wide. Come, I will show you where, and I will watch the babies while you bathe," he blushed as he took my hand. I checked the twins once more, and finding they slept deeply, I moved to follow him. As he led me around two large crates close to the steel door my eyes widened. There was a large silver galvanized tank, like the ones the farm supply stores back home sold for animal watering troughs. It was filled with fresh water, and I discovered it to be lukewarm as I trailed my hand in it. I could stand the temperature. Noah motioned to a small crate at the foot of the makeshift tub, and there were rags and towels piled up, and a bar of soap.

He left silently, to go and watch over the babies. I looked around and shuddered. The grating overhead offered me no protection against unwanted eyes, but no one seemed to be up there. I quickly shucked my clothes, holding my side and gasping as I tried to move. I grasped the sides of the steel tank, and struggled to raise my leg over, the pain prohibiting me from moving freely. I finally sank down into the water. I washed hurriedly, wanting to return to the babies as quickly as I could. As I soaped a cloth and washed my face, I winced, discovering bruises and faint swelling with my fingers.

"Miss?" Noah called out from the darkness.

"Yes?" I grabbed a towel and covered my chest over the water.

"I pulled your bag here. I will leave it so you can find what you need," he whispered, and then I heard his footsteps retreat. I climbed out of the water and wrapped two small towels around me. I quickly braided my wet hair over my shoulder, and then walked slowly back toward where I'd heard Noah's voice moments before. Tripping over the bag in the floor, I cried out as I grabbed my ribcage. My ribs were broken. I could tell by the constant searing ache and the piercing pains when I moved the wrong way.

Searching through my bag in the dim light, I found my familiar favorite pair of sweat pants, camisole and sweatshirt. I dug hurriedly through the bag but found no panties or undergarments. *Do Orcos not wear underwear?* I thought in irritation. I snorted…that was the last thing I needed to be concerned about at the moment.

There was nothing to put on my feet, so I slipped my feet into the boots that I'd worn since this morning, grabbed the rag I'd washed my face with, and two more rags that I wet in the water to wash the babies with when they woke. As I crossed the cargo bay to our pallets, I hurriedly brushed my teeth with my rag, trying to get the awful taste out.

Noah sat by the babies, his arm around them protectively. It was comforting to see his display of a protective instinct. He nodded to me as I approached, and started to move.

"No, stay there. Your presence is a welcome comfort," I murmured as he nodded at me once. I sank down carefully on the larger piece of foam, and placed my hand gently on Elly's back. She stretched and turned her head toward me, her eyes opening only briefly, and then shutting again slowly.

"Noah?"

"Yes?"

"What kind of blood was in the babies' milk?"

"Miss?" he whispered apprehensively.

"Was it animal blood?" I held my breath as I shut my eyes, dreading his answer.

"There are no animals on this ship, Miss." He answered softly.

My insides turned over. The Orcos had given my children human blood. I was horrified. Bits of a remembered conversation floated in my unconscious, something Everett had said about his father…*drinking human blood, never the same…changed him.*

I pressed my fist against my lips, holding in a sob. *What would all of this do to my children? Forget the blood thing…what would the hunger, the trauma…seeing me beaten, tortured…what would they remember?* They were so bright, already acting like they were a year old in so many ways. I prayed they weren't old enough to remember any of this. As I drifted to sleep, my mother's voice came to me, dreamlike and soothing.

"Chandler, you can't imagine the love you will feel for your own children. The urge to protect them is like no other feeling in the world. You will know that kind of love someday."

Chapter Twenty-Seven

The screech of the bolt on the steel door to my dungeon startled me awake. I pushed up, crying out as I sat upright. I quickly checked the twins, not believing they slept all night without waking. I was grateful they had, because the Orcos hadn't brought me anything else to feed them. Noah rose hurriedly beside me and ran to the door. An Orco female entered the cargo bay, carrying a basket with four bottles in it.

"Feed them and get them ready. Dante will be here shortly, and you will take care of them," she pointed to the babies who now lay awake on the foam pallet beside me.

As terrified as I was of Dante's impending arrival, the knowledge that Noah would care for the twins was comforting. After the female left, I checked the babies, both of their eyes glowing. I found disposable diapers in the duffle and changed them quickly. They were barely wet, no doubt because they'd been starved the day before. I left them on the pallet with Noah as I went to re-wet the washrags and put some soap on them. As I returned, Noah was already feeding them, Matty lay in his diaper on the foam pallet, nursing and playing with the blanket. Noah held Elly as she sucked hungrily on the bottle.

"Thank you, Noah." I said softly as I sat back down to clean them up.

"They were hungry," he replied simply, gazing down at Elly.

The twins finished their breakfast, and then after I'd dressed them in some of their footed pajamas I found in the bag, proceeded to romp on the pallet. Noah left without a word, disappearing behind the crates where I'd bathed last night. I could hear him moving some things around, and then he re-appeared.

"I'm sorry, Miss. It's time, I will take them now."

My eyes widened. I could hear footsteps coming toward the steel door. I nodded silently as tears formed in my eyes. Leaning over, I kissed Elly on her forehead, and then Matty. I shut my eyes briefly as I took in the scent of his hair, wondering if this would be the last time I would ever see them. When I opened my eyes, Noah grabbed the twins hurriedly and scampered off in the direction of the tub.

My stomach turned over. Whatever Dante had planned for me, Noah and the babies were going to hear. They weren't leaving the cargo area. I took a deep breath, and steeled myself for whatever lay ahead. The bolt screeched once more, and the large steel door swung open violently, slamming against a crate. I jumped once more, my nerves on edge from the obvious dread I felt as well as the venom still circulating in my system.

I refused to look in the direction of the door, but I could sense his presence. His large bulk filled the space around me, seeming to loom large over even the storage crates in the hold.

"You don't look happy to see me," Dante's deep, commanding voice vibrated through me like shockwaves.

I took a deep breath, and then glanced up at him. He was just as I'd pictured him... dark complexion, animal-like build. He appeared to be three or four inches taller than Banton, and his bulk indicated well over three hundred pounds.

"Look at me!" His voice thundered through the dark chamber. I could hear the twins whimpering somewhere in the darkness. Yes, they would hear everything that happened.

I looked up at him, not wanting to anger him further. I willed myself to stay passive as I repeated the mantra in my head, "don't fight him, don't fight him."

"Rise!" he commanded. I hurriedly pushed against the wall, and winced as my ribs protested against movement. He reached out to grasp my chin, and I instinctively ducked away from his hand.

My heart skipped a beat. Waves of emotion poured over me, startling me to my core. Unbelievably, I was connecting with this monster of an Orco on an emotional level, much as I had Brie or Banton. Sickness seemed to spread in my veins, as first one emotion after another struck me...loathing, despair, hatred, betrayal, and vengeance. His soul, or what was left of it, was tormented. He ached for something...what he was about to do to me, or to the babies. It was his sole focus in life, and I could feel what he felt. The sickening feeling was overwhelming.

"You will obey me, and you will tolerate my hands on you!" He bellowed as he struck me. His movement seemed like a swat,

403

but I found myself three feet away from the pallets, face down against the wall. He strode over to me in three short strides, and grabbed me by the hair, picking me up off the floor completely. I cried out, my hair feeling as though it were being pulled out by the roots. He dragged me around the corner of another large crate, and I paled, deathly still. In front of us was a large mattress covered in a sheet. He dropped me unceremoniously, and then sank down on his knees in front of me.

"So I finally have the fader. I keep you alive only to breed you, and for you to take care of my sacrifices. If you disobey me, I will kill you and let the crew have you. Do you understand me?"

My stomach turned over again, and I knew I was going to be sick. Think about your babies, Andie...only the babies. And Banton. Think about Banton. I shut my eyes involuntarily as I felt his hands on me. He yanked the sweat top up over my shoulders, and I screamed out in pain, my ribs feeling as though they'd just punctured a major organ.

"Quiet, bitch!" he roared as he shredded the camisole I wore. The tears rolled unbidden down my cheeks as I tried frantically to get my emotions under control. I was calm, my heart, without warning, detaching from my head, just as the day my parents had died...much like when Banton had been declared dead. I felt nothing as I glanced back up at Dante. Seeming to anger him once more, my actions brought another blow, this time his fist to my cheek. My last thought as my head bounced against the steel of the wall beside us, was Banton's beautiful face.

*　*　*

As I struggled to wake, piercing pains shot through my skull. I opened my eyes, and everything appeared upside down and out of focus. I moved my head slightly, and the motion sent waves of nausea through me. I heaved, throwing up violently.

"Miss...Chandler, please...Shhh. Be quiet, you are safe now. I am here," Noah's voice called out from the darkness.

"My babies," I choked out.

"They are sleeping on the pallet. What can I get you? How can I help you?"

404

"How long have I been sleeping?" My voice was raspy and hoarse.

"Almost two days. I was afraid you would never wake again." I could hear tears in his voice as he spoke.

I felt the mattress underneath my cheek. I was still on the mattress that Dante had dropped me on. What had happened?" I raised my arm and felt a sheet draped across me. I tried to raise my head, and my neck wouldn't allow me to move. During his assault on me, Dante must have dislocated something, or something was broken. I raised my other hand and placed it on my ribs. I was naked beneath the sheet. I moved my hand slowly downward, and stopped. My sweatpants were gone, and I could feel sticky, dried blood on my legs and abdomen. Trying to move my legs, I realized I was disjointed and sore. I hurt everywhere. Tears stung my eyes as the realization dawned. Dante had raped me.

"No...God, please...No!" I gasped out as dry sobs choked my throat.

"Miss, please don't let them hear you, or someone will come to hurt us. Please!" Noah's voice begged, his hands on the side of my face. I tried to jerk away from his touch, but couldn't move.

"Miss, let me help you, I know you are hurting. What can I do?" Noah's young voice pleaded again in my ear.

I needed to be clean. All I could think about was washing, scrubbing everything away.

"Tub...bath, please...oh, please!" I managed to cough out as I heaved and threw up again.

"I'm going to lift you, Miss." Noah's voice sent shivers through me, his breath in my ear. Although I knew he had nothing to do with my attack, I still shuddered at his touch. I wanted to die as I felt him hug my naked body against his as he carried me around the crates in the room and back to the tub. He gently lowered me into the water, and I cried out. I was raw, down there... everywhere. The water hurt. The steel of the tub hurt. My tears hurt as they ran down my face.

Noah wordlessly began to wash me, and I tried to focus on his eyes as he soaped the rag and ran it over my limbs. My skin crawled at the feel of the rag, but I was grateful for the bath. I wanted to bathe in bleach.

"More soap....please, more soap. More soap," I sobbed out, not even being aware of my choice of words.

"Okay, Miss...please, shhh. You are okay, now." He tried to reassure me as he continued to wash me.

I moved my hands to grasp the sides of the tub. Motion was getting easier, and I realized the water in the tub was warmer than it had been the first time I was in it. Numbly I thought it must be the warmth of the water that was freeing my movement. I tried to move my legs and cried out. For a moment, I thought Dante had crushed the bones in the lower half of my body. As I tried again, I was able to raise my right knee a small degree.

"Do you want this, Miss?" Noah offered the rag to me. I tried so hard to focus on the rag, and focus on his face. All I could see were shapes and shadows. *Had my eyesight been damaged from the blows to my head?*

I nodded and took the rag. As badly as it hurt, after soaping the rag heavily, I scrubbed my abdomen, my thighs, between my legs...I cried out in pain as I scrubbed hard. I had to get clean.

"Miss, are you ready to get out? You must get out now," he urged as I felt a towel brush against my shoulder.

"No, I have to get clean." I shuddered again as I soaped the rag.

"Miss, you are clean. You are making yourself bleed, scrubbing too hard. Miss, you are clean. Please, let me help you out," Noah pleaded again.

His voice sounded so young and desperate. Something about his plea sparked the mothering instinct in me. He needed for me to snap back. I shut my eyes tightly against the images that were threatening to come to the surface. I would not go there. I would not allow my imagination to go there. For the first time since I woke up, I was thankful Dante had beaten me unconscious before he violated me.

I pushed against the sides of the steel tub to stand and cried out again. My ribs wouldn't allow it.

"Please, let me pick you up. I have to pick you up," Noah urged me as I nodded to him. Before he could lift me from the water, the sound of the steel door opening startled both of us. Noah backed up, and I could sense his apprehension. I shook all over,

406

frightened that Dante had returned or Lucien was coming. Footsteps stopped beside the tub.

"So she survived? Lucien sent me down here to check on both of you and to make sure the twins were well."

That voice.... I turned my head slowly, and I could barely make out his form. He was strangely familiar. My fuzzy brain struggled with memories, flashes of scenes in my head. How could anyone else on the ship be familiar to me?

"Let me get her out," the voice was closer to me now as he leaned over the tub. A whimper escaped involuntarily from my lips. I didn't want Noah touching me, much less any other stranger. He slipped his arms under me and picked me up easily against his chest. Grabbing a towel quickly, he wrapped it around me as I reached out to grab another as he passed the crate by the tub. I struggled against his chest, shaking uncontrollably as I fought the fog in my brain. When we passed under the light, I gasped.

"Ben? Ben, is that you?"

He walked slowly back toward the mattress where Dante had attacked me.

"No, please, no...not there. Please take me to the pallet," I begged him as he changed direction. He knelt beside the foam as I drew the second towel over me. The twins lay sleeping peacefully on the small piece of foam. Noah stood behind him and reached down and pulled the corner of the blanket up and over me as I shut my eyes tightly, trying to shut the world and all that had happened to me out.

Ben stood over me, watching silently. I opened my eyes, trying so hard to make out his expression in the darkness.

"We thought you were dead. What have they done to you?" I choked out as I held my hand up to him. He knelt down beside me and touched my cheek. I winced, knowing my face was badly bruised and swollen.

"You don't want to know," he finally answered, his voice low and menacing.

"Julia will be so glad you are alive," I said, hoping that would spark some sort of positive response. I still couldn't tell if he would be friend or foe.

"Julia…yes, Julia." I could see him raise his eyes toward the moonlight. When he looked back down at me, I could see well enough to know his eyes glowed and fangs extended. He'd somehow been fully transformed.

"Oh, no…Ben," I whispered in horror.

"Yes…I'm Ben. Or I was," he snarled as he drew closer to me. "I thought I could do this, An…Andie. John called you 'Andie-girl,'" he whispered as if to himself. He muttered something else, and then moved closer. I shuddered, but didn't have the strength to move away.

"Wanted to…try…to help you. I've killed for blood. I've killed and I enjoy it. I'm in the dark," he hissed as he seemed to fight with himself.

"Ben, please! I know you are still in there! I could feel it, when you carried me just now. Please, help me? Help the babies?" I pleaded as I watched him study me, turning his head first one way, and then the other as if he didn't understand.

"The babies?" He looked down past me to their sleeping forms on the foam pallet.

"Yes. Banton's babies. You remember Banton?"

"Banton. Banton, Ty and John," he mumbled as I nodded furiously.

"Yes! You remember!" I tried frantically to reconnect with his human emotions.

He reached out and stroked my hair. Without warning, he dove at me, sinking his teeth into the flesh on the upper part of my right breast. I cried out weakly, unable to push him off. As he drank, I could feel the blood leaving my body.

"No, stop it! Stop, Lucien will be mad! Don't do this," Noah pleaded, trying to drag Ben away. Ben pulled away abruptly and wiped his mouth with his shirt sleeve.

I cried, closing my eyes tightly. He would be no help because he was more animal than human.

His eyes glowed even brighter as he turned violently around to face the door. He dragged his breath in, ragged and wet, making a hissing sound each time he breathed. I watched, horrified he would turn and come back for me or the babies. After a moment or two he turned back to me, seeming to be in better control. His fangs were still, no longer throbbing in thirst for blood.

"I won't come back here. I will keep my distance, and try to help, if I can," he said, sounding more like Ben. "I'm sorry, Andie. I'm not Ben anymore. Ben is dead," he stated coldly as he swung the door open and then slammed it behind him with finality.

I sobbed into the foam mat as Noah sank down beside me.

* * *

The babies' soft cries woke me. I opened my eyes and made out their forms in front of me. I couldn't focus enough on them to tell which one was Matty and which was Elly. Tears sprang to my eyes as I realized the last time I'd kissed them might have truly been the last time I would see them clearly. I pushed up and couldn't find Noah. I ran my hand down my stomach, realizing that Noah had dressed me in another pair of sweatpants and a t-shirt. *When had he done that?*

I focused on a brown form beside the pallet I lay on and reached out to touch it. It was the basket the young Orco girl had brought the bottles in. I felt around in it and located two full bottles. Pulling them out, I then held my breath as I pulled them over to me.

"Mommy," one of the twins had crawled closer to me and placed a hand on my leg. I knew it was Matty.

"Baby, here. I know you are hungry," I whispered as I placed a bottle in his hands. He lay back and nursed hungrily. Elly's form lay still across the pallet from him, and for a second, my heart stopped as I realized she wasn't moving. I reached over to pick her up and she turned toward me. I breathed a sigh of relief as I painfully placed my hands under her. I struggled and held my breath, but I couldn't lift her. My ribs were broken in such a way that I couldn't push with my arms enough to lift anything.

I began to sob as I realized I couldn't even pick my babies up. "Come here, Elly. Come to mommy. I have your bottle, baby girl," I urged as I sobbed. Elly flopped over and crawled toward me. As she reached my leg, I pulled her arm and managed to pull her up my body into my lap. I felt Matty's hand on my leg as I placed the

409

bottle in Elly's hands. I tried desperately to focus on them as they nursed. Elly began to whine softly, as if she knew I couldn't see her. I wondered if their eyes were glowing... with my eyesight compromised I couldn't tell. I placed a finger inside the edge of Elly's diaper to check if she was wet, but found her dry. Noah must have been here recently and changed them. I wondered idly where he was.

"Miss, are you hungry?" Noah's voice came out of the darkness.

"Noah! I thought you'd gone," I gasped.

"I'm sorry. I didn't mean to frighten you. You slept a long time, another day. You need to eat, I will bring you something," he said. I heard his footsteps retreating.

Another day! We'd been at sea four days. I wondered how many days it would take us to reach Somalia. I hoped at least as many more. My greatest fear now was the ship docking, and the Orcos taking my babies ashore. Fresh tears rolled down my cheeks as I searched again for the hundredth time for a way out of this.

I closed my eyes...they ached anyway from trying to focus. I buried my face in Elly's hair. I knew it was my imagination, but I smelled Banton's cologne. I cried silently as I pictured his face. Banton - my beautiful, loving husband. He'd promised to love, honor and cherish me all the days of our lives. I held my breath. How could he possibly ever want to touch me, after...

"Aargh!" A large sob escaped, my anger pooling and exploding. Anger at what Dante had done to me...to us. Yes, what he'd done to me, he had done to Banton.

"Miss?" Noah had returned and knelt down beside me.

I looked up at him, unfocused.

"Do you require blood?"

"I have to drink some animal blood, because I've almost fully transformed. Why?" I asked huskily.

"Because your skin is so pale, almost blue. I will bring you some, with the babies,"

"No! I can't. I won't drink human blood," I muttered as I clutched Elly close to my chest. *But you are making your children drink it*, I thought bitterly.

"Miss, you have to or you will eventually die."

"Noah, call me Andie, please. You had to take care of me. You bathed me. You can call me by my nickname, for gripe's sake," I retorted hoarsely.

Noah sounded relieved as he replied, "You are better, I can tell. You speak more words than you have in days. Here, please eat," he urged me, placing a tray beside me.

I shook my head. The thought of food was nauseating.

I faintly remembered Noah giving me water during my twenty-four hours of sleep.

"Noah, is there water to drink?"

"Yes, I'm sorry, here." He handed me a cool bottle. I ripped the top off and drank and drank.

"I'm sorry. I forget humans require water," he mumbled, sounding embarrassed.

"Noah, it's okay. You have taken good care of us. I can never repay you," I sighed as I sank back against the wall. I wanted to lie down, but the effort on my ribs was too great.

"Is it nighttime?" I asked him.

"Almost morning. As soon as the sun rises I will get some blood for you and new bottles for the babies."

"Noah, I can't drink it," I protested again.

"But you will die without it," he argued.

I shut my eyes. It would be a peaceful way to go. It occurred to me, I'd rather die than have Banton know what had happened to me. All I wanted now was for my babies to be safe.

"Then I will die. Just promise me, you will get my babies safely back to my husband or the SEALs. Promise me?" I asked wearily.

"No! An...Andie," he tried my name out and then continued. "Andie, do not give up. Do not think about what Dante has done to you. He will wait to see if you have bred before he tries again. He knows he endangers your life each time he does."

I shuddered and heaved, sick at the thought of his touching me.

"You are safe, for a time. Your husband and the SEALs, they come for you. Do not give up," he said adamantly.

"How can you know that?' I asked, knowing it was only hope on his part.

411

"Because I have a gift. I see things in my dreams. God gave me this gift, my mother told me."

"What did you dream, Noah?" I asked as hope sprang up inside me.

"I dreamed I would help you. I dreamed of this ship --and now, here you are. I dreamed last night the ship was sinking and there was fire. I dreamed of the Navy men and of Sam. Sam pulled me out. Sam and the Navy men saved the twins. They were safe," he said, with the most reassuring tone to his voice.

I realized I was crying. He said the twins would be safe.

"And Banton? What about Banton?" I cried out, needing to know he would be all right.

"Your man, Banton, he will be with them. He will try to save you," he assured me.

His words washed over me as I repeated them again and again in my head.

He will try to save you. He will try to save you. The words were heavy on my heart. *But he will fail*, I finished for him silently.

Noah was quiet, and I was strangely calm. The babies would be saved from the awful fate I'd been imagining for them. But the untold damage that Dante had done to me...I couldn't wrap my head around it. And instead of Banton having to deal with it, I favored death. Death would be easier.

My grandmother's voice came back to me as I fell asleep against the wall. *We'd been sitting in her old recliner as she read the bible to me. I'd ask her what happens to your body when you die.*

"Baby-girl, there are things worse than death. Don't ever fear death. As Christians, we should celebrate the day when we meet our Lord. What a glorious day that will be." She'd burst out in the old Baptist hymn of old. "When we all get to heaven, what a day of rejoicing that will be...when we all see Jesus, we'll sing and shout the victory." She smiled, her eyes crinkling at the corners as she cackled her loving granny laugh. Her tummy jiggled with the sound, and it always made me giggle. I laid my head against her warm, soft chest, playing with her antique broach she pinned to her apron.

"There are things in this old world that are much, much worse than death. Like watching my babies cry because they were hungry, and I had nothing to feed them; Like watching your own baby die in your arms, while the doctors can do nothing to help." She'd taken a deep breath, and stopped. *"Yes, there are things much worse than death. Don't fear death, baby-girl. And don't fear it for me! I can't wait for that great gettin' up morning!"*

Maw Maw Irene was so comforting. She always smelled of lilac face powder, pancakes and soap. The smells drifted around me as I dreamed of death. Death would be peaceful. Death would be comforting, my mother and grandmother waiting with open arms to greet me.

Chapter Twenty-Eight

Explosions rocked the world my cargo hold had become. Rapid fire sounded overhead, and the whining sound of a rocket being fired woke me. The ship shuddered, the engines falling silent. Noah sat up and turned to me, grasping my upper arm. I winced in pain, but said nothing. His touch was comforting.

"Andie, get up. I think your SEALs are here," he exclaimed excitedly as the door to my prison swung open.

"Noah, come quickly! Lucien wants you now!" a voice rang out. Noah rose and ran to the door and it shut behind him.

I was terrified of being left alone. *What if Noah didn't come back?*

It occurred to me that the ship was sitting still in the water. The engines were silent, and I could hear the shouts of the Orcos over and around me. Sunlight streamed down through the grating overhead, signaling it was midday. Another burst of gunfire rained over us, and I could hear bullets pelting the boxes of cargo in front of us. I pulled the twins closer to me, and they scrambled up into my arms.

Fully awake now, I realized this was it. I would have to be ready to fight if I had to. I tested my legs and could move a little easier than the day before, but I hadn't tried to stand on my own.

I placed the babies down beside me as I felt the boat begin to list in the water. *Were we taking on water?* I had no way of knowing how low we sat to the waterline, there were no windows. I pushed unsteadily up the wall. I was able to stand, but my legs were like jelly. Good. No broken bones in my legs, it seemed. I sat back down and noticed I could see Matty and Elly more clearly. Their eyes glowed with fear. I pulled them close to me again, and they both pushed up into my arms and grasped me around my neck.

"Get those babies in here with me, now!" I heard Dante bellow through the wall. "You, go and get them ready. I will restore my other half. I will retrieve my dead brother's soul. I will sacrifice them on the ship if I have to."

414

My heart stopped. *No! NO! What could I do?* I searched around frantically. I could hide, but they would find me easily. I knew our scent gave us away.

"What about the girl?" I heard a female voice ask.

"Leave her. Let her drown," His deep voice sent chills through me. *Let her drown?* I knew it, the ship was sinking. I couldn't panic now. My immediate fear was the babies.

I looked down at them, and it occurred to me.

"Elly, play peek-a-boo. Can you hide from mommy? Hide from mommy, Matty, please. Peek-a-boo!" I gasped, desperate for them to understand me. I wished silently we'd never scolded them to fade back. They were scared to do it.

"Please, please…babies…Peek-a-boo!" I said in as stern a voice as I could manage. "Peek-a-boo!" I ground out through my teeth. Elly looked up at me, her blurry image was clear enough I could see her eyes were wide and that I was scaring her. To my relief, both of them faded completely.

I whispered to them. Hide babies…that's good. Stay hidden," I pressed a kiss to Elly's head as the door swung open. I lay my head back and dropped my arms. A small female entered, followed closely by Ben. The female searched the pallet beside me.

"Where are the babies? What have you done with them?" she demanded as she walked closer. I prayed they wouldn't look at my chest too closely and make out their forms.

"Noah took them earlier…I don't know!' I cried out, hoping I sounded believable. She stalked back toward the door as Ben leaned over and dragged his gaze down my body. His eyes widened as I held my breath. He'd spotted their outlines. I still couldn't see clearly enough to gage his reaction. He stood upright, and then left silently through the door behind the girl.

I let out a sigh as tears pooled in my eyes. Ben was going to keep my secret.

"Oh, darlins', you are so smart. That's a good girl, Elly," I cooed to them as they remained perfectly still against my chest. "You are a brave, good boy, Daddy's boy," I praised Matty as I felt him look up at me. I kissed him on his forehead as I rocked them gently to and fro. I could hear more gunfire in the distance, and I could hear shouting, but couldn't tell if it was humans or Orcos.

415

I lay perfectly still, trying to get a sense of anything going on outside. I felt him. I could feel his rage...anger, love, devotion. I could feel his desperation. Banton was outside.

Tears burned my eyes as I looked down at my babies. "Daddy's here, darlin's. Daddy is here to get you," I assured them as I rocked.

I sat up quickly. I could feel the foam soak under me as my sweats became wet. We were taking on water. I watched in horror as the large crates around the room began to slide toward the back wall. *We'll be crushed, if they slide this way,* I thought. Terror gripped me. The water was pouring in fast from somewhere behind the crates.

I had to get the babies higher. Pushing up against the wall, I moaned. I still hurt all over, and with my ribs broken it made it almost impossible to hold Matty and Elly. I felt I was a little stronger. *Adrenalin rush helps too*, I thought. I searched up and down, covering every wall that was exposed enough to look. There were no ladders, nothing to get a foothold to climb up to the top. As I leaned against the wall where I'd been on the foam mats only moments before, I looked down in horror. The water was up just past my knees. I looked down at the babies...they were still faded. I'd never find them with my blurry eyesight if I dropped them in the water or got separated from them.

"Matty, Elly...where are you? Elly, come back to Momma! Ellyson Marie, fade back!" I called out frantically. She immediately faded in as she clung tighter to my neck. She sucked her thumb frantically.

"Matty, Matthew Gastaneau, fade back! Where are you," I admonished him. He finally came into focus. As I hugged them to me, I began to search again for something to cling to. Some of the smaller crates were floating, but the larger crates seemed stationary.

"Okay, babies...we have to climb. Hold on to Mommy," I gasped as I grabbed a wooden slat on the largest crate I could find. I pulled up and placed my foot on the fourth board. I moaned, the pain in my ribs was so great that I thought I was going to pass out. As I stepped back down, I panicked. The water was now waist deep and rising at a much faster rate. The horrible dream I'd had as

416

a child was coming true, except I wasn't in a car in the river. I was trapped in a ship's cargo hold in the Indian Ocean.

I looked up at the ceiling, almost completely covered in the grating. The water would pour through the top once this end of the ship was level with the waterline. I had a fleeting thought maybe some of the grating would be loose, and I could push through it once the water was that high.

I grasped the board and pulled again, crying out as I pulled my body up. Inch by excruciating inch, I pulled up, first one hand then the other as I checked to make sure the babies held on to my neck. They were deathly quiet, their eyes wide. Once again I worried about the lasting effect this terrifying ordeal would have on them. I pushed the thought out of my head as I reached the safety of the top of the crate. But it was nowhere near high enough to reach the grating. I still needed about ten feet or so.

I sank down on the top, exhausted from climbing. My ribs ached, and I knew if I thought about the pain at all, I would pass out. I struggled to hear any sounds outside. There had been no sounds at all except some shouting and the slow groans and moans of the cargo ship as it protested its inevitable demise.

There was a sudden jolt, and the ship listed hard to the right. The crate I was on moved unexpectedly and I realized it was now floating as well. Other crates and debris floated around us, and bumped into us hard as an explosion from somewhere deep inside the ship thrust everything sideways. I lost my grip on Elly, and she plunged into the water beside the crate.

"NO! Elly," I screamed, leaning over as far as I could to grasp her as she bobbed to the surface. I grabbed her pajamas and pulled her back onto the crate. She cried out as I pulled her up into my arms with Matty.

"Baby, I'm so sorry...Mommy's got you," I sobbed, heartbroken I'd dropped her into the cold dark ocean water.

"Mommy's got you, baby. I won't let you go again."

The water was pouring in now, sounding much like a waterfall. I looked up at the grating, now almost in reach. As we floated closer, I began to reach my arms up to push. Everything was solid.

"Chaanndller! Andie, can you hear us?"

"Chandler! Chandler! Where are you?" I could hear more rapid gunfire, and I could hear someone pounding on the ship's hull, farther away.

"I'm here! I'm down here, in the cargo hold! Please, we're here!" I screamed frantically, surprised my voice was so loud, considering how weak I'd been. "Please, the water is rising!" My shrill voice bounced off the walls and the water and echoed. I looked all around, turning first one way and then the other as my head touched the grating. This was it. The water would be pouring over our heads soon, and I could see no way out. I spotted a place closer to the corner where there seemed to be wide spaces between the grating, the panels separated with iron bars. I pushed and tugged at crates around us, trying to move us there.

"Arrgh!" I cried out in frustration at my protesting ribs, and the fact I couldn't budge us. I stood shakily with the twins, and started to jump across the crates to the corner. As I got closer, I was almost completely on my knees with my shoulders against the grating. I only had minutes before we would all three drown, trapped against the panels. I shuddered, my breathing becoming shallower as I began to panic. My lungs had been filled with water once before when I almost drowned in the river. My eyes stung with unshed tears as I thought about my babies drowning with me.

"Andieee, where are you?" John's voice was close.

"John! Oh, please, John! Down here, under the grating!

I pushed one last time and landed on the edge of the crate closest to the bars. The space was only about three feet square, with two bars that crisscrossed. I could easily push the babies through it.

"Over here! Please, she's here," I heard Noah's voice call out.

"John, Noah...please. The water is rising too fast, we're going to drown," I cried out, pulling my way across the top of the crate with the babies frantically clutching my neck.

A hand reached down and grabbed Matty's pajamas. I could see well enough to make out John's face.

"John! John, hurry, take them," I begged as he pulled Matty through the bars.

"Matty!" I could hear Banton's voice. My heart pumped so hard it hurt.

"Chandler, hand Elly to me," John commanded breathlessly. I pushed her up between the bars as I kissed her on the mouth. John grabbed her by the shoulders and pulled her to safety.

My babies were safe. I could see John above me as he stood and handed both babies to someone in an orange life vest. My babies were safe. I sank down on top of the crate as it pushed up against the bars. Water began to pour in behind me at the edge of the grating.

The adrenalin rush was gone and I had no strength left. Even Banton's frantic voice didn't move me. I fell, my body lying across the top of the crate. I could feel the iron bars against my back as the crate bobbed up and down in the water.

"Chandler Ann Gastaneau, don't you give up on me," Banton pleaded through clenched teeth.

The ship listed hard again, and the crate below me moved, sliding me off into the water.

"Chandler, where are you?" I could hear John and Ty calling out. I was about three feet away from the bars. I looked up at them passively. I could see their faces...John, Ty...and Banton.

John yelled, "Get that cutting torch over here, now! We'll have to cut her out!"

I knew his attempt was futile. There was no way they would ever pull me between those bars. I wouldn't fit. The squares were about six inches too small for my shoulders to squeeze through.

"Chandler, swim back over here!" Banton commanded sternly. He and Ty tried frantically to pull a piece of the grating loose. I swam back to the iron bars as Banton gave up and pushed his arms down to me.

"Baby, hold on. We're going to get you out," he said. Ty fell back to his knees beside him.

"It's not as scary as I thought it would be." I whispered, our faces only inches apart.

"What, baby?" he asked me breathlessly. He grasped my shirt, pulling me up against the bars.

"Dying. I think I always knew I would die this way. I knew I would drown. But what was so scary in my dreams was that I was alone. I'm not alone," I said. The water closed over my head. I

419

smiled at him, grasping at his hand as he lifted his face heavenward. I could hear him screaming my name.

Oh, no...Banton. It's okay. You are holding me, I wanted to cry out to him. I moved my mouth, and the water rushed in. He pulled me frantically, ramming my shoulder against the bars.

I could hear his muffled screams as John yelled, "We can't cut through this. Banton, pull her out!"

"Break her shoulders if you have to," Ty yelled, grabbing tight to my other hand in the water. I felt a pop as my right shoulder dislocated, and then as darkness closed in around me, I dreamed I felt Banton's face.

* * *

My Catholic grandfather, my dad's stepdad, was right. He'd joked with my mother on occasion that he'd meet all the Baptists in purgatory. This must be it. There was pain. Maw Maw Irene said there would be no pain in heaven. I wasn't in hell because I wasn't burning. I was chilled to the bone and my chest ached terribly. My head pounded. I fought and fought, but I couldn't move anything. My hands were tied down. Someone screamed my name beside me. *Please, please stop the screaming.* Someone picked and probed at me. I couldn't see.

Wasn't I going to go to heaven? I searched and searched, but I couldn't find a light. There was supposed to be a light. There was always a light in the movies. The cold, wet darkness consumed me. My lungs ached so badly. I wanted to take a deep breath. *Someone, please stop the screaming. My head hurts, please stop screaming.*

Voices came to me as if through a long tunnel - voices that faded in and back out again.

"...every one of her ribs has been cracked, some of them broken...surgery for her lung...get her back to the states before...time will tell us..."

More of the black, dark coldness. It was quiet and peaceful, but cold. I shivered, wanting someone to cover me up. *I need a blanket...I need...I need...*

"...lack of air supply. Even Aldon and half-breeds...brain damage...can't survive without oxygen...too much time..."

420

I could hear someone moaning and crying. *Why were they crying? I'm the one hurting! Please, stop their moaning! My skin is crawling! Please, no more.*

I could hear noises again, no longer from a dark tunnel, but in the room with me. Someone was breathing next to me. I could smell him…the warm, spicy male scent of Banton's cologne.

"There is no medical reason why she's still out. We can't do an MRI here. Have to wait until tomorrow. All her vital signs are stable."

A doctor? I didn't recognize his voice. I could hear a thrumming, an engine on board a ship. *Oh, no, I was back on board the ship. Dante would be coming for me, coming for the twins!* My heart raced as I heard loud noises around me.

"Doc, what's happening? Do something," I could hear Banton's voice exploding beside my head. I calmed down. Banton. Banton was here beside me. I wasn't on the Orco ship anymore.

I slept. I dreamed.

I floated. I was in the water, Banton had my hand. It felt so good, so familiar. *Banton. He could never know. I didn't want him to know what Dante did to me. Banton could never know. He would be so disgusted. It was vile…I couldn't wash it away…I needed more soap…Please.*

"No, please…no, don't touch…please, don't touch me. Please, no, I'm not clean," I writhed, trying to pull away from the sensations.

"Please, baby…please, come back to me. The babies need their mommy. God, please bring her back to us."

Soft voices pleaded with me. "Chandler, open your eyes. Open your eyes and look at me. I can feel you. You are safe, and warm, and loved. Please come back to us. We're here," Brie's soft voice drifted around me, making me smile. I tried and tried, but couldn't open my eyes. *Why can't I open my eyes?*

"Andie-girl, wake up. We're almost home, and everyone needs to see you. Brie's here, Chandler. She needs you. Please, please wake up." Someone kissed my forehead.

No, don't touch me. Please, stay away. I'm not clean, please, wash me again. Please!

421

"Chandler, Sweetheart, please come back to me. Doc, can she hear me? Chandler, I have to see your eyes, baby. You have to wake up. The babies need you, Chandler. Please, come back to us. Don't give up now. I'm so, so sorry. I had to break your shoulder, I'm so sorry. It's the only way I could get you out, please forgive me."

Blackness again. I floated in the water, face down. My lungs filled with it, making me sink further, further down. I touched bottom. *Good. No one will find me here. I'm safe here. Banton won't find my body. He'll never know what Dante did to me. I had to stay here and hide. Banton would be happy. He didn't know, and he has the twins. Everything is okay now.*

A   monitor   beeped   annoyingly   nearby. Beep…beep…beep…blip. Beep…beep…

Shut it off!

Why was I so irritable? I was never this short with people. *They are taking care of me, I have to be nice.*

"Pretty is as pretty does."

"Oh, Mom."

"Nice girls are polite and respectful. Do unto others as you would have them do unto you."

"I know, Mom."

I'm not pretty anymore, Mom. I can't be, Dante attacked me and made everything ugly. I want to hide. I want to die.

I was in overwhelming darkness again. I slept a deep, deep sleep.

Chapter Twenty-Nine

Normal noises…noises that made sense to me popped in and out around me. The sounds intruded on my sleep – the "squish, squish, squish" of rubber soles on a tile floor…a watch ticking, the "ommm-sheee" of a ventilator. I could feel something covering my face. I wanted to brush it off, but I couldn't move my arms. The great struggle to wake and open my eyes had begun.

The smell of Banton's soap, the clean fresh scent of him invaded my senses, calming me. He was sitting near. I could feel him under my skin.

His breath brushed my ear.

"Chandler Ann, wake up. Please," I could hear tears in his voice as he choked on the words. I pushed and pushed, but my eyes wouldn't open.

"Chandler, baby, the twins are here. They need to see you." I felt the bed dip, and I could smell Brie.

"See, Matty, here's Mommy. She's right here," Banton cooed. I felt a little hand on my arm.

"Mommy, see. Mommy," Matty's little voice mumbled as I felt him pat my arm.

"Elly, come here to Daddy. See, Mommy is right here, sweet girl. Mommy is here," I heard him choke on the words again as someone stroked my other arm.

I felt Ellyson's soft baby breath on my mouth as she lay her head down beside me. I could sense her sucking her thumb. She was watching me.

"Mommy," she whispered to me. Ellyson had never said my name before. She was talking, and I was asleep.

"Daddy," Matty said.

"Come here, Tiger," Banton's voice sounded more controlled.

"Banton, do you want me to take them and get them down now? It's late," Brie said.

"No, leave them in here and let them fall asleep with her. She needs to hear their little voices. If she won't come back for me, maybe she will for them."

He was crying. Banton was crying. He thought I wouldn't come back for him.

I will come back for you, Banton...I will! I'm trying, I don't want to die anymore. I want to be with you, I want...

I opened my eyes and scanned the room. Banton sat beside me, chasing Elly down the bed as she crawled on my legs. He pulled her back up to his chest and buried his nose in her hair. I smiled, thinking that was my favorite thing to do too. He turned his head to the side, sobs racking his chest.

My heart ached with loss. I realized I could feel what Banton was feeling. The feelings of desperation were overwhelming. As I gazed at him, I discovered I could finally see clearly as if everything had been enhanced with magnification and Technicolor. He looked so beaten, with several days of beard growth. I was surprised the babies knew him at all. He needed a shave and haircut. I'd never seen him so unkempt.

Banton continued to sob, his shoulders shaking as soft sounds escaped through his lips. Frustrated, I struggled but couldn't move my fingers to touch his face. I couldn't find my voice. I finally tried my left hand, and it moved.

"Mommy," Matty's voice called as I felt him touch my hand. I moved it higher, and felt his hair. He giggled his deep, belly giggle that I loved so much. "Mommy, see!" he giggled again.

Banton quieted and turned as I lifted my hand again to place it in Matty's hair. His quick intake of breath alerted me he'd seen me move.

"Brie, come quick! Get the Doctor!" he shouted. His voice was so loud, it made me wince.

"Banton, please...don't yell. It hurts," I rasped out as he cried out loud.

"Chandler, sweetheart...oh, God, you came back. You're awake," he sobbed, burying his face in my chest. I raised my left hand and placed it on his head, trying to sooth him.

"Banton," I croaked again as he pulled away to look down at me. He wiped the tears from his eyes with the back of his hands as Brie hurried into the room.

"You're awake! Thank God," she exclaimed as I winced. The noise hurt my head.

"Shhh, I understand, baby. Shhh, we'll be quiet," Banton murmured as he stroked the hair from my forehead. "Where do you hurt, Chandler? What can I get for you?"

"Shower. I need a shower," I begged as he chuckled.

"No, please. I have to get clean," I begged again as he tried to stroke my cheek. I pulled away from him, not wanting him to touch me until I was clean. The motion sent pain shooting down my neck into my right shoulder. I still couldn't move my arm.

Banton removed his hand and watched me warily.

"Banton, let me take the babies, and you can have some time alone with Chandler," Brie murmured.

Banton sat silently watching me as Brie gathered the babies in her arms. She leaned over to kiss me on the forehead, and I instinctively shrunk away from her. My neck stiffened again, and I screamed out.

"Okay, shh. It's okay, Chandler. You're safe. We can touch you. It's just me and Brie. You're safe," he whispered over and over as he tried again to stroke my cheek. I closed my eyes instead of trying to move.   "Chandler, I know you are hurting. Where does it hurt?"

"Everywhere. I can't move, Banton," I choked out as I opened my eyes again. A strange older man stood over Banton looking down at me.

"Well, it's good to see you awake. Your vital signs are good, and you are breathing on your own finally. You have multiple cracked ribs, and you've suffered from a punctured and collapsed lung. Both your shoulders were dislocated, one of them broken when they pulled you from that ship, but you are a lucky young lady. If you were a mere mortal human, you wouldn't have survived. I'm glad you are still here with us."

My heart sank as he told me how lucky I was. *I'm the lucky girl with the big, dark, awful secret.* Banton could never know.

"Sweetheart, what is it? Where are you hurting?" Banton kept asking me the question over and over. He was desperate to help me. He could see the pain in my eyes.

"I need a shower," I repeated.

"Chandler, I don't think you can manage that just yet. The nurse bathed you this morning and put a clean gown on you. We'll

425

see how that shoulder looks tomorrow, and we'll try to get you up. But right now, I need for you to try to drink something, and to rest. It took two transfusions to get you back to this shade of pale," the doctor shook his head and then winked at Banton.

"No, I have to have a shower. I have to…my head," I winced as I tried to move again.

"We can give you something mild. I'll send the nurse back in a few minutes. Drink, Chandler. Sange-Mele get dehydrated like everyone else," he said as he left the room.

Banton stroked my cheek again. Steeling myself against reacting, I tried not to pull away. I didn't want to upset him, but it was torture. I wanted to be near him, but I didn't want him to touch me.

He laid his head down beside me on the pillow, his breath brushing my lips.

"I've died a thousand deaths since they took you, Chandler. I don't think I've slept in over a week. I haven't thought of anything but you and the twins since I found your ring on the floor."

"You found it?" I whispered.

"Yes. I knew you had been taken then. Ava Grace found your bracelet and led me to the ring. I recognized your clues in the note, too. Good girl," he breathed, touching his lips to mine. His touch was exquisite, and I couldn't stand it. The tears rolled down my cheeks. I felt so unworthy of his love.

He reached up and wiped them away as he continued.

"You left good clues, Laurilee's name, calling Dan 'Daniel.' Everett and I had already picked up on those. You signed the note 'Chandler Ann' the name you say we only use when you are in trouble. Then Ava found your bracelet. We traced your cell phone to a dumpster by the loading docks at the Port Authority, and Brie and Everett could smell which slip had been infested with Orcos. Unfortunately, the ship had already sailed hours before we caught up to your scent."

I listened in mesmerized silence. I could listen to his deep, beautiful voice all day. He was here. Banton was here. He could never know.

"Chandler, what is it? You can tell me," he whispered softly as he pushed a strand of hair behind my ear. I wanted to tell him something, anything. I wanted to ease his pain, but I couldn't speak. I had to hide, so I turned my head to the wall.

"Oh, Chandler, what is it? I know I hurt you when I broke your shoulder. I'm so, so sorry. I had to. I just had to pull you out. I couldn't lose you! Baby, please!"

The desperation in his voice tore at my heart. He thought my silence and my reactions were because he hurt me getting me out.

"No, that's not it. You didn't hurt me, I promise. It's not you," I whispered.

"God, Chandler, tell me. What is it? I know you are in some sort of pain. Please tell me so I can help you."

I turned back to him. I loved him so much, and seeing him so tortured hurt my heart. His eyes burned, the flecks of gold were bright as his eyes brimmed again with tears.

"You can't help me Banton. It's nothing."

He continued to stare into my eyes, knowing I was holding back. The nurse entered and handed Banton a glass of water.

He placed his hand under my neck, and I shuddered at his touch. His eyes widened as he began to lift me slowly.

"Chandler, let me lift you a little so you can drink," he said softly as he watched me.

The nurse leaned over and grabbed the control, raising the bed under me as Banton pulled me up.

"Ahh!" I screamed as pain shot down my neck. From his touch or the muscles in my neck, I was unsure.

"I'm so sorry, Andie. I'll stop."

"Lieutenant Gastaneau, here is a straw. This will help," the nurse said softly as she handed a straw to Banton. He placed it in the glass, and then held it to my lips.

I took a long drink, the cool water soothing my throat. It felt good. I took another. I was so thirsty I could have sucked down a gallon of water.

Banton pulled it away, breaking my contact with the straw.

"Enough, we don't want it to come back up on us," he murmured, placing the glass on the table beside the bed.

I lay still, looking up at the ceiling. After several moments, Banton broke the silence in the room.

"Chandler, why won't you look at me?"

427

What could I tell him? I was so confused. *He couldn't know.* I felt as though if he looked deeply enough into my eyes, he would see every deep, dark memory I was hiding.

"No secrets between us, remember?" he said softly, placing his face back on the pillow beside me.

"I just want to sleep, Banton." I closed my eyes tightly, willing the images that were creeping in to stay away.

"You will obey me, and you will tolerate my hands on you!

"I keep you alive only to breed you, and for you to take care of my sacrifices. If you disobey me, I will kill you, and let the crew have you. Do you understand me?"

"Quiet, Bitch!"

The dam I'd held in place the last few days broke. Banton was offering me solace, comfort, and a love that I couldn't accept until I felt clean...until I faced the demon. I cried so hard and so bitterly that both the doctor and the nurse came running down the hallway.

"God, Chandler...what did they do to you, baby? Oh, Andie, please, shhh. I'm here, I'm here, and you're safe. I'm not going anywhere," he said over and over again as he tried to pull me to him.

"Please, Banton...don't. I can't stand it. Please don't," I pleaded as I sobbed.

"What, Chandler?" He sounded so wounded, so helpless.

"Don't touch me. I can't stand it." I pleaded as I searched his face through my tears. It came out wrong, I knew it did, and I knew it hurt him. He pulled away and looked down at me, horrified.

"You don't want me to touch you?" he whispered in confusion as the nurse fought to give me a shot.

"Calm down, Mrs. Gastaneau. We are going to give you something to help you sleep, now. It's mild and it won't hurt you. You need to rest," The doctor took the seat beside the bed that Banton had vacated.

The doctor had to know what had happened to me. I knew how much damage Dante had inflicted on my body, and the signs had to still be there. The doctor was my only escape. I wanted to confide in the kind, gray-haired doctor beside me.

428

I swallowed and stilled my breathing.

"Doc, please, can I talk to you alone?" I whispered. He turned and spoke to Banton and the nurse.

"If you don't mind, I would like to spend a few moments alone with Chandler."

"No, Doc…I'm not leaving her," Banton replied, taking a step forward.

"Lieutenant Gastaneau, please step into the hallway. Your wife wants to talk with me privately, and I will call you back in momentarily."

Banton looked betrayed. The nurse took his arm, leading him through the doorway with his shoulders hunched in defeat as he left the room. Several painful moments passed as I tried to formulate what I wanted to say. I could hear Banton's voice as he talked to John and Brie in the hallway. He sounded so distraught.

"Chandler, what can I do to help you?" the doctor broke the heavy silence in the room.

"You know about my condition? That I'm a Sange Mele?"

"Yes, Chandler. They brought me along to treat you specifically. And I know you're pregnant. All the tests indicate you are fine, and you haven't lost the baby. I haven't told Banton yet. I thought you would want to do that." He smiled down at me, and then his smile changed to concern as he watched my horrified expression.

"No. NO! NO!" I screamed, a blood curdling scream that could have wakened the dead.

The poor doctor seemed to age a hundred years. He placed his arms on my shoulders as he tried to quiet me.

"You have to get it out, now! Get that thing out of me, now!" I sobbed as he continued to try to reason with me. As I slowed my rant to drag a ragged breath, light dawned in his eyes.

"Chandler, you were attacked on board the Orco ship?"

I nodded slowly.

"You appear to be much more than a month along. You surely were pregnant before you were kidnapped. When was your last cycle?"

I calmed somewhat, realizing the baby could be Banton's.

429

"I...a few days before Will was killed. I don't know, maybe seven days before I was taken?"

"Did you and Banton have sex before you were taken?"

"Yes," I whispered.

"When were you raped, Chandler?"

"I don't know..." His questions hurt my head. "Maybe...two or three days before I was rescued. I'm not sure...I've lost all track of time."

He smiled down at me reassuringly. "I really don't think the tests I ran would have been conclusive if you'd conceived from the attack. I want you to calm down and consider you might possibly have been pregnant when you were attacked. I understand how you are hurting, and I understand your aversion to being touched."

"It's not just Banton, Doctor. I don't want to hurt him. It's anyone touching me," I sobbed softly.

"I understand that, Chandler. Yours is a common reaction to the trauma. I addressed your wounds when you came in, and suspected you might have been abused. I didn't say anything to your husband, but he knows."

"How? I don't want him to know," I sobbed as he tried to quiet me again.

"I can see it in his eyes when he asks you. He's tortured, Chandler, and he wants to help you. I know how much he loves you. He hasn't left your side for a second. I've never seen anyone cry as hard as he did when I told him both your shoulders were dislocated, one of them broken."

I nodded at him. I'd already guessed Banton was guilt-ridden about hurting me during the rescue.

"He saved your life, and he's trying to save it again. Tell him what happened, at least part of it. In the meantime, I will run more tests, and we'll put your fears to rest about the baby."

The baby. As if we didn't have enough to deal with. I had to know. I had to do something if it wasn't. I couldn't stand the thought if it was...

"Chandler, please, put this out of your mind, until we know. Don't do that to yourself. That is an order," the doctor said firmly. Then his gaze softened.

430

"Can I let your husband back in? Do you want him here?" he asked softly.

I nodded.

"Can you tell him about the attack?"

I shook my head and cried out at the pain in my neck and shoulder.

"Do you want me to tell him? That might be easier," he offered softly.

I nodded slowly. He patted my leg and then rose and opened the door.

"Can I see her now, Doc?" Banton pleaded in the doorway.

"First I need a word with you, and then we'll get you back to her. Brie, would you like to sit with Chandler for a while?"

John's voice interrupted. "Brie, go on in. I'll stay with the babies next door."

The door opened again, and Brie entered and closed it quickly. She sat down beside the bed and took my hand in hers. As I connected with her emotions, I was calmed enough to endure her touch.

We sat in silence for at least ten minutes or more. I finally opened my eyes to gaze at her, the tears pooling like I knew they would when I looked into her eyes.

"Oh, Chandler! What have they done to you?" she whispered as she stroked my cheek. "I know. I can feel your pain and self-loathing. Why are you doing that to yourself? Stop it!" she admonished me as I looked up at her.

"I think you know why."

"I have my suspicions. Chandler, I was attacked in much the same way before Lucien took my life. That was part of my struggle when I was trying to find my way back to John. Don't let this come between you and Banton, Chandler. The Orcos did this to you! It's not your fault and you did nothing wrong! You are beautiful, strong, loving…and Banton adores you. Let us all help you," she pleaded as tears rolled down her cheeks.

Lucien had attacked her like Dante attacked me. Only she could remember her attack. I was grateful I couldn't.

Her admission gave me strength and hope.

"I'm so sorry, Brie. I didn't know."

431

"Oh, Andie, it helps to talk about it. I know that now. Put it behind you. It will take time, but I'll help you."

I nodded as I gave her a weak smile.

"Thank God. We've all needed to see you smile."

I felt more normal, more human…more myself as I talked to my friend. I was talking to my friend who I had shared so much with already.

"Brie, there's a small problem."

"Honey, after all we've been through, it's bound to be a small problem. Bring it," she teased, stroking my cheek.

"The doctor just told me I'm pregnant."

She was silent. A thousand emotions ran through her hand and into my body in silent communication. The emotion I picked to cling to was extreme love and acceptance.

As tears gathered in her eyes, she whispered "Well, okay then. We'll deal with it."

I teared up again. "Brie, what if it is…"

"Then we'll deal with it. But it could be Banton's, right?"

I nodded forcefully.

"Then I'm sure it is. I won't have any other outcome. Are you going to tell him?"

"No, not till I know."

"Okay. Then it's our little secret."

Banton pushed the door open and stepped back into the room. He'd showered and was cleanly shaven. He looked like my Banton again.

"I'm going to leave you two alone. Call me if you need me. I'm just next door. I'm going to go and save John from a dirty diaper change now." She reached down to hug me and kissed my forehead as she left the room.

Her touch was uncomfortable but tolerable. It was getting easier.

Banton eyed me warily as he moved to sit down beside the bed. I couldn't tell from his expression if the doctor had told him yet or not. I was nervous. *When was that damn shot supposed to take effect, anyway?* I wished I'd fallen asleep before he'd returned.

"I'm sorry I was gone so long. John told me I stunk and that was probably the reason you wouldn't let me touch you," he said wryly as I smiled at him.

"You definitely didn't stink. I smelled you before I woke, and you smelled clean, like your soap. You smelled like my Banton," I whispered, smiling at him again. "But I'm glad you shaved. I can see your dimple again."

He returned my smile, and my heart melted. He raised his hand slowly, giving me time to decide whether I wanted him to touch me or not. I nodded once, and he touched the back of his fingers softly against my cheek as he shut his eyes.

I reached up and held his hand against my face as I turned to kiss his palm.

"Oh, Chandler. I love you so much," he whispered, cautiously keeping his distance. "I want to scoop you up and hold you in my arms, but I don't want to hurt you," he said huskily as he opened his eyes.

"I would love it if you would lay your head beside mine on the pillow. That was nice," I whispered up to him as he nodded. He slowly moved toward me, and then placed his head gently down on the pillow, leaving about three inches between us. I could smell his breath…clean and minty. He'd just brushed his teeth. I silently wondered how bad my breath smelled, having been asleep for how many days? I had no idea.

He continued to stroke my cheek as he gazed into my eyes. Finally, I felt my eyes droop as the medicine began to take effect.

"Sleep, sweetheart. I want you to sleep. I'll watch over you, and I'll be here when you wake," he assured me, pulling the sheet up under my chin. He tucked it in gently around my arms, being careful not to touch me too much. It was so calming. I drifted off to sleep.

Chapter Thirty

"Call my Momma and Daddy, and tell them Chandler woke up last night. Doctor Delsant called ahead and an ambulance is taking us straight to Renault. Call Singleton, and if he is back, have him meet us there." I heard Banton barking orders into his cell phone as I woke. It was a comforting sound.

I opened my eyes slowly and scanned the room. Banton stood in the corner, his hand over his ear as he listened into the phone again.

"Mr. Lon, it's Banton....yes, we'll be stateside sometime this afternoon...no, no...she's awake. Well, she's asleep right now, but she woke from the coma last night. She's doing as well as can be expected, under the circumstances...No, I don't, I'm sorry. I know you want to take the twins, but Chandler will want them near us. Will you come and stay with Claudia? Maybe we could let you take them there, so you can bring them to Chandler whenever she wants to see them. No, I don't know how long Renault will keep her...I'll call you when we get there. Thank you, Mr. Lon...for everything. Yeah, I love you too. Bye."

He hung the phone up, and slipped it in the pocket of his jeans. I realized he was in civilian clothes. He looked good. He wore a white T-shirt, a pair of faded jeans, and a white linen shirt opened down the front. He turned, and his eyes widened when he saw I was awake.

"Hey, sweetheart, how do you feel this morning?" He grinned, his million dollar grin that deepened his dimple. My heart melted in spite of everything. He loved me. Somehow I had to find the strength to make everything okay.

"I'm better. My head doesn't hurt today," I murmured, aware of the vile taste in my mouth. I pushed up, wanting to sit up.

"Wait, baby...let me help you," he offered as he rushed to man the controls on the bed.

"Just say when," he said, cautiously watching me for any sign of pain. As I came to about a forty-five degree angle I winced, and he stopped the bed.

434

"Enough for now?" he asked softly. I nodded at him and smiled carefully.

"I'm so glad to see you smile. I was so lost last night. I didn't know what to do," he said, a shadow crossing his face.

I still couldn't tell if the Doctor had told him I'd been attacked. He'd surely had enough time. I thought again about the doctor and the tests he mentioned. I panicked, realizing I would be leaving the ship today and going to Renault's in N'awlins. *I would have to tell it all over again!*

The monitors spiked, my heart rate increasing.

"Chandler, calm down. I can hear your heart racing. I'm sorry I said anything about last night," he said, sitting down beside me. "Is that it, or are you upset about something else?"

"I didn't know I would leave Dr. Delsant so soon. We'll be in N'awlins today?" I tried to sound cheery but failed miserably. His smile faded, and in a nanosecond he guessed my distress and knew I'd confided in the kindly Doctor.

His voice was choked, but controlled. "Chandler, Dr. Delsant will travel with us and stay at Renault's until you are settled in. Don't worry," he said, reaching up to touch my forehead. I winced, involuntarily moving away from him. His expression immediately registered remorse.

"I'm sorry, Chandler. I didn't mean to scare you. I know I need to let you know before I do that, I forgot."

The pain in his eyes was awful to see. I reached out and held my hand up to his face. He placed his cheek there, and I stroked it as he shut his eyes.

I had to dispel the tension in the room. I took a deep breath and tried to get my brave on.

"What did the doctor tell you last night?" I whispered.

"Enough."

I looked back up at his tortured gaze, the tears pooled in his eyes. I nodded slowly as he spoke.

"Chandler, please…can I hold you?" he whispered the plea that I dreaded most. I hesitated, my eyes opening wide with fear. I couldn't control it.

"Andie, baby…your eyes," he said as he stood abruptly.

"What?"

"When did your eyes start glowing?" he asked softly as he gazed down at me.

"What?" I asked again, mortified.

"Chandler, you didn't know? Your eyes...they're glowing, beautiful turquoise flecks just like the babies," he whispered as he reached out slowly, letting me know he wanted to touch my face.

I nodded, and he closed the distance, sliding his thumb across my jawline. "You are so beautiful, Chandler. Please, can I hold you?"

"Yes," I whispered back, terrified. He took a deep breath and sat down gently on the side of the bed. He methodically moved each hand behind me, one under my lower back, and one on my left shoulder. He slowly pulled me into his chest as I held my breath, his touch evoking shudders I couldn't explain. I could feel his heartbeat. He smelled so good, so familiar. As my nose brushed his neck, I melted into him. His arms tightened around me as he tangled his fingers in my hair.

"I love you, Chandler. You are going to be all right, I promise you. I will move heaven and earth to see you well and whole again."

He was holding me, and it felt good. I could let him touch me and not feel badly. I relaxed against him further as the damn broke for the second time. Minding the leads and IV's still hooked to me, he pulled me completely into his lap, gently stroking my hair and whispering against my cheek.

"Baby, cry it out. You cry all you want to, I'm here. I'm here for you, Andie."

I tightened my grip around his neck as he rocked me back and forth in the bed. He held me and rocked me for an hour or more as the sun rose and sent bright light across the foot of my bed.

I finally loosened my grip on his neck when the doctor came into the room.

"Well, Chandler, are you ready to try and stand today? Let the nurse take your catheter out, and then we'll get you unhooked from those IV's. We'll see if we can get some chicken soup down you before you have to take that ambulance ride."

I nodded as the nurse came around Banton to stand at the foot of the bed.

"Lieutenant Gastaneau, if you would step out for a moment," the nurse asked. Banton let go of me and nodded at her. He leaned over and watched my eyes intently as he silently asked my permission to kiss me. I nodded once, and he placed his lips gently on my forehead. My eyes filled again with tears as he pulled away.

"I'll be right outside."

I nodded again as he left the room. After the nurse removed the catheter, I felt so much better. Then she removed the IV's and leads, and I felt free. I slowly rotated my neck around and raised my left arm. I still couldn't raise my right, but I could move my arm a little, and move my fingers. I stretched my legs and then pulled them back up. I was sore everywhere.

"Do you feel like standing?' The nurse asked me as Banton swung the door open wide.

"Please, I've got this." He strode over beside the bed, and held his hands out to me.

"Chandler, will you let me help you?" he asked, keeping his distance again until I nodded. I knew he needed to help me and I needed to let him.

He gently placed one hand behind my shoulders as he took my hand, letting me place weight on his forearm. I stood slowly, my legs having to remember to work again. As I began to take small steps, he moved forward.

"How far do you want her to walk, Doc?' he asked.

"Down the corridor and back, if possible. If she can't make it," he began.

"I'll pick her up and carry her back. I've got this," Banton said as he opened the door and ushered me around it.

"Banton, my back," I protested. The cold air reminded me my gown opened down the back.

"Here." The nurse handed Banton a short bathrobe, and he helped me slide it on, being careful of my shoulders.

"Now. All covered. Shall we stroll?" he asked grandly, taking my hand again.

"Please," I answered back as I gazed up at him. He smiled, flashing the dimple, and leaned down slowly to place a chaste kiss on my lips. I held steady and closed my eyes, willing myself not to flinch. Mind over matter, Chandler. Mind over matter, I repeated.

437

We walked the narrow ship's corridor, and then back again. I wouldn't attempt it yet without his steady arms around me, but it was a start.

When we returned to my room, the nurse was back with my lunch.

"Just soup, crackers and juice, Chandler. Call me if you need anything," she said cheerily, pulling the door closed.

"Banton, go and eat something. I know you are tired," I admonished him.

"I ate a big breakfast next door before you woke. I'm good. Ty promised me the biggest steak we could find in N'awlins tonight if we escaped this scrape alive, and he's paying up."

He helped me into the bed and pulled the sheet up over me. After I'd finished, he carried my tray out into the hallway. I could hear the babies whining next door.

"Banton, can I see the twins?" I asked.

"Of course. I'll go get them." He leaned over and kissed me quickly on top of the head. Immediately pulling back, he looked at me with an alarmed expression, his eyes wide.

"I'm sorry, sweetheart...was that okay?"

I nodded. "Pecks on top of the head are most welcome and invited."

"Good. I'm committing the dos and don'ts quickly to memory." He grinned wider and dashed out to get the babies. I giggled as I watched him. He acted like a kid. *Just my smile returning had this effect on him?*

He returned in under two minutes.

"Here's Mommy...see, I promised y'all she'd be up," he said as he placed them both gently down on the bed beside me.

"Mommy," Matty said as he put his hand out to my face. I kissed it quickly and he giggled.

Mommy," Elly mimicked him, wanting her kiss as well. I pulled her up against me and hugged her close, burying my nose in her hair.

I remembered as I was waking up I heard Matty say "daddy."

"And who is that?' I pointed at Banton as he smiled down at them.

438

"Daddy," Matty grunted, lunging forward toward Banton. Banton swept him up in his arms.

"Yeah, big guy, I'm daddy. Took you long enough to say it," he pouted as he mussed Matty's hair up.

"When did he start that? I missed it," I said sadly.

"No, baby. You were there. You were just unconscious. We were in the helicopter, and as I was helping Ty tend to you, John and Sam were holding the twins. They kept crying for me, and when I was convinced you were alive and going to make it, I asked them to hand the babies down to me. I kept repeating, 'Daddy's here. Daddy's got you,' and then right out of the blue, Matty uttered 'Daddy.'"

I smiled as I watched the babies crawl around on me. "Hmm. That was a lot more dramatic than his first 'Mommy.'"

"Well, it was the helicopter and everything, you know. Boys are impressed with that kind of thing," he teased rather cockily.

Banton sat down on the bed beside me. He wrestled with Matty as he sat him back on the bed. Matty immediately crawled up to Elly, tugging at her to get her attention.

"They're so close already, always looking for one another if they're separated," he observed as Elly pulled Matty to her and leaned over as if to hug him.

"They clung to each other while we were…they never cried out, it was almost as though they knew." I whispered as I watched them. The memories came flooding back asking them to fade, clinging to me as I climbed the crates.

"Andie," Banton whispered. I glanced up at him over Elly's head.

"Thank you for protecting our babies. You took care of them under the most extreme circumstances possible. Noah told me how you cared for them, and hid them from Dante and Lucien." His eyes hardened, his tone becoming deathly quiet. "Noah told me what you endured at Dante's hands. He said you were brave." Tears pooled in his eyes as he reached out and touched my cheek.

I closed my eyes against the images. "Noah is sweet. I wouldn't have made it without his help."

Elly lay down on my chest as she sucked her thumb. As Banton reached over to stroke her hair, he noticed my breast

439

exposed above Elly's head. I glanced down to see what had caught his attention, and noticed the fresh bite marks. I looked back up at him and watched his gaze turn deadly.

"How many times were you bitten, Chandler?"

"Too many."

"Lucien and Dante?" he asked as he closed his eyes.

"Yes. And Miss Astrid."

His eyes snapped open, horrified as he considered what I'd just said.

"And Ben," I whispered. He searched my eyes, waiting for me to go on.

My voice broke. "Ben came after I woke from…the attack. He helped Noah lift me from the tub. He thought he could help me, but then he lost control. I don't know what the Orcos had put him through, but he'd fully transformed, and he was too close." I glanced back down at the bite above Elly's head. When I looked back at Banton, I could see fire and pure rage in his eyes.

"He told me when he left, he would try to help me and he wouldn't come close to me again. When the ship started sinking, Dante ordered Ben and another Orco to come and get the babies for the sacrifice," I whispered. "But I managed to get them to fade. The girl who was with Ben overlooked them, but I could see recognition register on Ben's face as he searched me." Tears streamed now as I thought about what Ben had done. "He left and never said a word. He protected the babies, Banton."

As I finished, he nodded, placing his hand on my cheek.

"Did you see Ben, when you boarded the ship?"

"Yes."

"And?"

"Just as John found your location, I was running toward him and Noah. An Orco leapt out at me. He let loose with a spray of gunfire at close range. The only thing that saved me was Ben. He jumped in front of him and then pulled him over the side. He took the bullets for me," he finished as he lay his head down beside mine on the bed. "He wanted to die. I could see it in his eyes."

I nodded, swallowing the bile rising in my throat. "Ben was fighting the demon. He had enough human emotions left to know he didn't want to exist that way."

440

"We can't tell Julia," Banton murmured. I nodded in agreement.

I winced as Elly moved across my breast. I was sore everywhere, but I recognized the soreness in my breasts as being pregnant. My eyes widened at the realization.

"Chandler, you look tired. Let me take them back to Brie for a while. They will be just next door," he assured me as he scooped them both up in his arms.

While he was gone, I wondered about the Orcos and if they'd killed them all. When he slipped back into the room moments later, I looked up at him.

"What is it, Chandler?" He could sense I wanted to ask him.

"Did you get them all?"

Banton pushed the chair away and sat down carefully on the side of the bed. He reached out slowly to my arm, waiting until I nodded before he touched me. As he caressed my arm softly, he spoke.

"Most of them are dead."

"What about Dante?" I whispered, hating to even whisper his name.

"John, Ty and I took care of him. He's dead, baby. He won't ever hurt you or the babies again."

I closed my eyes, taking a deep breath as I tried to put the evil to rest.

"And Lucien?"

Banton sighed as he raised his hand to my head, stroking my hair softly.

"One of the Orcos told us Lucien bailed before we got there. We think he got away," he said, his voice low.

"Banton, where is Everett? Did he come with you?"

He paused, and it was if a shadow crossed his face. He nodded once, and then answered.

"Yes, Chandler. He was wounded pretty badly in the fight. He's mending. He'll be all right. He wants to see you, but it will be a few days.

"How was he wounded?" I was alarmed Everett would still be down after all this time.

441

"Doctor Delsant had to re-attach his arm, and an Orco broke his neck. They almost got him, Chandler. He had us worried, but he's an Aldon. He's going to make a full recovery."

I tried to push up and winced.

"Baby, you can see him later, after we move both of you. I promise," he assured me, leaning over to try to ease me back down on the bed.

I shuddered at his touch as he startled me.

He pulled back slowly. I could see the hurt in his eyes.

"I'm sorry, Banton. I didn't mean to do that. It isn't you," I choked out as he placed his fingers against my lips.

"I know, Sweetheart. Don't worry about me. I can't even imagine what you must have…please. Just tell me what you need. I'll do anything for you. I'll do anything to make this go away."

He gazed at me, his eyes so full of love. He was so desperate to fix everything.

"It will just take time. Just you and time. Just hold me, and love me until I'm me again. You are all I need," I whispered, trying to keep my voice steady. "I love you so much."

He cupped my cheek with his hand as he gazed at me.

"Chandler, your eyes are glowing again. I didn't think your eyes could be any more beautiful, but I was wrong. The flecks of turquoise, the intensity…" he murmured as he continued to stroke my cheek.

"I want to see," I said. I hadn't seen them since they'd changed. I realized at that moment, my blurry vision the last two days of captivity must have been my vision changing. I could see clearly, everything was so vivid and bright.

Banton hesitated as I saw his eyes cloud with doubt.

"I don't know if we have a mirror around here," he murmured as he looked around.

"Go and ask Brie. I'll bet she has one," I urged him. He turned back to me, and shook his head.

"Andie, I don't think that is such a good idea," he argued. I cocked an eyebrow at him.

"Banton, what is it? Why don't you want me to see?"

He sighed, and left the room. A few moments later, he came back with a hand mirror.

"Just remember you are still swollen and bruised," he cautioned as I took the mirror from him.

My glowing eyes widened as I stared at the girl in the mirror. I didn't recognize the image looking back at me. My face was covered in bruises and swollen knots, two or three different shades of purple and blue that turned my flesh into a hideous mask.

I covered my mouth with my hand as a sob escaped. I looked as dirty and damaged on the outside as I felt inside.

"Baby, no...you are going to be okay," he whispered. Everything will heal and you will be back to normal in no time."

I placed the mirror down on my abdomen and covered my face with my hands.

"I don't know how you can even stand to look at me. I could barely stomach the thought before I looked in the mirror," I whispered. He grabbed my hands.

"Chandler Ann Gastaneau, stop it. You are just shocked, that's all. It's just bruises and swelling. It will go away, I promise. Please, can I hold you?" he whispered as I continued to hold my face in my hands. When I didn't immediately answer him, he slid his hands under me and raised my upper body against his, enveloping me in his arms.

"No," I whispered in protest.

"Baby, please. Don't do this to yourself. I love you, Chandler. Let me hold you. I have to hold you," he whispered into my hair as he stroked it. I willed myself to relax in his arms. I got it, in my mind, I was safe and the ordeal was over. But I couldn't separate the feel of Dante and Lucien's hands on me. I couldn't seem to let it go, and I knew it tortured Banton.

Chapter Thirty-One

"Lieutenant Gastaneau, we're in port now. The ambulance will be ready momentarily," the doctor said as Banton gently placed me back on the pillows.

Before I had time to process, the crew could be heard in the hallway, pulling a gurney into the room.

We'll be moving her now, Lieutenant," one of the attendants told Banton. I shivered uncontrollably as they both touched me, lifting me from the bed and transferring me to the gurney to move me to the ambulance. Banton watched, a look of helplessness crossing his face.

"I'm riding with her," he demanded as both attendants nodded at him.

"Banton, what about the babies?" I asked, my voice rising.

"Brie and John have them ready. They will bring them to Dr. Renault's," he assured me.

As they wheeled me out of the ship and into the sunlight, I shrank into the stretcher, the sun blinding me, seeming to scorch my skin. It seemed like weeks since I'd seen sunlight. The wind was blowing, and the chill in the air made me shudder, causing every bone and muscle in my body to ache. I cried out, the pain almost unbearable.

"Hold on, Mrs. Gastaneau, we're almost there," one of the attendants assured me. Once they'd lifted me into the ambulance, Banton crawled in behind, and draped another blanket over me, tucking the edges in.

"I'm so sorry, Andie. I didn't realize how chilly it would be out here," he said, fussing over my stretcher. As the attendants shut the doors and loaded in front, I panicked.

"Dr. Delsant," I protested.

"Shh. Chandler, he'll be right behind us. He won't leave you until he knows you're okay with it. He's going with us," he assured me as he leaned over me.

My heart raced. I was going to Renault's, and I knew it meant telling him everything, reliving the attack, explaining about the baby. Thinking for the first time about the tests they were about to run, I began to panic. I felt sick, dreading confirmation that the baby could be a result of the attack and not Banton's. I heaved, throwing up over the side of the cot.

Banton held my shoulders as he pulled my hair back. My stomach continued to convulse, but nothing came up from the violent empty spasms.

"Shhh. Calm down, Chandler. You're okay," Banton tried to soothe me as the attendant handed a cold rag to him. He bathed my face, urging me in soft whispers to lie back on the cot. He fought to maintain a calming demeanor as the ambulance bounced and swayed back and forth as we navigated the rush hour traffic.

When we finally arrived at Renault's clinic, I was in a full state of panic, my heart racing as my nausea reached a fever-pitch.

I could hear Dr. Renault in the hallway as we entered.

"Bring her in to exam one," he instructed the attendants. "Dr. Delsant, if you will come with us."

Banton held my hand as we crossed through the double doors.

Both doctors moved around the room as the nurse helped the attendants move me onto a bed. As the attendants left, Dr. Renault turned to Banton.

"Son, it sure is good to see you two alive. The Aldon owe you our eternal gratitude. You have dealt with our greatest problem in years, having taken care of the Somali problem and this Dante," he whispered as he glanced down at me. He shook Banton's hand. Banton pulled away first, turning back to me.

"Banton, we'll need for you to step out so I can examine Chandler for myself. Dr. Delsant will stay with her," he urged as Banton shook his head.

"No, Doc. I'm not leaving her now. I know about the attack, I'm not leaving her alone.

I began to shake uncontrollably, knowing they would have to do a vaginal examination and what that would involve. Banton couldn't be here.

"Banton," I began. I didn't even recognize the sound of my own voice, it shook so. "Please, go. I need for you to go, you have to," I pleaded with him as a shadow crossed his face. He leaned over and kissed my forehead.

"I'll be right outside, Andie."

445

As soon as the doors closed behind him, Dr. Renault pulled a chair up beside me.

"Chandler, Dr. Delsant has already filled me in on your condition. We need to examine you, and we need to do an ultrasound," he began.

I nodded, the nausea rising as I thought about them examining me.

Dr. Renault sensed my reluctance. "Chandler, this is Ms. Gary, your nurse, and she will be here the whole time to help you through it," he explained as I nodded.

"We'll give you something to calm you down before we start." Dr. Delsant patted me on the shoulder as the nurse gave me the injection. The three of them moved about, readying instruments and equipment, and after a few moments the nurse raised my bed a bit.

"I know you are in extreme pain, but I need for you to scoot forward, and bend your knees." She raised the sheet and helped me as I scooted down. I shut my eyes tightly, steeling myself against her touch and what I knew was ahead.

She helped me pull my knees up, and spread my legs apart gently as she fitted each of my feet into a stirrup. I began to sob.

"Shhh, Chandler, it's going to be fine. They need to examine you. They will be gentle," she soothed as she held my hand. I stared at the ceiling, willing myself not to panic. As I heard both doctors putting their gloves on, I began to cry. I could feel the medicine taking effect, my legs were relaxed and I was having a hard time keeping them bent.

Both doctors stayed silent as they worked. I could hear Dr. Renault muttering something, and Dr. Delsant answered him. When one of them inserted a finger and pressed down on my abdomen, I yelled out, "No, please, don't!"

"It's okay, Chandler. They have to examine you vaginally. This will only take a minute," the nurse tried to calm me.

I could hear angry voices in the hallway, and Banton's voice rose above the others.

"Dammit, let me in there! What the hell is going on," Banton yelled as Ty's voice and John's joined in with Brie's, trying to calm him down.

446

I caught bits and pieces of what the doctors were saying at the foot of my bed. They were both shocked at the amount of damage Dante had inflicted.

"Chandler, you are definitely pregnant. I suspect you are further along than you think, but we need to do an ultrasound to try to determine the length of your gestation. We need to do it vaginally, and I know that will be traumatic for you because of the state you are in."

"No, please. No, I can't," I protested.

"Chandler, we can do this to put your mind at ease. It's a small wand, and I will insert it just long enough to get a couple of pictures. It may hurt a bit, considering your injuries, but we will be quick and gentle, I promise. Would it help if we bring Banton in?"

"Oh, please, no! He doesn't know, not yet," I pleaded as Dr. Renault's eyes widened. He didn't know that we hadn't told Banton.

"I heard Brie outside. Get Brie," I asked.

"Okay, Chandler. Hold on," Dr. Renault urged, patting me on the shoulder. He walked over and opened the doors.

"Gabriella, could you come in and be with Chandler, for a bit?"

"Doc, let me in. Why won't you let me in?" Banton shouted. John tried to talk to him in calming tones.

"She needs a woman right now, Banton. Please be patient," Dr. Renault urged him as he shut the door.

Brie smiled at me as she took the nurse's place beside my bed. As the doctors wheeled the ultrasound machine around beside the bed, the nurse placed a chair beside me. Dr. Renault fired the machine up, and picked up a wand, sliding a condom on it.

"No, please, I can't do this, I can't...please, don't touch me again," I pleaded as Brie took my hand in hers.

"Chandler, calm down. You can do this. I know how you feel, remember? Look at me." She crossed around the bed, and placed herself between me and Dr. Renault. "Look at me, and hold my hand. You can do this," she coached me as I nodded at her, trying to be brave.

As I felt the fullness of the probe enter me, I involuntarily sobbed as my whole body shuddered.

447

"No! Please, Please, No!"

"Chandler, calm down. It's almost over," Brie assured me as her own voice began to shake. "I know how hard this is, Andie. It's over, we're okay. It's over," she repeated over and over as she kissed me on the forehead. I realized Dr. Renault had removed the wand and was printing out a picture.

"Chandler, the ultra sound indicates you are about eight weeks along. The baby is Banton's," he said softly as he handed me the picture.

"That isn't possible. How can you be sure? There isn't any doubt? Can you do blood tests? Please," I pleaded. I needed his assurance.

"Dr. Delsant told me you had a cycle about two weeks ago. How long did you bleed?"

"It's the only one I've had since the twins. I only bled about two days," I muttered.

"I don't think it was a real cycle. I think that was just break-through bleeding, because you were already pregnant. If you would like, we can do an amnio to be conclusive," he offered as I nodded furiously.

"Am I far enough along?" I asked.

He nodded. "It will involve using the ultra sound again, and as you know, the amnio is not without pain," he added.

I was determined to know. I felt a certain amount of relief and hope with the knowledge that he thought I was further along. I felt if I had genetic evidence the baby was Banton's, I could put part of the nightmare behind me.

"Please, Doctor. I need to know," I whispered. Brie clutched my hand tighter.

The nurse brought me some water as the doctors prepared for the amnio. I refused to look at them, at the needle they prepared, or the sonogram machine. As they raised my legs again, I took a deep breath, willing myself to stay silent. Brie continued to grip my hand as she stood over me, gazing at me with tears in her own eyes.

"We can do this, Andie. We've got this, no matter what," she continued to coach me as I gasped, the needle entering my stomach. As the pain of the fluid being drawn from my body took its toll, I focused on the fuzzy sleeping feeling overtaking my body as the medicine finally took effect.

* * *

Bits of a dream flooded back to me as I napped.

"Her heartbeat is stronger, and so is the baby's."

I'd dreamed about the first time Banton found out I was pregnant. As I opened my eyes, I hoped that was a good sign.

"Hey, Chandler." I turned my head to find Constance sitting beside me.

"Oh, Constance," I cried out as she hugged me close.

"Chandler, oh God, what have they done to you?" she gasped as she held me, stroking my hair.

I shook my head. I had no intention of ever speaking of any of it again.

"I'm so glad you're home safe. Momma and Daddy are right outside. Do you want me to get them?" she asked as she fussed over me, straightening my bedcovers. I realized I'd been moved to a private room, and someone had changed me into a regular satin gown.

I shook my head at her. I wasn't ready to see anyone, other than her or Brie or Banton. I couldn't face seeing anyone else.

She gave me a puzzled look and then her eyes widened as the realization dawned.

"Okay, Andie. I'll just tell them you'll see them later, that you are tired," she answered as she patted my leg. "I'm going to let you get some rest now," she murmured, placing a kiss on my forehead.

She quietly slipped from the room. My head throbbed, with all the memories and thoughts whirling around. I wouldn't rest until I knew the results of the amnio.

I heard the door open and shut again, and then I smelled Banton's cologne. I kept my eyes shut. I couldn't look at him. It was if all the progress we'd made on the ship had vanished since the trauma of the examination and the ultra sound. He sat quietly down beside me, and then I felt the bed dip as he rested his head on his hands. I opened my eyes slowly and found his gaze fixed on my face. He reached out and brushed the hair from my forehead.

"Sweetheart, are you okay?" he whispered. I nodded, remaining as still and silent as possible. As the medicine took over once more, I drifted off, Banton's eyes still on me, watching over me.

* * *

"Chandler, baby, wake up. You need to eat something, and you need to get up," Banton's soft voice urged me. I opened my eyes and found him hovering over me. He grinned at me, his dimple deep.

"Hey. You look much better this morning." He sat down beside the bed, looking clean-shaven and rested.

"You've slept," I murmured, placing my hand against his cheek.

"Doc put a cot in here, and I slept beside you last night. Best night's sleep I've had in a while," he said as he pulled a cart toward the bed. "We have oatmeal, orange juice and coffee. Can you manage?" he asked as I nodded. He took the control to the bed and raised my head. For the first time, my ribs didn't protest.

"I can actually sit up now without holding my breath," I commented as I let my breath out slowly.

Banton chuckled. "It's amazing what a good night's sleep and a good ace bandage will do," he said, helping me with my silverware.

I reached up and discovered someone had wrapped my ribs.

"You were really out of it last night. They must have given you some happy drugs," he said playfully. "The nurse and I managed to get you fixed up. I told her I thought most of the pain you were still in was due to those damn ribs and your shoulders," he said as he glanced sideways at me, a pained expression crossing his brow.

"That's not the real pain," I muttered as he sat down once again beside me.

"I know, baby."

450

I ate in silence, not really tasting anything. But I knew I wouldn't get out of this place until I was eating properly, so I pushed on, trying to eat most of what he brought to me.

"Banton, where are the twins? Where are our babies?"

"John and Brie took them to Claudia's. Your Aunt Sue and Uncle Lon are keeping them there with my mother and daddy."

I nodded and relaxed.

"Doc says you can leave the blood shakes off for a while. They're giving you injections again," he said, a puzzled look crossing his face. Then he grinned up at me.

"You do look so much better, Chandler. Would you like to see?" He rose and left the room. I shook my head. He was so eager to make me feel better. He came back momentarily with a large mirror he'd evidently taken off the wall somewhere.

"They will arrest you for vandalism in this state," I teased him as he grinned at me.

"I'd commit any crime for you, baby, to see you smile," he replied, holding the mirror up. To my surprise I looked almost like myself. The bruising was still there, but was much lighter. The swelling was nearly gone. I looked up at him, relieved.

"I told you. A beauty like yours can't be hidden. And you are beautiful, Chandler. The most beautiful thing I've ever seen," he tried to assure me as I smiled at him.

"Banton, I've been meaning to ask you," I began.

"What is it, sweetheart?" he said as he sat the mirror down beside him in the floor.

"Alexandra and Reece. Did you ever get the results of the tests?"

His expression changed instantly, and my heart sank. His reaction could only mean one thing, and he didn't want to tell me in my current state.

"We got the results, Chandler. I knew all along Reece wasn't my son."

I sat in stunned silence, staring at him.

"Are you disappointed?" I whispered, terrified.

"No, of course not. All of that turned out for the best."

"Then what is it?" I was puzzled by his reaction; he seemed unsettled.

451

"We are still unraveling everything. Mr. Lon and my dad did some digging while we were gone, and found out that we had video in the driveway on the garage camera. Apparently Astrid forgot about that camera. Astrid walked the twins out to the garage and gave them to Alexandra, and then she drove off with them. Alexandra was involved in the kidnapping," he said as I gasped. "Then Singleton called Dad. Evidently Alexandra was contacted by Reed months ago, not the other way around. Reed brought her here and put her up to all of this. Money exchanged hands in the process, beginning around the time I came home and the babies were born. We don't have a clue who Reece's real father is."

My eyes widened. All the tears I'd shed over her involvement, and it had been a setup from the start. I shook my head, unable to process all the revelations.

"Why would Commander Reed do that? What was he trying to accomplish?"

"I know it's a lot to consider. There's more, Chandler, but I think we can talk about all of that later when you are better. Just know all of this is finally over. You and the twins are safe, and Constance is out of danger."

"Yes, until Lucien shows up again. Banton, what if he..." I began.

"If he does, we will be ready. It won't be as easy next time for him to pull new recruits together. And if Everett has his way, we'll hunt him down long before he has time to regroup," he assured me as I shuddered.

"How is Everett?" I asked. I felt bad I hadn't asked before now.

"He's good. They released him this morning. He is at his grandmother's now, but he said to tell you he would be by to see you as soon as he can. Now, let's get you up and walking, so you will be strong enough for all the visitors knocking the doors down," he said, pulling my tray out of the way.

He pulled the covers back, revealing a beautiful pink and brown paisley gown. He reached beside the bed and produced a matching robe.

"Where did this come from?" I asked as he raised an eyebrow.

I went shopping last evening with a little help from Constance. I knew you hated those hospital gowns." He helped me to stand. "I couldn't have the most beautiful girl in the world wearing that awful blue thing with the snaps." He steadied me and helped me shrug into the robe. I shuddered as he brushed my shoulders, and I felt him tense beside me. Keeping his reaction private, he just placed his arm in front of me.

"Hold on to me, and I'm going to support you with my other hand," he said softly but firmly. I nodded without looking up at him. This was so hard, and I was so confused. I wanted him near, and I craved his touch. But when he touched me without warning, my skin crawled, almost to the point of being painful. *Would I ever stop feeling like this? Was this a result of the attack or my further transformation?* I desperately needed to talk to Everett.

"What is it, Andie?" Banton asked as we stepped out into the hallway.

"I know you want me to talk to you, but there are just a couple of things I need to ask Everett. I need to talk to him," I murmured.

"I understand."

We walked along, down the long corridor and then back again.

"Where is everyone?" I asked as we passed my doorway to go down the opposite hallway.

"Constance and Ty left a little while ago. I think they were craving a little alone time," he said, a twinkle returning to his eyes. I grinned up at him and he held me closer. I willed myself not to shudder.

"John and Brie are in the waiting room around the other side of the building with momma and daddy. They're all staying at Claudia's. Brie said they aren't leaving N'awlins until you can come home with us." He smiled down at me, his smile dimming a bit at what he saw in my eyes. I knew Brie felt she had to stay with me until we had the results of the tests.

"Chandler?" Dr. Renault called behind us. We turned to find him standing just outside my room.

"I need to have a word with you in private, if I could. Banton, would you go and find Gabriella for us?"

My heart sank into my stomach. If he thought he needed Brie to give me the results, it must be bad. I had to make myself put one foot in front of the other. Stumbling, I was light headed. *How could I appear to be so far along if the baby...if this thing inside me was a result of the rape?* Maybe Dante's genetics made it grow at an accelerated rate. I was nauseated as I held my abdomen, my body shaking from head to toe.

"Chandler, are you okay?" Banton asked in an alarmed voice.

"Just get me back to my room," I whispered as I searched Dr. Renault's face. He gave away nothing. As we turned the corner, Doc held the door open for him. As he helped me back on the bed I moaned, not knowing how I was going to handle this.

"Banton, go and get Gabriella," Dr. Renault urged as he pulled a chair across the room.

Banton left, and after we heard his strides disappear down the hallway, Dr. Renault rose and closed the door.

"It's...it's bad, isn't it?" I whispered as I closed my eyes.

"Only if you and Banton don't want to be parents again. The twins are young, I'll admit, but I know you want more children," he began.

I opened my eyes and looked at him. "The baby is Banton's?" I whispered as I clutched my abdomen.

"Yes, Chandler. The test was conclusive. The baby is most definitely Banton's. Congratulations."

I released my breath, all of the anxiety leaving my body. This was Banton's baby. I'd been pregnant way before I was kidnapped.

"Why...why did you call for Brie?"

"I needed for Banton to leave so I could tell you. And I know how you and Brie are. You probably needed a little girl talk to decide how to break it to Banton," he smiled at me as he winked.

I hugged myself, finally happy. The baby was Banton's. The relief that flooded through my body was unbelievable.

"Thank you, Dr. Renault. Thank you so much," I choked out as he patted my arm.

"Chandler, I know what a hard time you've been going through. I just want to leave you with this thought. I talked to Noah extensively yesterday about what he knew about the attack. He told me the attack was fast, and that not too much could have happened after you lost consciousness. Dante left in a rage. He also told me about the numerous attacks Dante inflicted on other women. He was rarely able to…let's just say that bruises and scars are the only thing he was ever able to leave behind."

I nodded, strangely comforted by his words. He rose and left the room, leaving me to consider all he'd said. I couldn't remember the attack. The last thing I remembered was him ripping my shirt off of me, and then striking me, the blow that knocked me unconscious. It was much like the attack in the tunnels, except that I woke naked and bleeding afterwards. My own imagination had done most of the damage. I took a deep breath. A good, heart to heart talk with Brie would do me a world of good. As if on cue, she opened the door and peered in at me. I smiled at her as she crossed over to the bed.

"Good news?" she asked as she took my hand.

"The best. The baby is Banton's." I whispered as she hugged me. There was no flinching at her touch this time.

"Oh, Chandler. I'm so happy for you," she breathed as she kissed me on the cheek. "Poor Banton…he almost put his fist through the wall when John made him stay in the waiting room," she said as she pulled away from me. "Are you going to tell him?"

I sighed, bone-weary. I couldn't think. I couldn't do anything but fall back into the pillows, too exhausted to make any decisions.

"Why don't we both sleep on it and come up with the perfect way to tell him. In the meantime, let me get him before he tears the waiting room apart." She giggled as I smiled sleepily up at her.

"Brie, I love you," I whispered as I shut my eyes.

"I love you too, darlin'! One more baby and we can each have one! I've got dibs on this one," she said, swinging the door closed. I barely got to shift in the bed and pull the covers up over me before Banton threw the door open and strode back in.

"Are you all right? What did Dr. Renault say?" he asked breathlessly, sitting down in the chair beside my bed.

"I'm better than all right. He just…he said I'm much better, and he talked to me a little. I'm so sleepy Banton."

Banton cocked his eyebrow, knowing I wasn't telling him everything. He reached out and pushed a strand of hair off my forehead. "Then sleep, baby. I'll be right here," he murmured.

"I need you near me. Please, will you hold me?" I asked as I flung the covers back, inviting him in. I opened my eyes briefly, and found him watching me warily, his eyes wide.

"Are you sure?" I could barely hear his whisper.

"I've never been surer of anything in my life. Please, I need you," I breathed out. His wide smile warmed the entire room as he kicked his boots off, pushing them under the bed. He sank down slowly beside me and pulled me into his chest as he lay back on the pillows. I snuggled into his chest, taking in his smell as I closed my eyes. I was home, safe, warm, and happy.

Chapter Thirty-Two

Good news and a nap can change a girl's world view. I woke, refreshed and feeling so much more optimistic than I had when we'd arrived at Renault's.

Banton still dozed, his arms wrapped firmly around me, his face buried in my hair. I tried to move without waking him, but my ribs protested too much, and I cried out.

"Hey, beautiful…you're awake," Banton breathed out, stretching. He pushed up in bed and then helped me turn.

"I'm just so sore, everything feels broken," I complained as he fluffed my pillows behind me.

"Well, you look even better than you did this morning. Dr. Renault says your ribs and shoulders are healing nicely. I'm going to go and get you something to drink and then I'll find Doc. I'll be right back."

He pulled his boots on and hurried down the hallway, leaving my door ajar. I pushed up further in bed and then adjusted it so I could stand. I needed the bathroom. After I'd finished, I checked myself in the mirror. Banton was right, I did look better, but my hair was a mess. I ran my fingers through it, and then tried to tie it up in a loose braid as I supported myself against the sink.

"Chandler? Where are you?" Constance's voice called out through the door.

"In the bathroom, I'll be right out," I called out. I opened the door, and found Constance sitting on the end of the bed, my suitcase in the floor at her feet.

"I thought I'd bring you some things from Claudia's. I know you like your own toothbrush," she smiled, flopping back on the bed. She looked great, tight tan leggings, pale pink sweater, leather ankle boots and pearls. She looked every bit the wealthy deb.

"Well, you certainly look classy," I remarked as she smirked.

"Umm, thanks." She looked down at her clothes, and then grinned back up at me as I sat down on the bed next to her.

"Going somewhere?" I asked as my eyebrow rose.

"What is it with everyone? Mom gave me the third degree when I left the house earlier. Cade and Drew whistled at me, and

Banton told me I looked really grown-up when I came down the hallway."

"Well, you and I have been living in a lot of tights and sweats lately," I sighed as she reached out to tuck my hair behind my ear.

"Well, it just so happens, Ty and I set a date, and we're going to pick out some selections this afternoon," she gushed as I leaned over to hug her.

She squeezed me a little too tightly and my ribs protested.

"Owh!" I gasped as she pulled away hurriedly.

"Sorry."

She reached to my unruly hair again. "Do you want me to help you with a loose braid?"

I nodded and she began to section my hair and loosely weave it.

"Chandler, Banton told Momma and Daddy on the phone you had broken bones, and one of your lungs had been punctured. He also said he dislocated both your shoulders, and broke one getting you out of the ship. He said you almost drowned. My God, it's a wonder you're still alive."

I closed my eyes.

"That isn't all, is it?" she whispered as I shook my head. I opened my eyes again to look at her and she gasped, losing her grip on my braid.

"Chandler, your eyes!"

I shut them hurriedly. Everett was going to have to give me some charm lessons, and quickly.

"I'm sorry, Constance. I should have warned you. I've transformed way past you. More bites, you know…" I trailed off, and then opened my eyes again.

"They're beautiful, Chandler…your eyes, I mean. I'm almost jealous," she whispered as she rubbed my arm. "You've been bitten again," she observed quietly, touching my neck. I shuddered.

"And more. You don't want to know," I gazed at her, and she nodded. I could feel her emotions. She was tortured, not knowing what to say or how to comfort me. It seemed I was sensing that emotion from a lot of people.

I took a deep breath.

458

"I'm going to be okay. I have the most loving, understanding husband, and the greatest family anyone could ask for. I'm just ready to get home now," I stated as she finished the braid, and then dug in her purse for a tie to secure it.

The door to my bedroom opened once more, producing my husband, his eyes twinkling with secrets.

"Baby, do I have some good news for you." Banton's grin deepened as Constance rose to greet him.

After he'd kissed her on the cheek, he moved around her and sat down on the bed next to me. "You look great by the way," he kissed me on the forehead as I smiled. He reached up and played with the end of my braid.

What's the good news? You got sidetracked," I reminded him.

"Um. Yeah, you can go home this afternoon. All your blood work looks good, and he said if you follow orders and continue your shots, you can go... on the condition that you stay in N'awlins at Claudia's for a week or so," he said as happiness spread through me like wildfire. I lay my head over in his lap and shut my eyes.

"Chandler, are you all right?" He stroked my hair, concerned.

"I'm just relieved. I'm so ready to get out of here," I whispered.

Sensing we might need to be alone, Constance waved at us.

"Well, in that case, I'd better get my derriere in gear and get home to help everyone. It's been a little chaotic with all the developments at Claudia's. I swear bad-ass dad has twenty five more gray hairs!" she said conspiratorially as she winked at Banton and then dashed out the door.

I turned my head and looked up at him. "What the heck is she talking about?"

"Oh, I think there's been quite a bit going on while we were gone. We'll fill you in on it as soon as we get there tonight. Let's just get you ready to get out of here, lady!" he said excitedly as he pulled me up into his arms. "I don't know what Dr. Renault said to you, but I'm so glad to see you back to normal," Banton whispered against my lips. I nodded, letting him know it was all right to kiss me. He touched his lips to mine softly, caressing them back and forth, breathing softly through his parted lips. I met his kiss, softly moving my lips to meet his. He tightened his grip around me, and then broke away to place his forehead against mine as he gazed into my eyes.

"God, I love you, Chandler Ann Gastaneau. Don't ever scare me like that again, please?"

"I love you too, Banton Matthew Gastaneau. Right back at you, now you know how I felt when I thought I'd lost you," I whispered.

He sat me upright, and then slid my bag around beside my feet. "Doc said you can shower and then get dressed. He will be in to give you discharge orders in a few minutes." He watched me warily as I rose to get my suitcase.

"Don't lift that, here, let me," he admonished, picking it up and placing it on the bed. He unzipped it and flipped the top back. I took out some clean lingerie and a long sweater and leggings. As I walked to the bathroom, I turned to find Banton following me.

"Andie, do you need me to help you in the shower?"

I shook my head. I wasn't ready for him to see me naked yet.

"I'll at least have to unwrap your ribs for you," his eyes darkened as he watched my reaction. I tried not to show it, but my heart began to race.

"Or I can get the nurse," he added quickly. He looked really hurt.

"You could help me with my ribs," I replied as he nodded cautiously.

I placed all my clothes on the vanity in the small bathroom, and then closed the seat on the toilet and sat down on it. Banton helped me remove the sling I had around my right arm that helped me support my broken shoulder. He watched me as he moved to grasp my gown to pull it over my head. I nodded, and he pulled it up slowly, grasping first one arm, then the other, to support them as he removed the gown.

I shuddered, feeling so exposed. He sensed my unease, and I could feel his nervousness as he carefully removed the bandages from my ribs. I held my breath as he brushed so close to me...I could feel his breath in my hair.

"Chandler Ann, everything is going to be fine. I'm going to take care of you," he whispered. "I know you can't move to do this, so let me, and then you can slip into the shower."

Reaching over with one hand, he turned the shower knob, and then moved back over me.

"Stand up, baby," he whispered. I stood slowly as he knelt down and slid my panties down around my ankles. I shut my eyes and steeled myself against reacting. My heart was pounding so hard it hurt my ears.

Banton stood up carefully in front of me and pulled me into his chest.

"Andie, please," he murmured. "Feel my heartbeat." He pressed my head against his chest, folding his arms around me. "This is me, taking care of you. I love you, baby. I love you with all my heart. Please, calm down for me."

I could feel the warmth of his skin through his t-shirt. Taking a deep breath, I inhaled his scent, pulled back and nodded at him, not making eye contact. I relaxed as he held me close. Slowly kneeling back down he commanded, "Step, easy now," as I slipped first one foot, then the other out. He stood back up and gathered my gown and the bandages. I opened my eyes, and his gaze never left mine as he opened the shower door and helped me in. As he closed it slowly, he handed me a rag and some body wash.

"I'm right here, Chandler, if you need anything. I'm right here," he repeated as I began to wash. As I soaped my body, I found bruises I didn't even know I had. My ribs were still so sore I could barely run my own hands over them. I discovered I couldn't move my arms to wash my shoulders or back.

"Banton, can you help me with my back and shoulders?' I asked.

"Sure," he answered quickly, opening the shower door. He pulled his t-shirt off to keep from getting it wet, and then poured a small amount of body wash into his hand. I closed my eyes...it was getting easier to let him touch me.

"Turn, please. Lean in to the water." He rinsed the soap off, letting the water flow down my neck and back.

"All done. You're doing great, Sweetheart," he murmured huskily. I opened my eyes as he leaned in and placed a kiss on my

461

forehead. He stepped away, and before I could ask, appeared at the door with a towel to wrap me in. He took another off the bar, and then as I turned, he held it up.

"Okay if I help you dry off? I know you can't raise your arms," he said as he watched me carefully.

I nodded, and he gently dried my shoulders and arms, across the middle of my back, and then my chest. I stiffened, my heart racing again.

"Still okay?" he questioned as he paused.

I nodded, and opened my eyes. He smiled down at me, and it was such a sad smile, full of emotion as he struggled with having to ask his wife if it was okay to touch her.

"Legs?" he murmured as he started to kneel. I nodded again, slowly as he reached up and ran the towel slowly and gently down each leg, rubbing the towel in circles as he went.

"All done," he whispered, standing up over me. Leaning over, he placed a kiss in my wet hair.

"Now, let's get you dressed," he said, reaching for my clothes. He knelt again, my panties in his hands.

"Step," he commanded as I placed my foot through the opening. I lost my balance just a bit, and I grasped his shoulder with my hand to steady myself. He looked up into my eyes as I placed the other foot in. He slid them up to the point where the towel ended. He paused. I held my breath and nodded down to him. He finished pulling them up, being careful to keep his hands on the outside of my hips, grasping my panties under the lace at the sides as he pulled them up. Not waiting for my reaction, he then turned and picked up the top. He gathered it up and then slipped it over my head, and then helped me work both arms through, being careful of my shoulders.

"You've had practice at this, Lieutenant," I teased him, trying to relieve the tension in the air.

He grinned down at me, seemingly relieved at my comment.

"Yes, I'm getting better at the dressing you thing," he murmured as he caressed my cheek with his fingers. After he'd helped me on with the tights, I was almost able to breathe normally. He knelt beside the bed to help me into a pair of fur-lined booties, and then finished packing my things in the suitcase.

462

Doctor Renault came in to see me off. "Remember, Chandler, to call me if you have any vision problems, cough up any blood, or have any other problems we've spoken of in the past," he instructed as he glanced over at Banton. I nodded, not wanting him to say anything further about the pregnancy. He smiled, and then turned to Banton.

"Son, thank you again. Please take care of this young lady. I don't want to see her in here again for quite a while," he said as he left out of the room.

"Ready to go home?' Banton asked as he held the door open for me.

"Ready for Claudia's, anyway," I answered as he followed me out.

* * *

"Don't we need to go by the pharmacy? I would think you need some strong pain meds," Banton said, watching me. He'd taken great pains to place pillows around me and between me and the seatbelt, and I looked like I'd been packed into the car.

"He didn't say, I'll call and check with him later," I said, hoping he would drop it.

"I don't want your pain to get too bad before you take something, and I know you have to be having problems with your nerves from all the bites."

I shook my head.

"I have stuff, from before that I can take if I need to," I rushed on, seeming to satisfy him. He continued to watch me cautiously as if he sensed I had something to tell him. I'd been mulling it over and over in my mind, and couldn't decide how I wanted to break the news to him about the baby. Nothing I could think of seemed special enough, but then it seemed silly to make a big deal out of it after everything we'd been through. Every moment was special with Banton.

My eyes widened at the display of vehicles in front of Claudia's when we pulled up. Banton wheeled around hurriedly, and then pulled to the ally beside the house.

463

"I didn't call ahead to let them know when we'd be here. I know after everything that's happened to you, you would prefer to keep this low-key, so I'm going to try to sneak you up the back stairs and keep you to myself for a while," he murmured as he leaned over and kissed my forehead. I nodded in agreement. My emotional state was not one receptive to a large gathering where I would be the center of attention.

Banton stopped me as I started to slide out of the seat.

"Chandler, let me carry you up. That staircase will be hard with your ribs and everything," he cautioned. He slid his hands carefully under me and around my back, and lifted me from my seat. He paused at the patio doors, checking to see if anyone was in view before stepping inside. As we slipped in Beau met us, his tail wagging furiously.

"Shhh, Beau, quiet now," Banton whispered as Beau followed us up the back staircase. Pushing the door open to our room, he crossed to the bed and sat me down gently.

"Do you want the covers pulled back?" he asked as he fussed over me.

"No, I'm fine."

He looked around the room and then back to me, a twinkle lighting up his eyes. "Seems as though we slipped through undetected," he grinned and flashed his dimple. "I'll run back down and get your bag, and I'll be back in a flash."

"'Kay," I mumbled, already scooting down into the pillows.

Faint footsteps padded down the hallway and paused at the bedroom door. As the doorknob jiggled, I thought we were busted.

"Beau, puppy! Beau, wherw are you?" Ava Grace called out. She swung the door open wide and stared at me for a moment.

"Hey, Doodle-Bug! Come here and see me," I urged her, recognition finally registering in her wide, saucer-like eyes.

"An Andler! Wherw did you come fwom?" She flew across the room and up on the bed. I winced as she bounced into my arms.

"Shhh, Bug, can you keep a secret?" I asked, pulling her hair back and kissing her forehead. She nodded at me enthusiastically.

"Don't tell anyone I'm here. I'm hiding. It will be our secret."

With a smile I placed my finger on her lips. She snuggled down against me as I stroked her hair.

464

"An Andler, no one would tell me wherw you were," she pouted up at me. "I heard An 'Stance say those mean men had you and my babies, an I cwied," she continued.

"Sweet girl, I'm home now and I'm safe. You don't have to worry," I assured her as she continued to gaze at my face.

"Does it huwt?" She reached up and gently touched my eyebrow. It occurred to me that my bruises were alarming her.

"Not too much, Doodle-Bug. I'm getting so much better, and with you to take care of me I will be healed in no time," I assured her. She reached to kiss each bruise on my face.

"Well, I see somebody found us," Banton remarked, quietly closing the door behind him.

"Unca Banin!" Ava pushed up and jumped off the bed to run to him.

"Shh, quiet now, Ava. We want to hide out right now, okay?" Banton asked as he swung her up into his arms.

"I'll be quiewet," she answered in her little girl southern drawl, her eyes wide.

"Good girl. I'll bet Aunt Chandler would love for you to snuggle with her while I get everything put away."

Ava nodded as Banton crossed the space between us and deposited her back on the bed.

"Gently, now. Be careful, Aunt Chandler has some broken bones, and she's really sore," he cautioned. She carefully snuggled down beside me as I placed a kiss on top of her head. My heart warmed as she gently rubbed her little hand back and forth across my arm as if to comfort me. I loved this little girl so much, and felt so blessed that she'd come into our lives like she had. I couldn't love her more if she was my own child.

"Pweese, An Andler, no more," she whispered as Banton came back into the room and sat down on the bed beside us.

"No more what, sweetie?" I asked as I gazed down at her huge brown eyes.

"No more cwying. I don't wike it when you and my Unca Banin weave. Pweese, don't go again," she whispered. She continued to trail her little fingers on my arm.

Banton stretched out beside her and drew both of us into his side.

465

"Little one, neither one of us has any intention of going anywhere. Everything is going to be okay now, I promise. You have my word," Banton assured her, leaning over and kissing her little forehead. After a time, he moved his face up to meet my gaze. His eyes were warm and beautiful as he smiled.

"I love you so much," he whispered, his face only inches from mine.

"I love you," I whispered back. Snuggling down against Ava, I placed my head closer to him as he pressed his lips into my hair. I closed my eyes and napped, feeling like I was finally home.

*   *   *

I woke and turned to find the daylight fading in the large window of our room. I looked down beside me, finding Ava was still curled against my side. Banton was gone and the door was ajar. I could hear him talking to Claudia in the hallway.

"I just didn't want to tell everyone and have them make a fuss. I sneaked her upstairs a couple of hours ago. Ava found us, she's napping beside Chandler."

"I thought she was with Mother, and when Mother came downstairs just now, I panicked,"

"I know. I'm sorry, I should have told you where Ava was. All I've been thinking about is Chandler."

My heart clenched, feeling as if it was in my throat. Banton was consumed with trying to help me adjust.

"How is she?"

"Fragile. She's trying to put on a brave front, but she's suffered through so much unimaginable..." he trailed off as Claudia murmured something unintelligible. "That's why I wanted to try to shelter her, to let her rest. She doesn't need a big scene, and I'm not sure about visitors, not just yet."

"I'll talk to everyone downstairs. Mrs. Sue is going to want to see her, though. She was so upset when Constance put her off at the hospital yesterday."

"I know. And I think Chandler will want to see Ev too. Maybe just the two of them tonight," Banton suggested. "Hey, how are you doing? I feel like we all abandoned you," he said guiltily.

"Don't be ridiculous, baby brother. You did what you had to do. Besides, the alone time I've spent with Ava, and with Momma and Daddy has been very special. We're all here for each other, now. I'm so glad you are all home and in one piece," she breathed, expressing her relief.

"I'll bring Ava down when she wakes," Banton said as I heard Claudia's footsteps descend the staircase.

A moment later, Banton opened the door and slipped back into our room. Finding my eyes on him, he crossed the room to the bed.

"Hey, beautiful, did you have a good nap?"

"Yes, I did," I breathed, pushing up in bed. I winced as my ribs protested, and Banton reached to grab some pillows to help me prop up.

"Do you want me to call Dr. Renault about pain meds?" Banton asked as he handed me a glass of tea.

"No, I'm fine. I will take some Tylenol, though."

He watched me for a moment as I reached to slide Ava Grace down from my shoulder.

"Chandler Ann, I know you are hurting. You've been moaning in your sleep. Why are you being so obstinate? Why are you so against taking something?"

"I promise I'll take something stronger if I need to. I'm fine, really."

He studied me for a moment, and then glanced down at Ava. She'd opened her big brown eyes when I'd moved her a moment earlier.

"Doodle-Bug, your mommy was worried about you just now. Can I take you down to her?'

Ava sat up and nodded as she rubbed her eyes. He reached down and swung her up on his shoulder.

"I'll be back as soon as I run her downstairs to Claudia. If the twins are awake, I'll bring them to you," he said, leaning down to kiss me. I raised my lips to meet his, and he softly stroked my cheek with the back of his hand.

As soon as I heard his footsteps descend the staircase, there was a knock on my door.

"Sweetheart, are you awake?" Aunt Sue's voice drifted through the door.

"Yes Ma'am, please come in," I called back.

Aunt Sue opened the door slowly and slipped in.

"Oh, Chandler Ann! What have they done to you?" she gasped as she saw me for the first time. She crossed the room to the bed and then sank down beside me. "I want to hold you, but I'm afraid to touch you! Constance told us you were terribly bruised, but I had no idea it was this bad!

"And here I was thinking I looked so much better today," I murmured as I smiled at her. She began to cry as she held her hand out to my cheek.

"I can't believe what those monsters did to you! Constance has told us a little, but it was sketchy. Thank heavens the babies are okay. They seem to have been untouched by all of this," she said as she fought to keep her emotions in check. "What did the Doctor say??"

"I'm healing fast. I still have trouble raising my arms, and I'm sore, but I'm going to be fine," I whispered. She reached out and touched the sling around my neck that held my right arm.

"That's for my broken shoulder. Banton and Ty had to dislocate my shoulders when they pulled me from the ship, and the right one is broken," I explained as her eyes widened.

"Mrs. Elaine said Banton was so tortured about hurting you when they rescued you. She said he cried in the waiting room at Dr. Renault's when they kept him from seeing you. He told them he almost lost you, that you drowned in that cargo hold, and they had to do CPR on you in the helicopter to get you back," she whispered, continuing to cry. "Banton thinks the CPR is what caused the rib to puncture your lung."

"He shouldn't feel guilty about any of that. He saved my life," I assured her as she nodded.

"I know, sweetheart. He loves you so much, and he is so worried about you. Is there anything else...that you need help with? Anything at all you need to talk to me about? Constance said there were other things that happened that you didn't want to talk about," she whispered as she stroked my cheek.

"Not yet, Aunt Sue. Maybe someday," I shook my head as my voice broke. I didn't want to shed anymore tears over the attack. "I just want to put it behind me," I finished as she nodded. She almost

468

looked relieved I didn't want to confide in her. I realized at that moment, watching the pain in her own eyes, an attack of this magnitude affected far more than just Banton and me."Well,   I'm going to let you rest for now. Banton should be back up here any minute, and I know you need your alone time. Everyone wants to help, but we understand your need for privacy right now. Everett just arrived and he and Constance are visiting. She said she will send him in later."

She rose and placed a kiss on my forehead. After she left the room, I lay back into the pillows. I could hear everyone talking downstairs. As I closed my eyes and sighed, I heard a car arrive in the driveway.

"Not so fast, come here, baby," Cade called out. I heard a car door slam, and then silence. Curiosity got the best of me, and I pushed off the bed and walked carefully over to the window overlooking the drive. Cade stood with his back to me, his arms around someone as he passionately kissed her. My eyes widened as I watched...who could it be? I wasn't aware he was even dating anyone. A slim boot-clad leg wrapped around his legs as he deepened the kiss. As he pulled away, I gasped.

Julia smoothed her hair, tucking some stray strands back into her pony-tail as she flushed. She gazed up into his eyes, and as he took her hand in his, he tucked it into his back pocket as they moved toward the back patio.

I shook my head, not believing what I'd just seen. Julia and Cade?

"Hey, you're up," Banton observed as he slipped back into the room with a tray of food. "I fixed you something downstairs." He walked over and sat the tray down on the ottoman beside the chairs and then turned to me. "Is something wrong?"

I looked at him. I was sure I still had that 'you could slap me down with a feather' look about me.

"I'm not sure...I'm not really sure if what I just saw was right," I shook my head as I sank back down on the bed.

"What did you just see?" he asked as he crossed to the window. He spied Cade's car, and then turned to me with his eyebrow cocked. "Hmmm, I suppose you just saw my sister," he chuckled as he sat down beside me.

"Umm… *yeah*, when were you going to tell me about that? Is that what Constance meant this afternoon when she said Uncle Lon had twenty five new grey hairs?"

"Here, lie back with me, and I'll fill you in," he commanded, gently pulling me back onto the bed. After he'd folded his hands under his head, I moved my head over on his chest. As his heart beat softly under my ear, I felt more relaxed than I'd felt since the attack.

"Are you ready for some shocks?' he asked as I nodded. "Well, for one, Drew came home while we were looking for you, and announced to your Aunt and Uncle that he'd enlisted with the Navy. He's dropped out of college."

He paused, letting me soak the information in.

"I'll bet Uncle Lon had a fit!" I exclaimed. I turned my head to look up at him.

Banton grinned his famous dimpled grin. "Yep, and Mrs. Sue said it was probably a good thing Ty and I were away, because he said a few choice words about the influence of some certain SEALs."

I shook my head and kissed his chest. "Drew could do a whole lot worse than to follow in your footsteps," I retorted.

"While they were still reeling from that one, Drew and Cade got into an argument, apparently over my little sister. They'd all been staying here at Claudia's, waiting for news about us. One night, Julia broke down and cried about Will and about losing Ben. Cade offered to take her out riding in his car, and as he was comforting her about your capture and her fears about losing me, well, things warmed up between them. When they got back here, Drew saw them kissing outside and he flew into a rage. Evidently, he'd already told Cade he liked Julia, and he felt Cade had betrayed him. The boys ended up in a little fist-fight in Claudia's kitchen. My daddy had to break them up," he finished as I stared at him incredulously.

"Wow, Constance wasn't kidding. Cade and Julia…it never occurred to me," I said as I eyed him. "How do you feel about them being together?" I asked warily.

"I think it's fine. Cade seems really crazy about Julia, and he's only three years older than she is. He's finished school, and he already has a job lined up here in N'awlins."

I sighed in relief.

"Were you worried about how I would feel?"

"You were just so protective of her when she was interested in Ben."

He stroked my arm lightly with his thumb. "I probably overreacted. I'd served with Ben, and he was so worldly, and I'd witnessed he'd lived a rather fast life with the girls," he murmured. "Anyway, Cade is different altogether. He comes from good stock," he said as he hugged me gently.

I giggled. "Now you sound like Dan," I sighed snuggling into his chest. "Speaking of, I guess I should call Laurilee. She's probably been trying to call me," I said wistfully.

"I talked to her yesterday. She called me to thank us for the honeymoon trip we gave them. I told her we'd had an incident, and I'd almost lost you. She wants you to call her as soon as you feel up to it."

I nodded, taking a deep breath. Banton smelled so good I buried my nose in his shirt.

He chuckled. "Baby, what are you doing?"

"Mmm. I'm just enjoying your scent. You smell so clean, my earthy, clean Banton smell. I love this smell," I said as I breathed in again.

"You never cease to amaze me. Now, are you ready to eat something?"

"Not just yet. I want to shock you for a change," I replied as I nuzzled his chest.

"Don't think you can top anything I've dropped on you tonight," he said playfully.

"Well, let's see. You know on my birthday, when you found me in the shower after I'd started my period…you asked me if I wanted you to start using something."

"Yes," he said as he continued to stroke my arm.

"Well as it turns out, it was already too late."

471

After a few moments, his thumb stilled on my arm. When he didn't say anything, I turned to look up at him. His beautiful brown eyes were wide as they searched mine.

"Andie, are you saying…are you trying to tell me…" he stammered.

I nodded as my eyes filled with tears. Banton sat up and held me cradled in the crook of his arm as he gazed down at me.

"We're going to have another baby?" he whispered.

I nodded. "Yes. Baby Collins will be here sometime next summer," I whispered as he continued to stare at me, open mouthed. "You're going to have another daughter, Lieutenant Gastaneau." I reached up to touch the dimple peeking down at me as he began to smile.

"How long have you known?"

And with that question, I knew I was going to have to talk about everything with him. I took a deep breath and shut my eyes. I could do this. I loved this man with all my heart, and I knew he could shoulder anything I shared with him.

"Chandler? Have you already had an ultrasound?" His voice took a worried pitch.

"Yes," I whispered softly, trying to decide the best way to explain everything. "Dr. Delsant told me I was pregnant when he asked you to leave the room the first night I woke," I began.

His brows creased as he processed what I was telling him. He tightened his arms around me.

"Is that why you became so hysterical? You were so distraught," he murmured as he brushed my cheek with his thumb.

"Yes. I was confused, and I had no idea I was pregnant. All I could think about was the attack, and when he said I was pregnant," I began to choke as I remembered how I'd felt.

"Oh, baby, no…you were afraid you were pregnant because of Dante's attack?" Banton's tone dropped to a dark, menacing level. I could see his eyes darken as his rage surfaced.

I nodded as tears formed and threatened to spill over. "I was terrified…sick with the thought I might…that he might have," I sobbed as Banton pulled me up against his chest.

"God, no…Chandler! Why didn't you let the Doctor tell me? Why did you go through all of that alone?"

"I couldn't bear the thought of having...of carrying a child from those circumstances. I was terrified, and I didn't want you to know anything about it. Dr. Delsant asked me several questions, and he thought from the start it had to be yours. I had to be further along than a few days. I had to wait until he got me to Dr. Renault's before they could run more tests.

"That's why they called Brie in, she knew?" he asked, seeming to be hurt by the fact I'd confided in Brie.

"Banton, she knew when she sat with me the first night. She sensed, just from my emotions, that I'd been raped."

Banton shut his eyes as though my words were too painful to hear.

"I had to tell her why I was so distraught, and to help me, she confided in me. She told me before the Aldon got to her the night she was attacked that Lucien had raped her. She knew the pain I was going through."

Banton opened his eyes and gazed down at me.

"When we got to Renault's, I thought they would do a regular ultra-sound, but they insisted on doing it vaginally. They called Brie in, to calm me down...it was painful, more emotionally than anything else. Dr. Renault told me immediately he thought I was at least two months along, and the cycle I thought I'd had must have been break-through bleeding. I was already pregnant then. I insisted on an amnio. I wanted to make sure the baby was yours," I whispered as I touched his cheek.

"If you had told me, I could have been with you through all of that. I just don't understand. Is it because I hurt you?" he asked, the tortured expression returning.

"Oh, Banton...no. That had nothing to do with it! I don't remember any of that. It has to do with me. I'm still struggling with it."

"Struggling with what, Sweetheart? Please, I want you to tell me," he whispered. I gazed into his eyes, the flecks of gold sparkled with his unshed tears. I reached up and touched his cheek.

"I didn't want to ever talk about it. But I know once I tell you, we can put it behind us. I remember the one thought I had after the attack was that what he'd done, he'd done to you as well as to me."

473

Banton nodded furiously, understanding my meaning. As I watched the emotion run across his face, I almost lost my resolve.

"No, baby…go on. You need to do this," he urged me.

"Dante sent Lucien a couple of times to bring the babies to me, and to check on me. Lucien is the one who broke my ribs, the first time, when he kicked me. Then he sent Noah, and food for me and the babies. That's something else I want to talk to Everett about," I said as he raised an eyebrow at me.

"I questioned Noah about what we were feeding the babies. The mixture had human blood in it," I admitted as a sick look crossed Banton's face.

I immediately choked up as guilt took over. "Banton, I had no choice. They waited forever to bring anything to feed them, and they were starving," I rushed out as I sobbed.

"No, Andie…I don't blame you. You couldn't help it, you're right. Shh. It's okay," he soothed as my hysterics ceased.

"I've been so worried about what effect drinking human blood might have on them, and what they might remember. Then the morning Dante came himself, he sent Noah to get the babies and take them back to another part of the cargo bay. Then he struck me several times, because I didn't obey him fast enough."

My breathing began to escalate as I replayed the awful memories for Banton. Drawing my breath in, I whispered, "He dragged me over to a mattress and ripped my clothes off. I tried to steel myself against feeling anything, hoping I could block it all out." I watched his eyes widen in horrified shock. "I guess that angered him more, and he struck me again, so hard my head bounced off the wall. I don't remember anything else until I woke more than a day later. I was sore and covered in blood."

I shook with sobs now, and I wasn't even sure Banton could understand me, my voice seemed so garbled.

"God, Chandler…I'm so sorry! I can't stand what that monster did to you!" he ground through his teeth as he tightened his arms around me even tighter. I winced as my ribs protested, he wasn't even aware of how tight he was holding me.

"I want to make it go away for you, baby. I can't stand that we couldn't have gotten to you sooner! I feel like I totally failed you.

474

It was the one thing I wanted to protect you from." He became silent as his tortured gaze fixed over my head.

"When Dr. Renault gave me the results of the amnio, he told me he'd visited with Noah. Noah told him he didn't think Dante had been able to do much after he'd knocked me unconscious. He said that he left in a fury soon after. When he told me that, I decided most of the horror, the revulsion...was in my own imagination. I'm luckier than Brie. I was unconscious, I don't remember the attack. Brie wasn't so lucky," I whispered as he nodded at me, large tears slipping down his cheeks. I reached and wiped them away.

"I told you all of this so you could understand why I've reacted to you, to your touch. From the moment I woke all I wanted was to scrub it all away. I begged Noah to take me to a tub they had in the cargo hold. I scrubbed myself with soap until I bled that night. When I woke with you and the babies, my only thought was that I needed to bathe. I didn't want you to touch me until I was clean. I imagined I could feel your revulsion as you touched me."

"No...I never felt that way! I'm so, so sorry," he murmured as he cupped my cheek in his hand. "I don't know what that son-of-a-bitch was able to do to you, but it was him, not you. Don't you think for one minute anything he could have done to you would make me feel differently about you."

I nodded and smiled through my tears at him. "A lot of it has gone away, with the knowledge the baby is yours. I'm just so relieved. I feel like the baby protected me in a way," I realized as he nodded.

Banton took a deep breath and placed his lips to my forehead. I tightened my arms around him. After a while, he loosened his hold on me, drawing back to gaze down at me.

"Chandler, your eyes are glowing. They're so beautiful, but are you upset? Why are they glowing?' he asked as he stroked my cheek.

"I guess I'm afraid."

"Afraid of what, sweetheart?"

"What you are thinking. You haven't said anything about the baby. I know it's a lot to take right now," I whispered as I searched his eyes.

"I meant it, when I said if it was meant to be...and I guess God knew best. And the amnio, it said it's a girl?'

I nodded as he broke out in a grin. "And you want to name her Collins?'

"It's a name you picked last time, remember? I picked the twins names, so it was your turn," I said as I reached up and brushed his dimple with my thumb. He shook his head and then placed a chaste kiss on my lips.

"Your poor body has been through so much. I can't believe you have to endure this again," he said as I shook my head.

"I actually haven't had any pregnancy problems, except the break-through bleeding last month. There are no tears, even after the attack. Dr. Renault thinks maybe because I've already transformed so much, I don't have that 'inner battle' going on this time. Although I told him in looking back, I have been fighting a lot of nausea."

"What did he say about that?" he asked, concerned.

"That the old-time doctors say the sicker the mom, the healthier the pregnancy and the baby. He said they might have been right," I sighed as he chuckled.

"Well, I'm sorry you have that problem, but I'm relieved to hear things might be more normal for you this time."

"So...you're happy about the baby?" I asked, holding my breath.

"Of course I am." He moved his hand over and caressed my abdomen. "Oh, Andie...the twins won't even be a year old when Collins gets here!"

"I figure they will be about ten and a half months apart," I murmured as I shook my head.

"Well...I guess this means Olivia and Patrick were right. You are fertile," he teased as he widened his eyes at me.

"Or I'm just married to a real-live stud," I retorted as he puffed his chest out. "Seriously, Banton...I just feel so blessed."

He nodded and leaned down and kissed me again, this time opening his mouth slowly as he explored my lips softly with his. I

476

opened my mouth invitingly, and he carefully traced just inside my lips with the tip of his tongue. I slid my arms up around his neck and tightened my grip. As he tugged on my bottom lip with his teeth, I moaned, the sound vibrating into his mouth. Still holding me in the crook of his left arm, he gently slid his right hand into my hairline, caressing the side of my face with his thumb as he continued his soft, gentle kiss. He withdrew and searched my eyes. I could feel his apprehension, the tension thick in the air.

I smiled up at him as I traced his lips with my index finger. "We're okay. You are really good at that 'loving me back to being me again' thing. You know just what to do," I whispered as he relaxed and grinned down at me.

"Do you know how scared I was when I realized you'd been taken?" he murmured, continuing to rub my cheek with his thumb.

I shook my head.

"All I could think of was I'd been so brusque with you about Texas and Alex showing up...Constance told me you saw me hug her on the porch. Then I didn't kiss you before I left. I was terrified I would never get the chance to tell you how sorry I was!" His voice was husky as if he were fighting a lump in his throat.

"I know, Banton. I was tortured about that too...how childish I felt after we'd quarreled, how selfish I sounded, whining about Laurilee's wedding when you had Will's funeral, your sister, Reed's murder...all of that on your shoulders! I'm so sorry," I whispered as he shook his head.

"We never fight," he said as I nodded.

"I know. And I don't want to fight with you, ever."

As he gazed at me, his eyes were so intense, sparkling with the flecks of gold fringed with his dark lashes. I could feel his heart clench. I could feel how much he loved me.

"Banton, may I come in?" Everett's voice drifted through the door.

"Please, come in. It's open," Banton answered.

Everett pushed the door open and walked slowly toward the bed as he gazed at me. His eyes glowed with an intensity I'd rarely seen as he saw me for the first time since the kidnapping.

"Bebe, you have no idea how happy I am to see you alive…in one piece," he whispered, leaning over the bed to kiss my forehead. I reached up and cupped his cheek.

"Thank you, Everett. Banton told me we almost lost you," I whispered, choking on the words.

"I have to say, next to the saber wound on the battlefield, this was the closest I've come to the pearly gates," he replied. "I guess God has other plans for me, sweet Bebe." He smiled down at me and sat down gently on the bed beside us.

"How are your wounds?"

"Healing. Lucky I'm an Aldon, or I would be working a bionic arm out of a wheelchair right now, if I was alive at all. I guess I'm not as agile as I used to be. I'm getting a little rusty. I let those Orco bastards get the best of me this time," he growled.

"Seriously, Everett, I've never seen anyone, SEAL or Aldon, take on that many Orcos at one time. You fought like a madman," Banton said as I watched him curiously. "I thought I'd lost you too, when that Orco snapped your neck and you dropped in front of him."

"He would have finished me off, too, if Sam hadn't appeared. He took that Orco out just as I heard you shout Matty's name. I knew at that moment the babies and Chandler would be safe."

"I almost lost her, Ev. I watched her drown right in front of me," he whispered as his eyes filled with moisture again.

I reached up and touched his face again. "Hush, I didn't drown. You saved me, remember? I have the broken shoulder to prove it. Thank goodness you didn't give up, and you did whatever it took to get me out." I smiled as a pained look crossed his face. "You saved all four of us. You are my hero…my knight in shining camo," I said as Everett chuckled. Banton shook his head as Everett cleared his throat.

"Um, Bebe…you said, all four of you?"

"Yes," I whispered as I turned to look at him. "Me, Matty, Elly, and Collins." I placed my hand across my abdomen protectively as Everett's eyes widened.

"Sweet Jesus, Holy Mother and the Pope in Rome! You mean to tell me… you and Banton…that we are…I'm going to be an Uncle again?" he squealed as Banton winced.

478

"Yes, Ev, and you found out before John did this time," I told him as his eyes twinkled.

"And who else knows?' he asked, the wheels turning in his protective, mother-hen, mischievous Aldon head.

"Just you and Brie. No one else," I said as he rubbed his hands together. "We'll tell everyone else when everything calms down."

"Well, I must say, when you Gastaneaus and LeBlances get together, things move along quite rapidly, indeed! Mr. Lon is still reeling, and I think this one might just do him in." Everett teased as Banton winced again.

"Mr. Lon's been good to me. I don't want to upset him anymore this week," Banton began as I gave him a sideways glance.

"He will just have to get over it, Lieutenant. It's a done deal."

"Yes, I guess it is," he murmured, leaning down to kiss me again.

"Well, I'm glad you are home and doing so well, Bebe. Mother and Grandmother will be so pleased to hear it. They would like to come and see you, when you are up to it." He rose and leaned over to kiss me once more.

Banton raised his hand, and as Everett shook it, he whispered, "Thanks for helping me save our girl. I couldn't have done it without you," he said fervently. "I love you, Ev."

"I love you too, dear boy. Now, I think I will go and see to my dear Claudia," he replied, warily casting a glance at Banton. Banton smiled and nodded at Everett. "Please do, Ev...with my best wishes."

After Everett had left the room, Banton turned back down to me, looking at me as if he hadn't been with me all afternoon. I shook my head at him.

"What?" he asked, a slight grin on his face.

"Just when I think I couldn't love you more, you show me more of the beautiful man you are inside."

He raised an eyebrow at me and pulled me up to his face as he kissed me softly.

Chapter Thirty-Three

Banton helped me slowly down the last two steps of the back staircase.

"Sweetheart, are you sure about this?"

I smiled up at him and nodded.

As I rounded the stone wall of the hearth, Julia squealed, "Chandler!"

"Hey, look who's up and around! Should you be walking?" Cade asked, rising to help me.

"I've got her...here, Chandler, sit down," Banton urged as he pulled a barstool over in front of the kitchen island.

"What would you like for breakfast, Chandler? I made omelets," Mrs. Elaine offered. I felt my face go green. Banton sensed my unease and squeezed my hand.

"Mom, maybe just some dry toast and coffee," he suggested. Constance's brow furrowed as she studied me and her gaze widened. As she started to open her big mouth, Banton caught her eye and shook his head. She closed it and then glared at him.

"Did I miss something?' Claudia asked, sitting down with a cup of coffee.

"No, just Constance being her usual, nosey self," Banton chided.

"Well, there sure is a lot of intrigue around this house lately. Just keep your little secrets. I've got errands to run. Just remember who's helping you out," Constance shot at Banton as she rose and headed out the back door.

I turned and gave Banton a quizzical look as he held his hands up.

"Well, you all are as entertaining as a morning show, but I have no idea what is going on," Mrs. Elaine shook her head as Julia rolled her eyes.

"And don't roll your eyes at me, miss. I had to cover for you two when you weren't back at two-o'clock this morning," she warned as she placed a piece of toast and a cup of coffee in front of me. "Your father might be aware you are twenty-one, but you are still his baby."

Banton stared at Cade, and he ducked his head and looked at Mrs. Elaine. "Um, sorry, Ma'am. We were here, just not in the house," he murmured as Julia elbowed him.

I took a few bites of the toast and drank a bit of coffee, unsure whether it would stay down or not. I glanced up at Claudia, and she was watching me silently.

"Be careful, Cade…just be smart and safe…she's my little sister and I don't want our families feuding," Banton warned as Cade nodded.

"Could you all be any more embarrassing? I'm in the room for gripe's sake," Julia exclaimed as she stalked off down the hallway. Cade immediately ran after her as Claudia laughed.

I couldn't stand it anymore and I giggled, immediately regretting it as I grabbed my ribs.

"Oh, I'm sorry. We should re-wrap those," Banton murmured, placing a kiss in my hair.

"See, here she is. Mommy's up," Aunt Sue whispered as she descended the staircase with Ellyson.

"Where's Matty?" Banton asked. Aunt Sue handed me Elly.

"He's still asleep. This little one just yelled out at me as I walked by the nursery so I brought her down."

"We just checked on them. She must have just woken up," Banton replied as he reached down and kissed her on top of the head.

"Mommy," Elly blurted out as she placed her hand on my cheek.

"Elly," I called back as I kissed her hand, making her giggle.

"Here, I have her breakfast all ready," Mrs. Elaine offered, holding her arms out to me.

"Please, I haven't fed her in days. I'll do it," I said as Mrs. Elaine nodded.

"I just don't want you to hurt your ribs," she admonished.

Banton reached out and took her from me. "Let me carry her into the living room and you can rock her."

I took the bottle from Mrs. Elaine as she leaned over and kissed me on the cheek.

"Welcome home, my dear. I'm so relieved to have you here and in one piece. We've had quite enough loss in one family for a while."

Claudia placed her hand on my good shoulder. "We love you so much, Chandler. Welcome home," she said.

Banton led me into the living room and then helped ease me down into the rocker by the fireplace. After he'd placed Elly in my good arm, he grabbed her blankie off the back of the sofa and tucked it around her as she pulled the bottle I offered up to her mouth.

I rocked her gently as I sang to her. She smiled crookedly, letting go of the nipple as she grinned up at me. She placed her hand lovingly on my cheek as I continued.

Banton knelt down beside the rocker and lit the fireplace and sat back into the floor with his knees drawn up and his ankles crossed. I leaned my head over on my right shoulder and gazed down at him. He looked so sexy in his tight white t-shirt clinging to his muscular chest, pajama pants that hung low off his hipbones, his bare feet...I looked back up into his eyes, and they were twinkling as if he was laughing at me.

"What?" I asked as I blushed.

"Ogling your husband, now, Mrs. Gastaneau?" He grinned at me and almost made me catch my breath. The sexy stubble on his face made me want to touch him.

"Well, he's such a hot stud and all...I was just checking him out," I retorted as Elly cackled to get my attention.

"And your daughter just thinks your funny," I added. Elly cackled again and dropped her bottle as she sat up in my lap.

"Ellyson Marie, come here and see Daddy. Can you say 'Daddy?'"

"Mommy!" Elly grinned and held her hand out to Banton. He kissed it and urged, "Say Daddy!"

"Mommy!" Elly cackled again and threw her head back against my chest. I winced. My breasts were more tender than ever.

"Chandler, is it your ribs? Sorry, here, give her to me," Banton urged as he reached to take her. As he placed her in his lap, she flipped over and began to climb up on his chest.

"No, my breasts," I whispered. "They're already sore and swollen," I said as his eyes widened.

"Wow, that's really kind of …hot," he murmured as he raised an eyebrow at me. "Mmm…bigger boobs!" He grinned devilishly.

"Banton," I scolded as the front door opened.

"Chandler! I'm glad to see you up, baby-girl." Uncle Lon came through the doorway with Mr. Matt. "How are you feeling?" He leaned over me and kissed my forehead.

"I'm good…much better today. Another day or so, and I think I'll be human again."

"And how are my grandbabies today?" Mr. Matt asked, leaning over and touching Ellyson on the cheek.

"They're hungry as usual. Here, Mommy, this one just yelled at me as I was going upstairs," Julia stated as she came down the hallway. Banton placed Elly in the floor at my feet and then took Matty from her along with a bottle she carried.

"Come here, big guy. Let's eat breakfast," Banton said, moving over to the sofa.

"Can you say Daddy?" Banton urged as Mr. Matt chuckled.

"Mommy!" Matty yelled as he held his hand toward me.

"What, not you too? Don't I rate anymore," Banton pouted as everyone laughed.

"Well, everything is squared away just like we wanted," Mr. Lon said as Banton shook his head at him and glanced over at me.

"What?' I asked.

"Nothing for you to worry about. Dad, I'll talk to you later," Banton said conspiratorially. His dad nodded.

Mr. Matt patted Uncle Lon on the back, and they both headed for the kitchen. I raised an eyebrow at Banton, and he grinned and then looked down at Matty as Matty sucked his bottle dry. After he'd finished, he threw the bottle in the floor and proceeded to wriggle out of Banton's arms and down into the floor to play with Elly.

"Why don't we take them back upstairs and let them play in their cribs while I help you in the tub," Banton offered as his eyes twinkled.

I nodded, and he rose to pick them both up from the floor. He grasped them both around their chests under their little arms, their legs dangling as they giggled. I shook my head and followed him up the staircase.

"You doin' okay?" he turned back to watch me as I climbed the stairs.

"Yes, but I will let you wrap my ribs today. It helps," I said as he nodded.

After he'd placed the twins in Elly's crib with a basketful of toys, Banton joined me in the bathroom.

I sat down at the vanity and dropped my robe to the floor as he started the bathwater. As he added bath salts and bubbles I cocked an eyebrow at him.

"Well, I remember when our relationship was new, and you were afraid to go into the bath alone…you felt safe after you were all covered in bubbles," he grinned down at me as I lifted my face for a kiss.

"You're very thoughtful, Lieutenant," I murmured against his lips. Drawing back, a serious frown crossed his brow as he reached down to grasp my gown. I nodded, and he lifted it over my head as he held my arm to support my shoulder. I stood and worked my panties down with my good hand and kicked them into the corner. Banton helped me down into the water.

"Mmm. This feels so good," I murmured, sliding down into the bubbles. I let the warmth wash over me, soothing my aching ribs and shoulder.

"Andie, you seem much more at ease with me," Banton whispered close to my ear. I opened my eyes to find him seated in the floor beside the tub, his legs crossed as he sipped on his coffee.

"I am. It's getting much easier. I think it's being home, knowing about the new baby…and you. You make it easy," I murmured, raising my hand from the water and tracing his lips.

"Do you want to wash your hair?" he asked. He tucked a stray strand of hair behind my ear.

"No, I'm good. I might get Constance to put it up for me or something," I replied, leaning my head back to gaze at him.

"What?" he asked as my eyes began to twinkle.

"I was just thinking about a night not too long ago, when we sat like this and you gave me quite a massage in the tub," I said as

484

he grinned at me. "I'm wondering if that is the night you got me pregnant again.

"Hmm...our first night together after the babies? I must be a stud," he teased, his grin deepening. Then he chuckled and took another sip of his coffee.

"What's so funny?" I raised an eyebrow at him.

"I was just thinking about something my grandmother used to say about my grandfather. "Every time he hung his pants on the bedpost," when she talked about their eight children.

"Eight! Holy cow. I think we'll do something to stop before that. Three will be quite enough, especially if they are all faders," I retorted.

Banton raised his head to listen as we heard something hit the wall, and then giggles erupted in the next room.

"Mommy!" Elly called out.

"I'm thinking Matty is throwing toys, and Elly is tattling on him," Banton guessed as he stood and strode into then nursery. When he returned, he carried both of them under their arms, their legs dangling.

I giggled as he rounded the corner with them, and Ellyson cackled out loud.

"I was just thinking, we might dunk them in there with you, and kill two birds with one stone,"

"Or clean two babies in one tub?" I quipped. "Sure, bring them here," I grinned as he placed them in the floor to strip their clothes off. Elly was cooperative as usual, and he quickly handed her in to me. I pushed up, and placed her in my lap in the water. She immediately began to squeal and giggle as she splashed me.

Banton cursed under his breath as he chased Matty's naked butt across the bathroom floor.

"He's like trying to handle a greased pig when he wants to get away," Banton muttered as I giggled. When he finally had him corralled, he leaned over and sat him down in front of Elly and sank down on his knees beside the tub. He helped me wash them with their baby-wash and rinse their hair. He then gently picked them up out of the tub, first Matty, then Elly, and wrapped them up in towels.

"Knock knock...Banton, it's Aunt Sue. Can I help with the babies?" she called through the door.

"Perfect timing, Mrs. Sue...here." Banton rose with them in his arms and opened the door. As he took them into the nursery to help her dress them, I finished bathing and then rose to get out. I managed to dry off by myself and stepped into our bedroom to find something to wear. After donning a short sweater dress and ankle boots, I wadded my hair up in a loose bun in the back and secured it with a clip.

"Chandler, I'm sorry, I got tied up with the babies," Banton began, pushing around the door into the room. He stood looking at me for several moments.

"You look great," he commented, walking around the bed to where I was standing.

"You say that all the time," I replied. He shook his head.

"No, really. You do! Almost back to normal," he added as he slipped his arms around me.

"I am almost back to normal, thanks to you," I said as I nuzzled into this chest.

"Well, if you'll be okay on your own for a bit, I think I'll slip into the shower," he murmured.

"I'm great. I think I'll go find the twins."

Banton picked my sling up off the bed and placed it around my neck, helping me work my arm through.

"Just don't overdue and let everyone else pick them up and hand them to you," he cautioned as he placed a chaste kiss on my lips.

"Yes sir," I retorted as I left to search for Aunt Sue.

I could hear Aunt Sue's voice in the kitchen as she and Mrs. Elaine and Claudia fussed over the babies. I smiled in contentment. My children would never lack attention as long as our families were around.

"Bebe, how are things with you today?" Everett's voice called from the living room. I rounded the large pillar at the base of the stairs, and found him sitting in front of the large windows, gazing at the trees outside.

"What are you doing in here by yourself?"

"Just enjoying a moment of peace and quiet, Ma Petit. Recent events have made me a bit introspective," he murmured, gesturing to the sofa beside him. I sat down and gathered my feet under me.

"It's a sunny day outside…it seems we are to have a few days of Indian summer before fall weather sets in," he commented off-handedly.

"Ev, there are some things I need to talk to you about," I began as he turned his full attention to me. He reached over and grasped my hand tightly, our connection stronger than ever before.

"What is it, Bebe?" His beautiful Aldon eyes sparkled at me.

"Something has been worrying me. The story you told me about your father…about him never being the same after he attacked Lucien and his family, and drank human blood," I began.

"Yes?"

"The Orcos gave me formula to feed the babies on board the ship during our capture. I asked Noah about it. I knew it had blood in it. He confirmed to me that it wasn't animal blood," I whispered. A sick feeling overwhelmed me. Just talking about it brought all the horror and anxiety back to engulf me.

"Bebe, it's okay. If it had been a prolonged period, they would have developed a craving for it, but I'm sure, at their age and no more than they consumed, they will be fine. It wasn't the consumption of the blood which changed my father, but rather the hunt and giving in to his baser, animal instincts. It's hard for the transformed to relapse and then recover."

My shoulders sagged in relief. Everett chuckled. "You've been worried, Ma Petit, about your precious little ones. You should have asked me sooner," he replied. "I still feel your unease. Tell me, what else is bothering you?"

"When Dante attacked me," I whispered. His eyes widened and then began to glow. "Ever since then, I've had trouble with people touching me. Even Banton…I was unsure if it was the venom, or if it is a reaction from the rape."

His eyes brightened in intensity as he pulled me into his arms.

"Oh, my dear, sweet Chandler. I'm consumed with a feeling I can't even describe. I hate and despise Lucien and Dante's followers with an intensity that has re-kindled brighter than ever after these hundred and fifty years. I would give all that I am, all

487

that I have to wipe this from your memory," he murmured, stroking my hair. "Yes, part of it is most definitely the venom, and I'm sure it had to have affected you more if it was done...as part of the act. I can only imagine how hard it must be for you to put this behind you." He pulled away and held my head firmly with both of his hands as he gazed into my eyes.

"It is getting easier. I couldn't even bear to let Brie touch me on the ship, and I was terrified to let Banton touch me. I think I was afraid he would be repulsed by what happened to me. But I'm mostly past that, now."

"Sweet Bebe, whatever we need to do for you, whatever it takes...we will do it. You know the depth of Banton's love for you? He is like a man possessed, determined to make everything right for you."

I nodded at him, unable to speak.

"Do not let this thing dull the bright light that is your spirit, my dear. I've never known a kinder, brighter, more joyful soul than yours. Yours is the light that draws everyone near...this group of family and friends that make up your world."

Everett drew me into his arms once more and held me, placing a kiss in my hair. I snuggled in beside him as we watched the Spanish moss sway gently in the trees on the lawn.

Banton cleared his throat behind us, and as we turned, he moved slowly around the sofa and sat down in a chair opposite us.

"Thank you, Everett. I heard part of what you said to her."

Everett nodded at Banton, his eyes still glowing brightly.

"That's the other thing I need to ask you. How do I control this new quirk I've acquired," I said as I gazed at him.

"Your eyes?" he asked as he looked deeply into mine. "Can you feel it when you are doing it?"

I shook my head. "Banton and Constance have told me. It scares me I might do this around others," I murmured as I looked down.

Everett took my chin in his hand and tilted it back up.

"Ma petit, it makes your eyes even more beautiful. You've been glowing the whole time we've been talking, although they've faded a bit. I want you to look at Banton, my dear, and pour your

488

love...all your feelings for him into your gaze as though you were sending all of your love for him in one look."

I did as he requested, and Banton gasped, I was sure in reaction to my eyes. I could sense it...a feeling that somehow connected to my heart, a feeling that felt strangely like the aching hole that opened in my chest whenever I was hurt or mourning.

"Now, try to calm that feeling, such as you do when you try to calm your heartbeat. Try to find your emotional peace," he instructed. "Sometimes it helps to shut your eyes for a moment or two and find the peace."

I closed my eyes and relaxed my body. When I opened my eyes again, Banton smiled at me.

"You amaze me, sweetheart."

"Why?"

"Because everything just seems to come so easy to you," he replied as he grinned at me.

"Chandler is exceptional at connecting with others as she seems to be with controlling her feelings. She is much stronger than she knows," Everett praised. I felt myself flush. "If anything, I think your heart has grown with all the attacks and venom...your transformation is one that continues to inspire Dr. Lane, Dr. Renault and me."

"What does not kill us makes us stronger?" I asked as I cocked an eyebrow at him.

Everett chuckled and patted my knee. "Something like that, Ma Petit. Just work on the control thing. Now you've made the connection, you will be fine."

Banton nodded and held his hand out to me to pull me up. "Let's go and see who is spoiling the babies now," he suggested as Everett followed us.

We spent the day playing with the twins and a relaxing afternoon with our families. Banton disappeared after dinner for a bit, and when he returned, he was placing his cell in his pocket.

"Who was that?' I asked curiously.

"Just some business I needed to take care of," he answered nonchalantly.

I shot him a questioning look as he sat down beside me and drew Elly up onto his lap. Cade and Ava chased Matty around the

489

coffee table in the floor with Beau close on their heels, wagging his tail furiously. I was amazed at the speed at which Matty was crawling.

"Banton Matthew, I think you'd better start baby-proofing all those cabinets and doors at home right away. They will both be walking in no time," Mrs. Elaine warned as he grinned and nodded at her.

Elly garbled her little baby jabber at Matty and he paused, sitting back and turning to look at her. Cade hid behind Julia's chair as Matty's attention was drawn away. Turning back, Matty looked for Cade.

"Boo," Cade jumped out at Matty as Elly cackled in Banton's lap.

Matty immediately faded as I knew he would.

"What on earth," Aunt Sue gasped. Uncle Lon stood up in alarm.

"Wait, it's all right," Banton held out his hand.

Beau sniffed at Matty and began to whine, upset by his sudden disappearance, and the fact he could still smell and feel him.

"Where's Matty?" I called out. "Where's my Matty?"

Ellyson laughed again and called, "Maaatty!"

Banton looked down at her in surprise. "That's another first," he said in wonder as he kissed her on top of her head.

"Matty, fade back!" Banton called more sternly this time. After several tense moments, Matty finally faded back.

"Holy crap, Chandler! When you play with these two you'd better be on top of your game!" Cade said in wonder as he picked Matty up.

"Chandler, should you encourage them to do that?" Uncle Lon asked in concern.

"I've worried about it, but it's something that comes naturally to them. We scolded them at first, and Elly seemed reluctant to do it again. But when we were…" I stopped as I glanced over at Banton. He immediately reached up and smoothed my hair back and placed his hand on my neck under my hair.

I continued, "The Orcos were coming for the babies, when the ship began to sink. I got them to play hide and seek and encouraged them to fade. It kept the Orcos from finding them – I

490

convinced them Noah had taken them. That bought me enough time until Banton and the SEALs found us," I was whispering now as I finished. Everything was still too fresh, too painful to talk about. "Their fading saved them. I somehow knew it would be useful. I don't want to discourage them. We just have to teach them to use it appropriately."

I looked up into the horrified faces of Aunt Sue and Mrs. Elaine. As it dawned on them just how much danger the babies had been in, Mr. Matt walked over and bent down, placing a kiss on my forehead as he whispered, "Thank you, Chandler. Once again, your faith and strength cause me to be forever in your debt."

I blushed and glanced at Banton. He sat silently watching me as he held Ellyson against his chest. I could see the pride and love in his eyes.

"Well, one thing is for sure. These kids will kick butt on the playground," Drew said with pride, picking Matty up out of Cade's lap.

"I think it will be a while before we can put them in school...at least until they can control their eyes and the fading," Banton said, rising with Elly. "It's been a long day. Chandler, are you ready to go up...I know you are tired." He held his hand out to me.

"Yes, goodnight everyone. Thank you for dinner, Claudia. It was wonderful," I said as I leaned down and kissed her on the cheek.

"You are entirely welcome. I enjoyed cooking this afternoon, with everyone around the kitchen. It made it so homey. I'll miss you all when you all go home," she sighed, her eyes misting.

"Well, Chandler and I will be in and out. I'm not coming to N'awlins to the base anymore without bringing Chandler and the babies with me," Banton answered.

"And that means I will be here too. I'm the official nanny, you know," Everett joked. He sat on the chair arm next to Claudia. I watched as he placed his hand on Claudia's shoulder, and Claudia placed her hand over his.

"Goodnight, all." Banton called over his shoulder, helping me climb the stairs with the babies.

The babies went down quickly, and as I came out of the bathroom, I smiled. Banton was backing into our room, pulling Elly's crib into the space at the foot of our bed, both babies asleep in her crib. He glanced up as I walked to him.

"I just can't leave them alone in the nursery, not yet," he replied. I cocked an eyebrow at him. "I need them near us."

I nodded at him. "I feel the same way. Thank you," I said as he leaned over to kiss me.

Beau settled down, curling up in the floor under the crib. Banton went into the bathroom to shower. As I heard him moving around the bathroom, I reached over to the nightstand and retrieved my favorite bottle of lotion, the one Banton had bought for me. I lathered my arms and legs, checking the bruises that seemed to be fading fast. I took in the luxurious scent of the lotion, remembering our magical night under the stars in the gossamer-wrapped pool house. The memories came flooding back...his hands on me, the oil and lotion, soft music playing romantically in the background. His fiery kisses, his mouth on mine, on my body...

For the first time, I didn't shudder when I thought about us becoming intimate again. I was ready for my husband to touch me. He hadn't even asked. He'd been so patient and gentle. I smiled as I imagined him drying off, the beads of water running down the muscles in his back. The bathroom door opened, and Banton quickly flipped the bathroom light off. There was only soft lamplight coming from his side of the bed.

"Chandler, I've got some bandages...do you want me to wrap your ribs for you? We forgot to do it earlier," he said as he sat down on the edge of the bed.

"Yes, please. It helps, especially when I try to turn over in the night."

I pulled the covers back, scooting closer to his side of the big king-sized bed. He turned and paused as he looked at me.

"You are glowing tonight," he murmured as he leaned over and kissed me softly. He seemed to still be a little wary of my reaction to his touch.

"Banton, it's okay. You can touch me now, I'm good."

"I just don't want to rush things. You are doing so great," he replied, stroking my cheek.

I pulled my nightgown up under my arms, and he scooted closer to me and began to wind the wrap around my ribcage. He tugged it tightly as he went, and I drew my breath in.

"Too tight? I can loosen it a little," he offered, drawing back to look at me.

"No, it's good. Keep going," I urged him as he leaned close to me again. I could smell the clean, spicy smell of his shampoo in his still-damp hair as he worked. When he finished wrapping, he reached over to the nightstand and retrieved the clasp to fasten the end of the wrap.

"All done," he said as he drew back to look at me. I reached up and slipped my hand around his neck, bringing his lips down to meet mine. As he kissed me gently, I opened my mouth, inviting him. He moved his lips slowly as he traced my lips with the tip of his tongue. I whispered a moan as I slid my hand down his neck to his shoulder, pulling him down with me on the bed. Sliding his hands around my shoulders, he eased me back onto the pillows. Our mouths were melded together, our tongues dancing and whirling when his kiss deepened. As he slid his knee up over my legs, I parted mine, letting his calf slide between them. I hitched my right knee up and over his, and pulled my thigh up against his as I pushed up to meet him. I could feel his passionate response.

"Baby, no. I don't want to push you," he murmured against my lips.

"You're not. I want this," I whispered back as I raised my lips to capture his again.

He pulled away and looked down at me. Pulling the covers back, he gazed down at my stomach and my legs. I followed his gaze, taking in the dark bruises that still marred my skin.

"I love you Chandler, and I want to make love to you. But not until I know you are completely healed, inside and out. I don't want to do anything to jeopardize your recovery. You are so brave," he said, stroking the side of my face.

"Banton, please...I need you," I pleaded as the familiar ache took over. I was surprised at myself. All I felt was my need for him, no self-doubt crept in. I had been afraid intimacy would be a hurdle for me, but I knew I could handle it. My desire for this beautiful man crushed any doubt that still remained.

"No, baby. Give it just a little more time." He looked at me sternly.

I nodded as tears gathered. I knew it was unreasonable, but I let the little bit of doubt creep in that Banton was having trouble with the attack, and he might be put off by the thought of Dante's having touched me.

"Okay, I won't push." I sighed and closed my eyes. I didn't want to cry, and I didn't want Banton to know he'd upset me.

I felt him brush his face against mine and his soft lips at my ear.

"Andie, don't do this. I know what you are thinking. I can feel you this time. Don't doubt my feelings...reach out, and feel what I'm feeling," he commanded as I opened my eyes and looked at him.

I was enveloped with the strongest desire, the strongest need I'd ever felt. My heart leapt. It was if I was feeling my intense love for him for the first time. I gazed back and forth into his eyes and to his lips as he lowered them to mine. He kissed me again, his passion apparent in his kiss as he drank in all of me. As he pulled away, I nodded.

"Can you feel me?" he whispered.

"All of you. There aren't even words," I replied.

"Good. Because the connection I feel with you, especially when I'm inside you, is almost mythical. I don't want anything to mess that up. I'm taking this slow, Lady...for both of us. As before, I want everything to be perfect."

I nodded, overcome with emotion.

"I remember a night when you were first pregnant with the twins; you'd been put on bed rest." He reached over and grasped the hem of my gown. As he slowly worked it up my body, I lifted my shoulders, allowing him to raise it over my head. He dropped it in the floor beside him. "I undressed and then I undressed you," he whispered as he shrugged out of his pajama pants. Then as he peeled his boxer-briefs down, he dropped them both in the floor. "I pulled you in against me," he whispered as he reached over and grasped me gently around the waist. As he pulled me up against his chest, he finished, "And I held you against my bare skin all night."

"I seem to remember something about your bare skin," I murmured as I snuggled into his chest.

He felt so good, our skin touching everywhere for the first time since the attack. I was so sensitive to him, and so aware of his every muscle, his every move, and it was heaven. I was home.

"Are you okay?" he asked as he reached to switch off the lamp.

"Mmm. Yes, I am. I'm perfect."

* * *

I was in a half-dream state, existing in that moment when you know you are dreaming, but you become aware of your surroundings. As my thoughts moved from the dream I was having about the twins playing on our front porch, I became aware of moaning, and the bed shaking. My eyes snapped open, and as I turned to look at Banton, a scream tore through the darkness.

"NOOO! Get her out now! God, no! Chandler!"

Banton fought the sheets as he thrashed around. I sat up quickly and reached to switch the lamp on beside the bed. Banton sat up, his eyes wild as he frantically searched around the room.

"Banton, you're just dreaming," I tried to calm him as I took his face in my hands. He was covered in beads of sweat, his eyes dilated.

"Banton, I'm here. It's me, you're all right. It was just a dream," I soothed, pushing the damp hair back on his forehead.

"Chandler, Oh, God...Chandler," he breathed in relief. He pulled me into his chest in a fierce embrace. I winced, my ribs protested against his tight arms.

He pulled me back to look at me. His eyes were still wide.

"Banton, you were just having a bad dream. Everything is okay," I repeated as his breathing calmed.

Our door opened abruptly, and Ty stood in the doorway.

"Is everything okay, Brother? I heard you yelling," he said. I frantically pulled the sheet up around our naked bodies. Banton nodded.

"Sorry, Ty...I was dreaming, I guess," he replied, a bit embarrassed.

"Okay, I was just checking," he said as he pulled the door to. As his footsteps retreated back to his and Constance's room, I could hear him talking to Claudia in the hallway.

"Well, that's embarrassing," Banton mumbled. He ran his hand agitatedly through his thick hair.

I reached up and touched his cheek. "Nobody understands nightmares better than I do, Banton. They can be pretty real."

He smiled down at me as his breathing finally returned to normal.

"Yeah, I guess you do know about those, don't you?"

I rose and grabbed my robe from the foot of the bed.

"Where are you going?" he asked.

"I'm going to go and get us both something to drink. I'll be back in a minute."

I hurried down the back staircase into the kitchen. Everett and Claudia were seated at the breakfast bar.

"What are you two doing up?"

"I couldn't sleep, and Everett has the uncanny way of always knowing when I'm stirring…we seem to be having a lot of these late-night chats," she smiled a wistful smile as she sipped on a cup of coffee.

"I just came down to get us something to drink. Banton had a nightmare and needs something to soothe his nerves," I murmured as I opened the icebox.

"A glass of wine might help. There are wineglasses to your right," Claudia offered.

"Um, no…I think I'll just get us both some water," I replied as I took out two bottles of Perrier and two glasses. I filled the glasses with ice and started back for the stairs.

"I thought so. Chandler, is there something you want to tell me? Claudia asked as I turned to her. She was staring determinedly at my tummy.

"How did you," I started to ask.

"I've been watching you turn green at every smell and every offer of food for the past three days now. You're pregnant again," she said as her eyes twinkled.

I nodded. "We haven't told everyone yet," I cautioned as she nodded. She looked over at Everett's guilty expression.

496

"You knew!" she said accusingly.

"Yes, and Chandler's secrets are the only one's I'd try to keep from you, darlin'," he assured her as he covered her hand with his. She continued to glare at him.

"Night, all!" I called over my shoulder as I retreated up the staircase.

When I entered the bedroom, Banton was nowhere to be seen. I crossed over to the bathroom, and found him standing in front of the vanity, splashing water on his face and over his head.

"Here, here's some sparkling ice water," I offered. He peeked at me from under the towel.

"Andie, I'm so sorry I woke you. I never have bad dreams," he stammered as he took the glass from me. I followed him back into the bedroom. Stopping to check the babies, I pulled their blankets back up over them, tucking them in around their shoulders. Amazingly enough, the commotion didn't wake them

We crawled back into the bed, and I reached up to shut the lamp off.

"Do you want to talk about it…what was your dream about?" I asked softly. Banton reached over and drew me back into his arms as he spooned behind me.

"We were back on the ship, and I couldn't pull you out between those damn bars. You were drowning again," he whispered, his voice thick with unshed tears.

I rubbed my hand back and forth over his. I turned in his arms and kissed his lips softly as I slid my leg intimately in between his.

"I'm here, and I'm safe. You saved me, Banton. Sleep, baby. I'll hold you all night," I whispered. I felt his eyelashes against my cheek as he closed his eyes.

497

Chapter Thirty-Four

"I know Claudia wanted us to stay longer, but I'm so glad to be going home. It seems like years since I've been in my own house," I said as I turned to gaze at Banton. The babies napped in their car seats in the back, Beau dutifully packed in between them. Every time one of them sighed or made a baby-squeak in their sleep, Beau raised his head and sniffed to check them. I smiled--Beau was their second nanny.

"I've been meaning to ask you something."

"What?" Banton asked as he checked the rear-view mirror, then signaled as he took the ramp to the interstate.

"When Astrid took me, Beau was nowhere to be seen. I didn't think about it until I was on board the ship."

"I didn't miss him either in all the commotion. After we left to find you, Dad went out to the garage to check the video camera, and found him locked in a room out there. Astrid must have locked him up when she took the babies out to Alexandra." As he mentioned the kidnapping his eyes darkened, a shadow crossing his face.

"That's another question I have. I remember you saying something, when you told me about Commander Reed and Alexandra...you said there was more. What else is there?' I asked.

Banton checked his mirrors again, and then set the cruise as we fell into traffic. He glanced over to me, and then took my hand in his, and lifted it to place a soft kiss there.

"Commander Singleton is conducting an investigation, and a lot of what he has found is classified. We're still not sure just how high up this went, and if others over Reed knew anything about the medical tests he was trying to run. But it's what they found in his files that disturbs me," he said as I cocked an eyebrow at him.

"What did they find?' I urged him to continue.

"The documents started around the time I called him out at the Christmas ball," he answered. "He was digging into my past, and he had my college records, information about my family...he had my dad's medical records from the Navy. Then there was

498

information on Hillary, Alexandra, my college girlfriends. And he had a file on you."

"Why? What was he looking for?"

"I don't know, but I have my suspicions. I think at first he was trying to mess with me, and dig into my past to cause trouble between us. Everett thinks maybe if he was able to upset you enough, you would leave, and he would have easier access to you…maybe to kidnap you for the Orcos, or to get medical information. Dr. Renault is suspicious of the Navy, and he thinks Reed's interest was your genetic makeup and in the twins for their own research."

"So you know for sure Reed was the one who persuaded Alexandra to come here?"

"Yes. He paid her a great deal of money. There were even e-mails on his computer. He didn't have to encourage her much, she had her own reasons for wanting to come back into my life, and she played right into his hands."

"Do you know what was in the e-mails?"

"Some of it. He just asked her if she could make me believe the child was mine. He encouraged her to make as much trouble as she could between us, and to try to draw you out. He also instructed her to make an issue of blood testing, for me and for you and the babies. She was supposed to go through his office, but of course I fouled his plans up."

"Will she be charged with anything?"

"Not if we can't find her. She's disappeared. Everett thinks Astrid and the Orcos probably disposed of her," he whispered as my eyes widened.

"What about Reese? What do you think happened to him?"

"I honestly don't know. I'm worried about that too, and Dad and Mr. Lon have some people looking into it," he replied, stroking my cheek.

"Baby, there's something else," he said as he glanced sideways at me.

"What is it, Banton?"

"In Reed's file on you, he had some things on your dad. Did you know he worked for a time, before he married your mom, with some sort of private security team?"

499

I frowned, and then looked up at him. "I seem to remember him or my mom mentioning that he had a dangerous job she didn't like, and after I was born, he stopped. He worked shift work, and sometimes two jobs when I was little. But they never talked much about his first job."

"Did your Grandfather Collins adopt him?" Banton asked.

"No, but my dad used his last name. Paw Paw married Mawmaw when my dad was almost grown."

"Do you know why she divorced your biological grandfather?"

I shook my head. "She never talked about him, and I don't think my dad remembered much about him. The only thing I ever heard my grandmother say was that she'd made a terrible mistake when she'd married the first time. Where is all this going, Banton?"

Banton shifted in his seat, and then changed lanes before he answered.

"There was a copy of your father's original birth certificate in the file, but there was no date on it. His biological father's name was Elan Samuels. Do you know who that is?"

I shook my head. As I mentally whispered the name again in my head, my skin prickled on the back of my neck.

"Everett says Elan Samuels was his biological father's brother. If it's the same Elan Samuels, you and Everett are cousins."

I stared at him incredulously. "That's extraordinary," I whispered.

We both sat in silence, lost in thought as the possibilities whirled around in my head.

"Banton, what are the chances…that I would come to Louisiana, meet Everett, buy the house on Rue Dauphine that was connected to his past, and then find I'm related to him by blood?"

"And the fact that your father brought you here when you were a child…to that very house. The picture on the fireplace, remember?"

I experienced chills up my arms, like I'd never experienced before. I was frightened beyond belief, and I had no idea why.

"Don't let this upset you. I just wanted you to know. We'll do some more digging, and we'll unravel everything. Are you okay?"

I nodded. "Except there's something else which might shed some more light on all of this. I need to talk to my Dad's lawyer back home. Did Everett tell you about the symbol?"

Banton shook his head. "What symbol, Andie?"

"There was a symbol on my parent's headstone. I saw it in the pictures Laurilee took for me. When I got them, Everett saw the pictures and he recognized the symbol, but he couldn't place where he'd seen it. Then the other day at my baby shower his mother was wearing an antique piece of jewelry Everett's father gave her a long time ago. It was the same symbol. Everett asked her about it, and she told him it was a symbol worn by Sange-Mele back as far as the revolutionary war. She called it the symbol of 'The Protectors.' They formed an alliance and many wore the symbol to identify themselves to each other, since they couldn't sense the gene like the Aldon could. They fought the Orcos on an organized level for years, sort of a vigilante force. Then they fizzled out after the Civil War. Everett's father fought as one of them for a time, fighting the hordes of Orcos in N'awlins at the time. He was bitten so much he finally fully transformed."

Banton listened, seeming enthralled.

"All of a sudden, I feel like a little genealogy lesson. Where should we start?"

"I think we should start in the unpacked boxes in the dining room," I replied as he nodded.

I couldn't wait to get home.

*　*　*

"Chandler, there's a lot more here than I realized," Banton commented, opening another box. It looked like a photo shop had exploded, family albums and boxes of records scattered about.

The babies' cries from upstairs brought me back to the present. I'd been pouring over old black and white family photos, hoping to find a picture of my grandmother with her first husband.

"I'll get them. I need to stretch my legs," I touched Banton's shoulder as I rose to run upstairs. I entered the nursery to find Matty and Elly both clutching the ends of their cribs, teetering on their little chubby legs as they waited on me to pick them up.

501

"Moooommy!" Matty wailed. I picked him up first.

"Little man, what's the matter? Did you wake up in a bad mood?' He looked around the room as I picked Elly up. I realized they were confused, they were still sound asleep when we'd brought them in the house and placed them in their beds.

"We're home, babies. We're home now. Let's get you both a bottle. I bet you're hungry," I cooed to them as I descended the staircase. I could hear the microwave running in the kitchen. As I walked down the hallway, I spied Banton in the kitchen preparing their bottles for me.

"I figured they would be hungry," he answered my raised eyebrow as I handed Matty to him.

"Hey, big guy! Are you that hungry? We're gonna have to start you on some red meat soon, buddy!" Banton exclaimed as he kissed Matty on the corner of the mouth.

"Daddy," Matty said tearfully.

"Yeah, Daddy's gonna feed you. Just hang on," Banton soothed him, retrieving their bottles from the microwave. He handed Elly's to me, and followed me down the hallway to the dining room. We pulled chairs out from the table, and sat down so we could continue to look through the files and picture albums as we fed them.

As I continued to flip through the albums, a sort of sadness descended. I hadn't looked at most of these pictures since my parents had been killed.

"Sweetheart, I can feel you. This is making you sad," he murmured, placing a kiss on Matty's forehead.

"No, I need to do this. It's just one of those firsts...life is full of them."

"Well, I think this album must be the East Texas/Arkansas bunch," Banton teased. He turned it to face me. I giggled as I looked at the obviously 1930's depression – era black and white pictures of shabbily dressed relatives, standing in front of dog-trot cabins, some of them missing teeth.

"Any of these your Uncle Earl?" he teased. Matty threw his bottle in the floor and pushed against Banton's chest, wanting to get down. Banton chuckled and kissed Matty once more before he sat him down on the rug. Beau was at Matty's side immediately, licking him in the face and making him giggle.

Banton started to pull the album back toward him when I exclaimed, "Wait!"

"What is it, Andie?"

"There! That man, he looks like my dad. He's holding a baby," I said. I pulled the album closer.

Banton stood and walked around to look at the picture over my shoulder. "The man standing next to him looks a bit like Everett...there's something about him," he murmured. I pulled the plastic away and peeled the picture off the ancient cardboard.

"Elan Lee and Jack Everett Samuels with baby Robert, May 1920," I whispered, reading the back of the photograph. I looked up at Banton in surprise.

"What is it, Andie?"

"That's not possible. My dad wasn't that old. My *grandmother* wasn't even that old!"

"Are you sure? Is it possible he was bitten...that your grandmother was Sange-Mele, and was older than you thought?" he reasoned. "I think this picture is what you've been looking for," Banton replied, placing his lips in my hair. He sat down in the floor at my feet, picked Matty up, and placed him in his lap.

"How could I not have known about this? Why didn't my father ever talk about his real dad? Banton, this means I inherited the gene from both my parents..." I trailed off as I shook my head.

"What, baby?" he rubbed my leg as he looked up into my eyes.

"My dad had been bitten. He'd transformed, he knew about all of this."

"Maybe your Dad's friend, the lawyer who handled everything for you...maybe he could tell you something."

I stood and handed Elly down to Banton, and then crossed hurriedly into the entry hall to retrieve my cell and Mr. Thomas' card from my purse. As I dialed the number, keys jingled in the front door and it swung open. Everett stood, grinning at me as he closed the door behind. I felt warm all over as I looked at him, knowing we were blood-related. His eyes immediately questioned me, feeling my emotions.

"Hey Everett, come and see this," Banton called out from the dining room floor.

I turned back to concentrate on the cell.

"Tyler Thomas," a voice answered on the third ring.

"Mr. Thomas, this is Chandler Gastaneau, Rob and Kelly Collins' daughter."

"Oh, hello Chandler! How are you?"

"I'm fine, Mr. Thomas. I'm sorry to bother you, but I've been going through some of my mother's things. I came across some family photographs and I have some questions about my daddy's past. Laurilee took photographs for me of the headstone on my parent's grave after they set the stone. The headstone you picked was beautiful, by the way. Thank you for taking care of it when I couldn't make decisions."

"You are quite welcome. I had a feeling you might be calling me," he replied, his voice sounding strange.

"You did?"

"Yes. Your father told me if anything happened to them, to follow his instructions for the funeral, your trust fund, and selling the house. There is a file, however, that he told me to hold for you, until you called me with questions about his past. He instructed me to mail it to you."

"What is in it, Mr. Thomas?"

"I'm not completely sure, he told me to keep it sealed. But I have an idea," he replied.

"What did you know about my father? Do you know anything about his past before I was born?"

Banton and Everett were standing in the doorway listening to me.

"Yes, Chandler. We were best friends."

"What kind of job did he have that was dangerous?"

"It wasn't a job of sorts, Chandler, but a group of us. Rob and I were hunting buddies, for lack of a better term. We did some vigilante stuff, on our own, during the late sixties. There was some trouble around North Texas for a time, and we…"

"You and Daddy were Sange-Mele, you were half-breeds," I whispered as total silence descended on the other end of the line. After several minutes, he cleared his throat.

"What do you know about it, Chandler?"

"Much more than I want to. But you have just confirmed much of what I needed to know. Was my father ever bitten?"

"Yes. We both were."

I took a deep breath, feeling a connection to him and to my daddy like I'd never felt before.

"Chandler, are you involved in something?" he asked, his concern evident.

"Yes."

"Mr. Thomas, the symbols on the headstone...the ones with the makeshift star. Why did you put that on the headstone?"

"That symbol was a source of pride for your father. You'll find something in the packet which will shed some light on all of this. It's in the packet that I will send you. I thought the symbol of the protectors was appropriate to put on the stone...in hindsight, maybe I should have buried it with him."

"Why?"

"Chandler, just be careful. I don't want something to happen to you too. Your family seems to draw trouble. You have a powerful gift, and it is a threat to many in that world. Don't make the same mistakes your father did. He tried to shelter you," he cautioned.

My heart pounded, a sick feeling washing over me. I whirled and looked into Banton's concerned face.

"Mr. Thomas, are you saying...are you trying to tell me the accident...that my parents were murdered?" I whispered as I held my breath.

"I can't prove it, but I have my suspicions. Chandler, your father told me he'd stumbled across some evidence of a lot of activity, things we hadn't seen in some time. He called me from Colorado, and said as soon as he and your mother checked on you, they were heading to Baton Rouge. I don't know what he was looking for, but he said he needed to connect with his past."

My mind whirled. My father had been involved in all of this, for how long I had no idea. I looked up again at Banton.

"Please send me the packet, Mr. Thomas. Can I call you, if I have any other questions?'

"Please do, Chandler. I'll tell you what I can, but be careful."

"Believe me, I will. Thank you," I whispered.

I switched my phone off and turned to Banton and Everett.

"Bebe, are you all right?"

"Yes. Banton, show Everett the picture."

Everett turned as Banton picked the picture up off of the dining room table and handed it to Everett. Everett's eyes immediately began to darken and sparkle. His eyes shot up at me.

"This is my father!"

"And my grandfather holding my daddy," I whispered.

He peered more closely at the picture. "Bless my soul…all this time…we're family." He shook his head, and then looked up at me with tears in his eyes, sparkling a deep beautiful turquoise.

I could feel mine doing the same. I crossed the room to him, and he folded me in his arms.

"I think I knew all along. We've always had this intense love…this connection," he murmured as his breath blew into my hair. He pulled back and gazed down at me.

"Chandler, what was that about your parents?" Banton asked.

I pulled away from Everett and looked down at Elly. She was pulling on my leg as she pulled up from the floor. I reached down and picked her up, wincing at my ribs as I stood.

"Chandler, don't pick them up, let me do it," Banton scolded, following me over to the chairs by the fireplace. I sat down in the chair and placed Ellyson on my lap. Everett sat down in the other chair with Matty.

"Chandler?" Banton asked again softly, sitting down on the arm of my chair.

"Mr. Thomas thinks Daddy was involved with something. He and Mr. Thomas were both Sange-Mele and fought Orcos for a time," I said. Everett's eyes widened. "Daddy called him from Colorado and told him something was going on. They were on their way home to check on me, and then they were headed here, to Baton Rouge. He told him he needed to re-connect with his past. I think he might have been coming to see you," I whispered to Everett as Banton leaned down to place a kiss in my hair. "Mr. Thomas thinks they were murdered. The wreck wasn't an accident."

The tears spilled. There was something about knowing it wasn't an accident after all, but Orcos had murdered my parents.

"Chandler, come here," Banton murmured. He enveloped me in his arms.

"This is all quite extraordinary," Everett exclaimed as he shook his head. "It's a lot to take in, sweet Bebe."

"I'm anxious to see what is in the packet Mr. Thomas has been holding for me. He's mailing it to me," I murmured. I glanced back down at the picture.

"Well, whatever it is, I hope it will put some of this to rest for you, darlin'. I know this has been unsettling for you, but I'm overjoyed to know we are related by blood. I can't wait to tell my mother," Everett said, his eyes sparkling. "Is that okay with you?"

"Of course, Ev.

He rose and handed Matty to Banton, then leaned over and placed a kiss on my forehead.

"I love you, my dear, sweet girl. I think I've always known our bond was more than friendship. I have much to talk to my mother and grandmother about. Right now, I'm on my way down to check the store, and then I'm headed back to Claudia's. I'll call you tomorrow," he said, walking to the foyer.

"Goodnight, Ev," Banton called, rising to close the front door.

I sighed and leaned my head back against Banton's body.

"Why don't I fix us a bite to eat, and then we'll go upstairs and give the babies their bath. It's been a long day and you need to rest," he suggested.

I rose with Elly as Banton quickly came around me and took her. "Let me carry them upstairs, then you can watch them in the bath while I fix something for us."

I followed him up the stairs, and then started the bathwater running. After he had both of them splashing in the tub, he helped me down into the floor beside them, and then ran back down the staircase. I giggled, watching the babies splashing one another. They squealed at Beau as he ran around me, first licking Matty, then back to Elly. I piled their toys in with them, battling to wash their hair as they tumbled and played in the water.

"Maaaaty!" Elly yelled at Matty when he splashed Beau.

"Are you yelling at your brother? Ellyson Marie, you'd better get used to that. You'll probably have to yell at him a lot." He splashed water on all of us.

"Ewwwwy!" Matty called back at her.

"Banton! Did you hear him?" I yelled down the staircase.

Banton came breathlessly around the corner. "I sure did. Hey, buddy; you're just full of firsts, aren't you? You said your sister's name," he said, sinking down in the floor next to me.

"Cold cuts and cheese okay with you?" Banton asked, placing a kiss on my shoulder. "I brought everything upstairs on a tray."

"Perfect. I'm not hungry anyway. I'm fighting the nausea today." I took a deep breath.

"I noticed. I'm sorry." He rinsed Elly's hair. Beau gave up trying to get to the babies, with Banton and me both in front of the tub, so he retreated to the bedroom to lie on the rug.

"What are you sorry for?" I asked. I took the pitcher from him to rinse Matty's hair.

"I guess for knockin' you up again, baby," he grinned, leaning over to kiss me. "No, I'm just sorry you don't feel well."

"I'll take this nausea over all the stuff last time any day, especially if it means it's a healthier pregnancy."

"Oh, that reminds me. I brought your medicine upstairs with me. We have to start your shots tonight."

"Hmm. I guess we do."

I tried to lift Matty from the water.

"I said don't lift them," Banton scolded. He reached over and took him from me. Playfully rolling him up in a towel in the floor, he then reached to get Elly. Matty grunted, fighting to get out of the towel. Then he was off, crawling as fast as he could across the tile floor into the bedroom.

"Banton, catch him!" I called. I dried Elly off.

Beau barked, and then growled low in his chest.

"Whoa, Beau...good dog," Banton gasped as I grabbed Elly up and stood.

"What happened?'

Banton knelt in the floor holding on to Matty. Beau stood in the doorway, blocking it, his head down.

508

Banton looked up at me with an incredulous look. "Matty was making a break for the doorway, straight for the staircase. Beau just blocked his way and growled at him to keep him here. Good boy, Beau! Good boy," he repeated, patting Beau's head.

"Banton, we've got to get a baby safety gate up at the top and the bottom of the staircase. Matty's gotten so fast at crawling," I said worriedly.

"Yeah, I know. I'll do it tomorrow," he said, kissing Matty on the head. He picked Matty up and carried him over to the bed to help me dress them. After we had their little footed pajamas on them, Banton left the room and then came back moments later with their pack-n-play.

"I thought we could put them in here and let them play until they get sleepy."

After I'd showered, I donned one of my silk nightgowns, and then flipped the bathroom light off. Banton lay on top of the covers in a pair of his boxer-briefs, watching the babies playing at the foot of the bed.

He rose and collected the syringes and bottles from the dresser.

"Ready for your shots?' he asked. I sat down on the bed.

"Yes, I guess."

"Here, lay back. Do you want to start in your legs or your hip?"

"I think hip for now. My legs are still sore," I whispered, glancing up at him. His eyes darkened, looking up and down at my legs and taking in the bruises that were still there. He nodded and sat down beside me on the bed. I turned over and raised my gown.

"Okay, here's the first one," he said, inserting the needle. I held my breath and mentally counted to ten like the first time we'd had to do this.

"Okay, that's one," he murmured. "Now for the bad one. Are you ready?"

I nodded, drawing my breath in again. He rubbed my other cheek, and then inserted the second needle. I began to mentally count as the medicine began to sting, then burn like fire. Just when I started to moan, he pulled the needle out.

509

"Sorry, all done. It's over, baby," he whispered, placing a kiss on my shoulder. He rubbed my backside, trying to soothe the burn. "I hate having to do that to you."

"It's the only way I can take the nutrients I need. There's no way I'd keep those blood shakes down with my nausea right now," I replied as I turned back over.

Banton's hand lingered across my backside, and when I turned, he left it there. As he watched my eyes, he slowly began to stroke his thumb across the lace at the top of my panties. My breath hitched as my heart beginning to pound. Reaching up, he grasped the bottom of my silk gown, and pulled it down my abdomen and legs.

"All done," he whispered as he leaned down to kiss me. I could tell by the fire in his eyes he wanted me, but he still wasn't ready for us to try to be intimate.

"You put the babies in here with us for a reason."

He chuckled. "Yeah, I figured with them in the room, it would be kind of like a cold shower…which I think I'll go take, now. I'll be back in a few minutes," he whispered against my lips as he planted a kiss there.

As Banton showered, I watched the twins playing with their toys. Elly settled down first, hugging a stuffed dog and sucking her thumb. Matty continued to play with some soft plastic connectable blocks, working them first one way, then the other, methodically popping them together. My mind whirled with all of the things I'd uncovered about my past today…finding out my real grandfather was a Samuels, that I was related to Everett by birth, wondering what other ties my family had to Louisiana, and why my father was returning here when he and my mother were killed. I shuddered, thinking about my parents possibly having been murdered.

"Andie, what's wrong?" Banton came out of the bathroom and flipped the light off. He sauntered over to the side of the bed as I watched him, sidetracked by the ripple of his abdominal muscles and the way his pajamas clung to him. He had on the white satin pajama pants that drove me crazy. Thank goodness they were dry this time.

I shook my head, and then looked back up into his eyes. "I was just thinking about my parents and the wreck. Banton, you don't think the Orcos were after my dad for a specific reason, do you?"

He pulled the covers back and slipped into the bed next to me, and then reached over and flipped the lamp off. As he pulled me into his arms, he sighed.

"I don't know, Andie. Maybe we'll know more when we get the package from your dad's lawyer. But right now, you need to get some rest. You're still healing, and I want you to get your full eight hours," he admonished, kissing my forehead.

"I need to move the babies to their cribs," I protested as he shook his head.

"No, leave them. Matty's almost asleep. I'll move them in a bit when I go downstairs to let Beau out. Go to sleep now, sweetheart."

My eyes drooped immediately as he gently stroked my hair, his heartbeat rhythmically rocking me to sleep.

Chapter Thirty-Five

"Wake up, sleepyhead. Sorry, baby, you look so peaceful," Banton murmured in my ear. I opened my eyes and stretched. Sunlight streamed through the bay window and flooded the room.

"What time is it?" I murmured as I pushed up and yawned.

"Almost nine. I let you sleep as long as I could, but I need for you to get up and dressed.

"Nine! The babies," I gasped. Banton handed me a cup of coffee.

"The babies are fine. They slept late too. I just got through feeding them both, and put them in their cribs in the nursery. Now, hop up and get that adorable derriere in gear. I have a huge surprise for you today!" He grinned his beautiful dimpled grin at me, causing me to catch my breath.

"What are you up to, Lieutenant?" I asked as I raised an eyebrow at him.

"Don't cock your eyebrow at me, baby...you have no idea what that does to me. We'll never get out of here if you do that," he said, leaned in to kiss me. As his lips moved over mine, keys rattled in the front door downstairs, breaking the mood.

"Helloooo, Bebe! Is everybody up and ready for the day? I have beignets," Everett's voice carried up the staircase.

"Come on, Andie! The quicker you get up and ready, the quicker I get this surprise underway!"

Banton's enthusiasm was infectious. I giggled and threw the covers back.

"What am I supposed to wear?" I raised an eyebrow at him again.

"Andie, there's that eyebrow again. Stop that," he warned as his eyes twinkled. "Anything you like. We'll be changing once we get there, anyway. Ev's here to pack a bag for you and the twins. Just put something on that's comfy for traveling," he said mischievously as he placed a kiss on my lips. He hurried from the room with Beau close on his heels.

I hurried into the bathroom and showered in record time. I decided since I had no idea what he was up to, I'd better shave my legs. After I'd dried off and lotioned up, I took the time to apply some makeup, eyeliner, blush and mascara. Still having trouble with my shoulder, I tied my hair in a loose braid and then knotted it in a messy bun, letting tendrils hang loose at my ears. I smiled sadly at my reflection, I'd lost weight since the attack, and my face looked tired. Rummaging through my closet, I found a lacy ecru dress that hit me mid-thigh, and then donned my favorite pair of leather and suede boots. I spied my grandmother's antique pearl earrings as I rummaged through my jewelry box, and decided I needed to feel her near, so I placed them on my earlobes.

I sighed as I descended the stairs. I still had my moments, when thoughts of the violation I'd suffered at Dante's hands and depression seemed to sneak up like an overcast sky. My spirits lifted quickly, however, when shook the mood off as I spotted the twins, tumbling in Banton's lap as he talked on his cell phone on the sofa.

"Okay, sounds perfect. We'll see you there," he answered someone happily as he touched his phone to turn it off. Laughing, he worked it back into the pocket of his jeans as Matty tried his best to grab it from him.

"You're a little young for that just yet, son," Banton said as he messed Matty's hair up. "You need a haircut, buddy."

"Oh, no. I'm not cutting one curl on that beautiful head until he's at least a year old. Maybe then...but you'll probably have to take him to do it," I said as I drew a ragged breath.

Banton chuckled as he turned to look at me. "Andie, his hair is longer than Ellyson's. Everyone will start thinking he's a girl," he teased as he placed them in the floor. He rose from the sofa and turned to look at me.

"You look adorable," he whispered as he stepped over Ellyson to come around the sofa. "You don't look old enough to have twin babies and another on the way," he breathed as he pulled me into his chest. He had on a dark brown plaid shirt and torn jeans.

"You look pretty good yourself," I whispered back as I grabbed his collar, pulling him in for a kiss. He softly explored my lips with his, and then placed a kiss on the end of my nose.

"So what do you have planned for today?" I asked as I nuzzled his neck, taking in his earthy, spicy scent.

513

"Well, Everett is upstairs finishing up the packing I started, and after we load, we'll be off. We need to pack your medicine and enough formula for the babies for three or four days," he informed me as I drew my brows together.

"But you aren't going to tell me where we're going?'

"Nope. It's a surprise."

I shook my head at him as he chuckled. As I rummaged through the fridge to pack everything we needed into the ice chest, I heard Everett and Banton talking in the foyer.

"Everything is loaded, so I'll be on my way. Safe trip, and take care of them," Everett cautioned as I walked up behind Banton. He grinned at me, tapping the side of his nose conspiratorially, and then running off to jump into his Mercedes.

"Okay, where are we going?'

"Just help me load the twins, Andie."

We strapped Matty and Elly in their car seats. I grinned down at them, and then grabbed my camera out of the front seat. Everett had dressed them in the most adorable outfits. Matty had on a lightweight cable-knit sweater and plaid shorts. Elly had on a jumper made of the same fabric as Matty's shorts, with a cable-knit headband and large satin flower cocked over her right eye. As I snapped away with the camera, Beau bounded into the front seat and then crawled between to take his place between them.

"All set?" Banton asked as I nodded. After I'd snapped my seatbelt in place, Banton turned to me and cupped my cheek in his hand.

"I have something for you," he said as he fished his hand in his pocket. Pulling it out, he opened his palm, revealing my wedding rings and diamond bracelet.

"These led me to find you." He took my hand and then slid my rings back on my finger. "I hope they never leave your finger again," he whispered, kissing the rings and my finger. Then he slid the bracelet around my wrist, fastening the clasp. He looked back into my eyes, and I leaned in to kiss him passionately. He tangled his hands in my hair as he responded, molding his lips to mine, drawing my bottom lip into his mouth as he sucked it gently. After a racing heartbeat or two, he pulled away and murmured, "We'll never leave the driveway at this rate. Let's make some tracks!"

514

Pulling out of the driveway, Banton turned to me with the silliest grin I'd ever seen, and I returned it, filled with happiness. As we drove through Baton Rouge, I busied myself with watching the twins and flipping through pictures on my camera. After a bit, I glanced up to see signs announcing our arrival at the airport.

"We're flying somewhere?' I asked, surprised.

Banton just flashed his dimple, giving nothing away.

He pulled past the main terminal and down to a private runway. A man came out of a small building to greet us.

"Everything is ready, Mr. Gastaneau. You can go ahead and board. Your pilot will be aboard momentarily."

"We're taking a private plane?"

"Yes, we are. Good deduction, Mrs. Gastaneau," he teased as he leaned over and kissed me. He jumped out and began helping the man who greeted us with unloading our bags. After I had both babies out of their seats, Beau jumped out and followed me to the plane.

"In you go," Banton gestured to the small jet as he took Matty from my arms. I climbed the stairs ahead of him and then turned to take one of the seats. The small plane seated eight, with a large sofa and two small tables at the back.

"Here, let me help you. They have safety seats for the babies and a secured crate for Beau until we get airborne," he informed me as he showed me back to the left. After we had both of them strapped in, I remembered their formula.

"Banton, we'll need the ice-chest up here, for their bottles," I began as he moved past me. He pulled it out from under one of the tables.

"Already taken care of. Now, sit down, relax, and enjoy the ride, please." He sat down beside me, and then leaned over and placed a kiss on my forehead.

"Why didn't we just fly on a commercial flight?" I asked.

"Well, with the twins and Beau, I figured this would be a lot easier on both of us. Besides, I can afford it," he said, shaking his head.

I started to question him further, but the arrival of the pilot and co-pilot interrupted me.

515

"We'll be underway momentarily, Mr. and Mrs. Gastaneau. This is Jean, and she will be your flight attendant."

A slender young blonde with a pixie haircut motioned to us. "If you will both buckle your seatbelts, please."

After Banton urged Beau into his crate underneath a seat at the back, he sat down and secured his seatbelt and then reached over and tugged on mine.

"What are you doing?" I asked as I cocked an eyebrow at him.

"Just making sure you are completely safe, sweetheart. That's my job, you know," he whispered as he leaned over to kiss me.

The engines revved, and the noise and vibration seemed much more dramatic to me in this small plane. I grasped the armrests tightly as flight attendant Jean went over the routine safety instructions, and then indicated the emergency exits. She then made her way to the back part of the place where the small galley was located.

"We're fine," Banton assured me, clasping his hand over mine. I nodded as I felt the wheels of the plane leave the tarmac.

Once we were airborne, the engines seemed quieter, the ride smoothing out. After a few minutes the seatbelt light went off over the cockpit doorway, and we both unbuckled our seatbelts as our flight attendant Jean returned.

"Can I get you anything? wine, beer…a soft drink?"

"I'll have a beer…Chandler?' he asked softly.

"Sprite or ginger ale, if you have it," I replied. Banton's eyebrows furrowed as he gazed at me.

"Morning sickness?"

"Morning, night…motion…you name it, I've got it," I said as I shook my head.

He reached up and stroked my cheek softly with his finger. "I'm sorry. Do you want to recline your seat or lie down on the sofa?"

"No, I'm good."

Banton rose, and checked the babies as I turned my seat to check them. They were both fast asleep, and after Banton let Beau out of his cage, he settled at their feet. As the flight attendant returned with our drinks, Banton sat down in his seat, and then reached down to grasp my ankle, pulling my foot up into his lap.

"What are you doing?" I opened one eye questioningly.

He pulled my boot off, and then began to rub my foot. I moaned and kicked the other boot off and placed my other foot in his lap.

"If you are trying to get lucky, Lieutenant, I'm a sure thing. You don't even have to say anything." He grinned at me, flashing the dimple. "All you have to do is look at me like that and I'm yours."

"Why didn't you tell me? Here I am, trying to romance, dazzle and rev you up, and all this time, all I had to do was look at you? How long has this been going on?"

"Since the day on the sofa in the living room, when you proposed that you and John move in with me. You ran your finger back and forth on the sofa, and I wished it was my skin you were caressing," I breathed as his eyes widened.

"Really? That far back?" He leaned closer as his eyes twinkled.

"Actually, the first time I met you, when you hit me in the head opening the back door. You could have had me, right there on the kitchen floor," I whispered. I looked back and forth into his eyes.

"Hmm. Kitchen floor…sounds interesting," he murmured, nuzzling my neck. My heart quickened at his touch. Placing slow deliberate kisses down my neck and shoulder, all the while sliding his hand slowly into my hairline and pulling me closer, Banton lit fires that had been smoldering just beneath the surface for days.

"Darlin', we are on a plane," I whispered.

"Private plane," he corrected. "One of the reasons I didn't fly commercially."

He stood and scooped me up out of my seat. I giggled as he continued his assault on my neck as he settled down with me on the sofa.

"Now I have you where I want you," he murmured as I tightened my arms around his neck. He slid his hand up the lace at my thigh, and then played with the elastic lace of my panties with his thumb.

517

"Mmm," my purr of contentment vibrated into his mouth as he assaulted mine. This magic, the way our mouths danced, our tongues playing chase as he explored, mesmerized me as always.

"Your kisses never disappoint," I muttered against his lips.

He chuckled, and then pulled back to look at me. "I could kiss you for hours, Chandler. I'm like a thirsty man, the more I kiss you, the more I crave you," he whispered as he slid his hand higher, rubbing his thumb across the bare skin at my side.

"Please tell me, wherever it is that you are taking us, you will finally make love to me?"

"Chandler Ann, if you are sure you're ready for that, then yes. I want you, I just want to be careful, and take things slowly." He placed his forehead against mine and sighed.

"Mommmy," Matty wailed from his safety-seat.

Banton chuckled. "I'll get him," he said as he rose to unbuckle Matty from his seat. No sooner than he'd handed him to me, Elly's cries joined Matty's.

"Okay, I know what you two want," Banton said as he picked Elly up. "Daddy's got you. We'll get you something to eat," he soothed her as he reached over and grabbed two bottles from the ice chest.

"Sir, do you need for me to warm those for you?" the flight attendant asked as she stepped from the galley. Her glimpse of Elly's bright, hungry gaze stopped her in her tracks.

I drew my breath in as Banton straightened. "Please, if you don't mind. Just a few seconds," he added, watching her warily.

"Banton," I whispered as I panicked.

"Shh, it will be all right," he tried to assure me. He sat down with Elly and placed her in his lap to change her diaper.

I continued to gently rock Matty against my shoulder as I worried about what the flight attendant had just seen in Elly's eyes. When she returned a few moments later, she acted as if nothing had startled her.

"Here you go, Mrs. Gastaneau."

"Thank you," I answered as I took the bottles from her. She retreated discretely, and I let out a sigh of relief. She must have written what she saw off as her imagination.

After we had the twins dry and fed, they played in our laps for a while with Beau at our feet, sticking his nose in frequently to join in the fun.

"Um, sir...if you will return to your seats, the captain has turned the seatbelt lights on. We will be landing in a few minutes," Jean informed us.

Banton rose and carried the babies back and strapped them in. As we both settled back into our seats, I could feel the plane begin its descent. We hit a rough patch of turbulence, and I tensed as the plane pitched and jumped a bit.

Banton covered my hand with his, and a warmth spread over me as he tried to convey a calmness. I smiled and nodded to him as he leaned over and kissed me on the forehead.

"Find your happy place, baby. I can hear your heartbeat, and your eyes are glowing," he warned in a whisper, glancing back at the flight attendant who was strapped in a seat next to the galley.

I nodded and closed my eyes, taking a deep breath and trying the technique Everett had suggested. When I opened them again, Banton smiled at me.

"Good girl," he said, kissing me again.

The plane touched down, and then slowed as it taxied around to another runway. I searched out the windows for some clue to where we were. When I spotted a cluster of tall palm trees, I turned and raised my eyebrow at my smirking husband.

"Figured it out?' he asked, his eyes twinkling.

"You are taking us for a glimpse of our new beach house," I guessed as he grinned.

"Well, with this little warm spell chasing the fall weather away, I decided this might be the perfect weekend. I don't know if we will want to dip in the ocean, but we can certainly take some barefoot walks on the beach and let the twins play in the sand for the first time," he answered as his lips brushed mine.

"I hope your stay here is a pleasant one," Jean said as we unbuckled our seatbelts and rose to get the twins. As we stepped off the stairs to the runway, a white SUV pulled up to greet us. A young man jumped out and walked over to Banton, handing him the keys.

"Mr. Gastaneau?"

Banton nodded.

"Your rental, sir. May I help with your luggage?" He followed Jean back into the plane, and then emerged with the ice-chest and Beau close on his heels. I stood holding Elly as Banton secured Matty's safety seat. He then took Elly and walked around to the other side to load her.

"Come, Beau…load up," I commanded. Beau jumped into my seat and then settled himself between the babies as usual. Banton finished loading our luggage in the back and jumped in beside me.

"Ready?"

He grinned, fairly jumping in his seat with excitement. I had to laugh at him. He was like a small boy on Christmas morning.

* * *

My jaw dropped. Beach house, my ass! The place looked like it was worthy of a Kennedy summer gathering.

"I thought it was a condo," I whispered.

"It is. It's actually three houses in one. All of these in this beachfront community are built that way. They're built to look a bit more vintage and homey," he commented as he pulled into a stall of covered parking to the side.

The house was painted in peach tones with bright, blue shutters and built high off the ground on tall pillars. A wide staircase led up the front to a massive wrap-around porch. Oversized wicker furniture welcomed us from the porch. I could envision spending many, many happy summers here.

"Banton, I love it," I whispered.

"You haven't even seen the inside yet," he chided.

"I don't have to. It's heaven on earth!" I exclaimed, gazing out at the ocean, visible between the parking shed and the house.

I jumped out and opened the back door to retrieve Matty. Banton did the same with Elly, and as Beau followed us, Banton turned and stopped me.

"Here, give me Matty. I'll carry them in, stay right here," he commanded sternly.

"Why?"

520

"Just stay here," he called over his shoulder as he climbed the stairs. He sat the babies down on the porch as he unlocked the door. Disappearing into the house, he returned quickly and then ran down the stairs and across the yard to me.

"Now, this is what I wanted to do," he gushed as he swung me up into his arms.

"Banton, please. You don't have to do this," I grinned goofily at him.

"Oh, yes I do. Your house was yours before it was ours. I bought this for us," he said as he shook his head, his eyebrows furrowed. "Did that make sense?'

I giggled. "Yes, funny enough, it did to me. I love you, darlin'."

"And I you, Mrs. Gastaneau," he murmured against my lips. He pushed the screen door open with his foot and swept me into the entry and set me down on my feet. Both walls were lined with whitewash bead board and benches with pegs for wet swimwear and hats. Baskets lined the floor under the benches, handy to store flip-flops or beach toys. I wandered through to the great room. The walls were the same bead-board, with a large white stone fireplace at one end, and a galley-style kitchen at the other. A large island with a wrap-around breakfast bar separated the kitchen from the living area. Furnished in over-stuffed sofas and wide armchairs covered in white slip-covers, it was homey, beachy and perfect. Pale blue floral and check throw pillows were tossed about, and light throw rugs were scattered on the white-washed pine floors. The entire back of the house incorporated one long line of French doors, opening to a large deck overlooking the beautiful turquoise water.

Banton watched me curiously as I turned back to him. I launched myself at him as I squealed in delight, and he caught me mid-air in his arms.

"I take it you approve?'

"I love it, Banton! It's breathtaking," I said as the twins began to yell out at us from their seats, wanting to be unstrapped.

"Okay, okay...keep your diapers on," Banton mumbled against my neck. He threw me down playfully onto one of the overstuffed sofas and then knelt to unstrap the twins. Carrying them under their arms with their little legs dangling, he dropped them one at a time into my lap.

"See the wonderful place daddy bought for us? Isn't it beautiful?" I turned both of them around to gaze out the windows at the ocean. The sun was sparkling on the turquoise water, turning it a deeper shade of blue as the waves washed toward us. The babies seemed mesmerized by the water.

"I can't wait to take them out to play in the sand," I said as Banton grinned at me. He dropped the suitcases, one by one inside the door as Beau followed him back and forth to the car. After he'd finished unloading all our stuff, he came back in and closed the front door. I'd placed both babies on the rug so they could explore, and they'd both headed straight for the French doors, pulling up to stand as they gazed out at the water. They jabbered at each other, and then pointed back to the beach as if they were carrying on their own little secret conversation. Beau ran through the house exploring, and then back into the great room with us. He barked at the twins as he sat down between them as if he were joining in their conversation.

"Chandler, have you seen the rest of the house?" Banton asked as he dropped down beside me on the sofa.

"In a minute. I'm in love with this view," I sighed as I looked up at him.

"The kids seem to be too," he said.

"I sometimes have to remind myself they're just barely four months old. They're already crawling, pulling up…saying their first words."

"I know. I think we are only days away from Matty taking his first step."

I looked at him, and nodded. He smiled and pulled me into his side, wrapping his arms around me.

"I guess that's a good thing, now that we have another one on the way," he said as he nuzzled my neck.

Elly sat down and whimpered as Beau stuck his nose right on her behind.

"Oops, looks like somebody might need changing," I said as Banton chuckled. I rose to get her.

"Don't lift her from the floor," Banton scolded.

"Banton, I'm fine. My ribs are much better and they hardly hurt me. I'm almost healed," I answered as I stood with Elly. Banton picked Matty up and followed me into the foyer.

"I'll get their bag. The bedrooms are down that hallway to the right, the master is at the end of the hallway," he instructed as I made my way back.

There were two large bedrooms with king-sized beds on the left with a bathroom in between, and a large bedroom on the right with the same. All of the rooms were decorated with natural wicker furniture and fluffy pastel duvets and throw pillows. Large double doors opened to the master at the end of the hallway. Decorated in shades of white gossamer and cottons, it was furnished with dark carved teakwood and dark-stained rush furniture, giving it a Caribbean feel.

"This just gets better and better," I breathed as I wandered around the room. To the right of the massive four-poster bed, another set of double doors opened to the master bath, complete with sunken stone bathtub and hammered copper fixtures. There was another set of French doors in the bathroom that revealed a small, private enclosed deck and courtyard for sunbathing.

Banton walked up behind me and placed a kiss on my shoulder.

"No matter how much time we spend here, it will never be enough," I breathed, gazing at him wonderingly.

Elly squirmed in my arms and I remembered the task at hand.

"I'm sorry, baby girl. You need a change," I murmured as I kissed her on top of her head. Banton helped me change both babies, and then I placed them on the thick, soft carpeting to let them explore as I began to unpack their things. Banton carried their pack-n-plays in and set them up in a corner of our room. After I had most of our luggage stored in the closet and in the bathroom, I chased the twins down the hallway back to the great room.

Banton stood in the kitchen, putting the things from the ice chest in the refrigerator.

"The staff stocked the kitchen for us, and placed bottle of white wine in here. I know you can't have much, but would you like a sip?" he asked as he took the bottle out and placed it on the counter.

"I'd love a sip, then some sparkling water, if we have any," I said as I joined him. As he opened the wine, I settled on a stool at the breakfast bar, watching the twins as they crawled back toward the French doors again.

Banton laughed as he uncorked the wine. "I see where their favorite place will be."

"So it seems. I hope the staff left me a lot of window cleaner," I noted as I watched them placing little finger prints and baby slobber all over the glass.

"Chandler Ann, that won't be your concern. The cleaning crew will handle that. I pay for a service to clean twice a week while we are here and once a month when we're not," he informed me as he poured the wine. He handed me the glass half-full, and then lifted his glass to touch mine. I raised an eyebrow at him, and he shook his head.

"That is a rule, and I'm not budging. No cleaning while we're at the beach house. And you only cook when you want to," he admonished. I grinned at him.

"I can live with that, Lieutenant."

"To our family beach house, and many, many years of happy memories here," he said as I lifted my glass to my lips.

I sipped the cool wine slowly, and it tasted wonderful. After the second sip, I handed my glass back to Banton.

"Finish mine for me. I'll have some sparkling water."

He smiled, and drained my glass as he reached for a bottle of Perrier. Refilling my glass, he came around the bar, sat my glass in front of me, and then folded me in his arms.

"Why don't we take the babies out on the beach for a bit, and then we'll come in for an early dinner," Banton suggested as he kissed my neck.

"That sounds great. Just let me go and change into something more appropriate."

"I'll watch the kids, take your time," he called as I made my way back to the bedroom.

Once in the closet, I opened my hanging bag to find that Everett had been shopping for me once again. I shook my head as I rummaged through the new clothes, finding several pairs of linen capris suitable for beach-combing, three maxi-dresses, two new long cover-ups, and two beautiful new swimsuits. It was certainly warm enough outside to wear them, but I doubted if the water was warm enough to go swimming. I frowned as I took the clothes out of the bag and hung them in the closet…my bridesmaids dress for Laurilee's wedding was packed in the back. How on earth did this get in there? Everett must have forgotten it was there when he placed everything else in. There was also a beautiful backless dress in pale peach, with crystals on the tight bodice, and then a wispy tulle skirt that almost resembled a ballet dress I wore once at a dance recital. I smiled as I plotted a place I could wear it. *Banton must be planning to take me out somewhere special!*

I opted for a pair of tan capris and a pale green camisole, and brushed my hair out and tied it over my shoulder in a side-swept pony-tail. I then located a pair of sandals and slipped them on as I hurried back down the hallway. Banton had removed the twins' clothes and put them both in little cotton onesies.

"Banton, I didn't think about sunscreen," I worried as he smirked at me.

"I don't think Aldon babies will sunburn, but just in case, we have large beach umbrellas out there. We'll keep them in the shade," he assured me as we picked them up.

Once we were on the beach, it was if the last of my worries drifted away across the water. There was only me, my beautiful husband, and my two precious babies to play at the edge of the vast ocean. We sat together, scrunching our toes in the sand and building small sand castles, which Matty flattened like a wrecking ball as Elly giggled at him. I lay back on a beach towel and shielded my eyes as I gazed at Banton. He leaned over and murmured, "I'm pulling you closer, Chandler. You are in the sun, and I don't want you to burn."

Déjà vu! I remembered the last afternoon I worked at the dress shop in Texas when I was dressing the windows, dreaming about beaches and expensive bikinis and waiting for my life to start. As I gazed into Banton's beautiful eyes, I smiled.

At Banton's chuckle, I raised an eyebrow. "You are grinnin' like a Cheshire cat, Mrs. Gastaneau. What are you thinking?"

I shook my head. "I was just thinking about a daydream I had in Texas my last day in the dress shop. It was pretty much like this,

525

except I was in a red bikini, and you weren't nearly as handsome, in my dream…"

"You daydreamed of me?"

I shut my eyes, absorbing the late afternoon sun. "Mmmm. I did, Lieutenant. But you have exceeded my hopes and dreams in a way that still overwhelms me."

I took a deep breath, and as I opened my eyes. He was over me, his lips hovering over mine.

"I'm glad I overwhelm you. I'd like to see just how overwhelmed you can be," he murmured as he gently moved his lips back and forth over mine, teasing as he breathed slowly into my mouth. I reached up and drew him down hard as I passionately returned his kiss, running my hand up his bare chest between the lapels of his open shirt.

"Daaaddy!" Elly called. We broke apart and laughed. Elly sat on the end of Banton's blanket, her thumb in her mouth, her little head resting on Banton's leg. Matty sat on my blanket, picking up handfuls of sand and dropping them on the blanket around him. He seemed mesmerized, and then I realized he was barely holding his eyes open, fighting the sleep that was about to overtake him.

"They're wrecked. I think it's early to bed for them tonight," I observed as I rose to pick up Matty. Banton gathered Elly and our blankets and bag, and we headed back up the sand and through the smattering of grass and reeds to the boardwalk leading up to our deck.

"I think we'd better strip them out here, or I'll be sweeping sand for a week."

"That's what this is for, Andie," Banton observed, kneeling down beside a showerhead I hadn't noticed before. I'd passed it unnoticed in my haste to get to the beach. Banton stripped Elly down to her diaper, and then as he removed it, dumped a sand pail's worth of sand out of it. I giggled as I did the same with Matty. Banton switched the water on, and thankfully it was warm from sitting in the pipe warmed by the sun. We rinsed them off and then wrapped them in clean towels.

"Now you, baby," Banton said, a sexy tone to his voice. I slipped my sandals off, and he rubbed my feet and ankles, sliding his hands up to my knees as he rinsed the remaining sand that clung to my skin. As he caressed my ankle, his eyes sparkled up at me, the flecks of gold intensifying against the brown, causing my breath to hitch in my throat.

"Get me inside, darlin', or I might jump you right here."

"My thoughts exactly," he said, his dimple deep. We both giggled and grabbed the babies up and swept them through the patio doors into the great room. I was a woman on a mission, for the look in Banton's eyes at that moment held promise. I hurriedly warmed the twins' bottles, and then we carried them down the hallway. We never said a word to each other, we just worked in unison, diapering the babies and then slipping their pajamas on them. I took the only rocker in the room, rocking Elly as she took her formula. Her eyes were closed before she finished as she dropped the bottle and fell into a deep, exhausted slumber. I looked up at Banton, who rocked Matty back and forth as he sat on the foot of our bed. Matty soon followed Elly, and Banton placed both of them in their pack-n-plays, covering them with their blankies.

He turned to me, grinned, and pulled me down the hallway back to the kitchen.

"I'll heat us something up for dinner," he murmured against my neck as he pulled me into his arms.

"I'm not hungry...for food," I replied as I leaned my head back, giving him more of my neck to explore. I felt him grin against my neck, and then he swept me up into his arms and crossed over to a large chaise lounge that was wide enough for two. He sat me down carefully and then sank down beside me, stretching his body out, twining his legs between mine as he played with the lace at the top of my camisole.

"Now that I have you alone, I want to look at you, Chandler. Your body is changing again," he noted, tracing along the top of my breasts with his finger. My breathing accelerated as his thumbs slid down my ribcage to the hem of my shirt. He grasped it and pulled it up as his lips traced kisses along my collarbone.

Pulling my camisole over my head, he reached up to support my broken shoulder.

"It's good, it doesn't hurt anymore. Accelerated healing, you know," I mouthed against his lips as he smiled.

527

"I'm so glad," he breathed as he threw my camisole into the floor beside us. He pulled away, and swept his hungry gaze down my body. My breasts were already beginning to swell; they'd been tender for a while now. The lacy, see-through bra I was wearing was a little tight, and they flowed over the cups.

Banton whistled through his teeth.

"Sweet Dixie," he breathed, burying his face between them. I giggled as I tried in vain to push him off.

"You are such a guy! Why do boobs fascinate men?"

He pulled away and slid his hand up my ribcage to cup one as I gasped.

"Hmmm." He shook his head. "Beats me," he said flippantly.

The doorbell rang.

"Who on earth could that be?' I asked as he shrugged. I retrieved my camisole from the floor and slipped it back on as Banton rose to walk to the door. "Maybe it's the cleaning crew to check to see if we need anything," he called over his shoulder as he reached the door. I stood to follow him, and as he opened the door someone shouted, "Welcoming committee! Where's my sweet Bebe?"

"Everett!" I gasped in surprise.

Everett swooped in holding Ava with Claudia close behind him, followed by Ty, Constance, John and Brie.

"What are y'all doing here?' I squealed as Constance dropped her bag and ran to greet me.

"Surprise! You didn't think you were going to get any alone time now, did you sister?"

I glanced at Banton with mixed emotions. I loved that they were all here to share the excitement of our new beach house, but a small pang tugged at my heart at the thought our "alone" moment had dissipated. Banton smiled knowingly.

"You had this planned all along, didn't you?"

His dimple deepened as Everett placed his hand around Banton's shoulder.

"You don't know the half of it, Bebe. Now, let's get this party started."

Everett sat Ava Grace down, and she ran to me with her arms opened.

"An Andler!" her squeal could be heard back in N'awlins.

"Shh, Doodle-Bug, we don't want to wake the twins," I cautioned as I hugged her to me.

"They're down already? I was hoping for some Aunt Claudia time," Claudia pouted as she hugged me.

"They were wrecked. We wore them out on the beach earlier."

Noises from next door traveled through the kitchen wall, and I heard patio doors opening next to us.

"Hum. Sounds like we have neighbors this weekend," Banton commented as he grinned. I turned to look out the French doors as Cade and Julia appeared, grinning as they knocked on the window.

I turned and cocked an eyebrow at Banton.

"Daddy bought the place next door. We have a really big family, you know," he said as he slid his arm around me. "And don't cock your eyebrow at me like that, or I'll have to be rude to the guests and drag you back to our room," he whispered in my ear as my eyes widened.

Slapping me playfully on the rump, he stepped around me to let Julia and Cade in. Drew and Aunt Sue soon followed.

"Chandler Ann, this place is absolutely enchanting! I'm so happy for you," Aunt Sue gushed, pulling me into a hug.

"I'm still a little overwhelmed," I replied. I sat Ava down on her feet, and she immediately ran over to the doors to look out at the ocean.

"Come on, Doodle-Bug...let's take Beau and walk on the beach," Cade suggested as she nodded enthusiastically at him. Taking her hand, he led her out onto the deck and down the steps to the sand below.

"Don't go too far. We've got etouffee for dinner," Everett called after them.

I turned and grinned. "Grandmother Wellington's?"

"You know it, sister! They sent two big pots full, along with some bisque and a boatload of gumbo. We won't need to cook for a day or two, at least," he said animatedly as he kissed my cheek and then waived his hand at us. "We'll unload everything. You ladies just go on and take the tour."

"He just rocks my world," I shook my head as I looked at Claudia.

"Yes, mine too," she whispered as she blushed.

I opened my mouth to say more, and then taking in Constance's expression, I closed it. It was too soon to go there.

"Come on Drew, we'll help Mrs. Sue and Mr. Lon unload their car and help Everett get all this food squared away," Banton called. Drew followed him and Ty out the door.

"Okay, give us the grand tour, Andie!" Brie said excitedly. I grabbed her hand, pulling her down the hallway as the others followed.

"Two bedrooms here," I motioned to the left, "and one here, all with adjoining baths. And this is the master," I announced as I pushed the double doors open. Everyone followed me in as I checked the twins in the corner to make sure they were okay. They both slept like hibernating bear cubs.

"Chandler, this is beautiful," Constance breathed, stroking the gossamer draping the four-poster bed. Aunt Sue peeked around the corner into the bathroom.

"Ralph Lauren would have designer envy in this place," she noted, stepping back into the bedroom. Constance disappeared where Aunt Sue had just been, and then emerged with an incredulous look.

"You have a private sunbathing deck? Holy shit!" she exclaimed as Aunt Sue whirled to face her.

"Constance Clarice LeBlance, I swear if you don't get control of that mouth, I'm going to wash it out with soap," she admonished as Brie giggled.

Julia wandered around our big master suite, and then asked off-handedly, "So, where is everyone going to sleep?"

"Your mother and I have discussed that, and you and Claudia and Ava Grace will stay next door with us. We'll let Ty and Constance, Brie and John, and the boys and Everett stay here with Banton and Chandler," Aunt Sue answered her as Constance rolled her eyes. I noted Julia's shoulders dropped a bit as she followed us back down the hallway.

The night had turned into the circus it usually did with both families and our friends around. I smiled at Banton from across the room. He stood in the kitchen with Everett and John as they laid out the food for dinner. It all seemed so wonderfully normal--our first family vacation together. Tears pooled in my eyes. I was so overcome with relief...with love...with gratitude. A little over a week ago I was resigned to death, my only hope was that the twins survived the ordeal and found their way back to Banton. Banton noted my emotions, and hastily made his way through the throng of family in the living room to where I stood. He folded me in his arms and pulled me into one of the bedrooms off the hallway.

"Andie, what is it?' he asked as he stroked my hair.

"I'm just so happy. Everything just kind of hit me at once. Just a few days ago I thought my world was ending, and now everything is so blissfully normal," I choked out as the tears threatened to spill over. "I'm being silly," I said as I wiped the tears from my cheeks.

"I know this is all a little overwhelming, and you have every right to be emotional. You know what venom and pregnant hormones do to you," he teased, kissing me on the forehead. "Everyone just wants to celebrate having you home alive, most of all me," he continued as he wiped my tears away with his thumbs. He lowered his lips to kiss me, enveloping me in his arms. I sighed as sweet contentment washed over me.

"Sorry our alone time has been curtailed, but we do have that big master bedroom all to ourselves. I'll make sure I let everyone know you are tired, and we need to go to bed early," he whispered playfully in my ear. I smiled against his neck.

"Promise? You be sure and do that. I'm countin' the minutes."

We joined the rest of the family and ate our dinner, everyone scattered around the great room and out on the deck. As the sun set, Banton lit the fireplace, and Ty and Constance left out the back doors to take a moonlight walk on the beach. Brie and John decided to follow them. As the house emptied, Aunt Sue and Uncle Lon and Banton's parents opted to go next door to play dominoes, and Everett, Claudia, Julia and Cade settled down in front of the fireplace to watch a romantic movie. Banton grinned at me and started down the hallway, my hand tucked in his. Before we could make it into the bedroom, little wails greeted us.

"Oh, man...the babies are up," he said in an exasperated voice.

"They have been down for more than four hours, Banton. They're probably hungry again."

"Can't we contact Renault about starting them on some solid food?" he asked, reaching down to pick Matty up.

"Ddaaadddy," Matty blubbered as he touched Banton's face with his hand.

"I know big guy. We just can't seem to get you full these days. Let's go and get you a bottle," he murmured, planting a kiss on Matty's forehead.

Elly held her little arms up to me and then snuggled down against my breast, her eyelids heavy. She didn't seem that hungry, she just woke when Matty did. Banton warmed their formula up in the microwave as Claudia came in the kitchen.

"Can I feed them, please? I've missed having them around," she said as tears gathered in her eyes. Her loneliness at William's loss was palpable.

"Sure, we'll bring them in to you," I said.

After we'd handed the babies off to Claudia and Julia, I went to make sure the bedrooms had everything our guests would need before they returned from their walk on the beach. When I'd finished I wandered out on the deck. Everett stood, muttering to himself and scowling.

"Everett, is something wrong?" I asked him softly. Everett was never in a bad mood.

"Oh, everything is just divine! Everett's everybody's best friend..." he flipped his hand out in the air as he turned to me, his eyes fiery. "I'm the happy go-lucky, gay, everybody's best friend-- Everett will fix it--fairy godmother, right? Everybody loves Everett! Everett, let's snuggle! Well, it's all warm and fuzzy, the spooning thing...until somebody gets a hard-on! I should have stayed blissfully in my make-believe closet," he muttered to himself disgustedly.

I pressed my lips together hard, trying not to laugh, and failed miserably. As he turned to glare at me, I heard another chuckle in the darkness, evidently John and Ty had returned with Constance and Brie from their walk on the beach.

"I need a little baby time," he muttered, returning to the living room where Claudia and Julia had the twins.

"Is it just me, or is Ev having a hard time adjusting to the hetero twenty-first century?" Ty asked as John chuckled.

"You could say that, and don't tease him whatever you do," I warned in a serious voice.

"It's obvious he's in love with Claudia," John asserted. Ty's jaw dropped.

I sighed. "I guess it was obvious to everyone but me. He doesn't want to push her. Will's death is too fresh and painful. He's in love with her, but he just wants to be there for her right now."

"That's a hard position to be in," John answered and then shot a glance at me. Brie blushed, and placed a hand on John's shoulder as she slipped inside the French doors. After a moment of awkward silence, Ty followed her, leaving me with John and Constance.

"Well, is someone going to address the five-thousand pound elephant on the deck?" Constance quipped.

"NO!" John and I both exclaimed at the same time.

Constance looked back and forth at us, and then shook her head and followed John inside. I stood for a few moments, trying to shake the sad memories John's comments stirred. I leaned on the railing, enjoying the cool breeze wafting in from the water and the sound of the waves lapping on the shoreline. Flashlights fanned back and forth down the beach, moving to and fro as some kids chased sand crabs.

I returned to the living room to retrieve the twins, but Claudia and Everett had already taken them to our bedroom. As I entered, Claudia was watching Everett as he leaned over and placed a kiss on Matty's head, and then Elly's.

"They're down, Bebe." Everett crossed the room and kissed me on the forehead.

"Thank you for feeding them and getting them back down for us," I responded as Claudia hugged me.

"You are entirely welcome. We both love doing it. We needed a little bonding time with them," she whispered as she kissed my cheek.

"Okay, back to our movie, my dear. We'll have to rewind," Everett fussed, waving his hands in the air as Claudia rolled her eyes at him.

533

"Oh, where is Banton?" I called to them down the hallway.

"He took Ava Grace out to catch sand crabs. They should be back in a minute," Claudia called as I smiled. The flashlights I'd seen on the beach were Banton and Ava Grace. Banton was just a big kid at heart.

I decided to use the time in the bathroom. I slipped out of my clothes and stepped down into the tub, taking the time to pin my hair up on top of my head. I used some sugar scrub to exfoliate and bath oil to make my skin glow, hoping to distract Banton's attention from the faint bruising which still marred my skin. After I'd bathed, I rubbed some lotion on, and then spritzed on some of the insanely expensive perfume he'd bought for me on my birthday. After applying a bit of mineral makeup to give me a soft glow, I pulled my hair down and brushed it out, then flipped it back to make it look fuller. Some soft pink lip gloss finished the look. I stood back and looked in the mirror...perfect. Now, to find something sexy to sleep in. Surely Everett had packed something for me. I searched through the suitcase and found just the thing...see-through lace panties with a sheer camisole to match, with delicate white crewel work embroidered on it. I slipped the panties on, and then looked in the mirror. You could see everything but my colon in this lingerie. Good. Then I slid the camisole on, and my breasts strained against the fabric, my nipples looking rather large under the sheer fabric. A year ago, I would have been mortified at this outfit. Now, knowing I would have to persuade Banton to make love to me, it was perfect. As I gazed at myself in the mirror, doubt began to creep in. Could I do this? Was this too brazen, after everything that had happened? Would it put him off?

My heart began to pound as I heard Banton's voice in the living room. Too late now, sister, I thought. This will just have to do. Instead of standing here waiting for him, I'll dim the lights and get into bed. Yeah, that's a plan.

This is so stupid! He's your husband, you've been married for almost a year, and you've had two babies together. Why are you so nervous?

My heart's pounding increased, flooding in my ears as Banton opened the door. I was nauseated, thinking he might reject me again, afraid it was too soon after the attack.

"Chandler? Sweetheart, are you ill?" his voice sounded worried as he crossed over to the bed. The only light in the room was moonlight bouncing off the ocean outside the long French windows. He sat down on the bed beside me and leaned over to switch the lamp on.

"Hey, do you feel okay?" he asked as I turned over to face him. The sheet slipped down my arm, exposing part of my chest. Banton's eyes darkened, his pupils dilating as he gazed down at my breasts straining against the fabric of the camisole.

"Chandler, you look beautiful," he whispered as he reached up to stroke my arm.

"Come to bed, please, Banton! Before something else calls us away," I whispered. He nodded and strode over to the bathroom and shut the door. As the seconds ticked away, my nerves became more jangled and raw. Finally the bathroom door opened and Banton came out, wearing only the white silk pajama pants I loved. He walked around to the dresser and switched the music system on, and then cracked the French doors so we could hear the ocean. After he'd checked the babies, I threw the covers back as he eyed me warily. He slipped into the bed and slid across the sheets, pausing as he propped up on an elbow.

He gazed at me for several moments as if he were making his mind up about something. I drew my breath in. I wanted him so badly. I felt once we were intimate again, we would put everything to rest. I wanted him to put his hands on me, his mouth on me, to erase what had happened. I knew in my heart I was ready, but I was anxious about how Banton would respond. I could see him clearly in the moonlight. I searched his eyes, wide with what? Uncertainty?

"Chandler...you are breathtaking. I'm a lucky, lucky man," he murmured as he leaned in to place a kiss on my lips. My breathing was shallow as I held my emotions in check. I wanted him to take the lead and take us where he wanted to go. I wanted to make sure he wanted this.

535

He placed his fingers under my chin, tilting it up so he could study my face in the moonlight. As the melodic piano music played softly in the background, Banton caressed my chin, and then ran his thumb down my neck to the dip at the base of my throat.

"I can hear your heartbeat, and you're shaking. Chandler, please don't push yourself. I know you aren't ready for this. I understand. You were attacked viciously in the worst possible way. It will take time for you to heal, and I will wait as long as it takes," he murmured as he bent again to place a soft kiss on my lips.

I shook my head at him. "Believe me, I want this. I'm just nervous about your reaction. I need to know you still want me," I whispered, tears gathering in my eyes.

Banton gazed down at my ribs, grasping my waist with his hand. He slid the fingertips of his other hand into my hairline, pulling me in to his lips.

"Don't doubt my desire for you, Chandler. I need this too," he whispered. I've never wanted you more. I want all of you, to be inside you."

His kiss was fierce as his tongue invaded my mouth. I responded fervently, our tongues twisting and dancing as we melded as one. His hands explored my body, gently at first, and then when I didn't shy away, he became bolder, pushing the camisole I wore up under my arms as he stroked my chest, my breasts…every inch of my skin felt alive. Placing slow, languid kisses beneath my earlobes, his hands continued to stroke, to massage…lower until he hooked his thumbs in the lace at my hips.

"Please tell me if anything feels wrong, if I hurt you," he murmured, his concern evident in his voice.

"You won't hurt me, Banton. I crave your touch, and I need you," I whispered. "I need you to make me whole again. Please, love me," I begged. Grasping the waistband of his bottoms, I pushed down, freeing him of the garment.

Gently stroking my abdomen, he drew back in the moonlight to look at me.

"Another baby," he whispered as he shook his head. "I didn't think it was possible to love another child as much as I love Matty and Elly, but I was wrong. I already love this little one." He leaned down to touch his lips gently to my belly. I twined my fingers in his hair as he continued to kiss my skin, running his lips over my abdomen, lingering there. I grasped his face firmly in my hands and brought his mouth back up to mine.

"I don't know how I would have survived if I'd lost you. I miss you even when you're not in the room, and I long for your touch, more so than before. You are so precious to me," he murmured against my lips. His eyes were so beautiful in the moonlight, shining with love... with a longing I knew he only had for me. We lay for the longest time, just exploring each other's bodies with our hands, our mouths, skin against skin.

As he watched me intently, his eyes on mine, he slowly rose over me, taking my hips in his hands as he covered me with his. As he began to move, I closed my eyes, losing myself in the feel of him.

He whispered softly, his breath in my hair, "Chandler?"

"Mmm. Yes?'

"Are you okay?" He pulled away slightly, his body tensing.

I opened my eyes as I nodded. "Banton, I'm perfect. Love me," I whispered back. He placed one hand under my neck, holding my head in his hand as he held my hips with the other, slowly entering me. I held my breath. It had been such a long time.

"I love you, Chandler. I love you so much," he murmured as he began to move. I sighed as contentment washed over me. It was if he was banishing all the hurt, all the pain and violence as he made slow, sweet love to me.

"You are what I need. You are my everything," I whispered up to him as his gaze intensified. As my own body responded, I could feel the relief flow through him. He moved deeper, and I met him stroke for stroke, the heat building inside me as I opened up for him as our bodies became one. We connected once again on that level only few achieve. I cried out against his neck as he drove in hard, both our bodies throbbing together in sweet release. Our breathing stilled, our bodies glistening with sweat in the moonlight, clinging to each other as we floated back down to reality, sated and fulfilled.

Banton rolled over on his back and pulled me with him, positioning me so I lay on top of him, my head on his muscular chest. He wrapped his arms around me and pressed his lips into my hair. We lay silently, listening to the waves break on the beach outside in the darkness. The breeze had turned cooler, and I shivered as he pulled the comforter up over us.

"Are you cold?' he asked, his lips still in my hair.

"No. I'm perfect. I could lie here forever."

"So could I. As long as I could touch you."

I fell asleep on Banton's chest as I listened to his precious heartbeat, wrapped in his arms, our bodies still connected.

* * *

We woke to the sound of giggles at the end of the bed. Matty pushed against the mesh on his little bed as Elly pushed her hand against his, laughing at him. Both of them turned to look at us as Banton chuckled at them.

"Dddaaaddy," Matty yelled as Elly pulled up to stand at the foot of her little bed.

"Mmmaaattyy," Banton answered him playfully as he sat up in bed beside me. We were still wrapped around each other, our legs intertwined.

"Mommy, up," Elly called out.

"Okay, okay...we're up," I sighed as I pushed up to sit, my back against Banton. He slid his arm around my naked torso and planted a kiss on my neck.

"Good morning, baby. Did you sleep well?'

I tilted my head back against his chest, looking up into his eyes.

"Umm, yes...I did. Someone kept me warm and satisfied all night," I replied silkily as his gaze darkened.

"Mmm. I was a little worried about round two, I couldn't get you to say much," he murmured as I turned to grin at him.

"I was too satisfied and exhausted for talk," I answered, pushing up to retrieve my robe. As I tied the sash, he pulled me back down on the bed.

"I wish the twins would have stayed asleep just thirty more minutes," he grinned down at me. I reached up to kiss his nose.

"There's always naptime...and tonight."

Banton growled, rolling out of the opposite side of the bed as he retrieved his pajama pants from the floor. He shrugged into a t-shirt and then brushed behind me, placing a kiss on my shoulder as I leaned over to pick up the twins.

"I'll go and get their formula ready," he offered as he opened our bedroom door.

After I'd changed both diapers, kissed their little tummies and had our morning romp, I carried Matty and Elly down the hallway to follow Banton to the kitchen. All of our guests' bedroom doors were still closed. I checked the clock over the fireplace, to find it was a little after eight. Everett lay on the chaise lounge, seemingly in a trance, a book perched across his chest. When he heard the babies jabbering away, he sat up abruptly.

"Good morning, kids. You're the first ones up. "

"Morning, Ev. We'd still be asleep if it weren't for the squirts," Banton said, popping their formula in the microwave.

I walked over and handed the twins to Everett.

"Ev, if you'll watch them for a moment, I'll start some breakfast."

"Chandler, you are not cooking breakfast for everyone," Everett admonished.

"I most certainly am. I'm hungry, and I know everyone else will be too," I said, moving into the kitchen and around Banton. I located biscuits in the fridge, and popped them in the oven. I then found eggs, cheese, onions and peppers, and some frozen hash browns in the freezer, so I proceeded to improvise on a breakfast casserole. Before Banton and Everett finished feeding the twins, I had everything baking in the oven.

I sat down on a large ottoman across from Banton, watching Matty take the last of his bottle. As I sipped my coffee, I heard a tap on the French doors.

"An Andler?' Ava's little voice startled me. I turned to find her face pressed against the glass.

I rose and opened the door.

"My mommy said if you and my Unca Banin were up, I could help wif my babies," she announced, bounding through the door.

"Of course. You can play with them, Doodle-Bug."

539

She jumped up on the sofa and settled between Everett and Banton. Everett leaned over and kissed her on top of the head.

"Good morning, my precious Ava. What are you doing up so early?' Everett asked her as he finished feeding Elly. Elly pushed up and immediately crawled over into Ava's lap. Ava's eyes lit up like a Christmas tree.

"Wewl, I had to feed my cwabs Unca Banin caught for me," Ava explained as she wrestled with Elly. I giggled. Elly was almost as big as Ava.

The front doorbell rang, startling everyone. I couldn't imagine who it could be; everyone had been coming and going through the patio doors to the condo next door.

I rose, re-tucked my robe at the top, and tightened the belt as I went to answer. As I opened the door, Laurilee launched herself at me.

"Chandler!" she squealed as I held her, a stunned expression on my face.

"Laurilee? What are you doing here?" I stammered as Dan pushed in the doorway behind her.

"Chirpy, when Banton called and gave us another chance at a beach get away, we just couldn't refuse!"

As I continued to gape at them, Dan picked me up and swung me around. I winced as he grasped my ribcage a little too tight.

"Oh, sorry, Banton said you were still bruised up," he apologized as Laurilee placed her hands on my upper arms to study me.

"I can't believe you are here! I'm so glad to see you," I gasped, finally reacting to the surprise as I pulled her into a hug.

"Banton called us a couple of days ago and explained everything that had happened. He said you were still torn up about missing the wedding. He and Everett suggested we come and get married again on the beach, so you could finally be my matron of honor. Now I ask you, how many girls get the chance of having the big hometown wedding, and the get-away barefoot beach wedding to boot?" she said as she cocked her eyebrow at me. I turned to look at Banton.

"That's why I found my bridesmaid's dress in the dress bag!" I exclaimed as Everett and Banton grinned at me. I turned back to

Laurilee, shaking my head in disbelief. "Now, everything is perfect. Everything," I whispered as she hugged me again.

"Come on, we have to have a little girl talk," Laurilee urged as she took my hand. I nodded, and pulled her down the hallway toward our room.

"I'll show Laurilee and Dan where to put their bags," Banton said as he rose. "Good to see you again, Dan!" I heard Banton say warmly as I pulled Laurilee into our room and shut the door.

"Oh, Chandler...are you really all right? Banton called us right after you got home. Please tell me this whole thing is over?" She pulled at the neck of my robe, exposing a still bruised shoulder and arm.

"I hope so, Laurilee. Banton and the SEALs killed the leader and most of the group. There is one who got away, and I'm sure we will have to deal with him at some point, but for the moment, we're good."

We both sat down on the foot of the bed as she looked around.

"Chandler, this place is beautiful. Banton said it's yours?" she asked in awe.

"Yes, he surprised me with it on my birthday, but this is the first chance to come and stay here. The whole family is here, but I guess you already knew that," I said as I narrowed my eyes at her.

She nodded. "Banton called as soon as he knew you were on the mend and planned everything. Dan is working for his dad right now, and it was easy for him to get away. I don't start teaching until January, so here we are. It was really sweet of Banton to fly us down here, and the honeymoon trip! Really, Chandler, that was too much!"

"Banton felt really bad about not letting me come to Texas. I felt so guilty about it. I let you down," I said as she shook her head.

"You didn't let me down, Chandler! I was sad you weren't there. But this so makes up for it! Just think of all the beautiful pictures we'll have on the beach!" she exclaimed as I laughed.

"Chandler...um, what is up with your eyes?" Laurilee wondered as her own eyes widened.

"Oh, gosh..." I closed them, paused for a moment to gain control, and then opened them again.

"How did you do that? Are you…" she stammered as she moved away from me.

"No, Laurilee…it's okay!" I pulled her back to me and hugged her. "It's something I can't explain to you, without telling you too much. Just know I'm still me."

She studied me for a moment, seemingly frightened of the changes in me.

"And you may see the babies eyes do this too. They're fine, and we can't infect you. But until they're older, we can't take them out in public."

"Infect us? Chandler, please tell me…what are you? What has happened to you?"

"I can't, Laurilee. Please, let it go. Just know you and Dan are safer not knowing everything."

Laurilee stared at me for several minutes, and then finally nodded.

"Oh, I have something to give you." Laurilee turned and pulled a packet out of her purse. "Tyler Thomas gave this to me when I told him we were flying to see you this weekend."

My eyes widened and I took the packet from her. She watched me warily.

"Chandler, what is it?"

"I've been doing a little research into Daddy's past, some questions I had about my real grandfather. Mr. Thomas said he had some things for me…" I trailed off as I looked down at the packet again.

"Well, why don't I go and see where Dan's put our bags, and I need to see my babies!" she exclaimed as she stood. "I'll give you a little alone time," she murmured as she leaned over to hug me, and then slipped quietly from the room.

I hurriedly tore the package open. An intricately carved medallion with the symbol of the protectors on a silver chain slipped from the envelope and fell to the bed as I pulled the documents out. As I glanced at the papers, it was if I was seeing my dad for the first time. After looking the documents over, I folded them neatly and placed them back in the envelope. As I held the necklace to my chest, I unfolded a letter and began to read.

Dearest Chandler,

I never wanted for you to have to read this letter, Puddin. I've always known someday I might have to explain all of this to you, but I'd hoped to do it in person. I lived a different life before I met your mother, and I've been fortunate I was able to leave it behind. You must know by now if you are reading this you have inherited a trait from me that puts your life in danger, and plants you right in the middle of a super-natural world that you didn't know existed. I'd hoped the private battles Tyler and I waged in our youth in Texas put an end to the madness, but I was wrong. We've been able to live for so long in peace, hiding in our little town away from the creatures who could seek you out. Our family history, the Samuels' family history, has only recently come to light, and if you need answers, go to them. You will find the documentation that you need here to find them in Louisiana.

I was drawn to your mother from the moment I met her, and I've loved her with all of my heart. Now I know the love we share was destiny, and your destiny is a more special meaning than we could have ever dreamed. Stay close to your Aunt Sue and Uncle Lon. They know nothing of this madness, but if you must, confide in your Uncle Lon. He will help you.

I fear my past will come again to haunt me, and I've failed to protect you from that life. I only hope you can stay safe. You have been the most precious part of our life together, and we will love you forever.

Daddy

I sat staring out the window for the longest time. I'd felt so alone for so long, and all this time, my dad had known. My momma and daddy had been trying to protect me, even beyond the grave. Somehow I'd always known. The documents the envelope contained confirmed much of what Everett and I had already figured out, and I would give the information to him. It was such a revelation, that Everett and I were family. I'd always felt that way about him, now it was just official. There would be much for his family and mine to talk about, but for now just having the missing pieces somehow brought me closure I didn't even know I needed.

"Sweetheart, are you all right? You've been gone a long time," Banton said softly as he pushed the door open. He crossed over to the bed and sat down beside me. Studying me as he took my hands in his, he leaned over and kissed me gently on the forehead. As I handed him the necklace with the symbol of the protectors, he held it up to look at it, and raised his hand to stroke my cheek with the back of his hand.

"Are there any surprises in there?" he asked as he motioned to the envelope. "You don't have to tell me if you don't want to," he murmured, tucking a strand of hair behind my ear.

I shook my head. "There's just a letter from my father, explaining everything…and some documentation about Everett's family… property I evidently own. There was a trust, set up by my grandfather, which my father had only recently discovered."

"What property, Chandler?"

"Some property in Louisiana. I need to give all of this to Everett for him to sort out. Evidently my father was on his way here to do that, when my parents were killed in the accident."

"Do you want to talk to Ev now? I can go and get him," he offered as I shook my head.

"There's plenty of time for that later. We have guests, and I want to enjoy this time together, in the here and now."

"Well, why don't you shower and get ready, because there will be a little ceremony this afternoon on the beach I think you won't want to miss," he announced with a twinkle in his eye.

"Today? We're doing this today?"

"Yes. Everett and Constance have been busy planning for days, and we'll have quite a party afterward on the beach. I'll send the girls in here to get ready with you."

Everett had picked dresses similar to mine for Constance and Brie, and they were to be bridesmaids at the second ceremony with me.

No sooner than Banton had slipped out of the room, Constance, Brie and Laurilee burst in the door, just as I was slipping out of my robe to get in the shower. Loaded down with dress bags and make-up supplies, they were giggling as they came around the corner into the bathroom.

"Get it in gear, Gastaneau, we've got a wedding to get ready for," Constance chided as they began to lay everything out. I hurriedly showered, and then jumped out as Brie brought in some stools from the kitchen, so we could all sit at the large mirror. I dried my hair, and then Constance insisted on braiding it and then running a flat iron down the braids, giving me what she called "beach waves." It turned out beautifully. I couldn't stop looking at it.

"That's a great look for you, Andie! You should wear it like that all the time," Laurilee commented as Brie worked on her hair. After Constance had her makeup picture-perfect, she turned to me.

"Let me play make-up," she begged as I nodded.

"We have a professional photographer out there, you know," Brie said.

"You're kidding," I retorted as she grinned.

"I can't believe I'm going to have two sets of wedding pictures. This is so cool," Laurilee said as she bounced in her seat. I'd never seen Laurilee this excited about anything.

Everett called out from the bedroom door. "Ladies, are you decent? The photographer would like to take some of those cute 'bridesmaids before the wedding' pictures, and I have something for you!"

"Come on in, Ev. We're decent," I answered. We'd all donned robes while we fussed over our makeup and hair.

"My lovelies, you are a vision," Everett breathed, handing each of us a large latte and then placing a tray of beignets and pastries on the counter in front of us. The photographer followed him in and began snapping pictures of us, candid photos of us applying makeup, silly pictures of us posing, and close-ups of our faces when we were ready.

"Now, if you ladies will step into the boudoir, I will snap a few special shots just for your men," the photographer offered as we all looked at each other. "Oh, don't worry, I'm as gay as a rainbow parade on Judy Garland's birthday," he said as Everett chuckled.

"I'll leave you ladies to it, then. Call Uncle Everett if you need anything," he said as he closed the bedroom door. Brie and

Constance walked over to the bed and gazed down at the beautiful lingerie that had been placed there.

"This all looks like something from a Victoria's Secret runway shoot," Laurilee wondered as she picked up a lacy corset.

"Come on, this will be fun. And it's for our guys," Constance grinned as she held a garter belt up around her waist. Carrying the insanely expensive items back into the bathroom, we all donned our new lingerie, and then blushed as we looked at each other.

"Well, all I can say is that our men are some lucky sons of bitches," Constance exclaimed as she turned to look at herself in a full-length mirror.

I eyed them all warily as the photographer pulled a chair over closer to the window. He opened the window, and then pulled the sheer drapes together, making them billow slightly toward the chair. He turned to us.

"All right, ladies…who will be first?"

I wasn't altogether sure about this lingerie photo thing, so I was more than happy for Laurilee to go first. As the elfish little photographer snapped the first few photos of the new bride, I relaxed. They were tasteful, a "giving the groom a glimpse of the bride before the ceremony" type thing.

I was the last to go. As we were finishing up, the others had gone back into the bathroom to dress. Brie picked my phone up off the dresser.

"Chandler, wait. I have an idea," she grinned as she held my phone up. I realized what she had up her sleeve, and I nodded at her. I sat in the chair beside the window, just as I had been in the last picture. I looked over my shoulder at her as she snapped a picture of me, my legs crossed to one side of the chair, my thigh-high silk stockings showing, and my hair draped over one bare shoulder. She walked over to me and handed me my phone.

"I'll let you type your own message," she said conspiratorially, flitting back into the bath.

I typed quickly, "Even when I'm not with you, I'm thinking only of you," then I hit "send."

I'd forgotten how beautiful the bridesmaid's dress was that Laurilee had picked until I slipped it on. The dress was the exact cocoa brown of my eyes. The sweetheart neckline of the fitted bodice accentuated my bust, making me look bigger than I really was. The fabric was pleated and crisscrossed across my breasts with a smattering of crystals at the waist, giving it the effect the fabric had been gathered and pinned with a broach. Then wrapping around my waist, it flowed into a skirt of wispy shredded tulle. The ballet length of the skirt would be perfect for the beach.

"Chandler, that dress is beautiful on you," Constance breathed as my phone pinged, signaling a message. I grinned as I picked it up.

> *Wow. I love this picture, and I*
> *love you. That is some*
> *beautiful lingerie...I can't wait*
> *to see it up close!*

I giggled as Constance tried to look at my phone. I shook my head at her.

"Nope, just like the picture I texted him, this is for my eyes only," I told her as she glared at me. "All right, here," I handed the phone back to her.

"Crap, Chandler...could y'all take it up another notch or two? You still act like newlyweds!"

"Well, we are. We haven't been married quite a year yet," I corrected her.

"Yeah, but you've already got the normal American family with two kids," she retorted.

"Um, that would be two point five, and yes, we do..." I trailed off as I smiled at her.

"What does that mean?"

Laurilee and Constance stepped into the room, Laurilee dragging her train of ruffles behind her. I smiled at her as I teared up.

"Oh, come on, Chandler...Cowgirl, up! You've seen me in this dress before at the fitting," she scolded, always the one in control with no tears.

"I know. It's just...so perfect," I whispered as the tears flowed.

547

"I'll ask again, what did you mean by two point five?" Constance repeated as I smiled bigger.

"Well, the two are here, and the 'point five' will be here sometime next summer, making a full three," I whispered as I cradled my abdomen.

Laurilee's mouth jaw dropped a full two inches as Constance shook her head. Brie just smiled at me.

"I knew it! I just knew it, the way you've been turning your nose up at food since you've been back. Studley do-right might want to tuck that thing away for a while. You *do* know what causes that, sister?" Constance cocked a perfectly arched brow at me.

"Yes, and for your information, we want another baby. We just never dreamed we could get pregnant again this quickly…we didn't think we could," I retorted as Constance smiled conspiratorially.

"What?" Brie asked as she looked back and forth at us.

"I was just thinking, maybe this fertile thing runs in the family. There might be hope for Ty and me after all," she said.

"Well, I hope so, because the two of you are just going to have to share," Brie said, her eyes glistening.

"Well, before anyone else jumps on the baby bandwagon, can I get married one more time?" Laurilee asked as we all giggled.

"Ladies, it's time," Everett called out as he pushed the door open.

Chapter Thirty-Six

John, Ty and Banton stood with Dan, waiting on us at the makeshift altar in white linen shirts, washed blue jeans and bare feet. Banton's tanned skin glistened in the late afternoon sun, beautiful against the crisp white of the shirt. They all smiled broadly as we stepped out on the deck. First down the aisle was Brie in her pale cream dress, her beautiful red hair a fiery match to the sunset. Constance followed, her blonde hair perfectly curled in beach waves like mine, the blonde beautiful against the pale pink of the dress. I came next, slowly making my way down the aisle to stand across from Banton. As I turned into my position I glanced up into his eyes, soft and warm as he seemed to envelope me with his gaze. My breath caught in my throat...I still couldn't believe this beautiful man was mine. *When you look at me like that, everyone and everything around us seems to fade away,* I thought as I met his gaze. He smiled softly, his dimple peeking at me from the corner of his mouth as if he'd heard my thoughts.

Soft guitar music played in the background, joining the waves in a slow rhythm. The tempo changed, signaling Laurilee's walk toward Dan. Everett had agreed to walk her, standing in this second time for her father. I was strangely calm. Things like this usually made me nervous, even if I was just a guest in the audience. I took in everything...every moment...the way Laurilee's dress hugged her slender frame, the way it dipped low in the back, accentuating her long, linear form, the way the antique lace of the ruffles in the back billowed out with the breeze.

Everett had enlisted a local free-lance artist to build sandcastles at the altar, and there was even a replica of the Alamo, his tip of the hat to our native Texas. I smothered a giggle behind my bouquet as I watched Dan. He was never without his cowboy boots, and somehow Everett had talked him into going barefoot today. He nervously squished his toes in the sand the entire time they were exchanging their vows.

As the minister proclaimed Laurilee and Dan "husband and wife" for the second time, Dan grandly swept Laurilee up and then dipped her as he kissed her. The look in his eyes said there had never been a more beautiful bride.

As everyone clapped, Ava jumped up and asked, "Unca Banin, can I pway in the sandcastles now?"

"Doodle-Bug, they're all yours," Laurilee answered her as Dan swept her up and swung her around. Aunt Sue and Mrs. Elaine rose with the twins and turned them loose in the sand with Ava Grace. Matty giggled as he tried to stand up at the walls of one of the castles, immediately bulldozing it down, causing Elly to break into a fit of giggles to match his. Banton moved to stand beside me, encircling me in his arms as we watched the kids play in the sand.

"Okay, you win. This was a beautiful wedding here on the beach," Aunt Sue proclaimed as Ty and Constance walked over to her. "Just one condition," she cautioned.

"What condition?" Constance asked warily.

"That Everett does all the decorating, and you still let me do the over-the-top flowers," Aunt Sue replied.

"Momma," Constance warned as Ty placed his hand over her mouth.

"Agreed," Ty answered for her as Uncle Lon threw his hands in the air.

"Finally!" he exclaimed. "Now, maybe a little less drama and no surprises."

As Ty pulled his hand away from Constance's mouth she grinned wickedly at me.

"Oh, Daddy, you know better than that, with Chandler and Banton in the family now. If Chandler is going to be my matron of honor, we will either have to postpone the wedding to late summer, or move it up to January."

"Why would Chandler have anything to do with when the wedding is?" Aunt Sue asked innocently.

As it dawned on Julia what they were talking about, she jumped up and down as she clapped her hands.

"What the heck is going on?" Cade asked as he snaked his arms around her waist. She leaned back to look up at him as he kissed her forehead.

550

"Chandler's going to have another baby," she giggled out as Drew laughed.

"Oh, man…here we go again! I get to be here for this, too! This ought to be good."

"What are you talking about?" Julia asked as Constance continued to smirk.

"The last time she told my Momma and Daddy she was pregnant, she was summoned to the study by 'Bad-Ass Dad'," Drew retorted. I glared at Constance.

"Don't look at me. They had to find out sooner or later. Besides, Banton's here to protect you this time."

Aunt Sue and Uncle Lon's stunned expressions were as expected. But this time, Uncle Lon just shook his head. As before as our news sunk in, Aunt Sue's eyes began to mist as she pulled me into her arms.

"I'm so happy for you, Chandler. I was afraid you and Constance wouldn't be able to conceive now you've both been bitten. Maybe there is hope for her, too," she whispered as I smiled knowingly at her.

"I was thinking the same thing," I whispered back.

"Chandler, your little body has been through so much, I hate to see you do this again so soon," Uncle Lon scolded.

"I'm worried about that too, Mr. Lon, and I assure you we will take the best possible care of her," Banton replied, pulling me back against his chest and placing a kiss in my hair.

As everyone congratulated us on the new baby, Everett spoke up.

"We have food on the back deck. Everyone let's toast the happy couple and celebrate being together." He guided everyone back toward the beach house. As the deck filled with our guests and the champagne was passed around, Everett held me aside.

"Bebe, I am so happy for you. You have been through so much physically and emotionally. Are you truly okay?

"Ev, I've never been better." I smiled as Banton paused to look at me from the deck, his eyes shining as he flashed his dimple at me. "I'm married to the most beautiful man in the world with the most beautiful soul. I have two perfect babies, another on the way, and I am blessed with family and friends. I never dreamed when I left Texas my life would be so full, so perfect. And now I have you," I whispered as he smiled at me.

"Ma petit, you have always had me, since the day we met. Knowing we are related by blood just makes it sweeter."

I reached up on my toes as I hugged him around the neck.

"Banton said you received your confirmation from Texas?"

"Yes, evidently my father was on his way to find you and the Samuel's family. And there were some things in the packet that puzzled me," I said. He cocked an eyebrow at me. Banton walked back over and slid his arm around my waist.

"What else did you find?'

"Some notes, about my father's knowledge of a cell of Orcos operating out of Baton Rouge, with connections in Colorado and Texas. There was a letter that looked quite old, a plea for his help."

"Who was the letter from, Chandler?" Banton asked softly.

I turned and looked up into his eyes.

"The return address on the envelope was 505 Rue Dauphine, Baton Rouge," I whispered as his eyes widened. "It was signed H. DeLee," I said disbelievingly. Everett stared at me, speechless.

"That's impossible," he said finally as he found his voice.

I smirked. "After all this time... meeting you, meeting Everett, falling in love with you with both of us being Sange-Mele, being drawn to our house and buying it, my mother's spirit, the soldier, the existence of Orcos, Aldon, and a Tariq stalking my dreams for gripe's sake...and now we aren't going to believe something we have right in front of us?"

"What was the postmark on the letter?" Everett asked.

"March 15th, last year. Two months before my parents were murdered by Orcos," I answered him.

"Well, I guess we have some more research to do, Bebe," Everett said as Banton placed his lips in my hair. "Oh, how I love a good mystery," he gushed as my news soaked in.

"Sweetheart, you said something about property deeds in the paperwork, some property your father found out he owned?"

"Well, that's some more research we need to do. If my calculations are correct, my grandfather bought the land the Old Catholic church was on, which would encompass the old cemetery and the field beyond it."

"Bebe, it would seem our stories are even more intertwined than we knew. He must have bought it when Mrs. Johnson sold part of the land after the war. "

"Do you think he knew about you and Marie-Claire, and wanted to buy some of the property for you?' I asked.

"I don't know. We may never know," he said as I nodded and leaned over to kiss his cheek. He continued, "Unless we can find them and ask them."

I pulled away and studied him. "What do you mean? Find who?"

"My father, and your grandfather," he answered simply as he shrugged his shoulders. I realized my mouth was hanging open, and I shut it.

"It never occurred to me they could still be living."

"They were both bitten, my father fully transformed. It is entirely possible they both still live."

"Where would we start?" Banton asked as he looked back and forth at us.

"That might be a question for my mother for another time," he paused, seeming to weigh the consequences of a search for our relatives, and then he added, "Well, let's get back to our party and the guests. We'll have much to talk about later," he said as he moved to join the crowd on the deck.

"Come with me," Banton whispered as I began to protest.

"Banton, the babies," I began as he crooked a finger at me, the biggest grin I'd ever seen plastered across his face.

"Um, no worries about them, little mama. Look there. Mr. Lon and my daddy have them fully under control," he nodded in their direction as he continued to pull me into the beach house. They each sat with a twin in their lap, feeding them wedding cake and letting them play in the icing. Elly giggled as Matty mashed a large handful of icing into her hair.

"They will be fine for at least thirty minutes or so," Banton urged me as he continued to pull me down the long hallway into our bedroom. He pulled the door to and then locked it. Turning back to me, he grinned wickedly at me as he pulled me into his arms.

"You, my hot, sexy wife, are stunning in that dress. You upstaged the bride today," he murmured, sliding his lips down my bare shoulder. "I could hardly breathe as I watched you walk down the aisle toward me. I could never tire of that vision."

"You are really sweet, Lieutenant. I would have to say you were definitely the most handsome man in the wedding party, to me, anyway," I whispered back.

"I'm glad to hear it, Mrs. Gastaneau. By the way, your little text before the ceremony was really a tease. We'll have to do something about that little indiscretion," he murmured playfully, fingering the crystal beading on my dress. He slid his hands around my ribcage, stopping to grasp the zipper in the back and unzipping it slowly.

"Now, Andie, about that lingerie …"

Epilogue

We lounged in the sunshine, soaking up the warmth of a beautiful April afternoon. Banton rested his head in my lap as I lazily curled my fingers in and out of his hair. We watched the twins as they scampered back and forth across the blanket, first chasing Beau, then back to chase the butterflies flitting around the edges of the bushes beside us in the flower bed.

"Don't you have a meeting with the developers this afternoon?" I asked.

Banton hired a team of contractors and bought several properties around us to develop the neighborhood. Since the SEALs were once again inactive, Banton entered into several business ventures that, according to his father, were surprisingly lucrative. He seemed to have his father's touch when it came to business.

"No, we handled everything by phone this morning. I'm all yours this afternoon, baby."

"Will you ever have to go back to…the SEALs, I mean. Are you still officially on leave?" I'd been dreading his answer for months.

"This isn't not like being a regular SEAL. They could call us back anytime, when there is a threat of the Somali's or Orcos. I guess if the threat ever rises again…" he trailed off.

"So you're my Batman," I teased as he grinned up at me.

"Sort of. But without all the cool toys," he retorted as he leaned up and kissed my ever-expanding belly.

"Oh, by the way, what was that interesting little conversation I overhead earlier? You were on your cell when I came out here," Banton questioned, raising an eyebrow.

"Well, I guess you might as well know. Constance called for advice."

"Oh, Lord…what now?"

"Well, it seems our dear Constance is having a bad bout of morning sickness," I revealed as Banton raised his head inquiringly.

"Really? That's great! That's really great! Seems you two are truly unique," he exclaimed as he sat upright and pulled me in for a kiss.

"Well, you know Constance. We're really going to have some family drama now."

Constance and Ty married in February on the beach, complete with sand castles, ice sculptures, and enough bridesmaids to line the beach for a country mile. Constance got her barefoot wedding wish, and Aunt Sue got to spend enough of Uncle Lon's money to put him in a tailspin for months. I giggled as I thought about the wild weekend we'd all spent together.

"What are you thinking about?" Banton whispered as he touched my cheek.

"I was just thinking about their wedding and all the drama after," I murmured as I watched Elly toddling back and forth, picking flowers and handing them to Matty.

Banton smiled at the memory.

I stood at the French doors, watching Everett as he held Ava's hand, picking their way through the sandcastles that had escaped the wrecking ball that was our son. She skipped happily along beside him as they approached the door.

"Bebe, you are looking radiant today...doesn't Aunt Chandler look beautiful in her dress?' Everett asked Ava. She nodded enthusiastically at me as I picked her up in my arms.

"My An Andler is the most beautiful, cept for my Mommy Cwadia," she whispered as she leaned into Everett's ear. I smiled conspiratorially at him as I put Ava back down in the floor. Everyone sat gathered around the fireplace, enjoying the left-over champagne and resting their feet.

"Unca Ebret?"

"What, my princess?" he asked her as he took a place beside me on the ottoman.

"Wiwl I eber hab another daddy, wike my Daddy Will?" she asked as she looked inquiringly at Claudia.

Claudia spoke softly. "No one will ever be able to replace your Daddy Will. But maybe someday," she answered as her eyes misted.

Ava then looked up at Everett, who was watching Claudia intently.

"Unca Ebret, wiwl you pweese marry my Mommie Cwadia, and be my new Daddy? I wuv you aweady," she said simply as Julia choked on her champagne. Mr. Matt chuckled as Mrs. Elaine covered his hand with hers.

Everett cleared his throat as everyone waited with baited breath.

"My dear, sweet Ava...now that sounds like a good idea. We will have to think about that one," he answered as he continued to gaze at Claudia. She blushed. Ava ran across the room and jumped into her lap, burying her head in Claudia's chest.

Of course, that would be a moment to write in our family's history, to be recanted again and again. Everett and Claudia had already given in to their feelings and had been dating ever since.

"Yeah, that was something. Thank Ava for breaking the ice between Everett and Claudia."

"I'm thinking we'll have another wedding before the year is out."

"Humm. So it seems," Banton muttered as he rose to get Matty, who had wandered too far away from us.

After several moments grinning as I watched the twins, a thought occurred to me as sadness swept over me. Banton scooped Matty up and swung him back to the blanket. After depositing him beside Elly, he sank down beside me and pulled me into his side.

"Sweetheart, what is it?" Banton asked, drawing his eyebrows together. Lifting his hand, he caressed my forehead as to erase the worry lines. "What are you thinking?"

"I was just thinking about Elly," I responded, releasing my breath as I blinked up at him. "The kids are Aldon, Banton...it hadn't occurred to me before, but..."

"But what? Yes, they are Aldon."

"Aldon women can't reproduce. Ellyson won't ever be able to have children," I muttered sadly. She toddled back toward me with her hands outstretched to show me a butterfly that had landed on her arm. She giggled as I touched it, causing it to fly away. The tears gathered in my eyes as I pulled her into my lap.

557

I gazed back at Banton, and I watched as tears gathered in his eyes. As he took a deep breath, he seemed to come to a conclusion, shaking his head to clear his eyes.

"But here's the thing, Chandler. They're still an unknown. They may be transformed Aldon children, but Elly's still half your daughter. She is half fader, one of the fertile as Olivia puts it. She has your and Constance's genetics...and we both know you have proved Dr. Renault wrong." His eyes warmed as he grinned. He leaned back slowly, and then placed his hands gently around my face, drawing me down for a kiss. After several moments, he moved his hands down to baby Collins, snuggled safely in my belly. Caressing it slowly with his hand, he gazed back up into my eyes.

"Maybe it has something to do with my virile mate," I quipped as I traced the outline of his lips.

"She looks so much like you, except for my dimple," he murmured. His eyes darkened. "Hmm. Maybe I'd rather she couldn't...the thought of..." he sputtered as he tried to put his fear into words. "There will be too many teenage boys. They will come sniffing around, wanting to date her, wanting...Oh, God...I'll have to be ready!" he exclaimed in the most adorable manner possible. "I know, I was a teenage boy once...and they'll be like me!"

I grinned, my heart so full of love for this man...the father of my children...my love, my entire life. I placed my hands gently on his face and pulled him to my lips as I murmured, "Oh, Banton, don't worry. There isn't another male like you on the planet. I promise."

Author's Notes

What a journey it has been to write The Southern Series! I have so many people to thank. First and foremost, the most deserving of my thanks are my husband and my boys, who understand my crazy need to write and support me through my fits of seclusion.

Then there are the crazy ladies who make up Shelley's Southern Street Team. Linda Lambert and friends…you ladies are the best, and have helped to put The Southern Series on the map in the book blogging world.

Last, but not least, are my main beta readers. A gigantic thank you is in order for Julie Lama, Ashley Ward, Cindy Henry, Amelia Cato, Angela Turket (my comma Nazi), Katy Hardin, and Audrey Schaffner. Being an Indie author with no budget, I couldn't do this without you.

"Southern Spirits" was supposed to be the last book in the series, but as I sent this book to print, I decided I'm not ready to leave the family and friends on Rue Dauphine behind just yet. So watch for announcements about upcoming projects. You can follow me on Facebook on my author page, Shelley L. Stringer, Author, on twitter and Pinterest, or you can find me at www.shelleystringerauthor.com.

Made in the USA
San Bernardino, CA
15 January 2015